GLOUCESTERBOOK

GLOUCESTERBOOK

JONATHAN BAYLISS

DRAWBRIDGE PRESS

Copyright © 1992 by Jonathan Bayliss

First published 1992 by Protean Press

First Drawbridge Press paperback edition 2019; contains minor corrections by the author

All rights reserved. No part of this book may be reproduced or transmitted in any form or by any means, electronic or mechanical, including photocopying and recording, or by any information storage and retrieval system, without the permission of Jonathan Bayliss Trust. Requests for permission should be made in writing in care of Drawbridge Press, PO Box 833, Gloucester MA 01930 or info@drawbridgepress.com.

Library of Congress Catalog Card Number: 92-062216

ISBN: 978-0-9974641-5-3

To Lois Henderson

MICHAEL CHAPMAN'S APOLOGY TO THE POSSIBLE READER

As a matter of personal integrity, in resistance to the times, and in the interest of efficient information, it was impossible for me to render this transfiction in the demotic language of contemporary American literature. Possible systems of experience, like technology, can best be represented on the page not by reducing or simplifying the complexity of English but by fixing more dimensions of abstraction that commonly intersect as prose. Thus the value of my construction is proportional to the number of right angles at which the unrealized concrescence makes its place.

Robert Burton says "our style bewrays us":

> To dunces, what indeed have we to say?
> And yet bar none: bid all and sundry in:
> Stranger be doubly welcome, friend or foe!

CONTENTS

PROEM

FIRST MOVEMENT

1	Rafe Opsimath's Disquisition Log	*15*
2	The Van	*35*
3	Rafe's Log (2)	*49*
4	The Harbor	*67*
5	Rafe's Log (3)	*111*
6	Rocky Bay	*139*
7	Rafe's Log (4)	*189*

SECOND MOVEMENT

1	Lore of the Saints	*227*
2	Caleb Karcist's Current Curriculum Vitae	*239*
3	Acorn Pasture	*241*
4	Beltane Hill	*257*
5	The Rectory	*277*
6	Poet's Corner	*295*
7	Avalon Reefer	*309*
8	Rima Vocalis	*335*
9	The Resistance	*353*
10	Quinquagesima: Offertory	*379*
11	Ember Wednesday: Consecration	*411*
12	Lady Day: Communion	*433*
13	Lent	*459*
14	Moonfeather	*483*
15	Magic Mountain	*501*
16	Matter a Priori	*531*
17	Lustration	*553*
18	Lore of the Angels	*571*

GLOUCESTERBOOK

PROEM
(IN LOCATIVE VOICE)

Some have held this to be the best of all possible worlds purely because it's the only possible outcome of all the causes that produced Adam and Eve. Under the circumstances, mankind can't be blamed for its own failures. Others believe that things have been needlessly unsuccessful, and perhaps that whatever we bring about will always be anything but the best possible. The most liberal view of our particular case is that we have simply made a lot of mistakes on our faultily named continent.

Mistakes are usually topical in motive. Chicago for instance, the way it was allowed to play the spider with our railroads. Before surveying parties started for the Mississippi all reins of investment had been gathered at Chicago. World capital flowed to Chicago, and thereupon it ossified as properties that will never be relocated. All northern lines began or ended in Chicago, where furthermore the smallest wills prevailed in seeing to it that each company had to build a different station. So it was hardly possible to skip Chicago on your way across the country, or to sleep through it, unless you had a private car that could be shunted through the freight yards. This inexpungible web of negligent polity was graven into the earth itself before anyone realized that there might have been a more efficient alternative to the spoils system.

Thus the political principle of least resistance historically inverted the economic principle of least action. Many jobs materialized when capitalists and local politicians took advantage of each other. No one in Washington tried to shape the imperial skeleton by which organs would be placed and sinews strung at various distances from their inchoate lakeshore Venice. Far-flung ekistical nuclei rooted themselves in the landscape as knots in Chicago's farflung net. Even if the ganglionic marshalling yards of the new metropolis were paved over with asphalt and parking garages, and all rails extirpated, that rawhide town built upon a mushy portage between the lake of the Illini and the tributaries of the Mississippi (which Fr Marquette tried to name Conception) would remain the de facto hub of our inland trade routes.

For such were the expediencies that those few kilohectares of wild garlic swamp began to produce larger goods from the small goods brought in from many distant places, as well as dressed carcasses and smaller chunks from large living wholes. Soon all lodestones pointed there. They still do. For after a century of railroading the nation's commitment to Chicago was reaffirmed with a deuterocanonical enlargement of its fixed assets by construction of the world's most attractive airport. By preestablished magnate force it was made the hemispheric pole at which to break the transcontinental rhumb lines even of air carriers elsewhere based. As late as 1960 it still could not be bypassed aloft by most passengers between one ocean and the other.

Raphael Opsimath had no business in Chicago, but airborne again in the daily reflux of pioneers and gold-seekers headed against the sun, their backs to the Pacific frontier, he was accustomed to having lost an hour there on what happened to be a straight line between his westerly origin and easterly destination. At least the airlines all shared the same airfield; and he had nothing to say against refueling at the center of the continent so long as he was not obliged to transfer himself or his baggage to another airplane.

But if the nineteenth century political economy had been guided by a central nervous system, and the railroad corporations less partial to "Strong-town", many a western city might have located itself according to incentives put forward by reasoning experts. One of the modern consequences might have been that that generation's busiest refueling airport was situated near the city of Cairo, which would have been firmly established at the navel of our waterways, without mortgage to the New York Trust Company and possibly called Eden instead. But then Eden would have been off the crow's course between his ports of departure and destination, both of which were placed geologically.

Opsimath had often pondered the ironies of inefficiency sowed by the invisible hand. Our enterprise is often justified only by its meeting of some small unanticipated requirement. Waste or redundancy can be made to seem wise for the long run. As a citizen of history he had always found it intimately painful to contemplate the casual stupidity or creative perversity with which mankind has usually abused its rare opportunities to shape things from scratch; but to him as a businessman aware of the modern weakness for experts, our most excruciating failures usually were the planned projects in which form was left to specialists. He approved the literary theory that form determines content. As he was yet to be told, Henry's worst abuse of power was to allow Archbishop Cranmer to form the *Book of Common Prayer*.

But now, once more launched from the most transitive of airports, his mind was engaged with aspects of error and failure at the personal level of management: his own numberless opportunities in the recent past and proximate future to improve or prevent. Not for the first time, he was examining his own habits and methods of responding to privately motivated responsibilities for fundamentally impersonal matters. Without repenting the past he meditated corrections to the series of actions (including words and intonations) by which he continued to make himself felt in the affairs of his Tubalcain Manufacturing Company.

Though he rarely worried about his policies or decisions after they were made, he was sometimes discontent with the way he got things done. Nowadays the aspects of tactics were called style, and the term was extended to strategy as well. But the best style must be thought of as the only way you can accomplish a purpose, which is modified by the means of bringing it about. As he stared down at the steel mills along Indiana's lake front his larynx faintly rehearsed a proposition that it was not his lot to have occasion to discuss with anyone: style is the form of function determined by content.

Opsimath was aware of his fault in employing spare time to relish such abstract questions. This habit impaired his style; yet it would be impossible to perfect his style without doing violence to his psyche—thus necessarily altering the very motive (whatever it was) for all his chrematistic efforts. On the other hand, he might well resolve to watch himself more closely and hold his tongue more often.

His superficial difficulty in management was unfortunately more significant than the prevalent intellectual defects of business leaders in the new Atlantis. It betrayed a dangerous boredom with the more or less repetitive quotidian duties of a chief executive, which despite all pretense to the contrary were mainly operational and defensive. He had to force himself to face the merely preventive or socially lubricative duties that most Atlantean managers regarded as their least irksome obligation. Aside from continual analysis of the persons he sold to, bought from, conferred with, placated, or bossed, all his zest for the going concern seemed devoted to negotiation and development—where he was likely to find odd details as interesting as the schemes themselves.

The worst of it was that his principal colleague and corporate partner, whose genius was engineering, diffidently refused to assume burdens of general administration. "You're the maestro of paperwork, Rafe. You know how to handle money and lawyers. I got my Master's in Business to please Mother, but it all went in one ear and out the other. I'd never make a good president." Walter Edenfield was too sweet a man to be scornful of anything, but to him, upon whose technical talents the firm depended for its unique position in the market, management was nothing but tedious "paperwork", which he was quite serene about not being any good at, like a Noble laureate declining to head the whole School of Arts and Sciences. But Rafe, without any degree at all, and without the capital to buy his way in, had risen through the hawsepipe on sufferance of the Edenfield family, and one consequence of the scion's deference to the hireling was that as president he worked much harder than any other stockholding employee.

So whenever he knew a trip was coming up he tried to concentrate on operational matters for a few days, tossing the work he preferred into a briefcase that was always open for the purpose, looking forward to the pleasure of constructive studies in peaceful airplanes and quiet hotels. In the course of usual events at the office he had perusal time only to cull his perpetual stack of magazines and journals for future reading—time only to postpone actual attention to the books on management or technology that might hearten his struggles or stimulate his enthusiasm for progress. For there were always financial reports to analyze, with pencil and paper, from many different angles. More urgent yet were the crucial documents that he alone could draft, and could draft only alone. He was chronically starved for time to record his ideas and resolutions with sufficient care, or his critical response to others'. His memos could come tumbling in pent-up profusion only during blissful respites from desk and telephone. And only at manifest remove from his clamoring factory could the future of everything he managed lie malleable under the visible hand that held his swift fine pencil, not so much a stylus as a tool.

He always hoped to clear up the chaff before he left, marveling that so little of it could be delegated; but he never quite cleared up the odds and ends that couldn't be taken with him. The pressure of particular meteorological conditions fluctuated with his willingness to acknowledge or challenge them, but there was no remission of the general weather in his office. The more attention he devoted to trivialities the more he fertilized their proliferation; and the more gratefully they responded to his licks and promises the more often he was obliged to deal with them as Gordian knots—except when he brutally smothered their cries in the round file, muttering his forthcoming trip as shopworn excuse.

Yet over and over again he found to his amazement that under guilt-ridden neglect a remarkable percentage of unattractive problems quietly dissolved. Fading under his bravado of irresponsibility, the tangles loosened themselves. Complaints died of old age as complainants suffered a procession of new ones. He learned to guess which anxieties were the most likely to evaporate, and to sweep those least tractable under the rug of one department or another. Most of the rest he managed to dispatch, talking furiously right down to the minute of his departure. Upon his return he rarely found himself beginning the new cycle at any more cumulative disadvantage.

On a plane the trouble always was that as soon as he settled down to work, all full of zeal for reading or writing, his papers classified on the folding tray above his knees, a crisp pad of blue-lined paper inviting the neat inscription of sharp black ink—if he wasn't interrupted by the business of eating or pleasantly encumbered with a drink in hand to quell his ravenous anticipation of a meal to come, and if not engaged with some friendly fellow at his side—he fell into reverie over what he saw outside the window. For unless the route was entirely too familiar he habitually sought an outboard seat far enough forward or aft to see ground under the wing, a laughably childish compulsion quite beneath the dignity of a college sophomore even in those days when flying was still measured by landmarks. Already by 1960 all but virgin air travelers were looking more to their insulated comforts and the significations of their watches than to their geographical perspective.

He liked to read the country by mapping its rivers, or at night by analyzing the way its orange jewels were flung. West of the Rockies his nearly constant sensation of temporal stress had been prolonged by stubborn carpets of Sunnyside vapor, which, except for a few glimpses of wrinkled sierra far below, redirected his eyes to the simple blue heavens; but he was at last able to pick out one or two branches of the great Mississippi oak, and at last joyfully discern the trunk itself, whereupon the patch of hemisphere below him became clearly defined by the railroads converging toward their roots in the short side of the gnarled treetop like an industrial equivalent of mistletoe.

Now on the cloudless afternoon out of Chicago he unconditionally surrendered himself to the temptation of vision. Without compunction he pondered from his slowly advancing epicenter the hazy-edged scroll that unrolled and rerolled a mere five miles from his face. It was barely near enough for identifications—yet it was much too close. Staring at the sharply bounded colors of fields and plotted nests of buildings, he indolently imagined a vantage so far elevated above the details that the whole misshapen pinheaded dinosaur stretched out with all its flaws and blemishes under the plane's attenuated shadow. Had United States teratology made as many mistakes as United States business? Incorporating lower Ontario and the Maritimes its lines might easily have matured more handsome. And with Baja California the beast would have had a tail. With all of Mexico it would have been a deal more shapely. Better yet, with Yukon and British Columbia to complete the imperial pattern, if tolerably balanced by the complement of New France, it would have been all in all a Leviathan more noble. Then, governed by a larger Senate, no wetbacks but more voters. Add the isthmus down to Nueva Granada: dearer bananas by now, no doubt, and more expensive Presidential campaigns, but a safer and perhaps wider Canal.

Of course by the first two laws of thermodynamics some other things would have had to turn out worse in compensation, so Opsimath didn't waste his time protesting schoolbook boundaries. Yet after fifty or sixty centuries of experience with civilization, Indo-Europeans had had the freshest possible start for their New World empire. It seemed to him that at the Renaissance epoch of mercantile evolution, considering our heritage of Oriental literature and Levantine categories of speculation, we'd truly possessed (without Adam's handicaps) the means of grace and hope of glory. There will never be another new beginning for North Atlantic nationality.

The size and shape of this unmated creature was eventually

delimited not by ontogenetic possibility but by geohistorical conditions that may be said to have been determined long before it was begotten upon the chthonic continuum. The great animal's language, however, offered our will much greater freedom. It is true that most acts and common entities had been well enough verbed or nouned in Europe, and the Indians (as we called them in our first mistake) generously distinguished for us all the plants and animals still unbooked. But old Adam had named few places, and Indian proper names were not always available for the stealing. We were wondrously free to pick and choose, to invent, the names of landmarks and settlements.

Capitalized names, rehearsed and then recorded, soon seem as natural as labels for genera and species, or for all the fundamental components of syntax. In fact our onomasticon ends up as a gazeteer of style, a phenomenon of imagination, or at least of the parsimonious freewill engaged in making mere decisions. Since names have meaning, different mistakes in naming would have led to different mistakes in our interferences. Our history would not have turned out to be the best possible.

Or else the names on our map have fallen into place insignificantly and the historian should be indifferent to their accidental signification. The lineaments of paths and crossroads get worn into the land by a people's consensual convenience over the years; and in a new world any topological or ekistical name may be arbitrarily fixed, before it's critically pondered by the body politic, by the epithet of a single invader, uttered in his passing mood, whether advisedly or unbethought. Even when the scouts and surveyors of western landgrant corporations scientifically recorded their coordinates and elevations, they were often as free as Adam to choose labels for cuts fills tunnels bridges and work camps perhaps destined to flourish as the seeds of cities. The proper names they attached were likely to be more capricious than those inscribed upon the coastal cartographies that had to be approved by Tudor sovereigns or papist viceroys.

To my contemplative traveler it seemed strange that so many of these names entered history without remark. He would have been interested to hear what Sam'l Purchase had said, friend and consultant to Captain John Smith: "History without that so much neglected study of Geography is sick of a half dead palsy." But here what's more to the point, given Opsimath's 1960 relativity in all four dimensions, is the question of distinguishing possible fiction from palsied fantasy. No matter how deterministic your universe, you must allow that the attribute of plausibility is not limited to actual history and geography, even when your credulity is confined to the possible as only a special case of the conceivable.

A successful art of management tends to aggrandize its purview, like the statecraft of a dominant sea power. Opsimath was accustomed to informing and manipulating a corporate body organized by himself. Perhaps at another time he would not have been averse to imagining maps of various national configurations, idly speculating on what might have happened in war and politics. But gazing down upon the actual country he felt no desire either to juxtapose real parts surrealistically or to imagine the parts themselves anew. It was more interesting to imagine a system differing from history in another way.

No one can compose a new republic from the ground up. Who could match God by dreaming up a world of etiologically consistent details organized parallel to Evolution's in time and space yet novel in every correspondence? No cell could be a real cell, no crow a real crow, no axe a real axe, no street a real street, no politician a real politician, no feeling a real feeling—to say nothing of the thoughts within our thought. Why, it would take a mortal lifetime to imagine the handful of items mentioned in a lyric poem! And even if you were indeed blessed with ability to elaborate all the requisites, what a fatuous abuse of God-given time, to toil over a set of alternatives to common sense! Any synthesis as interesting as reality is impossible to conceive.

But a style that makes free with history's nomenclature may suit a busy man's penchant for pragmatic speculation upon the pseudo-possibility of alternatives in certain veins or segments of our accidental world, one who takes special pleasure in pretending to persuade himself that some of its details might have turned out a little more interesting, slightly more manageable, at negligible expense to the truth of his experience in the infinitely meshed net of reality. Having neither time nor appetite to tinker with the whole geohistorical scheme (nor of course competence), we are bound to exploit the compendious facilities of language in our probing thought experiments. We know that if our procedures are too rigorous we won't get very far in making up anything that God hasn't anticipated. A free and easy method is wanted: for the most part taking things as they come, in God's idiom, and accepting common report for everything outside our idiosyncratic spots of focus.

In any case, Opsimath wouldn't be ascending far enough into the stratosphere to take in the grotesque U S A all at once. Only a mind's eye trained in unbiased projection could limn that vulnerable amphibian in her entirety, hoofless stumps and all. But a West Coast thinker coming eastward into the past, how could he help gestalting his prejudice?

The national anxiety seems to intensify with one's approach to its central organs of intelligence. The neck grows mean and crabbed as it narrows. Though admitting his grudged respect for the seedy undersized brain, and for its vestigial dominion over the entire endocrine system, he was unable to shake off the invidious opinions of a born Cornucopian. He was heading in seven-league boots for a pate hoary with grime. Rejecting a West Coast prejudice that the northeast end of the country was corrupted by its bad weather and obsolete machinery, he nevertheless couldn't deny a measure of wholesome contempt for what he and his colleagues regard as the decadent pretensions of "the East's" superannuated "culture".

Yet when the Atlantic was still an hour away there began to grow in his heart the desire for an anthropologist's short perspective of all the works and habitations he ever passed over—the places of his country that he would never get to know although he had flown to every state in the Union and traveled some of them many times over. Most of what he had seen (from cars restaurants and hotel windows) was replicated commercial artiscape, because he never had time to go about on foot. Till now on this trip he had savored the detached locomotion of his airplane with an appetite for the poetic satisfaction of unbidden questions, and it was almost with distaste that he had deferred consideration of his goal—yet without having taken the opportunity to finish the work that was all the more important to get out of the way because the special purpose of this journey required him to forget business as soon as he reached his destination; but as he crossed into the atmosphere of Wellingborough Redburn's North River watershed he was suddenly seized with the craving to possess every local sensation of aged Nova Anglia, the northern reaches of Elizabeth's Virginia.

In fact he was nearly overcome by a visceral impatience for the stolidly droning plane to land. It was a passion without particular object—except perhaps lungfuls of salt air right off Vinland Bight, where the most educated colonists in the history of the world had excelled the feat of Troy's remnant; or rather a vague desire for recreation, already percolating up through the interstices of more sober concerns. His joy in the particular places he was going to revisit would probably pass with the occasion, as it had in other parts of the country, like a mania for strange women; but the further experience he wanted of these unfamiliar little states would foster the topological urge by extending his emotional repertory rather than simply rehearsing it.

My dyed-in-the-wool Cornucopian had no great liking for Chauvinist religion or Yankee virtues; but as he drew near the base of Cape God, bending itself out into the sea under a shroud of blue haze like the maimed claw of a lobster fossilized in the act of scratching its cheek, he curiously envisaged Vinland's eastward-gazing countenance. He had been informed by his Controller, a native of the little Commonwealth, that this Epimethean coastline (from the Kerouac River to Kites Bay) was longer than that of his own majestic state, which occupied 800 miles of purple-mounted latitude claiming the world's noblest trees and longest irrigation arteries as well as more voters and twice as much of the earth's crust as all six New Armorican states blocked together!

In the diminishing scale of eastward passage the aircraft seemed to decline long before it yielded altitude. Opsimath began to feel a boreal shadow from the Markland forehead invisibly beetling the upper horizon, hanging out over the granite brow on his fantastic map like a sperm whale's macrocephalus. At the same time he grew more and more conscious of the concentrating differentiation of the physiognomic crease he was going to land in. Even along the shores of his own Yerba Buena Bay, with its kinds of splendor that excelled all the worndown cities of the East, there was nothing in Cornucopia of such cerebral intensity. Irony here was too crinkled for the happily deeuropeanized mentality.

With little preliminary flourish—no more than a tilt and a change of tone—the sealed featureless cannister, half full of docile adventurers and homecomers strapped to their seats in hermetic transit exactly like thousands of others all over the world at the same moment, makes one swift descending turn of a gyre over the aquamarine shoals that refracted celestial light to the retina of Leviathan's backward-squinting eye. The map rapidly expands itself into a clarifying chart of necks and islands, some connected by bridges and causeways. It looks as if the oldest metropolis of North Atlantis still relies upon an archipelago for protection against a motherland long since outdistanced and renounced.

The magnifying glass encloses faster and faster as it precipitates onto the vastly enlarged mainland, until it gets horizontal bearings on Botolph's skyline, which lies just across the inner channel left for ocean shipping at the very edge of the immense flat blank that has been bulldozed out of the great harbor's former string of Gibraltars to fill a dozen square miles of polluted shallows. This sea-level desert (closer than any other city airport to its mart) usurps the urban function of railroad terminals and steamship berths by attracting a ceaseless screaming circus of containerized human cargo: imported exported and domestic, professional commercial and peregrine, infant youthful mature and moribund, genial and morose, libertine and ascetic, black yellow red and white, female and male. It's an extravagantly smooth platform driving all the others out of business.

Framed by Opsimath's finally slowing portside window a magnified seagoing tanker skirted the westerly border of the field as closely as a canal boat (nearer and higher than freighters seen from the old World's Fair grounds at about the same sea level on Golden Horny Island, before Yerba Buena too had begun its maritime degradation), every detail of its superstructure (though mounted on nothing but a cistern full of homogenized bitumen) more complicatedly interesting and personal than any streamlined monoplane with differentiated cargo. Compared with the ship, in his opinion, still fastened to the seat, his plane, like each of the other knights returning and departing every minute in emblazoned armor, required too many attendants and made too much of a din.

The supercilious Trojan horse in which he sat, now helpless in the hands of its servants, dwarfed and disdained the pettily ambitious vehicles of land. All external structures seemed diachronistic or out of scale, like the ships and ill-assorted vehicles of the cities he had assembled to support his model trains and warplanes before he got more interested in girls.

The noise of coming to earth fell abruptly into sweet silence. Passengers shook themselves free of dream. Opsimath stood up and looked about at his random fellows as they stirred a muted bustle. Presently they would be assuming the vapid cinematic self-importance of performers in the vanity fair that gathered and scattered at every airdrome. But it always seemed to him that the crowd at Bot's Guy Winthrop International was not quite typical.

FIRST MOVEMENT

1
RAFE OPSIMATH'S DISQUISITION LOG

White Quarry College
Yeovil, Mt.
24 Aug 60

[Ad mentorem]

Ipsissimus Charlemagne insists that I keep this diary of my project. Otherwise, he says, he won't accept a banausic thesis. "It's a liberal arts degree we grant," he says, "and our granary is not supposed to be available to the likes of you: so we've got to make it seemly. You'd better find a literary title too."

I suggested "An Atlantean Redaction of the Labyrinth Metaphor", but he said "No use trying to make it seem precocious, young man. You're still an undergraduate. If we attract attention with a title like that, somebody in the office might want to read it. Then I'd get fired and you'd have to shop elsewhere for your degree. Let's just wait and see if and how the text emerges."

I set down this directly attributed quotation to assure myself that he will keep secret this running confession so degrading to one who's too long in the tooth to suffer such humiliation gladly. The struggle between us goes deeper than the issue of my expedient Degree, especially when we're drunk.

The reason I get away with my duplicitous strategy is that it gives him an opportunity to subsume Economic Man along with all the other kinds of men he's always subsumed. He'll go to his grave with the upper hand over every branch of Wissenschaft. I'm pretty clever at letting it be known how smart I am, but I play up to the experts—whereas he does so by playing them down. With "morphological understanding" he masters the history of everything. He can afford to be generous in the appreciation of his nominal peers because he classifies them all as specialists.

No doubt he'd have made a reputation in management or politics if he hadn't left the honors to those who owe him a living for the sake of his elite contribution to Atlantean culture. His distinction as the world's greatest Director is betokened by ungodly hours and clothes safety-pinned together like John the Baptist's lion skin. But this prophet of the Last Testament is so alert in his recognitions, so charming in the kindnesses of his personal address, and so openhanded in the fist-clenching matters of everyday life that he seems not only unselfish but also unselfcentered. People mistake his sympathies, despite magisterial dismissal of every symbol and institution they believe in. He'd be lionized by a certain minor category of the public if his keen and faithful discriminations were not so confusingly digressive. But his friends know that the only job he'd ever put himself out for would be that of top dog in the Theater of the World. And even for that he wouldn't condescend to take out nomination papers.

I'd hate to be his employee or employer—yet he's just the kind of teacher I need. He knows more than I do about everything except steam cleaners, and I must admit that he understands me better than I understand him.

25 Aug

Ippy was as tactful as a woman in getting me to yield to this undignified collateral assignment. When I hinted that keeping a diary would make me feel like a schoolgirl, and that he might as well take attendance at his classes if he wanted to demean a mature businessman who'd volunteered in good faith and paid in advance to sit at his feet, he softened me up with the plea that "It's no diary I want: just a journal to prove that you found your abstract labyrinth on a real journey." With tolerable tolerance he bent my stiffnecked pride. My instructions among others are to comment upon his following justifications for treating me like a child, and to offer myself respective apologies for putting up with his tyranny.

First, I've never taken the Common Course in Expository Writing, and if I'm to be excused from that abuse of my maturity (under some other instructor), my Mentor (Ippy) must vouch for my Proficiency on the basis of written discourse more expressive of my humanity than whatever I may produce in what he calls my "muckraking journalism of Churchyard monkey-business". (He affects to remember The Street of the financial district as "Churchyard" rather than Graveyard.)

Second, this pot that calls the kettle black seems to be suggesting that the toil of circumstantial writing may purge my poetic libido of its weedy tendency to obfuscate the analytic process by play of mind. Indulgence of my imaginative impulses in a chronicle of the scaffolding will make it easier for me to keep a tight hand on construction of the Senior Research Disquisition itself. He's even in hope that this log of my navigation will forestall unnecessary scribblings in the Opsimath correspondence he's paid to cope with until I graduate.

Third, I should welcome this homework exercise as a means for springing loose the metaphorical faculties of my misdirected mind. This remedial screed is to be a well-grounded perfectly confidential lightning rod.

His fourth proposition clinches my acquiescence. If I don't like to write about the provenance and context of my inhumanistic treatise I'd perhaps be happier purchasing my sheepskin at a business college in southern Cornucopia, or maybe someplace in Ohio, where my mean ambition would be sincerely respected.

It has taken a heap of sifting to extract this orderly list from all his friendly ramblings in the classroom, on the grass, and in the cafeteria, and in his room or mine so late at night that even West Coast insomniacs are asleep. Like everything else at White Quarry College these sessions often take place in the presence of other students. I'm the only one who stands up to him, taking my lumps without a flinch. For all his charming camaraderie, I soon divined that it's an insolence to disagree with him unless your protests are couched in appreciation of his own previous utterances or in the zeal to protect his line of thought. I save face by virtue of the fact that he's old enough to deserve customary respect.

26 Aug

As soon as I promised to keep this log he showed his warm motherly side again. Once more he was helpful in every way, nicely sympathetic to my divergent interests, delicate with my indelicate sensibilities. To be sure, I'm only a mouse at the cat's big cheese, and he saves his claws for the rats. With this log I can make believe I'm getting in my nibbles—even though I'm pretty sure he's bluffing when he warns that he may check up on my fidelity by actually taking a look at what I'm writing whenever he feels like making a stab at his tutorial duty.

Ippy declares that the promise was exacted even more directly for my own benefit than the rest of this White Quarry self-discipline. Much to my amazement, after these few pages, I already think he's right. By forcing me to consider my perspective at each reach and narrows of my progress, especially at times of flagging will or expired inspiration, this continual review will help me recall the gamut of dim and headstrong visions that started me chugging up this Amazon. And successive surveys of my progressive discoveries (which will attain to no eminence from which to view the whole of the watershed) will forearm me against the doubts of an armchair critic who has never seen either the forest or the trees.

At the outset (before gathering my data) I am expected to explain my motives for choosing the subject. But I must remark that a most gratifying indulgence of this ancillary obligation has been Ippy's tacit permission to reserve any statement or recapitulation of my theme for the Disquisition itself, which will be the sole surviving monument to all this work. I'm always grateful to a boss who doesn't insist upon knowing what I'm going to do before I do it. I so love Ippy for such latitude in the journalistic function that I shall now go out of my way to set forth ultimate purposes as frankly as such amalgams can ever be sorted out (short of psychoanalysis), in case he should sometime really take it into his head to become my reader. Hereinafter I shall be studious to account for my prejudices and predilections.

My entelechtual destination is a Master's degree in Business Administration. *Sine qua non.* But the longer I postpone the Business part of my curriculum the less life I'll have wasted to approach that achievement. It's a joy to find the White Quarry way. You can't get an M B A without first getting your Bachelor's ticket, but thanks be to God it's not necessary to go through the fraudulent tedium of *undergraduate* Bus Ad.

On the other hand, my particular Senior Research Disquisition, which so mootly meets the requirements of Ippy's Atlantean Studies program, may economically justify the self-indulgence of buying my first diploma at the world's most expensive correspondence school. For it will address elements of genuine financial edification as well as provide the foundation for a future Master's thesis therein! Without being wasted, my Liberal Arts matter can be alienated and used again more properly as advanced groundwork at some singleminded institute of Business ambition.

Once I can call myself an M B A I won't get too many questions about my academic history. If people don't probe for dates they'll assume that aforementioned undergraduate Liberal Artistic studies were an excusable indiscretion of my flaming youth, subsequently redeemed by the presumably undivided vocation of maturity.

In short, Mein Hochst Geehrter Privatdocent, yours is the most efficient way for your pupil toward the defensive credentials a man nowadays needs for passwords. The truth is that I'm a little anxious about my future. Within two or three years destiny will make itself definitely known to the Tubalcain Manufacturing Company, Inc.: we'll either be going broke in compulsive anticipation of growth or facing radical changes of equity structure. Whatever the event, in any contingency, I'll need my M B A .

27 Aug

You ask why a Master's degree in Business should be wanted by one who's already the president of a company, especially in a countereducational society where he's already reaping more gain than Johann Wolfgang von Goethe?

I remind you that our business culture has now forsworn its native doctrine. It has come to the sorry point that it accepts without debate the academic assumption that you can't learn anything without taking courses. And you have to take them "for credit". Wafers of knowledge must be swallowed in quarterly finales of devotion, but they are consecrated only ex post facto at a grand retroactive communion— wherein the years of tentative assimilation are consummated all at once. The whole of education is regarded as infinitely greater than the sum of its parts, none of which in any case can be acquired through the untutored sweat of your own brow or through your independent experience of the very same books and more besides.

The funny thing is that even the remaining autodidacts among managers of large-scale "economic tension" have become touchingly diffident about their own judgment in personnel matters. By misappropriation of the principle of delegation they leave most of the choice of their assistants and successors to a winnowing process largely controlled by the very schoolmen whom they despise as "theoretical" (an epithet more scornful in their dictionary than their otherwise synonymous term "academic")—though they should be aware that the catechism used by the professors to "train" their students is founded on nothing sounder than dogmatized opinions as to more or less recent business habits. It seems to me that my vocation is an art that needs as its critics theoretical artisans, practicing in its ateliers, not blackboard business scholars engaged in the counterproductive pretensions of profession.

But as long as the conquistadors of commerce and industry piously defer to these priests in the unnatural selection that so largely determines managerial evolution, few sports will survive unsterilized. So if I want to rise further in our country's least exclusive calling I must take on the docility of a serpent and the cunning of a deferential peasant. When I finally submit myself to the pedagogues of Business I'll keep a straight face, chew on the jargon, and excrete the bullshit.

Nevertheless, I own to weakness in the financial specialties, and there must be some interesting tax accounting or useful usurious mathematics in a few of the M B A courses I'll eventually have to face. When the time comes I won't be loathe to study quantitative prosody, learn everything I can about form and technique in the international art of numbers. "Money is a kind of poetry." says my favorite poet (whose essays Ippy told me to read)—one who ought to know, being counsel to a Charter Oak insurance company. By classroom simulation I can master boardroom metaphors in dollars cardinal and ordinal, in vaticinations of "present value" (a recondite calculus of relativity which so generalizes classical accounting that it computes the affect of time upon one's prehension of the dollar), and in caesural lines of credit.

Of course I'll abstract my own principles from the textbook cases, without letting on that my mnemonic crutch for examinations is imagistic; and by mouthing the idioms of our chrematistic trivium and quadrivium I'll be able to pretend that I'm not too proud to bow down and worship also at the feet of "marketing" pundits. I'll close my eyes and repeat whatever rosary the professors like to hear. When I'm inclined to reason with them—I'll learn how to hold my tongue; I'll find ways to express my doubt by statistics. That kind of homage will be far more galling than my present ignominy at the hands of His Grace the Cardinal Director of Dramatic Poesy, who at least doesn't set himself up as a Doctor.

Yet if Walt and I go broke, or otherwise liquidate the Tubalcain corporation, I'll be forty-one or forty-two and fading into the welter of executives and salesmen "between jobs" who, without the advantage of certified specialization, feel less secure than migratory field hands. The value of my incomparable experience in extemporaneous ad lib leadership can hardly be imagined by potential employers who have risen a corporate thermometer and have never had to save a payroll from extinction or assume sole responsibility for uncontrollable circumstances (as well as the problems they cause), such as those irreconcilable or unconscionable conditions of history geography or psychology that awaken no interest in academic model-makers. The few at the top who know what I'm referring to are the most likely to recognize me for what I am, but they are usually not quick to offer a foothold to the kind of rivalry they have reason to worry about; and the penultimate officers of a big company naturally can't stomach at the antepenultimate level a past master who's accustomed to overseeing and evaluating men like themselves.

And so, whereas most suppliants claim the experience of responsibilities they're really innocent of, I shall have to bowdlerize my résumé, or at least tailor several narrowed versions, in order to downplay my career as a Commander-in-Chief. (It goes hard to hide my light under a bushel!) Only the ballast of an M B A will compensate for the priceless phrases I'll have edited out of my suits for a lucrative command.

By the same token, any small company that might want me as president or general manager—distinctly for those same unceremonious qualifications—would be obliged to satisfy its bankers; and bankers are rightly wary of crude simpleminded producers who haven't understood the need for educated formalities as a business enlarges itself. Nowadays for hardheaded sponsors an M B A is the only evidence of enlightenment.

If on the other hand we sold our outfit lock stock and barrel to a conglomerate or large manufacturer, even with contracts to keep our jobs, without the commonplace M B A cachet to back up my humble opinions, I'd die on the vine. I'd suffer all the bitter frustration of subordinating myself to educated staff officers at corporate headquarters—with never a chance to display my style of coordination.

Supermerger is therefore a more intriguing possibility than merger or submerger. The theatrical genius supervising what he calls my "Senior Parenthesis" will surely grasp this third alternative for a small company short of working capital: survival by expansion, and expansion by acquisition. The more assets and the larger your base for growth, the better your credit. In our case more capital would energize the quantum jump to an orbit of self-perpetuating success. Aggrandizement in turn attracts more capital, just as whistling in the dark proves that you're unafraid.

So I'd do well to seek out a tired and undermanaged outfit, perhaps an old fully amortized metal working plant here in the East, larger than Tubalcain itself, with assets or credit lying fallow. If I could induce the owners to put up their stock against ours at some mutually interesting ratio, I might parlay our joint properties into something much more important than the sum of two parts. But of course they'd have to be convinced in advance that I'd be better able than they to employ their formerly accumulated wealth.

It's not a case of the smaller swallowing the larger. Their people would hold majority stock in the succeeding new corporation. (After all, the Edenfield family owns most of the firm that I already preside over.) As a matter of fact, when everything's said and done you might whisper that it amounted to having them buy us out. Of course any deal must guarantee Walt and me our present jobs in the larger organization. It would have been my leadership and Walt's engineering (as well as our invigorating share of the steam cleaner market) that had interested our new associates in the first place. I'd have made them glad to absorb our liabilities and provide the cash for multiplying our efforts, in the expectation of improved net asset value per share and a better rate of return than they got under their own management.

But mine alone, who came to the company as a sweeper of floors and walloper of acid drums, is the burden of seeking out such luckily rich and diffident strangers, to say nothing of negotiating an improbable (but not unprecedented) amalgamation and thereafter maintaining the necessary ascendancy over a wary board of directors. As an educated professional, Walt has no appetite for any responsibility beyond that of his own personal performance.

Naturally it would be even harder thus to persuade Protestican stockholders to swap their known shares for the mere hope of greater gains than it would be to get a new job somewhat worthy of my self-esteem. If I need an M B A for the executive-recruiting agencies, I'd need it all the more for the Tybbot credit reporter who'd be nosing around our Tubalcain premises to evaluate my management capabilities. The dynamically friendly but unorthodox personality of Raphael Opsimath certainly requires the putative stabilization of M B A culture. It would not always be remembered that I wasn't born to it.

Anyway, life's too short not to regard every task as a millstream.

I don't like to squander my kinetic energy. I dam it up for swimming or fishing or watering my stock—and then make it turn a workwheel as it runs down to the level of my destiny. But that means that my motives are mixed; and even on the pleasure principle I can't put one before another. A logbook is not the place to analyze my psychical drives or evasions, which are none of Ippy's business.

28 Aug

However, if I can't give a single real reason for choosing the PARITY CORPORATION as subject of the study that will satisfy a final requirement for Liberal Arts on my way down the flume, I can at least offer several good ones. They may be discussed in provisionally ordinal terms.

Permit me to label as ultimate the motive I have already mentioned—to wit, some preliminary milling with the grist for a future Master's thesis at whatever dismal institution my Body of Fate may find expedient. This level of intention relates strategy to a choice of tactics.

Next, my ulterior motive derives from the hypothesis that Parity befits my extramural plans uniquely. Or rather that Tubalcain may find a place in their extramural plans—if I play my cards with the savvy I hope to cultivate in the next couple of years. Perhaps my real-life business with Parity will be to save the enterprise that I've spent twelve years on. Assuming that the intelligence I'm about to gather proves indeed propitious.

Thus to my ultra motive for working on Parity. The exploration of Tubalcain's future possibilities is a matter of perfectly legitimate business expense. Walt fully agrees that I am justified in improving the occasion of my private education by charging much of this trip to administrative overhead. The Convocation is not a business convention, but it's one stop of an Eastern itinerary on behalf of the Tubalcain Corporation. Even Internal Revenue will allow that most of my travel expenses should not be taken out of my own pocket.

Leaving Parity aside, I have plenty of company business for this reconnaissance. To be or not to be, to liquidate or merge, to borrow or to sell: these are all sacred questions recognized by law in the life of even the tiniest fictitious person. The problems of our corporation are always with me. In my unremitting preoccupation with the talents entrusted to me—to make them compound faster than average in a growing economy that no one understands save in retrospect—on any trip to the archaic but populous East I keep my eyes open for some well located floor space. Since New Armorica's high freight rates, expensive weather, and endemic resistance to change all reinforce the national opinion that it barely survives as a backwater of the industrial current, the prices of fine old manufacturing properties in these quaint little states are mostly depressed. If we can't finance a virgin facility closer to the center of the Eastern market, I may find a good mature widow who could be fixed up to serve us at a bargain-basement rent or token real-estate taxes. There's still cheap skilled labor in many of these old mill towns.

Even up here in northern Montvert I look around wherever I go, talking to everybody. There's even the remnant of a one-track railroad that wants to stay in business. I believe one might wheedle better tariffs by playing it against the truck lines in petitions to the Interstate Commerce Commission.

Of course I don't expect to find anything near here—Yeovil, Yeovil Corners, Yeovil Flat, Lower Yeovil, Yeovil Bend, or Yeovil Summit (which is little more than a siding of the French River and Champlain Bay Railroad, where the eastbound to Bournemouth used to wait for the Montreal train to pass and the freights had their extra engines taken off after the steep pull up from Hector Falls). Not counting dairy production or lumbering, there's never been any industry in the Yeovils; and there's no longer any to speak of down in woolly Joppa (which still looks as open to sin and shootouts as a placerville in the Cordillera, though bereft of half its population), where all the granite-cutting sheds used to be and where two or three small sawmills now have less than they can handle from the logging that remains. White Quarry, up this way, was never a success—maybe a spurious vein, or too deep and narrow; or too soft for anyone but sculptors, yet without the plastic qualities of the truly white lacustrine sublimestone quarried twenty miles to the southwest.

In fact there's nothing of industrial interest on the entire "French side" of this piedmont divide, where the French River starts winding toward its pass through the Green Mountains to Lake Van Luck (which Monsieur Charlemagne tells me is named with a redundant Anglo-Dutch corruption of Champlain's *Lac Van + Lake*), draining naturally into the Atlantic by way of the St Lawrence. But there is plenty of industrial archeology on the "English side" of this ridge, watershed of the English River, a tributary of the Pequod (named from the mouth up), which reaches the same ocean about seven thousand miles of coastline further south. Starting at Hector Falls (after a French Anglophile), still the base of world-renowned Hector Valve & Gauge Company, the old waterpower sites are scattered in charming irregular digs as far to the east and south as I care to drive my rented Little

King. Therefore my business expenses resume as soon as I cross the saddle of this misnamed Marble Mountain, not a quarter of a mile from here by foot but a mile and a half by wheel.

29 Aug

So I don't need the Parity excuse for most of my delightful travels. But in a few days I head south to the heart of power, before swinging back up to Botolph where I take my plane home seventeen days from now. I've got all I can out of Parity's stockholder reports, and the next step is to start my real research at the Securities and Exchange Commission files in Washington. Archives are not to my taste, but it can't be helped, and I'll take some time off for education at the Smithsonian and for amusement on the Senate subway. Scholarship will be tolerable if I can learn to read between the legally reduced lines of blooming buzzing paratruth.

But I'll also spend a day or two in the Port Campion area with Jim Riata, the Midatlantic manufacturers' representative who still condescends to handle our line, and Fred Tracy our salaried Eastern service man, who has failed to make himself into the field sales manager we gave him title to, shaking down instead into nothing more than a philosopher-slave to Jim and three or four other independent gentlemen who loathe their mechanical and administrative problems and are always well pleased to have him perform special demonstrations or emergency repairs on their behalf, seeing that he doesn't mind getting dirty or talking to technicians.

At the S E C I'll just blindly start a card file of past and present Parity interests, principal stockholders, directors, and all the other names of friend or foe that I can glean from the statutory 10K disclosure reports of this singularly enigmatic closed-end investment trust. Thereupon I'll take a nice parlor car ride up to New Uruk and visit the Curb Exchange library to see if I can pick up any further clues. Only then shall I make up my mind whether or not to beard the mastermind (if there is one), or his collaborators, in their Smart Avenue headquarters. I'd like to test their reflexes anyway, in case Tubalcain someday offers itself to one of their distal "affiliates".

Northerly on the way back to Botolph I have other more proximal prospects and problems to pay my way. For one thing, I'll take my first tour through the wealthy little state of Pequod, keeping a couple of promises I've made to Ted McKee our Sales Manager, who's been imploring me to visit Tractor Equipment Distributors in Charter Oak and try to dissuade them from holding out for an exclusive franchise.

(One of the absurdities of our tiny ancillary industry is that the dealers are often more powerful than the manufacturer.) Ted thinks that if we can just sell them a gas-fired Model 360 for their own shop they'll be impressed enough to agree to handle the entire line according to our cardinal sales policy, on the same terms as everyone else. T E D is the best in its field, exactly the kind of first-class distributor we've been shooting for in that trading area. They'd open the whole Pequod construction equipment market to our high-pressure machines. And so forth. It's an old story, which I've heard more than once from every one of our territories: the Sales Department wants help from the president to sign up a princely jobber who controls a key clientele! But of course it's worth a try. And it's always important to encourage Ted's optimism.

Yet I do wish he had more heart for the less glamorous automotive trade. He may be right that it's a limited segment of our potential market; yet, despite his lofty goals, that's still where our bread and butter is. He comes out of the materials-handling business and he knows all the mill supply houses in the country, but when he's bending over backwards to avoid overemphasizing his familiar trade channels (which are the least important to our growth) all he can get excited about is the maintenance requirements of earth-moving and farm equipment. His unacknowledged distaste for lowly automotive jobbers, who don't want to understand the machinery they're involved with and whose language is limited to the argot of auto parts, can't be concealed from the old automotive reps we still depend upon for thirty or forty percent of our volume.

The automotive jobbers are more like jackals or hyenas than cooperative wolves. Next to food, the market for auto parts and basic tools (but not for its sidelines like steam cleaners) is probably the broadest and least orderly in our consuming civilization, a conflation of wholesale and retail sales wherein the terminal vendors are always scrounging for credit, starving for collections, and cutting prices as the chief means of competition—in open violation of their "Fair Trade" agreements with honest manufacturers like Tubalcain. It's an unsavory jungle for a decent rational sales manager with business ideals who preaches the doctrine that "clean" sales and adequate profits are absolutely essential for dealers who are expected to provide their customers with factory-approved installation and service—just what most of them fail to do for us. But there are times when Ted should turn a blind eye to the chiselers who shave their own margins to sell our small Model 101, which is a simple unit, more or less comparable to our generic competition's but famous for sustaining all kinds of abuse in shops and service stations. (My double standard is a hypocritical secret that can be confided only to my diary and perhaps hinted to our next sales manager, whom I think I've already got my eye on.) Ted truly believes that our missionary work for A NEW CONCEPT IN STEAM CLEANING is going to revolutionize the maintenance of machines and structures all over the world. Until that great day arrives, however, we're in no position to rigidly scorn every small customary irregularity among the cynical villains who labor in our vineyard with churlish indifference to our honor. The brutal truth is that our best apostles are soldiers of fortune who have consented to wear our colors into the fray while they're really fighting for their lines of auto parts and accessories, and are as likely as not to emerge from battle shamelessly bearing the gages of our rivals.

It is embarrassing but fortunate (in the short run) that our Northeast manufacturers' rep makes no bones about his opinion that it's a stupid affectation to go around talking about our Simon-pure sales policy in his scrabbling ruins of nineteenth century power. Ray Lagniappe is sincerely proud of our line as the creme de la creme, but he admits that after thirty years he remains a compulsive two-bit automotive equipment peddler, and he's chary of highsounding "industrial" and "construction" trade channels out of his depth. Every month his commissions lead all the rest (and he knows it) because he understands that the proles who run garages and gas stations—the only demographic group already acquainted with primitive steam cleaning—are not enamored of complicated engineering. To them new equipment is nothing but a necessary evil, and the main question (after price) is how much downtime they'll have to put up with.

So Ray's one sales theme is RELIABILITY. There we all agree that our older steam-vapor models are paragons. One clause of our policy he enforces better than any other rep (to his own immediate benefit): he insists that his jobbers buy several 101s for initial goodfaith "floor stock."

But we can't break him of doing their work for them—beating the bushes, conducting all the demonstrations with his own trailer-mounted unit, and actually closing many of their orders. Instead of making a serious attempt to motivate and train the jobber's salesmen he does the selling for them. I certainly agree with Ted that Ray works much too hard without multiplying his personal efforts. (Even doctors have learned to use parallel consulting rooms.) But I wish Ted could understand why Ray laughs at all our hopes to modernize his methods. He knows that enlightened policies are designed for long-term growth, and that we'll replace him with company salesmen as soon as we no longer need his labors with the small-fry.

Nevertheless Ray will be delighted to see some of our big machines on his commission statements, if we can help him sign up Tractor Equipment Distributors, the largest and best-financed of their kind in all N A . He'd begin to realize the benefits of a well-managed retail sales force, and he might be persuaded to live longer than his present life expectancy by taking a vacation every year or two.

In any case, to have T E D flying our flag would strengthen my hand in any higher level corporate negotiations.

30 Aug

As to my Eastern terminus, Ray has been pressing me to spend some time on his stamping grounds at the very hub of our national past in order to consider at first hand his most persistent request. He wants us to maintain stock for his territory in some public warehouse that he can draw upon. It's all very plausible from his angle: with an ever-renewed carload of units at his immediate disposal he can overcome the disadvantage of being three days' delivery time from Brotherly, where we already keep an East Coast inventory from which to fill small orders that we don't ship directly from the factory back in Londonbridge. Customers in a hurry are glad to pick up merchandise at their own expense. He says he could save the sales we're now losing to competitive quick-fix artists. He hints that we wouldn't have half Jim Riata's lazy Midatlantic volume if it weren't for the advantage of a local warehouse down in Brotherly.

The intercoastal steamship line we use for those consignments still serves Botolph too. Shipping all the way by water, he argues, we can save enough on freight to absorb the costs of storage, handling, and short-haul trucking to the hinterlands. The Sales Department backs him up on this one. There's no doubt such an arrangement would stimulate New Armorica sales. So I have agreed to accompany him on a visit to the Atlantic Market and Terminal Warehouse.

In the end I'll have to find a way to let him down easy. We need Ray's loyalty. But my Controller has armed me for the debate, in which I'll eventually be forced to disclose a foregone decision. Ray will sulk for a few days, but he'll probably come around. He's a good-humored skinflint, and when I finally give him the solid financial reasons I wouldn't be surprised if he accepted my refusal with a better understanding of the problem than his educated clean-cut high-minded sales manager has so far evinced.

It's a typical four-dimensional situation. I marvel that even most blue-chip companies haven't until recently fully grasped Pierre DuPont's analysis of industrial usury. He enriched the First Law of Talents (conservation of dollars) with a Second Law that establishes something like an inversion of entropy called *Return on Investment*. All businesses calculate net profit as percent of sales, but it doesn't matter how much profit you make if it takes too long. R O I is the measurement of economic power, proportioning both mass and energy to time, which is no less costly in itself. *Zeit an sich* is the Controller's motto. As it is, we've got too much capital invested in the Brotherly inventory, considering its limited velocity (known in business as turnover).

We're not offering fungible commodities. My most important achievement as president has been to get our line reduced to half a dozen basic models; but we are still obliged to provide for a number of contingent requirements: oil-fired or gas-fired boilers (for either natural or manufactured gas), electric or gasoline motors, stationary or portable mountings. It's very difficult to predict the assortment of specifications that will be called for. The Controller must judge from misleadingly small historical data, resisting but not rejecting the self-serving hope with which each field rep estimates his own favored component of the Eastern regional sales forecast. Obviously the variants we assemble and ship for inventory should be those at the center of the demand curve; but at best some items lie idle too long, while we lose sales when others have not been made available.

But the worst of it is that these packets of potential energy (though frozen dollars, already spent to bring them into existence at their point of sale, plus the margin required to pay their share of everything else) can none of them be liquidated as cash kinetic energy for at least seven weeks—the time it takes to get an economical carload accumulated from our daily production, transferred to the pier, loaded into the ship according to its sparsely dated schedule, transported around North Atlantis through the Panama Canal, navigated up the South River to Brotherly, off-loaded, drayed to the warehouse, and speculatively stowed where it can be released or trucked one unit at a time to various points of display or final installation. Even then we won't get our investment back for another ten days (when our 2% cash discount expires); or else we'll wait at least twenty more (usually over fifty) to get our return. The Controller calculates that our East Coast turnover is now less than a quarter of what it is in the eleven western states. Yet Ted is willing to duplicate the Brotherly distribution system at Botolph in order to gain a mere two or three days in the delivery time for local orders in a single territory!

What we really need is an Eastern plant. Our business east of the Mississippi has grown to two thirds of the total. Walt might agree to hire the kind of production manager we need for standardized manufacturing—at that sufficient distance from the fountainhead of "improvements". Somehow I've got to break Walt of the elegant jobshop innovations that sometimes still inhibit efficient production runs. Walt and his old gang won't be so traumatized by assembly-line techniques if the full conversion takes place on the far side of the continent. I might be able to evade the appallingly fundamental conflict with my dear friend against which I've been steeling myself for all too long.

"Reminds me of Roosevelt's boys against Churchill's, on the Combined Staff, about the best way to use our manpower for a second front." says Ippy, beginning one of his fascinating digressions that lasts a hundred times as long as the brief allusion that touches it off, and leaves me breathless with a sense of his intuitive typology. His way of flattering me.

On the other hand a second location would present me with whole fields of management problems in which I've had no experience. For instance, to make any such leap we'd have to justify ourselves to canny lenders or investors. Walt and I must both be prepared for a curtailment of the freedom we're so accustomed to—he in his experimental engineering and I in everything else!

Under the singleminded scrutiny of money men interested only in R O I for the capital at their disposal, he must master his moral and aesthetic compulsion to specify expensive parts and materials of the best possible quality when they will obviously out-excel and outlive the mechanical ensemble to which they contribute, and give way to systemic considerations of the entire commercial enterprise. By the same token, my own more or less uncriticized plans and sometimes impatient decisions will have to find rationalization more plausible than *ad hominem* psychology; they will be probed and ratified by some procedure more formal than a preoccupied nod from Walt, who so imprudently trusts me as his attorney in all affairs of management. Even without losing our legal sovereignty, we may have narrowminded financiers looking over our shoulders, asking for budgets and long-range plans, insisting upon reasons for everything we tell them.

They won't be nearly as sympathetic as Ipsissimus Charlemagne, nor settle for a journal of whatever may pass through my mind while I'm on the job.

31 Aug

But there's something we need more than a Master's degree or a new distributor or a second factory, and a successful quest for it would repay the expense of a degree in Atlantean Studies for all our employees. We have an acute defect at the very heart of the part that's the heart of the machine at the heart of our recent success: an unreliable diaphragm in the high-pressure water pump of our Model 360. I'm as likely to find the solution in New Armorica, by some quirk of Yankee ingenuity, as anywhere on earth. Western consultants and engineers have failed us; patent searches have revealed nothing to suggest the solution.

To this engineering problem Walt is almost willfully blind. He refuses to admit that we have an essential technical difficulty with his pride and joy, which has otherwise projected us far ahead of all competition. The machine's extraordinary performance depends upon his hydraulic system, the basis of all our exclusive claims to the new market we've been spending so much money to develop.

Tubalcain's previously nurtured reputation for "reliable trouble-free steam cleaners" has been the foundation of our sales strategy; yet this pump is still giving our customers more trouble than all other service problems combined. For the first time in company history we have chronically angry users. Our technical and marketing effort has been concentrated on the 360 for five years: everything hangs upon its continuing acceptance. Yet as its field population approaches a thousand—most of the machines no more than two years old—our pump failures are becoming a byword in the trade.

The production people begin to balk at the series of modifications that Walt has said would clear up the trouble. Much as they love him, they've suffered cascades of frustration at his unending design changes. But they may be choosing precisely the wrong occasion to rebel against his so-called perfectionism. He continues to assure me, with that sweet humorous smile of his, that "it's only a matter of finding rubber with a little more woof to its warp!" He makes gentle jokes, but I have nightmares of catastrophe. I must anticipate the consequences of a possible flaw in Walt's basic design. Has he dreamed up an heroic heart that requires supernatural tissue to endure the pounding fatigue of its early youth? Does the whole NEW CONCEPT IN STEAM CLEANING hang upon a fairy tale invention?

It may be that we need a whole new concept of PUMP! If we're going to keep going even long enough to sell out, it will be absolutely necessary to triple the longevity of the organ that drives water through the heating coils under high pressure. It's too late to fall back on our line of vapor-pressure machines, good as they are. They may support Ray Lagniappe in New Armorica, but they can't generate our national outreach. Unless Tubalcain remains a High Pressure outfit it will revert to the secondary regional status in which it dwelt back in the days when I was hired as a maintenance laborer, down at Eden Grove—practically at land's end, in a shed near the old S P turntable—before we moved up to a proper factory on the industrial margin of Golden Bay.

Oddly enough, it's at the opposite land's end that I'm going to finish off this excursion with a busy vacation, and for reasons related to much that I have touched upon. It will be a chance to chew my preliminary cud of Parity notes and lay out the lines of my Disquisition. Dogtown happens to be my Controller's birthplace, and he says I'll find it "interesting" to compare with my native San Ricardo (adjacent to Eden Grove), which is also an old fishing port on a small cape. I guess he's aware that I sometimes think him too romantic for his job, and that I don't dare encourage his impatience for improvements by praising him to his face; but I try to drop him hints that I take little heed of the complaints I hear about the systems and procedures he's installing. I'm glad to be able to please him by accepting his advice about my personal sojourn.

Dogtown's only an hour north of Botolph. I can always change my mind after I see the place and smell it. I wouldn't be loathe to find an excuse to come back up here for my scant rustication. New Armorica's not as cramped as I used to think it was, and Montvert has taken better care of itself than the other states—formerly through sheer cussed Protestican reaction (even when almost every other federated commonwealth was voting for solidarity), but recently by way of deciding to live off the lovers of its greenery and snow, many of whom have come to stay, including educated Catholicrats who are about to tip the balance toward a liberal cultivation of conservative prohibitions. By proscribing the kind of rugged individualism that expresses itself as billboards they have preserved charming foregrounds that magnify the continuous ranges of small pasture-footed mountains close behind them.

But I suppose the uniqueness of the beauty here is no more or less extraordinary than a lovely woman whose voice you'll never hear. Many goodly homesteads have I seen; everywhere between Pacific and Atlantic I get soundless glimpses that pierce me with nostalgia for places within places that I've never seen before and will never take the trouble to see again—usually details more interesting than beautiful: a skiff tied to its muddy river bank, a platform in the branches of an oak, the bay window of a country railroad station, a homemade suspension bridge for pedestrians over a creek, a grass-lapped rock at the turn of a path, the tiny brick library of a prairie village, the second-story pulley clothesline of a shabby gray house with broad verandas, a ledge I'd like to climb above a meadow, a cat creeping along the pickets of a weathered fence. Two weeks in the hollow of this incomparable valley, my second Convocation here, haven't reduced my nameless yearning, nor quenched my wonder at what no one possesses.

When I forget my dread of the winters here, when I ignore the community opprobriums of small-minded individualists, I'm sometimes bemused with insubstantial schemes for acquiring a permanent right to the breathtaking peace of this discretely recultivated state, which as a striving congeries of lawless clearings at the bottoms of forested hills once fought off two sovereign colonies to become an independent republic. I must ward off such foolish dreams. These visual loves make me promiscuous. I should remind myself that Montvert has already sold some of its beauty to the skiing culture, in order to preserve the rest of what its independence has been traded for.

"The beauty of my business is that it doesn't depend on beauty." I told Ippy today.

"It's the beauty in your business that you've got to guard against." was his instant rejoinder. It was a mistake to have shown him my poems. "You haven't fallen far enough yet." he added.

"I haven't always been a president!" I retorted, and made him smile most disarmingly. He affects an opinion that the poet is my true self.

Well, if so, I'm warped beyond redemption, because as this workbook will no doubt prove, I'm more likely to notice ditches and culverts than wildflowers. Up here I spend more time hanging around the waterpowered sawmill than gazing at the fantastically clarified sunsets on the French side, behind those purple-shadowed alps of green that have superseded the overwhelming Rockies as my touchstone of skylined beauty. It's because the artifacts of husbandry have so long refined the lower mountainsides that I love landscape here the better. I'll stop anywhere to contemplate a working barn.

The value of a place lies in its works: that's the belief of mine that saves me from aesthetical apolaustics. Ippy Charlemagne has no quarrel with me there. Atlanteans spend more of their lives at works than at loves and leisures. For the most part, like other peoples, even as colonists and pioneers, they've added their works to what has been left behind by others. Amid all the insolent destruction and careless deterioration, it's the diachronistic manifestation of human investment that excites my desire for a place. Every poem I've thought of writing is about either the stratification or the juxtaposition of a community's spent capital.

There are no tempting mountains in Dogtown, but, from what I hear, plenty of ruins. Since as my mentor's refuge it's the place I mail my homework to, I've often tried to visualize him there receiving my weekly opinions about his lessons. I wonder if he's ever off guard. As he refuses to install a telephone, I must beard him in his lair, with a bottle of Scotch, and take my chances. I hope he'll consent to go out to dinner with a student.

Because he says there's a man in town who may be able to solve our pump problem. Well it's another excuse for me to indulge my undisciplined curiosity about Charlemagne's supersagacity. Even in a small town, how can the exiled sage of the stage be smart enough to know the kind of sage I've been searching for?

But I also have some honest company business there. I promised Ray to look into our garbage-cooking problem on some pig farm.

2
THE
VAN

Before the end of the three-minute cab ride from the station Opsimath was determined to alter his vacation plan. Making his reservation on the telephone he had been cautious enough not to commit himself for more than one night, though it was in his nature to respond more generously to such a cooperative welcome of his patronage. Without surprise or interrogation the very nice lady had promised him a large room with the furnishings he required. Well, he could use the occasion to pay one call on Ipsissimus Charlemagne, make one inquiry about nineteenth century pump ideas, and take one glance at the garbage-boiler; then he'd return to the metropolis, scan the Norumbega Business School library, and go on back to the peace and beauty of Montvert for his studious solitude. He sighed at the unsurprising disappointment, for his luggage was now full of heavy paper and he had hoped to flop down in one place for the rest of his time off. The tired wanderer seeking beautiful comfort was in no mood for the likes of Dogtown.

Riding a forlorn train into this dark place (with such weak lights in streets and houses), his only evidence of concentrated energy had been the same luminous unsleeping squared-off cyclops in fireless hearths that he saw through curtains of all qualities when he walked the night streets at home or anywhere else. By shielding his eyes at the coach window he'd made out shabby back fences (high trails for urban cats) behind cramped and crooked houses. From a short drawbridge without superstructure high over narrow water the roadbed cut through a granite ridge collecting rubbish and junk which seemed to have been jettisoned by several generations of the dwellers on its jagged bluffs. Before coming to a stop the diesel hauling two or three cars as old as Opsimath himself had emerged from the ravine like a hesitant behemoth bleating harshly to the opening silence; brushing with its starboard skirts a tiny windowless variety store beveled to fit the oblique intersection of a local thoroughfare where it dipped and bent between two rises; shouldering past on its left the gate-tender's embankment with his grimy windowed sentry-cube and heap of coal just outside the door; clanked across the street between striped yellow crossing barriers lowered for its arrival with red kerosene lanterns suspended at their centers; and screeched along a canopied platform much longer than necessary for present purposes and hardly better lighted than the deserted obscurity in which it was situated, with puddles from no very recent rain still unevaporated in the hollows of its buckled asphalt.

The wornout depot itself was a good enough specimen of the ample wooden style—peaked roof overhanging all around; trackside bay window still with a telegraph key on the shelf inside—but it was closed for the night, before the last two or three northbound trains, and the baggage facilities looked abandoned entirely. The obsolete semaphore mechanism above the ticket office had never been removed. There appeared to be junked automobiles in the parking lot. So few were the passengers to be dropped—four or five night school students and late-working commuters—that the train's brakes had hardly stopped groaning when it was rumbling away again with the last couple of riders, hooting hoarsely on its way to rest at the Land's End terminal.

The regulars scattered like Virgilian shades, ignoring the one listless battered taxi parked in deepest shadows. It would have made no claim to anyone's attention if Opsimath hadn't been looking for some such. But as he caught a fleeting whiff of peculiar salt air the ununiformed driver did jump out and help him with his bags, apparently more delighted by meeting a stranger than by having a fare. The young man's face and hands were freshly clean, emblems of a sweet cheerfulness that Opsimath had never found among those who served the public in Botolph; but in his dress he looked no more prosperous than his threadbare hack. He struck the canny visitor as a part-time extra, filling in when little business was expected. When he helped his passenger unload, less than half a mile away, he seemed amused to get a tip with his unmetered fee.

During the short trip there was nothing for the curious Cornucopian to see but crooked unswept streets and narrow unrepaired sidewalks crowded by ageing low-ceilinged houses of cracked clapboard that must have been densely packed with families ignorant of grass and trees. Seldom had his topological zeal been so abruptly depressed.

The attentive cabby however was particularly pleased that a man of affairs should be arriving by train and staying at the place that most townspeople had forgotten was a real hotel. "It's mostly gypsies go to the Van." he remarked. "Sometimes Customs men. Down there you'll get to know things about Dogtown that the pilgrims never dream of!" The crypto-pilgrim mumbled his gratification at that prospect. Whereupon he was handed a wallet-worn business card. "Here's the number to call when you need another ride. If you want to see the real thing, ask for me. I can show you scenes the artists never have sense enough to paint."

On the lobby window at about eye level he reconstructed by light from a corner street lamp the sign of the inn against a whitish curtain: an arc of black letters (and stained outlines of lost black letters), decipherable as REDBURN'S NEEDLE, semicircling over a faded facsimile of the flat wooden shuttle used by fishermen to mend their nets; and across the bottom, like the base of a schoolgirl's protractor, the substantive *CaraVANsary*. The cab moved away with a discreet cough or two and Opsimath was left waiting for response to the night bell at a deserted counter.

"You're the feller that called." The old man appearing from the depths was short and thick and very broad, with close-cropped gray hair on a round brown skull. "Could have saved you the long-distance: always plenty of room here because we don't yet have devilvision for the guests. Did the wife tell you that? She said you got our name from the Chamber of Commerce. That means you made two calls. But I guess you can afford it."

Opsimath signed the register, glancing around as the formalities were concluded. Except for a few chrome chairs upholstered in yellow plastic, each with an ashtray stand, the lobby was bare. Telltale traces of red design in the discolored white ceramic floor—precisely small hexagonal tesserae defined by the blackening of dirt at their boundaries—suggested that this entrance lounge had once been much larger, and that the opposite corner had originally been occupied by a diagonal main entrance. A grated rubber mat lay at the foot of straight oak-bannistered stairs.

"She's gone to bed. I take care of things at night. Ring anytime, I don't care, if you need something. Here's an alarm clock, in case you want to get up early. There's phones in the rooms but we're too shorthanded to guarantee to call you exactly the right time." He gestured toward the tiny switchboard and an old upright telephone with the earpiece hanging at its shoulder.

The guest now noticed that all was not quiet beyond the inner wall of the cheerlessly silent lobby. Just as the host was picking up the two suitcases to lead him upstairs the muffled surf of men's laughter resonated in a dim corridor. "That's an entrance to our bar down the other end. In case you're ever desperate. Mostly lumpers and gypsies. But you won't hear them upstairs very often. My son has the liquor license. I tend bar when he has to go to the head. He doesn't like to use the customers' Men's Room, being so stout you know. —Sorry our elevator's on the blink. State inspector won't let us turn it on."

Opsimath insisted on taking the heavier grip, his bulging office carpetbag, and together they stumped up to the third floor, pausing at the middle landing—not so much to catch their breath as for the landlord to get a better look at his customer from under wispily beetling eyebrows like antennas which seemed to grow more and more sensitive as his curiosity ramified. The guest was vividly regretting that he'd turned in his rented car at Botolph just for the sake riding to Dogtown on a train. After one look at the outside of the Van, if he'd been driving, he could have shrugged off his oral contract and perhaps found doorstep comfort at some beach motel on the edge of town.

"I notice you signed in from Londonbridge, Mr Opsimath. I was out to Golden Bay once—mostly over in Yerba Buena though. Worked on his boat."

"Whose boat?"

"Jack London's you know. Had it built across the Bay. The *Lark*. I couldn't stand the way they robbed him blind. Tried to warn him after I quit; but the foreman, he told him I was crazy. Who ever heard of a Jewish ship's carpenter? By the way, the name's Schlossberg—Shelly Schlossberg."

"It was the *Snark,* Mr Schlossberg."

"*Snark,* was it? Something like that. Yes *Snark* I guess. It was no lark, that job. I thought they'd never make it as far as Owhyee even. Interesting times out there before the First War. I just missed the earthquake. No bridges then of course. You took trains and ferries everywhere. For a couple of years I was out at the Iron Works. Got to be a patternmaker. Railroading got into my blood for a while, but I won a contest to be the first one to fly an aeroplane off Double Beacon Peaks, to pay my way back East. Didn't amount to much more than gliding 'cause I made my engine too light. Poor guy, you know, he put heart and soul into that gold-plated little ketch, and he had to give up before he was halfway around the world. She ended up in the Trobriand Islands. They say Malinowski wrecked her."

It was hardly to be expected that Opsimath's former vision of doing his homework in a stately old inn would be revived by any cell in Schlossberg's; yet presently he was shown into a lofty corner room, indeed spacious, out-of-date but clean, with plenty of large thick towels and extra woolen blankets, a floor fully carpeted in worn green, and a vast Continental-looking tile bath in the converted room adjoining.

"The wife said you wanted a writing desk. All I had was this table I used to make models on. I have a workbench now, when I'm not welding you know. This is nothing to look at I realize, but good and sturdy enough I should think. I glued on this linoleum top to make it nice and smooth for you. Hope the lamp's okay. It's got a hundred and fifty watts." Schlossberg also assured Opsimath of all the hot water he wanted, and of steam heat in case of unseasonable chill. Nothing in the room was fresh, except the linen, but it was clear the management had taken pains to satisfy his functional requirements.

"I never went over to your part of the Bay very often. For some reason I was always going the other way, up the river to Baghdad. Funny thing, that's how I learned to make sails—for the hay barges. Fine time in history to take up that trade!" For the first time he chuckled at his wasted life. "I don't like working for yachts." he added. "Here they call them toyboats."

"Got time to sit down and rest a while?" Opsimath asked his host. "It must have been quite a job getting that big table up here." There were arm chairs on either side of the blocked-up fireplace. He displayed three bottles of Scotch whiskey taken from the largest suitcase. "I brought these to drink with a friend of mine, but I think it would be a good idea to crack one of them right now." He fetched glasses and water from the bathroom.

Schlossberg sat without leaning back. He was fond of Scotch but it wasn't the center of his attention. "We're not so backward that we don't have liquor stores here you know. Never been a drought in Dogtown, not even during Prohibition." His taut posture and alert chestnut eyes belied the vacancy with which he conducted business and the absentminded air of his self-revelations. He'd been talking about himself to prime the pump, preoccupied with the formulation of hypotheses about this guest who was making himself host for the nonce. "But that couldn't be the only reason your bag was so heavy. I think I'm getting old. This is no elegant room you know, and I've got to admit it's the best we've got. But we always like the idea of a writer staying at the Van."

Opsimath felt guilty for having to disabuse a touching trustfulness as he explained that the "research" he'd alluded to on the phone with Mrs Schlossberg, in explanation of his special requests, was not sociological or literary but financial, and that it had nothing to do with the charms or crimes of Dogtown. To make amends he began to speak a little more about himself, and straightway found that his friendly inquisitor was pleased enough with the truth. It wasn't Rafe's habit to assume the deportment of a prudentially reserved businessman, and he saw no reason now to deny himself the openness he preferred whenever and wherever it was not of definite advantage to shroud his condition or his purpose.

Moistened with the water of life, Shelly accepted his client's substitute for a profession, and did so with smaller surprise than Rafe's when discovering there was no need to explain that steam cleaners had nothing to do with the cleansing of unwashable apparel. It wasn't even necessary to point out the similarity of purpose and difference of method between steamcleaning and sandblasting.

"Oh I worked on a couple of your 202s over at Murphy's pig farm. Rigged up as boilers to cook the garbage. Never could get half the stuff boiled. Nothing wrong with the machines—plenty of capacity and all that. Not your fault. It's the cooking tank that's wrong. Poor guy's just a little pig farmer who believed the experts, and instead of going out of the business he went and invested all he could borrow just to comply with the new law—and he's stuck with the Dogtown garbage collection contract. I understand the same thing's happening all over the state. Everybody's worried about trichinosis, but unless you can feed pigs on fish gurry that new cooking law is going to drive them all out of Vinland. There's no pig lobby to get it repealed. Public opinion is against hogs anyway."

"Our sales people thought we were going to cash in on that law. They called it an 'ideal special application'! The word got all the way to our shop floor that we were going to expand production! Made for a lot of good farmer jokes. But all of a sudden nobody's talking about it anymore. After all the work Ray Lagniappe and Fred Tracy have done to excite the engineering department! I hate to think of the special expenses I've okayed for this great new market, not to mention the little clusters of hidden cost that have been buried without the gravestones to call them to my attention. Ray persuaded us to send him a special trailer-mounted 202—against my all-too-indulgent better judgment—and then he personally went all over the state to make demonstrations, knee-deep in pig-turd while the jobber salesmen watched with distaste. Now he's putting out disclaimers as gracefully as possible. But I wish we could do something about Murphy's installation. Of course we can't take back the machines. Ray's still hoping for some simple solution."

It dawned on Rafe as he spoke about the problem that even dear old Walt Edenfield, abettor and guardian angel for this "market of opportunity", hadn't mentioned "the garbage-cooking application" for some time now. He smiled at being surprised. He could hardly expect a creative partner to bring up the conclusive technical frustration of a pet project just because he the president scrupulously refrained on his more than few occasions from saying "I told you so!" To Shelly he said: "What do you think's wrong with the idea?"

"You've got to spread the garbage better, or keep it moving. But now the farmers can't afford to replace all the cookers they've built wrong from listening to the engineers. It's a shame I didn't pay more attention to the stories in the paper a year or two back. Everybody just assumed that batch-cooking was the way to do it—the way they make fishcakes and clam chowder here at the Yard."

"Were you in the fish business too?"

"For a while I competed a little bit with one of the Mercator-Steelyard sidelines. I learned a lot about batching when I had that codliver oil business. Used a propellor to mix it in a twenty-gallon drum. Found a way to homogenize it with honey. Had to add a tenth of a percent of benzoid soda to prevent spoilage and fermentation you know. Poured it out in eight-ounce bottles. I had some red white and blue labels made up with the tradename DOGTOWN SOLARPURE; imprint said 1500 units of Vitamin A, 85 units of D. I'm talking about modern times now, but it was before synthetics. All the smart mothers made their kids swallow codliver oil by the tablespoon. I had a touch of peppermint in my formula, but it didn't help the taste. Sold all I could make, practically, to a wholesale house in Bot. But I couldn't make a go of it because my line wasn't big enough. That's when I went into natural foods retail you know. Had a store in Bot called Raw Food Products Company. Every week we had an open forum discussion about healthy eating. But there wasn't much interest in the long run. Swill is different. But I got called in on this too late." Mirth spread across his round face and he slapped his thigh at an old thought: "Only a Jew could have saved the pork industry!"

Rafe reminded himself of the many euphoric cycles by which one "innovative application" had replaced another in the buzz between Ted McKee and his ad agency. The latest HUGE POTENTIAL (not limited to a few anachronistic swineherds in Vinland) was for pairs of the high-pressure 360 flanking automatic car-wash conveyors, AN EXISTING AND RAPIDLY EXPANDING NATIONAL MARKET in which numberless small businessmen were investing all they could borrow and to which the agency was sure that Tubalcain's patently superior equipment could be introduced by putting two or three grand into just one more monthly "book", *Auto-Wash,* a journal known to be read religiously by all operators in that specialized sector of the so-called automotive service industry. To Sales Manager Ted McKee this plan promised a groatsworth of the glamor he missed in the unedifying pages of *Automotive Jobber.* The weary president of Tubalcain now carelessly eased his anxiety about advertising costs by mentioning this impending decision to his disinterested drinking companion. It wasn't the kind of thing an ophelimitous executive could talk to Ippy about, and as yet it would have been indiscreet to speak of it to anyone in contact with the trade.

"Can't beat your machines for carwashes." said Shelly. "I know a place that's been using a couple for fifteen years, one on each side of the washing bay."

"Those are the same old 202s that we modified for garbage cooking. It's a funny thing how most of our hot new applications seem to call for our oldest machine. It has no white enameled cabinet, and it still looks like a plain old boiler. In the footnotes to our ads it's called THE WORKHORSE OF OUR STEAM-VAPOR LINE. In Cornucopia, if you look out in back of truck garages and construction equipment yards, you still see a lot of them chugging away every day at engine blocks and fifth wheels after twenty years. The sales department thought they should have been taken out of production five years ago!"

"I saw something about your new high-pressure units in some literature Pat Murphy had. They reminded me of an idea I got when I was a Water Tender in the Navy: a better way to evaporate brine. Recover the salt too you know. There was a time when people needed salt, especially right here for the codfish. Which they still dry some of, over at the Yard, every once in a while; and you'll always be able to smell the ghost of it here when the wind is right. The next town down the line is a snooty place that calls itself Felicity-by-the-Sea you know, and the conductor's big joke on the up-train is 'Felicity-by-the-Sea, Dogtown-by-the-Smell'. You heard that one already? The first settlers tried making their own salt, but in the end they had to bring it in from Hispania to get enough, right up until they started using freezers. Of course here on the Cape there's always been plenty of fresh water. My little still would have been just a kind of hobby for self-sufficiency. What I forgot about was fuel consumption, because I was used to the dairy sterilizers I sold before the war that didn't take many B T U s. Never did have mechanical aptitude." He slapped his thigh. "My Gentile friends always said I went off half-cocked!"

"Forty years ago my company was started to make dairy sterilizers." Rafe replied. "Cornucopia had passed a sanitation law! We still make a few steam generators more or less under that heading for one national dairy supply house. Ever hear of Hafnia-Iona?"

"That's the one I peddled for. I had the New Armorica territory."

If Shelly hadn't been growing uneasy about his duty below stairs they would have talked all night. "I'm supposed to be within earshot of the night bell and the phone." he said, reluctantly refusing a third drink. "I've got a conscience. Once in a blue moon, this time of year, there can be a call . . ."

He rose with stiff joints, still preoccupied with his interest in Rafe Opsimath personally, and apologized for not being able to help him with whatever financial research it was that had brought him to the Van. "I don't know anything about finance. The wife runs our checkbook, does the tax returns, everything. It's only for fun that I started our investment club you know. It doesn't amount to anything. We meet in my old Malfunction Room downstairs next to the bar. I never have much to say but I like to listen to their research reports on the Industrials. Don't care much for Financial stocks and nobody ever mentions the Rails anymore. When I sold mutual funds my heart was never in it. Customer pays a big loading charge but he's dragged down by averages and the shares are never worth more or less than market Net Asset Value. Seems to me if you go into investment companies because you don't have enough money to spread around on your own, or the time to study each trade, you might as well buy into a closed-end one that's got some play of its own. But the guys are in the club because they want to fool around with a portfolio. They're like kids at a picnic when it comes to making out a Buy or Sell order by parliamentary procedure!"

As the chunky little salt-mill of experience regained the balance of his stocky limbs lurching to the door he turned to Rafe with a last appeal of apologetic curiosity, by the desperate look of his face dismissing as mere preliminary chatter everything that had been said so far, like a suitor obliged to say goodnight before having gotten up his courage for a demonstration of personal interest: "Who's your friend?"

Rafe was so tired that the whiskey had gone to his head. For a moment the bewildering question upset his confidence in the entire architecture of his situation. "What friend?"

"The person you brought the bottles for."

Person? Rafe glanced at the big brass bed. Does he think I'm tracking down a woman? Or suspect that I'm a solitary drinker? "My college teacher lives here."

"Lots of them around."

"The one I'm doing my thesis for."

"Oh I see. I was wondering why you'd come to a place like this for research. I thought maybe you'd heard about our financial library."

"I didn't expect that convenience!"

"The FEEL we call it. Free Enterprise Education Library. One of Richard Tybbot's answers to the New Deal. It's even got a ticker and a broad tape. Like a poor man's brokerage house, except some of the people who use it aren't exactly poor. Pretty handy for registered reps and traders when they're too hung over to get to their office in Bot. But mostly just locals hang out there to watch the tape and read the *Graveyard Chronicle.* Not much other excitement in center city. Main thing is it's got all the looseleaf stock and bond books. Recognize the name Tybbot?"

"Nineteen twenty-nine? The all-time master of short-selling? After him F D R changed the rules! Isn't he the same Tybbot that started the financial news services and credit reports?"

"There's only one, the Duke of Dogtown. Great prophet of business statistics, and for Dogtown a philanthropist all over. Born here from a long line. Humphrey Tybbot was the first Troglodyte or something like that. So Richard wanted to enlighten the whole Cape and make it famous too. Don't get me wrong: he was no phony. Did a lot of good before he died a few years ago. There's a nice quiet reading room in back that you could work in while the maid's up here during the day—from what I hear."

"Why, haven't you ever been in there?"

"I snuck a quick look at the front part once. But don't ever tell the wife. I promised her never to go in there you know. She's got the idea that Tybbot was antisemitic. He was never for Hitler or anything like that—at least not after about '36—but she thinks he was too Yankee. It doesn't bother me if he didn't like Jews, but she's an Etruscan and she *feels* for me." He looked keenly at Rafe. "But maybe I'll duck in just once more to take a gander at the Tubalcain credit rating. They've got the Tybbot Bible on a little table all by itself."

"But that's supposed to be a confidential reference book for subscribers!" Rafe was shocked to be so casually disillusioned. "It's damned expensive too."

"Nothing's confidential in Dogtown—unless you try to tell the world about it. We can read financial letters that rich people pay twelve hundred dollars a year to get by airmail."

"But that's an illegal breach of faith, equivalent to copyright infringement!" Rafe exclaimed, mocking his own surprise.

"Who's going to worry about Dogtowners? They've been called the Lawless Innocents of North Atlantis for three hundred and fifty years. Besides, most of those financial services were started and owned by the old man himself, just like the credit Bible; and he set up the FEEL trust so that all the registered voters of Dogtown are shareholders of the corporation. A corporation's a person in the eyes of the law you know, and that person can be given a personal subscription to anything, it seems like."

"But I'm not even a resident of Dogtown."

"That's a point I got the Chamber of Commerce to go to the Attorney General about as a matter of cy-pres the year I was president. It's enough to be using our sewer system. We encourage people to vote in every election, wherever they come from, and that's all Tybbot really cared about—the eugenic franchise for all owners of property, real or personal, local or off-island, regardless of race color or creed, even Jews and Catholicrats."

"—Ippy, you say? I don't know any Ippies here."

Rafe raised his elbow and put a hand to his brow, wondering if he was agile enough to follow this Arethusian transition. But he now remembered that his tipsy lips had earlier slipped an *Ip*. "Ipsissimus

Charlemagne. Used to be in the Ur theater but was too big for the stage. I get the impression he's a native returned. He said he'd give me the name of a mechanical genius for my pump problem."

"You mean *Doctor* Charlemagne!" The robust round face relaxed into the continuously benevolent coruscations of which all the darting concentrations at his eyebrows were nothing but expressive modulations, as if the solution of a riddle had suddenly accomplished what the whiskey could not. "Didn't come here until after I did, and it was only fifteen years ago I bought this place you know. I never heard him called anything but *Doc*. Looks like a tramp but he's got a Doctor's degree from Norumbega."

Now that was something that Rafe happened to know wasn't true because he had impertinently questioned Ippy on that very point up at White Quarry College, where an instructor would have every reason not to understate his academic qualifications. Since it was inconceivable that such a man would falsify himself anywhere else, and indeed in certain circles would have been offended by academic ranking as a discredit to his artistic integrity, Rafe presumed that the mistaken title was accepted as a jocular honorary degree granted by friendly Dogtowners presumed to know that he had held his brief teaching appointment at that great university only while declining to submit to normal supervison of his idiosyncratic studies.

"Whenever he comes into the bar Jake calls me. I like to go talk to him and give him something on the house. He's the only customer we have who drinks Scotch. Naturally he's a little uneasy with the locals because he knows some of them resent him for not working. But he gets along great with most of the gypsies. They take him as part of the waterfront landscape. I know it isn't his favorite bar, but he has to pass by on his way home from eating, and sometimes he drops in after the restaurants close. We've got to put in a DV though, and then we'll probably never see him again."

Standing with Shelly at the open door Rafe was prompted by some imp to turn the tables on his interrogator. "You from Brotherly?"

"Say, how did you know? My accent still give me away? Dogtown seems to have a special attraction for people from Brotherly."

"So do most other places, according to the comedians. It's too bad the Brotherly wharves are so run down—worse than Yerba Buena or Botolph even. But it looks like a fine city."

"To come from." Shelly stared at the floor smiling slightly in his recollection of the most distant past yet mentioned in their conversation. "That's where art got in my blood. Only I didn't know it. Never gave myself the right education. All I thought about was girls. But in Brotherly they all seemed to think of boys as brothers. So I lighted out for golden Cornucopia and found out you don't have to be a lawyer. But it was only after I settled here that I took up sculpture you know. Realized I'd been trying to do it ever since that one sabbath morning kids' art class a friend of mine took me to before my father found out. Should have gone to the Academy when I was young. Would have had a different style."

"You never would have known Jack London." Rafe remarked.

"That's true!" He lifted his face to Rafe again, grateful for the reminder. "But I was too late learning everything. Never saw an adze until I was sixteen, never used a welding torch until past forty, never thought of picking up driftwood until I was sixty-six. Imagine that. Well at least I got into forestry when I was an instructor in the C C C. You remember F D R's Civilian Conservation Corps?"

"Best program we ever had. Even the Protestican have stopped maligning it by now. I thought of joining, but I was too scared of tough guys."

"I'd like to see it come back, for kids who don't want to be drafted into the Army. Should have girls in it. Service for everybody. My boy could of used the discipline you know.

"—Well I got to get back down. I hope no one woke up the wife with that bell. She deserves her sleep. Runs this whole place practically without help, and without being too efficient anyway, which makes it harder than you'd think. That's why I do our cooking. Feel like coming down to have supper with us one of these days? Being a practical man, you might be interested to see how I've fixed up the boiler room. Looks more like a welding shop than a studio. I'll show you some of my abstract schooners. That there is only one of my more realistic ones." He pointed to the mantelpiece. Rafe hadn't noticed the misshapen wood and cloth model of a fore-and-aft-rigged vessel with two stumpy sticks for masts and stiff cloth sails. "Schooners were invented here you know. Makes up for everything else. You probably won't like my women: they look like me too. Or like lobster boats. Or lobsters. Too rugged for people around here, most of them. But times are changing. When I went to Florence I saw some things that would knock your eye out. And there's a few guys in Dogtown who do some good work too. But you can tell none of them ever held an axe in their hands."

Rafe pretended an indifference to art, warning the innkeeper that he knew nothing about sculpture and was no collector.

"Oh mine isn't what you'd call art. I never sell much. Anything I really care about I'd rather keep here in the city. I'd give it all to my friends except if they got it for nothing they'd treat it like nothing: the whole trouble with Dogtown. That's why these people need so many historians around here—to tell them what they've missed before all the relics are lost.

"—He probably means Buck Barebones."

The guest wiped his brow again, this time without any pride of perception. "What?"

"The man for your pump problem. Didn't know Doc knew him. Good friend of mine. I'll take you to see him anytime you want. Pat Murphy should have called him in right at the beginning of that pig thing."

Rafe watched the primitive landlord hurry down the hall, rolling like a cowboy sailor on short bowed legs, which would have made him as tall as anybody but Doctor Charlemagne if they'd grown in proportion to the arms and torso.

Making an effort to remember why he was standing there, the disoriented sojourner turned to use the sewer facility. He looked again at the nautical model and wondered if there really was such an apparent distance between Shelly's reach and his grasp. Going to sleep he tried to think up compliments that would be gracious in that line of art, having accepted the invitation to a meal three days hence.

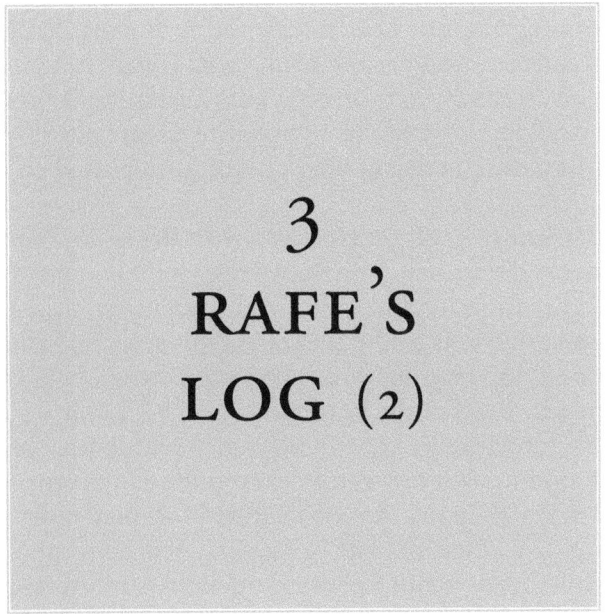

3
RAFE'S
LOG (2)

The Van, Dogtown, Vd.
Dictated 9 September 1960

I hope the sporadic and discursive mode of this all-too-human narrative will compensate in Doctor Charlemagne's eyes for the unhumanistic efficiency of having it typed by a secretary 3000 miles from its origin. What with Ray Lagniappe's importunities to me in Botolph, following the fatigue of research in New Uruk and some heavy entertainment at Charter Oak on the way up, I was way behind with my schoolwork when I got here. If the expediency of dictating this nuisance-log hadn't occurred to me as I was unpacking my portable Bardic recorder, I think I would have found myself balking the Doctor after all (if that's really what he likes to be called on this soil).

I always lug the little machine around with me because it inscribes the same plastic disks as the somewhat more convenient equipment in my office. I must admit it was a long time before I let the Controller modernize our written communications. It was a hefty capital expenditure for mere paperwork. As he tirelessly insisted, the basic system couldn't be installed piecemeal, and it required compatibility or interchangeability among all the field and office units. Even after the Bardies were installed I refused at first to participate in the network of progress. But now he's proved to me that dictation-and-transcription (once you get the hang of it) is easier than shorthand bouts with a secretary, not only for sales correspondents who write letters all day long, or salesman who write them half the night, but also for a footloose manager who's never gotten used to office discipline.

I'm not entirely unsympathetic with Irma for fighting this improvement: she is such a first-rate stenographer, when we can sit down together in peace and quiet, and she can assimilate my afterthoughts or corrections before she starts typing, that nothing short of a telepathic editing machine with a magic typewriter could match her skill and speed. But I'm the bottleneck, and her other talents are far too valuable for her to be kept on the bench with poised pencil while I flounder around with my words or respond to interruptions during office hours, which in my case are ill spared for the written word anyway. I'm uneasy when she has to be away from her phone and sit waiting while I answer mine or wind up conversations with whoever may be keeping me from doing the dictation when I said I would. It's hard enough in any case to batch my letters only once or twice a day, and in a small office like ours I simply cannot keep the poor lady running in and out to gratify my whims. This new method is forcing me to economize my time and hers for the good of the company.

And Doctor Charlemagne won't have to wait for the next Convocation to be apprised of how I've obeyed him. Irma's a whiz with carbon paper. After I get back we'll start sending him copies as soon as each fragment is typed. It's even possible that this modernization of pedagogic method will please him. The Lucifer of Limeway was renowned among intelligent actors for his electric imagination; now he needs technology more than ever as THE DIRECTOR of some new Pandemonium in a smaller pit. By the same token, however, I risk his unnecessary irritation with my comparatively efficient ways. (Only comparatively. To my Controller I seem as inefficient as Doctor Charlemagne seems to me.)

And while we're on the subject of efficiency, it's time to be blunt about a certain expediency of my grotesque world that I will not renounce in my storming of the liberal arts. The scowling reader of this journal and of the Disquisition for which it's camouflage must put up with some of the abbreviations acronyms and codes of everyday life. I'll try to remember to define each one at its introduction, but instead of translating it at subsequent appearances—which would defeat the purpose of easing my task, Irma's, and eventually the readers—I'll build a table (as computer programmers say) to be attached to the end of both documents as a glossary. I have already introduced several widely recognized labels. As I write more and more about my object Parity Corporation, for example, the convenience of its Curb symbol PAR will become apparent to those still innocent of financial jargon; but even professionals need a lexicon when it comes to many of the other ticker codes they don't happen to be familiar with, not to mention nomenclature outside the parochial communications of Graveyard Street.

Don't forget, ye literary polymaths, mine too are provinces of "Atlantean Studies"! If you want to keep me out, call your Program something lesser.

The search for PAR's rhyme or reason will be instructive. So far the fascination is more tantalizing than promising. There's greater mystery in PAR than in other fictitious persons with the divine attributes of immortality and limited liability. I can't yet see the governing principle or significant pattern; I can't yet distinguish teleological unity in the apparently sporting welter of evolutionary agglomeration. The history of PAR acquisitions and divestitures would be work for a doctorate. It's hard enough for me simply to describe its present state. Even experts find the company extraordinarily complex. Their impatience with the difficulty is the only thing that accounts for its persistent undervaluation by the stockmarket. And for its neglect by S E C lawyers.

Is it the very purpose of this maze to baffle investigation of the Minotaur? There's no reason not to assume a mastermind, or not to assume that the mastermind is Arthur A. Halymboyd, President of Parity and president or chairman or at least board member of all the companies in which PAR has significant interest—a few well-known firms listed on the G S E (via the Big Ticker) but mostly less conspicuous companies traded on the Curb Exchange (C E), like PAR itself, and obscure industrial financial or insurance corporations traded "over the counter" (O T C). For these twenty years he seems to have been planning ultimate power rather than immediate personal profit, like an epic poet who spends most of his life on the acquisition of learning, construction of his system, and private drafts, instead of dissipating his libido in quick and famous lyrics. Not that he's a failure meanwhile, but his reputation is confined to the intersecting circles of colleagues and enemies.

He appears to be both more of a speculator and more of a manager than other imperialists. The Parity Corporation is registered under the Investment Company Act of 1940 as a "non-diversified management investment company". It professes to emphasize long-range growth and capital appreciation through "consolidation of and concentration in industrial properties", but apparently it's not expected to cleave literally or singlemindedly to this desideratum. In ordinary parlance the word *industrial* refers in the first instance to manufacturing and processing; yet for a long time, perhaps from the beginning, PAR had a large somewhat fluctuating interest in Financial Usufruct (FU on the Little Ticker), a holding company for investments in banking and insurance which seems to have been the satrapy of one Zane Capstick. How FU sorted with PAR's truly industrial holdings is hard to see; and if it's a mere investment, either for speculation or income, there has been an apparent violation of the Act. Perhaps PAR is perpetually anticipating some legal reconfiguration *tending toward* compliance with its own manifesto that will pacify the Commissioners for a few more years.

In financial imperialism, where the fourth dimension is so prominent and so obviously irreversible, transition and process are always at the forefront, architectonic images of equilibrium are always receding into the future like justice, and plenty of allowance is made for the inertia of the status quo. The reports of an entity are possibly valid only in terms of formalized past states and aspired future possessions. In this case the future is a sum of Halymboyd's intentions, perhaps not frankly represented even to himself. That leaves me with a decade or two of the ostensible past, which is hardly less secret than what it foreshadows, at least to a remote outsider with too little time to scrape beneath its evanescent pentimento.

Yet every day I find myself more interested in this imperfect superorganic artifact. The large orthodox investment trusts can be scrutinized with little uncertainty; but in exploring this complex of portfolios I feel like Theseus, and my dominant motive remains unacademic. PAR's most recent quarterly report, under the heading "Policies and Objectives", contains this bait for country churchmice like me: "Parity offers growth-oriented companies the kind of financial and advisory assistance that is not normally available from the banking community."

Though I'm aware that this enticement is not meant for eyes as mean as mine, the attraction for Tubalcain is that PAR has subsidiaries and affiliates which also have subsidiaries and affiliates, and they in turn their own, sometimes even unto the fifth or sixth generation.

Somewhere in that house of many mansions must be a place for the world's best line of auxiliary H_2O machines whereby the Edenfields and I through exchange of stock may end up with a few ingots from the palatine treasury. An operating vice-presidency might not be too much for me to be offered. (If I knew more about finance I'd aspire to the Praetorian Guard.) Heady matters for an Opsimath!

Today I got a small glimpse of the ambiguities I'd have to master at the highest levels. I met an intriguing dipsomaniac who admits to having known Arthur Halymboyd. At first I thought he was going to cadge drinks from me, but it turned out that he bought mine, and lunch besides. Before this sitting is over I'm going to thumb through my "Names Mentioned" cards and see if *Jason Anacoluther* was one of those I copied mechanically while poring bleary-eyed through 10K reports and other purposely tedious data filed with the S E C and the stock exchanges.

You see, after the first hour or two in the Washington archives I decided to bite fast, for future mastication, rather than ruminate on what I was abstracting. I resolved to set up a rote and become an automatic amanuensis without evaluating the numbers and words I swallowed. I hoped only to steep myself in the notes passing without remark through my central nervous system and providing content for future deliriums of intellectual despair.

When I heard the name Anacoluther it was hard to visualize myself having seen it on a 3-by-5 card in my own writing, yet it didn't sound unprecedented inside my skull. Not remembering to have encountered it since I shed my clouds of glory forty years ago, I inferred that I was experiencing only the déjà vu a platonist might postulate for any cognitive event. Ever since I began this precipitous project my head has gone round and round with strange and sometimes fanciful names that are almost entirely uninformative (although every now and then I come across a public name of the second rank on this or that PAR-related board). I've grown highly suggestible.

But as this is supposed to be an exercise in first-person narrative and not a ledger of hypotheses, I'd better tell the story of how I made my new acquaintance. Before settling down to business I wanted to get the lay of the land around the harbor, which I gather is the womb of Dogtown's gestations. One thing I'll say for this place: it's got a good one—something my home fish-town was not endowed with. Right up to the end of Hispanic hegemony in the nineteenth century, San Ricardo's freight had to be beached with small boats in the bight of a wide parabola open to the north (as if without need for protection from that pacific ocean), and our latterday breakwater doesn't amount to anything.

It wasn't until I'd bought a map at the drugstore that I perceived the greater part of Dogtown to be an island, though so littorally continuous with the mainland that it is also considered a promontory named Cape Gloucester. The waterway I crossed last night on the "Dogtown Draw" is called the Namauche *River* despite the fact that it has two tidal mouths serving as counter-sources, like the Estuary at Londonbridge that insulates my present urban platform at home, except that the inland sea of Cornucopia is a sight warmer than the unpacified cold blue ocean that lies in perpetual siege of this poor city—two waters as different as the Aegean and the Arctic.

Here the streets seem dirtier and the smell in the air (when I stop to notice) even fishier than San Ricardo's when I grew up near the sardine canneries, where there was hardly any tidal corral to keep the wastes from dispersing. But perhaps it's only that I respond like an old horseman, accustomed to the royal aroma of stables, suddenly entering the cloven-hoof stink of a cowbarn, which on the contrary is sweeter by far to a dairymaid. The gulls here are always scolding the dogs, and there are dogs or dogturds wherever you look. Without the enormous population of scavengers this town would be unfit to behold.

As you know, however, nothing can dampen my zest for exploring any place that's new to me—not even a dismal ceiling of high gray clouds. After breakfast I set out westward on Front Street, the most promising way to escape the downtown jumble on foot. My purpose was to skirt the northern strand of the outer harbor and try the broadest view from Salt Cod Park.

When I crossed the harbor end of the Janus brine-washed Namauche on the short double-bascule bridge at the center of the esplanade, where the river narrows into a short granite-lined canal to pierce the seawall, I saw that Dogtown's principal part may have been made into an island artificially. The cut that makes it such, severing what looks like a natural connection to the city's mainland reaches, is trafficked with fishing boats on the way to and from inshore grounds (labeled Smith's Bay) north of the Cape, and I suppose that before Labor Day it's clogged with pleasure cruisers. I was glad to see a public institution that still gives right-of-way to things that float. It's an issue you can appreciate when you see the long lines of cars that quickly form on either side when the bridge's two skew jaws are open. The bridge tender told me that he's opened for boats as many as forty-nine times on a single shift in July.

By ignoring the dilapidation of masonry set in living granite, beer cans in the shrubbery, broken glass in the glades, paper scattered everywhere, and discarded condoms in the nooks, even a stranger as hostile as Myles Standish would see that the grounds of the park were once admirable. You try to imagine the fresh thrill of that prominence when it was a hillside meadow footed by those bare knobs of massive rock, smoothed by millennia of weather but plasmatically articulated with the continent's foundation, which still guard the crescent horns of a tiny delitescent beach like miniature doubled Gibraltars. From the lowest oak-dressed ledge of one of these sunbleached chthonic exposures I walked the eroded earthworks of a small iron-cannoned fort that reaches unpretentiously into the harbor. Then, climbing the opposite crag by goat-tracks and crannies contrived or exploited by informal granite-masons, I reached a peak that the devil could have used for Christ's temptation. It's lower than the ridges of horizon that screen the distant west and south, but looking out over that harbor at the city on its three hills you can easily forget the surplus value that's littered all about the land.

Some blue was beginning to show among the clouds. The baroque City Hall clock tower is high lord of the builded slopes, and he has two or three slighter deputies among the belfried or aspired churches. I was surprised how vivid the dun town looked from across the water. Her supple dress is a ground of white dashed with pink and blue but aproned too with kitchen colors and petticoated with a thousand lines and smudges. From the embracing green arms that define the basin's sky her swelled and hollowed fabric keeps its hold along maternal lines but with textural gussets and gores, looking alive with unheard rustlings as it drops to a bottom of flattened drapery down at the level of the ewered sea. The blank whitewashed walls of the freezer plant on a thin hem of beach, in the center of this all but motionless scene, smote me with primitive feelings of my childhood during the Depression, when I hoped for war and dreamed of every life except business, in a San Ricardo of situated lines and shapes not dissimilar.

Far more distant on my right, demarking the greatest visible expanse of bluing ocean, based at a lighthouse on the last rocky point of opposite land, the long straight breakwater ends with what looks like a miniature white tower on a truss-mounted platform, almost half way out to the opposite shore of granite a mile or so south of where I stood. To my left, where the mainland's green ridge recovers much of its elevation and foliage after its interruption by the winding valley of the river, among a perplexing mixture of structures and vegetation, I picked out above the imitation skyscraper tacked onto the flat roof of the brick high school (which looks newer than any other building in the city) a more distant cable-rigged steel derrick certainly worthy of my investigation. The Chamber of Commercials puts out a pretty good map, but it doesn't identify the landmarks for an industrial archeologist like me.

Not far to the right of the white freezer straight before me, separated by a piled thicket of houses and fish plants on low black rocks, the peaked red NET & TWINE MANUFACTORY which I'd glimpsed from Front Street guards the water's edge in a different neighborhood entirely, below residential shade trees on the rocky bluff of Mother's Something-or-other that I can't remember without the map at hand. If there'd been no boats going in and out, if I'd had no map at all, if I hadn't spent a night beyond that shore of the harbor, I'd've had no suspicion of the cleft that opens between those two landmarks into a fecund inner harbor. By land and water that dilating ventricle is the whence and whither of Dogtown's traffic, enfolded in viscera and concealed at a distance by the draped facets of mother's clothing. By contrast, San Ricardo is epicene and naked.

There you have my first impression of your city, Doctor Charlemagne. You asked for subjective journalism. That means jumping to conclusions, if you don't mind. Irma won't be offended; she's accustomed to the passive vagaries of my male mind. (Her husband's much worse in public than I am.) But there'll be no more of the like. A true account of my psychic condition (merely to counterbalance the objectivity of my Disquisition on banausics) would take too many Bardic disks, and I'm also already running short of time. Every outer harbor has an atmosphere and every inner harbor has a mouth.

Back toward town, once more aware of ordinary vehicles (unquiet and unharmless), I walked again along the esplanade, where the city's sea wall and ancient access to the coast road seems to have been improved by some fluke of farsighted statesmanship. I wonder what that strand was like before its frenchification. It looks as if the frame houses that line the inside roadway facing the breakwater were surprised by their full exposure to the broad length of the harbor. Their roofs and their view are overlooked by a steep shoal of larger and smaller dwellings in jumbled tiers of unadorned homeliness, a few spruced-up crystals distinguishing themselves for tastelessness in the unarchitectured throng. There's a bandstand at a widening of the pavement, and the famous green bronze statue of a fisherman with his wife mending a net while their dog points out to sea, which was now a keen blue under half-cleared skies.

I decided to stop for lunch at The Windmill, an inn I would have chosen for my lodging if I'd had the mischance to look around before I decided, which stands conspicuously on a sea-cliffed knoll where the broad promenade abuts the gnarled old business district of the inner harbor. Sure enough, I liked the looks of the Millstone Bar off the dining room, so even though it wasn't yet noon I went in to quaff a bottle of the ale I can't get in other parts of the country. It's rare to find a light and spacious drinking counter. I sat looking through large plate glass down the longitudinal axis of the harbor and past the breakwater to Vinland Bight's horizon. By this time, under perspicuous sky, I had to shield my eyes from the blue glare.

But I took the opportunity to go through my pockets, as I try to do whenever I find refreshment alone in some idle well-lighted place with an uncluttered surface to work on. I began to sort and consolidate the scraps I'd been accumulating on this trip as usual. The ashtray was soon stacked high with tiny-torn bits. The bartender kept it empty with a sympathetic smile. People here are nice. I feel sorry for them.

Business suits were beginning to arrive for lunch in the next room, and some of them slipped in to sit first at the bar. I hadn't consciously noticed the dazzling noontide brilliance of the blue plain outside the windows until a row of quick drinkers obstructed my view and relieved my squint. It was no great surprise that my one remaining precursor at that pleasant horsehoe trough spoke to me from my left when the bartender got too busy to prefer him as a conversational favorite. I knew this neighbor had been watching me out of one eye, and with half my mind I had automatically hazarded the idea of a local character fallen from metropolitan eminence on account of one weakness. I've learned how to take care of myself in all kinds of bars, but I was prepared to spend ten or twelve bucks on a talkative confidence man to get the feel of Dogtown's big names.

But it turns out (if I'm any wiser in my second judgment) that his world is more cosmopolitan than micropolitan, and that what I mistook for misfortunate necessity is nothing but congenial liberty arising from a large range of choices as to the means for increasing his wealth. So late in life, however, moneymaking seems to remain his chief intrigue only by default, simply a habit from earlier and larger conditions, or rather (as a fallacy of misplaced concreteness) an addicted comfort that palliates the nightmare of death. At his level that vulgar preoccupation seems aristocratic. His independence is arranged to accommodate the one thing he's dependent on. In my opinion he sticks to business because it affords a variety of social occasions, insufficient but necessary events without which his stock of private sorrows would have rendered the ruling passion immediately fatal.

Yet often enough I've been wrong about people I marry or hire or conspire with. In this case it appears that I'm the confidence man, if either of us is. His appetite for new company yielded me a hundredfold from my few seeds of self-revelation. He's so interested in life as he has experienced it himself that he had too much to talk about to ask many questions, glossing all topics with first-personal anecdotes of unflagging interest to me, pacifying my own *cacoethes loquendi* with the unspoken implication that I was a person exceptionally capable of appreciating allusions to the larger world of his autobiography.

In reply to one of his few inquiries I told him I'd come up for a little vacation after some grubbing in the sloppy files of the Curb library. That's hardly the kind of revelation a prudent businessman would volunteer to a stranger unless he wished to invite further questions; but my indiscretion was intended to probe his knowledge, and if possible to get him going in a useful vein. When I gave him my card he made no return of his own, but I wanted him to see how far I'd come from home and how far I was from being a securities analyst or reporter or IRS agent. Thus I stimulated his unintrusive interest in me as a social phenomenon worth his while, and tacitly invited him to gossip about matters that the companions of his retirement were probably too provincial to appreciate.

He responded by speaking of the Curb Exchange restaurant, which he likes as well as I do, where many a nefarious conspiracy has been discussed and where he claims to have hobnobbed with many a magnate and magneto, many a politician incognito. I learned something about his knowledge (or notion) of how to trade large blocks of stock off the floor. Then he reminisced about Graveyard Street at large, and such fellows as the father of the Senator who's now running for President. But he wandered superficially; his stories never went deep enough to satisfy the curiosity he aroused.

His teasing nevertheless seemed anything but deliberate as he stuttered and stumbled without embarrassment in continual darting motion to release incipient logojams like a happy-go-lucky lumberjack absentmindedly impatient with the proleptic requirements of a sentence. The effort to convey thoughts he found was often too much for his sputtering tongue and salivating lips. He would sometimes offer a bridling smile at his success in spitting out the words, boy-blue eyes brightening with friendliness athwart the vertical creases of his jaundiced rosy-cheeked face.

I'm sure he was meanwhile trying to figure out whether I was looking for investments or investors. All through lunch I kept him guessing on that score, as with discriminating and respectful questions I played the switchman whenever he needed direction or went too far on one track, thereby ever renewing the hint that I was as competent to interrupt as to admire anything he chose to disclose of his history. I was getting used to the way he'd start to assemble and then break up his partial trains of thought without even finishing the definition of what he was talking about, as if expecting of me a boundless clairvoyance. His lips would puff experimentally at every outset, and his rather high voice trail off vaguely without ever finishing a paragraph, rarely returning to successive points of departure.

This manner of speech, with all the appearances of reflecting a muddled thought-process, would have disqualified him for any Atlantean business career that started below the top, less for its idiosyncrasy of subject than for its confusion of objects. I conclude that I was witnessing his most careless off-duty behavior, when he indulges his alcohol in laziness of address and relaxation of motor control while reserving to himself the mnemonic and contemplative functions. Perhaps, rivaling Hesiod, he does his whole day's work before noon. The explosive consonants were amiable, and the sibilants candid, because his diurnal rest begins at a time when other men are pausing to recruit their strength. Although his fine sandy hair is hardly graying about the ears, and more of it than necessary still adorns his long high dome, he smiles with raised eyebrows and his moist pink lips expose the nicotined yellow buck teeth of an aged man. It's the humanly rugose face of an old horse with squirrel cheeks and the dewlaps of a cow. I chose to take the name-dropping boasts as humorous self-mockery of his clumsy struggle with language and of his mottled physiognomy—as the waning sprezzatura of an imperfect gentleman.

By the time we came to cigars and brandy I was imbibulated with good feeling toward him and making no effort to mark all the jumbled boards he's sat on, all the unlikely companies he's presided over, or all the celebrities he's befriended—until he mentioned that back in the old days he'd served on the Catholicratic National Committee. As I made sure that he noticed my particular admiration for his political associations, he dwelt for some time on his pickings from that memory-bag. His politics are personal rather than conceptual, but they happen to fall into the best tradition of persons. He rambled for instance into a story of how he'd helped Adlai Stevenson raise extraordinary money for a crucial broadcast speech, and made allusions to his longstanding friendship with the present candidate's family in mentioning that the Senator and his two brothers had spent the last weekend but one at his house over on the Foreside.

Yet when I somewhat excitedly evinced my curiosity about the private relations between these two latest Catholicratic nominees for our country's Presidency, he faded out on me—as he had previously done whenever I tried to get him to address the heart of a matter, or even to express a value judgment. It was as though he'd lose the thread of his story—or reach the bottom of his knowledge while he was still on the surface. It appears that these New Armorican eupatrids consider it gauche to take sides in any true argument. When up against one, those glistening eyes wandered the dining room impartially, his stiff wattled neck swiveling slowly. One might think he was the Windmill's proprietor pondering his fixed overhead. But in that wagging interval, as he grappled for a discontinuous new remark, his eyes were scanning faces not present and events unknown to anyone anywhere near there.

"They both like my paintings." he finally brought out, as if that explanation was as good a sampling as any from his spectrum of experience beyond the telling. "Roomful of Impressionists I've pick—picked up over the years in Europe. A lot of Ex—Expressionist stuff too; but they don't count so much: collected them when they were cheap just because I liked them, be—fore they were ap—appreciated by the market."

By that time I was wise enough to know it would be futile to pursue that waggish conflation of ophelimic apology and aesthetic diffidence. It's possible that his engaging words inverted the asymmetries he had in mind. But the matter prompted me to ask him if he'd ever heard of his fellow citizen Ipsissimus Charlemagne.

It was a lucky throw. He stared at me as if he was surprised that I should think he and I could share distinguished acquaintances even of a class neither his nor mine. Of course I said nothing about being a student in search of his teacher. I trusted that as a man of the world he wouldn't ask questions about my background or about any associations that might embarrass me. At the same time I thought he was wary of a name I might know something about *in vivo*. For a minute I was afraid he suspected me of bringing it up to probe him for name-dropping humbug. But as we broached Charlemagne his eyes wandered with a new animation; they were now shining with pleasure, pausing again and again to regard me with a smile of recreational happiness that flattered my insignificant presence if not my worthiness, his spirited stammer fondly conjuring the personage in question.

"Why—why that silly—why that silly bastard! I try to catch him around here when—whenever I can! He thinks he's a—a monk keeping the idea of theater alive in our new Dark Ages! I love him for it though. What an anthropologist! I could—I could listen to him till the cows come home. I'd rather drink with him than any man alive!" His eyes welled with affection and he turned away to gaze out the window for an instant of privacy. "I'm only—I'm only afraid he won't outlive me. Doesn't take care of himself. People come here from all over the world to see him." His lips quivered with the effort to do justice to his goodwill. "It's always nice to know he's around here somewhere most of the time. I don't want him to leave us, dead or alive . . ." He glanced at me with a another passing flicker of immediate interest. "Did you know him as an actor or something?"

"Oh no. I've read some of his essays. I subscribe to a little theater in Yerba Buena, and I met him once when they had him there to direct a play." If they're really drinking companions Jason will no doubt hear the truth about me sooner or later, but I didn't want to put myself at an unnecessary disadvantage by confessing the ambitious inferiority of adult education.

When there was no more to eat or drink without a positive decision to prolong the lunch absurdly, he rested his hands on the edge of the table, covering the check, and moved slightly sideways to indicate by gesture that he was about to say "Shall we go?", if it was necessary to make me understand that he had other things to do. It would have been much too late to come to the point of an ordinary arms-length business lunch, but as I responded appropriately to his polite dismissal, assuming the manner of a man himself at least as busy, I tried one last dash of salt, while I still had the chance, to see if I could precipitate a little sediment of useful information from my tankful of murky new experience. I asked him if he knew anything about the Parity Corporation.

Did he think me trying to take advantage of his generosity? For an instant he was as silent and motionless, impassively florid, as a portrait on some boardroom wall; but I couldn't tell whether it was astonished suspicion or the search for prudent words that accounted for an effect so much more pronounced than I had bargained for. Certainly he was trying to read my mind. There was no doubt about the hiatus of goodfellowship. Was he disappointed in me for provincial ignorance of protocol, as if I'd asked a lawyer for legal advice at a cocktail party? In febrile confusion (which I concealed in the motions of rising from my chair) I reviewed the sound of what I'd just said to see if I'd misspoken my intended words—only to assure myself of no neurological error. Flustered by the tilt of his long nose I added: "Or did you ever hear of Arthur A Halymboyd?"

Around the blue eyes from which all moisture had disappeared the humorous palimpsest of wrinkles had hardened coldly. The slack pouches of his cheeks began to work like gills, exhibiting their microscopic network of tiny red and purple veins. Once more he looked slowly around the restaurant, this time as if appealing from side to side for witnesses, while with mouth inert he weighed his options of reply. I almost began to expect some witticism at the expense of my presumably two-bit financial interests. But at last the long upper lip agitated itself once more and the pause waxed spluttery. Various words were formed but got no further than the teeth before they were swallowed half alive, whether out of courtesy or caution I don't know to this moment. The illusion of having made a new friend was utterly disabused.

Searching abstract horizons with constricted vision the mind at last mastered the tongue. He started to answer me when he was facing twenty degrees to my left and still swinging away, but he seemed to change his mind, for the actual response, finally spit out on the opposite tack, was defensive: "Wha-what d'you want to know?"

You can well imagine that I have a great many questions about PAR, but I was quite aware that my time was up, and intimidated by his refusal to tell me frankly that he was or was not privy to inside information about that obscure establishment. I cast about for the one question that might best expose the degree of his cognition. Hoping for the tone of a modest speculator who assumed that the financier would know all about a stock which was generally overlooked, I asked: "Why is it selling at half its Net Asset Value?"

"Is it?" I couldn't tell whether he questioned the postulate, doubted that I could have figured it out for myself, or accepted it as a fact he hadn't been aware of.

"That's just my estimate," I said. "I can see why an investment company might sell for more than the sum of its parts, but I can't understand why it should go for less than its market value. Maybe I've overlooked something in my arithmetic. But I wonder if you know why traders are neglecting it."

"My—my dear young man, they may have certain—doubts about—about what they don't know."

"You mean the Financial Usufruct spinoff? Is Capstick still in the Empire, or is there going to be a separate Byzantium from now on?" Without expecting any direct answers I assumed an innocence that I hoped was plausibly poised between amateur intelligence and parvenu fatuity. I wasn't clear about my main purpose, but I wanted to demonstrate that I knew enough for him either to take me seriously, and perhaps tell me more, or to admit to himself that he might learn something useful if he helped me along. I might ascertain the level of his interest and guess whether or not to rely upon his implicit confirmation of Halymboyd as the Daedalus (if not Minotaur) of this maze. Or at least it was a way to assay his degree of sham, in case he knew nothing whatever about PAR, hadn't even heard of it, was instinctively faking just to keep up his front with a stranger. "Parity's investment in F U has been reduced by three quarters during the past year. It used to be called one of the main 'Subsidiary Companies', but now it's only listed among 'Other Affiliated'. It looks like an all but final divorce. Who took the initiative? Both parties seem to be happy about it. They're already reproliferating separately, unwedlocked."

"Professor Capstick is a competent man. He'll do well on his own."

Professor, eh! I remembered reading that Capstick had been a general in the Army during the war by virtue of his civilian position at a dental school, but none of the documents or financial reports I've seen ever use that title. Already I'd learned something about the erstwhile co-emperor, as the kind of man who is addressed as Professor (rather than Doctor, Dean, or General) after he's opted to become a Mister; and about Jason Anacoluther's authenticity. "But I'm interested in the industrial side," I said. "I hope Parity's now free to follow its imperial destiny—like England, when it was liberated from an ungovernable young wife by our Revolution." I introduced this anachronistic simile advisedly—for it's not the kind to which most Atlantean men of commerce are accustomed—because while I'm at it I always like to sound a man's historical boundaries.

I would have been better advised to notice that I was making myself unnecessarily disagreeable to my host. His drooping worn countenance, now oscillating more rapidly back and forth across our common axis, lighted up with a fake smile of culminating irony, neither at me nor against me. "Be care—careful, sir. Take my word for it!" Leaning forward slightly but without glancing either at the table or pausing on my face in the sweep of his eyes, he drew up the bill with the flat of his hand and pushed back his chair. This time the body followed the swing of the head as he rose. For a couple of seconds he gazed out over the refulgent blue of the afternoon. I could see very clearly the rocks I had climbed on the main. "Atlantic Fleet used to anchor out there. And J P Morgan's yacht."

He moved without haste toward the cashier. I trailed him like a retainer to whom adequate instructions have been issued. He dropped the check on the counter without a signature and grinned at the meek-looking proprietor near the desk, elevating a forefinger three or four inches from his hip with an air of recidivistic acedia. "I'll buy you a drink in the other room, Busty." he drawled to the innkeeper. In the lobby he turned to give me my leave at the front door. Having espied him sneaking a look at my card, I made bold to ask him for his, resolved somehow to make up for my offense to his sensibility. "Never carry one," he said. "I can always be reached through my office at the bank. Nice meeting you, Mr Op—Opsi—." I thanked him for his hospitality to a sojourner; he allowed me to touch a limp humid palm. He had started to saunter back over to the Millstone Bar with the other hand in his pocket, blowing sibilant puffs of air through narrowed lips by way of an absentminded whistle, when he suddenly turned and stopped me as I was halfway into the vestibule. Either he repented of the way he'd treated me at the end, reconsidering some suspicion, or he decided to teach me a lesson. Now his broad twinkling smile was cordial, and his generosity struck me as unrelated to the alcohol of which it had never been deprived.

"Hey, Raph-a-el! Tell you what: there's a fellow may be able to help you. Hangs around the Curb a lot. Very nice guy, a priest. Fa— Father, Father . . . something or other—Father Lucey! Manages a fund for the Lab—Laboratory of Mel—Melchiz—Melchizedek, out in East Harbor. Look him up! Let me know what you find out." For the first time he hoisted a wave of his whole arm, like an immensely confident politician who never has to worry about public relations.

Walking back here to the Van I made a very simple determination of Jason Anacoluther's local importance, if not of his credibility. At the third and largest bank I went into—Cape Gloucester Security Trust—I found his name listed as Chairman of the Board. In the Millstone room, long before he mentioned the bank, he'd identified himself as the operator of a freezer; and that, I soon discovered, is Atlantic Market & Terminal Warehouse, said to be the city's largest taxpayer. Thus I learned that he couldn't be accused of vainglory as far as the micropolis is concerned.

* * *

I have just interrupted this dictation to go through my cards again. All along I've given most of my attention to the current reports and records, among which the name Anacoluther does not appear, but now I find it prominent enough in the old ones that I had been tempted to ignore. Five years ago, though holding only a few qualifying shares, he was nothing less than Chairman of the Parity Corporation!

Once you get a taste of old-money eccentricities, it's not too hard to image him as an inborn paladin sitting with other boardmen, even presiding over them by virtue of interlocking influence—but to visualize him at the active management of anything productive is laughably difficult. Was he a figurehead chosen to make investors underestimate Parity's intentions? Or was his election a regretted mistake? Considering all the trouble they've had with the Governors of the Curb, it even occurs to me that he might have been put there as a representative of Catholicratic interests to satisfy old man Kennedy's S E C , especially to alleviate suspicion of Halymboyd as the eminence rouge who declared far less than a controlling interest (even counting all his "associates" and trusty relatives). Why was Anacoluther then deposed as front man by Halymboyd and/or Capstick? Was he simply found to be an anachronistic Titan, and shoved under the mountain by Zeus and Poseidon as a hindering conservative?

Chairman of the Bar is more like it.

But he left me an opening for another talk with him, if I make up my mind to stick it out here.

* * *

Don't say it, Your Honor! This method of journalism makes me too longwinded by more than half. Even as Doctor of Letters you don't want an existential diary out of me.

My reader (not to mention Irma) would have me write from an inkwell, standing up, like Mister Justice Holmes. Well, technology can't be reversed. Fortunately I didn't bring many enough disks to accommodate much more expatiation. But I'll try to be more compendious from now on. Imagine, all the students of composition in this country who can't think of a single thing to say!

cc: I. Charlemagne
RO:i

4
THE
HARBOR

ast of the Van less than half a mile, where the oddly terraced city fell off to the contours of the inner harbor, Leviathan Court dove directly down the underfall of Spirit Hill into Front Street's shabbiest depression. Looking up that byway, a short double-dead-end T, Rafe faced a gross of souls domiciled in a dozen disrepaired multiple-dwelling Census units. The tallest of the gray clapboard tenements, all occupied on at least three levels, were backed against the base escarpment of the hill he'd surveyed from the park as apparently the most populous quadrant of city. Above the shelf scraped for the head of the tau from jagged granite (rusted and blackened by two hundred years of exposure to over-salted air and smoke) the brightened houses on the higher ascent, open broadly to the sky, although set as close as possible to each other at every possible angle and level, gleamed clean and neat. But Rafe climbed only the lower alley of stoops and windows that lay in the afternoon shadow cast on his left by a spur known as Federal Hill, which introduced the lower end of Back Street at the highest point of Front. A single bed of wavy potholed asphalt served the steep of Leviathan alike as sidewalk street and gutter.

Awareness of the orient ocean conflicted with his native expectation of a westering sun. When he turned as he caught his breath to look over the rooftops that delineated the inner waters a segment of the nearly circumferential sea-plain was visible beyond the broad breakwatered valley of the greater harbor. It emanated a peculiar luminosity that terrestrial rotation didn't seem to account for. With no white afloat in the sky to draw attention to its background, the pellucid atmosphere purified his previous distal impression of the panorama he now explored, without denying the broken glass and wastes of packaging that were more profusely strewn upon this paved ravine than upon the rocks and grass of the abused park.

"Who are you looking for, Mister?" He was running a Dardanelles of porched and windowsilled women whose conversation across the gully had ceased at the apparition of his puffing ascent though the squealing tumult of their children had not. Impertinent demands to account for himself were no sweeter to Rafe than to anyone else of his dignity and means; but as an affable traveller, tolerant of everyone's motives, mindful of his own original neighborhood, he as usual forestalled resentment by trying to make friends. And anyway the fishwife's harsh challenge proved opportune rather than gratuitous, for he would have had to ask directions of one of the women and in any case this unabashed monitor of the Court would have arrogated the reply. At the sound of her hectoring voice even the busy children stopped to watch his humiliation. Was he being treated to unanimous attention merely as a sociological novelty, or was the vibrant solidarity calculated for mutual defense against bill-collectors?

Few of the doors displayed numbers, but he had passed 7 and 14 on the right, with none between; and nothing else was to be made out except a 5 on one of the four lintels further up at the left corner of the T. But Rafe betrayed no haste or surprise. "I'm looking for number 10."

"For God sakes they took it away from here twenty years ago. Who you want?"

"The man that lives at number 10."

"What man?"

Rafe had no choice but to reveal his hope. "Mr Charlemagne. Very unusual-looking man."

"I know what he looks like. What you want him for?"

"Just to see how he is."

"He's fine."

Rafe weighed the question as to whether they were hostile to Ippy and all his visitors or only protective of his privacy as one of their own. "Is this your boy?" He nodded toward an immobilized one gazing up at him with fascinated soft black eyes. "He's going to be a heart-breaker! Was it very hot here this summer?"

"Why you want to know?" She was relenting a little, realizing perhaps that a man on foot carrying a heavy paper bag at his chest and asking for the least propertied of citizens, though dressed in the kind of business suit in which her distinguished neighbor had seldom been seen to be sought, was more likely to be an intellectual in disguise than a sneaky real-estate lawyer.

Without either disclosing his background or stating his business Rafe ascertained that Ippy was indeed known as Doc, and that he lived on the top floor of the further side of the patched-up wan green stack at the trailing extremity of Leviathan's portside fluke.

The gauntlet run, at the top of the Court he turned right and looked to his left where the pavement petered into dirt. This time it was the voice of dogs that challenged him, from the middle deck of the house he wanted, but he didn't pause to let them fix his scent. They seemed to be the only imprisoned dogs in town. Their jailer—a seedy codger with skinny arms and no shoulders in a stained undershirt with suspenders hanging looped below the pockets of his yellowed black-checked knickerbockers—inspected him from the window he had to pass on the unshipshape balcony leading across the facade to the foot of Doc's inside staircase, which was bareboarded and much too narrow for any building code, seeing that it had been divided with the domicile next door by flimsy partition. The stink of dogshit rose perpetually to the top; but the baying of the hounds subsided, as if from usage it had degenerated into merely perfunctory duty.

After slowly responding to several knockings it took Charlemagne a few seconds through his bifocals to identify the visitor; but he showed no surprise. Rafe was glad that two bottles remained intact. Pointing to the bag he said "Whenever you have the time: one for you, one for the two of us. I was afraid they were going to be confiscated on the way in."

"Did Mrs Laplace harass you?" Bent to peer intently at his student he finally smiled. "If you stay more than ten minutes she'll know you're okay by me and next time she won't bother you. I'm under her protection. She thinks professors need peace and quiet."

"Is she the one that named you Doc?"

"It's a waggish city. I suppose you're in town on Yahoo business?"

"Right now I'm here to take you out to dinner, if it's not too late for you to change your plans."

"Never mind plans. I just finished breakfast. Let's think about it a while. My housekeeper won't be back for a few hours."

As he was led over creaking floorboards to the back of the house, through the congested study and a small windowless chamber likewise scattered with books and papers, Rafe wondered what the housekeeper spent her time on; but when he had more chance to look around while they were drinking at the kitchen table he came to the opinion that no one could have done much better for this master in circumstances not at all resembling the mise-en-scene that over the last couple of years had idly fixed itself in his mind's eye as the setting in which his homework was read and replied to.

The student soon understood that Ipsissimus demanded yet more attention in his own motte than at large in other places. But how far from this citadel of symposium were the outer walls? How great the real extent of his barony? Certainly his authority as magus was bound by no less a circle than the equator, though acknowledged only by the few who appreciated the autonomous learning with which the sage conflated confounded and subsumed the categories of art and science; but as for the blooming and buzzing of the exoteric world, was he recognized as an actual lord even in the bailey of Leviathan Court?

"Have you found a title for your dreary Parenthesis? What was the name of that company again? Something to do with justice and motherhood—and farm prices. Yes of course—I remember! How could I forget a straightfaced joke like that? I've been thinking how slyly you hooked me. I hope you've come to tell me you want to change the subject. But as far as the logbook's concerned, don't dare ask for a dispensation."

"So far that's been taking as much time as Parity itself. But you told me to take in everything along the way and that's what I've been doing. Sometimes it leads me astray."

"Astray from your way is just what you may. I want to get you wandering out of the great game. But see that you wander down to reality, not up and out into Socratic clouds. Clever fellows like you have too many answers, and you're all too ready to deliver yourself of them. But Mr Opsimath has got to be more empirical if he wants to get at least halfway to Existenz."

"Corporations are fictitious, but persons! Why aren't they human enough for an arts degree?"

"The human embryo is a fictitious person too. White Quarry College shouldn't allow your conception of it."

"But if I psychoanalyze my protagonist in vivo?"

"I'm more interested in the mind of the analyst. You understand how things get done in the world. It takes a lot of doing to make a galaxy like Parity. I'll accept your paper if you can get the kind of action into it that nobody else capable of writing would know anything about. 'Action of a certain kind.' No literary stuff, mind you: just discoveries and connections. Parity's a parcel of still palpitating shards and you're the archaeologist. Your experience is what's interesting."

"Then I'll turn in my journal as the Disquisition itself!"

"No siree! The cofferdam's for your own benefit, to keep your cesspool effects outside the work. What I want from you formally is the unified *effect* of other men's diachronous trans-actions that is knowable to a disinterested reader only through writing yet sufficiently interesting to justify the considerable action of writing it . . ."

It was not so bad to be subsumed as a man of action by his graciously dominating elder, but as so often before (at Convocations) Rafe was annoyed at his teacher's unwillingness or inability to speak plainly and consistently even when there was no new ground to break. Act your experience of the object as subject of fossilized action, forsooth! Once again he found that the advice of His Imperial Majesty (H I M) could not be applied without the negative capability that was supposed to be the end-result of a liberal education rather than its prerequisite. It made him doubt his own wit; yet also, in self-defense, it made him suspect his teacher of histrionic irresponsibility. And he was beginning to get a little hot under the collar at Doc's quizzical attitude toward psychoanalysis.

But Doc continued on a more agreeable tack, dropping smile and banter. "As a matter of fact, you've got what it takes to push experience a greater distance against pressure than any student I've ever had. The President was in one of my sections at Norumbega. A Petrine Scholastic of latter generation, born not to fear the Pope, with a debonair precocity that always carried the day without effort care or knowledge. I remember him as a kind of Lamarckian stand-in waiting for dynastic assignment, but he never made his own experience the way you have. Nothing but his own personal limitation stood in the way of success at anything."

"But why give Kennedy the dickens for being no better than Roosevelt?"

"Because he was just following his old man's determination to make the family into Irish Roosevelts, for one thing. The Law School was coming next according to patriarchal schedule. For a Kennedy education was nothing but the most noncommittal way to further general ambition."

Rafe now had no objection to the commonsense prudence he'd scorned in his youth, and had always been too far from privilege to resent any 'Bega man for a father who had the means to confer it; but he thought it was a good idea to get along with Charlemagne, like most of that man's interlocutors, by refraining from argument against his cranky or persnickety pronouncements. "Parity's mastermind came out of the Norumbega Law School."

"Sure. Law's our modern substitute for divinity as the honorable school of rhetoric."

"Be thankful it isn't the 'Bega Business School that attracts the ablest. Atlantis hasn't sunk that far yet."

"Don't speak too soon. But meanwhile the priest-at-law, once he's acquired the vestments and the language, if he's rich and Irish too, can very well represent all three estates without being obliged to actually take the cloth of our national religion—unlike his recent opponent, who's just a hollow mean-spirited Cornucopian shadow, neither rich nor Irish, called to the bar from vocational school."

"But the Law has saved us from ourselves. The Constitution, the courts—"

"That's what religon's supposed to do. In a legal culture your defense and competence is the governing lingo, like Norman French among the 12C Anglo-Saxons. In law every word can be construed inclusively as well as exclusively. The axe is Janus-faced: it's more likely to nullify the action than to double it, but it cuts both ways. If you must study for a vocation, my boy, prepare for law school." Doc grinned in peroration.

Rafe was accustomed to this advice from those unaware of his intolerance for boredom; but under the circumstances he ignored it as insulting. Yet as always he marveled at the convergence of symbols. "Parity's corporate seal bears a double-bitted axe!"

"Mind you don't fool yourself with Gnujian symbullisticism. It's probably some kulak's grubbing mattock, not Arthur's double-axe. There's no spider that spins the kind of labyrinth you dream of. The innocence of production management is perpendicular to that carnivorous arachnidicity of the higher financial mind."

Did Ipsissimus Charlemagne think he was tutoring young Galahad? If it hadn't been for the whiskey (without ice) the affable student pro tem might well have been nettled by this gratuitous preaching from an erstwhile showman who probably didn't know watered stock from summer stock. But in the generous sunshine of Doc's attention, which was as alert as a child's to the peripheral interests of them both, Rafe waived most of his opportunities for a peer's reprisal. Better now to make use of the gossip, at least to test the teacher's grasp of local reality. In the process maybe this kitchen table would gradually spin itself a rounder shape.

"Did you know that Jason Anacoluther used to be Chairman of Parity?"

To give the devil his due, Doc never made any pretense of conceal-ing his pleasure at offerings of new information more savory than the commonplace sacrifices he otherwise had to make the best of. "You don't say!" He always peered attentively at the person he was addressing, or stared dominantly, but this time his eyebrows were high with amazement. Joining the pursuit, he abandoned his usual subsumptive approach to the topic of conversation, and became plainly informative to the best of his knowledge, quite frank about his interest in Rafe's interpretation of the facts about Jason, as if for the nonce he and his pupil, as colleagues in selfless research, were nearly of the same rank.

He assured Rafe that Jason was no humbug, contrary to what might be heard in some quarters, and that his art collection was well advised as well as cosmopolitan. He characterized him not so much by his boasting as by his lechery toward females younger than himself and lower in the social scale—i e , most women. Jason's public flirtation always seemed a jocular matter on both sides, but nobody could be sure that the liberal spender was never successful. His disinterested kindnesses and charities were less ostentatious and less uncertain. "Jason's a philandering philanthropist, the only one from the Foreside who ever seeks out any of us. Morally, aesthetically, he's a money-man who doesn't care about power. He owns the bank but he doesn't try to run it, and he lets good men manage his warehouses. He knows he's as weak a captain as his namesake, but smarter. I've never told him that Heracles was acclaimed as superior by all the war chiefs and virtuosos crewing the Argo but had sense enough to turn down the command and join in the rowing. Jasons never take an oar."

Doc was more encomiastic about the other friend of his that Rafe now also mentioned by way of testing his local witness. They were both glad to sing the praises of Shelly Schlossberg, but Doc furthermore wanted Rafe to appreciate Edie Schlossberg when he met her. "She's a little peach, his second wife. Fifteen years ago she was top space-buyer at a Monroe Avenue agency; came up here on a spinster vacation, spotted his driftwood sculpture, saw the error of her way—

which had been exceptionally successful, considering her looks: plainer than Jayne Eyre and twice as old. He swept her up with art, and they've been love-birds ever since. Etruscans and Jews often get into bed with each other. Shelly always was a handsome dog, and he had plenty of women to choose from when he was a widower—especially in the summer of course. Who could be more intriguing to schoolteachers on holiday than the U S A's first modern primitive? Everybody discovers him. Now she's mistaken for the jejune Yehudi business manager of a vitalic Florentine!"

"Apparently she's chambermaid as well as manager." Rafe commented. "Anyway I don't see how they could afford help. He says he has to make boat models to keep the Van going. They fetch good prices, and that's what he resents. He grudges the time they tempt."

"He doesn't grudge it as much as she does. She complains she isn't working her fingers to the bone just to let him make money. Edie believes in art for art's sake. She puts on a Yiddish accent to say she didn't give up her brilliant career just so he could imitate the Yankees." Doctor Charlemagne beamed at the thought. "'In the needle trades one of us is enough.' she says."

"The garment industry?"

"When you darn a net the flat wooden arrowhead that shuttles the twine is called a needle. Looks like a pointed sail-batten, about nine inches long, with a spindle carved out of the middle." Doc put down his cigarette to make clumsy descriptive motions with his two forefingers. Rafe recognized the device on Shelly's lobby window, but in his San Ricardo youth he'd never known what they were called, where the purse-seiners were not easily accessible to the common run of Anglo children. "The needle's in Dogtown's corporate seal. An enlightened commercial element wants to change our trademark into something more attractive to pilgrims—along with the Civic Instauration that's going to wipe out our waterfront. They think they can get rid of the unsightly poor with wrecking balls and bulldozers. Look what they're doing to your hometown!"

Doc stared hard at Rafe, forcing him to understand what was to follow. "But we lawless innocents won't let them clear any slums on this side of Front Street!"

Rafe wondered why THEY should bother, now that he was beginning to estimate the futility of Dogtown reformation. But "them" and "they" had been on Ippy's lips back in San Ricardo itself, during the first drink he'd ever had with him, when White Quarry was holding its West Coast Convocations amid pine-sheltered dunes at the nearby Isogloss Conference Center (in a precinct which to him as a native child had been as mysteriously forbidden as the Presidio or the sumptuous grounds of the Hotel Delecto). At the time in that bar he had been much less alarmed than his visiting instructor by the continual verification of Robert Louis Stevenson's statement that "The San Ricardo of last year doesn't exist. Alas for the little town, it is not strong enough to resist the influence of the flaunting caravanserai, and the poor, quaint, penniless native gentlemen must perish like a lower race, before the millionaire vulgarians of the Big Bonanza." Though cherishing hardly paradisiacal memories of his childhood Rafe thought it taxed nobody's imagination still to see the calyptic beauty of San Ricardo, while mourning its abuse, as R L S did when the railroad people hadn't yet even laid the cornerstone of their speculative hotel; or to cherish its distinction as the former capital of Cornucopia at every international stage before the Gold Rush; and now in Dogtown he recalled his previous impatience with some of the Eastern master's crabbed little historical crotchets, which might have been labeled monomaniacal by a cosmopolitan like himself if there hadn't been so many more than one.

The epitome of his own nostalgia was not uncommon in essence: the abandoned S P line from Yerba Buena, which had ended at a turntable in Eden Grove where kids were sometimes allowed to help the fireman push the engine halfway around the circle to head it back toward Golden Bay up the coast more than a hundred miles. The energetic ride itself was a rare and dear excursion. By the time he'd finally got to go to college—in fortnights of homecoming vacation—the journey was by road or air. The branch line's demise had lifted the last inhibition of the motel boom. And when the schools of sardines vanished—this time perhaps forever—THEY the rising generation of nonproducers learned the Panatlantean leverage of borrowed money. Migration and toil were indeed outmoded there. But surely, to invest in *Dogtown's* modernization would be throwing good money after bad!

"All the old livelihoods from or for the schooners used to be called the needle trades, after sailmaking, the elite art. Not just carpenters', coopers', smiths', and all the other artificers': also the chandlers' and victualers' and providers' of shore comfort. But nowadays 'needle trades' is our mockery of all that, like sealskin handicrafts in Terra Nova or diving for coins in the Caribbean; or at least it was a mockery until the Pilgrim Division of the Chamber of Commericals ignorantly adopted it as a solemn term for the yacht and tourist business. Edie says that Shelly's models for schooner-cult shrines remind her of the Sacred Heart of Jesus preserved in Valentine samplers. She keeps trying to convince him that grasping sentimentalists are worse than hardhearted developers. She knows that in the end anything more than two people can get to like will be put out for advertising—especially talents like Shelly's. But you can't teach a primitive the value of his art without turning him into an art-lover. Poor woman took the veil to do penance for the songs of New Uruk, and now she's found they're beginning to sing them in her convent!" Doc glared at Rafe as if defying the whole damn civilization and daring any citizen to cast salt on holy prophecy.

"Some convent!" Rafe sighed.

"Well there are still four or five sweatshop payrolls. Dogtown's full of cottage skills and uninsurable lofts. Low overhead and cheap labor make up for obsolescence. It used to be logistically logical: oilskins and foulweather gear, and the bidding for winter jobs ashore—instead of making shoes at home like the earlier fisherfolk of Hardmarble and some of the other towns in Gloucester County. Then during the war we got contracts to export sailor hats and dungarees for female bluejackets. That's how we got into the fat-ass stuff. Now its mostly fucking sportsware. But this little terrace got its name from the real kind of needle trade."

For a moment Doc forgot his glass, both elbows on the table, his mouth dragging cigarette smoke, eyes fixed intently on the the saucer he used for an ashtray, deeply absorbed in what Rafe took to be another speculative interpretation of facts, as if rethinking this story. "Old man Levi Nathan bought up the tenements in this Court on what he made in that business, competing on a cash-and-carry basis. His family understood R O I long before your people ever heard of it, from their century under the Czar, and to this day they're plus roialiste que le Roi. But Levi was so well estimed for his benevolence to Jews and Gentiles alike that twenty years ago the city fathers renamed this alley for him. Originally it was Potter's Lane, but that name no longer had any constituency. The City Clerk elided LEVI NATHAN to LEVIATHAN, a sound that satisfied Christians.

"The son Benlevi still runs the Factory Store you passed on the water side of Front Street just before you turned up this hill. It's an unadorned dry goods emporium for the poor and thrifty where I buy my mittens. Ben lets people think it's his own factory's outlet, but in fact he buys most of his merchandise in Bot at auctions and fire sales; sometimes drives all the way to New Uruk in his converted 1950 Frontenac hearse, which he says he bought because he needs room behind the wheel: weighs more than any man in town and likes his luxuries. Now his father's dead he's coming into his own. He's still got about thirty women cutting and stitching up on the third floor. That part of the business can't last much longer, but he's too haunted by the voice of his governor to lay anyone off. For fifty years the skinny old man jeered at every move he made."

"Feel like eating now?"

"Is it dark yet? Yeh. I've got to put out the garbage. I'll show you the old Whale Wharf. You'll see the crotch of the harbor where fifty schooners used to berth—where there's nothing now but shit." He had risen to his feet, tilting, and pointed vehemently downhill. "The Chamber of Commercials wants to cover up her shame, but the filth is in their grubby minds . . ."

Rafe would have liked to decline the favor of local history in situ, or of anything else that might further delay his dinner, but he feared touchiness at any sign of imperfect fidelity.

Doc hoisted to his back a gray tweed overcoat with splitted seams, knotting the arms around his neck. It was a warm night, Rafe remarked. "The weather has nothing to do with it," said the big man with one of his charming unexpected grins that always flattered the heart of a companion. "It's my cloak of respectability, for going downtown. In your honor." Spreading his palm on the breast of his undarned purple cardigan he made a leg with soft-shuffled ankle-high gunboats, bowing politely, took a stuffed brown paper bag from beneath the sink, and led Rafe out the dark back door.

They went down a short gangway connecting the third floor to a sloping irregular ledge, a shelf of weedgrassed scree on beaten earth in the inhabited scarp of Spirit Hill, and without enough light they cautiously picked their way down a series of rickety wooden steps and galleries around the end of the house to the street. In the diminished noise of evening a litigation of gulls and barking of distant dogs was peacefully revealed. Two nightwalkers had stolen right by the resident hounds.

"Come up the back from now on, if you stay in town. You won't have to pass the inspection of that brokendown actor. I go without central heat in order to get that apartment with the private postern."

Doc twisted the skirt of his coat over the bag of garbage. The concealment was as conspicuous as an evil shepherd spiriting off the baby Jesus, but the Court was empty even of kids. "Devilvision cooks their little brains and keeps them off the streets when I'm out prowling. These generations will never grow up. That wouldn't be so bad if the irradiation sterilized them, but they'll conceive their own children under that evil eye, and their children's children will be born within eyeshot."

Down on Front Street he pointed to Benlevi's Factory Store. "It used to be the largest ship chandlery on this coast." But instead of turning before it, after Doc had disputed the sparse traffic to cross the thoroughfare they headed down a dirt ramp to the waterfront behind it, passing a few abandoned sheds and the foundations of others, and came out on a broad tapering pier rotted full of dangerous holes and splattered with guano.

Deftly, daintily, Doc stepped to the side, dropped his paper bag over the edge, and returned to Rafe with a new air of relief, putting behind him the silent feat of legerdemain that he had just pulled off with the cooperation of a witness delicate enough to be looking the other way and not to be asking questions about sanitation ordinances.

To Rafe the planks on which they stood were undistinguished details of the generally ruined waterfront, gray by day and dark by night, but Doc tugged his shoulder to reverse the direction of his gaze, making him look landward whence they had descended, up the hill to the poor lights of Leviathan Court, which could be picked out like an exiguous constellation in a sparse patch of crowded sky. "See— we're treading the head of that whale! See how he dives under Front Street?" Like Matisse with long brush lashed to arthritic wrist he traced and sketched with an arm extended straight.

"Whaling here was always a dark ambiguity. It wasn't 'Fishing' and it wasn't 'Commerce', the Harbor's two recognized investment cultures. Except for one or two of the small-scale ventures from this wharf, serious whaling was a failure here. The men in our fisheries were too horny and the owners too short of capital to go hunting at sea if it took more than a single season. Our commercial capitalists preferred Dutch Guyana to India and China for the quicker turnover too. Somehow, among all the other New Armorican ports, they'd preempted that trade after the British and the French shut the U S out of all the rest of the West Indies. Dogtown was Guyana's most favored nation: that's the ugly mystery I've got somebody working on. Between unloading cargoes of salt fish and cabbage and ice and manufactures in New Leiden and loading return cargoes of rum-sugar to make their legitimate domestic fortunes on they apparently had time to pull off a much faster R O I than anyone could ever net in whale oil: certain maritime services for the Plattdeutsch planters that could only be performed with a guilty conscience. As far as I can make out, only a few ever actually tried the quick unmentionable run across the South Atlantic, probably because the abolitionists at home, mainly their own good womenfolk, made most of them too nervous about breaking the law on that account; but they were pretty sensitive about being sutlers to that trade. It was considered indelicate even to admit that the salt fish they carried went to feed the slaves already there. Anyway, 'whaling' became a euphemism for such enterprise. But for a hundred years the codfish aristocracy here has been praising itself for having refused to invest in real whaling, which was said not to have been up to its commercial expectations. Not very different from the theater industry: 'It may be good—but is it commercial?'"

Doc's finger swung slowly counterclockwise from jumbled waterfront buildings defined only by their occlusion of more distant city light, past the black gap of the outer harbor, along the elevation of treetops close across the water on Mother's Neck (much of which was blocked in the foreground by the massive septum of a freezer-warehouse on Beauport Fish Pier which divided the slot of deepest water from a broader cove where boats of business and pleasure lay intermingled at other wharves and anchorages), around to the night foliage of East Harbor's ridge, the highly peopled shin of stately Harbor Foreside, and back to the ramshackle structures on their right. Having boxed the compass in reverse, like two parallel magnets in a swinging ship, they again faced the nightlighted hill. "Dogtown will be barren. They want to scrape her womb smooth! Then after Whale Wharf's torn down, along with all these sheds and sail lofts, they'll even stuff her twat with real estate to keep the tide from its bourn."

The act of starting back to the ancient shoreline road, so long deferred by recitations of little interest to a hungry stranger, somewhat encouraged Rafe's patience for historical entertainment. It also diverted annoyance at the teacher's preemption of his own more delicately descriptive imagery which a couple of hours before had been mailed to Cornucopia for the transcription that would prove his poetic invention. But perhaps all men given to mapping were likely to visualize this fold of the harbor at the lower rather than the upper end of the seaport's spinal cord.

Yet this gathering of her sights and sounds, when he seemed to feel her own seeing and hearing, was mainly cerebral. Without Doc's tutelage he could no more have interpreted the planeless picture of presentation than he could have decoded the signals of the fire whistle. Against the stationary white and yellow lights that limned the land, varying in altitude magnitude clarity and signification, burning at fixed distances from each other and from the unlighted whale's head which centered the much dimmer heavens known to be wheeling, others of random or deliberate inconstancy made a theater of the unwalled mural with moving and intermittent jewels of independent electricity, red green or colorless: navigation lights in motion, shore and channel definitions, glancing beams of errant automobiles, the wandering stars of airplanes taking turns toward Botolph below the southern horizon.

Dogs were quiet now, and most of the gulls retired to Parliament Island, or to the coves they favored when shunning crowds of their own kind. Rafe listed to the civic continuo: a susurration of pulsations fainter than throbs from stationary and mobile power plants, from hearts at rest or still at work—a panoramic rhythm. He identified the bottom of this vale, whose level changed around the clock with tides, as the very center of the soft nightlong vibration that at the Van calmed him into deep sleep and then wakened him before the day's noisy melodies started up again.

He remembered no such primitive music in the body of San Ricardo, an even older settlement of Christians, from which vast territories had been governed. On Cannery Row (even in its heyday unimaginable either as an invaginated haven or as a lumen of consciousness) everything was nakedly passive to a vaster Ocean. He could remember no electromechanical hum in the night-breath of his own hometown.

Now Charlemagne pursued a more romantic line of poetry. "You've been standing in the hollow of my ship." he said, lingering again in his tracks (to Rafe's hungry consternation) and once more turning full circle, looking hard in all directions, but this time with his hands swinging loose. "At night I take the anchor watch." Up on the street without his bag of garbage Raphael's Virgil was little less conspicuous.

The Cornucopian himself had yet to be disputed by dogs on liberty. Two of them coming down the slope of Federal Hill crossed to the other side in passing, evidently not in fear or enmity but simply out of habitual respect for the largest nightwalker they knew, now superfluously reinforced by a somewhat smaller one of blander scent.

Only from the top of this acclevity (where Back Street spliced into Front) did they first catch sight of neon colors—and then not many: too few in fact to cheer the heart of a ravenous bigspender who'd had his bellyfull of chophouse disappointments all over the most charming parts of North Atlantis. But Doc assured him that the Windmill would still be serving.

They stayed on Front Street, past the Van, along the dip and bend, up the rising double row of storefronts to the wide place called Morality Square where it's intersected by Pleasure. Until they reached this summit of the second wave (longer than the one at Back Street), Dogtown's busiest crossroads by day, everything was closed for the night except the dimmed City Lights Theater (which had already swallowed the last show's last spectator), a couple of liquor stores, and half a dozen ill-lit bars. Not a soul was to be seen coming or going on foot—only a few soul-directed cars attracted or released by the brightly lighted prism of Pound's Drug Store on the crest, the illumination from which was choked by divers streamers and posters affixed to the glass of its modern doorway at the chamfered corner but which nevertheless now dominated the darkened Yuleworth chain store and two bank buildings on the three corners that overshadowed it before dusk and after 10 PM.

Into Pound's quick as a wink ducked the honorary Doctor, courteously furtive, a fish skipping out of water, coins ready in hand for a fast transaction, to snatch a copy of the *Dogtown Daily Nous*, only to roll it up without inspection and carry it as a baton on the rest of their way, sometimes tapping his own chest and thigh, or Rafe's head and shoulder, and extending the sweep of other gestures. "My dessert." he explained. "My midnight entertainment, the quotidian resolution of civic uncertainty and renewal of suspense, the herald of local surprises: Dogtown's weekday letter to yours truly. On Sunday I have to use the *New Uruk Testament,* but its coverage of Dogtown ain't what it should be."

Front Street narrowed as it dropped again, bent northerly, and then veered to opposite bias in a canyon of business blocks that looked the taller for facing each other so closely along the curve, the abbreviated barely lighted markee of another picture theater making a salient on the harbor side. Just beyond it came the only stretch of priceless architecture, early 19C gabled brick or granite, originally residential, which being little prized was given over on ground floors to disfigurements of beauty in the interests of what looked to a Cornucopian like very cramped retail commerce—barbers, cobblers, a locksmithy, more than one Tuscan bakery, a secondhand furniture store, and other such Old World shops, all now darker within the darkness of the street than comparatively they were by day. Front Street's remaining taverns betrayed very little of their animation because it was still too early for argument to burst the doors.

"These are the ones they're keenest to tear down. They love to fill up the coves with bricks and slabs like these; they say it's just what's needed for the best construction footing. These buildings were put up by housewrights trained in making schooners who knew how to improve all the curves and angles of shoreline lots with Federalist simplicity. In those days water frontage was too precious to waste on stables: their kitchen gardens went for ship stalls; spars and cooperage were kept in their backyards. But now even this unpolished gem"— Doc patted the curve of granite they were passing—"offends the Earldermen because its upstairs windows are broken and the landlord won't keep it in repair otherwise either. It seems that the pilgrims turn up their noses at this end of the street, and that frightens the merchants up there." His thumb jerked toward the business establishments they had passed on higher ground, from which this Tuscan West End was hidden by no more than the littoral twist instituted by a colonial footpath.

He waved at the storefronts. "Naturally these Etruscans don't give a damn what Dogtown used to look like. They always build their nests from the inside anyway. They care about their cooking equipment—most of them have two kitchens—and their furniture; and cars of course; but they don't have the Yankee obsession with neat and clean externality. They came here for the fishing, by God, and for each other! Better the Europeans mess up lower Front Street by making it a neighborhood, after nobody else saw the good of it anymore, than have it disinfected of life and modernized for the needle trade! Mess and stench has always been Dogtown's best defense against the landsharks—and against the goo-goos too—who haven't yet discovered what's under the shambles. God bless our dirt! Preserve our politics!"

Doctor Charlemagne wheeled to address not only Raphael Opsimath but also the entire bourgeoisie of the upper city, thumbing a nose elongated by the rolled newspaper, a magnified lightly fantastic faun too old to prance very lively. "Reformers, beware! Belletrists, go away! Enlightened businessmen, invest your loans someplace else!"

"As long as ignorance keeps wages down!" Rafe teased him with the dark Satanic conspiracy of Dogtown mill-owners whose messuages were well removed from Dogtown's tolerated litter and variably provocative stink. Doc looked sharply at him, and smiled, falling silent, as they came to the end of the lumbar curve at the bottom of the city's stunted backbone.

Sacrum Square, a bleakly exposed slope of cobblestones, was the source or sink of Front Street and five others, each of its asymmetrical radiants rooted on a different level of the original town-landing hollow. The island's circumferential road that Rafe had crossed at the end of his train ride, Cod Street, wended down to anchor from its highland course, below the old settlements now fused into a single city shaped by the cincture here knotted. All paths still met at the irregular hexagon, into which Rafe and Doc now emerged from between two corners that brought an end to the fine old brick opposite the more adorned concrete sales garage of an automobile dealer.

Divided from the unlighted showroom by a continuation of Front Street called Serpentine Avenue was a triangular tongue of wooden family houses overflowing from the surface of population that decked every hill and glen of the city's torso. What might have been the sixth and broadest corner of real estate was the head of Landing Cove, an indentation of the inner harbor jammed with moored boats and crowded on its flanks by fish wharves. Down on their left, next to the thicket of masts, they faced the Key Street maw of the Casbah, a villainous-looking hammerheaded fortress of Tuscans guarding the introitus of the inner harbor in opposition to the tranquil barbican of Mother's Neck across the channel. On their immediate right, between the steep rectangular descent of Cod and the tiny diagonal of Bevel Street shortcutting down from the west end of Back Street, a cluttered little MONOCO gas station clung to its strategic gore, half lighted and obviously neither opened nor closed at uncertain hours.

Rafe had walked this course already, and noticed these features, but he hadn't yet divagated to the right or to the left, and he was already beginning to worry that he wouldn't have time to see everything on the map. "Dogtown leaves me no rest." he said. And neither now lagged the other in their quest for dinner.

They picked a straight way across the unbitumened knobs of gray stone still embossing this pitched locus of six streets each long since repaved everywhere else with asphalt. "When there's no moon this is the brightest spot in the city." said Doc. In fact it was like walking onto the bare stage of an empty house. This slippery misshapen square diffused mutually reinforcing glare from half a dozen high-hung public lamps, the reflecting lids of which delimited a hanging ceiling of opaque darkness above the cars dogs and men who nevertheless here exposed themselves one or two at a time to the thousand eyes of night.

At this hour, however, but for themselves there were no dogs or men, or even cars—the few of which at this hour were alarmingly self-absorbed, careering unbaffled through the spacious traffic star, slowed only by its jolting bumps, where on schoolday afternoons hundreds of them milled with trucks and buses in a melee differentiated only by the individual temperaments of their pilots—unless governed by some indigenous code of customs impenetrable to Rafe—who was prompted to remark "It's a good thing I didn't rent a car in Dogtown. I'm not used to anarchy in the streets. Aren't there any rights of way? It looks like first-come-first-serve at every intersection. Stop and go at will! All drivers seem to rely on other people's brakes."

"But pretty cute psychologists. They don't kill many, and then it's mostly themselves or dogs. Nearly all of us left in the infantry are fearless; the cars themselves are intimidated, even if the drivers aren't, and they're aware that jaywalking is our inalienable rite de passage. Horses have always been more sensitive than horsemen."

"I'm not worried about insolent pedestrians, or the dogs I see in the streets. They're as disdainful as cows in India. Judging by the multitude, there seems to be a good measure of survival. But what shocks me is the way your cars treat each other! Aren't there any conventions of war? Look: even in this intersection there are no traffic lights!"

"Everybody says signals don't work in Dogtown. Whenever the State engineers succeed in sneaking one in there's such incredible confusion that they're forced to take it out again. So the prophecy is self-fulfilling, like Sam Adams's warnings against the Stamp Act. Dogtown is ruled by public outcry. One car, one vote! The Earls content themselves with ordaining one-way streets—usually because two-way traffic threatens to interfere with random double parking. Sometimes they post nominal stop-signs."

"The West was never so lawless!" Rafe marveled. Doc's worry about progress in Dogtown seemed misapprehensive. Civic virtue had apparently left the place untouched. Perhaps untouchable.

They put behind them the tilted astigmatic carousel (as if turning their backs on the vacant and deanimated stage set of an operetta with no janitor to turn out the lights and lock up), climbing the short pass between car-stable and people-houses, a third offshoot of the upland, this one bearing them to their goal: a small beach-hemmed headland halfway down the Serpentine's twist—the very coccyx of Front Street's sacral curve, or the very codicil of Cod.

Now at nighttime on the mainland side of the island's westermost ridge, beneath a hillface open to the bay—where the neck of the serpent descended abruptly to flatten out at seawall level below the Windmill, sharply straightening out beneath the perpetual surveillance of inland windows mounted in tiers, and broadening uncharacteristically into the outstretched boulevard—Rafe understood the anatomy he'd only seen by day. All he could look at now was a stately line of streetlights, which to a foreign captain on the cold dark sea would seem the raiment of civil pleasures. Instead of a genteel pavilion with statue bandstand and drawbridge, denuded of greenery and devoid of style but designed for a comparatively undenatured view of a demilandlocked roadstead clean outside the slovenly overworked inner harbor, Rafe now contemplated a shorn and bastioned causeway to the continent. Across the Gut, where a string of lights lost itself in Tansy Hill, the road recovered its old unimproved sinuous way down the coast to Felicity-by-the Sea, Beggarly, Bethsalem, Swanfen, Liverpool, and all the other towns he'd passed in the dark on the railroad's straighter course along the inside of the coast.

Crossing a line of residual elms that resembled pillars of a ruined cathedral on the nearly deserted parking garth they went up some steps into the fenestrated clapboard barn set broadside to the harbor on its walled bluff. There on the inn's bucked-up spit of rock the Serpentine's mouthpiece was presented to the southeasterly winds that swept the open Bight of Vinland, the worst seas of which for the last fifty years had been chastened two miles off by the breakwater of chthonic granite hewn and transplanted by direction of the U S Corps of Engineers to provide coastal craft a pasture of refuge outside the inner city's crowded corrals and paddocks. But long before the breakwater was projected the sails of a great windmill on this knoll had been reefed also for northwesterly gales blowing down the Namauche River valley from John Smith's Bay, and driven by all the world's other airs that were broken or swayed by hills and vales of the islanded Cape.

* * *

They were the last diners, and not very welcome to their waitress (who probably had trouble enough to get home at a decent hour); for as they awaited someone to greet them Rafe caught sight of her at the kitchen door catching sight of Doc. Striking her forehead with the heel of her palm she spun right around and ran right back inside—whether to give the alarm or to compose herself. But in due course she approached them with a sprightly smile outstretched.

The restaurant that on Rafe's previous visit had been aglare from the waters below was now dimly lighted by ocher-amber table lamps, which warmed the ocher-brown carpet and rendered as cordial frozen flames the ocher-red napkins tented in pairs and double-pairs amid gleaming silverware all over a forlorn field of larger and smaller tables caparisoned in thick snow-white linen. "My ocean liner." said Doc. "I like to eat after all the other passengers have retired to the saloon." At this time of night Busty Pacioli relinquished supervision of the dining room, though he could always be found fraternizing with customers in the Millstone Bar. At Doc's insistence they were led to one of the tables least convenient to the kitchen where he could occupy his favorite vantage at the great plateglass windows. "This looks like the Queen Mary's tourist-class dining room in the middle of the night. Being as wide as the whole deck it had to serve also as a passageway and was kept half lighted at all hours. But you could see out both sides."

Doc wouldn't let the woman simply drop the menus and depart straightway with a plain order for the drinks. "Pull back those drapes all the way will you dearie so I can show this stranger our harbor." She obeyed docilely in the manner of one who had previously suffered the gentleman's whims.

The divaricate gulf of Dogtown's nightsprawled loins was sparsely punctuated with an ensemble of dissonant lights—clear red, sharp green or blue, weaker sparkling white—each darting its own assignment in abstract display without sound or vibration to reinforce its warnings, without the percussion wind or string of mechanical motion: an electric thrill bleakly devoid of the inner harbor's haptic throb:: fixed stars, unfixed airplanes not so distant (not even so distant as two or three lighthouses flashing faintly over the horizon on Vinland's principal reefs), and mimic buoys quick with spates of warning::: but all predominated by the red beacon in the foreground at the navigable end of Parliament Island and its distant gemination in the doll lighthouse at the end of the breakwater. Even unmanned stationary warnings were not to be understood all at once. On the extreme right, for instance, halfway down the esplanade's straightened crescent of landsmen's lights, Rafe's eyes were drawn obliquely to a horizontal pair of steadfast unfaltering red eyes that at first he did not recognize as the target and barrier for boats seeking the Gut bridge, portcullis to the tidal prairies of the Namauche and shortcut to northern waters from the outer harbor.

"Sir, the kitchen wants to close soon." the waitress timidly apologized, after Doc made a big fuss about being asked for his dinner order before he'd had a couple of rounds of the same stuff they'd been drinking in his kitchen (only at five times the cost per ounce to Rafe). As the big customer beetled at her she made it worse by hastily adding "It's slower tonight than usual. You're the last one left." She was so possessed by fear of Doc that her attention and her second-person pronouns were singular, as if she addressed the parent of a mute.

"You're always pulling that one on me, sister! —What does your watch say, Mr Opsimath? —It's still forty minutes to the advertised closing time. The cook can't object to staying on the job. I wonder if Busty knows how you treat his best patron." And by way of threat he glanced toward the bar.

Rafe had never sailed across the Atlantic, nor had he frequented polite circles in his native land, but he was easily able to put himself in the place of a servant in any society. It was still but a few years since he'd acceded to the personal service of a secretary, whom he would have coddled even if he hadn't found coddling more expedient than abuse. Southerners and salesmen may be courteous because they reckon to catch more flies with sugar than with vinegar, but with Rafe, abhorring rudeness because he sympathized with its victims (until they proved themselves willfully hateful), it was not a matter of policy. So as a bystander he conveyed his compassion for the handmaid with an understanding smile. Yet he was well aware that sympathy is often misguided, and that he sometimes failed to grasp the self-estimation of willing inferiors. He also knew that an infuriating Director might well be better than himself at revivifying salutary anger in a dead soul. Maybe Doc's bullying was intended to goad the waitress into rebellion against the very idea of serving any man for pay. Though without renouncing creature comfort, Doc himself had refused to serve Mammon. And that was a virtue which Rafe was not inclined to pretend to claim to even fancy the possession of.

By this time Doc was condescending to a paternal tone with his servant, gazing at her treacherously. "A business loses its good name you know if it doesn't keep its word. We might have come all the way up here from Bot. Do you ever come home on the train when it's almost empty? Have you ever been the only one on a bus?" She had to nod her head like a trapped schoolgirl. "Well then my dear how would you like it if they decided not to make the run just because your fare alone didn't make it pay?" She smiled in spite of her fear. "I guess you wouldn't like it. Their franchise is a sacred trust to take the bitter with the better—and occasionally forget their goddam Return on Investment!" Here of course he grinned maliciously at Rafe, as if he'd just trumped Rafe's partner.

There was a giggle. A new waitress had appeared, summoned no doubt by the terms of a mutual assistance pact. To her, as to the first, Rafe did his best to communicate silent disavowal of his companion's attitude. This one was more amused. Perhaps she'd never borne the brunt. "Hello there!" she was greeted by the infamous customer. "Come to help handle the terrible infant? Well there's two of us too, so the problem's reduced by half." He turned back to the primary attendant: "Milly, are you willing to split the tip?"

Both women laughed this time. Thereupon, asserting the authority of host, Rafe intervened to negotiate a compromise whereby Doc agreed to study the menu, as long as the first remained poised with pad and pencil, while the other took care of the bar order. When the whiskeys arrived Milly was still waiting for Doc to end his vagarious observations and asides, mentally tapping her foot and physically staring at the carpet. Her poverty of spirit only prolonged a cross-examination of the chef's methods and materials and the final cantankerous instructions that made free with the sets and categories printed in the bill of fare.

"There now, you see? We've given you everything you wanted and it's still hardly past the closing time for arrivals. We'd be within our rights, practically, if we came in the door for the first time right now! But you're a good girl, and I thank you for giving us time to breathe. Thank you, thank you. You have lovely blue eyes, and I bet you've laid them on sweeter sights than me!" Doc was smiling at her with ingratiating joviality as she bent to retrieve the menus. Rafe was afraid he was going to pat her on the ass, but he only touched her arm, just as she was about to swing into action at last, and slowed her down once more. Peering solicitously up into her face he gently asked "How are the kids, Milly?"

Wanly she pulled a fleeting painful smile—"Good, thank you Doctor."—and finally escaped at a run down the long emptied room to the kitchen door. Doc appealed to her colleague, who was cheerfully enough helping with the various small accoutrements and garnishments required by the formulas chosen. "Tell your sister I meant no offense. I'm no worse than many a celebrity—and you know I gave up a glittering career at first base in order to live in Dogtown." She was older than the other, newer to the Windmill, and as it happened not averse to a little eccentricity, but wise enough to respond with nothing more than a genuine noncommital smile; and Doc soon ceased to notice her. "I gather that our girl doesn't like to be called Milly." he said to Rafe.

"Is she a Mildred or a Millicent?"

"I don't know, but it's a reasonable diminutive for Windmill. Or for Millstone; sometimes she works in the bar. I never thought she minded. It's not as bad as Sally-In-My-Alley. I suppose she thinks I'm a brokendown doctor of medicine, an abortionist or something. God knows what legend she makes of me. On this island of cynics and gullibles that's one thing they all have in common: not the legends themselves but the faculty for making legends. Kids aren't allowed into high school until they've written up one (which goes with them in their dossier); and they aren't allowed to graduate until they've compiled what's known as a Gloucesterbook, their geographical cross-section of extant legends—their personal canon of historical outcomes—from all over the Cape. Their meretricious paradigm is Faust's exploration: *Doctor Foster / Went to Gloucester* and fell in a puddle, et cetera.

"Dogtown's always had a capacity for negative patriotism—the nearest it gets to prophecy. Take Meriwether Sterne, the Royalist counterrevolutionary priest. Merry Sterne was fed up with Monmouthshire and full of zeal for the New World. He'd lived in France for a while and gotten corrupted by secular literature. Over here the Separatist divines called him the Anglican Rabelais. Of course they couldn't distinguish Rabelais from Montaigne. The *Mayflower* people drove him out of Bensalem, and in Botolph the Governor sentenced his manuscripts to the stake. He was lucky to get out of there alive.

"The only refuge was Dogtown, never in good odor with authorities. He presumed that it would be more susceptible to his interpretation of the City of God. All who heeded him were to get something like immediate return on their investment in this hard life of fishing and scratch farming. He hacked out a little homestead over there across the Gut, just above Old Bethsalem Road. Very few came to his Cranmer revision of the Lord's Supper (which was still too Scholastic for Separatists), but some listened to his sweet and reasonable sermons in defense of goodhumored tradition; and they began to flock to his celebrations of life when he set up a Maypole on Tansy Hill—in Fisherman's Field, the flat you saw at the top of Salt Cod Park, where visiting circuses and carnivals are staked out nowadays.

"That was too much for the Overseers. He was ordered to confine the merrymaking to his own land and thereto fined for every occasion thereof. So on the crown of the much higher hill in back of his house he trimmed a standing pine thick enough to belong to the king and cleared the ground around it, making a Maypole far more prominent than the first one. When the maying season was over he hoisted a yardarm and turned it into a cross, which was the last straw even for the latitudinarians. A gang came and chopped it down. He lost his remaining followers, relieving them of the intolerable freedom of conscience preached by the official parish, which in any case had demanded their free time and surplus money all along. And the town fathers raised his taxes—an amercement they knew he couldn't pay because he'd used up the last of his patrimony on said devlish vanity. There was no bishop within 3000 miles to appeal to.

"I believe he was a lovely man, not yet at middle life. He'd married, here, a thrilling young witch who kept his spirits up and made him start writing all over again. She was very good at helping him recall things he thought he'd read or heard. No one knows what happened to the second batch of manuscripts, but his doctrinal seed had fallen on ground that was not wholly barren. Nothing could have entirely prevented antinomianism of one kind or another in a bastard colony like this; but I hold that the denomination of General Individualism would never have been founded in Dogtown—as you know, a century later—if his inspiration hadn't survived subliminally in the town libido. It ain't surprising that a partiality for universal salvation should incubate in congenitally lawless roughnecks ruled by puritannical oligarchs."

In his sightseeing of the U S A Rafe habitually skipped or slighted historical monuments and inscriptions, but he now remembered catching a phrase or two of the bronze plaque set into living rock at Salt Cod Park to the effect that Dogtown fishermen, defending their immemorial but unrecorded industry by squatter's rights, had stood off Myles Standish, up from Bethsalem to police their commerce, long before the settlement submitted even to its voluntary self-government.

"Anyway it was the General Individualists right here in Dogtown who eventually forced genuine freedom of religion into clauses of the Vinland constitution, finally disestablishing the Separatist disestablishmentarians. That fostered the misapprehension that they were otherwise liberal, and has fooled the Humanist Divinity parish into a poverty-driven merger, which is now about to be followed on the national level. It's to be called the Divine Individualist Church: an ill-starred marriage here at least, greased by the accidental blandishments of language. But thank God they keep up the old Bulfinch meeting-house on Halibut Street . . ."

The hearty course was served by both waitresses, who seemed trained to ask diners if everything was all right exactly as they began to chew their first big mouthful in the midst of animated conversation, as if response was necessary at that very moment to reassure a diffident conscientious chef. "Yes yes," said Doc "this steak is fine. Seeing that we seem to be taxing the patience of this organization by showing up at all tonight, I'd better tell you ahead of time that I'll be wanting another one." With wagging eyebrows he challenged them impartially, the principal having willingly shared power and responsibility with her selfless auxiliary. "I want you to get home early to your boyfriends. All you've got to do is repeat my order, verbatim, the whole works. Can you still read the slip you wrote before? I'll eat this one reasonably fast. Run and tell the cook right now, so he won't hang up his apron until it's quitting time, but don't bring it so soon that it'll get cold on me. And Happy New Year to him! —Mr Opsimath, will you be joining me in a second helping?"

It looked as if Milly had been dreading just such a contretemps as this, fearing the chef as much as her public tormentor. The other woman went off stifling a shriek of laughter.

"But what happened to Father Sterne?" Rafe asked, averting his eyes from the spectacle of Doc as trencherman, head down, elbows out, fork in one fist and knife in the other.

"Please excuse me for anticipating, by the way. I didn't want to keep the staff late. —Oh yes, Merry Sterne: except for a few hooligans, the people of Dogtown didn't persecute him after he was forced to quit corrupting their religion. After all, his wife was no stranger. But their general bigotry would have killed him if he hadn't sold out and gone back to England with her. He was finally granted a living in Yorickshire, on the strength of having defied the Roundheads, and there he bred a congregation of his own kids (like Bach's family choir); but the poor guy was so deranged by his experience here that he tried to preach universal salvation in the wrong temple. He was no radical, and he knew perfectly well that the Tudor church was just as terrified of wiping out Hell as the schismatics were, but he died practically defrocked, driven mad by Dogtown—the first of a long line. The widow returned, leaving her male children in England. You can see his genes in Tristram Shandy. Forty or fifty years after that book came out there was finally a Dogtown shipowner gracious enough to name his brig the *Uncle Toby*. As a matter of fact she was famous in trade with the Continent, from the Baltic to the Mediterranean. Turner painted her portrait, which you'll find at the Atheneum. The Scientific's been trying to steal it ever since academics started calling Turner civilized, on the plea that they'd had first refusal of the gift way back."

The Dogtown Atheneum is the Free Library, and Rafe had already learned that "The Scientific" is the usual abbreviation for "Cape Gloucester Literary, Scientific, and Historical Lyceum", which was long since ossified into a genteel museum by its paternalistic benefactor. But he continued to wonder at Doctor Charlemagne's assumption that such historical commentary would be of interest to a transcontinental geographer like himself.

"The Atheneum's less Platonic than the Lyceum, despite its name. It's naturally where they keep all the Legends and Gloucesterbooks, by the way. Some day the Scientific will also be claiming those. But we've got a honey of a reference librarian, with the energy of a puppy. She's indexing and cross-referencing everything in the Gloucester County Room. It takes an Irish off-islander to appreciate what we've got. She probably wouldn't have known a needle before her husband brought her here from Montvert. She's started a new collection on the Depression too, which she doesn't think should be forgotten; but a lot of people here are still as much embarrassed by the hard times they had as by the stories their kids write. She's a good little Locofoco.

F D R's picture is still pinned to her wall calendar. Gets her spunk from being brought up by the only Catholicrat family in a little town of rugged Protesticans. Some day posterity will bless Gloria Keith—if the Library has sense enough not to neglect her archives after she leaves."

On this line of rumination Doc kept eating, eyes turned inward as his dragging grapnel found a purchase on what he was getting warmed up to talk about. Rafe recognized the prodrome of something that might last all night long if he went back to Leviathan Court afterwards. The pleasant steadily confidential matter-of-fact voice, full of modest subsuming respect for all his companions in history (present company included) and for all the competencies from which he had turned aside in favor of his unique one, was always too interesting to interrupt much or to argue with; and such references to his personal experience as then ensued were as absolutely fascinating as productions of *Hamlet*.

"She remembers, as you and I do, that first F D R's P W A and then his W P A saved us. It was a recovery of the true concept of public works by an emergency Works Progress Administration. The antithesis to market economics. In those days we didn't have an Offense Department to promote merchants-of-death prosperity. The Navy built most of its own ships, with tax money directly, and the Army ran its own arsenals; they were still professional 'services' of public policy, not Government-guaranteed angels for secret procurement from private industries addicting all employees and employees' vendors to entropic affluence. Under Roosevelt our res publica's works were a national liturgy that took in many *urgies* of society, not just the waterworks and roads of ditch-diggers. Harry Hopkins was a genius of implementation, like General Marshall in the war, who may have learned from him. He wanted to employ all abilities for the sake of society itself—though of course the W P A always had to be justified in terms of jobs for the sake of wages, even when it hired accountants and engineers and lawyers and doctors of medicine and teachers of everything. All through the devastations of the Depression and desperations of the war he and F D R instinctively understood that civilization without culture is no society.

"The secret truth is that by Federal action Roosevelt wasn't merely trying to save the economy. That was unconscionable enough to make him Private Enemy Number One to most of the income-taxpayers in the country. If they'd realized that he hoped to encourage the idea of society for its own sake they would have taken to arms with the Veterans Legion. They were suspicious enough, you remember, about all the musicians painters sculptors and writers getting bread from the W P A for doing their own work, especially when it was the first time many of them had ever made their living with art and when no one evaluated their output commercially. Worse yet, none of them made more money than the others!

"All you ever heard about was freeloaders leaning on their shovels. So what? The waste was negligible compared with the waste in most of the elements of our Gross National Product, under Eisenhower or anybody else. The principal product of W P A art projects was artists.

"But I couldn't make it with drama-*turgy*. I wanted to be F D R's assessor in his office of Archon Eponymos, and make myself archchoregus for the Theater Project at the expense of the U S Treasury; but they gave me the degrading title of Senior National Creative Consultant, out of Washington, supposedly a sort of advisory dramaturge to the local directors, with no archon's authorization to insist upon the repertories I was hoping for. In the long run it always has to be what the people want—even when there's no box-office excuse and the President isn't one of the people. It's all too easy for a schoolboy like Whoreson Sells to make himself famous in films. In those days I was a tenderfoot at democracy in the arts and I still believed in politics. I meant to have an Abbey Theater in every neighborhood—and without the O'Casey degeneration! I considered myself a Hermes to Roosevelt from Yeats!"

"Yeats! But after all I've heard you say about idealistic—"

"I met him in London when I was playing Cuchulain in some dance-studio productions of the plays. We couldn't get him to come look, he'd been so often horrified by the artistic corruption of his admirers. He thought we might be doing *Baile's Strand* in football suits. So I went to visit him at his hotel. Of course he didn't give me any message, but when I arrived in Washington I had some beautiful Yeatsean sentences. However, by the time I finally got to see F D R I was so absorbed by power politics that I didn't waste any of my minutes on synthesized advice from a name that he was probably vaguely aware of as someone in ditherland who once got a Noble Prize as a literary anachronism who made Irish patriotism a little more troublesome.

"There was just time enough to have an unscheduled cup of coffee with him, but I was too het up about my scheme to drink a drop. It was the only chance I'd have to put it directly before the king. I suppose he was amused by youthful enthusiasm. Anyway he was very friendly, tilted cigarette-holder and all. I must say I got a better reception than Niels Bohr did from Churchill after the war.

"I'd just been put onto Meyerhold's work in Russia, which bolstered my own theory of a director's authority as creative artist and all that. I'd written a scenario of F D R's life and as an experiment I wanted to distribute it to all the Theater Project directors and let each of them work it out his own way." Doc chuckled without slowing down. "It seemed just the thing to unify a spectrum of vanities, which even at that age I'd known would be the Project's greatest problem, and at the same time to educate the country in politics. F D R was one character that indigent actors under those directors might subordinate their personas to."

Rafe tried to visualize Ipsissimus Cuchulain starring in that role at a White House command performance, under his own direction, paragon for a thousand others.

"I went so far as to ask the President if he had any tips to give me about the drama of his life. Naturally he was just waiting to laugh me out of court. 'Nothing doing, young man!' he says, roaring with goodwill and charming the shirt off my back. 'Can you imagine what the Cans would do with the slightest whisper of a hint that a thing like that ever crossed the mind of one of my friends? THAT MAN is in trouble enough, thank you! What a job the cartoonists would do on me! Especially if they got wind about your interest in that Russian fellow. They already know I was an editor of the Crimson. F D R ORDERS RED TO STAGE CAMPAIGN BIOGRAPHY IN ALL W P A THEATERS! Not to mention what some of the local hams would do to me in the role, accidentally or on purpose! Do you think I want to let them use Federal funds to lampoon me? Speaking of that, what an embarrassment it would be to Fairy Norumbega! You'd ruin my last hope for an honorary degree after I hang up my spikes, which I've got my heart set on just to spite the ghost of old Kittybardmonger who wouldn't give me a gentleman's C in Coriolanus.'

"He laughed all the while but he was serious enough when he turned to Harry and said 'Find this precocious boy a better job, where he won't be so dangerous, and swamp him with responsibility so he won't have time to dream up any more social experiments. Meanwhile, if so much as a wild guess of this gets into even a gossip column I'll fire you both and sic J Edgar Blacklist on all your loved ones.' He wasn't frowning though as he wheeled himself back to his desk."

Doc wasn't frowning either, for all the world like That Man himself, charming the shirt off Rafe's back. None of his other topics had ever been as interesting as this one. Rafe started asking questions raised by the belated admission that the F D R interview had not been entirely private. He was overtly curious about the Presidential staff system, covertly curious about Doc's personal relations with Harry Hopkins and his comparative status among all the juniors pressing for attention. Charlemagne had had the obvious advantage of being conspicuous. But how many others were present at the meeting, and was it really in the Oval Office?

Rafe was still trying to keep this monologue on track when the second steak arrived and broke the thread that was apparently no more precious to the spinner than a hundred other narrative and speculative lines. Not that Doc noticed the service when he was pursuing something historical or dramatic. At first he only interrupted himself to say "Don't rush me! Can't you see I'm still eating?"

"I'm just clearing a place for your seconds, when you're ready for them!" Milly retorted resentfully, as if she'd had a drink in the kitchen for the courage to remind herself of the extraordinary job she'd been doing. Doc was impressed by the sign of spunk. He came to a full stop, looked at her with comical admiration, and suddenly softened into the most winning gentleman Rafe had ever seen in a restaurant. There was something apologetic about his irresistably respectful intimacy, which soon had her laughing; but Rafe couldn't overhear it because he was busy taking advantage of the hiatus to uplift morale with more substantial reparation, and to anticipate the extraordinary demand upon his wallet, by arranging with Number Two that the dessert orders should be taken and served prematurely, along with a giant pot of coffee, using space on the nearest table as forward supply depot; that betweentimes he and his guest should be brought two more rounds of drinks in a single delivery; and that he should thereupon be presented with the bill without further ado, written up for the Atlantean Impress credit card he was now handing her in advance: then the ladies could go home long before Doc discovered that the coffee had become tepid and that they had been dismissed—provided only that the two gentlemen were permitted to sit as long as they liked, leaving the midden to surprise another crew in the morning. (His plan to exonerate himself and mitigate underclass resentment called for a ten dollar bill and two fives on the spot, in case it was too late for Milly to collect currency from the cash register that night for the tip he included in the amount above his signature, which was going to be an additional twenty percent of the principal.) The conspiracy brought on a final flurry of anticipatory service—with Doc's surprisingly tacit acquiescence—and the customers were soon left swilling at their scattered mess like a pair of deserted pashas while almost half the champion's meal still awaited the full justice he was in course of doing it, surrounded by platoons of crockery and glass.

Rafe wanted Doc to continue with his Washington anecdotes. In an election year his ears were preternaturally attuned to the political overtones and undertones of every intelligence—whether public opinion poll, economic statistic, crime report, culpable accident, Congressional appropriation or other vote, Presidential veto, procurement contract, expert commentary, or nostalgic reminiscence of Catholicratic administration. But as the self-made manager of a Protestican enterprise in the milk-and-honey civilization of Cornucopia—an agricultural commonwealth of such commercial ambition in every category of its inferiority to any other part of the country that all its stores were open on Sunday and business was the only culture outside the University (and almost dominant even therein)—he seldom had the pleasure of discussing the Catholicratic Party with anyone who knew anything about political institutions.

Until four years ago, in fact, when he was clearly becoming the indispensable leader of Tubalcain's owners and felt secure enough to confess his faith as undefiantly as Joseph in Egypt, he had been as guilty of keeping his own counsel among business associates as an Elizabethan Papist. During the first Stevenson campaign, like Peter, he had denied the master he loved—at least to the extent of evading political topics in order to conceal his passion—being then a mere foreman, with the excuse to his conscience that the Catholicrats could win Cornucopia's electoral block without the two or three employees' votes he might have converted at the cost of the Edenfields' personal confidence who then still held all the corporate power. Because he had kept secret his allegiance to the egregiously intellectual politician regarded as soft by hardheaded sentimentalists, however, it was slightly the easier to conceal his patriotic despair and personal sorrow during business hours on the morrow of election day 1952.

But in 1956 he joined the brave little band of BUSINESSMEN FOR STEVENSON who pledged their names under newspaper advertisements attempting to convey the impression that they'd been convinced pragmatically by four years of Eisenhower's ineffective performance, and giving readers to understand that they remained among those who subscribed to the self-serving cant then promulgated by Protesticans that neither party nor ideology should influence the preference of an independent mind. In that campaign there could be no doubt that every last Catholicratic vote was a pearl of great price. But though his hope was weaker his dejection would have been yet deeper at the people's confirmed judgment, after a full term's proof of Protestican motivation, if he hadn't by then been so absorbed in the responsibilities and anxieties of meeting his own payroll.

Rafe had never so desired personal success as he did Stevenson's. Yet in 1960, after those two disappointments, he had transferred allegiance to his second choice without great difficulty, seeing that the Convention had of necessity endorsed the soi-disant new age of Atlantean realism, trusting that his most beloved Catholicrat would be employed by a Catholicratic administration at next to the very top, for the world's larger good, in affairs that most cried out for the very kind of wisdom twice rejected by the domestic electorate.

But he was already aware that Doc deemed it a wisdom with "no clutch", "too Sunday-schoolmarmish". There seemed to be nothing more definite against the wit from Illinois than that he'd been educated at Princedom and never graduated from the Boy Scout level of Divine Humanism, and still believed in the True the Good and the Beautiful. To the accusation of transcendentalism was added the charge of aspiring to oratory without the ability to write distinguished sentences.

It wasn't that Ipsissimus Charlemagne preferred any of the losers at the last three Conventions, and ostensibly he didn't disbelieve in the possibility of great men newer than F D R or H I M ; nor was it that he affected to expose monumental feet of clay, for on the contrary he was famous for discovering heroes and heroines cherished by no institution school or claque (unless on ironically muddled grounds): he'd cite their "passion for reality" or "action despite vision", or some other virtue, thereby more or less assimilable to their appreciator. Most of them were failures, obscure or famous. So it nettled Rafe that he grudged Stevenson—even as an anachronistic goo-goo—any of the praise with which he was so ingeniously generous for "men and women of gut material". But you can't refute a savant who ignores a statesman's jokes, and you can never much argue with the negative preciosity of a leader in his own right who has actually operated in Washington and won't be pressed for evidence or reasons.

Rafe was practiced enough to mask most of his annoyance that the old braintrusting New Dealer misliked Stevenson as much as Kennedy for what appeared to be opposite reasons. It seemed to him, a shirtsleeve psychologist from the realm in which Doc's kind of existence was least honored, that the man withheld praise from any living person esteemed by the best of liberally educated citizens or honored by any of the other categories in which he himself might be anthropologically classified—as conversely with the praise he did render. Thus F D R , now much criticized, having died soon enough not to be resented for residual praise, survived as Doc's paternal peer; but Churchill, the western world's most general living hero, was an "histrionic old woman" little more to be valued than hammy Whoreson Sells. Rafe had been as shocked as Doc's other students to hear that W S C was a "rhetorical fraud" standing on the shoulders of quiet able men, "bawling the gasp of fame", who had "no call to degrade the art of masonry to aristocratic dabbling"—"not to mention what he did to painting" when he was in a God-given position to transform the old Empire into a sempiternal galaxy of English-language arts far more liberating than a futile British Commonwealth or a nationalistic United Nations.

Rafe had forgotten that so much larger a mass could absorb an equal dose of alcohol with much less affect than his own. While Doc was polishing off the last of his steak in a sort of continuous operation probably unlike the comparatively dainty batch-processing of eaters like Henry the Eighth (that is to say, more like fluctuation of wave energy than sequences of discrete particles) Rafe got up to go to the Men's Room, far from half starved on account of having passed up a duplicate dinner for himself. Never thereafter was he sure of what he had been listening to, but as he eased himself before the porcelain gutter with a deep sigh of limited relief, stiffening his knees to keep from collapsing under the weight of his heavy head and stuffed stomach, he gathered the notion that while he was rising from the table Doc had come back to the point with an incoherent gripe either that Mrs Stevenson, a patron of the arts, had withdrawn her financial support of *Dromenology*, the little magazine of which Ipsissimus Charlemagne was founding editor, or that Mr Stevenson had divorced her for not having done so.

The pisser's satisfaction at the insight gradually dawning from this recollection was not without an element of self-congratulation—as he acknowledged with amusement—having come to think of it in the pause between passing water and turning on water in the wash basin. Psychological analysis was most useful in reconciling oneself to an undeniably admirable rogue elephant who refused to accord one the status of rival or peer. On the other hand, Rafe admonished himself, only a fool is jealous of his teacher for being wiser than the face smiling wryly in the mirror; and there should be no pleasure in finding anybody's wisdom alloyed with clay. In any case it was despicable to grudge Doc the superiority he had earned by the renunciation of success instead of blaming himself for squandering a profusion of similar talent. I, said Rafe, indulged my Ipsum by scorning college when all my comrades submitted proudly to the yoke, and of course that's the only reason I'm too uncultivated to understand the greater mind.

Though enteroception overwhelmed introspection and peptic disquietude made a churl of his reason, Rafe sniffed a familiar posey of rue in assuring himself that if he hadn't merely amused his own sweet mind when everyone was urging him to apply it, he might have become a peer and rival capable of subsuming Ipsissimus Charlemagne in duel, capable of putting H I M in his place. But the truth was that Doc, for all his self-indulgence, had been singlemindedly about the investment of his talents and had compounded them many times over—not as a prudent steward but as a megalomaniac going for broke.

Thus his envy of The Director's success subsided into the old grief which he had learned how to suppress in this case by criticizing the homage that was offered by the others who didn't regard this slumdweller as a failure. Perhaps to Dogtown's people also, Doctor Charlemagne was either nothing or the most.

Drying his hands under a noisy tap of electrically heated air, he took heart once more and reminded himself that there was fun ahead still. His education at the hands of Doc wasn't over yet, and he shouldn't carp at his doyen until he'd experienced more knowledge of certain kinds. Besides, you shouldn't judge a mind by its manners. If there was bullshit, what kind of floor did it cover? The fact that an ageing artist of an embattled art wished to differentiate himself from all men at all points might be the innocent symptom of an absolutely superior intelligence that can't help being self-conscious and is therefore too full of itself only in innocence of heart.

On his way back to the table, pausing to look at the harbor from a new angle, he shielded his eyes against the image of himself and the soft ocher innscape projected into the outer night by the long bank of black transparent mirrors now shared with no living soul but Doc, whose perfect double could be seen reading the paper in an isolated mess far across the dully gleaming field of properties arrayed at parade rest for tomorrow's lunch crowd. Beyond, excluding or ignoring immediate apparitions, he watched with a renewed thrill of perspicuity the confusing harmony and counterpoint of lights, near and far on waters blacker than the glass—each either steadfast or constantly coded in dots and dashes of apodictic self-identification—all action measured by the red bass in the foreground on Parliament Island, a metronome for soundless orchestration. Then yonder he noticed an unclamoring emerald that had been pulsing all the time—and another and another, almost alloys of sapphire, each so fleeting, so apparently irregular in relativity of period, that if he hadn't known they were ruled by a rigorously positivistic Coast Guard score he would have doubted that their positions in the real field of night were absolutely fixed.

At this moment of review from a slightly altered standpoint he was more aware also of a concentrated pulsating aurora australis—equally indefatigable and monotonous but less parochial and parsimonious than the others, the only illuminating signal of the entire scene—which revealed itself as if from beyond a rood screen in tirelessly recurrent flashes and sweeps behind treetops on the distant arm of land that obscured the head of the breakwater. Earlier he had missed this flux of Foreside Lighthouse (called Foreskin Light by fishermen), which he knew would be keeping a separate faith for those on the open sea, in charted coordination with other white powerlanterns marking rocks and havens far off in Great Vinland Bight.

Beyond Dogtown's airspace, where they didn't belong in sight, landing-lighted planes at the end of their rhumblines still picketed the starry sky as if it was their bay, patroling like heavily laden wasps as they awaited admission to the Guy Winthrop International nest.

Nights of ocean held at bay by the works of man are not strange to a portdweller from West or East; but in such spaces, owing to the tidal and seasonal agencies of time, even master mariners coming home, by day, with every hydrographic instrument and chart, need pilots for their navigation; and for an unprepared pioneer like Rafe there were neither memories nor portolanos to explain anything out there that deserved one's study.

* * *

"Prospero is dead!" he was told when he returned to his seat. Doc thoughtfully tapped the newspaper spread out on a fragile bumpy bed of dishes and glasses. "I once had hopes. In spite of his dilettante Neognosticism I thought he might stake me to a school of Dromenology and get Dogtown College going. But these last few years he's been too much of a psyche-seeker. I bet there's been a deathbed conversion for the Scholastics. He always did affect an ultimate orthodoxy. But a chunk of his money will still go to the Gnujies. They've been hoping to buy one of the white-elephant estates out on the Foreside for a therapy barn. These days they've even begun to subvert some of the Scholastics. Wouldn't they love to be one of the Retreat House neighbors! It would be easy to hook consecrated hosts for their experiments."

"If I hadn't outgrown my gnostic phase and weaned myself of Alt I'd probably still be walloping drums of chemicals on the Edenfield warehouse dock, consoling myself with preterconscious symbols." said Rafe. He was beginning to suffer a crapulous fatigue and wanted to make himself as agreeable as possible in order to forefend any friction or boredom that might aggravate the remainder of their bout. But Doc's animation had been waxing and was just now hitting its nocturnal stride. Rafe was beginning to believe that nothing in Dogtown ever got bruited in straightforward fashion to or from the point. The familiar sensation of time under pressure clasped his head like a diving helmet, and the sense of a vacation wasting, yet without the pleasure of laziness or sleep. But that wave of private dismay was gathered in and transformed by the lines of force that drew all attention to any immediate object of the Director s interest.

"One advantage Ozzie didn't have. He never had to do anything he didn't want to do. . . . This picture must have been filed in the *Nous* morgue thirty years ago. He hated reporters and he spent a lot of money keeping himself a secret. I'm surprised they got this much this close to the truth." Doc handed Rafe the paper.

PROSPER OZONE DEAD AT 80, headlined the paper in a front-page box, which included a smooth unsmiling side view of a lean young patrician with closely shorn wavy hair and sloping forehead looking down a long arched nose, giving the lie in advance to any image that Rafe might have conjured up by himself from what he read in the article, which was so terse in proportion to its prominence that it hinted a secret reason for the biographical brevity.

Ozone, who had died at home after a short illness, was "an electronics wizard, holder of more than three hundred patents", whose inventions, though unknown to the general public, "underlie many devices essential to modern communications and control systems. Born to independent means, he is said to have turned down numerous awards and honorary degrees in order to avoid publicity. He served at various times on the boards of OHM (Old Homestead Manufacturing Corporation), EG (Energy General), CRF (Cash Register and Forms Company), PCA (Panharmonic Corporation of Atlantis), PI (Photon Incorporated), and other electronics-based companies."

The second paragraph stated that he was born on July 4, 1880 to the former Miss Alice Beacon, of "an old and socially prominent Botolph family", through whom he inherited the controversial New Albion Claim, and her Hungarian husband Syzygy Ozone, a professor of mathematics at Norumbega University. "He graduated from Vinland Institute of Polytechnics in 1898, and went to Strasbourg, then in Germany, as assistant to Karl Ferdinand Braun, who was to share the 1909 Noble Prize for Physics with Guglielmo Marconi, the father of radio."

The third paragraph told of Ozone's return to the United States in 1910, and of his purchasing in 1920 an estate on Prudence Point in the Taraville ward of Dogtown, "where he built a large residence and laboratory called Joyous Gard. As a patron of the arts, he founded and supported the Theater on the Rocks, which earned an international reputation in the 1920s and 30s."

The fourth paragraph mentioned his assignment in Europe for the S I S (Strategic Secret Service) during World War 2, as a result of injuries from which he became totally blind in 1953, "the year he changed the name of his estate to 'Chateau Noir'."

The last paragraph announced that there would be no public funeral. "Please send no flowers. Donations in Prosper Ozone's memory may be made to the Beacon Institute for the Blind, Quinobequin Falls, Vd."

As Rafe read the story Doc was pondering it with the relish of a disinterested gossip. "Notice there's no mention of survivors. The public's final clue to all the mystery he made of himself will be who gets his money. I don't think the sightless bairns will get too much of it. I wouldn't put it past him to leave Distard Undershot Noxin a personal nestegg."

"Noxin!" Rafe howled. "How could any New Armorican brahmin stand the sight of that rancorous selfserving hollowed-out evilminded vindictive belly-crawling basilisk!"

"Tut tut, Mr O . Don't lose your head until after the revolution."

"Besides, hasn't Noxin had trouble enough with private grubstakes?"

"No trouble at all. He pulled it off in 1952, and Father Eisenhower approved. That DV trick crucially tested our degradation of the democratic dogma. The Dred Scott case could be undone with blood, but that one was judged by all the people. The politics of DV is irreversible. In this campaign even the philosophers are more worried about the Pope than about our soul."

"Maybe Ozone thought slush funds would mollify Noxin's love of pelf." Rafe suggested. With White Quarry students the teacher had always made much of Toqueville's essential insight about Atlanteans' "love of pelf."

"No. Oz took satisfaction in the debasement of democracy. That was his main reason for continuing to support the Cans after they began to make themselves out as in favor of Social Security, Federal Deposit Insurance, collective bargaining, the GI Bill of Rights, and other elements of socialism.

"But with him hatred of the Crats really went back to Wilson and the very idea of an income tax. Among cleareyed Protesticans always cherchez les impots. Noxin's the cleverest they've ever had at concealing the fact that that's what they're protesting—not the national debt in itself, not government inefficiency, not encroachments upon freedom, not the decline of patriotism—but the disproportional diminishment of maximum income that they consider a confiscation of assets. In their hearts, they abominate any tax based even on linear ratio.

"Ozzie literally hated Roosevelt worse than death, even back in the early '20s when F D R as Assistant Secretary of the Navy was encouraging EG's PCA deal, which was originally suggested by Oz himself, he claimed, to keep Radio Atlantis out of British hands. But he wasn't cleareyed. The poor boy was brought up in blinders, and he half disinterestedly believed the cant about free enterprise, commercial liberty, self-reliance, and the invisible hand—versus pampering the poor, creeping socialism, and the communist conspiracy.

"But he was more than a typical dupe of your economic R O I-alists; he was one of their financially intelligent loyal life-member New Armorican patricians who are quietly charitable and tolerant in private affairs, which for him included art and learning. He collected icons, admired Henry Adams and all the good Medievalists, yet also encouraged the avant-garde. But he knew only the unexamined life and never grasped the principle of society or the notion that commonwealth is a Ding an sich.

"Allowing for the ideology in his mother s milk, plus roi-alties and capital gains from his military gadgeteering, he was a tolerably honorable technologist. In his own trade he naturally hated DeForest as an opportunist and liar, but saw a sort of pure antidote to F D R in Noxin's vulgar ambition. He didn't have much use for Eisenhower as the puppet of his Griping Old Party, but he did give him credit for picking its epitome as his V P . His admiration for Noxin's willful malevolence was technical. I think he was envious of the lovelessness. Before he fell totally blind, when he was still a consultant to the Offense Department, he went to several semi-official lunches with Noxin, but he missed the chance to see through the hollow man's mask of conservative virtue because like almost everybody except maybe in their own professions he wasn't educated against sentimentality either by his family or by his schools. That illustrates the only reason why the Dogtown College charter will prohibit degrees in technology . . .

"I suppose now there'll be no new numbers of *Dromenology*. But Oz kept us afloat for a few good years without reading what he'd abetted or worrying about sociological inconsistency. In the old days his mother was a distinguished patron of the Botolph arts, you see—all the while she was hissing venom at the Squire of North River. It was from her that he absorbed as an axiom—not merely as an objective metaphor or fact—the epithetical idea of F D R as 'a traitor to his class'. Oz always solemnly approved his mother's oath that she wouldn't forgive That Man for such treachery even if God elevated her to Queen of Heaven; and that's no light blasphemy from a cultured High Church pietist of the old Dutch family's adopted communion."

Rafe wondered if his hatred of Noxin was worthy of comparison. But he was too tired to weigh the sin of being glad that Prospero had died. Instead he only asked what the inventions were that might justify a career so blindly hateful. It was a question that he wasn't surprised to hear Doc already answering in his own way.

"Ozzie's language was electromagnetic circuitry. Kirchhoff schematics to imagine by. There was nothing sentimental about the poetic means of that symbolic logic. He thought it was hopeless to talk about his work with anyone who couldn't read those ideograms. It's no mean lingo. It'll be the lingua franca of superorganic systems too, if they're ever visualized in AC-DC analogs. It applies a certain range of mathematics, of course, but he soaked up as much math as he needed the way a Medievalist steeps himself in vulgate Latin until it becomes a transparent medium: simplified, clarified, easily intelligible—yet debased from the classical. But unless he had to write things up for reports or journals he wasn't much more likely to translate his circuits into mathematics than into English. They're both too abstract for genius like his. He called himself a pragmatical black-box engineer, and at bottom he despised mathematics. In that deadly heart of his dwelt a rebellious libido."

Rafe again asked what the fellow had invented.

"Mostly, I take it, small improvements that made good ideas feasible. I think the first few had to do with telegraphic relays for submarine cable. Later, after he invested in a full-fledged laboratory, he got credit for the work of his hired consultant. Which he probably deserved. It's usually the structural synthesis, the ideas for nexus or overlay, that count most in crucial developments: the imaginative application of other people's conceptually limited inventions. But whereas a scientist, for example, might connect information theory and thermodynamics by noticing the similarity of equations from two entirely separate natural philosophies, Ozzie would build his metaphor on the analogies between circuits being used for entirely different purposes. . . .

"He's best known for his details of multielement vacuum tubes—which is what they call those with at least three biases or modulations.

The one celebrated by specialists, which probably added the most to his riches even though the market for it has always been pretty esoteric, is still catalogued as the Ozone Sexode. Then there was his superheterodyne beat receiver—though I gather he lost out on the major patent. You understand the technology better than I do."

Rafe knew nothing about electronics, and he knew that Doc subsumed as much.

"But his most important work was with audion triode oscillator devices for remote guidance—first tested right out there in the harbor on a torpedo-boat-destroyer—and it led to his authority in servo¬mechanisms for Navy fire-control systems. Aren't they the precursors of analog computers? In England way back before the War he got wind of the radar project, and I think he was the one who proposed the magnetron that finally gave it enough power to make it generally practicable. He sold his rights to Polytheon Electronics right here in Vinland and they produced them for all the Allies at their Millhampton plant. The paper didn't mention that company because he stayed off the board to avoid the appearance of what they call conflict of interest, seeing that he was a technical advisor to the Navy, but I happen to know that he's been a major stockholder for many years.

"He also helped come up with the so-called 'electronic password'—you know, the transponder carried by our ships and planes to prove to our own radars that they weren't bogeys. That sort of thing got him interested in espionage, and he went into the S I S as the least vulgar way to prove he wasn't as timorous and effeminate as he knew he seemed. A man that looks like an incognito prince who couldn't possibly know anything about the lives and manners of common citizens, let alone electronics, was the kind of spy the Germans might least expect."

"That wouldn't make him any less conspicuous."

"He'd never tell me how he covered himself, but he professed to be uncircumcised; and of course he was very good at the language thanks to his early years apprenticing with Braun on cathode ray tubes.

"And I think that's where you have to look for the constant through all his adventures: his first and last love was oscilloscopes: rigged-up cathode ray tubes. He kept improving them and finding uses. His own super-scope was his computer. Wouldn't you agree that the oscilloscope has been the most important lab instrument of the century? As a matter of fact, radio plus magnetron plus cathode ray tube equals radar. I called him Father Cathode."

"Then you might as well give him credit for DV. Superheterodyne radio plus photography plus oscilloscope equals devilvision."

Doc stared at Rafe for a prolonged second, all animation suspended. With hands thrown up mouth open and eyes expanded he was the mute snapshot of a broad comedian. Rafe couldn't tell whether this transitory physiognomy was accidental or histrionic (or perhaps the former in transition to the latter), but there could be no doubt about the keenness of interest. It wasn't quite comfortable to enjoy the unexpected pleasure of having surprised his teacher's so distinguished attention without being aware of its special significance.

"Holy Codfish!" The savant gave a whistle. "Wow." he confirmed in a level voice, gazing with noumenal thought into the face of his clever adjutant, who couldn't help averting his eyes from the phenomenon of approbation. "I get you. It never occurred to me that Prosper Ozone might have been responsible for the sugar cone. I should have called him Father Phisto!"

There followed the longest silence Rafe had ever known his tutor to let fall, who had taken up his knife and fork again; the hands that held them rested on the tablecloth, but the eyes on a space beyond the heaping plate. Once or twice while still solemnly abstracted he opened his mouth again as if in underwater reverie. Suddenly he looked at Rafe and grinned. "I've been a spy in the house of Dis! A double agent without knowing it! Almost a collaborator, as a matter of fact, by accepting all those invitations to the Chateau!"

Doc resumed eating with the crudity always so dissonant to the courtesy of his learning, then paused once more, absurdly appealing by look and tone, and whispered a dramatic question. "Do you suppose he could have known all along about me and the Resistance?"

Rafe's heart faltered in dreadful instantaneous astonishment at his own stupidity. His fatigue vanished. The entire map of his acquaintance with Ipsissimus Charlemagne rapidly revised itself in every contour.

It was very late in the day to be warned of the Resistance. For a moment it seemed to him that an existence he had put behind him was glaring out of the past and threatening to obliterate his hard-earned social integration. Fortunately, while he rallied his wits, it wasn't difficult to get Doc off again on local history.

It was still soon enough to bethink himself of downtown appearances with the maqui during business hours. At the same time the more he sweated about his nascent reputation in Dogtown the more he was ashamed of himself for sweating. In principle, though weakly of will, he remained a fellow-traveler. But the time was not yet to use up his credit on any losing cause, and it was too late to spend it on one already lost that was also in his heart outworn.

In openly asking the rhetorical question was Doc presuming too much of the student who had presumed too little? Rafe's sympathy for the Resistance turned to anger at being taken for granted as practitioner or accomplice. But a tide of embarrassing memories flooded his brow as he was listening to Doc launch into an apparently inconsequential canvass of the various stories about Dogtown's missing sea serpent. What he remembered was from old forays into select society, in the days of his youth before it had dawned on him that he might be destined for respectable responsibilities in the organization that was paying his wages as a laborer. He had hung around the Beaut parlors of Yerba Buena and Hume where those who haunted the edges of arts or educations sometimes met poets or scholars and where the samizdats of the Resistance had found a tiny West Coast readership.

In Dogtown memory is revelation. Antipater! Furtively disclosed at a winey candlelighted gathering of Beauts he had once seen a tattered copy of the underground manifesto by DOCTOR ANTIPATER! Without reasoning or doubt, without even looking for postmarks in retroactive imagination, he realized that he was now entertaining that old legendary hero of the very few—whom he found not awfully infallible, but yet more admirable as leader of the remnant fewer.

As an affable businessman Rafe's sense of guilt was not unfounded. Even in those days six or eight years earlier, when there was still some small hope of raising a partisan defense among the older and educated generations, resistance had been inconceivable or ridiculous to all but the fewest in precious few places; and those of a mind for such a possibility were mostly willing only to finger the notion ironically, having already lost the faith they still claimed among their old comrades. Then and even now the sickly movement had occasional ad hoc sympathizers, usually in accordance with limited or special aversions, Rafe among them; but he had never detected a fully committed member, and the Resistance had seemed to have faded away, or perhaps to have retreated across the Atlantic to some enclave like Unaford, the home of academic freedom and other lost causes. It was only by stumbling upon the source, having chanced into the Vatican of the Resistance, that he now knew the Atlantean opposition to remain alive at all, despite the uncalculated hostility and vigor with which it was still being stamped out.

Although resistance had always been a less likely epidemic than, say, celibacy, it was generally feared as a viral danger to the new republic, and it always showed up among the most scurrilous innuendos preferred by Cans like Noxin against Crat intellectuals, who were chronically discomfited by the charge most of them could truthfully deny. As resistance was officially rejected by both parties, and by default barely tolerated only by one of them, it should be no matter of surprise that Doctor Antipater had withdrawn from the apparatus of democracy.

It was in this connection that revelation brought a contributing memory—both a subliminal cause and a subsidiary effect of Rafe's sudden enlightenment, alleviating one of the irritations that had been giving an edge to his attitude toward Charlemagne ever since one of the recent White Quarry "seminars" on Atlantean political history. One of the students, a woman notorious for her tactless insensitivity to a man's prickly zones, had hurled Ippy the pointblank question of whom he'd voted for in the 1948 election. It was the only time Rafe had ever seen the master squirm or hesitate, and most of the class was acutely embarrassed at this effrontery. He had always insisted that citizens of the U S A were morally bound to form and exercise political judgment as the expression of their values or in defense of their cultural freedom. And he pressed for continual reference to the Constitution in critical discussion of society itself. So he could hardly plead the sacredness of privacy when confronted with the application of his own franchise by a student to whom he'd freely vented his personal opinions of public figures and from whom he'd expected candid exposition of dissident views. He was forced to respond. "Oh I can't vote." he'd mumbled with feigned impatience. "I'm not registered." And immediately turned aside the bull of the session by bruiting the question of how the political archon of a small city might have been qualified not only to select the rich men to produce the trilogy and satyr play for each day's festival but also to appoint the competing poets.

The ultimate motive for this social dereliction—which seemed to Rafe inexcusably shameful in the peculiar case of this New Deal loyalist, archenemy of misplaced idealism, pundit of liberal polity, master-hater of commercial tyranny, champion of resistance, artist of action—would never be admitted. But knowledge of it rankled in Rafe's heart by whom the regal attitude of grand subsumption was subtly understood and in this instance secretly execrated.

Rafe's displeasure was nevertheless somewhat alleviated when he began to acknowledge that the private person Antipater might have a very good excuse for not registering to vote: to wit, the sorry reception accorded his doctrine by both sides of the aisle, by the floor of the house and by its balcony, by every rank and every file. And he began to marvel anew at the absence of bitterness and illwill in Charlemagne's truly Jovial temperament.

Meanwhile however there was his own craven temperament to be ashamed of. Now he'd never claim entertainment of The Director (under any of his titles) as a business expense, even if he were using an occasion to develop contacts with local pump-problem-solving geniuses. But the danger was worse than an I R S audit. At home when it served his purpose he sometimes made bold to pass himself off as a maverick among industrialists, but on the road he was a cautious explorer. And yet here he was, foolishly contaminated—first only as Charlemagne's student but now as his extravagant host!—like an innocent progressive blundering into the toils of a callous Communist. How could he be sure the Tybbot Bible credit reporters weren't wise to Antipater's identity and watching all his contacts? Rafe would have cared nothing for official scowls or social disapprobation, he told himself, if it hadn't been for his duty to protect the good name of the Tubalcain Corporation and especially to further its interests on this very vacation.

He didn't charge Charlemagne with duplicity. No one blames Descartes or Newton for failing to trumpet their traffics with magic. It seemed more likely than deceit that Doc's fault lay simply in too much trusting his assumption of perspicacity on the part of his cleverest and most congenial student. In such an intimate pedagogical situation how could any mature pupil mistake the drift in all the radical metaphors with which he was lectured? Short of an overt and literal proclamation, it was now clear, Doc had been frank enough in their private relations right from the beginning. So, as he chided himself now, Rafe was willing to exonerate his friend of haughtiness in refusing to vote and of cunning in the omission of superfluous confession.

Hoping to finish off the evening as covertly as possible and weighing all the risks he could think of, he decided to take Charlemagne home in a taxi. As they waited for two or three minutes on the front steps for response to his call, the visitor again gazed down upon Serpentine Avenue, which Doc had just explained was named not for the musical instrument it resembled in overall shape or evoked by association with the parade space and bandstand of its magnified and straightened sector but for the famous observations made from its shoreline at a time when the first windmill was still new. Benjamin Franklin and other men of science had sent a delegation there to join the sober magistrates and notaries of Dogtown in successfully waiting upon further appearance of the Atlantic sea serpent, which in those days seemed to be hailing this harbor as its home port.

5
RAFE'S
LOG (3)

The Van, Dogtown
Dictated 14 Sept 60

You can't size up a town just by blending the views of an exorbitant old Jew, an alcoholic euplutocrat, and a classless operator of the dramatic arts. None is a native; none lives the common life. Whatever they observe in this place or perceive in its history—and no matter how much or how little property they own to—they can't teach me what I want to know about its center. As I keep telling my partner: always attack a muddle in the middle. The middle class is the only one that bounds two others. *Cherchez le bourgeois moyen.*

To this end I was lucky to hit the second Wednesday of the month. For an explorer of this continent there's no better way to collect and distribute business cards than to attend a Turntable Luncheon. He can be sure that any House of the Turntable will be of genuinely middle class, however petty by European standards. The gilded International membership card can be very useful to a Knight on quest. It's better than holding privileges to a monastery guest-house chain.

I've been a member ever since I got wise to the silent hints of all my business acquaintances in the Bay Area. Knowing that no one is ever invited to join unless he takes the initiative in asking to do so, I finally mentioned my interest to Walt Edenfield. He was as pleased as if I'd offered him the chance to save my soul, after all those years in my irreverent company! He's an easygoing unpretentious guy, amazingly tolerant of deviants (as long as they're self-reliant); but for his own part he would never have dreamed of shirking the bourgeois oblige of belonging to a few of the fraternal associations that cement the several bricks of self-interest which make up the wall regarded as the community's bulwark. His gratification at my voluntary effort to normalize my reputation, and to demonstrate that I'm neither too proud nor too churlish to bother with the title of Gentle Knight Roturier (without yet knowing that term for my postulation), was clearly so profound and so affectionate that I began to wonder if I was getting into something Rosicrucian, or at least spiritual.

Almost immediately my fears proved unfounded. There happened to be a vacancy at one of the tables in the Londonbridge House and I escaped the usual ordeal of eagerly humble probation during which the supplicant is expected to ask a lot of questions about the club heraldry. After my initiation, when I saw that there's nothing deeper to Turntable than there seems to be, and that my irenic undemonstrative partner had no more to say to me than before, I was touched to find him moved rather by the idea of us being fraternity brothers than by the salvation of my soul.

WELCOME TO THE HOUSE OF SEVEN TABLES says the sign hung once a month on the wall of Lothario O'Toole's function room at The Doghouse here on Front Street. I'd already passed that establishment many times, right on the chine of the business district a block from the Van, without suspecting that it aimed to be the city's modern restaurant and only night club. Under previous management it must have been a fine old tap room, but the two long windows that once closely inspected street traffic right opposite the Alma Mater Department Store have been blanked out with a facade ostensibly resembling the vertical weathered gray boards of a village fishing shack, the studding for which has not yet been walled up on the inside.

But the Reunion Room, hollowed out like an underworld headquarters from the cellar of the storefront house next door—an expansion that recently attracted Turntable Lunches to the Doghouse for the first time—admits not a trace of fenestration. Nor does its decor acknowledge the parochial theme announced by a large netting needle that transfixes ocean waves over the outside of the street entrance on what would be called the entablature if this were really Greek Revival instead of Main Street architecture. With its pretension of costly-looking plywood veneer paneling and low flush ceiling this sunken cenacle and club room is a first departure from Dogtown tradition, according to Loathey O'Toole himself, the unctuously friendly proprietor and Knight Victualler pro tem. During the winter he's going to finish his adjacent public dining room in the same modern style, to make even oldtimers forget the propinquity of fisheries. By perfecting his progressive participation in the national installation of fungible interior designs he hopes to dominate the businessman-lunch business. He claims already to have the only "full-service" restaurant within stepping distance of most of the city's stores and offices.

There are two others elsewhere in town that have enough auxiliary space for the Local's seven roundtables—84 members, plus guests—as well as a staff expansible enough to handle such a spread of mouths on comparatively infrequent occasions at the very hour of the day most devoted to fast turnover of regular independent customers. Thus once a month the encumbent Knight Victualler plucks from his competition four or five dozen lunches in addition to his normal share of the market.

I met Loathey's two rivals, also Knights of course: his cordial pals awaiting their respective triennial (formerly biennial) bonanzas. The unassuming Busty Pacioli, whose Windmill could accommodate seven times seven exceptional tables, gave no sign of having seen me as a customer of his own. Saturnine Sammy the Mouth Samouthropolus, proprietor of the Town-Ho-On-The-Wharf, goes all-out for the pilgrim business.

Which in truth also gives Loathey and Busty a seasonal margin of lucrative cream. One reason the enterprising faction of Dogtown wants to clean up the harbor and give it over to the needle trades is that pilgrims encourage the kind of restaurant that prosperous residents like to have on hand all year round. Furthermore, a year's Turntable franchise brings in many a Knight International on vacation with his family who is glad to trust any public house appointed by his unknown brothers—not to mention other travelers who notice International Turntable roadside signs wherever they go.

At most Locals in this country the commissary quid pro quos are more transparent—that is to say less conspicuous, less prominent in the Club's collective consciousness. The present Victualler was modest enough the day I attended, merging himself with the less dynamic

Knights like an undistinguished guest who would have been content to sit below the salt if the formalities had not required equality; he never seemed to prompt the service, or in any way to presume upon his backstage power over the proceedings: yet the principal beneficiary of the event hardly needed pointing out. Even on his good behavior you can always spot an entrepreneur of goodfellowship, especially if he's the town's pioneer in modern hospitality.

Feeding comes before the burden of the meeting, and watering before the feeding. By the time everyone took his second drink to the table I was pretty well acquainted with the September Knight Commander, a very friendly carpentry contractor by the name of Slim Willard Boxshaw. He's thin in face and limbs, and his hair's still auburn, but I think his belly's troubled about the management of an expanding business that he inherited from his father. Like many of the people I've since met around here, he's an indefatigable talker when you're buttonholed but a shy one when it comes to public speaking—which is not only the main educational purpose of Turntable for all its members but also especially his particular duty as the day's master of ceremonies.

Slim covered his embarrassment as ex officio preprandial guest-greeter by paying undue attention to the level of liquid in our two glasses. Some anguished sense of tact prevented him from asking me anything about myself, and impelled him to scatter the throng to its seats with amazing punctuality before I had time to put him at his ease. We both knew his awkwardness was of little consequence, however, because it's an adjuvant purpose of a Luncheon, by International charter, to give any stranger Knight ten minutes or so to introduce himself to the membership as a whole and reveal his motive for being there.

I got the feeling that Roundhouse Knights of Dogtown especially welcome Knights Errant because they delay the next notch in rotation of Roundhouse speakers, seeing that visiting Knights (if there are any) substitute on the rostrum for Roundhouse Knights during the time allotted between Business and Outside Guest Speaker. But it's a double sprocket: there are two prongs at each notch. As the sole visitor that day I spared only one of the two By-Speakers.

But any local new member goes to the head of the queue, and that day I was lucky enough to get the benefit of a reality-estate prophet's maiden address before I had to make myself public.

Hastings Mooncusser is a handsome and precocious graduate of Norumbega who seems determined to realize Doc's fear that Dogtown will be sold. If I should ever want to take a hand in anything here I'd damned well do it before this young shark gets much further along his way to maturity. There'll be no advantage to doing business here when labor and property overtake mainland prices. This harbinger of the inundation—a type of Reality-operator no longer new elsewhere—means to ride the first Cape Gloucester tidal wave.

But that's not what discomposes the unenlightened natives who listened to him. To them it's a future too deferred either to worry about or to cash in on. Although young Mooncusser has condescended to join their club, what secretly bothers them more than his educated ambition is that he's trying to lead them—before he knows his cod from his halibut—on the strength of an almost disdainful manner of charming superiority, with no sign of emulating his elders in their immemorially osmotic ways of doing business. I don't think they put much stock in his claim to be a native by virtue of the fact that his family paid taxes here for all the summers of his childhood. In every way he's two cuts above their own children, and three above themselves.

Having just opened a Dogtown branch office of his uncle's big-time Botolph firm, Mooncusser, Coneycatcher & Company, which he would have us believe is known among sophisticated moneymen as "MC^2"—especially well known for industrial development but not too exalted to list domestic real estate as well—the debonair young nephew is nominally in competition with thirty or forty independent agents, probably including at least a dozen Knights Roturier. It's easy to get a real estate license in this state, and apparently many a feverish housewife with time to spare likes to drive young couples around town looking at nests ready-made for feathering. The 'Bega man probably wouldn't scorn to snatch such menial sales, but his vision is directed toward something greater than anything his preestablished colleagues can yet conceive.

He offers a remedy for their tacit hard feelings. In his talk he graciously vouchsafed the proposition that if everybody works together to enlarge the pie there'll be a bigger piece for everybody. Probably even before college he learned to magnify commercial cliches without embarrassment. A rising tide lifts all boats, etc. So he was well applauded, and I heard no word against him or his communal dream; but I can easily imagine the inner skepticism with which the old-timers must have entertained his exhortations to consensus. I was already aware that there has been no unity in Dogtown since Captain Faustus mustered his fencibles to drive off a British sloop-of-war in the summer of 1776.

Hastings Mooncusser minced no words in crying out for a more intelligent exploitation of the Massachusetts Felly, informing his new brothers that Botolph's "forward-looking" circumferential highway has "revitalized" the metropolis by dispersing most of its profitable industry to the suburbs, where factories can be served efficiently by over-the-road trucks instead of boxcars, and where automotived workers need not be indulged with a public transportation system. He was politic enough to pay lip service to Dogtown's leaders for bringing the northern end of the Felly to Dogtown, but even I know that nobody here deserves any more credit for the route of this final segment than for the original bulldozing, which began soon after the war, near the Indian hill it's named for, fifty miles overland to the southwest. I haven't yet traveled this famous wagonwheel of commuters and gypsies, but I've had a glimpse of the picture-postcard steel-arch bridge that lifted it high over the Namauche less than ten years ago and blessed this moated town with an unguarded gate. Mooncusser was hardly original in referring to the Felly as a "freeway to prosperity" for the city that now anchors it to a harbor.

In his thirteen minutes the "young man on his way up" (as I afterwards heard him called by Clint Clifford the tolerant leader of local housing sales, the city's most reputable appraiser and V P of the Dogtown Home Bank which finances a majority of everybody's sales) also managed to urge that the City's trademark, and eventually its official seal, be changed from a netting needle to a schooner under full sale. The logotyped claim to the invention of that romantic machine would foster the recognition of Cape Gloucester's "sentimental heritage" on travel pages from coast to coast.

Whereupon he was boldly seconded, out of order, by Loathey O'Toole, who, though he couldn't resist confessing that he still somewhat preferred the fouled anchor motif he's apparently been touting on his own hook, or even some simplified version of the Fisherman and His Wife (sans Dog), nevertheless offered to start the ball rolling by using any new symbol as a prominent device over his main portal to replace the homely old needle when he resumed his remodeling this year or next.

After this cordial interruption, following the land-shark's address I took nine and a half minutes to introduce myself. Then came the Outside Guest Speaker, who gets most of the postprandial time. This one was refreshing to me and embarrassing to the local Knights.

I am told that Garibaldi Ghibellini was brought in as editor of the *Nous* a couple of years ago to modernize and professionalize Dogtown's journalism. One gets the feeling that he's shaken things up a little too vigorously, and there seems to be a general doubt that he'll last much longer. I gather that everyone had been surprised at

Slim's selection of such a controversial didact. He later explained his indiscretion to me as a desperate expediency: he couldn't get anyone else at the last minute. I had already sensed that Slim has the reputation of a procrastinator.

Judging by what Gary said at that lectern and by an editorial I saw yesterday, to jeopardize his *Nous* advertising revenues the bête gris of Front Street doesn't have to go much further to the left than aligning himself with the "bunny-lovers" who wish to protect from development that almost mystic moorland in the interior of the Cape that I hear is called Purdeyville after a vanished village last inhabited by a witch named Perdita—the very tract of upland moraine that the young new land-lusting Knight Realist had just been urging as a site for Dogtown's own airport. Yet between his lines the editor seems to be challenging not only progressive fur-traders like Mooncusser but also the goo-goos who categorically oppose the peregrination of industry. It's not hard to guess Doc's opinion of this highminded commercial equivocation so much like my own.

But Gary is quixotic enough to buck modern diction by claiming to be a conservative on the strength of his belief in conservation. He proves by definition that conservatives (as all good Knights call themselves) must oppose development of the town's old commons: landings, pastures, and remnants of woodlots once set aside by sufficiently enterprising individualists for the joint use of themselves and their posterity in perfectly respectable tribal self-interest. The poor fellow fails to understand what I've learned from my college professor: that his inborn European assumption of the corporate nature of society, a residual sense of which remained even to the Deformation colonists, is no longer shared by the individualists of an economy that incarnates deformed Christianity. Nothing he argued of general import hasn't appeared over and over again in the liberal press opposing the party that derives from the liberalism of 18C republican merchants; but Knights don't read much besides newspapers (except those who take an interest in the official historical foundations of Arthurian railroading as reflected in Turntable's vague nostalgia for the Knighthood of the Iron Horse—which, by the way, seems to be ignored by this Local in its enthusiasm for all the kilroys pulling into town on the Massachusetts Felly, and in its apparent indifference to the fate of their Vinland & Markland Railroad service), let alone leftwing magazines.

I think he impressed us all with his conservative delivery, once he had laid aside his chin-curved pipe, solid and stocky as himself, and stood up at the podium like a swarthy Florentine merchant prince representing civic virtue. In conversation as in public address his pronouncements follow each other without hesitation in the effortlessly loud deep voice of a born herald, wagging the black ledges of hair over his eyes in the expressive frown of a thinker as well. Among Dogtown admirers, when he's the champion of some common cause, his ponderous aura is probably taken as the manifestation of scholarly deliberation. Better-read critics may pass him off as a pompous anachronism. Yet his demeanor is really nothing worse than the unwitting outward manner of an inwardly honest public mask. But he's possessed with weakness for sarcasm, which sometimes raises the pitch of his voice to a whine. He's not nearly as phlegmatic as he appears. I liked him as a misfit.

I also liked his theme: the essential conflict, recognized by our amended Constitution, between democracy and private rights. He piqued my interest by remarking that in practice the rights of personal freedom depend upon property rights for the protection of their institutions as much as property rights depend upon due process of law for protection against majority rule. I suppose that to the few Knights who listened with unfeigned attention this analysis sounded like a sour intellectual (not to say Marxian) criticism of Atlantean polity. But it was evident that most of the audience hadn't even tried to make out what he was talking about, because he got a nice round of applause for finishing in a reasonable time. Misled perhaps by the professional identifications of lawyers and dentists on Turntable rosters, he may have misapprehended that Knights are inculcated with a higher order of values than ordinary economic men.

It's not claiming much for my public-speaking ability to note that they'd liked my short talk better than his long one. I've been made too much of, in fact. My popularity of course can't last, unless I leave town tonight. Sooner or later I'll betray my interest in this rather than that—admit a preference, ask one question too many, suggest a first step toward something, or otherwise show the ragged edge of my colors. At that point one begins to lose the intriguing uncertainty of a Knight Errant and become the less unpredictable freelance whose quest deserves less assistance than that of a local Roundhouse Knight in the competitive economy's web of quests. But coming between Mooncusser the self-appointed spearhead and Ghibellini the enemy of the people I must have seemed easy to get along with.

Whatever the impression I made in publicly accounting for my presence, and despite the fact that I had to decline many consequent personal invitations I won't have time for, once again I'm uneasy about my air of self-assurance. It always appears when I find myself with willing listeners. It would have been better to evince no opinion at all about Dogtown. I must cease drawing specious comparisons between Dogtown and San Ricardo, my knowledge of which hasn't been much extended or confirmed since I was too young to pay any attention to the kind of similarity or contrast that might interest this seven-tabled House. I suspect that the rocks of Cape Gloucester are strewn with wreckage of Mooncussers and Opsimaths bearing cargoes of wisdom for the relief of Dogtown.

In any event, I haven't yet accomplished anything here. I'm riding on a turntable that hasn't yet stopped long enough for me to steam off on any of the tracks. Yet one of the promising consequences of my exposure to these Knights is that on Friday I'm going to have lunch with the man who may be able to help with our pump problem. Not that I told the whole assembly all about Tubalcain's technical difficulties; but I did emphasize that my company is always seeking improvements in "hydraulic pressure-generators"! The reason he came up to me afterwards, however, was to disabuse me of a misconception.

My ears burn as I recall the fatuous tone of condescension in which I'd alluded to Dogtown's unenlightened attitude toward industrial cleaning, delivering in my casual avuncular tone a friendly kindergarten chat on the advantages of high-pressure superheated solution for purposes of sanitation, maintenance, and general efficiency. In a glow of benevolence I had gently hinted my criticism of fish-processing plants for the enormous labor costs of washing down the production lines every night with garden hose and tap water. Fortunately there were probably few in that room who have any notion of the routine inside those buildings on the waterfront; most Knights evince little interest in the manufacturing component of the economy they do so well by. But Buck Barebones (whose card says Baucis Barebones) gently explained to me that even ordinary steam vapor cleaners are not regularly used on production-line equipment because their heat takes off the necessary machinery grease as well as the unnecessary germs and gurry.

Now there's a revelation that hasn't yet percolated up to Tubalcain's sales manager, who's never been able to account for our dismal record in the food processing industry. I wonder why no one in any tier of our sales organization has ever appreciated this rational sales resistance. They know by now that I don't shoot the bearers of bad news. Then is it too abstract for salesmen to articulate? Maybe nobody in the field infantry has ever tried to find out from a prospect's maintenance department why it rejects the suggestion of its own company's purchasing agent, as I've so often heard. I shudder at the waste of our misguided ads in industrial maintenance magazines, and it annoys me to find the "research" in Ted McKee's "total marketing concept" so inexcusably superficial. Maybe this is something that would have shown up in the call-report system ("just more damn paper work") which the Controller has been pressing him to install. It's certainly an argument for hiring the direct sales force that we can't afford.

In any case I was so impressed by Buck's grasp of the application problem that, knowing he runs a machine shop specializing in developmental work, I took him to the bar for another drink or two and gave him as many details as I could of our engineering weak point, hoping that a fresh and objective technical view would stimulate my imagination for an entirely new approach to the function of pumps in steam cleaners.

Ostensibly he's interested in getting jobs for his shop, but what makes me like him so much is the same self-forgetful love of mechanical design that so often bemuses my partner Walt Edenfield— except that Buck is even less aggressive, certainly less ambitious. His weaknesses make him interesting to talk to. He's probably had many good ideas on all sorts of machinery that he's lacked the capital—or the drive for capital—to realize. In short, a lovely and sympathetic man. I expect to see more of him.

With all the others I had been as adroitly evasive about my lodgings as a frank and open Knight well can be when something not quite respectable in his circumstances is concerned. I simply gave out a private phone number that I'm lucky enough to have at my service, thanks to the generosity of the Schlossbergs. Edie has patched the switchboard so that their unlisted second line always rings in my room without interception. Of course that means there's never anyone to take messages in my absence; but at least I get them directly when I'm there, and I'm able to make my own calls anytime I wish. Those two innocents seem to think nothing of leaving me on my honor to use a credit card for long-distance, and they charge me nothing for this trustful arrangement.

It's a phone number that's fallen into desuetude with the decline of the Van and should have been canceled long ago. Shelly and Edie warned me that I might be annoyed by calls from a few old customers or vendors from the distant past. But right from the first I was getting far too many of these to square with expectations. Now it happens that my Controller has somewhat educated me in the devices and options of AT&T, so upon investigation I discovered that the Schlossbergs had never been aware of the invisible "hunting" mechanism which was still automatically diverting incoming calls to my line when theirs was busy. The upshot is that they're now alarmed at the unnecessary equipment they've been renting all these years, lumped into the unitemized entry on their monthly bills. After I leave they're going to take out both the extra line and the otiose switchboard. Edie talks as if I'd saved them from an old age in the poor house—and she refuses to charge me for supererogatory services. The whole question has set her to wondering how much else they don't know about their business.

Meanwhile I keep my line so busy when I'm here that I protect myself from the few remaining calls that are truly misplaced. I average two or three hours a day on the phone, although as much as possible after 7 PM when the rates go down here but offices on the West Coast are still open. In the morning after breakfast, before I go out for the day, I try to work on my Disquisition, which I'm afraid is falling further and further behind schedule. My evenings are now taken up with social life of one kind or another. After all, this is supposed to be my vacation.

Because of all my meetings with Sirs John Doe and Richard Roe, John Stiles and Richard Miles—and carousings with more distinguished characters—I had neglected my search for help, which should have occupied my attention sooner than anything else. My dislike of the all-important hiring process is subconsciously conditioned by past misjudgments, by regret for all the time wasted (if not worse) in trying to educate or motivate the nitwits and passive learners who have befuddled Tubalcain with topnotch credentials and uncanny skills at being interviewed. After a few years of conscientious and extremely time-consuming efforts to recruit by rational methods you tend to get either too impulsive or too fatalistic in taking whatever comes along at a moment of need. By that time you're only too glad to delegate all the hard work of attracting and sifting (though it won't be done cleverly enough) and reduce your own part to one or two brief questions followed by a snap judgment whether or not to veto the nomination and let yourself in for another.

If the truth were known, that's pretty much the procedure followed by most executives in all their functions, budgeting included. In the business schools they call this process "decision making". By reducing it to the form of games they're trying to turn the art into what they call a science. For that matter, if I were a shrewder degree candidate I might now be reconstructing the putative Decision Tree of some typical lumber company's harvesting plans instead of trying to draw up an astrology chart of the Parity

Corporation. I'd be better off if I could bring myself to squander psychic energy on case histories. But I'm not yet sorry it's too late to back out of this swamp.

Thus when Brother Bill Babwell introduced himself to me at Turntable as the proprietor of PERSONS LIMITED, a local secretarial firm, I was inspired to commission him as my employment agent to get hold of Caleb Karcist, a young man that Ray Lagniappe was convinced did a marvelous job running his sales office in Novantum for a while and was supposed to have moved up here a year or so ago. I thought he might be available for some temporary research work.

Bill has beautiful prematurely white hair and acts like a paradigmatic butler liberated from humorless taciturnity. He had to keep talking for quite a while before he could absorb the idea of this novelty in his business, which was designed to deal in typists and typing; but at last he perceived that he was agreeing to "screen the applicants". He was once an office manager in Bot, he said, and he knew what I meant, nodding blankly as I attempted to accommodate myself to his mores by specifying the kind of talent I was looking for, in case he had to find someone else. But I knew all my eggs were in one basket, being in a hurry, being in Dogtown, and I began to repent my rashness as I became convinced that Bill would fail to communicate to Karcist (if he could find him) the interest and value of the experience I was promising him, and perhaps so misrepresent my offer that it would be declined out of hand.

* * *

But much to my surprise the third person appeared before the first person at eleven o'clock this morning, having been found, baited, and committed to interview by the unruffled second person. It didn't take much persuasion to hire Caleb on the spot, for he was evidently trying to persuade me. He happened to be looking for a job, so he had nothing to lose by signing up for an odd scrap of uncertainty. He has absolutely no knowledge of the market to start with, nor any experience in finance, but I think he can pick up what he needs to know as he goes along. At least, I judge, he can read and write, a competence that you can't assume of college graduates these days.

In earlier jobs he seems to have produced useful statistics on his own initiative. Perhaps he's a little too unrealistic about his scheme for "total sales control", which makes a bushleaguer like me distinctly uneasy. But any outfit needs one mind like this, just as we need our Controller at Tubalcain. I differ from most of my colleagues and counterparts in believing that administration can be improved by the discipline of systematic reason, little as I myself relish the prospect of submitting to it. Yet in an interesting discussion Caleb agreed that the art of management can't be reduced to quantification, but said his purpose is always to reduce complexity to its irreducible, so that managers won't have to waste their time on what systematic administration can deal with. When I remarked that he seemed reasonably theoretical in his approach to business he retorted rather defensively: "There's nothing wrong with theory if it's based on the facts of your own situation." But thereupon he smiled sheepishly, as if belatedly realizing that he wasn't up against the usual hostility toward Creative Mind, and blurted: "I may be theoretical, but I'm not academic!" Needless to say, I'm partial to anyone capable of appreciating that distinction, to say nothing of an employee who finds it out for himself!

I would have liked to spend much more time probing his worm's eye view of management, but I had to go meet Frank Bacon for lunch. I handed Caleb pencils and paper, told him we'd buy anything else as soon as he knew what he needed, and left him at Shelly's big table to spend the rest of the day with my raw materials. I don't deny my moral uneasiness at leaving him to flounder without definite instruction or goal. It's an assignment that I myself would have found intolerable.

But off I went to call for Frank, one of the best of my new friends and not the kind of gentleman you're likely to meet at a Turntable Luncheon. He's known around here, when he's known at all, as Frank Bacon the Younger, because he's a nephew of the famous Frank Bacon who originated food-freezing techniques (using brine, I believe), one of Dogtown's legendary dead. Frank is almoner of the Tybbot Eleemosynary Disbursement Service, which is enantiomorphically homologous to the centralized purchasing department of a corporation with disparate subsidiaries, except that he has much more relative power than any purchasing agent. One of his dependencies is FEEL (the Free Enterprise Education Library, you remember), and it was there that I was introduced to him the other day when he happened to drop in to speak to the curator during my exploratory visit.

A rash physiognomist might take him for an old Yankee C P A —tall and thin, with short hair, rimless glasses, and a long nose— until she heard him speak. He's a scholar by training (PhD in Assyro-Babylonian philology from Henry Adams University) but singularly unambitious (he says lazy) by temperament. Frank is lucky to hold the only chair he's suited for outside the academic pale. Today I came to the conclusion that he's the most objective person I've ever met. But he got his job through posthumous nepotism.

The elder Bacon, he told me, died in bankruptcy, leaving nothing to his widowed sister and her children whom he'd been supporting at the highest level of available culture. His sleeping partner, old Richard Tybbot himself, after forty years of exploiting the inventor in special ventures, had refused to save him from the classic imprudence (whatever it was) that wrecked him—simply because it was his own fault.

Apparently his nephew the younger Frank was spared the academic consequences of destitution by the charitable intervention of my quondam informant Jason Anacoluther—banker and warehousing Dives, friend to both parties, Bacon's executor and later Tybbot's too, Chairman of the Board of the Tybbot Philanthropic Foundation from its inception ten years before the donor's death—as follows.

Jason persuaded the Trustees to concentrate on the management of income and relinquish disbursement decisions to someone who understood Dogtown itself as well as the sciences and humanities. This city had been genuinely loved by its richest native, notwithstanding that most of his posthumous estate was devoted to the world at large. In his lifetime Tybbot had been known as the Duke of Dogtown (in a mixture of gratitude and resentment), and after his death he wanted to be known as its patron saint and guardian angel. He wished Dogtown coupled to his surname, as if with a *von* or a *de,* so that all the outside benefactions for which he was given credit would bring notice also to his birthplace. Long before the Foundation was set up he had been giving land and money for various farsighted public purposes, such as watershed conservation (being a true conservative as far as his native ground was concerned), which for the most part are not yet appreciated. To this day, eight years after his death, few of the locals (though vaguely aware of his lordship and sainthood) have any idea that he was also the prophet of their Domesday Book. "God will let us increase everything we have but land." he preached.

Having won his point, Jason nominated the young Bacon, who he knew might have been heir to a fortune collaterally related to the much larger one that had been multiplied by investment in lots of other shares almost only to end up in various Funds of the Foundation. Of course the name Bacon never appeared in the documentary history of the Tybbot trust, and perhaps none of the other Trustees knew any of the people in Tybbot's home town. But Jason's rectification of the Duke's blood-guilt, even if known to them, would have been no cause for scandal: such arrangement (which may also have served for Jason's own atonement) is a mechanism often employed to repair the web of families that still binds culture to wealth in the New Armorican republic. Frank himself confesses the bland corruption.

Yet he's probably the perfect spending agent for a foundation. He's so conscientious that he studies every field in which he makes grants—even business! (As a subject of education, business qualifies as a tax-exempt object of charity. Even business books are educational in the eyes of regulators—I suppose because it takes an education to read them. But shouldn't that make them consider all business educational—and therefore charitable?) FEEL, however, is the only Tybbot charity that has much direct bearing on business.

Frank also distributes half a dozen other Funds of the parent Foundation. In Dogtown itself there is the Open Dictionary Endowment (ODE), which supports a small museum to encourage the use of lexicons by exemplifying the history of these conveniences in many different languages and disciplines. Tybbot's stated purpose with ODE, in defense of Atlantic English, was to forestall jargon by expanding the nation's general vocabulary. Frank donates several hundred thousands of dollars a year worth of variously appropriate lexicons to institutions, sailors, indigent college students, and all Dogtown school children. This Fund also supplies gratis the vulgar but usually virgin dictionaries found in the bedside drawer of every hotel room in Atlantis.

Frank is therefore much courted by lexographing publishers, and he's truly in a position to influence our linguistic morals, in writing at least, seeing that Atlanteans tend to become passively pedantic when they're forced to consult the good book. He's disturbed by the general indifference to etymology, which he thinks should be taught in schools when Latin courses are dropped.

But he spends most of his time granting money from the other Funds, always keenly diffident about his ability to distinguish true merit from mere professionalism. "I'm not creative myself," he told me, "and I distrust my conservative instincts: so I'm apt to give the benefit of my doubt and fall too readily into the danger of mistaking novelty for originality." I observed that his alleged fallibility is more to be trusted than the common practice of yielding the power of selection to juries made up of the applicants' orthodox peers or jealous rivals. But he demurred at my invidious opinion. Perhaps under the sway of his familiarity with referees of scientific journals, he believes that on the whole nowadays the professional panels serving other foundations are to be admired for their disinterested awards; and he says that he would gladly avail himself of specialists' judgment if he were not forbidden to do so by stipulations of the deceased benefactor, a Pauline individualist in every particular. Frank is a Petrine Scholastic with six kids under his control. I think he's uncomfortable in exercising spiritual power without historical authority.

At lunchtime I went to pick him up from his office on the ground floor of the narrow brick house he lives in, which stands without shade or buffer in a tiny triangular plot at the acute corner of Bevel and lower Halibut Streets, hard by the thicket of mostly whitish frame houses covering the ridge between Sacrum Square and the Windmill. It's on a slope just below the lofty statue of Perdita and her goat in Purity Square.

He works in a high spacious room (across the hall from his ample unrushed staff) furnished with mahogany and oriental rugs, his restoration and modification of the elegantly simple parlor installed by a 19C sea captain after the hull of the house was dismembered in Botolph and moved up here by barge. Even then Dogtown was penurious in architecture, compared with the other old seaports of the North Shore, thanks to its history of commercial misjudgment, anti-intellectual disputation, and fires.

My afternoon was very absorbing—from there to the Town-Ho for lunch on the wharf among a few idle fishing boats, and back again to his office (where he brews a fastidious cup of tea); but the only outcome relevant to my research project is that he will prepare the FEEL librarian for Caleb's ensconcement at a work table for what I hope will be an effective use of the various financial services which poor old Tybbot expected to be in great demand by his fellow townsmen. I'm told that the reference material is scantly consulted, even by the Dogtown Investment Club that Shelly belongs to. The only thing that's popular is the obsolete little stock ticker. The Library never has to dispose of the rubbish it produces. At closing time the spent tape is always salvaged from the festooned wastebasket by one or another of the wistful mock-traders and taken home in coils. There was a time when the tape got snitched before everyone had a chance to see it; but then the machine was moved to a conspicuous outer position near the factotum's desk, leaving the reference room nice and quiet for the bulls and bears of long-term investment.

The real brokers and traders who live in Dogtown rarely avail themselves of FEEL's facilities because smoking isn't allowed and there are none of the privileged professional conveniences that afford boardrooms even in the quiet city of Bot an insulated imitation of the Ur-island's tempo, and probably because they'd dislike being jostled by the little clique of dreamers that gathers around the magic glass dome without the means to act upon its information. So it may be that Caleb will have the back room all to himself for studying in objective tranquility the world's economy as reflected anticipated or falsified by the hurly-burly of its symptomatic transactions.

In preparation for which Caleb was still going through my cards when I returned to the Van. As it didn't take much psychology to surmise that he had no commonlaw wife cooking for him at home—and as he looks halfstarved anyway—I asked him to dinner with me at the Doghouse. He hesitated at the thought of his dog awaiting him, but he was eager to discuss the job.

He went out to get some stationery items while I put in my usual call to the office in Londonbridge. There wasn't much doing with Walt or the Controller, so I was off the phone almost before he got back. When I brought some ice up from the bar and broke out the Scotch he began to relax a little. Despite his years in sales departments he's no smalltalker, and seems to prefer politeness to breezy familiarity. I'm too friendly with most people, but at first with him it was hard work to get friendly enough. After he began to trust me, however, he grew rather animated on a variety of topics. We both had plenty to talk about for the next five hours, before I let him run home to his famished dog.

He's rather reserved about his private life, but from the résumé I knew he went to college at Hume and lived for a while in Babylon Oaks, so we had Cornucopia to talk about. He seemed normal enough in his impressions. But by the time we got to the Doghouse he couldn't help reverting to the subject of his new employment. He was determined to talk business—just the sort of dinner guest the I R S pretends to believe in. His enthusiasm for analysis entails the conviction shared by all cocksure young staff men that it requires rarer talent to find out what's wrong than to act on the basis of that knowledge and correct the problem. He overestimates the scope of his own experience and underestimates the value of experience acquired by others in mismanaging imperfections.

Caleb's modesty is not intellectual. He was at pains to let it be known that his ideas are his own, even when they happen to converge with academic doctrine. "Pride of authorship"—as Ted McKee calls this characteristic weakness of creative people, who are likely to remain immature in this respect until they are overloaded with general executive responsibilities—will hinder Caleb's career more than the attributes he is modest about, namely his weak voice and unimpressive appearance. I like his spirit well enough, and I'm inclined to meet it on its own overeducated terms, though it must go hard with him when he's trying to impress less sympathetic managers. I suppose I'm the only mustang president in the U S A who regards an employee's mind as more important than his "personality". Maybe I've got reason to be more sensitive than most C E O s to certain agonies of self-confidence.

But I must say it's a trifle irritating to be nipped back to my subject, whatever I happen to start with, by a bold little whippersnapper taking advantage of my indulgence. His unspoken apology is that he's so interested in what I was going to say that he can't help wanting not to let me forget it for a topic that's not quite equally relevant to his hot pursuit. It's true that my parenthetical digressions occasionally grow a mite too heavy for the main stem; after they're broken off under their own weight I'm afraid I've been known to forget what tree they ramified. Some may say I'm prone to gratuitous explanations.

But I think it's a bit premature for Caleb Karcist to verge upon the liberties of an old friend (though now and then I'm myself a little guilty of the same with Doctor Charlemagne). The risk of too much familiarity is a drawback of my careless informality. So far he's been tactful enough not to presume too often, and to disguise his slightly insubordinate impatience at extended intervals of listening, but I don't think it's mere dignity on my part to complain that he's got the bad habit of interrupting his elders. He's still an untested employee, after all, and I should be leery of adopting him as my little brother. Especially when I don't yet understand his motives. It's one thing to discern a man's character but quite something else to learn his secrets.

In any event the agenda wasn't very personal. I gave him a short course in the stock market—practically everything I know. It's a pleasure to teach someone who can grasp the heart of a matter by imagining the intersection of a few compendious abstractions. It's the leverage of a common reader with a liberal education. We were able to cover a lot of ground totally new to him.

I also touched upon the principles of accounting, urging him for his own sake to master the lingua franca that makes any businessman a common reader of any other. I think I succeeded (where his previous associates had failed): I got him interested in the theory, which is mechanically practiced almost solely by inarticulate and suspicious bookkeepers who never can or never will explain their closing entries and trial balances. All too well I know the source of Caleb's prejudice against the medieval accounting mentality, of which I too was a fuming victim until good fortune put me into a position where I was unconditionally obliged to learn their Latin. By setting before him the latent "accounting equation" that his previous informants had likely forgotten (or never understood) as a mere kindergarten tale, I aroused his actual enthusiasm for learning the classical tongue. He now delights in the beauty and power of double-entry mathematics as what he calls a lovely model for the First Law of Thermodynamics!

Inasmuch as Caleb is looking for a permanent job, I expressed the kindly hope that he didn't talk that way at his other application interviews. He only laughed. His résumé suggests that he's got sense enough to discriminate among his interlocutors. If he can learn to bridle his enthusiasms and not to talk so fast when he gets excited, he may get away with some kind of a business career. I advised him to learn how to program computers. Programmers are going to be the intellectuals of business, antithetical salesmen—and that's exactly what Caleb is: a negative salesman. Such a fellow, once he happens to get a job, must work twice as hard as everyone else to get anywhere at all with his boss.

But he's so cheerful that I don't think he's yet conscious of the odds against him. I suppose he still assumes that business careerists are as interested in the work itself as he is. The fact escapes him that colleagues and superiors are motivated almost exclusively by their personal prospects, and care much less about their corporation than he the oddball does who criticizes its stupidities.

I asked about the approach made to him by PERSONS LIMITED. He said that Bill Babwell had interviewed him with a sort of jovial self-deprecation, apologizing for his aggression, and in fact joking about the hazard of becoming known as one of the LIMITED PERSONS gathered in Dogtown by the most limited person of all. Hearing about this below-stairs aspect of Bill's personality I forgave him for acting like a butler to my face. I said to Caleb: "Stick with his agency and you'll meet a lot of girls!"

"But I can't type!" he moaned. I hadn't expected any reply. It sounded as if he'd actually thought of offering himself for temporary office jobs. Was his desperation economic or sexual? I think he was blushing as he added that Babwell's office didn't look very prosperous. When I mentioned my surprise that Limited Persons could stay even in limited business in this limited place he told me that, contrary to that supposition, the problem in Dogtown is not lack of demand for trained office help but lack of such helpers, despite the high rate of unemployment and an ample supply of women seeking an income of their own. "Around here" he said "a good typist is considered well educated, and secretaries are ladies of awe-inspiring quality."

I remarked that in Cornucopia everyone goes to college nowadays.

"In Gopher Prairie too." he said. I was then given his inside view of Dogtown. "Marooners don't like to cross the Gut Bridge. Many of them have never even been to Bot. . . ." He complained about xenophobic antibodies who sooner or later put an end to any intrusive germ of public improvement or political enlightenment—yet fawn upon every petty capitalist who offers to make money off their birthright with the immeasurably overstated promise that his property assessment will alleviate their tax burden. "And now the natives are breeding their own carpetbaggers to join the off-island predators in summertime milking of pilgrims and in winter retirement to Poncedeleon, where they batten on cream in fragrant orange sunshine, putting behind them their annual contribution to Dogtown rubbish."

I was still finding Caleb uncomfortably pejorative. But this island does seem to generate a fearful mixture of willful ignorance and progressive scourging that I can't help comparing with San Ricardo's.

"They're trying to persuade voters that this country's going to be eating more and more beef every year: fishing's all washed up, they say: there's no longer any money in producing what's good for people—"

"*They* again!" I laughed. "The conspiracy! You may have been born here but you sound like an Ippy. Do you know Doctor Charlemagne? He says enclosure of Purdeyville will always be the main issue. I don't see why: the cows and sheep are long gone."

I think I detected a little hesitation when Caleb allowed that he had read a couple of Charlemagne's essays. He seemed genuinely surprised to hear of the Director's Dogtown residence. I'd swear he was suppressing some kind of agitation at the news.

My suspicions about Doc have withstood the tests of further cogitation, but my personal alarm had subsided after a couple of days among these innocent insulars—especially when on second thought I reflected with some surprise (having been too preoccupied the last few years to notice the increasing self-confidence of our nation's invisible hand) that Leviathan is no longer really worried about feckless bugbears. Whether or not J Edgar Blackbook already has a dossier on me, he must know I'm a free-enterprise capitalist, and my Dogtown associations won't make any difference. As long as he keeps his information secret I don't care anyway, since I have no need for a security clearance; I don't do business with any of the broadcast industries.

By way of experimenting with Caleb, therefore, in light of his admission that he reads belles lettres, I offered to take him to Charlemagne's court if I can find the opportunity before I leave town.

"He'll give you heart," I promised. It may be embarrassing as well as amusing to witness the revelation that I'm a student of Doc's (which could hardly be concealed), and Caleb's just the kind of kid to take advantage of such leveling, so I won't necessarily keep my promise; I'll ponder it further. But I wanted to test his reaction to the proposition.

My qualms about his honesty were alleviated when he accepted my offer, though evidently torn between eagerness and shy reluctance. For why should the two of them stage a phony making of acquaintance if the whole scene could be easily avoided? I confess the absurdity of my inklings. But if I decide to follow through with this meddling I'd like to find out why this clever young bachelor has returned to a hometown so poor in prospects for livelihood or liaison. I've been told by everyone I meet that once they get over the Gut to college the talented children of Dogtown generally stay away forever.

I don't dream up paranoid hypotheses just to extend the recreations of my vacation. I'm much too busy. My imagination was stimulated by annoyance at echoes of Doc's automatic horror at any new construction or demolition. Like him, Caleb wants all fully depreciated artifacts to perish only in the fullness of archeological decay.

Nevertheless, I sheered off from the subject of Charlemagne by pursuing Charlemagne's subject. I asked Caleb what he thought ordinary taxpayers thought about industrial development, as distinguished from the exploitation of pilgrims.

"The people may hate change but they'll approve any selfserving blue-sky promise of more jobs and lower tax rates, never questioning the analysis or the forecast. They think it's all gravy, like war contracts. No one understands the long-term costs of expanding city services because bond issues are deferred and painless, and the lesser public expenses are vaguely diffused. Right now they're about to level the loveliest old pastureland on the Cape, right on the edge of Purdeyville. The city's own Industrial Development Economic Agency will bulldoze an 'industrial park'—'park' they call it!—and dispossess the world's best view of the harbor—all on the strength of an unverified expression of uncommitted interest by Fourier Associates Inc, which has learned how to expand production in towns along the Felly by trading glass beads for trapping rights. We flatter ourselves that we're unique because we're at the end of the line, but we swallow the same nostrum as everybody else and issue tax-free municipal bonds to 'develop'—'develop' they call it!—what's known as unproductive land, by blasting ledges, flattening hills, and filling marshes.

Meanwhile acres of abandoned industrial property are falling into ruins at the city's center!"

These goo-goos irritate me. What the hell does Chicken Little know about industrial economics? My erstwhile San Ricardo might still be a generously unprettified city of real workers and loafers if the people had sought new industry instead of settling for quaint tourist-prosperity. No old seacoast town can resist both pressures for very long, unless it turns itself into the kind of nesting colony that Doc and Caleb would hate most of all. I was tempted to argue with him, but it's useless to talk sense to liberals who live by reaction; and I didn't want to abort Caleb's nascent confidence in me by taking the side of Satan. So I asked him other questions about his city.

In 60 years its housing has expanded in irregular retreat from the shambles at its center without increasing the population. But Caleb can't tell me much about the people. Until a couple of years ago he hasn't lived here since he was a very young child; and I think he shies away from people anyway. He doesn't know a single fisherman or plant worker in his bluecollar ward; nor on the other hand did he know so much as the names of Jason Anacoluther the chairman of all things, Shelly Schlossberg the innkeeping sculptor, or Buck Barebones the toolmaker, still less of Slim Boxshaw the contractor or any of the other Turntable locomotives I mentioned. He wasn't even aware of Frank Bacon the almoner of endowments. Since he's never taken a taxi in Dogtown he couldn't know Sam Craigie, my first acquaintance here (who by the way turned out to be a poet, and a friend of Doc's, when he drove us home from the Windmill). In fact, having no car Caleb doesn't know any mechanics or gas-pumpers even by sight; and he doesn't like bars, so he's never talked to a bartender or drinker, as far as I can make out. He doesn't know a single doctor, lawyer, minister, rabbi, priest, salesman, shopkeeper, clerk, or elected official.

Comparing my social permeation with his, I begin to see what draws such a diversity of mariners Marranos marooners maroons and cimarrons to Dogtown, and divers originals in the great chain of being. The city's not so big that anyone can't know anybody if he wants to, but it's big enough to absorb a delitescent idiopath who wishes to remain unremarked and unremarking. Caleb sounds satisfied with invisibility when he tells me that he's always overlooked at counters and ignored at parties. It's hard to imagine him being invited to a party.

But even Caleb can't live in Dogtown without knowing somebody that's known to the public. He is acquainted with the librarian that Doc admires so much at the Atheneum, because she happens to be his landlady—or at least the housewife of his landlord, who happens to be the City Planner. Thus he is known to at least two public servants.

And I suspect that in general he's less anonymous to the people of Dogtown than they are to him. For he has met and may be recognized by both a veterinarian and the Registrar of Dogs at City Hall.

Fortunately, he says, he's had no occasion to meet the Dog Warden. But I wouldn't be surprised if that citizen knows where to find Caleb, inasmuch as Caleb's dog seems to be much admired by Cynics (the dogloving pilgrim-hating faction) and much feared by Puritans (doghating pilgrim-lovers). He tells me that Cape Gloucester is the origin and principal habitat of a Viking Shepherd breed, of which his specimen is the noblest scion, going by the name of Ibi-Roi and weighing more than his master. I asked Caleb how he came by such a valuable protector, and that's how the fact emerged that he isn't entirely unconversant with Dogtown's highest class.

"Ibi was given to me by a blue-blood I did some work for. After gradually going blind on the verge of old age he'd given up the idea of guide-dog training when he couldn't be bothered with learning his own part in the teamwork, even though he helped endow a free school for others to do so. But he was an inventor and he thought he could find a better alternative for his own case. He was working on an electronic dog when he died. Have you ever heard of Captain Ozone?"

"Not as a captain" I said. "What was he a captain of?" It's an equivocal rank, especially around here, where it often means skipper of any fishing vessel down to a singlehanded dragger; in the Army and Marines it's no higher than company command, in police and fire departments it's just a sub-lieutenancy, and even in the Navy it's below Commodore, which any yacht club could have dubbed him. It seemed odd, because I had the impression that Ozone, though secretive, was obliquely as imperious as General MacArthur.

Caleb assumed the story true that Ozone had bravely refused to accept any rank higher than Captain in the quasi-military hierarchy of the S I S during the war, but personally witnessed his haughty insistence upon local recognition of the title in perpetuity.

"Why that title? I thought he was a baron to start with—heir to a Royal land-grantee—who still kept lawyers working on his claim to a strip of parallels all the way to the Pacific Ocean? He could have been knighted by Hoover or made a peer of the realm by Eisenhower. Why only Captain?" Was there some special image from childhood reading that had never been dislodged? A war captain is young enough to lead men in action and too young for desk duty: was that the idea he cherished, to gainsay maternal mollycoddling?

"I think the old glamor of schooners. He told me he'd wanted to go down to the sea but his family sent him to prep school."

"They all say that." said I, without examining my personal pronoun.

"But when he was growing up here, mostly summering of course, highline schooner captains were heroes for everybody in commerce and industry, not only for romantic boys. He always had a wistful streak when it came to the sweaty folks he was cut off from, first by wealth and sensibility, then by the nature of his work, and in the end by blindness—which inspired more wist than ever."

"The Lord of New Albion must have owned a lot of souls."

"The souls of Dogtown are emancipated by birth. The rich weren't here from the beginning, and most Dogtowners have always been too cussedly independent to make good domestics. Yet transpontine servants go stir-crazy here, especially black ones. So Captain Ozone thought he had to pay higher wages than anyone else. He hated trouble with the help. His only interest in the Cape economy was its effect upon the slave market. He wanted to keep Dogtown just the way it was mainly because if things got too depressed he'd be swamped with appeals for charity and if they got too prosperous he wouldn't be able to get any menials at all. The only thing he asked of the city government was that it enforce the restrictive zoning up around Prudence Cove in Taraville."

"I suppose the enclosure of Purdeyville was nothing to him?"

"Oh yes! Of course he didn't want anybody messing around his quarries or putting up radio transmitters that would interfere with his experiments."

I asked Caleb what kind of work he'd done for Captain Ozone, seeing that it wasn't itemized on his résumé under "freelance consulting", the occupation listed as most recent.

"By the time I knew him he'd dropped all his other research to work on devices for the blind. His first step, when he found out he was going to lose his sight, had been to buy a CRF paper-tape machine and start teaching himself to read the 5-hole chords with his fingers. But almost immediately he converted to the new 8-channel communication equipment—which incorporates parity-checking—and retrained himself to sense with his fingertips the Hollerith code that's used in tabulating cards. He had CRF make him a set of keys with embossed symbols and learned conventional touch-typing from a private tutor.

"As his helper I got to know what can be done with punched tape. Eventually it will replace OHM cards for all data-entry; CRF Tapetypers and Computapers will make keypunching obsolete!"

Since Parity controls CRF (Cash Register & Forms Company), I was respectfully attentive to this sanguine vaticination.

It's a company that started out many years ago in the forms business, as primarily compositors and printers; and it's still the leading supplier of manifold business forms that are too complex in construction for most of the trade—chiefly those used in "dedicated" teletypes, bookkeeping machines, computers, etc . That original component of CRF business is now relatively phlegmatic (though attracting more competition with the expansion of the market). Having accumulated a lot of cash the company was able to diversify by integration. It acquired and developed a manufacturer of cash registers and office equipment, most of which at the time still had no connection with paper or printed forms. Their rotary desk calculator became standard equipment in offices and laboratories—and I have reason to know that it's very expensive. But then they brought out a fast ten-key adding machine that prints on a roll of plain tape—which has recently led to the first printing calculator on the market.

Meanwhile another of their acquisitions was producing the mechanical guts of electric typewriters for OHM and others. And all along they were making a quiet splash in the retail trade with a truly analytical cash register.

Their R & D was so successful, and their technology so far ahead of undefined competition, that when they came up with the Versatility line of Tapetypers (for "writing" and "reading" the aforementioned paper tape as input and by-product of transaction documents— invoices, bills of lading, etc —as they are being "created" on automatic typewriters with built-in programmed calculators; and even for controlling machine tools), they had to themselves a whole horizon of new markets that OHM couldn't match them in; yet CRF machines can sense or punch OHM cards, and are otherwise usefully compatible with OHM's tabulating machines.

Thus Caleb enlightened my banausic interest in the CRF blackbox. What potential for growth! This small office equipment—merely "peripheral" to the high-volume batch-processing of unit-record OHM cards—can accomplish multistage business transactions without the orthodox duplications of "data-entry" that he reviewed for me (though in far too much detail). He has no doubt that these mechanisms are only the beginning of a new industry in wired communications at the input and output ends of "automatic data processing".

He used the words *flexibility* and *efficiency* over and over again—until, as layman with headache coming on, I fully appreciated the drift of his excitement, which was much enhanced by his new mastery of accounting.

His inspired eloquence wholly diverted attention from himself. He grew as animated as Tubalcain's sincerest sales rep, and I must admit that his ingenuous enthusiasm might well be infectious to bureaucrats. It's nice to know that it will go a long way in motivating his work on my project; but there's a danger he'll be carried away by preoccupation with this particular star in the firmament: after all, CRF represents only about 15 percent of PAR's assets.

But when it comes to CRF's marketing, Caleb's as querulous as an outside director from OHM or I C E Corporation. Despite its engineering lead, plentiful working capital, brilliant designers, excellent research and development facilities, sound quality control, all kinds of patent protection, and famous industrial relations, the company has not been doing as well as it should. Whether or not the faltering is really due to misguided marketing organization and sales policy—as Caleb angrily complains, it relies upon independent franchised dealers for all sales and technical services—the stock market has been disappointed with its profits. Yet as PAR's largest single investment CRF is obviously the keystone for any plans that Arthur Halymboyd may have to integrate potentially related manufacturers into a major new empire.

Just lately CRF has jiggled upward a little on the Big Ticker, but that may be due as much to a mention in the press of Parity's recently increased interest as to any signs of financial improvement. Halymboyd is never inactive for long. Now that he has strengthened control of CRF we expect him either to attempt some managerial correction of its operations, as may be hoped, or just to encourage the stock market to bid up the price so that he can spin off some shares as a bonanza dividend to PAR stockholders (including of course his own trusts and holding companies)—which would certainly deflate Caleb's emotional commitment. And mine too, truth to say. Or what would be even more disheartening, he might sell CRF to one of the big companies that wants to compete with OHM, so that he can realize profits large enough to start all over again at a higher level of pseudo-managerial investment with some other black box.

As an instant admirer of Parity herself, the alluringly fictitious person synthesized by her own sale of her own ownership, Caleb prays that Halymboyd will use Parity's increasing Net Asset Value (N A V) as lure for exchange-of-stock mergers, if anywhere, in the electronics and office equipment fields. I don't disagree, but secretly I also hope for the expansion of one of her less conspicuous yet not entirely unrelated smaller constellations, such as that of the Cook Evaporator Company, which suggests prospects for Tubalcain.

With bold liberality, just inside Loathey O'Toole's blocked-up street window, we juggled the possibilities like two highly liquid millionaires.

However, I wonder about Caleb's sense of proportion. At the end of our dinner he was fervently expatiating on a patented office file tray that he had already been delighted to discover was the product of one of PAR's small possessions at a fourth remove from the mother kingdom (though itself possessing two colonies at a fifth). This formerly independent manufacturer (as if almost all Atlantean manufacturers weren't formerly independent!) is called Cold Steel Office Equipment Corporation. Among its wholly owned subsidiaries are Categorical Looseleaf Products and Thanatron Rectification Company.

As a fundamentalist in every fibre of my being, on the theory that Halymboyd's putative industrial objectives may best be detected by looking away from all his feints and obfuscations on the Street and examining every one of those unnoticed little black boxes of production from which most of the real value of this inorganic molecule ultimately derives (since apparently the structure itself has as yet contributed little more than the propinquity of working capital), and that jumps in its superorganic evolution may be anticipated by the affinitive valences of the divers atoms actually or potentially in bond, I asked Caleb to find out all he could about the products of the Cold Steel arsenal, which seems to be a microcosm of Parity herself in its odd assortment of constituents.

Still bemused by his recollection of the Cold Steel file tray, Caleb gladly made note of this sub-assignment. You'd think the managerial selection and deployment of this desktop convenience made a difference between profit and loss, the way he raves about the design and quality of Cold Steel's version, a modular unit with scalloped openings in the bottom and on all four sides, so mounted that one can grasp the entire contents of papers from any direction by thumb and forefinger of one hand without interrupting the paperworking rhythm of office motion! He's enchanted to find no structural limit to the number of storeys that can be erected atop office surfaces—in single or multiple columns—by virtue of the neatly detachable stacking posts and rubber-capped foot-pieces that are provided with each unit. He's fascinated by the idea of building a tower on his desk!

Poor Caleb argued his unopposed case as vehemently as if he was trying to get me to approve the appropriation for a new office building. He clinched his brief for the functional superiority of Cold Steel file trays by swearing that a stack of three or four is strong enough to bear the full weight of an office visitor leaning on both elbows.

I was bound to acknowledge that even at poor little Tubalcain's paperwork-stations I'd noticed more than one partly buckled stack of inferior articles. Caleb's prophetic sensibilities disquiet me nonetheless. They augur a culture fraught with paper. He's an engineer of the coming age. I don't know anything about the administrative problems of firms like insurance companies—in which paper itself has always been raw material, work-in-process, finished product, and inventory—but clearly Caleb would belong in such an atmosphere if it weren't so chary of open flames.

In any event our conversation suffered no lapses, and I didn't notice that he'd never answered my question about his job with Captain Ozone. Caleb too, was he guilty of forgetful digression? Or of sly evasion? But then, one must never ask a consultant much about what he's actually done for the clients he claims.

When we got up to leave the Doghouse it wasn't very late, but I wanted to come back to the Van and catch up on my dictation. My vacation is so busy that this diary gets harder and harder to keep up. It seems to lengthen of its own volition. And I haven't yet been outside Harbor Ward!

"Well I'd better let you get back to Ibi-Roi," I said. Caleb tells me that in Dogtown it should be pronounced Ibi-Roy.

cc: I. Charlemagne
RO:i

6
ROCKY
BAY

"Our Jack will take Vinland even if we don't lift a finger." said Tessa Barebones. "Nowhere can he be discredited either as an uneducated courthouse pol or as a milksop, and in this state he has nothing to fear as a Petrine Scholastic. Besides raising a widow's mite for the National Committee, there's nothing much we can do to help win the rest of the country. But the campaign's a good excuse for having a party with my friends. God help you if you're not a Skinny Crat, because you're wasting your time if you're just a spy for the Fat Cans looking for Premature AntiFascists. We may not discuss politics at all tonight. I almost didn't invite you, but I knew Buck wanted me to."

"I'd crash anybody's dinner if I thought it would help keep Noxin out of the White House." Rafe replied. "Cornucopians are sensitive about having fostered his career."

"Well I'm glad I took the chance: you seem to be pretty handy in a kitchen. But there's nothing more to help with at the moment, so sit over there on that stool and tell me more about the great world."

"I hope I'm not in the way. I really wanted to go upstairs with Buck and see him put the kids to bed. I wouldn't mind reading them a story."

"And see my private housekeeping? Not on your tintype!"

"I could tell right away that your little girl is a genius, as well as a ravishing beauty."

"At that age we all are. Fatal characteristics for a woman. Buck spoils her. But please be patient. There'll be more work for you pretty soon. People will be coming in half an hour. Thanks to you I'm readier than I expected to be. You're a lot more helpful than a wine-taster. Have more Scotch. It isn't often that I can combine entertainment for Buck's business with my own convenience."

"I won't talk any business that you haven't brought up. Was this house your idea?"

"We had to wait until the children were old enough, and I'm not sure they are. Many's the time I've almost repented the worry of it. But at last both kids swim like seals and climb the rocks like sea-goats. Now that I've recovered my equanimity I'm beginning to enjoy the stone jail I've made for myself."

From where he was perched in the gleamingly equipped kitchen of gray granite, a few steps lower than the oak floor of the beam-ceilinged living room that was once an unceilinged machinery shed, and not many feet above the highwater mark of the Atlantic Ocean that lapped the barnacled rust granite of the barge wharf upon which the building was planted, Rafe could watch lobster boats and pleasure-sails pass more or less slowly from left to right or right to left inside the unfinished and abandoned Seamark breakwater. It was half a century since that half-sunken public work had been prolonged without beginning or end a mile or two from land in an attempt (inspired by the success of Cherbourg) to make Seamark not only an anchorage for Teddy Roosevelt's Great White Fleet but also an international harbor. Though otherwise only loosely embraced by the headlands out of his sight on either hand, Rocky Bay was deep and broad enough for the protection of a thousand ships. It was to have been the nation's most expedient port for North Atlantic freight, breeding prosperous piers warehouses and grain elevators; passengers were to save a full day's sailing between Europe and New Uruk by connecting with a boat train at the Land's End terminal. But as speedier ships reduced the economic disadvantage of this coastally extended sea distance between Britain and New Uruk, as the V & M made no improvement in Dogtown's access to transcontinental railroading, and as Congress began to balk at the the Corps of Engineers' cost overruns, the lodestar of local wealth gradually faded; the city ceased spending its limited political influence (vitiated moreover by the usual internal dissension) on romantic petitions for perpetuation of the port-barrel. With much of its length invisible beneath the surface as a proven hazard to navigation, the incomplete breakwater, like an isolated half-mile of Roman wall against oceanic Picts, though flanked by nothing but level cavalry plains, was indeed a stumbling block to dangerous easterly seas. But the bay remained too exposed from the north for the Eurotropic jaws to be designated even as a Harbor of Refuge, and Seamark's artificial inner harbor, where stones had been piled for the protection of small boats, was a pharynx too crowded to succor even the smallest craft unless driven by individual accident.

So much and not much more did Rafe already know about the green and white Fifth Parish of Dogtown, photographically clean, settled down so neatly for all the rest of time. Tessa had just told him that Seamark, once an independent village of fishermen and saltwater farmers, had been mediatized by Dogtown in 1842 when it refused to cooperate in extending the V & M Railroad's Gloucester Branch all the way to Land's End. The annexation was accomplished nearly without bloodshed by calling out the Sea Fencibles while offering to relieve the vassal of its debts and grant it the status of a "liberty". It thus became a socially autonomous enclave within the larger township (which was not incorporated as a city for another thirty years). To this day Seamark and North Village—the Sixth Parish, co-product of the Fifth's own fission—have together enjoyed disproportionate representation in Dogtown government, though they lack the popular votes to put up a mayor. They have continued to exercise a liberty's prerogative to ban sales of alcoholic drink within their frontiers, as much in order to demonstrate their distinction from the rest of Dogtown as to contend with drunken driving.

To many Yankee oldtimers, Tessa warned him, the Squarehead Compromise (a euphemism for the treaty of submission incorporated into the Dogtown city constitution of 1873, to which they were forced to acquiesce by the voted defection of their own naturalized Scandinavian townsmen, the cannon fodder of Seamark and North Village militia) was still a bitterly inherited experience of collective shame. She admitted that it was too easy for her, a native of New Uruk City (Borough of Lagash), to laugh off the talk of secession with which the diehard troglodytes were beginning to infect Norman newtimers. Not that she didn't join them in complaining about the factious and smelly hegemon that collected taxes from them by a kind of mob rule.

Now Rafe had spent most of the day over in the city with her husband Buck at his machine shop, her senior by about fifteen years, a source of intelligence neither witty nor ironical, and knew from him that contrary to present appearances Seamark had once flourished on its own productive industry in unprivileged interdependence with other wards of Dogtown. It was the sly infestation of vacation visitors, many of them evolving into "all-year-round summer folks", that finally crowded out most of the sweat-producing establishments, spruced up the ruins, and suppressed the feuds among bitter Scandi tribes. In the evolution many lovely elms were planted along the dusty streets, old houses immaculately restored to what they'd never been, lawns and flowers cultivated to the New Armorican ideal.

But who could help being charmed by the townlet of Seamark and its northern villagette, so disparately better kept than the city they belonged to? The Barebones lived in the march between Seamark and North Village, which was considered the latter's Sixth Parish territory by virtue of its quarries. It displayed rather fewer houses of the prevailing white clapboard and rather more of the distinctive rusty granite; but in both wards of the liberty the living body-rock of Cape Gloucester was washed nearly naked to the waist by the sea it confronted.

Nearby above the Barebones house, at the southern boundary of the Village, slightly inland, jaggedly blackened desert-red cliffs enclosed the largest of numerous vast hollows blasted by men now quiet. In order not to interrupt this bluff-mounted segment of Cod Street in its circling of the island they left a narrow ridge of granite between the great seaward pit and the like-hewn shoreline. Two hundred years before the rock was scratched the circuitous highroad around the upland heaths of the interior had found its northern path more or less sixty feet above the ever-besieging sea, and it was forty feet above the level of the fresh water that now filled a hundred feet of the excavation, which was deeper perhaps than the briny anchorage outside. But to make an obvious shortcut for shipping the quarry's yield, a gap had been pierced in the isthmus of living granite and a keystone arch of its own refitted bone planted over the embrasure as an all but natural bridge. Two hours before he'd been invited by Buck's wife to stay for quasipolitical buffet, Rafe and his host had walked the bottom of that canyon passage, along the remains of an ad hoc railway formerly running down to its private quay, which was likewise built of the Cape's cooled magma, protected from

Poseidon's horses by the mine's own inshore breakwater of gigantic granite rubble.

The Bareboneses' rehabilitated wharf—like the other squarely constructed of massive blocks—lay more exposed in the next inlet to the north, a tiny obtuse cove too steep and poppled for barefoot bathing. This separate portlet, with nothing to shield it except a small storm-tossed arm of cut stones, had been built by a different company to moor sloops exporting the production of its own inland pits and importing coal for the powerhouse, which Tessa was to convert into a distinguished homestead as compensation for her lot. The boiler had occupied the kitchen space where Rafe was integrating bits and pieces of Barebones history.

Beneath the greenery of little more than a single generation, which now lightly cicatrized the scarifications of ruthless industry (headlong right-of-ways from the trepanned hills to the invulnerable sea), a steep drive of granite chips sidled down the shore's bluff from Cod Street to the laved foundations of the Cape, serving on its way a few other houses half hidden on their shelves. Tessa had a tangled garden on the soil-covered mole, and small trees had grown up around the house, which—wharf, garden, and superstructure alike—were walled with consanguineous rectopolyhedrons unalike in size or weathering only: rusted loaves of bone sawed and split from the depths of maternal earth.

Rafe did not need to be told that this masculine domestication was of her design. Buck was proud enough of what she'd done, and pleased with her pleasure in it, as if thereby absolved of certain obligations to his family; for obviously the pretty conversion had cost his fortune, and he was no nest-builder at heart. Worse, neither was she, at heart, Rafe was beginning to surmise—if any woman wasn't. The eccentric little messuage was already her last year's work of art. She was getting bored with waves.

Rafe was envious nevertheless, curious about the industrial origin of the property. This spontaneous spark of interest in local history met with the damp tinder of her technological ignorance and her courteous determination to scotch incipient illusions about what he was missing in life, apparently under the compunction to set his mind at rest about the superiority of his unmoored independence.

"It's lovely here now, with the big doors open in the other room, on a warm afternoon with a nice blue sky and no wind to whip up our halcyon high tide; but in the winter that o'er-beetling cliff which you'd think would shelter us from cruel Boreas only makes this house as gloomy and cold as a witch's teat before the day's half westered, no matter how much money we burn in our furnace. It's no mere mistral that makes us crawl in and out the leeward postern like Eskimos at an igloo and wear ski suits for pyjamas." She was sure Rafe had forgotten about winter, which right here wasn't like two or three weeks in a cozy snow-sunned chalet.

"For the sake of four good months of zephyr or sirocco" she drawled, without a trace of Lagash accent (having been trained for the stage), "we go without mountains, lakes, forests, cocktail parties, playhouses, air strips, fast cars, and all the other things a footloose woman takes for granted. And during those few hoarded weeks that are supposed to make up for all our suffering we can't step out the door without bumping into queues of pilgrim chariots. The Greeks used to say that honey tastes bitter to the jaundiced."

"You don't look yellow to me." protested the visiting knight.

"Between the devil and the deep blue sea, there's not even a Crat to talk to, except a mathematician up the road who's invented a calculus that improves upon Newton and Leibniz, or some traveling salesman like you who drops in with flattering illusions. Don't be mistaken about this part of Dogtown just because it's been purified: this is no paradise."

"Neither is it hell!"

"Purgatory then. Perhaps all my grievances will vanish with maturity. No doubt my soul is tried for a purpose. The worst of it is that people around here don't like dogs. The neighbors snub poor dear old Praisegod, who faithfully guards everybody's lambs from wolves and octopuses. They say that sheep dogs come from wolves, not from sheep. They cut him dead. They look right through him when he smiles and wags his tail at the mere sight of them."

The well-brushed family collie had already been admired by Rafe, as he was by most warmhearted human beings. He was now trustfully flung out in sleep at a locus that would have been common to all Tessa's paths about the kitchen if she hadn't stepped around him. The sad import of her remark impelled Rafe to descend from his stool and again stroke the good dog's narrow Pictish brow, and his generic affection was acknowledged by a melancholy thump or two of the aged tail.

"Some of the Village Protesticans are against Evolution as liberal."

"Well I have my own reservations about it." said Rafe.

"But you just mean the natural selection part of it."

"How did you know?"

"Because I can see that you're a strong manager, even though you come from Cornucopia and aren't working on a hardhead degree."

"But you and Buck go over to the Harbor every day. Isn't there a whole different bunch of talkers to choose from? Maybe I could give you one or two introductions."

"I need cunning evasions more than ingenuous leads. But it's true, we must keep running back and forth over the hill to consort with our kind of fugitives and failures. Yet over there you keep getting entangled in the endless political squabble, and most of the aborigines are perpetually defending their grubby little jobs or screaming about their piddling little taxes. It's no wonder that the whole city was once excommunicated and the county seat taken away. Pilgrims flock here for the wicked thrill of our lawless history. This summer my children saw license plates from thirty-nine states and five provinces. —By the way, let us know if you ever see one around here from Parthenia. For some reason that's the only Eastern-states gap in our list of sightings. I suppose they still resent the time George Washington spent with the Continental Army in Vinland.

"But instead of playing geography games I should be doing what you are doing!"

"I don't think you're Narcissistic enough: what I'm doing is gaping with admiration at what *you* are doing!" Rafe was truly fascinated by the unpondering efficiency with which she coordinated fancy cooking while carrying on a conversation that she had to think about.

"I mean going to college. I didn't take advice when I was young. White Quarry may be just the thing for me now. Two vacations every year in Montvert! Skiing without the kids! Singing folk songs with scouts almost my own age! I had my babies late in life advisedly, but do you know the result is that I'll be forty in very few years!" Rafe would have taken her for thirty, but as thin and keen as a medical student. Her smooth Old World face, olive and aquiline, closely capped by straight short black hair, was always tossing back aslant to evade the smoke of a cigarette expertly suspended in her thin lips while she worked with both hands under the autonomic supervision of lowered eyelids, except when it was taken thoughtfully between two momentarily disengaged fingers and she turned to face him.

"Next February's Convocation up there will be my last." he said. "They have central heat. As long as the snow is fresh and deep, things won't always look bleak and miserable from inside the glass. But I couldn't survive a whole winter month up there. Why not live where it's always pleasant? Spiritual discipline is tough enough in a land of milk and honey! Where it's summer all year round you can save your energy for contemplation—where it's the normal assumption that all industry flourishes as a matter of course. But up there when the snow gets dirty, before the mud is rid of ice, White Quarry's probably just as mean and disconsolate as all the other cold places of the earth. Still, it's easier to excuse pride-of-place in Montvert than elsewhere in New Armorica—which seems possessed by various peculiar forms of that mania, don't you think?"

He tried to explain why he liked that northwest corner of the puritannical region in which he did not wish to dwell during its season of adversity. "I swear the borders of Montvert were drawn by God. On the west south and east you can practically see the state line, the mountains are so distinctive. But my feeling for the state comes as much from what I've learned as from what I see. It's 19C archeology. The slopes are forested wherever they're not cultivated by cows, yet there's not a virgin stand among them. Second and third growths have advanced the woods, and one knows they obliterate the sites of a waterpower prosperity that was starved when cheap steam began to turn the wheels of industry everywhere else and the railroads were getting through to the easy ploughland. Now they've got nothing to ship to market but immature pulp logs, some reforested hardwood, and tons of milk. Only depopulation made it possible to survive on those rocky little dairy farms in the southern part of the state."

"A friend of mine you'll meet tonight, Gloria Keith, is from one of them, where every acre's on a cold little mountainside and none of the mountains are majestic. I know the landscape's more generous up north around White Quarry, if not greener. Yet you can still tell it's the same pastorale, I agree. But beauty and revelation are rarely correlative. By now I'm inured to landscape. I'm less joyous with cold citizens than with cold weather. After all, the snow's an insulator against the terror of retracted warmth, which beneath the snow differs only in degree from the same season in your fabulous promised land. You can't pull the wool over my eyes. I've lived in Yerba Buena. I've also been down the Messpot Valley in wintertime as well as summer, and it's not like the Garden of Eden. The cold is as cruel as the heat when those naked vines are pruned to the quick—lines of stacked crutches converging by rows and columns in any perspective, or ranks of gnarled dwarf crosses balancing each other at the hands like totalitarian paperdolls. I must admit that in hells like that I miss the kind of beauty I pretend I'm now indifferent to. When you can't even see the mountains as horizon there's nothing but a few riverbank willows to baffle those long sere winds. The houses are as low and drab as their addresses, like Avenue 39 and Road 15-1/2, and hunkered down forlornly they can't hide any slattern detail of flimsy ugliness. You can bet that under their flatly replicated antennas not a single book is sheltered! Those air-wave fingers: rootless tacked-up parodies of the mutilated vines, which at least are wired to each other! What could be colder than such a naked snowless flat?

"But cold as it is, the people who live there are human like you. So are the Aleutian walrus-hunters and the winter-wheat farmers of Itasca and the Jefferson sheep ranchers and the loggers of the Upper Peninsula. It isn't the weather that freezes New Armoricans; it isn't the temperature that turns involuntary bleak white hardship into self-discipline and keeps their fever down to zero! Montverters believe that maximum virtue per capita is bred by the abortion of all nature's attempts at happy-go-lucky selection! To hear them boast, you'd think they've chosen the rock pillows of their necessity and banished luxury by free will! Yet when the gods boil us all down in their try-pots state by state you'll find just as much residual value in the teeming morality of the Cajun bayous."

Rafe remembered marveling that it was still before Mardi Gras season when of a brilliant afternoon in a dining car he'd glided along white-fowled swamps on the approach to New Arc. The wings of grounded water palms were spread like green birds just alighting. In those amaranthine suburbs winter did not betray to passengers the tree-huts of children or expose to each other the secrecy of lone cats prowling.

Rafe said that he didn't know any of the people who really lived their lives in Montvert, but he told her not to worry about the inhabitants of the colony at White Quarry College being sympathetic with or acceptable to the local society, especially the distinguished members of the faculty, least of all the one she'd like the most.

"Good. If I were to go, it certainly wouldn't be to admire the Monvert character. But Doctor Charlemagne would be worth knowing." Her friend Gloria, none other than the historical librarian mentioned by Doc, and Caleb Karcist's landlady, had got wind of Ippy's famous doings out of town, which to this Frau Knight seemed to render him less inaccessible in Montvert than in Dogtown. "Years ago I was in and out of theater. I always thought that if I made it in a few leads I'd call him in to cast me Off-Limeway in something of his own. But I knew he refused to be commercial, and I never was able to be. I recognize him on Front Street when I'm driving by, but not because I've ever met him. He must have fallen upon hard times, or he wouldn't be on this side of the Gut Bridge—but not so hard that I'd dare ask him to give a master class at the Hoof and Mouth School!"

Buck had told Rafe that his wife taught theater.

"I call it coaching voice." she drawled. "My sister handles dance and another woman the visual arts. They'll both be here in a few minutes. We hire men for handicrafts and musical accompaniment. The studio's a downtown loft that used to be a boxing club next door to a sporting house. We're trying to raise the professional level by calling it the Troika Arts Center. It was named after the quarry we were swimming in when we got the idea one moonlight night."

"Then Russians also settled here! Red or White?"

"Only three. They drowned themselves all together after chopping three separate holes in the ice—the man and his wife and his mistress. I guess the pit was already abandoned: otherwise it would have been pumped out. Haven't they told you that this is where Mitya and Grushenka ended their days, with Katya to boot? The framed convict escaped to Finland, you see, resolved to do penance for the rest of his life by following a trade among the people. That's how he learned to pass as one of the Finns—though he found them rude—and immigrated with a boatload of them when they heard about jobs here in stonecutting. Mrs Karamazov was with him all the time; Katarina came later, when she found out where they were, bringing her money, what was left of it. That's what they bought their little acre with, over in Taraville. It was the day they got their U S citizenship that—". She drew a finger across her throat, smiling brightly at her boggled guest.

"What happened to Ivan and Alyosha?"

"Oh they never came to Atlantis. —But you still haven't told me what brought you here to the dead beginning of the northern New World. I'm sure it wasn't just to butter up your rusticating professor. I don't believe your story about being on vacation. I'm quite aware that you're picking Buck's brains about something. Everyone who's smart enough does that. But you couldn't have known about him before you came to Dogtown."

As usual, Rafe explained his situation circumstantially, more than sufficiently; and he couldn't help himself even when he perceived that she had half ceased listening to his distinctions and differences. But he wanted to be honest about his intertwined motives, and they entailed several judgments based on ill-defined facts. On his way to the answer, therefore, he found himself clarifying the subject of steam cleaning with some of the locutions Ted McKee had repeated hundreds of times in sales meetings and advertisements, and on a thousand daily occasions of oral honing, to promulgate the awkward idea that the term *steam cleaner* was a misnomer for the advanced "jenneys" [from "engine" or "gin"] offered by the leading company of the steam-cleaning industry. "Steam doesn't clean. It has simply been the means of providing mechanical force and thermal energy—impact and heat—for the third element, a chemical solution. Detergent—"

"Any housewife knows that!" she interrupted, with a smile that looked a trifle impatient. "Applied thermodynamics is our vocation."

Now it was perhaps true that a sensible woman might have saved Tubalcain a great deal of trouble in communicating its science to the trade, and he now so acknowledged. But he wanted to be sure that she understood exactly the kind of cleaning he was talking about (since most laymen did not). Only then could he get to the pump problem; and it seemed to him very important that she appreciate the significance of his interests. "You must have seen our 1500s working on the Goat Island Bridge when you rode the train across the Bay. There are four of them working all year round, rolling on their own trolleys, and each one has four cleaning hoses, blasting away at dirt and rust and flaked paint to prepare for the new coats of paint, beginning at one end as soon as the other is finished, five or six miles of steel girders. Or maybe you've seen other models on trailers in the street, or on scaffolds, cleaning the facades of buildings, especially stone ones, maybe of imported Dogtown granite. . . ."

He was surprised by the interest she evinced when he finally touched upon the HP360 pump problem for which her husband had become accidental consultant, and he now discerned that her appreciation of Buck's "genius for gadgetry" was neither mocking nor bitter; but he couldn't yet make out whether the irony of that phrase of hers lay in aristocratic meiosis of his talent or in her estimation of his clients' underestimation. At any rate she was pleased by Rafe's praise. "It's nice to hear the good opinion of a qualified critic." She smiled encouragingly and encouraged.

"But I know you won't laud him for his businessmanship." she continued. "He took you to the shop, didn't he? We haven't half paid for all those lathes and milling machines yet. And any day that old shed's going to blow down or go up in smoke. It won't be as exciting as a big wooden summer hotel, but fire is still a principal diversion for our populace. It's for very good reason that insurance here is almost too expensive. There's more respect for floating property. A different principle applies to the water-death of fishing boats. That usually occurs only when the insurance is sufficient, and the cause instead of arson is what our fisherman Wat Cibber calls 'floating rocks'. Him too you'll meet tonight, Buck's oldest friend here, and not the least waggish.

"For years I've been trying to get Buck to incorporate. He wouldn't lack for investors. The business ought to be expanded. For one thing, he's too passive about his inventions, his excuse being that they aren't *basic* (which I take to mean *generic*—is that right?). But patents are troublesome and expensive—a damn nuisance when you're already thinking about the next one. So I've been pestering him at least to get a patent lawyer. He's persuaded himself that his designs are protected by his obscurity and by the promised discretion of his client gentlemen—yet he himself will speak as freely about his ideas to curious strangers as if he were an astrophysicist at an international conference of cosmologists!"

"I didn't pump him!" Rafe protested. "He volunteered to help me!"

"That's what I mean." she half-smiled laconically.

In this matter Rafe was confident of his ability to estimate her hyperbole and ellipsis. He had spent several hours before and after lunch at Dogtown Machine and Design Company with Baucis Barebones her husband. Buck's shop was housed in a shabby dun building of framed wood whose upper storeys retained the shape of an old-time agricultural feed store. Judging by appearances, as well as by Buck's emotional preoccupation with unique final products, the firm was oblivious of public relations.

The half-empty ill-adapted plant stood under a knoll of creased gray granite ledge known as Fuckintired Rock, which but for thin skullless hair of crag-flat blueberry bushes suggested the exposed brain of a whale petrified by millenia of weather. This eminence commanded the narrowest and deepest bend of the Namauche River like nature's toll-castle, about half a mile in from the Harbor, hard by the railroad drawbridge that viaducted trains at a level halfway between tide and summit. And Rafe discovered in amazing daylight the causewayed embankment crossing a broad marsh of tidewater on which he had so blindly entered the island.

With pleasure too he identified just across the double tracks from Buck's machine shop the steel derrick he had spotted from Salt Cod Park. It was planted at the crest of a steep bank dividing the courtyard of the Dogtown Smithy & Iron Works between the elevated level of the railroad and the level at which barges once were moored. On the upper plateau, blocking the foot of Coalyard Lane, a spacious brick machine works with windows as tall as a power plant's housed the company's huge engine lathes and other titanic machine tools. At the waterside below, in the latticed shadow of the drawbridge tracks, a much larger and loftier shed of patched and rusty metal sheltered the furnaces and forges in a theater of colossal hydraulic hammers and chisels, where square logs of steel were rounded and cuffed into rough shape for the machinists above to finish and ship out as customized freight.

Between these two stages of work-in-progress the derrick's rotating mast, guyed by steel cables fastened to four quarters of the yard, suspended on a pivoting boom at variable distances from both levels the massive electromagnetic discus that bore enough direct current to raise swing and stack like sawn or unsawn timber a variety of ferrous beams, columns, and made-to-order shafts, each often distinguished enough to require its own flatcar. The spur of the V & M Railroad, which by penetrating the enclave connected the Iron Works with private sidings all over the continent, came to an end over the edge of the bank on a trestled coal-pocket which hadn't been replenished since the furnaces were converted to oil sometime after the war.

The firm had been founded when its Hephaistos was a sculptor of ships' iron anchors, modeled on the riverside and handled with the hoists and carts of human labor assisted only by steam; but now a few men controlling more sensitive machinery pounded and circumcised steel propulsion shafts or papermill rollers that might well have been tapered pillars for the temple of Dis. But on working floors the overhead cranes couldn't be called upon to handle all the tasks of lifting and locomotion: some work-in-progress was still trundled from station to station in wheeled Paul Bunyan cradles on home-made rails, for reduction or improvement, in or out of fires.

Buck had courteously given the visitor enough time and commentary to take in this impressive metalworking plant across the tracks. It dwarfed his own in everything but complexity precision and art. But on the inside, to such a connoisseur, Buck's shop wasn't bad at all. Although some of the machine tools were rather old to the eye of a modern Cornucopian, they seemed efficiently laid out and well maintained. Only a few of them were in use at any time, Rafe noticed, since it was a job shop (not a production plant like his own) and the men took their work from one to another. The floor was remarkably clean, considering that the day was more than half over. There were about a dozen cheerful and unhurried employees, but apparently not a loafer among them. Only Buck's business desk betrayed conflict and procrastination.

In Rafe's professional view, as he inspected the outfit with benefit of the proprietor's exegesis, it was an exceptionally capable jobshop (much like those in basements devoted to the service of university professors when mechanical experiment was still the first resort of engineering), however dreary it might have looked to bankers lawyers or guidance counselors who judged by housekeeping and financial statements. He had at once recognized the enterprise as a cult that renounced architectural and fiscal formality for dynamic functional forms, usually in steel but otherwise not necessarily related to each other, though most of them—either as single parts or as subassembled articulations—were commissioned by freezers or fish-processing plants. Obscure ingenuities were the Barebones bread and butter. Buck met the payroll for his cadre by dealing with inconspicuous areas of problem.

But Buck's shop, Rafe had found, was also, like his body, a personal laboratory. There was a drafting room partitioned off from toolmaking benches, hand tools, machine tools, and assembly floor, but the whole atelier was equally sentient to the speculations and the actual commissions of the engrossed maestro. Contracts and assignments continually interfered with the independent conceptions and experiments that remained his sole and weakening fortification against the mild sadness betrayed by his homely goodnatured countenance.

Perhaps Tessa feared that the process was beginning to work both ways, and that the problems set for Buck by others (like Rafe's cursed pump) were gradually getting more interesting because of the Bourbon they did nothing to discourage, because they left him less and less time to risk failure in the great projects of his heart—one of which, Rafe had shamelessly wormed out of him, was a radically new device for the desalinization of seawater. Unlike his good friend Shelly Schlossberg, some of whose sculpture decorated the Barebones properties, Buck's pursuit of this ancient quest (as of several others) had never been displaced by other arts, despite the additional disadvantage of never having overlooked the question of thermal efficiency.

"If we'd had Buck as consultant a couple of years ago we would have been spared the Vinland garbage-cooking fiasco. Before I said ten words about our 250 pump he realized that it's to other water circulators what the magnetron was to primitive radar tubes. He immediately suggested that we might dispense with our troublesome neoprene diaphragm by trying a new single-ply synthetic put out by Bonjour Rubber, because he'd noticed that their advertised 'flexion endurance' somewhat goes to waste on the conveyor belts he's worked with at Mercator-Steelyard. He's going to experiment with the 'woves' best suited to drumhead assaults."

"You see," Tessa replied "his casual ideas are worth a million dollars, but he always ends up trying to prove them for nothing! It's like a guy he knew in China who kept the Air Corps going against the Japanese by substituting slices of buffalo horn for plastic distributor caps: not so much as the Medal of Honor, let alone flight pay! I know he'll refuse to bill you for the advice. He'll say his advice wasn't worth any more than the lunch you bought him, because it didn't take any of his working time! Besides, he'll say, his solution hasn't yet been tested. Right?"

"Right. But trust me. I'll think of some way to pay him. We've been much too unimaginative in our purchasing department, but it's worth a lot to me to know he thinks we have no basic design flaw. Unfortunately I can't invite him out to our plant for a per diem consultation without raising the hackles of my placid partner."

"Well I'm pretty resigned to not being rich. You're no worse than the others. Everyone carries off some of Buck's ideas, but many also steal his billable time. Rest easy in your conscience."

She told Rafe that her husband had originally come to Dogtown to work for Frank Bacon the Elder. "Buck worshipped him; and, since he was an all-round entrepreneur without any compunctions about financial motivation, I thought we'd soon be living almost as high on the hog as everyone thought he was. He took Buck under his wing all right, but it turned out to be broken!"

"In the shop office I saw some old steel file trays made by a company I'm interested in, and when I remarked to the secretary—Mrs Doloroso?—that it was an uncommonly good design, she told me that Bacon had sketched it offhand one afternoon and immediately sold the patent—the same man who took years to invent the food-freezing process!"

"He had a clever patent engineer. But he didn't invent frozen foods. The Neanderthals froze their meat for winter. A hundred years ago the Dogtown fishermen were freezing their bait in the Maritime winters. Frank Bacon inherited the idea of freezing food from Francis his corrupted cold collateral ancestor. It was a matter of finding the way to freeze things unnaturally fast. Buck won't hear a word against him, but Gretta Doloroso—who'll be here tonight—can tell you that old Bacon didn't deserve the credit for inventing the priceless method of sealing glass to the base of radio tubes that his plant was producing over at the Casbah long before the war. It was one of the fishwives that worked on the line. She got a fifty-dollar 'Suggestions' award for it. But of course the tube bootleggers didn't pay any attention to patents anyway, once they learned the secrets; and somebody would have conned him out of that business anyway. Probably Tybbot."

"Dogtown ought to be able to support a whole bar of patent attorneys."

"If there'd been one in Turntable and handy as a drinking companion we'd own all of Pilot Hill by now, and I'd be playing with a portfolio of stocks while supervising nannies and footmen. The reason we now live on a stone wall is to keep from having a lawn that I couldn't afford to have mowed. But Buck's still bemused by the business. Tonight is the first time in a year he's tucked the kids in. I do thank you for that. He wanted to give me someone new to talk to.

"Let me tell you something," she continued, lowering her voice: "You very rightly admire that man. But despite the fact that he's a practical genius, a more or less respectable employer, a loyal customer of local merchants and bankers, even a fundraiser for Turntable charities, he's not one of Dogtown's real burgesses. He's a sweet gentle otherworldly Yankee without the slightest Chauvinistic urge to dominate anybody, least of all his family! He's the kind of sage that shouldn't be burdened with wife and kids. I'd drink twice as much as he does if I were half so generous and tender, half as much in conflict with my talent. He belongs at T-Square luncheons even less than my brother-in-law does, who'll also be here tonight. You're a member for reasons of policy, and you're tough enough to laugh about it; but Buck lives in a saintly kind of unrequited brotherhood!"

Rafe began to disclaim the acculturation he was accused of, but she stopped him with a raised finger and another half-smile. "I was unconsciously waiting for him, to have my babies late, and I'd do it again in at least one more life if I had it. But I worry about putting them through college. That's why I keep telling Buck he ought to work for some easy company with a pension plan and stock options. He's had plenty of good offers—not just local either—and God only knows how many he doesn't bother to tell me about. He hates to wear a tie and join country clubs. Of course I love him for his inoffensive honesty and all that; but I'd put up with corporate Mrs Grundy, for his sake, even in Cleveland, if I only had some servants!"

Just then Buck descended into the kitchen. "What's the conference about?" he asked his wife with the diffident smile of a Natty Bumppo as he moved autonomically to his only familiar corner of the cookhouse and busied himself with the pauseless task of getting cocktail ingredients ready for the guests and providing meanwhile for himself. "Have another drink." he added, without looking at their glasses.

"I'm half drunk trying to prepare Mr Opsimath for our other visitors, while he praises the kids. He thinks I'm too modest about them. It's nice to get an objective opinion from Cornucopia, the fountainhead of educational psychology."

Finished with some task she wiped her hands on a towel, dragged on a cigarette, and sipped at her drink while facing the two men vivaciously. "To sum up the briefing: they're all either nice or interesting people."

She and Rafe carried trays up the rough gray granite steps to the long living room on the other side of the granite chimney, where sixteen-inch-square oak beams supported the ceiling and oak panels covered the walls wherever granite was not exposed. Along one side magic casements opened out over the edge of the wharf on the forlorn strand of tidal stones. At the landward end Tessa's main portal was flung wide to the green tenderness of a warm windless twilight cast by the loom of the Cape between Powerhouse Cove and the sunset. High oaken doors half the width of the house stood open for life of any kind to wander in.

"First there's my sister Cora, the gifted member of my tribe. She's the dancer, and if she hadn't married too young she'd have become famous—perhaps will be yet. She's still not too old or too local to make a name as dance master and choreographer. She's got enough followers, and soon she'll have a company of her own in Bot. I'm lazy: she is not. I've already mentioned her husband, another gentle man, the only Knight I allow in my uncourteous house, present company excepted, Thad Kryothermsky—"

Rafe cried out with pleasure. "What luck! He sat next to me at Turntable. A prince of technology! He's apparently the director of all engineering and development at Mercator-Steelyard. But also research, quality control, packaging, sanitation, and maintenance—as well as product development! That's a whole portfolio of ministries!"

"It's just another case of the Yard's pennypinching. His only staff is some kitchen help. The company adds one practical scientist to the payroll to answer for three or four vacant departments. He's not happy there."

"He seems interested in it all."

"He's worth his weight. If the company had any brains they'd let him do some real research, instead of commercial calculations. There's no end to his competence. He's got a doctorate in food technology and a master's in mechanical engineering. I know because I typed his résumé."

"He said he's been in Dogtown only three or four years."

"Buck got him the job. If Mercator-Steelyard can't get Buck Barebones himself they'll take anyone he recommends."

"Oh Tess, you know I couldn't handle any more than the machinery." Buck finally intervened, patting her on the head as if her complaints about the Yard (his principal client) were the incorrigible crotchets of a fiercely partisan wife. "The Masterson sisters are known for their poetic license." Looking down upon her like an awkward bird with bulbed unaquiline nose, no chin, deeply creased cheek, and great bentforward ears paying fondly embarrassed homage from the top of a pole, he might have been the ungainly father from whom she'd inherited her skinniness only. His balding hair was still dark, but at the age of fifty he looked altogether close to sixty winters. "It's mainly the administrative side that Thad's not crazy about. Same as me. But with him it's because he's too well educated, and with me it'd be because I'm not educated enough."

Rafe remembered that Thad Kryothermsky had at first identified himself simply as "a sort of technical sergeant". It took a lot of questioning to find out what he meant by being "chief cook and bottlewasher". His quiet Slavic grin suggested nothing less ingratiating than undeceived goodwill toward his employers and equable cheerfulness about all his functions. Rafe marveled at the managerial ingenuousness of the world's leading fish-packer in amalgamating under one executive—and, at that, a babe in management—the several functions pertinent to quality control that should have been checking or balancing each other. Thad personally could hardly be called a fox in the chicken coop, but the author of a process or product naturally has little incentive to discern and report its defects. The human psyche can't help the selectivity of its impressions. It was as if the company had made the chief accountant his own auditor.

Rafe was afraid the Bareboneses didn't understand their brother-in-law's selfconflicting position. As he already felt so affectionate toward his hosts that he wished nothing significant to be lost upon them, he began to explain: "What Thad's real difficulty is . . ."

Clairvoyant Tessa sweetly interrupted, forestalling an excessive exhibition of her guest's overweening proclivity. She had already learned that this humbugless follower of all lures was not one who minded being turned aside. She understood that he was as alert to unexpected data as to the patterns that had already formed his opinions, and that he wouldn't stand upon his dignity even if he saw that she was criticizing his insensitivity to the boredom of others, herself included. "Thad's preoccupied with the local smell. The company wants him to work on batter-fried fish bricks, but he'd rather solve the atmospheric problem of by-products. There's no longer any salt cod drying in the sun. Nowadays most of our Dogtown stink comes from the Yard's fishmeal plant."

"Except every now and then" Buck amended "when they have to

air out a wet batch of cod from Terra Nova. Most of us don't notice the smell. To me it's just the east wind. But it bothers the sisters. That's why Cora settled over in West Marsh and we moved out here where the air is sweeter."

"He teases me for suburban sensibilities. I bet Thad would be the culture-hero of Cape Gloucester if the Yard let him spend his time the way he wants to. But Buck thinks that project is doomed to failure."

"There's no mechanical solution." Buck solemnly replied. "Oil and meal make very efficient food for animals, but you can't help giving off gases when you cook trash-fish and gurry to render them."

"Unless you neutralize them with the ambergrease of whale." said Tessa.

"Personally, I'd rather see him working on the dogfish project." Buck continued. "We might have a whole new industry here if we found a good way to extract the living oil for vitamins and pharmaceuticals. It would fill the place of the old codliver business. I'm sure we could export the dogfish meat, to the Japanese or somebody, if we could learn how to get at it economically. Those fish have skins like chain mail, and they look as if they're nothing but gristle, yet like all sharks they have no bones. I think I could build a cutting machine to do it. But they say it's mostly a marketing problem, like trying to sell rattlesnake meat. Even Wat Cibber wouldn't grudge the Yard credit for pulling that off!"

"You'll probably hear how Wat stands vis-a-vis imports and exports." Tessa commented. "He's our ornery isolationist. He talks politics like his dead father, who must have been the Cape's ruggedest Protestican; but he's heartbreakingly innocent of national affairs—except when they touch fishing! His wife Teddi is my adored mother superior."

The three of them had just finished loading the sideboards when they heard the first car coming cautiously down the steep approach. "Now it's too late for more biographies. Of course I'll introduce you to everyone with whatever mnemonics I can slip in, but I'm afraid you'll have to figure out each one for yourself. We all talk at once, usually about our own hobby horses, and there's always plenty of new public gossip, so I'm afraid I won't be able to watch over you as protectively as I should. Please try not to shock anybody with your urbanity and tolerance."

Rafe was nothing loathe. He said he trusted his own friendliness and perspicacity, without adding that he was accustomed to making himself the most impressive guest at any party by his technique of articulately appreciating an interlocutor's bent without directly boasting of his ability to do so.

"But I must warn you about some of the language you'll hear." Tessa went on. "We have our own modus loquendi, and the city's mutually tolerant lies are descended from many different Herodotuses. The trouble with an ecology of legends is that they can't be as consistent as any one kind of truth."

But Rafe had not yet accumulated enough evidence to take in the panoramic scope of her anthroposophical meaning.

* * *

The first who hove into the open haven was the aforementioned Gretchen Doloroso, like a genial tugboat, already known to him as the one who actually ran the business of Dogtown Machine & Design. She was greeted like a sturdy kingpost of the family, and in the manner of a born grandmother she immediately went down to the kitchen with Tessa to slice up some tomatoes she had brought from her vegetable patch.

Before long six or seven cars had crowded the wharf, besides the Barebones two, all cunningly fitted into the flat grassy space between bluff and saltwater garden. None was new or polished, but the one driven by Eric Vanderlyn, hesitant photographer husband of the Troika's unhesitant "visual art" partner Beni, was imported from Deutschland. That couple looked like respective fairhaired models for each other's own work, equally covetable for both body and behavior by a casual observer of the opposite sex.

To these two and others Rafe was liberally introduced by Tessa as "an affable angel incognito. He's in Dogtown for the cheap labor, but thanks to the poverty of his youth he's no Fat Can, and he's still mourning Adlai Stevenson. So you can speak somewhat freely before him, even though he plays the market." Or "Mr Opsimath has come East seeking gold. He's got some romantic notion about the treasure buried on this island. But he's given me to understand that he regards the Atlantic Ocean as pretty tame." Or again: "Huck and Sally, this is our fairweather friend. He's brought it with him. . . . I'd like you to meet one of Buck's sales prospects. . . . Mr Opsimath is an economic royalist on our side, but claims he was a charter member of Tammany Hall, and has come to explain Return on Investment. To him R O I is king. . . . One of Buck's industrial pilgrims that he's dragged home for some respite from the noise and litter over on your side of Birdhouse Hill, to see why John Smith called Seamark the Paradise of all Virginia. He's a New Deal Skinny Crat who nevertheless pretends to sympathize with your Village Rights movement. . . . This man's company tried to save the Cape's pigs. . . . He's hatching some mysterious Graveyard Street takeover scheme; but if I'm any judge of character he's going to fail—because all the successful financiers I ever knew were insensitive bores."

The carpetbagger was gradually instructing himself in the self-perpetuating emotional heritage that allied the Markers and the Villies of this northeast liberty against the other parishes of the micropolitan confederacy. "I'm still confused," he'd say—modestly enough to start with—when resisting efforts to overcome his impartiality between the two geohistorical factions, which his host and hostess seemed to represent between them. For the most part he softpedaled his predilection for the working wards, just as he usually concealed his preference for geography to history.

It was interesting to hear that in the days of steam—when waterpower was no longer required (only the transportation of coal), but before wirepower was available at points better for distribution—Seamark had existed for some years as a true mill town. (The cotton factory burnt down one winter night about the time competition was rendering it unprofitable.) And that as long as cod and halibut still pestered the coast an inshore fishery (now surviving only as a carriage trade in lobsters) had sustained an important population of working small boats.

Best of all, to his ears, North Village, the most charming ward in all of Dogtown, erewhile denuded of trees as rape by pirates and quarrymen but now sprucely redressed with green and white paint—its naked dusty slashes of quarry works (except for the pits themselves) readorned with shrubs and lawns—still tolerated a daily routine of deafening bangs from the mechanized hammers of the Cape Gloucester Forge Company, the closed-die plant founded as a toolmaking smithy for the granite industry but long since employed in forging steel parts for manufacturers all over the country. That small community of craftsmen laborers shopkeepers and clerks, less than a mile north of Powerhouse Cove, tucked into the vale of a rust-granite quay in yet another tiny hewn-stone harbor where one of the other quarry railroads loaded granite onto coastal vessels broad of beam and blunt of bow, had been a gathering place of single-masted "stone sloops" when Dogtown Harbor was a concentration of nobly battered two-masted fishing schooners. Save for the raucous obsolescent forge, now so anomolous in the waterside hollow alongside a few moored lobster boats and below the most decorous of dwellings, North Village had irrevocably resigned the swarming sweaty class of work. Most of its present inhabitants lived on an income previously or never earned, or else they commuted for good salary somewhere down the line they lived beyond this end of.

The most sensitive of those residents, however, one John Vole, who lived close to the factory in an 18C homestead of framed white clapboard, commuted no further than Harbor ward, to the Clavier Temperament Manufactory, where he had been making pianos and harpsichords for concert musicians since he gave up experimental physics at Los Alamos in 1945 as penance for the abuse of his education. Rafe was shown a letter this pacifistic friend of the Barebones crowd had published in the *D T D Nous,* contributing to the environmental controversy between retiring or aesthetic reformers (who had welcomed him as neighbor these fifteen years) and those whose interests lay with the payroll or profit of the Forge nuisance (few of whom were Village voters):

> *The recent talk of forcing Cape Gloucester Forge to build a soundproof wall around itself is very disturbing. I herewith enter my plea against such an idea.*
>
> *Everyone knows the Forge makes a ground-jolting racket, and there aren't many North Villagers who can remember a time when it didn't. Yet how can it be that those who are neither deaf nor psychically bruised have lived comfortably within its earshot all their lives?*
>
> *As one who has long consorted with music and its instruments, I think I have part of the answer. It has to do with the type of noise being made. If just one hammer at the Forge were to bang incessantly and at a constant rate, with exactly the same sound emitted from each stroke, everyone in the Village would go berserk.*
>
> *But that isn't the way it is. Each hammer beats out a sequence of blows, then rests as a new piece of hot steel is drawn from the furnace and thrust onto the die. And each hammer stroke is different. The blows first roughly form the metal with great crunches, and then gradually develop into smart whacks as the dies actually close around the fully shaped piece.*
>
> *This kind of variation about a seemingly steady pulse is the stuff of which music is made. Jazz, for instance. I submit that there is something musical about the sound produced by the Forge. It's comparable to the night sound of forest insects in late summer. Next time you go past the Forge during working hours, instead of thinking what a fool Jack Vole is for writing this public letter, ask yourself if there isn't something appealing in that sound.*

While you're at it, you might also ask yourself why it is that so far North Village has avoided the Seamark syndrome of pilgrim gift shops and the smell of money. It's very simple: The Forge is what prevents Seamark from coming to North Village.

Its bark is much worse than its bite. It looks like Soviet Socialist Heavy Industry, but in fact it's just a small company working an old trade under anachronistic conditions. Quite apart from jobs and tax revenue, it differentiates the traditional North Village character of guts. It keeps our settlement real in a way that Seamark keeps no longer. I'm for that kind of reality, and I'm against any public action that could work a hardship upon the Forge or precipitate its demise.

Thus was Rafe apprized that in some matters the Villagers saw eye to eye with each other and with Seamarkers almost as imperfectly as with the Dogtown majority. Thanks to the situation of the Barebones wharf halfway between the center of Seamark (now given over almost entirely to the delectation of pilgrims and photographers) and the nucleus of their quaintly schizoid Village, from which they were separated by Pilot Hill and its sea-thrust shoulder, Buck and Tessa excused themselves from the vehemence of partisanship; but one of their guests was a lobsterman by present trade who kept his boat in the granite basin of Pigeonhole Cove at the Forge not far from his own house, which served not only his family but also his vocation, for to it was attached his stone-carving shed.

This Huck Salter was so immediately congenial, parallel in age and growth (albeit muscular and calloused), and apparently in temper, that Rafe would fain have called him his twin—the complementary opposite in talent condition and place. But they shared little in knowledge and less in experience.

"Lobsters are consumable jewels, seaweed scarabs for pilgrims Normans and the export trade. They're the nearest thing to a granite fish. But even granite was never a necessity. Being as how I hardly ever get work as a stonemason, I'm sometimes willing to build a brick chimney, if that's what it takes for family necessities. My grandfather was a quarry blacksmith, but, like everyone else living at the end of the past, he too ended up in the carriage trade, as farrier to the gentry while they still kept horses on the Cape. That's the moral price you pay to stick it out here."

Huck's lean jaw tugged on an unlighted pipe, but hardly paused, making the most of a fresh off-island ear. "Yet in grandad's time the Village had been as ugly as Placerville from ruthless strip-mining. They tried to sell anything granite but the noise. Road contractors bought the chips, and the dust went for fertilizer! Not until sixty years ago did people start planting shade trees along some of the naked streets. Now there's sumac and scrub oak sprouted from the grout strewn all over the land between the abandoned pits. Unfortunately everything's getting nicer every year, and the cost of individualism keeps rising. Sally and I could never have afforded to live here if I hadn't inherited my father's mortgage."

Sally didn't say much, but any man who felt no aversion to housewives of carelessly youthful figure and flaxen complexion would glance at her as often as he dared. The experience of fatigue was no longer quite erasable from her face, but it was defined as an attractive suggestion of the fairest chiaroscuro. Rafe immediately guessed that she was not bred to be an unassisted mother but that she was trying to put her past behind her. After ten years with Huck, whom she'd met only several years after finishing Cistern College, and whose work (except for the boat part of it) was even less comprehensible to her family on the Eastern Shore of Magdalene than her occupations at the Sandwich Village school she'd fled to in New Uruk, she seemed to have diverted her unintentional glamor also by some incongruous commitment of the mind.

But she did say, with friendly enough smile, "Dogtown has more sculptors than skippers, but Huck's the only troglodyte in the whole bunch." By this statement she meant to boast that her Mithra was born and raised in the granite armature of Dogtown's most exposed liberty, his blood bluer than a Tidewater planter's, and that the other artists were none of them chthonic sons of Gaia.

With a mechanically triggered mannerism Huck snorted at what had been a bitterness in his youth, before he'd earned local toleration of his local character. "There aren't many of us real Villies left in any walk of life—and damnsight fewer Crats! In the Village they still think I belong at the Harbor, or over in Taraville, if not in hell—'cause I'm half Finn, half Square, half Viking, a quarter Loosey, three quarters Irish (where I get my black looks), and only one tenth Yankee. But so help me Lord Jaysus, I'm going to keep running for Ward Earl until they finally elect me!"

By this time everyone was gathering food from the buffet, and Rafe had no further opportunity to probe with Huck his puzzling sense of brotherhood. And delayed by the business of the glass in his hand, despite Tessa's efforts to promote him as guest of honor, he was too late through the line to find a place among the ladies, who had a lot to say to each other and tended to cluster like mussels on a rock, the hostess included—once she had given up the hope of making her party urbane. Plate in hand, he sat down next to the least urbane of characters, Captain Wat Cibber, the group's sole Harborside aborigine, whom he'd been prepared for: a shy stout Yankee, carefully draining his beer before attending to his food. "Pleased to meecha," he'd mumbled when Rafe was introduced at the door, the fingertips of his handshake like wooden handles ventured not much further than his prominent beltline, elbow hunched under his shoulder.

Wat now resumed acquaintance as if nothing had interrupted. "This was a dram-come-true." he said, holding up his empty glass. "I don't belong here because I ain't a Crat, but my wife's too aristocratic to learn how to drive, so I'm her show-fer and I work up a long thirst. Buck and I are old friends and dissociates. He's the finest kind. Cognominious fellow too. He taught me a lot about machinery. Once in a while he goes fishing with me just to get away from intelligent people."

Wat lived and fished from Mother's Neck in East Harbor. Rafe would have liked nothing better than to be invited out for a day's observation of what John Smith called "the great business of the sea"; but he was cautious about the allocation of his small remaining hoard of Dogtown time. "How long do you go out for?"

"Just long enough to whistle up enough wind to put an end to dragging. At the most I'm only a day-tripper. That way I can work alone, and not starve more than one family. Over at the Cervix they conspire to keep me tied up with good excuses not to go out, just so's they can get in some good days for theirselves. You see, I always seem to stir up half a gale for everybody whenever I try to serve the hopeless cause of earning my living. A Cibber was one of the first six year-round fishermen over there to the stage at Crosspatch Beach, before any of the Tybbots ever crossed the Atlantic—which don't mean a thing except it gives me the right to complain piteously."

He spoke softly yet in a measured declamatory tone, as if he'd memorized all his lines; but suddenly he made a face at Rafe, playing the fool with his cheeks. Rafe realized that he was practiced in thus interpreting his own unsmiling assertions for polite off-islanders who didn't know how to take his humbly selfconscious pleasantries. "When I first got my boat I dubbed her the *Weather Breeder*, because I like to call a spade a spade, but fishermen are stuporstitious you know, and they got me to change her name. But it didn't make much difference: if I don't sneak out in the fog or dead of night it still breezes up the minute I get outside the breakwater. So for the sake of my colleagues most days I stay ashore and listen to the weather forecasts. Always plenty to do, fixing to go fishing while I wait for the prices to go up to the slave-wage level."

"So the name you changed it to wasn't any luckier?"

"Now she's registered as the *Motion*." Wat's explanation was well honed for the edification of curious city slickers. "My old man always used to quote Isaiah to me: 'Took unto the rock whence ye are hewn, and to the hole of the pit whence ye are digged.' He was always bidding me to get over my idolatry of fishing, and if I wouldn't listen to him about a sensible trade in carpentry ashore at least I should remember the land of my mother up at Taraville. Her people were farmers from the beginning, but in off-season during the great Granite Rush, like everyone else up this way on the Cape, her grandfather used to take out some stone and split paving blocks in his spare time, with only one helper at the most. He'd find a ledge up in the hills, scrape off the topsoil, set up a mast and boom, which they called a stick, and start his own private pit, like digging a boat. All through the woods and along the old roads there were these little shallow quarries—*motions,* in their lingo. In some places slabs have been motioned out of the bare rocks even right down along the shore, which the pilgrims think are Greek theater seats to watch shipwrecks from. Making motions was like drilling for oil in a pasture—except you had to work just as hard in the end as you did in the beginning, and it was never any bonanza. The same way with me and the holes I make in the water: most of the time I can't get enough fish to hire any help. So I stick up my own rig and work my own hours. "Too bad I've only got a one-Watpower engine: can't go very far in my motion before it's time to turn around and come home for tea. Should have christened her the *Slow Motion*."

Captain Cibber evidently trusted that the wit of his entertainment would sooner or later dawn on anyone who stayed in Dogtown long enough to learn of his reputation as the skipper of a one-man dragger who so loved fishing that occasionally he hired out himself and *Motion* as pilot and workboat for odd little towing or research jobs "to support the privilege of unmaking a fortune in Dogtown's uncommercial fishing industry".

"They say all those motions in the woods around Purdeyville are filled with water or covered with catbrier now." he continued. "But I wouldn't rightly know, because I haven't strolled up there since I was in Grandma School." Wat didn't look like much of a walker. His arms and legs were as thick as oak trees. "We used to go for the blueberries. A lot of people still do, but not the kids. They don't go anywhere they can't ride. Nowadays boys won't even take girls for a walk."

Wat's last sentence touched more general interest. All at once Rafe was aware that several of the men eating off their plates were standing by them. And Thad Kryothermsky, who sat smiling on the other side of him but had seemed too unobtrusive to volunteer any remark, leaned into the huddle to say: "When I first took my little kids up there all I could think of was those secluded glades and grassy patches in the bushes. In Susa where I grew up there was nothing but city for twenty miles, and the countryside we could have got to on the rest of Elam Island was all closed off with barbed wire, or else just ploughed-up potato fields. A guy would have given a season ticket for the Dodgers to walk a girl into a park like Purdeyville!" Thad's benign frame, otherwise dedicated to the responsibilities of maturity, was alight with a mischievous enthusiasm for the idyllic experience he'd missed. Rafe wondered if he would encourage his daughters to walk in Purdeyville with their admirers.

"In my time we didn't all miss out." said Huck Salter, the privileged native. "A buddy of mine used to swear a thousand couples could be hidden among those stones and juniper bushes while half the town was out picking berries with the schoolmarms! That's an exaggeration, because I wouldn't say I knew even a hundred good spots. What I hear though, there's still a lot of birdie business going on, from our Village side at least. Some of the big kids over here still use their legs, and maybe some of the older folks too. Many a finch has been plucked between a rock and a cedar."

"That's right." Wat agreed, the older aborigine from the other side of the moor. "Nobody ain't ever heard of a virgin from the Village."

"If there are any they don't last long when they get over to high school at the Harbor." Huck replied. To Rafe he added: "The only reason I keep involved with Dogtown politics is to make them build us a high school of our own before my children need one."

Tessa's attention was attracted by the men's turned backs and low conspiratorial voices. "Gentlemen!" she called. "Finish your jockey stories and come over to the table for dessert and coffee."

Thus at last did she succeed in mixing her people coeducationally. The great double doors had been swung shut against insects and the cool of the evening. The ladies made spaces for the men around an immense oblong coffee table of polished oak mounted on granite pedestals. There was room for everybody on three extraordinarily long rectangular sofas set perpendicular or parallel to each other in front of the six-foot fireplace now cheerfully ablaze. Lamps here and there behind their backs shed little greater light but steadied the fluctuating effect of the flames.

Before Rafe perceived Tessa's will at work he found himself in the center of symmetry, facing the fire across a courtyard of brandied desserts and cordials, between the very two women he would have chosen if he'd had to choose only two after the hostess herself: her sister Cora and her best friend Gloria Keith. From her place at the extremity of the right wing, whence she could hop out of the square to fetch things from the kitchen, opposite Buck on the left, where he could tend the burning log and see to the supply of bottles, Tessa smiled at Rafe with a roll of eyeballs and a flutter of eyelids to call his attention to what she had compassed: not a single wife sat next to her husband. In the kitchen beforehand she'd mentioned her despair of ever getting Dogtown couples to risk the symbolism of broken yokes when traveling in parties or sitting with friends. Looking away from him she smugly kissed the inner fingertips holding a cigarette to her lips ever so nonchalantly.

"This is always the best venue for our playreading ensemble." said Gloria, crowned with a pageboy's fluffy yellow hair, who in an open-eyed selfsubordinating way at first seemed pregnant with enthusiasm, altogether the vivacious type of a slightly freckled undergraduate, notwithstanding the fact that one of her children was already in high school, but beneath whose frivolity as time passed he began to see an almost feverish devotion to her duty as the official curator of legends for a town full of devoted historians in which she hadn't yet lived ten years, and perhaps to other duties as well; and deeper still an ultimate melancholic distrust of her own and every other ambition. It was the memory of her that he was to carry back to Cornucopia as representating his regret for the exteriority of his ambivalent explorations. She may have felt there was something superficial about her work, for later that night, when he asked what it was that made Doctor Charlemagne call her Goody Keith (which obviously pleased her), she told him that like Nennius she wouldn't take credit for interpretation—only for making a heap of all she could find.

From Cora Kryothermsky on his left, Tessa's grave and unvivacious sibling, he learned of Gloria's energetic initiatives, not only in organizing the playreading club but also in encouraging her three friends' Hoof and Mouth Troika studio as a practical response to the frustration of action in their merely literary drawingroom amusement, and at the same time as a means for testing Cora's own profession of dance with the word and thought of which it had been stripped by centuries of specialization. Cora had been excited by the most theatrical modern dance (studying and performing with various companies in New Uruk) only to discover what she now termed its self-imposed artistic limitations; and she told Rafe that she was exceedingly grateful to Gloria for stirring up local support of the Troika's paying school, which might make possible certain experiments in a drama of dance.

Tessa must have been keeping an ear specially tuned to her sister's quiet voice, amid all the eddies of conversation, because just then, in a low but precisely resonant tone cutting across or under the blooming buzzing confusion that would have blocked anything less than a shout from anyone else, she interjected a defensive answer to Rafe's unasked question. "We're not maenads by choice. None of the men who've been interesting enough to invite—starting with each other's husbands—are willing even one evening a month to so much as listen to us do a reading, let alone take part. They all have more important things to do with their superabundant leisure."

"Like playing with their toyboats or attending to devilvision." said sober Cora with a straight face.

Gloria laughed with the shrill gaiety of a happy maiden released from classes to extracurricular activity. "I was so het up by the dearth of male voices that I even screwed up my courage to ask Mr Charlemagne! I told him he could be our Euripides! You should have seen the stare he gave me! For weeks afterward he wouldn't come near my desk at the Library. I didn't realize how touchy he is about the theater. Now I don't dare talk to him about anything but Dogtown history."

Tessa was unable to audit them any longer, for of course as hostess her intervention was occasionally required by sets of others; but Cora continued in the vein Rafe might have expected of her sister, though both face and voice were somewhat less feminine in their peculiar attraction for a man who told himself that he valued masculine attitudes in female psyches. ". . . yet as far as playreading goes we found certain advantages in art-without-men, and now we wouldn't hear of having a man imitate a male part. For one thing, by ourselves we can be more satirical. But it's mainly that beforehand, afterwards, and aside we say things incomprehensible to men. It's been an accidental liberation. Each meeting grows longer and longer, at somebody's house, after we've finished the play. It won't be long before we're out all night howling on the moors. The Troika Art Center serves a different purpose; it's no substitute for bacchanalia."

Rafe felt the guilt of a spying satyr. But his speculation along this line was broken off by his consciousness of an approaching silence. It was never quite attained, yet it almost seemed that everybody was about to cooperate in the initiation of parliamentary procedure. For a moment he thought they were going to have a political caucus after all.

In the event it appeared that this band of friends was used to a kind of unspoken cooperation that easily brought forth the same results as protracted democratic expediency. It was as if these parents of children—all busied and harried in their daily life—had learned what they taught. There was a delicate balance of spontaneity and sensitivity that struck Rafe as habitual. By tacit consensus they were entering into one of the largest general conversations he'd ever witnessed. Bilateral talk ceased in the common impulse to honor the guest of honor's velleities.

The council thus made him its focus, not in inquisition but in a curiosity of which he was subject more than object: they were curious not about him but for him, as if trying to imagine or remember what a disinterested stranger would wonder about their cape of marooners. The two natives Huck Salter of the Village and Wat Cibber of East Harbor were comparatively indifferent to any history except that which touched their own families, but their contribution to Rafe's civic education was magnified by their respective crystals of distilled salt.

As an experienced traveler with much to say about his appreciations, Rafe was not slow to improve the occasion, perhaps here and there taking a little too much advantage of their polite goodwill with strokes of impertinence that would have ill beseemed a less affable guest. "Everywhere else in this country I've heard more local history than I wanted to know. Geography usually suffices. Other towns have quarries and fishing, railroad lines, even degraded sloops and schooners; but here there's too much left to explain."

"You mean the rogues mavericks and idiots?" asked Huck.

"He means the has-beens and failures." said Wat.

"No, he means the pirates and refugees." the hostess tactfully corrected.

"Maybe the names explain everything." Rafe offered. "If I could keep track of all the names."

"But then what explains the names?" Theodora Cibber said serenely, Wat's wife who sat straight as a queen, older than any of the princesses attending. "Perhaps that's what would most interest you."

"Gloria's our little saltmill of names." said Gloria's husband the goodman Dexter Keith, City Planner, a romantically dark giant with whom so far Rafe had hardly exchanged a word.

"Each name has its own field of explanations remaining to be explained." the custodian of legends responded with a smile of warning. "No matter what you ask, the question is begged! Answers are offered by every child in Dogtown. Not to mention the poets. We have more poets than policemen. Poets even come in from the outside to make something of us. Like T S Chittering, the one who celebrated those reefs you can see from here." she giggled. "Doctor Charlemagne calls him 'the transpontine pontifex, greatest groaner of them all.'"

That afternoon Rafe had noticed three small patches of white surf in the offing beyond the southern end of the discontinued breakwater; but in his reading of the expatriate Antidisestablishmentarian he'd never paid any attention to the title note of his favorite Quintet in the famous *Quadrivia* that now at Gloria's hint identified them as the Three Griefs: Father's, Savior's, and Holy Ghost's—all awash at flood tide.

"Yes indeed, old Tough Shit Chitterling!" came the booming drawl of Huck Salter. "They used to read that poem to us in Sea Scouts." Rafe learned later that he was referring to his wartime hitch in the Coast Guard. ". . . *nagging mock of rested quarters!* In the service I got special consideration for having been raised within sight of the Griefs."

Rafe chuckled a little uncertainly at this irreverence toward the Noble laureate as he turned again to Gloria, resuming his more comfortable exploitation of the forum. "There's geography and history in any name. For instance, why Cape *Gloucester?*"

"I suppose that question is no more or less controversial than all the rest. Nennius says that in British it was *Caer Gloiu:* Gloiu's Fort, built on the Severn by his four sons; but in Old English it's said to mean a splendid spot for the legions to build their castra."

"I thought it meant the camp of Claudius!" Tessa exclaimed.

"Or a bright place." added the clear cheerful voice of Teddi Cibber, a small plainly adorned Demeter with flat Irish features of the kindliest dignity, who seemed only a generation or two removed from Anglo-Irish soil. It was still hard to associate her with slyly awkward Wat her piratical-looking steersman. As soon as he was introduced Rafe had wanted to stay at her side if only to overhear her speech, sweet pure English clarified by German and French studies at Zurich but still as virginal as matronly in its warm simplicity. "You might say a shining place. A place for Gloria!" Everyone took pleasure in her smile, and Gloria blushed at the compliment. "But of course that was in England. You'd naturally also like to know why the name was brought over here. Wasn't it because the first settlers were from Wales or the West Counties and didn't much care for the East Anglian Separatists on the South Shore? It must have been a theological protest against the Jerusalem Colony and a demonstration of loyalty to the Tudor Church despite their own disagreements with the Archbishop of Gloucester.

"Even so," Mrs Cibber merrily continued, "I believe it was their quarrels among themselves that made Dogtown the mother of quite a few other settlements in New Armorica, especially in Pequod and Markland: it was comparatively easy for counterdissidents among the dissidents at a place like this to pack up and re-emigrate by sea. But the theocrats continued to complain about the 'ill-carriage' of Dogtowners long after the Casterbridge Company had given up its fishing stage at the Harbor. When the time came to incorporate the remaining voters a majority couldn't agree even on their background, so they had to adopt the least common denominator of local parlance for the Dogtown name of their town. Meanwhile the charts of all the world's navigators had us geographically established as the Bishop's *Cape* Gloucester.

"Isn't that the orthodox story, Gloria? But I've always felt it doesn't do justice to anybody's sense of humor. For one thing, as you've hinted, it doesn't explain why the name Dogtown was the only consensus. I wish you were officially appointed Superintendent of Shanachies and Bards so that you could declare certain truths once and for all!"

"Don't ask that, Teddi!" Tessa laughed. "Gloria would be burned at the stake as a pedant. Dogtown has no use for canons or academies of any kind."

Gloria laughed too. "It's impossible to distinguish and disentangle the various threads of . . . "

" . . . traditional truth." Wat murmured.

" . . . but it's the vainglory of my job to benefit from the earnest kids of Dogtown. They're the ones that shine! One of them discovered that to the Naturals—as the Atlindians were always called in Vinland" —she explained to Rafe "this was *Glooskap's Dwellingplace,* the god's sea-ground. *Gloucester* was a typically garbled transliteration by some English cartographer who scratched out the older *Cap-aux-Isles,* maybe hoping to win from Champlain the title of Great White Father for King James. Glooskap was the Naturals' Man-from-Nothing, their Adam, and their Prometheus too. But the Algonquin name Glooskap was literally cognate with 'the sound of tasting juice'."

"Fermented, I'm sure." said Eric Vanderlyn the formerly Apollonian blueblood photographer, wishing to forestall his wife Beni's private reproach for not trying to conceal his defensiveness about the cups he was always in; for she was his one abiding prize, the envy of ambitious men, a daunting gold and tan girl of congenital self-confidence, though absorbed in art. She was his rock, his motive, his exclusive model: the incentive for his aesthetic profession, which he acknowledged was mere creation-without-toil, compared with her painting, but which still kept him in intermittent communication with respectable elements of the outside world. Beni's ostentatiously intelligent beauty—slenderly nulliparous yet more sexually differentiated than the dark leanness of her partners the two matrons of the Troika—might have been the scourge of any man, but it was insufficient scourge of her husband's other craving.

"Champlain and Smith both called it the Cape of Islands. Have you seen our island's islands, Mr Opsimath?" asked Gretchen Doloroso, Buck's conscientiously managerial secretary, who'd been reconciled since childhood to the figure she cut in the world of appearances and for many years amenable to the disadvantages of weight. "They don't amount to much—if you think of Mona or the Isle of Manannan or the Isle of Mass, or even of Aran—but one of them has the oldest and tallest twin lighthouses on this side of the Atlantic, which Seamark has made into a trademark. But it's not yet copyrighted, and pilgrims like to take their own images of it."

Rafe could see that Gretta, a Jew who'd once been married to a Tuscan, was as Britannically oriented as most of the other lorists of New Armorica.

"Pinnace Woe on the charts, but I'd hate to tell you what fishermen call that island." said Huck.

"Tell us!" hissed Tessa, turning all eyes upon Wat for authentication.

"I ain't saying." Wat croaked, staring straightfaced before him, horny hands curled in his lap like a furless muff. "But that's where T S Chitterling's ancestor drowned before there was anybody around here with the spare time to build lighthouses."

"A Chittering family tale." scoffed Huck the cynic.

"I wouldn't know, Ma'am, not being a lit-er-ary scholar." Wat replied to both Tessa and Huck, swiveling his head with a jerk from one to the other while looking at the floor. "But somebody forgot to tell Mr Opsimath that the Vikings came before the French. As far as they're concerned it's still the Cape-of-the-Cross, where Thorwald was buried as a decent Christian." Having evoked smiles by gruffly redressing an injustice, he clammed up like a ventriloquized statue.

"But the Irish of course were first, my dear." said Teddi with the thoughtful smile of a Celtic abbess.

The humorous bust closed its eyes and unclammed its pressed lips with a sighing exhalation: "My wife's going to be the most educated woman in the cemetery." Rafe gathered from the general laughter that it was an aphorism from his stock in trade, amusing rather for its place in a pattern of familiar situations, and for its connotative congruity with Wat's conjugal incongruity, than for any immediately apposite wit that might be appreciated by a visiting knight.

Gloria was called upon for gloss: as follows.

In dim uncertain times the Irish had bucked the current of Western civilization by looking eastward for gain or adventure, repeatedly invading Britain and old Armorica; but St Patrick turned their thoughts away from plunder and revenge. When Ireland was still called Scotia, long before the Vikings sailed even as far west as Iceland, the Irish had a name for this blessed Land of Peace—far far to the west of their own Western World—a lost island that St Ita said could never be found by looking for it, any more than enchanted pigs could be counted or holy tombstones measured. St Brendan however, resolving to disprove her (his foster-mother), though heeding her advice that it would be impossible to happen upon Perdita by sailing in a coracle made from the skins of slaughtered animals, cut down the last seven oaks in Galway and built a longboat.

And find it he did, planting a little colony of monks but neglecting to lay upon them the vow of chastity (seeing that no females had been taken along). Leaving them without a priest, he hurried home to Innismor and told his mother that despite her unchristian pessimism the lost had been found. But what with one thing and another, that was the last voyage he ever made. The monks naturally married Naturals and began to lose their grasp of theology. When the Ericssons got here a couple of centuries later they didn't realize how strange it was that some of the inhabitants had wispy beards.

The continent attached to this island came to be known in Europe as Great Ireland, but with matrilinear discretion the Irish marooners made no attempt to impose their prophecied appellation upon the blessed isle itself, Nama-Auche, which was Glooskap's Place. The name Perdita was thenceforth preserved in the person of the first among their daughters, schooled to preserve the lore of the Western World after everyone else had forgotten most of their Latin and much of their Gaelic. The name was passed down the generations from mother to daughter in almost a thousand years of unbroken succession, until the English came and drove them underground, just as their Hibernian ancestors had come from Sumer (by way of Hispania) to drive the Tuatha De Danann (themselves invaders upon the savage Firbolgs) into so-called Tir-Na-Dog.

Huck Salter was getting warmed up to the communal pleasure of enlightening an openminded stranger. "It took the Georgios two hundred and fifty years to kill off the last Sumerian genome."

"But Sumer had icumen in." mumbled Eric Vanderlyn, who remembered a bit from having attended some of the best prep schools. "—going to the dogs in Perdita-ville, to put it in French. When the last known Perdita died without recorded issue the Old Irish were nothing but our embarrassing remnant of a chiefless folk. By that time she had naturally preferred dogs to mankind. Then within fifty years they're commissioning Auguste Rodin to put up a statue of her in front of the Veterans Legion! Yet the city fathers were still so ashamed of the truth that they told the sculptor she'd kept a goat instead of a dog—their bigoted euphemism! Later, when Rodin heard the truth, he disowned the piece, said it was done by his worst imitator. I laugh everytime I drive through Purity Square. The damn fools still don't realize how much we've lost!"

"Oh there are still plenty of Irish around." Cora said. "You'll see when you're trying to find someone else in the phone book!"

"They're all Salt-Irish or Doiley-Irish—and even so, far too few." Huck retorted. "But I'm talking about the Irish of Purdeyville, before they assimilated. I'm talking about the Irish that were hated for their speech and their religion, and worked the quarries before any of the Squares could get up their courage to cross the Atlantic, but were always the last to be hired and first to be fired. The owners thought they were superstitious devils with green horns that would never live in peace with honest Paulines. And yet the Finn strawbosses would privately admit that they'd rather have one lefthanded Purdeyville Irishman than three righthanded Yankees!"

"Wait a minute, Huck!" warned Sally his wife with a slow smile to deprecate her earnestness. It happened that she was working on a poem about the witch of Purdeyville, as it also happened that she was attracted by the spells of Petrine Scholasticism so much feared and hated by her fairhaired Low-Tudor parents and anathematized by more reformed Paulines in Magdalene, the one Colony of the Crown that had been originally chartered as liturgically Christian. "By now almost everyone up here in the North seems to have some black Irish blood, just as practically all Southerners have a drop or more of Moorish black; but up here the Irish are more insidious because they can disguise themselves easily, so we can't stop our ears to their artful English. In their decadence they've made us sentimental. But let's not give our innocent visitor the impression that the Yankees were wrong about Perdita. She wasn't merely a lapsed papist. When she took up with Colonel Riley the union was consecrated by Hobbomocco, great adversary of both Glooskap and Christ. It was Riley who wanted to die in the faith, and that's why one of the Harbor priests began to go up and say Mass in Purdeyville as a missionary duty."

"Well," said Huck—not to Sally, who must have been tolerably informed of his knowledge and opinions, but to the rest of the assembly—"I'm not a religious man myself, and I don't rightly know what makes Mass so important, but my Quarry-Irish blood won't let me forget the old wives' talk I grew up resenting. I don't take offence at Perdita's blasphemy."

Again Gloria (who boasted railroad workers among her latterday Irish forebears in Montvert)—explaining to Rafe, recalling to the others an obscure book of the apocrypha:

Riley was a renegade of the Mexican War who had come to Dogtown about 1850 after losing a damage claim against the U S Government for having lashed and branded him under General Winfield Scott's mitigated sentence for desertion. He had already deserted from the lowest ranks of the British Army in Canada before joining the American, in which he became such an impressive drill sergeant that he was once detached to New Uruk as a recruiter. Then, while serving in Lonestar—before the war began (a fortunate legal technicality that was to be taken into consideration by "Old Fuss and Feathers" in reducing the court martial doom of hanging)—he got fed up with Atlantean anti-Scholastic bigotry and crossed the Rio Grande to join the Mexican Army, where he was welcomed as a Lieutenant and soon rewarded for good service with a brevet captaincy. Before long he was second in command of the San Patricio Company, a band of mostly Irish deserters. It was finally wiped out by the Gringoes (including those of his former unit), assisted by a troop of Mexican deserters, only after an extremely valiant defense of the Convent of San Mateo on the river Churubusco. But the Mexicans were so grateful to these Petrines under the labarum of St Patrick that before General Santa Anna would sign a peace he insisted upon the outright release of the captured deserters who'd been spared execution. As soon as the war was over Riley went right back into the Mexican army and rose to the rank of Colonel. In the end he was asked to leave the country when he irritated one of the juntas.

But he hadn't escaped perpetual punishment. All the rest of his life he carried a double brand symmetrically disfiguring his famous good looks. The maladroit man executing the sentence had at first branded the two-inch D on the right cheek upsidedown; whereupon to correct his error he applied the iron literately on the left. The resulting "butterfly mark" made Riley's cheekbones look like the terrifying double blades of a prehistoric battleaxe. It wasn't easy to get a job north of the border.

Perdita was said to be the widow of a hundred men, and perhaps of beasts and demons too, but Riley was the last and truest of her husbands. He prolonged her youth by twenty years but then got himself killed by powder blast in a pit above Scape Cove when he was cutting one of the big olive-green slabs for Winfield Scott's cenotaph in Washington.

"One of the great unknown marooners!" cried Huck. "Not even mentioned in the Index to the Journal of the Gloucester County Society for Nonrepresentational Historiography! But there's a monument to the whole company of San Patricios just outside Mexico City—a cross inscribed with a fighting cock, a pair of dice, and a skull-and-crossbones."

"What d'you spect?" Wat Cibber suddenly spoke again. "Does Dogtown ever know the finest kind while they're still alive? Sometimes we honor them when it comes to obituaries and ex post facto memorials. That's what we mean by loving our history."

Rafe listened for wit or sarcasm, and with anxious uncertainty also as to the relevance of this undisguised emotion, whether befitting or displaced. The pent-up words were loosed with almost breathless fervor, yet in the measured tones of rehearsed recitation, as the bulky fisherman looked fixedly into level space like an entranced oracle. Wat's friends showed no surprise, but what had at first impressed Rafe as humorous histrionics was shockingly clarified as genuine passion released by Huck's off-hand recognition of a single injustice that the speaker believed far less deserving of attention than those suffered by the stalwarts of sea hunting.

For Wat fishing was at least as ancient as fighting, and simply essential to the history and geography of Dogtown—infinitely more important than the ephemeral industry of stone-cutting (howsoever old elsewhere), which for its own profit far from nourishing had undermined Mother Gloucester's stronghold. His grievance however was with present issues of political economy. "The people won't know what fishing's done for this city until after the harbor's been paved over with bituminous concrete for the reefer trucks to park on, and they read the obituary of fresh fish in the *Goddam Daily Nous!*"

For the sake of converting a disinterested stranger to his reactionary faction, Wat was taking advantage of indulgent friends who had long since ceased to weigh his inveterate complaint. But he now made clear to Rafe the dichotomy to which he must be exposed as a serious anthropologist hitherto only vaguely aware of the razor that in Wat's mind divided the world into two faiths. The fission had begun little more than ten years ago—but it would last until Dogtown was wholly given over to the decadent polity of pilgrims aestivators and Normans. All Wat's public and economic emotions were defined in terms of a bitter conflict between the local fishers and cutters of fresh fish, on the one hand, and the large frozen-fish plants (with all their ancillary services) on the other. The latter brought raw material to a modern concrete wharf in refrigerated freighters from the Maritimes and other foreign ports as solidly packed cargoes in the form of compressed and frozen cartons like uniform flagstones: slabs of fish-flesh larger and flatter than paving blocks but far smaller and somewhat less dense than the curbstones and structural granite that had once been exported from other harbors of the Cape.

There was no pretense of disinterest in Wat's tireless preaching of the proposition that the "seafood corruptions" (especially Mercator-Steelyard Incorporated) were conspiring to extinguish 350 years of Dogtown's most virtuous industry by taking over the waterfront, flooding the market with artificially preserved fish, and driving down domestic prices. Yet his motives were selfless to the extent that as one of the few remaining Yankee individualists in the present fishery of Tuscans and Lusitanians he spoke on behalf of all competitors or dealers who owned, manned, supplied, or purchased from Dogtown draggers gill-netters or purse-seiners.

Thad and Buck, on their part the least disinterested of his friends, looked at each other with faint smiles and fainter shrugs, having been enticed into the old argument once too often. Everyone looked for Dexter Keith, the only public official among them, to take up the gauntlet, at least to acknowledge the outburst, if only to alleviate Teddi Cibber's burden.

She had been listening as attentively as if she was hearing a fresh point of view. With irenic tact she reverted to her husband's initial generalization: "It's true: until you read an obituary you may never know that your neighbor or old acquaintance, or someone whose name is familiar as a writer of letters to the editor about local affairs, was the inventor or discoverer or author or creator or donor or leader of something important to all mankind—maybe even of the wheel or the sail!" On her pale smiling lips common words were pure, like those of an empress taking uncondescended delight in the language of her favorite kingdom; but the hands folded in her lap were rough and reddened with work for which there had never been servants.

Nevertheless it would have been cowardly for the one City Hall insider who inspired their confidence not to protest the kind of Luddite attitude toward progress that among enemies frustrated his rational efforts to save Dogtown from the garish or genteel destiny of Botolph suburbs. The City Planner, Gloria's bedlord, Caleb Karcist's landlord, and by virtue of his gifted aspect a lord withal of all who beheld him, hesitated only a moment between diplomacy and conviction. Dexter Keith was a towering blackheaded leader of men, with voice and visage for women to dream on, yet of friendly candid manner in the sincere practice of his vocation, as sympathetically light of touch with each individual as the best of politicians. So he now defended a theorem to which he was professionally committed (though in public he was obliged to pretend neutrality in the value-judgments that usually underlie debates about the greatest good for the greatest number), namely that the bulk raw imports of frozen fish were both cause and effect of investments in facilities that would preserve the port of Dogtown for the old as well as for the new fishing interests, fresh and frozen, therewith providing steady year-round payrolls and major property-tax revenue for the common good.

" . . . Our lumpers are more efficient than the stevedores in Botolph or Bournemouth; and our continental trucking too, connected by the Felly, via the Berkshire Turnpike (our new canal to the West), all the way to the Nether Land Throughway without a stoplight. Dogtown can become a general cargo port, for exports as well as imports. That's why Atlantic Market & Terminal is willing to invest so much in new freezers along the waterfront and also in a dry warehouse up at the railroad yard.

"Of course it would be a lot easier if the teamsters, horse dealers, harnessmakers, livery stables, wheelwrights, wagonmakers, and other selfinterests a hundred years ago hadn't joined the Irish-haters to prevent the railroad from laying track down to the waterfront while the going was good. Then in the next generation it was the trolleycar people and the coastal sloop-owners who kept the quarries from joining their rails and building a spur around the tip of the Cape to connect with the V & M at Land's End—as a result of which Dogtown couldn't compete for many big inland contracts, simply because we had to sail granite down to East Botolph just to get it into the national system! In both cases it was the shortsighted opposition of perfectly useful economic elements that throttled their own prosperity in the long run as well as everybody else's."

Dexter Keith spoke so competently and wore his parts with such charm that he would have overshadowed Raphael Opsimath from the start if his position among the women here—whatever it was—hadn't long since been settled, or if he hadn't so modestly effaced himself until baited by the fisherman. The Cornucopian industrialist himself was not sorry to hear the rational warning not to oppose all industrial development, lest Dogtown degenerate like San Ricardo into commercial otiosity. He would have spoken up in support of Dexter (and perhaps reclaimed the preeminence of his untrumpable intelligence) had he not been hoping that Wat would invite him out fishing. He wanted to see how ingeniously *Motion* had been rigged so that one man was able to do the work of two or three.

Then Dexter's peroration: "If we weren't so dependent upon the fishcatching industry now we wouldn't be so vulnerable to beefeaters—and we'd be better able to keep waterfront facilities for fishermen until the freshfish market improves, as I'm sure it will when consumers start paying attention to nutritionists."

Everyone looked at Wat to see how he responded to Dexter's long patient riposte to the gravamen of his old internecine quarrel so gratuitously summoned up before a guest of honor. He sat head up in sullen silence, his thick hands interdigitated like a plowboy's in Sunday School, staring fixedly at nothing, his face clouded with anger, refusing to acknowledge the calm counterattack. Mistrusting the eloquence of his passion, he wouldn't let Dexter get his goat. Wat was more easily appreciated by off-islanders than by most of his fellow townsmen. Rafe flattered himself that he divined Wat's resentment of the Normans who affected to love Dogtown better than he did who was privileged to have been born there. The native fisherman played up to those who presumed his uneducated insensitivity due to picturesque charm and poignantly envied him the memories of his breeding ground, forgetting the advantages that had placed them in a position of condescension; but (as Rafe would explain to Tessa at the first opportunity) Wat grudged the presumption of psychological friends who tacitly understood his reactions as determined by ineluctable strictures and oppressions of his particular childhood.

Embarrassed by the silent reply, Dexter put an end to the unintended brief by slowly getting to his feet, unintentionally enhancing his unintentional dominance of the scene. "Gloria and I must go now. I'm sorry to have disburdened upon you the conflicts of Lilliput Hall. The Mayor and most of the Earls never wanted a city planner. They don't know what planning is, and they'd abhor it if they did. But they had to ordain the office in order to apply for Civic Instauration funds from the federal government. My bosses trusted that I would do nothing but advise the Planning Board on technical details and rubberstamp any project that claims it'll increase the tax base. Meanwhile the publicspirited denizens who've pressed for rational planning all along (and are now under the illusion that they have a majority on the Board of Earldermen) only make it tougher by expecting me to come out categorically against industrial expansion. Yet it's the fish plants and other manufacturers that keep this town from becoming nothing but an amusement park for pilgrims or a pleasure garden for Normans."

"Better whorehouses than sweatshops!" muttered Wat without altering his posture but thereby restored to his usual ambiguity of humor, preferring the less dramatic attention of his audience. "There was a time when just scriptors and pictors came on purpose to see the piscators, but now that the Felly funnels all the other pilgrims here the only artists that show up are the ones who can't afford to go as far as Markland. That's true. I guess you can't blame the Yard for that."

But Gloria had made no move to rise, and neither had the host or hostess. Stepping therefore no further than the fireplace, bemusedly jingling his car keys and pausing a few seconds to give the historians a chance to change the subject, Keith leaned against the smokestreaked granite and, with the dazzling smile of a champion one could count on, confidentially resumed, as if he never ceased pondering his job.

"In Washington and Bot, whence all the public moneys flow, supposedly on the basis of informed reasoning, Dogtown is known among the bureaucrats as Tall Tale Town. And are we not generally considered the most fractious city since Dante's Florence? The poets may call us a polis of 'collective singulars', but to prospective benefactors the infamous Dogtown mentality seems more like willful stupidity. You all make fun of me for being a politician, but I tell you it takes a diplomat to make them forget that we're a tribe of wrangling black sheep!"

"Without a Gulliver we'd be lost indeed." Tessa allowed. "We'd get nothing back from our taxes to Washington!"

"I have no power. I'm no more than an ex officio advisor with the license to issue certain visas. If I'm going to do any good I've got to pretend it's in somebody's economic interest—not necessarily everyone's. I can't breathe a word of moral judgment, unless it happens to agree with the consensus—not to mention aesthetic opinion. Since cultural questions are more vulnerable to majority rule than anything else, you must try to avoid them entirely. Otherwise you risk the loss of the beauty that remains to us out of neglect or accident or oversight, or because some imagination exceeded its powers before it could be frustrated. We've got a nice beige trim on City Hall, for instance, instead of cliche-white, only because the painter thought my offhand suggestion was official! I almost got impeached. Fortunately the earls didn't want to spend any more money to correct my misunderstanding of public opinion! I can't very often pull off triumphs like that. It's taken two years to allay doubts of my professional sanity!"

Rafe was beginning to see some of the crosswinds blowing upon all the tides of controversy represented by the civil disagreement of Dexter and Wat. There was a whole climate of controversy. All history aside, he thought, it's not as simple as it was in San Ricardo. There the undertows and currents were not so disturbed by the eddies of a complicated shoreline. And maybe this lucky bedfellow of that happy energetic blonde is no mere clothes-horse after all. He seems to have critical faculties.

But Dexter's command performance was turning into a sermon. "It's sheer luck if anything built on Cape Gloucester is not in bad taste. The best we can hope for is the tasteless. So one must keep up the pretense that credentials are required for any kind of aesthetic judgment, which must be delegated to referees—who of course can only be outside consultants, since nobody willing to join the city payroll could possibly be deemed qualified to make evaluations. So we're always being ground between the millstones of popular taste and blind trust in academically accredited professionals. But to my mind it's better to risk the wisdom of fatuous arbiters than to keep asking the people what they'd like to see on the Acropolis. Whatever influence one can muster is best spent on the process of selecting specialists and on implanting in them the subliminal seeds of what you personally want!

"Bear in mind that if step-by-step questions were put to the voters in such a way as to elicit the real preferences of a majority, Purdeyville—next to the harbor itself our most precious public possession—would be sold off to any airport entrepreneur or Panderland operator who promised a local payroll. For the present, there's enough solid granite under the moraine to make the blasting difficult for roads and utilities, but the time will come when nuclear bulldozers are available to anybody who can borrow money and pay real-estate taxes."

There was a general sigh at this pessimistic reminder, and Dexter's homily dwelt sympathetically upon the matter most troubling to marooner patriots. "What's more likely in the meantime is bums and squatters. It doesn't take Irish to make a shanty town. Purdeyville could become a colony of unwashed Beauts. But that's the least of our worries. The horror is that it's becoming an unofficial dump. There are already junked cars and mutilated refrigerators; piles of trash and demolition rubble line the edges of any Purdeyville road passable for a kilroy. If we don't do battle against the waste-vandals right now, the city fathers—if they don't sell off the land entirely—will make it a dump officially. Consider the civic incentive: it would give us an irresistible advantage over other towns in attracting new industry if we could offer practically unlimited waste space as space for waste! Other towns would pay to dump their trash here! The blueberry-pickers and bunny-lovers would be outvoted three to one in any plebiscite for lower property taxes.

"Otherwise—domestic real estate! Houses are already beginning to encroach. The pastures of Maiden Lane are being filled up with worse-than-tasteless prefabrications. All the approaches to Purdeyville are about to be populated. Even the ridges above Haw Avenue are under seige! The skyline's changing every month. Construction without architecture—every bit of it! That's what makes me sick. Some development is inevitable, some can be prevented; but nothing can stop the immoral synthesis of ugliness. Mortgage-prosperity is going to turn decent hardworking Catholicrats into smug Protesticans. The fruits of the New Deal are its own destruction!"

Rafe warmed to the man, approving Tessa's sober observation: "You're working harder than we deserve, Dex. Especially considering how easy it would be for you to make a good living in the big city. I wonder how many good men of Dogtown have given their lives in vain."

"Not to mention women." Cora grunted.

"At least once a month I tell Gloria I'm going to quit!" Dexter laughed. "Which I would have done twenty times over if it weren't for the view of the harbor from my office in City Hall tower!" But he couldn't stop. "I've never been so close to it as I was this afternoon. The bankers and lawyers are complaining to the Mayor that I block all development. I keep hoping to make him into a leader. In many cases he's got enough power, but he's afraid to use it: their arguments are too political."

He hesitated, looking at his watch and down at all the faces still attending him, though one was his wife's, and then allowed himself to confess more of the thoughts that consumed his professional reveries and lucubrations and sometimes tormented his very sleep. "Politics is a function of morality, but morality's no less a function of aesthetics than aesthetics is a function of morality. Either way, short of criminal conduct, they're equally impossible to argue by. That leaves economics, which you can pretend has nothing to do with morality or aesthetics because of its requirement that value be measured by money. Money at least introduces the logic of accounting, which impresses people because they think it represents the true financial state of the city. But the accounting system is deeply faulty, and the city's financial officers don't understand even its formal equations and inequalities. So without the apparatus of reason you are forced to rely upon the unjustified politics of persuasion as a means of gaining the power to do something that is justified morally and aesthetically only on your own authority. But I have very little legal power even to launch persuasion.

"So I'm satisfied if two days out of three there's so much as a chance to lay a single brick. After we finish all our title searches there may be a way for the city to get funds for buying up all the Purdeyville land and forestalling private desecration until the deed's irrevocable. But that's not incompatible with using other unproductive land away from the waterfront for new plants in industries we haven't had before. There are three hundred fifty-one municipalities in Vinland, and we have more land area than almost all of them. I'm afraid it's true a city's got to grow, or die; and when it's surrounded by water on three point nine sides it can grow only by intensification. If new industry is ruled out, the Normans will win, and fishing will survive only to titillate the pilgrims. When all the bad smells are banished the waterfront will be given over to toyboats and needle trades. Dogtown won't be a working city. It'll end up at best as a Bot suburb with the native population subsisting on kitsch. We don't even have enough old architecture to foster a cult of preservation like Bensalem's or Newessexport's. Even a return of the Irish can't save our soul if the only jobs are for shopkeepers and lackeys. When all the tastelessness is spread out evenly there'll no longer be any neighborhoods to sweep the dirt into, and there won't be any gurry in the harbor to keep the gulls around here that we depend upon to clean the beaches! The gracious rich and the harmless old aestivators will sell out to reality speculators. Then what will happen to the lovely little museum wards like the Village and the Plantation? There won't be a town landing left anywhere, nor a foot of open shoreline—not one untended plot of grass from the beaches to Cynosure Rock! That's what happens when you stop industrial development!"

Pace Doctor Charlemagne! said Rafe to himself. This Dexter Keith is a man I should get to know.

Tessa relieved the ensuing silence. "Yes, I understand why you've got to slither like a serpent."

"There's no moral way through the swamp of imperialistic individualism." said Cora grimly. The dancer's Marxism or feminism, or whatever it was, could be laughed off by her sister, Rafe thought, but it must be a radical embarrassment to her poor husband's career at the Yard.

Their host spoke up for the first time. Having finished all possible service with bottles and glasses, Buck had been following the conversation with the look of an emaciated bear awakened too soon from hibernation, mournfully unable to assist in the wintry forests and fields outside his hollow tree but conscious of a duty to warn the foxes and squirrels. "Lent is what I'm worried about. They say the Pope may abolish fasting."

"Thirty percent of our calendar is meatless." said Kryothermsky of the Yard. "Some say liberalization of the Church will be almost as deadly to the fish business as asphalt was to granite. People found it unpleasant to drive automobiles over granite paving blocks, and the masses think it's rough to eat fish when they can afford meat."

Ever since arriving in Dogtown the curious visitor had noticed adversions to Lent in the talk of businessmen and consumers, but it hadn't previously occurred to him that most of the year's frozen fish production would have to be kept in storage for a peak selling season, for which reason Jason's warehouses were the city's largest private investment. It now appeared that Dogtown's citizens were not mouthing a merely religious sensibility.

"But eating fish is considered fasting, the equivalent of vegetarianism, only because meat was once the sign of a feast." Thad went on, looking around at everybody with the cheerful selfdeprecating smile that characterized his irony. "It's not a matter of faith or doctrine. Unfortunately fish is still stigmatized as penitential food because it's cheaper than meat, though livestock has the advantage of storage on the hoof, without the inconvenience of a chase—for movable feasts as well as fixed. But now, thanks to freezing, fish too is available at times of need or stress, all year round, for what anthropologists call high-quality protein. We're trying to make it more attractive. We call it seafood and cook it up in advance with all sorts of coatings and garnishments to make it taste like mammal fat. Of course that costs more labor and more advertising, thereby raising the retail price. That helps take it out of the hardship category; and in the long run, if all fasting is done away with, we might end up with a steadier demand, reducing our logistical costs so that we can spend more money on advertising!"

"For God's sake, don't quote my husband outside this room!" said Cora to Rafe, as if to supply Thad's wry intelligence with its missing sarcasm.

Gloria remarked that it wasn't only the Scholastics. Early in Elizabeth's reign Lord Burleigh—Bacon's uncle who never helped him much—got Parliament to pass a sumptuary law requiring fish on Wednesdays and Fridays. He wanted to encourage fishing so that England would have experienced sailors. "If he hadn't, we might not be speaking English now!"

"You see how commercial the Deformation was!" Sally Salter exclaimed.

Thad returned her a smile but persisted in a sweet-tempered exposition. "Still, Buck's right. Ever since the U S started raising a lot of beef Dogtown's relied too much upon ecclesiastical discipline. Forty percent of our sales are for the Lenten trade. If the Pope lifts all fasts, or if the Friday distinction between fish and meat is rescinded, we'll have to keep praying for drought in cattle country, or wherever chickenfeed is grown. Fish must be a great deal cheaper than meat before people think they're getting as much for their money, because it's obvious from the bite of it that a pound of fish weighs less than a pound of beefsteak. It'll take years of marketing to overcome people's association of fish with self-denial, which is obsolete.

"On the other hand, don't underestimate the inertia of our Holy Mother Church!" Thad's broad smile and gentle voice disarmed any possible doubt about his goodwill toward infidels and apostates. Rafe knew from Tessa that he never urged her sister to respect his religion, and was even willing to disregard canon law by honoring the right of his children to share their mother's prejudice against superstition. "Rule or no rule, I think a lot of people will stick to the custom of eating fish at Lent, and on Fridays too."

"The demand for meat is totally unscientific, cruel, and economically inefficient." said Cora calmly in support of her husband's position on grounds of her own. "But even in wartime we're convinced it's essential for the population. Caesar's legions got along without it."

"So do the Loosies." said Huck. "Of course they eat fish. That's why they've always done better than anybody else at fishing. They don't eat up the profits on butcher bills. Catch their own protein. When they've made enough money most of them sell their boats to the Tuscans and go into some respectable profession."

"Fish would be everybody's gour-mett food if we had better ways to take it out of the boat." said Wat, now quietly jumping at the chance to talk about his metier. Known as the most cooperative proponent of fishery research among Dogtown practitioners, he sometimes chartered himself and his *Motion* to parties of scientists for offshore sample-hunting or small-scale experiments. "We do too much damage with pitchforks and baskets. The fish would keep better and the yield would be higher if we had quality control at the lumping stage of the food chain." Then his voice rose and his words accelerated with the unsmiling self-parody familiar to most of his listeners: "I try to tell them, but you know—an unprofitable prophet is never known on his own strand until his boat's sunk by an insurance policy!"

When Gloria at last rose to accompany Dexter, reluctantly dissolving the party's spell of cohesion, Tessa called out at large: "Tell one and all we'll have our caucus next week."

Rafe yawned. But the narcissistic discussion of Dogtown still showed no sign of approaching a limit. Everybody's standing and stirring raised further undisputed points, as they all talked at once. Rafe recognized the behavior of guests gathering before a long mirror on the way out: they did not wish to disperse. But what this madding allopatric clan saw in the glass was their exasperating Mother Gloucester herself, not merely themselves as the chosen people of a site for the Second Coming. Rafe wondered whether he should make bold to share this insight with Tessa, or even with Doctor Charlemagne. But in the end he was more concerned with maneuvering for his last crack at the strongwaters that Buck and Eric had pretty much had to themselves during the trunk of the evening. While everyone milled about in the general leavetaking Praisegod came out of his corner and stood patiently by the door to wag his tail goodbye to each and every guest, often prematurely.

Rafe made arrangements to follow up new friendships, principally with the aborigine of the Harbor and the troglodyte of the Village, as well as his schedule allowed—aside from his further business with Buck—in the short span remaining to him on the Blessed Isle.

The duration of a crack-of-dawn appointment with Wat was contingent upon the weather, but at least they'd "check the Foreskin" together, riding out to Crow Point in the fisherman's "horseless wagon" to auspicate sea and sky for a contemplated day of fishing. He had finally requested the privilege point-blank when he realized that the invitation would never be tendered by a shy old salt so highly skeptical of any worldly person's sincere interest in the cranky livelihood that he said he couldn't have afforded to pursue had he not been born with an incapacity for anything else.

The hope of seeing Huck's work in North Village was broadened by Sally's dinner invitation in accents much softer than her husband's powerful twang, though purged of Southern locutions. "Don't expect to see much indigenous stone." said the sculptor, clearly happy that she'd volunteered. "It's strong enough to survive Judgment Day but too hard and persnickety for anything halfway fine. If I want to work in granite I usually do what the decorative carvers here have always done: I import some Markland pink. I help Wat with a couple of days' dragging along the way and he takes me up there to fetch a little deck cargo. But—I hate to say it—my finely worked stuff is mostly white marble fetched from Montvert, which is a good excuse for rolling off to the mainland every now and then."

"In Colonial times up here all heavy rock was called marble." Sally told Rafe. "Granite was '*dog*-marble'. That's my theory of how Dogtown got its name—when the Cape was still almost completely forested except for stone the farmers thought too hard to work. Seamark already had its Viking name: Forest-in-the-Sea. No one dreamed of cutting quarries until all the King's masts were lawlessly squandered on firewood and timber, mostly to benefit Botolph."

"Our most beautiful poet says that even when the Cape was dressed in trees men could see her naked ankles at the waterline and guess what her body was made of." said Huck. "For two hundred years they contented themselves with what they chanced to glimpse of it, the lines say, until some Irishmen in drunken passion offered the first disrespect and showed them how to expose gleams of flesh here and there; but their desire was quenched before they stripped her naked, and it will be the end of the world before God sees her in all her beauty. Meanwhile the scratches made in their brief blaze of lust are already healing over as monumental scars, and the excoriated bare spots are redressing themselves with kinds of trees that were never there before. That's only my crude paraphrase. I can't remember the poetic words."

"Let's go home!" said Sally, tugging at his sleeve.

"In another poem the same poet refers to Hosea's Ledge—the last pit still worked occasionally and not yet filled with water—as an inverted cathedral carved by god-men out of dog-marble; yet you can see that the altar at the bottom has been hewn from living rock to defy Yahweh in a low place that will outlast all worshippers and their fleches."

"I'd like to read that poet." the foreign student said. "Who is it?"

"I'm not at liberty to tell you who she is. I'm her Swiss banker until she decides to publish."

By this time in the heel of the evening Rafe was quite ready to call it a day. With a new batch of ludicrous facts echoing in his head, or the shades of facts, he was glad to get a ride back to his Schlossberg with the oddly levelheaded Kryothermskys on their way home to West Marsh, hoping that as experienced ultrapontines not long habituated to the island they might change the subject. As Thad drove up the steeply oblique drive to Cod Street, passing several individualistic houses no longer lighted from within and almost invisible in the bosky shadows cast by brilliant moonlight, he nevertheless found himself looking for the massive blocks of granite that Buck had told him were scattered upon the formerly bare face of the sea-cliff by careening flatcars that more than once broke loose on the old "gravitation railroad" in transit to the powerhouse wharf from their birthplace up behind Pilot Hill. There had been a flagman at the highroad crossing, posted by the Seamark Granite Company to ward off worser accidents.

He tried to feel the sweaty patience of Clydesdales hauling empty cars back to the top. Meditating upon the abuse of horses, which was now happily eliminated with the unhappy extinction of the horses themselves, and thence upon the labor that remained to humans, he suddenly remembered that he hadn't asked the Bareboneses if they knew anything about the clue in his Parity research that slightly dampened his prospective joy in the maieutics of field work. "Do you know of a religious house in East Harbor called The Laboratory of Melchizedek and the Mesocosm?" he asked the Cora and Thad. "I'm looking for their investment manager, a Father Lucey—and I don't even know how to address him!"

"I've heard it's an order of Tudor revisionists." Thad replied.

"*Revisionist* antidisestablishmentarianism is oxymoronic!" Cora retorted. "But more likely Petrine High than Pauline Low. Not that it makes much difference. They all clip coupons to preserve the spiritual life. You'll probably find them serene and aesthetic. It's as if Marx never lived!"

Thad raised his voice as Rafe had never heard it raised before, affecting to overcome the noise of the car he was driving in order to head off her indiscretion: "Cora's a radical Modalistic Monarchian heretic, and she can't stand halfassed schismatics! Now that the Sabellian Humanists have joined the Arian Generalists she's been merged into a Nestorian melange of anticults called Divine Individualism. At least they're not prejudiced against fish!"

"Oh shut up, Thad. I don't believe any of that stuff." But the family skeleton consented to the covering of her politics, accepting the head of the family's warning with an angular smile on her boney equine face. Without having seen her dance or met her children, Rafe unhesitatingly concluded that her career was a deliberately unrelated displacement of social action. But he was to have an opportunity to reexamine this conviction, for she too now invited him to dinner on his last day in town.

To help dispel the embarrassment of divided religions, the last thing he said to her as they drew up to the Van was: "I'm very grateful to Thad. He's about the nicest guy I ever met. He refrained from exposing me as a damned fool at the Turntable lunch when I was holding forth about the stupidity of not using steam cleaners in his own fish plant. He was sitting right beside me and he never let on!"

"Well only because you got me thinking that maybe we ought to try your high pressure cold water system." Thad replied. "Cleaning is a problem I've neglected."

7
RAFE'S
LOG (4)

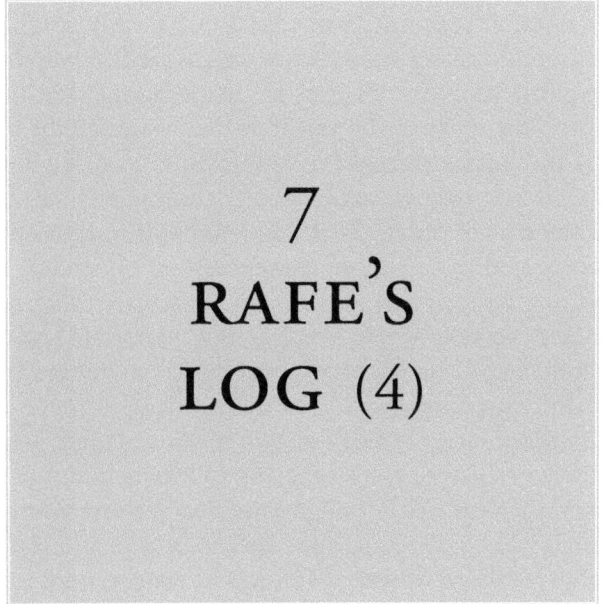

The Van
Dictated 18 Sept 60

Saturday I finally fly home, two days after my deferred deadline, having uneasily availed myself of the presidential freedom that helps compensate for the cares of total responsibility. This past week my reveries haven't attracted much thought of Tubalcain. I've been preoccupied with the Parity business. My homework turned into a lucid dream of action much too densely kinematic to be recounted fully in this last convulsive attempt to entextualize a journal (or semainal?) of my research. No other fortnight of my life has been crammed with such a variety of discovery, and I fear that some of my new experience has been wasted merely from my incapacity to assimilate everything in time to remember it. But hereinafter I'm going to be compendious about what I do remember. Even though I was able to bring back from Botolph a bountiful supply of recording disks, I haven't left myself time enough to develop themes or to indulge interesting digressions. So caveat mentor: I have a whole hasty little history to tell!

At first I wasn't sure I'd done the right thing in hiring Caleb Karcist as my research assistant. Not that I was greatly troubled by the moral question of buying statistical as well as clerical help for my academic assignment. Don't professors use doctoral candidates and secretaries too for most of the research they claim credit for? I don't go as far as the justices who have opinions written for them by law clerks. I wasn't asking anybody to do my thinking or writing for me: just to put the data in order. The bibliography of a paper on any other subject is expected to be full of references that do no less than that. There's nothing wrong with subsidizing the research that one should have been able to take for granted as raw material. So I don't feel guilty of abusing White Quarry's confidence in my academic integrity. Nor do I especially fear I C ' s disapproval.

As a matter of fact, for a day or two it was the inefficiency of that move that I worried about. It's sobering to hire help out of your own pocket when the cost neither augments nor protects your assets and yet can't qualify as a tax-deductible expense; and in an improvised situation it always takes a wretched amount of time to train the cleverest most willing person not already skilled or expert at your task—even when you yourself know (as I didn't) exactly what you want.

But I must admit feeling a little guilty about the cowardice of sloughing off the dogwork that's the underside of revelation. The boredom would have profited my conscience, which is pragmatical, not academic or moral. Unlike most other executives, I'm more uncomfortable about the delegation of cognition than of operating power, because perception is determined by thought. But there just isn't time for all levels of direct experience.

I was already so busy with appointments and social explorations that I despaired of finding even the time to take in what a pilgrim sees of Dogtown's geography, when I was suddenly drawn into a waterspout of more congenial research than the kind intended for Caleb. I might have gotten a glimpse of that vortex in any case, mechanically following a clue I was given at the outset, but I probably would have pursued it too late to partake of its excitement if I hadn't first indulged my casual interest in the personality of Gary Ghibellini, the editor of the Dogtown paper whom I'd heard speak at the Turntable luncheon, by finding a pretext to call him up. There were so many other people I wanted to see that I'd given up the hope of time to take him out to a meal. I was almost as busy as I am at home.

Luckily I reached him by phone in a cubicle whither he sometimes hides from the interruptions and inhibitions of the open newsroom. From the part of our long conversation that was relevant to this journal I infer that he's an off-island second-generation anticlerical Tuscan who'd like to be taken as a man of the world. To the best of his ability he assumes the manner and language encountered among cosmopolitan academics when he was earning his Master's at the Ur School of Journalism, while at the same time affecting the radical individualism supposedly characteristic of New Armorican Yankees. His passionate revolt against the Petrine tradition has landed him among the quasi-transcendentalists of the Insubordinate General Church on Halibut Street, which I suppose represents the best of capitalism, the point of the very nail I was trying to hit.

For the question I put to him was bourgeois. Becoming more enmeshed in Dogtown matters, each day I had looked further into the back pages of the *Nous,* until I noticed that it carries in a little box the latest market closings of about fifteen "Selected Stocks of Local Interest" on both Exchanges, most of them dominant Blue Chips or large Vinland companies—but including our little friend Parity! I asked Gary how in the world such an obscure issue could be of special interest in Dogtown.

In truth I was wondering if Jason Anacoluther yet retains some financial connection with the company he once unsuccessfully headed, or if perhaps some local outfit has been acquired by PAR. I hoped the editor would be willing to discuss whatever soi-disant facts a fulltime student of Dogtown couldn't help stumbling upon. Private talk is the only thing that saves such men of character from saying too much in print. As a journalist he couldn't be expected to know much about how things really work, but I thought he might be induced to express his impressions. I guessed that he's a man to pride himself on his frankness. My intuition still functions well enough, even here in Dogtown where it can't keep up with all the enfabulations.

"That daily listing was one of my least unpopular innovations!"

I also had praised his Turntable speech. Listening over the phone to his chuckle at the low-pitched end of a loud spectrum I visualized the bridling complacency of Meerschaumed Algerian briar pressed against blunt chin retracted into Angus neck with eyebrows wagging. But allowing him no time to deprecate his scholarship in anachronistically conventional terms, I made him keep to the point, knowing what a busy person any Dogtown editor must be.

"We've been accused of being a non-newspaper—printing too much about the past. And some say we harp too much on the local.

So I thought that little token might help make counterweight to the parochial sine qua non. As for Parity in particular, I stick that in just for the fun of it. A friend of mine who teaches at the High School tried to make his civics class tolerable for the so-called terminal students by suggesting that they chip in and buy some shares to see how the free enterprise system works. He gave them a dozen penny stocks to pick from, and they chose Parity because the investment club which one of the kids' father belongs to was interested in it. They bought seven shares, and they've gone way up. We ran their picture holding the stock certificate—all the boys in their R O T C uniforms. I dabble in the market too, so I bought some Parity myself. Why not learn with our youth? It went from four and a half to six. Of course it's leveled off since then. Anyhow, it's not as obscure as you might think. I hear that the president of Parity had a summer place out on the Foreside some years ago."

Was it indeed to Arthur Halymboyd, the chief executive officer, that he ignorantly referred—rather than to Jason Anacoluther, the erstwhile Chairman, who now lives on one of those estates, whom I refrained from mentioning but whom he probably would have recognized if there was merely a conflation of two titles. This rumor may have arisen as a bit of folk misintelligence from Jason's history as a semipublic figure in the off-island world. But if Halymboyd was once a Dogtown landowner, it might help explain special local interest in the unfamous name of PAR on the infamous Curb in New Uruk.

Almost by the same token, after all, Generic Victuals Corp is the best known Blue Chip around here—as the company that acquired Bacon's fish-freezing outfit after the war and applied its patents, reputation, and trademark to a line of frozen vegetables produced at harvest centers. I wonder how many of the odd lots on Graveyard Street are bought for nostalgic reasons. Many a small investor buys into some multifarious corporation simply because it owns part of the local scenery. This transferred fealty is almost as foolish as the superstition of betting on horses by the private symbolism of their names. I may be slightly romantic about the products I invest in, but at least I'm cosmopolitan enough to be wary of absentee landlords.

In order not to seem tendentious in my initiative, I spoke of other things before hanging up. For instance I sounded him on politics. He's suspicious of Kennedy's professed loyalty to Petrine Scholasticism, and still loves Stevenson who softpedals but refuses to deny his Divine Humanism.

The next step was to beard Jason in his den at the Atlantic Market and Terminal Warehouse Company headquarters, a spacious office overlooking the inner harbor, on the floor above a large room full of clerks and teletypes where all the receipts, bills of lading, and invoices are issued, recorded, or filed, according to the standard procedures of commercial storage facilities.

Half a dozen trailers were backed up to the trucking dock on the inland side of the building, and there was room for as many more. At the waterside a small freighter from the Faroe Islands, looming very large, was discharging pallet-loads of frozen codfish blocks in corrugated paper cartons. Elsewhere under the same roof, at the furthermost insulated wall of the vast zero-degree (F) cavern, forklift operators dressed like Eskimos were scooting similar raw material on other pallets out of deep hibernation in the silent nave—through the huge padded double posterns of the crowded narthex called the Holding Room (entrepot of exchange between the public warehouse and its one special customer)—out into the subtropic atmosphere of Mercator-Steelyard's noisy production lines. Jason's corporation financed and owns the whole building, half of it for arm's-length "public" cold storage of anybody's frozen goods, but leases the other half to the Yard for its principal frozen fish "processing" plant. There the imported bricks of fused and frozen fish fillets are sawed into regular pieces of various shapes and sizes (as cobblestones used to be made from granite, but in vastly greater quantities at vastly greater speeds); cooked and/or breaded on moving conveyors, or batched by trayloads, in automatic vats or ovens, on various levels of the factory; then packed by avenues of female hands and gaudily packaged by extremely clever machinery. But hot or cool, before the dressed and metamorphosed fish-cobbles can be encased in shipping cartons and returned through the same purgatory to Jason's custody, they must be instantly rehardened in blast-freezing "tunnels" that circulate Jason's subzero fluid of condensed gas, which is pumped forth and back through the common wall at a billable cost proportional to the weight of flesh thus drained of the thermal energy it has just been forced to absorb. Stored in Jason's symbiotic temple, arrayed by bays and stacks, a hundred different products (made from half a dozen species) await eventual plucking out the other end of the building for transfer by bill of lading to highway trailer-rigs that purport to be equally refrigerated.

But although the Yard enjoys a special relationship at Jason's back door, A M & T W C remains a public storage business at its other two portals, and many food merchants or processors, local or international, avail themselves of its docking and shelter for lesser volumes. Thus Jason's establishment (since it also includes "dry storage" space) is the lazy susan for any export trade that Dogtown can hope for in further exploiting the cargo-handling facilities originally developed exclusively for the importation of fish. It's a remarkably flexible system for absorbing overhead.

By this time I knew something of Jason's local reputation. There's little said against his warehouse, or his bank either, and still less against the discretion with which his left hand distributes the benefactions of his right. Doubtless I could find disgruntled employees, ex-employees, debtors, or would-be debtors, if I searched them out; and anyone who hates the established order must consider him an enemy: but for doing business and charity Jason seems to be generally trusted. Yet not much for anything else—least of all for his amaranthine libido. While tenderly loving his wife of thirty years, they say, he remains devoted to the quest for a succession of golden fleeces that won't turn gray with age before his eyes. It's his more public vice, however, practiced so largely at the Millstone Bar, that divides cognizant citizens into mockers and sympathizers.

It was late in the forenoon, but before his earliest likely start for preprandial appetizers at the Windmill, when I dropped in without an appointment, on the chance that he'd be at his warehouse desk rather than at the bank or out of town. I found him vaguely staring at the harbor view and lightly drumming his fingers on that idle work station. My story was that I happened to be passing by and thought I'd ask his help to get in touch with Owen Leary (a name I'll account for presently), whom I thought he'd know, perhaps as a sometime neighbor. Owen had invited me to call on him anytime he was ashore at his summer palace, but I'd neglected to ask him for his address here, and the telephone directory doesn't list him. I tried to sound casual in my inquiry because Jason knew as well I that this noted yachtsman could have been tracked down without his help, if indeed I'd really been distinguished by the invitation to do so.

Somewhat to my surprise, Jason welcomed me with a smile and, after I'd offered my prosaic narrative as faineantly as I was able, took me at my word. My real purpose was to ascertain my present standing with him, and to prove that I could carry on a conversation without so much as covertly alluding to Parity and without appearing to remember our previous exchange, like a man on vacation whose only concern for business was some good news he'd heard about his own little company in connection with Owen Leary's.

The fact was that I'd just had a call from my sales manager Ted McKee informing me that my visit to Tractor Distributors in Charter Oak two weeks ago was not after all for naught. In my own mind I had written off the effort to sign them up on behalf of our territorial representative (Ray Lagniappe) as nothing more consequential than a planting of our name at the highest level of the New Armorica construction equipment trade. Owen Leary is the inheritor and president of that model dealership. He was my dapper and ever so slightly effeminate but very congenial host at the best lunch in the state of Pequod. I made my main pitch to him and two lieutenants, his sales manager and his executive vice president, believing he would ratify whatever they recommended and therefore speaking at first to their narrow fields of interest; but during the meal I began to realize that despite his dandyish attitude toward company operations he makes all the decisions as to the product lines they'll handle. Later the sales manager told me that Owen also personally brings in most of their large sales contracts, usually negotiated at the yachtclub or statehouse level, and never on terms unfavorable to Tractor Distributors net margin.

The reason I thought I'd failed (as one expects to do in two cases out of three) was that Owen Leary would hardly let me talk business at all. I supposed afterwards that he'd already made up his mind to refuse us, but that simply as a courtesy (like the lunch itself) he baited me into talking too much about the subjects he himself broached so gemütlichly. And later it crossed my mind that our personal compatibility in matters of politics and poetry, far from throwing us into business together as fellows in a tiny minority (a distinction of which he pretends to be unaware), might have deepened his suspicion of Tubalcain's reliability as a supplier. Maybe he'd seen the Tybbot report estimating our financial strength, and had gathered that, unlike himself and neither a graduate of the Laurel Amphictyony nor a scion of wealth, I had no business dabbling in commercially counterproductive amenities. I myself would never trust an unhypothecated aesthete! For what we ended up talking about, leaving behind his two employees (who finally began an important interdepartmental conversation between themselves, such as you sometimes see at table between colleagues who have been too busy with their several duties during regular hours to coordinate matters of more general import), was T S Chittering's poetry. Owen had read it at Norumbega College with the Petrine sympathy of a Scholastic, especially the *Quadrivia*.

Yet just before my visit to Jason Anacoluther's warehouse Ted McKee out in Londonbridge had been handed a letter with Owen's signature accepting our terms—no exclusive franchise but sole Tubalcain appointment for the area in T D 's class of trade—and enclosing a purchase order for six Model 101s and two 360s: the largest initial stock order we've ever had! Ted was already talking to Ray Lagniappe in Botolph and Fred Tracy in Smithsburg about going to Charter Oak to set up a sales meeting with T D ' s men while the iron was hot, and that very morning he released a couple of the 101s from the Brotherly public warehouse (heated, not refrigerated!) for quick hot transshipment. The Controller has probably frowned upon this unnecessarily expensive partial delivery of a firm and unurgent order. I'm sure Ted didn't go out of his way to tell him what was going on before it was too late to prevent it.

It's not entirely irrelevant to explain as follows the timeliness of this windfall on Ray's current and future commission statements as consolation for his recent successive loss of several heartfelt battles with Ted and me.

When I arrived at Botolph on this trip, fresh from Charter Oak and only pausing on my private way to the White Quarry Convocation, I made what at first I thought was the mistake of getting in touch with Ray before even opening my suitcase. He insisted on showing me the town—which means the inside of some night clubs that replicate those of Cleveland and Kansopolis. In spite of the fact that most of its hills have been truncated and its inlets filled, Bot is much more interesting outside than inside the buildings I've been into. I would like to have gone aboard the frigate at the Navy Yard, sister ship of White Jacket's. But our crusty old star producer, as burly and gruff as a rogue bull bison, with the crunching broken voice of a frontier badman, is anxious to draw attention to everything "modern" in his native city, and Tubalcain is in no position to offend him. He points out anything that emulates the youthful vigor of Cornucopia, which he visits every year or two at his own tax-deductible expense, seeing that he's in no position to offend us.

I thought it strange that he said nothing about his plea for a carload consignment in Botolph, but, as he wouldn't talk any business at all until he'd had a chance to soften me up, I was willing enough to postpone the issue. When he finally exposed his heart, at our second dinner, what came pouring out was an entirely new scheme. All along I'd sensed that he regarded my visit as a godsent opportunity to bypass Ted Mckee, which is the sort of insubordination that as a rule we discourage.

In brief, he was now enthusiastic about making money on our "soap"—the detergent compound that we sell through Tubalcain jobbers under our own label merely as a convenience for any user of a steam cleaner who hasn't taken the trouble to make arrangements with some chemical supply house. He'd found a concern that could make it for us in the New Armorica market at a much more competitive local price, with instantaneous delivery, etc , etc .

As I've hinted, it's difficult to turn down the latest pet idea of a resourceful fifty-eight-year-old salesman who's ceaselessly hustling your steadiest volume, especially when you're about to veto his previous one. We can hardly less afford to discourage than replace him. So I had to spend six hours explaining the reason we can't do business that way: our national sales agreement with Holystone Products (out of Nineveh)—which has often enough been rehearsed with all our Reps and is no secret from anyone in the trade. It's an uneasy modus operandi, to be sure, but Holystone is the largest such supplier in the country, our only transcontinental dealer and by far the largest account receivable, yielding us a couple of hundred machine sales we can count on every year (including a disproportionately large share of our heaviest equipment), most of which would never come our way through any ordinary jobber.

Holystone's in what Leo LeFranc our Western Regional Manager calls the razorblade business. Detergent is necessarily and continually expendable, and they're interested in steam cleaners as devices that feed on their cleaning chemicals. At first they took us on only because they were having maintenance problems with Thanksgiving jenneys, the line they sold for many years. (Thanksgiving Fabrication Company is our industry's market leader. Our reps deny spreading the etymology that Thanksgiving salesmen must be sharp to polish off those turkeys.) But in order to promote our superior equipment in its own right, Holystone has hired service specialists at all their branches. Leo did a good job training their sales force. Now they're even running in-house sales contests to move our razors as a major direct source of earnings. Furthermore, they faithfully keep machines in stock, stick to our pricing policy, and discount all our invoices.

Of course their coast-to-coast bureaucracy gives us headaches proportional to their size, and some of their aggressive salesmen have brought on justified as well as unjustified complaints from our locally competitive jobbers. In our company the subject of Holystone has endless ramifications, and it's the one marketing relationship that I'm obliged to monitor personally. But I hated to rehearse with Ray the whole long dreary diplomacy of a difficult arrangement that must be accepted as necessary, at least until we dominate our market.

Now Ray our Northeast man has been loyal to Tubalcain for many years, and he has worked very hard to make us famous. In order to mollify his disappointment at our reaction to his suggestions, Ted and

I perhaps occasionally confide in him a little too much. He likes to be recognized as our diamond-in-the-rough elder statesman. Fortunately the old skinflint is one salesman whose appreciation of net profit is nearly as keen as his eye for gross income, and he's genuinely sensitive to our fiscal constraints. But naturally I don't want him asking too many questions, because one confidential and ostensibly separable term of our alliance with Holystone is that they manufacture for us our private brand of cleaning compound, which we sell at an uncompetitive price to unHoly users who don't wish to start out with any chemical dealer.

In order to divert Ray from the conversational course he had charted for the entertainment of his company president, I decided to relieve one of his unspoken anxieties with a more or less frank explanation of why I was poking around in his bailiwick.

"I don't have to tell you it's nobody else's business." I concluded. "I wouldn't want the word to get around that I'm concerned about my lack of education."

"I never went beyond the eighth grade myself." he grinned. "Education is a topic I never raise. But I don't guess you've got any objection if I tout Parity's stock. Maybe I can run it up for you a little!"

"This is no tip." I warned him. "I'm not investing in it. It just happens to be the company I'm doing my thesis on. In fact it's a pretty suspicious outfit. You'd better not recommend it to anyone you like. For God's sake, keep it under your hat."

Needless to say, I did not mention the possibility of Tubalcain making a connection with Parity, nor of course my personal apprehensions about the future; and I allowed not the slightest hint that a possibility of selling out had ever even flitted to the edge of my mind. It was foolish to have mentioned Parity by name; but he's no gossip, and I think he appreciated the revelation as a gesture of my particular confidence in him. Perhaps I indulged a faint curiosity to find out if he'd ever noticed the stock. It's generally known that he plays the market, and at every Company sales meeting he's full of suggestions for his comrades.

Anyway, as I had hoped, the name of an unknown penny stock sidetracked all his respectful complaints and advices about our mutual means of livelihood. He probably didn't believe that PAR is not a major investment of my own. I was plied with conspiratorial questions about its speculative prospects. Whether or not I was successful in dampening that vision for his own account, however, Ray is authentically disinterested (when not actually interested) in the subject of making money—and on that subject only. He's always glad to discuss applied chrematistics, and with histrionic facility he can easily assume anyone else's personal viewpoint in any instance of this dramatic struggle, which he deems second not even to sex in mankind's common fascinations. Yet he makes no pretense that Lagniappe self-interest doesn't transcend the intellectual beauty of the art and rule every fibre of his being in the special cases that seem potentially relevant to his own fortune.

I'm generally pretty free with advice, but far be it from me to offer investment counsel to anyone who has had to work for his nest egg. I tried to snow him under with all the risks and dangers he would share with thousands of ignorant widows and orphans who put their trust in an unpredictable management with a portfolio full of pending legal actions. "Aw go on! Every company has lawsuits and S E C decrees!" he protested with a cynical laugh, as if I was trying to keep a good thing for myself.

I was racking my brains for a new lure to get him off that scent when I made the passing remark that I was overwhelmed by the numberless facts I had already gathered, and that if I had Aladdin's Lamp I'd use it first of all to get the services of a clerical genii. Maybe my allusion escaped him. He's the kind of man who's unlikely to have had a traditional childhood. Moreover he's getting a little hard of hearing. But whether it was a lifetime's deficit or the long-deferred emergence of humorless wit, I got the homophonic benefit of a pun. "I know a paperwork genius who lives on Cape Gloucester." he said. "I don't know where he works now, but maybe he'd do some moonlighting for you. Come to think of it, he knows a lot about Tubalcain too, because he worked for me a while! I wish I could have kept him."

Ray told me that during business hours the little guy had occupied a sunporch desk in his house, handling all the "details" of his multiple-line sales business to such good effect that for the first and last time in his career he had been relieved of the dreadful burden of office work that haunts the sleep of every manufacturers' representative, and especially one like Ray who prides himself on exploiting the economy of our postal service for sales promotion, as compared with that of personal travel and long-distance telephoning.

It was thus that I first heard of Caleb Karcist, before I ever got to Dogtown. Ray's no mean judge. He may not understand the demands of scholarship, but his critical faculty is highly developed in the estimation of persons connected in any way with the expansion or contraction of his profit, and his only animadversion upon Caleb seemed to suggest academic virtues more appropriate to my project than to the causation of automotive equipment sales. At the time his remarks didn't interest me much, because it's as a pennypinching husbandman of his gains that Ray makes most of his managerial judgments, and it seemed likely that Karcist was nothing more than any ordinary college graduate poor enough in spirit to do the work of a girl. On the other hand, I knew that Ray was continually torn between his Depression-impressed parsimony and an ambitious hankering to establish himself as the respectable proprietor of New Armorica's most progressive independent equipment agency, with his own salesmen to assist him in the field and an office manager to coordinate and control the organization. So if he spoke well of someone not producing sales yet carried on his own payroll as outright overhead, he must have been recommending a ciphering scribe par excellence.

And that's the praise of a maestro. Ray's own memos, hacked out on a 1936 typewriter, are sometimes vivid and ingenious masterpieces of insubordination that force their way through Ted to my attention—such as the six-page brief in which he justified his claim to split commission for an HP1558 (the largest unit we make) sold on a Corps of Engineers bid developed by a Holystone salesman out of Kansopolis Missouri and shipped to Rock Island Illinois, on the grounds that the procurement officer, a Major So-and-So, had attended one of his personal demonstrations as a Captain attached to the Millhampton District in Vinland two or three years earlier. Ray probably smiled to himself when he lost that decision, knowing it would come in handy as a moral quid pro quo in the subsequent disputes to which he would be party either as plaintiff or as defendant. Even when it's not a matter of equity, hardly a month goes by that he doesn't argue about some solecism on one of our invoices to a jobber, seeing that every last line-item of parts and accessories shipped into Territory 10 earns him a commission, and every penny of a credit memo diminishes the delta of silt that extends his private estate into the gulf of commonwealth.

If such a precisian of selfinterest and selfreliance—Protestican-elect from the instant of conception—was so positive about the exceptional qualities of a scrawny timid Catholicrat daft enough to take up residence in Dogtown, the kid must have been an office wizard! With wry tolerance Ray suggested that Caleb, while too meek to have the makings of a businessman, as a docile egghead might be just what I need to take care of the drudgery. Even Mrs Lagniappe, an old dragon of Christian Health Docetism with nothing to do all day but keep her overstuffed house spic-and-span while gazing at moving picture broadcasts of simulated human beings, vouched for him as a perfect gentleman who had volunteered to take out her garbage and always cleaned up after himself in her kitchen.

Not that Ray wasn't still piqued at his inability to fathom the motives of such a clever hardworking assistant, for Caleb had left his employ not to go on to better things but apparently to disclaim all ambition.

Anyhow, in the warehouse office overlooking the inner harbor Jason Anacoluther admitted that he had known Owen Leary for many years. They had sat on several boards together. But, said Jason with a malicious grin, stuttering as usual, Owen wasn't here; he was taking his boat south to winter quarters. He didn't spend even many summer days in Dogtown now that he had a cruising schooner, though there was a time when he'd taken enough local interest to get elected Commodore of the Foreside Yacht Club and unofficial spokesman for the aestivating members of the Foreside Association.

And so my pretext served at least to ascertain that Jason was tolerably friendly when he had a good excuse for not giving out his neighbor's unlisted phone number. But the fortuitous revelation of my brief visit occurred as I was leaving. Its significance dawned on me only after I had walked half way back to the Van. At the last moment in his office I noticed on his desk a loose-leaf binder that had been taken from the mahogany bookcase behind his highbacked leather swivel chair. I recognized its embosssed label as that of the Aggrandizement Advisory Reports, an expensive series of research letters on capital-gain opportunities in the stock market.

This highly esteemed service is provided from the backwoods of Pequod by the reclusive Ambrose Merlin, whose reputation for timeliness, if not for infallibility, has survived every vicissitude of the Tybbot Industrial Average. His avowed specialty is to search out stocks that are undervalued by the Street and worthy of special attention, assuming that securities should sell at more than their book value when everyone is bullish, regardless of the party in power. The rise that follows is due in part to his own prophecy.

Now there are numberless investment advisories that a man of Jason's means might subscribe to, and probably he gets many of them at the bank or at home. But, as I tardily realized, whereas no other market letter seems to have paid any attention to Parity, this one had issued a very favorable two-page analysis of the company just a few days before I met Jason at the Windmill. No wonder he responded so oddly to my mention of the stock on that truly accidental occasion! At first he probably suspected me of searching him out in the vulgar attempt to pump an insider—of trying to steal a march on honest speculators!

Or perhaps he thought I was deceiving him for purposes of even more dishonorable espionage. If so, is it solely because he still benefits from Parity's market performance that he fears investigation of his enemy Halymboyd's web by government agents or journalists—or because he's guilty of having collaborated with the spider in earlier phases of its spinning?

Apparently, in either case, his suspicion of me had been somewhat allayed—whether by some quick transcontinental identification-check or simply by cogitation. Yet he still wasn't thoroughly convinced of my innocence. And indeed by then I was no longer half so guiltless, thanks to Caleb's research at FEEL. Somehow before I leave town I should find a graceful way to assure Jason that when I first met him I had had no inkling of that particular Aggrandizement report (which I now see must have been responsible for PAR's rise at the time)—even if the disclaimer obliges me to reveal the nugacity of my financial wardrobe.

Dictated 19 Sept 60

My next appointment came none too soon, considering how important it's proved to be for my academic project and for my current joie de vivre. I regret the procrastination with which I initiated it. If I had sought out Father Lucey a week earlier, by this time his wake would have been so much the wider. It was from cowardly aversion to piety and sanctity that I had kept finding excuses to defer action on Jason's plainly valuable suggestion. I'm ashamed of how much harder it was for me to telephone the mysterious Laboratory of Melchizedek and the Mesocosm than it would have been to crash Parity headquarters with a person-to-person call to Arthur A Halymboyd. It turned out to be an absurd hesitation. It's easy to talk about worldly matters to the Father Economist, who manages the investments of the Classic Order of the Vine, of which the Laboratory is chapter house and sole real estate. He's also the Registered Representative of a Graveyard Street broker.

On the phone he immediately said he'd be especially delighted to talk about Parity, there were so few who knew anything about it. He did not invite me to his monastery, so it was arranged that he would stop at the Van before lunch the next day on his way into Bot. Accordingly, soon after my return from Jason's, while Caleb was away at the library, he knocked on my door. Half an hour later I was riding down the Massachusetts Felly in the Lab's big Nicolet sedan, swept up by his cordial invitation to spend the afternoon with him at his brokerage office.

"I'm a worker-priest." he says. "We have no Pope to forbid it." He smiles brightly at every such statement. "Some think I'm in as much danger of secularization as the French ones were, and our bishop doesn't like the idea very much. Since the public prefers not to see priests doing the work of the world, and I don't like to make a scandal for the church, I wear my canonicals when I'm going to be seen in Dogtown, but usually change my collar when I get to the office. Not always, though. Sometimes it's of distinct advantage to do business as a priest. Of course it's all for the benefit of the Order."

Most of his commissions are from trading the Order's portfolio, but he earns a little more by handling the transactions of friends and a few others who ask him to do so. He says he's considering serious pursuit of his customer business, but he obviously has little heart for risking other people's fortunes. By dint of very active trading, which is what he delights in, taking full advantage of the fact that the Trustees of the Classic Order of the Vine (a charitable corporation) are exempt not only from the short-term capital gains tax but also from practically all other tariffs, and encouraged by the fact that his share of the commission costs is returned to the fund as capitalized income, in the last eighteen months he has doubled the paper value of his Order's assets.

At the time that Father Superior Duncannon took his vow of poverty in starting the Order about twenty-five years ago, I was told, the Trustees (including himself) put the conservative securities he had inherited from his family—greatly contracted by the Crash of 1929—into the hands of an investment counselor in Botolph. When Father Lucey took over its management in 1958 (without a great deal of previous experience) it contained several thousand shares of Parity. He never made much effort to find out why, he admits. "I'm more or less a behaviorist in the market." he says. "Parity had been fairly profitable, what with the aggregation of small gains, spinoffs, stock dividends, and so forth. In view of its reasonably predictable undulations, I've always kept at least four or five hundred in the portfolio, buying large lots from time to time when the technical situation looks promising. But for churchmice it takes too much time to make a lot of money on it without putting all our eggs in one basket. The work of the Order is too important for me to take big chances sitting in one nest" he laughs, "— as long as I can make our capital grow fast enough by diversification. It's bad enough to be criticized for being in the market at all.

At every Chapter meeting I'm in the dock. According to most of our members I should be investing only for income. But it's usury to put money even into a savings account, and I think it's making a distinction without a difference to feel more guilty about direct than indirect participation in the economy as we find it. Most of us in the Order would be happy to see a day when capitalism's no longer necessary for human liberty; but you can't contribute to mankind's redemption if you affect to extricate yourself from the world's present moil. Still, it's no fun suffering the gentle reproaches of true Christians, especially when you know how dangerous is the practice you're preaching!"

Like some of the noblemen in centuries past who have taken holy orders because the church alone remained civilized, Father Christopher Lucey is diffident about his social adjustment. Even a lone Knight Templar among pacifist pilgrims may be sensitive enough to appearances. And in fact he's an alumnus of Princedom's best club and the scion of a Nashborough family that probably owns a percent or two of the state of Cherokee. Perhaps it's his very success at finance that spares him unequivocal censure for what he calls his avocation within the vocation. His pleasant forthright sophistry is calculated to disarm both pietists and cynics.

As for me, neither one nor the other, I was candidly told that he's protected politically if not spiritually by his Superior, whose power is supreme among the financial Trustees (when he cares to exercise it), and whose rule of the Laboratory is of course absolute—even though the Order he created, for the sake of which both Trustees and Laboratory were established, is theoretically democratic. It's not at all clear who owns what, and Father Lucey is rather vague about the tax-exempting trust instrument. But few Members seek the "Regular" life of the Laboratory, and he is apparently the only one who has been willing to follow the founder in a cenobitic life at Dogtown, where facilities have been provided for a much larger religious community. Under the three vows of poverty, chastity, and obedience, as the one Member therefore absolutely submissive to human authority, he should, I guess, be as secure in his position as Father Economist as in his success in the market.

All others in the Order are Members Secular, men and women living "in the world"—all over the world—though only a few dozen in all. A majority of them are married priests of the Tudor Communion, in parishes or missions, and most are of course under various bishops of the Pauline Apostolic Church in this country. (The Laboratory itself—a monastery of two, chapter house of the Classic Order of the Vine—is under the uneasy jurisdiction of the winking broadchurch Bishop of Eastern Vinland, to whom the two Fathers must nominally report at least once a year. Father Lucey tells me that the Order is shielded from too much scrutiny by its ambiguous classification as "High Church", or "Classic", as if it belonged to the faction sprung from the Unaford Movement, and nowadays made literarily famous by T S Chittering, which is never suspected of anything more scandalous than reactionary aestheticism.) Other members are professors or scientists, or ordinary soldiers of the laity.

Father Lucey asked me nothing about my religious nurture or predilection, but when I volunteered that I vaguely sensed the tenor of never-established antidisestablishmentarianism from having been sent to Sunday School and Scouts at a church in San Ricardo that was one-eighth Petrine and seven-eighths Pauline in its use of the Book of Common Prayer, lower than Luther in its ceremonial but higher than the mean in its moneyed fellowship (for which my family's condition never prepared me), he understood that he was free to speak within the immense latitude of Tudor tradition. The purpose of his Order he says is to reform the church's ritual. If I were ever to be interested in the need for that, I told him, I'd first have to be convinced that the survival of the Tudor church was of any importance at any level of churchmanship, T S Chittering to the contrary notwithstanding. There Father Lucey has been as pleased as I to let that matter rest, and he seems content to be relieved of the obligation to say anything further about the anachronistically feckless purpose of his Order, so long as it gets the benefit of ecclesiastical prestige among both those who respectfully mistake him for a powerful Petrine Scholastic priest and those who are aware of the freedom for good works afforded by the residual wealth that putatively sustains Tudor vagaries even in Pauline Atlantis.

At the Weatherglass, Neatherd & Company branch office, sheltered in the arcade of what was once the city's largest office building, Father Lucey has space on a small mezzanine overlooking the projection screen of the Translux ticker and eight or ten desks of the manager, customers' men, and clerks. Like a private prince he's ensconced with his own bookkeeper and a third table for the use of his personal advisors, clients, friends, or other visitors, of whom there are usually too many for the furniture. The Weatherglass leasehold, vacated less than a year ago by some expanding haberdashery, next door to a flourishing florist, is altogether too small for the investors and traders who avail themselves of the Botolph services provided by that venerable Street name. It's no first-class storefront—and the manager makes no effort to decorate it as a choice location—but it's the only temporary space Weatherglass could find when it decided to cash in on the provincial rush for stocks that most of its New Uruk competitors had already begun to meet by opening branches hundreds or thousands of miles from the exchanges.

In short, this experimental mission of the conservative old brokerage was hustled into a shabby situation that will probably loosen up its mores quite profitably. Its Botolph trade, unlike that of its Ur board rooms, seems to be largely Jewish, and so is the local headman, Pryce Factor, whether by cause or consequence. Father Lucey was imposed upon Bot operations by the Ur partners primarily as a lucrative private trader, but Pryce has no objection to the additional odd business he brings in like so much gravy to overlard the branch's meat and potatoes. Having few customers besides his own Trustees account, the priest is glad to share his commission with one of his stablemates if there's a trade to be made in his absence.

What with such a popular Christian among the cheerful majority of Jews, and all the strange characters who come in to talk to him as Father Lucey, Father Christopher, or Father Chris—notably three or four young "advisors" or semi-retainers eager to make their marks as financial scholars or prophets—it's quite an informal atmosphere. He doesn't keep his nose to the grindstone. The young and intelligent, whether or not they are believers in the stockmarket, alight on Father Lucey like birds on St Francis, and he reassures them all with unfailing consideration of their self-esteem. They are attracted by his courteous liberality, his warm interest in persons of every estate, his unassuming intuitions, his intelligent kindnesses, and his gallant complementarity of professions.

After ten years as a priest, he regards himself as more of a therapist than a broker, accepting fees only for the cure of moneyed souls, according to the schedule established by the Ur stock exchanges, though none of them is aware of being a patient. But I give him credit for modesty in his role as unbeknownst doctor. He's wise enough to appreciate the ambivalence and delitescence of his own psyche as well as everybody else's. His Master's degree in psychiatric social work was granted by the Petrine Scholastics at Botolph College a year after his stint at the Pauline Apostolic Divinity School in Unabridge. For all his tact and savoir-faire, this shepherd of lost sheep was not born to be the pastor of a flock. He'd rather be a Luke than a Francis. Yet neither of these saints is cited by the Order he serves; his outreach seems to be supererogatory and amateur.

As Father Economist—investor or speculator—he's expected to

weigh the relative degree of immorality with which listed corporations earn their profits, and he would probably never buy a stock that represents armaments or devilvision; but he makes a plausible case for the notion that such distinctions are arbitrary or illusory when you fully understand that money is always the prima and ultima materia of economic conversions, the fungible measure of all elements in the Gross National Product, and that unless you keep your liquid assets under the mattress it's blended into the investments of the banking system in such seamless continuity that you can't logically discriminate usury from any kind of production.

Several times during our meals and journeys together we have discussed my aesthetic or even romantic view of business (for I find myself closer to Caleb than to Father Lucey in my emotional evaluation of securities), as against both the financial and the moral. My criteria of productivity are sensuous and temperamental rather than objective or ethical. Yet if I were a Member Secular I'd ask the money-manager more questions about his investments than he would like to answer. Aside from vague classification of product, in his urbane calculations a corporation is but a black box of stockmarket behavior. Like all good financiers he's more interested in phenomena than in the Ding-an-sich, and he subordinates manufacturing to a much larger set of economic transformation, the paradigm of which is the Street's perpetual double-auction of supply and demand, where all desiderata are outcomes of the principle that since capital naturally expands with the usury of time its value also increases with the anticipation of that expansion, whence it follows that present value is determined by parimutuel betting on future anticipation.

Still, Father Lucey's infernally practical outlook has made a great impression upon my Weltanschauung. He has modified my fundamentalism. In particular, under his undidactic influence, I have learned to look at Parity in new perspective. Whereas, like Caleb, I had been mesmerized by PAR's complex holdings, Father Lucey has taught me to question its mysterious root system. Why was I so obtuse as not to have seen that the key to my Disquisition is Parity's *ownership?*

The question is not how PAR ramifies and climbs above the ground but how its roots are branched. Though it's true that Arthur A Halymboyd's basic scheme is to control a sorites of larger and larger corporations with the smallest possible equity necessary to do so at each nexus of investment, and that by this kind of leverage (which the law pretends to discourage) he wields pecuniary power thousands of times greater than his personal wealth, his complex is not a simple pyramid with Parity at the apex.

The system, shaped more like an hourglass, or a Mississippi with its delta, is much more organic. Halymboyd himself is the tap root of an axon with several acropetal dendrites augmenting his personal resources; but an analyst of the afferent underground tangle is bewildered by other tuberous ganglia, cabalistic circuits, and adventitious anastomoses. Moreover it appears that PAR, though the main trunk of an exfoliated ramage in the air above, is not the only public stem. Doctor Zane Capstick's Financial Usufruct Incorporated (FUI) is still a living branch of Halymboyd's banyan, but it seems to have taken root for itself also as another tree.

Furthermore, one presumes that most of the people who have shares in a corporation that owns the company that holds controlling interest in PAR also have stock in other enterprises; and it's undoubtedly a fact that nearly all direct PAR stockholders are nutrients also of Atlantean capitalism at large—the same being true of the outside stockholders of the companies that PAR controls at first second third or fourth hand. I'm obliged to admit that my tree is only a uniquely gnarled thicket in the bejungled hedge.

Dictated 20 Sept 60

A couple of days' discussion with Father Lucey on the road, at meals, in his office, convinced me that my heedless oversight of subterranean roots must be remedied by some research at the Curb Stock Exchange library. At the same time my industrial fundamentalism had somewhat modified his hitherto purely "technical" habits of evaluation, thereby reinforcing his interest in the Parity enigma, which already happened to have been reawakened by the Aggrandizement Report. It looks as if he's always been remiss in searching out details to anchor or justify his inferential imagination. So of one accord we decided to drive Caleb down to lower Ur (where the North River is joined by the Hell) and turn him loose in the files while we made an attempt to gather some intelligence at PAR's midtown headquarters.

In my presence, using his full title and affiliation, Father Lucey telephoned for an appointment with Parity's president, carefully hinting to the secretary at the other end that he would be interesting to Mr Halymboyd not as a solicitor of donations but as the representative of an investment fund. The top man was reported out of the country, but the distinguished caller was immediately connected with the Executive Vice-President. It soon transpired that Hamilton DeCamp Jr, whose name appears on the board of almost every PAR company, is an elder fellow alumnus of Princedom, a graduate of the Pale Law School, and a yachtsman with memories of Dogtown Harbor that probably mean nothing to a resident monk practically indifferent to landscape and artifact.

Of course everyone in the financial District knows that the church is still rich and that its secret riches are subject to less scrutiny perhaps than any other riches in Atlantis, but on Ur island few are aware of the distinction between a freelance priest representing the resources of a tiny Pauline Apostolic community and one who might be acting for international bodies of the Holy Petrine Scholastic hierarchy with real estate holdings mortgagable for stockmarket cash. A priest is an awesome priest; he wears a round collar.

Father Lucey's openhearted manner implied open-handed familiarity with blocks of shares. He said nothing to misrepresent our identities or wealth, but he omitted to mention that I am a mere student of the game and that half the purpose of our trip was my edification. The result of this unhasty colloquy was not only an appointment for the very next day but also an invitation to lunch.

It's refreshing to me that Father Lucey loves to act so swiftly. Operators in the abstract world of finance are not inhibited by chains of command. There is little inertia in financial acts. Triumph and disaster are all too easy, compared with success and failure in the organizational kind of management where stupidity is better protected. Swift action is just what I need on a vacation, especially when bogged down in boring scholarship at the sedentary end of the spectrum. Sharing the motion but not the mass, it's a joy to behold Father Lucey's cinesthesia. He drove us down to New Uruk in the fast Nicolet that same afternoon.

Although he often wears his canonicals when he's particularly to be seen in the financial circles of Botolph, New Uruk, or Washington—sometimes beneath a black cape lined with red—when shunning hometown or ecclesiastical notice in Ur he steers clear of the Cape Gloucester Hotel, which offers special rates for Dogtown travelers. He took us instead to the New Uruk Ascetic Club (for men only), housed in its own convenient building full of steam rooms and gymnasiums, with bar service at the huge swimming pool. The next day Caleb worked down at the Curb files, and finished what he started, but had his dinners with us. We then enjoyed a pleasant drive back to this island, talking to beat the band, arriving home little more than forty-eight hours after we'd left.

Father Lucey would accept no reimbursement for my room or Caleb's. "This trip has been of far greater benefit to me than to you.

You and Caleb have rendered the Trustees an invaluable service by sharing your research, and a generous kindness to me personally." I would have reversed subjects and indirect objects, and on occasion I have tried to do so. But he always proves that my time is more valuable than his and that I have magnified his contribution at the expense of my own (which in truth consists entirely of Caleb's underpaid services to myself). "You have led me to see Parity in a new light," he says. "I wasn't competent to judge the industrial value of Mr Halymboyd's conglomeration, but you've shown me what to look for as his possible aims. I'd always thought of him just as a smart lawyer who makes opportunities to extend his leverage at every level, Parity being merely his accidental instrument. But you've set me thinking about the company as an incipient web of industry—which may suddenly strike the market as a machine for catching fliers. As far as Parity's concerned, thanks to you, I'm beginning to see past the dogma of technicians!"

So said he—just as I was almost coming round to the black-box view of business! I warned him of the wishful thinking in my expositions. We agreed that it would take a deal of further study even to assemble the published facts on which any fundamental interpretation of Parity should be based. We'd have to see at least what Caleb could array of the data he extracted in his inspection of the reports filed by entities listed on the Curb: Financial Usufruct (FUI); United Gear and Machine (UGM), a major subsidiary of PAR that owns the Cold Steel Office Equipment group and several other manufacturing concerns; Venture Corporation of Atlantis (VCA); Bunyan Wood and Resin Products (BWR); Whirleybird Aircraft Corporation (WAC); Atlantean Arnheim Industries (AAI); Container Technology Corp (CTC); Carborundum & Bituminous Machinery (CBM); a few other small industrials; and of course PAR itself. For verification or amplification of my notes on PAR's Big Ticker holdings—Arnheim Electrical Industries (AEI), Associated Electronics (AE), Bardic Corp (BC), Public Operations Corporation (POC), Laclede Aircraft Co (LAC), et al — we've been satisfied to rely on the business publishers whose reports are filed at the FEEL in Dogtown; but when it comes to the thousands of Little Ticker stocks accepted by the Curb with greedy indulgence and hardly supervised thereafter, the advisory services can scarcely afford to look deeper than the routine financial reports intended to disclose as little as possible, as late as permissible, which are countersigned no oftener than necessary by public auditors no better than they should be in the competition for clients.

When Caleb complained about the sloppy state of the Curb library, Father Lucey told him we were lucky to have any files at all to look at. He said if it hadn't been for F D R 's reforms (under the wolfish elder Kennedy, then but lately decked in a sheepdog's ruff), the Curb would still be a den of bookmakers and moneychangers where sporting men could bet on anything, from baseball teams like the Chicago White Sox and horses like Pep Pill to tickets for Limeway musicals and defaulted bonds of East Indies coal companies or Latin American railroads. It had been so lax that many of the stock-companies traded thereon were embarrassed to admit where they were available, and respectable financiers never boasted about their seats on the Curb (only recently come in from outdoors). All too often its tickertape had been "painted"—churned with false volume—by its own manipulating incorporators.

It wasn't such history, however, that made those two days so significant in my education. Today the Curb Exchange dwells in its own building just across the graveyard from the most respectable of all Pauline Apostolic churches, and we don't worry about the legal mechanics of the risk it houses. Father Lucey took me through the capital of uncertainty concentrated in the skyscrapers of old Bartleby's Street itself, where the brokers are, and uptown to the unspecialized Cartesian grid of offices where counselors are domiciled, and a lot of the traded corporations. Many an insider must I have seen, walking their pavements and riding their elevators.

The senior partner of Father Lucey's brokerage, Jonah Weatherglass the Third, to whom I was introduced as a prospective customer for their new Yerba Buena branch office, treated me like a celebrity for about fifteen minutes, until my friend and I took a cab up to Smart Avenue for our Parity appointment. Joe Weatherglass is a younger man than I, extraordinarily relaxed in manner, with a complex view of commerce and shipping from his fortieth-floor corner office. The visit gave me little more than a whiff of Urtown business, but the experience will be useful in my rhetoric of extrapolation. The back room of Weatherglass, Neatherd & Company is a typical node of the world's Graveyard Street switchboard.

The Dutch did a good job in starting the globe's ultimate city, compared to which our other municipalities are only neighborhoods or specialized congestions—mere suburban attenuations of a few real blocks, or elaborations of a few features only. To millions of women as well as men New Uruk is a machine for all of life, an airship too heavily fraught with its power plant to be sustained aloft in the event of engine-failure by gliding floating or standing still. But the motion in its privileged cockpit is exhilarating to a breezy stranger on the wing, and I wish I were a passenger more often.

Yet even at the Royalist Club lunch, with four or five liveried waiters standing in a row to attend each table gleaming with redundant silver and crystal for half a dozen wines, offering the best Havanas, only one underside of that culture's most insulated stratum was exposed. I'm sure that at his leisure in the club and elsewhere our host moves freely at the top, but the fact is that for what seem to him (or once seemed to him) sound financial reasons he has chosen to spend his business hours sitting in on a game usually dealt from a deck of face cards in the innermost room of the Curb's semidemimondain, the oligarchic court of a traditionally disreputable subculture whose best men also possess far dearer seats on the Graveyard Exchange where all the brokers are reputable. The Curb has grown more respectable of late, but it remains a marketplace for skim-milk wanting the fat to keep a place as cream at the center of the quern.

DeCamp had no way of knowing how much PAR stock Father Lucey controlled (since it might be held by any broker "in street name"), but he took no chance of slighting a potentially troublesome friend or foe. I suppose he enjoyed the novelty of entertaining a priest at the expense of the company and the I R S .

I was presented as a small provincial industrialist fascinated by PAR and looking into it for a group of friends while out this way. Beyond the questions invited by a business card, DeCamp is prevented by noblesse oblige from inquiring into the curriculum vitae of inferiors, so he never asked when or where I went to school. Nor did he ask his eccentric peer (ten years younger than himself) anything about the Order's affairs that one gentleman wouldn't ask another about his private fortune. I was the only brash one, advisedly. I found out, simply by the asking (as if I were his equal), that he commuted every day by train from Mussel Harbor out on Elam Island, thereby inferring that although he lived among the very rich he wasn't rich enough to have himself driven to the office in his own limousine.

No: he's in some degree dependent upon Mr Halymboyd and/or Dr Capstick (the FUI magnate), we conspirators later agreed. The job of Executive V P is not particularly flattering to a fifty-year-old Princedom man well born of old money. His ruddy ungroomed moustache represents neither vulgar ambition nor crisp vanity. The thick half-disciplined head of hair is more youthful than mine, but the face is fleshy and a little flushed. He's a methodical Anglo-Norman trencherman, without the affectations of a gourmet, and probably never loathe to take two and a half hours for lunch with someone like Father Lucey to match him drink for drink before and after meat. If he weakened the other's guard I don't think he was in any better condition than I to improve his advantage. Yet even two against one our advances were neutralized by the bland defense. Without volunteering a single hermeneutic or prophetic word he readily confirmed most of the information we offered for the testing, and as if among friends once or twice slipped us a bit that might have appeared in Tybbot's *Graveyard Chronicle* when there was a dearth of important news.

But we benefited from more than pleasant smalltalk while Caleb was downtown slogging his way in solid matter and having his maiden adventure of lunch alone at the Curb restaurant. As one thoroughly imbued with the managerial ethos I am charmed (and sometimes alarmed) by the way Father Lucey, for all his financial strategification, makes no attempt at tactical coordination. Judging by my experience with him, he never prepares his allies for meetings with others or tries to influence their performance. He prefers the dramatic uncertainty of experiments with people. Perhaps he simply wishes things to fall out as God wills. With DeCamp he let me ask some questions about industrial subsidiaries that Caleb had primed me with, while he himself played the part of an earnest investor fully trusting in the Christian purity of a multifarious will-to-gain, asking his financial questions as a pragmatic steward—without once touching upon the ownership side of PAR's equation. As DeCamp is wise enough not to lie about facts or immediately incipient events, in the end we profited by a few new tidbits that helped guide the picture I'll be offering you in my Disquisition (q v).

The pretext and agenda of our conversation was of course the Aggrandizement report that had spotted Parity as an obscure closed-end investment trust available at an inviting discount. Father Lucey made much of the fact therein brought to attention that PAR had already distributed to its stockholders, in addition to the usual cash dividend, almost two thirds of its shares in Financial Usufruct, Dr Capstick's Byzantium. Would it be reasonable to hope that Rome in the coming year would spin off to PAR's stockholders its last twenty-five percent of FUI?

"I think we've been rather generous already. The Aggrandizement Report didn't mention that Parity and Usufruct have been very closely associated for many years. Usufruct still owns half of Management Services Corporation, which maintains the office and pays all our salaries at 103 Smart Avenue . . ."

This indifferently creative contrivance to throw flour into the eyes of amateurs, who were only asking the same questions that professionals ask about Parity's corporate mysteries, wasn't even peripherally enlightening; but the fact he adduced—footnoted in every quarterly report to stockholders—was certainly evidence of the marriage between PAR and FUI. Management Services, wholly owned by the two investment companies, is nothing but a paper corporation specially created to allocate the shared costs of executive overhead: an apparatus whose neutrality (contingent upon the rationality of the imperial pair) is obviously crucial, but whose intrinsic value is so nominal that the net tangible assets claimed by a 99 percent owner would be negligibly greater than those of the minority interest. Whether PAR would now be getting and paying for an unequal share of its ministrations (including the executive services of Halymboyd and DeCamp themselves, other corporate officers, the accounting staff, and the general secretariat), now that the balance must have been altered, was a small point of conversational obfuscation that left begging the question of incestuous divorce, separation, annulment, capitulation, reinvestment, or mere redistribution of entailed property. He was legally obliged to turn aside any speculator's request for inside information. Even so, as an innocent, I for one might have probed for managerial clues if I hadn't heeded my tutor's behavior as a hint.

For Father Lucey cheerfully accepted DeCamp's evasion, and without resentment shifted his ground. "Do you know Ambrose Merlin?" he nevertheless then asked, serving notice that there was a method in his madness. In the tone of his voice there was neither frivolity nor impertinence, nor yet indiscreet seriousness! It was as if as inconceivable that an honorable man like Hamilton DeCamp could conceive the suspicion of being suspected of vulgar manipulation as it was that Father Lucey could be animated by any such suspicion. Yet I confess that the very notion evoked in my mind the outrageously inappropriate proposition that it's useful to have for friend an influential public analyst capable of pointing out the present if not future worth of one's saleable securities. Did I only imagine a hypersensitively deepened flush flickering across the exposed zone of DeCamp's ravaged forehead?

"I don't think anybody knows him well." he dryly replied. "Somebody told me he lives all by himself in a lonely old farmhouse out in the Pequod hills, with Baskerville hounds and quicksand to keep out bad influences. But once I spoke to him on the phone and he sounded sensible enough. My policy is to take no more than one call a year from each of those fellows."

In the effort to rescue Father Lucey from DeCamp's displeasure (if such it was), I sheared off with a non sequitur meant to keep the game going, blurting out my perfectly natural curiosity about a topic he had somewhat unnaturally chosen to ignore, although the point that we were from Dogtown must have occupied his mind from beginning to end. "Were you with Parity when Jason Anacoluther was Chairman? He seems to have settled in Vinland for good."

"Mr Anacoluther resigned just before I joined the company. Took over Arthur Halymboyd's old place up there. I understand he always preferred Botolph to New Uruk. I sometimes envy the Fate Street crowd. In my cruising days I was so charmed by Cape Gloucester that I often thought of relocating. But nowadays I never seem to have time to sail that far."

It was interesting to learn that Jason and Arthur Halymboyd had not so absolutely severed communications that they couldn't conclude a private real estate deal with each other. As if this was exactly the information he'd been awaiting, Father Lucey beamed at DeCamp like a deferential junior alumnus. Against the bright afternoon light of windows two stories high his translucent ears stuck out from the narrow nearly naked white scalp like a hayseed's.

As we were finally leaving the Club, I asked DeCamp bluntly as ever if he knew my new acquaintance Owen Leary, owner of Tractor Distributors in Charter Oak. He looked at me thoughtfully. Perhaps he was suddenly brought to reflect that grubby businesses in provinces forgotten on Street and Curb were the ultimate sources of his noble livelihood. "A very fine yachtsman. Won the Guyana Race last year. New Uruk to Nieuw Amsterdam: neat piece of navigation. He's been our Honorary Commodore several times. Also a marvelous tennis player, and a good hand at bridge; but won't touch a golf club! Wonderful family he has too. His daughter just had a lovely wedding at the Old Haven Yacht Club. Married Dr Capstick's nephew. . . . "

So it is that one learns a thing or two in the byways of an arms-length lunch with someone whose guard is not infallible—or whose method is too subtle for immediate detection. His championship of Owen Leary's talents was so warm—compared with the temperature of his other commentary—that Father Lucey and I afterwards agreed it might have been either to assure us of his tolerant respect for Catholicrats and Petrine Scholastics or to imply his alignment with the Capstick party, in which case he was unlikely to be representing Parity much longer—leaving us further to deduce that he is no longer privy to Halymboyd's strategic plans. Yet I wonder if Father Lucey reads too much into DeCamp's words when he takes them as an innately honorable gentleman's subconscious apology for having been so reticent with his artless guests on other topics.

In the view I expressed as we were driving home, DeCamp's

message was perfectly conscious and deliberate, but more of a warning than an apology. Yet now I think I may have been too much under Father Lucey's influence in discerning any message at all. I would be the last to scorn psychological inference, but managerial experience teaches that all linguistic behavior is modified by chance and lapse. Many an artifice, unconscious or not, exists only in the mind of the detective.

In any case, between then and now we've been through several waves of self-doubt. After lunch, taking leave of DeCamp out on a broad sidewalk of what was left of Gansevoort Hill (whereon Smart Avenue rises nobly from Vanderbilt Station, which is still my favorite building in Ur), I had been disappointed that we weren't invited back to see more of the combined headquarters on the fourteenth floor of the building jointly owned by Parity and Usufruct through their 100 percent control of the Realization Corporation of Atlantis. But that night, forgetting our serendipitous successes, which we would have missed by adopting a shrewder more cautious policy, and without which our uncertainties would have remained less defined, Father Lucey cheerfully criticized himself for the imprudence of having been seen there at all—not only seen but also introduced to two or three of DeCamp's colleagues as we'd waited for the elevator before lunch. It was bad enough, he said, to have his name in the secretary's appointment book. He had rashly associated himself with one of the dissident Turks—whether Young or Old!

In my indicative moods it's easy enough to see another's paranoia in suspecting suspicious intelligences all around one's own funny little strategems! Of course there's always a chance of being watched. But what I merely allow for Father Lucey is likely to assume. The information of the District is so detached from life—its systems are so far abstracted from matter and sweat—that schemes of espionage and counterespionage, if not literal conspiracy, are as easily sketched as castles in the air. In these cases the difference between simulation and action is merely money, which anyway has no mass. And the difference between appearance and substance is so subtle that a man like me can have a good time close to the seat of power (or close to the luncheon seat of one close to the seat of power) without so much as being asked his alma mater!

Still, "One hand washes the other." Why did DeCamp take us to such a good lunch? If it wasn't merely to indulge his own appetite, we provisionally concluded, it was to neutralize a potentially inconvenient enthusiasm on the part of clumsily inquisitive stockholders at a moment of corporate transition as delicate as the old consummation it was about to annul. Instead of responding to our conjecture that Halymboyd was synthesizing an integrated industrial organism, this family attorney, perhaps now representing only the wife, had expatiated upon some of Financial Usufruct banking and insurance holdings, which obviously had no such destiny. And maybe he wishes to be free of his entangled position as Janus-lawyer before dealing with any eager new faces, whether friendly or hostile. Probably his sole purpose was to put us off without either encouraging or antagonizing us, while dispelling our scruples at any conceivable prospect of sailing with him to Byzantium.

But on our part the objective wasn't sole and it wasn't unified. I didn't know what Father Lucey's was, yet I now realize that I'd lost sight of mine in linking it with his, after having been the one to draw him into this beguiling syndicate of speculation!

Dictated 21 Sept 60

Not unlike most investors, I believe, we spoke with Hamilton DeCamp as if we knew what we were talking about when in truth we had only the haziest notion of the interconnections among black boxes, to say nothing of their contents. We were only aware enough of the reports to be confused.

For instance, some entities in the Parity patriarchy seemed to own shares in other entities that owned shares in the parent, and some owned shares both in their subsidiaries and in the entities that their subsidiaries owned shares in; and in a few cases the coopted corporations of the clan owned shares in the parents and grandparents of PAR itself! One wondered if the intellects of the co-emperors (Halymboyd and his erstwhile tanist Capstick), as well as of their expert palatines, were like those of angels, grasping with precision and clarity, simultaneously, the entire structure that is publicly documented only by the congeries of S E C [Form] 10K reports filed severally over time with the stock exchanges, each prepared exclusively from its own uniquely prehensive point of view.

At any rate, English words and Arabic numbers cannot reconstruct what Halymboyd may or may not have envisioned in the making. It takes a graphic scheme like Caleb's. If only we'd had his beautiful chart before we talked to DeCamp! Our comprehension of imperial affairs might have shocked him into confidences or useful introductions. At the time, alas, our only weapon was the implied possibility of taking a significant position in the PAR market, with the proxy of the Trustees of the Classic Order of the Vine as a star of unknown zodiac.

It may as well be confessed right here that Caleb's map—a compendious crystallization of all current data—has become the table of contents, the index, and the bibliography of my Disquisition, and the armature upon which all my discourse hangs. He's a laborer worthy of his salt. I praise him to the housetops for the way he has organized on a single sheet of paper (though so large that it must be rolled) all my essential raw material. My gainly essay, three or four months from now, will be founded upon his comprehensive mastery of the ungainly details.

The amazing thing is that he has drawn up this cabal of colored lines and circles without understanding very much of what they represent in financial terms. It's unnecessary for him to interpret his structure for bankers. In New Uruk he gleaned what I had missed in the 10Ks, and revised my card file. On the way home Father Lucey and I were given no hint that he contemplated a diagram of all those names and numbers. I hadn't told him what I wanted—partly because I didn't know, partly because I hoped not to inhibit or repel his peculiarly creative motivation (which I give myself credit for divining in advance); but I'd half expected him to convert the names and numbers into many pages of dreadful paragraphs and tables. Back in Dogtown, when Father Lucey dropped him off at his house before taking me back to the Van, I was still wondering if his employment had been nothing but an interesting waste of my money.

I hadn't fully realized what can be wrought from reality's blooming buzzing confusion by a noetic psyche. Two days later, having extracted numbers without understanding the terms in which they were imbedded, still undomiciled in the culture of money, he unrolled before me the 18 by 22 sheet that he'd worked on all night at home. He said it would have been easier to read if he'd been able to find a larger piece of graph paper. The grid was used merely to align the layout; it would be impossible in a single such document to represent in proportional sizes all the disparate quantities of dollars and shares in which the relationships of capital are measured—as he had found to his disappointment, he told me, when he made a first hypercartographic attempt to calculate, calibrate, and spatially deploy his countless diameters! But never had I seen such an ingeniously composed nosegay of variously radiated circles: a map of unequal blossoms intricately interconnected by ligatures of straight wire—gossamer diagonals of ownership far more truthful than the rectangular lines of authority on militaristic organization charts.

The circles are of three or four different sizes, PAR itself being the single largest, two thirds of the way up the center of the paper, with the lesser companies asymmetrically arranged at various distances down and across the field below. Above PAR are small circles in simpler but redundant configuration showing the entities of primary possession through which Halymboyd and Capstick exercise their unequal control of the PAR nucleus—as of six months ago, the latest date for which the Curb files are as complete as they'll ever be. Parity and its organelles are in red. The early stage of mitosis is clearly evident from the greenness of all circles and lines centering upon the FUI alter-egg not yet extricated from the mutual bonds. There is also an intriguing strain of blue that stands for the Arnheim interests (of European emanation) in which and with which Parity shares some investments. At first glance I was dismayed by the unfamiliar picture, but from it (after a few minutes of holding my tongue) I grasped the Parity enterprise in its entirety, as a Gestalt that I could never have formed from long alphanumeric scrutiny of the documents.

Until I saw his chart I had been inclined to regard Caleb as an overeducated clerk somewhat too scornful of common practices. And even now that I know his talent I still feel sorry for him. He's reached the age of twenty-five with no definite career, no cathexis in the business world that he's apparently drifted into for lack of a profession. And on our return to his tall white house next to the cemetery near the railroad station I was witness to the fact that his covert love for Ibi-Roi was as vulnerable as Ibi's overt love for him.

Caleb had left Ibi in care of Gloria Keith the landlady, of whose family it seems the dog is well beloved. "I sometimes help her out with the rubbish and things like that when Dexter's away." Caleb told me, blushing. "She likes dogs." I would have been glad to catch another glimpse of Gloria when we paused there on the opposite side of Cod Street just before dark on a fine evening; but none of the Keiths were to be seen.

The noble animal lay on grass above the sidewalk with his nose on his paws as he inspected the whizzing traffic with sadly swiveled eyes, favoring the cars into town from off the Massachusetts Felly. But he'd been watching long and his hope was low. At first, distracted by a spate of decoys, he didn't notice that our car slowing down across the street was the one that had taken Caleb away; but all at once he raised his head like a chief, displaying the broad mane of his chest, his pointed ears directed like radar antennas at what suddenly seemed to be just what he'd been looking for in all his spare time for two long nights and days. Yet he'd been fooled before by the parking of power-cages, and for a moment he made no motion. When the expected one started across the the street—a figure whose movements looked familiar—he stood up in cautious interrogation, and I glimpsed what a handsome dog he was—not gigantic like an Irish wolfhound but greater than a wolf: perfectly suiting his name but quite unconscious of the phenomenal contrast he made to his scrawny unprepossessing master.

Who as we were approaching had joyfully pointed out to us "There's my Ibi!" But as soon as we'd slowed to a stop he cried out "Oh my God!" in a rising voice of alarm, and scrambled out of the car on the street side before it had come to a stop. The dog's tail was waving hard. "No!" Caleb screamed, dropping one of his bags and raising his right palm toward the dog still hesitating across the street. "No! Stay! No! Stay where you are!"

There had been a lull in the traffic, but now kilroys from both directions were entering the broad reach in front of the house. Just as the dog bounded toward Caleb, a comet of joy mindless of command, heedless of safety, Father Lucey gunned the black Nicolet broadside into the middle of the thoroughfare, curving leftward as if to make a 180 turn in the face of dual onslaught. Hardly across the center line, however, he swerved back to the right lane and dropped to proper speed. The feint was effective. It slowed down the two oppositely approaching trailer-trucks in high gear that were about to pass each other in front of the house.

In two seconds Caleb was safely reunited with the ecstatic prince, who whirled and surged around him on the Keith lawn like a fuscous circle of waves at Eddystone Light. As we dipped out of sight to cross the tracks Ibi-Roi was racing around the front yard in curlicues of joy, bowing to his man at every turn, teasing and laughing and weeping like a foolish puppy relieved of all anxiety.

With a trembling sigh I expressed my admiration of the priest's impulse and envy of his reflexes. "That was quick thinking." I said. "You're a born sky-pilot!"

"I'd never be an ace. It was my fault in the first place. I should have turned around and parked on their side of the street. I thank God for correcting me. We're not supposed to believe that animals have souls, but it seems to me that the love between Caleb and Ibi is perfectly Christian on both sides." He laughed lightly, as if ever confident of grace, and returned to other matters. But the next day I heard from Caleb that as soon as Father Lucey got back to the Laboratory he telephoned his fervent apology at great length and asked for Ibi's forgiveness.

That incident was especially remarkable because Father Lucey is not himself interested in any species but the human. And even at that, his service to God's noblest creation, if I'm not mistaken, centers upon devotion to Father Duncannon personally, to whose wellbeing all his strivings are dedicated. He trades in the market to support the Order because it is Father Duncannon's life-work. I believe he is thinking only of his Superior's personal happiness when he says that the object of his stewardship, having regained the Depression losses of what used to be Father Duncannon's private fortune, is to make the capital grow at three or four times the rate of national economic growth, after meeting all the Order's expenses, thereby contributing to the eventual redemption of the world, while taking upon his own head any blame for the usury entailed.

It's my impression that he's always practicing and experimenting with his defense against that charge of usury, and he enlarges his freedom to do so by making jokes about himself as the C O V ' s official casuist. "We share the risk. We don't stipulate a rate of return. I never buy bonds or even preferred stock. If I exploit the economic system of the fallen world, at least I don't do it smugly and safely! If our profits are greater than some arbitrary standard, it's more like gambling than usury! The work of the Order can't wait. Of course I admit that my moral scruple at conservative securities is reinforced by temperamental impatience, perhaps a fault with which God blesses me lest my other frailties be too sorely tested. Yet I like to make investments that are productive—that is to say socially useful rather than merely usurious."

I rarely challenge him, but at that point I did remark that although he and his trading friends sometimes took notice of Net Asset Value they seemed to have little interest in yield. "If you're interested in your own productivity," I asked, "shouldn't you measure in terms of overall R O I ?"

"Oh but I do—in one form or another! I speculate on future yield. With an investment trust Net Asset Value is a reflection of composite opinion about future profits of the component parts."

Of course this ontological conflation of cash with paper profits is what makes the system work, like the physics of complex numbers, where the mixture of real and imaginary quantities is pragmatically indispensable. Many a tangible property—castle, swimming pool, or gentleman's horse ranch—has precipitated from illusory concoction. I only said I hoped at least that Arthur Halymboyd's blend of values was not deliberate malarkey, notwithstanding the suspicion that PAR's holdings were undervalued by market standards.

"Even classical usury," he replied, "is nothing but a recognition of the fourth dimension of capital. To leave time out of chrematistics is as absurd as to omit it from physics. In anticipating gain one merely recognizes the future aspect of Relativity as well as the historical!"

In the end we both always laugh at his hair-trigger defenses and eschew the deeper arguments. When I'm with him I find myself less and less concerned about products—about what their market value represents. When I asked Caleb to show Father Lucey the chart, at the hour we'd become accustomed to seeing him in my room on his way in to the Botolph office, his enthusiasm for that pretty picture was abstractly aesthetic. My assistant's graphic compendium is incomparably useful to me in setting boundaries to my present inquiry; but for the Father Economist, bearing a responsibility that immerses him in the welter of technical possibilities on all stock exchanges and over-the-counter, it proved to be the only possible lure to a fundamental interest in this "special situation". He was as elated by the chart as Caleb must have been at his acquisition of Ibi-Roi.

After poring over it for a full ten minutes (perhaps all that he'll ever require) he straightened up with an air of decision. You'd think something new had just taken place, visible to second sight alone. "That settles it!" he said. "I thank you and Caleb for the most extraordinary assistance. And I thank you on behalf of Father Duncannon. I believe that you have furthered the work of God!" And with beaming solemnity he shook the hands of us both like an envious sovereign as he decorates a couple of field officers for having proven themselves in the heroics of war.

"Why, what are you going to do?" I indiscreetly asked.

"I don't yet know what I'm going to do." he smilingly replied, taking a couple of turns around the room in loping strides and staring at the floor in dramatic excitement. "Except that I'm going to start buying more Parity as inconspicuously as possible. Very conveniently, it happens to be dropping. I'm going to watch nothing on the tape but Parity and its present or future affiliates! Meanwhile I've got a lot of thinking to do. Perhaps after Father Duncannon has approved my plans I'll call you in Londonbridge. There may come a way to repay your generosity in sharing this brilliant analysis of the Street's most quietly notorious mystery. I hope I can reciprocate in an equally solid mode!"

Does he think I'm about to take a plunge with him, in the courage of my academic convictions? Well, why not—come to think of it—if all still looks well when my Disquisition is finished! I may be an expert by then. Making money out of this project is an unlooked-for incentive! I'm no Caleb Karcist, to be content with intellectual speculation. Maybe Father Lucey can further the work of Raphael

Opsimath too, by introducing a more existential pique into the study of Parity—just where this humanistic account of it leaves off!

Which it does herewith. I'll be lucky enough if I find time to start and finish the Disquisition itself: there will certainly be no leisure for continuing this self-explaining narrative. That laborious construction will be far less weightless than Father Lucey's transactions. If it weren't for the chart—seeing how little leisure the management of Tubalcain leaves me—the inertia of my academic matter would be well nigh insuperable!

I'm taking it with me, since I paid for it, but I'm leaving with him a rather splotchy black-and-white photostatic copy, reduced in size and clarity. In my own hand I will annotate all the circles on the original with locations of corporate offices and principal plants in order to survey PAR's geographical penetration of the economy. That exegesis should satisfy my mentor that I'm not a merely passive consumer of images. It only remains, while I'm still in this literary phase, to adopt a title for my banausic thesis that will disarm the liberal artistic mind. I propose "DAEDALUS OR MINOTAUR: An Arthur as Postfabulous Artificer".

cc: I. Charlemagne
RO:i

SECOND MOVEMENT

1
LORE
OF
THE SAINTS

In breeding as much as they dared after initial marriages with aborigines, Brendan's abandoned sea-monks strove to retain their Celtic culture even if their Christian learning faded. By settling at the very heart of Glooskap's Camp (instinctively withdrawing from a seashore vulnerable to raiders) they unmindfully profaned the interior upland of that god; but after a few years, the god having refrained from striking down the white strangers, various bands of Naturals had resumed their summering at Nama-auche and accepted barbarian occupancy of the divine precinct as itself an act of god.

[Caleb Karcist was acquiring Dogtown history from a series of columns in the Nous *by his landlady and by locally educated contributors.]*

Simply by staying where they were, repeatedly approached by encampments of various fishers and clamdiggers, the Irishmen had their pick of nubile girls and widows, most of whom were quick to learn a wuthering Gaelic. But after the first generation or two the Irish-Natural Irindians grew partial to their own acculturated women. Halfbreed married halfbreed. Pure Naturals were taken to mate only when the population of sexual valences was uncomfortably out of balance, or when passion overruled reason in cases of idiosyncratic attraction. The unlucky scions too ill-favored for their own kind but unwilling to labor in celibacy were free to join roving mainland tribes, if they didn't kill themselves with vice.

The Celtic blood of these founding brothers from across the sea had thus diminished from the half to perhaps no more than a quarter by the time Thorwald Ericsson appeared, Lief's brother, and the average no doubt further dropped to an eighth or less before it was reinforced by Irishmen Manxmen Welshmen Jerseymen Bretons and other Old Armoricans serving English kings six and seven centuries later.

Yet there never had been a single fullblooded Irishwoman among them, and the Irindian heart craved queens of its own making—an unbroken succession of Perditas. Though sometimes invigorated with alien alloys, Perdita's blood was never weakened. Thorwald introduced a violent tincture into the artery of gynocracy without leaving much trace of the Vikings among common Irindians.

The monks were also dog-breeders, and the wolfhounds they brought with them were both male and female. On almost all occasions they were too big or too proud to mate with wolves or indigenous huskies, but an exceptional Norumbegan strain began to improve their hardiness their independence and their tails, and with the admixed confidence of beauty they were soon governing their own behavior as the colony's dependent but protective corps of fencibles. When mobilized under the personal command of Perdita they were stalwart against war parties from inland nations and white sea-raiders, of whom Thorwald proved the most doughty.

He would as lief have massacred the Irindians and seized their place as merely sacked it and carried them off, for he found the lovely landscape truly a purpled Vinland. The dogs he admired almost as much as Perdita, recognizing in them the descendants of Bran or Skolawn, great twin hunting hounds of Finn MacCool the most feared foe of his forefathers and the only one they envied. In the longship he always carried his own sea-dog, the greatest of his time at stud and battle, ironically baptised Saint Cynewulf—as the unpromising single whelp of a gravid bitch Thorwald had captured in a raid on the late Alfred's subjects, herself obviously derived from the Danish side of Britain, more domestic but no less powerful than the tall dogs across the Irish Sea. Thorwald was a humorous enemy of decadent Anglo-Saxon poetry, and he had been pleased to express his contempt by naming the pup so delicately.

But Saint Cynewulf, born at sea, was misbegotten as an ugly duckling is. He grew larger than his mother, faster, and at least in some matters twice as cooperative. His sire must have been a shaggy working dog of Carolingian provenience. Filiation was usually difficult for mothers themselves to determine in the defenceless marches invaded by Lochlanners and Dani, especially in a species that raves for love and keeps no records.

Thorwald was fonder of his brave war-dog than of any young woman he'd ever kidnapped for his colonies. He probably spent as much time training St Cynewulf as in his opinion the dog's namesake had wasted on religious kennings. But love of the mock-saint resolved his equivocal Christianity. As he lay mortally wounded from the skirmish following his rape of the ravishing Perdita (having mistaken the word *desirable* for *desirous* in what he'd been told of her temperament, and at the same time unconsciously avenging himself upon his bastard half-sister Freydis who had tricked two of his brothers to somewhere in Vinland and killed them there, axing also all their wives and daughters), he negotiated truce enough for his obsequies by promising that instead of sacrificing St Cynewulf, to be buried with him, his men would leave Perdita that heroic dog who alone had saved the Vikings from utter extinction by her pack of giant hounds. He asked to be buried under a cross on the headland (which would be known as Crow Point long before the breakwater was projected from it nine centuries later). Thereafter in Viking memory the dog-place of Vinland was always the Cape-of-the-Cross. And in modern times Perdita's enigmatic dog-call could still be heard now and then at night among the Purdeyville cellar holes.

Thus Dogtown's fame among cynecologists as the source of Viking Shepherds. For St Cynewulf soon made friends with Perdita's proud braches and despite an occasional hitch of inferiority engendered an aristocratic new race in which the beauties talents and motivations of several distinct evolutionary emanations from primordial wolf were anamorphically reunited in complementary nobility under unique circumstances of community and freedom in a Celtic culture. Proving himself an imperialistic ace in erotic dogfights, he won droit de seigneur, and none disputed his priority when those big females came into heat. His loins grafted the new breed, splicing dam and daughter and granddaughter, leaving little creative opportunity at the highest level for native wolfhound younkers, most of whom gradually wandered off inland or died without issue. But St Cynewulf did not compete with his own children, and they multiplied until his genes asymptotically approached the half in all canine blood at the hunting grounds of the fish-place, which was coming to be known instead as the village of dogs.

In late Renaissance times, when Champlain called at this "Beauport" to gather wild rosehips for the scurvy that plagued all French crews, while his shallop was being caulked on the tiny beach of the tidal island later connected to East Harbor's inner shore as Mother's Neck, he found Perdita's leading ward-dog even more remarkable than Perdita herself, though he'd never heard of a white woman anywhere in Drogeo. Yet he was sadly befallen with the necessity of converting that saint into an angel with his own arquebus—not for taxidermic trophy but in accidental self-defense.

This apparently magical casualty brought to a halt the Irindian attack upon Champlain's misunderstood rose-foragers. But his sensitive ear and gallant delicacy revealed themselves while playing the peacepipe with Perdita. Having now heard a little of the native speech, he eulogistically referred to the dog whose blood was on his hands as Ibi-Roi, which was his unstudied rendering of an appellation he took to mean "King-of-the-Place", worthy of the most solemn honors. His plausible transliteration was not far wrong, and it was thereafter accepted locally as one of those dynastic titles that descend through posterity as surnames.

Like that of *Caesar* and *Perdita,* the derivation of *Ibi-Roi* is worth knowing, though ultimately false. Irindian Latin had long grown faulty in ways easily undetected by a French seaman too old to have been schooled by the rising Jesuits. But the French were better anthropologists than other European explorers, and he had no difficulty grasping the Irindian feeling for their situation in an immemorially sacred locus ludi, nor in accepting the genius of their treasureless Delphi (which he'd laconically labeled merely Cap-aux-Isles). He understood that the essential place could no more be named to a stranger than Yahweh to Jews themselves. *Glooskap's Place, Namaauche,* and other demotic toponyms for the aboriginal shoreline campsites were mere penumbral periphrases for the name that was unspeakable either because it had no vowels or because any utterance of it was regarded as promiscuous. In their remaining Latin the Irindians had devised for the place proper a pronoun as generic as the Naturals' noun Ishi, "man" (which was used without particularity to conceal their given names)—a sound which happened also to have been similarly used by Eberews and prehistoric Celts.

For Perdita's people were not satisfied with Indo-European discriminations of the third person. Their peculiar place could hardly be referred to as *he she* or *it*. Being so far removed from Irish centers of learning there was no one to protest the formation of a fourth personal pronoun from the Latin adverb *ibi*. The ibicity of Glooskap's Place was not to be characterized by any of the three sexes, and in its (ibi's) intensive there-ness this sempiternal locus of unlikely intersections belonged in a category decidedly less psychical than the mobile and ephemeral *you* and *I* or *we*. But the locative pronoun *ibi*, invariant in all cases yet as unique as the place for which it stood, was of course rejected only a little later by the supervening strangers in sheer Pauline bigotry against everything Natural, Irish, or Scholastic, and therefore did not enter the English language.

What a pity that our speech and writing have never enjoyed the pronominal precision for which a concept of historically identified space cries out! It's a sloppy expediency to slough off the burden onto the feminine simply because that gender may seem grammatically underloaded, as we do in indicating such entities as fatherlands; the neuter third-person singular is ridiculously indiscriminate; and the masculine pronoun would be absurdly catachrestic for a stamping ground of matriarchy. But at least one place in the Milky Way of places has claimed the right to a topological "gender", though it's no longer more than vestigial.

Under the rule of the English colons, in contempt for everything French, Champlain's pronunciation of the one derivative proper name was scornfully altered to Ibi-*Roy*. Under the incentive of a bounty, Viking Shepherds were almost totally extirpated, as sheepkilling "wolves". But loconymic kingship was revived and preserved in its original spelling by the heraldic documentation of the modern Viking Shepherd Society, scriveners and notaries to the surviving nobility.

The occasion of Champlain's appellative bequest troubled his dreams thereafter. Except for his later battle with some Iroquois on the Nether Land side of Lake Van Luck, it was the only time this rather mild French imperialist had any real trouble with the Naturals—or any sense of personal attraction. The braves who placed themselves under Perdita's command at the time were from the nation of Mahicans (the "man-eating" Mohawks), just then taking their turn at the Algonquian fishing site. At the sudden appearance of the Great White Father's winged village they had besought the protection of Perdita and her otherwise irenic Irindians (who despite the disquieting agitation of their dogs believed that as invisible highlanders they had little to fear from preternatural raiders).

The defenders having taken to the warpath, Champlain, seeking fresh water, was obliged to turn them back with an an ambuscade distasteful to himself. It was that one lethal thunderstone flashed at Perdita's leading saint that broke their hearts for the nonce, and immediately brought repentance to the heart of the godlike stranger, whom they nevertheless propitiated with all the peltry they had on hand. Champlain sadly left "Les Chiens" in peace as their funeral procession mounted the hills to burn Ibi-Roi on the ashes of his ancestors under the loftiest of the boulders set down by the last glacier. It lay split asunder on overgrown ledge as if the hand of God had flung it down against the granite sternum of a Titanic sarcophagus. The cape's breastbone was not then bared to the grass by woodcutters and cows, but the towering gray jag of cloven tooth was nearly as smoothed as it is today by geological weather, scarred by sky-knives and opened like a whale's jaw by the tiny prisings of repetitious frost.

Something of this event, vague and garbled, reached the ears of John Smith, the next European inspector on record and the most effective geographer of these parts, though he never went ashore at this the place he afterwards said he'd rather live in than anywhere else on earth. From his barge, late in the season, pressed for time, with the shore to his lee, he scrutinized the rocks beaches and trees without seeing any Naturals, not to mention Irindians that no Englishman believed in, taking the word of Squanto, his shipboard guide from another part of the coast, that the local tribes had been wiped out by pestilence and famine, and that their dogs had gone wild, living in the hills as a pack and driving away all who would come again for seafood on the shore below; but he did spot a few of the handsome Viking Shepherds and seriously consider a plan to return some day and capture a couple.

Reminded anyway of his own earlier romantic adventures by Squanto's version of Champlain's encounter with Perdita, he wistfully named the cape Tragabigzanda, after the princess who'd freed him from the Turks when he was enslaved on the Black Sea not far from the goal of the Argonauts or from the mountain to which Prometheus was chained.

In place-naming, however, all cartographers gave way to political influence. Prince James, who disapproved this penciled label for its tongue-twisting outlandishness, cleverly responded to the suggestiveness of "Glooskap's Castra" (with which the sub-location of the Nama-auche midden was mistakenly tagged on the chart he was shown) by strongly suggesting that this conspicuous North Parthenia promontory be renamed to flatter his worship the king-making

Archbishop of Gloucester. He was unaware that the Hispanics (who still fecklessly claimed "North Poncedeleon") had long since named it for Saint James!

As for the eventual name of the settlement there, its origin at about this time is lost in the mist of merged and conflicting doubts much too pondered. Certain it is at least that although none at all appeared on the dense and careful map for the first three editions of the Admirall's *General Historie of New Armorica,* the site was shown as "Dog Towne" in later states of the engraving, prints of which were used by the Casterbridge Adventurers when they obtained their royal patent in the name of Elizabeth herself.

Some say the by-name was slipped in ex post facto by John Smith in order to discourage planters from choosing the Eden he meant to return to, by hinting at haunts of diabolically socialized were-dogs far more parlous to Christian souls than a population of merely voweling wolves or lions without the barking ability to consonate fatally cunning coordination, seeing that they'd frightened off even the Natural brothers of indigenous predators. The first English farmers, unaware of the Irindian remnant lurking in the interior like the Sidhe of Erin, lacked not the courage to assay this terror; but they did lack Smith's creative imagination in adapting their georgic vision to such rocky woods, and after a brief trial they confessed the place unfavorable to their ambitions, moving down the coast to thicker soil at Bethsalem, whence they could also seek out Naturals as objects for the Word of Paul. That left Dogtown to be occupied by less evangelical Englishmen more willing to extend their toil to fish game and timber.

To these permanent colonists, who still didn't believe in the Irish presence but were somewhat disquieted by barking saints with curled tails, the granite that set the shape of Cape Gloucester and made its landmarks was known as "dog-marble" in a belief that the chthonic rock had been discolored and hardened by dog piss. The great cloven Marking Stone had still not been reached by the settlers' peripheral clearings, nor its part of the forest yet allocated as a woodlot. Its domestication was to require nearly a century, and they knew nothing of its monumental significance as the venue of Mayday Eve's cynods; but its site happened to serve as a natural trivium for paths connecting the three settled ridings of the town, from Churchhouse Green to the northern shores of the east and the west. (The sulphurous-looking waterline of uric acid all around the base has since been almost as blackened, by reaction to the waftings of combustion, as the tidal strata on rocks of the inner harbor.)

As the forest was at last converted into a common weald for the pasturage of cows and sheep in later more puritannical times (when orthodox Separatists had gained absolute control of public opinion), this menhir, apparently having been blasted by heaven and targeted by every leg-lifting saint on the cape, when fully exposed was primly christened Cynosure Rock. The ungovernable felling even of pines branded with the King's broad arrow, along with all the lesser trees sold as firewood for Botolph, left this cynotaph the dominant landmark of a denuded moraine. But it was still hidden from masthead eyes by a rim of copsed ridges, and it was in its shadow that the colonial strangers gathered as suppliants to God when the sails of pirates or Frenchmen were descried in the offing, like their terrified ancestors in Dorset at the sight of Viking sea-dragons.

The surviving saints were housebroken in course of time. The first Ibi-Roi's matrilinear male descent was further blended with the best genomes of Cabotland, Terra Nova, Scotland, and especially Alsace. Yet thanks to an innate sense of caste—and decency in incest—the main Viking Shepherd line had been stabilized for many generations when Richard Tybbot, himself a descendant of one of the first bounty-hunting strangers, applied for formal recognition of the nobly mongrelized race which his family (and a few others of the codfish aristocracy) was culling protecting and educating. It was 1930, and he was the magnate who'd been most enriched by the Crash, so he got his way with the impoverished Atlantean Kennel Club.

Before that national college of heralds could regain the strength to insist upon its standards of purity, Tybbot had endowed and staffed an office on lower Front Street as permanent headquarters for an institution dedicated to the certification of individual Viking Shepherds and to the advancement of their collectively venerable status from parochial beatification to catholic canonization. Such investiture calls for a hundred years of probation, but meanwhile within Dogtown's own purlieus the customary usage of "saint" continued to be tolerated—and not only for the chosen ones but also for all the others of their species.

A Viking Shepherd Society office served the coadjutant purpose of putting to work a few deserving strangers. In those hard times Tybbot foresaw that his home town would be reduced to prizing the pilgrim trade, and in a spirit of bourgeois oblige he was glad to find a way to add to its special attractions. While he sincerely loved the V S saints he kept in his own house, and relished the merit of employing some impoverished clerks, at the back of his mind he expected to gain eventually from a bullish hagiophilia in the national market. When recognition of the pedigree was finally withdrawn in a burst of moral courage at the A K C 's New Uruk curia (about the time of Kristallnacht), there were dedicated V S S members in all states outside the Deep South except New Sweden, where the DuPont family disapproved of ethnicity.

So it was a tribute to Tybbot's eccentrically rugged individualism that the Society held out as a tiny independent—nay, competitive— institute, domiciled perpetually in Dogtown under endowment of the Tybbot Eleemosynary Disbursement Fund and Management Service directed by Frank Bacon the Younger, who didn't much worry about arresting the progression of impurity, for he was aware that the aristocratic instincts of V S saints, fostered by acculturated self-discipline, had flourished on discriminating miscegenation. The Society's free lending library was the focus of its specialization, often cited for its Cynical philosophy, sacred dogmatics, and historical cynocology.

Dogtown's genealogical authority was the Registrar of All Saints, whose records in the office of the Ibicity Clerk went back three hundred and twenty five years, and the municipal Board of Heralds by whom she was appointed, which by ordinance comprised the Reference Librarian (ex officio) and six other representative strangers (chosen by the mayor for staggered three-year terms and confirmed by the Council of Earldermen): a veterinarian, a dog-tutor, a truckdriver, an automobile owner, and two mothers of small children. The Registrar's main duties were to enroll all sacred residents without prejudice, issue their birth certificates and vital tags, and collect their poll taxes. The Board's function was to adjudicate paternity cases and to certify the V S coats-of-arms occasionally drawn up or examined by the Registrar.

In principle at least, a patient researcher could trace any bloodline step by step to its first apparition in Dogtown, as far back as 1623; wherefore, though the Shepherds were now a small minority, their records remained the most voluminous of all those kept in the Registrar's special sunken vault, which had been designed into the new Ibicity Hall in 1873.

According to the usage of pre-Salic Celtic custom (ultimately derived from Sumerian canon law), every successor to Ibi-Roi had been the firstborn legitimate dog of the latest firstborn royal bitch. Though many left town or went to sea, especially in wartime, the males remained generally endogamous. The only incest taboos in Dogtown were Oedipal and Electracal; but usually inbreeding was also forfended by prolonged happy puphoods, for Viking littermates were too familiar with each other to feel much mutual romantic attraction; and for thirty years Mrs Sirius the Registrar, like most of her predecessors, had arbitrarily refused to publish banns not only for egregiously miscegenous engagements but also for any half-blood matchings of degenerate characteristics. She was the strongest personality in public office, with the rasping voice of a kindly bosun's mate, and except when passions ran high her judgments were accepted by all concerned.

These and other rulings were enforced as far as possible by the harried Dog Warden, Sergeant Proctor, the town's most self-effacing conscientious sympathetic and overworked public servant, who tried to absorb into his duties half a dozen functions formerly performed by four or five different departments, whose heads he all now nominally answered to but actually ignored. Paid no more than any other police sergeant, he bore all the legal and operational responsibilities of the following offices anciently established by local ordinance or Commonwealth statute: Dog Captain (originally Dog Constable) and Dog Prosecutor, both under the Chief of Police; Dog Tribune (defender of the saints and prosecutor of persecuting strangers), under the Ibicity Solicitor's jurisdiction; Inspector of the Blessed, under the Board of Health; Canine Agent, under the Welfare Department; Superintendent of Sacred Education (mainly obedience-training), under the School Committee; and Curator of All Animals: performing euthanasia at the scene of accidents and picking up other dead bodies, retrieving treed sinners, and admininistering or promulgating all matters relating to the safety or control of birds, rodents, saurians, reptiles, and otherwise unspecified mammals, for the benefit and convenience of featherless bipeds, reporting directly either to the Mayor or to the Council—no one was sure which.

The reason for this oppressive burden upon one unassisted officer was that the poll taxes paid for the saints had fallen further and further short of the budget for these services, and in any case were about to be entirely outlawed by the U S Supreme Court. Soon after World War 2 the property-taxpayers in full flush of new prosperity angrily caused the several appropriations for those dispersed services to be reduced or eliminated, forcing the consolidation of previously discrete jobs without abolishing any of the mandates. So the Dog Prosecutor, most popular of said functionaries, had been promoted without a pay-raise to the new position of Dog Warden, and all the old positions were vacated on the payroll.

But Sgt Alvin Proctor, despite his erstwhile vigor in law enforcement, surprised everyone by emphasizing, among all his officially conflicting interests, the elements of social equality and sacred rights. His tenure was secure, thanks to great popularity among Cynics (the liberal majority of voters who were willingly affected by dogs), despite grumbling by pilgrim-worshipping promoters of the needle trades and other Puritans that he was betraying their portion of law and order. Also among the saints themselves he was the most generally beloved stranger in Dogtown, notwithstanding the mutterings of delinquents at his dogged pursuits and blessed investigations.

But even this little round man with steelrimmed spectacles and a sharp nose—amiable jailer of the visible elect yet intercessor for saints in the forums of strangers—would not have dreamed of offering to attend the sacred Thing at Cynosure Rock on the high place of Purdeyville heath. In a thousand years not even divine Perdita had been privileged to witness the Walburga Eve parliament of howls, with its Dance of the Night-Mark, at the crowning stone of every anointed Ibi-Roi.

2
CALEB KARCIST'S CURRENT CURRICULUM VITAE

240   GLOUCESTERBOOK

Caleb Karcist 165 ⅓ Cod Street Dogtown, Vd. (Tel) ATlantic 3-2674

Objective: Staff administration or consulting (methods & procedures)
Education: A.B. (Liberal Arts), University of Cornucopia at Hume, 1955
Experience:

7-60 to Present *Business Consultant,* Dogtown, Vd. Assignments in special situation investment analysis and various aspects of organization, methods, and control.

1-59 to 7-60 *Sales Analyst,* Zoroaster Lamp Works Corp. (product: incandescent, fluorescent, and mercury vapor light sources, with national distribution), Bethsalem, Vd. Design and implementation of sales control system, including routine product-performance reports, input/output analysis of field sales force, and comparative efficiency indicators; sales planning and graphic itinerary studies; solution of administrative problems for Sales Manager; design and execution of statistical operation reports to top management.

6-57 to 1-59 *Sales Correspondent,* Vinland Supply Company, Inc. (regional packer and wholesaler of groceries, frozen foods, and paper products to the New Armorica trade, including private brands for the institutional market), Liverpool, Vd. Voluminous sales service and general customer relations by dictated correspondence and phone; expediting and troubleshooting of orders and traffic; office liaison with salesmen and vendors; coordination of sales with warehousing and distribution functions; preparation of material for direct mail promotions and sales meetings.

9-56 to 6-57 *Assistant to Manufacturers' Representative,* Ray Lagniappe Associates (exclusive New Armorica sales representation of 6 industrial and automotive product lines sold through distributors, jobbers, and industrial supply houses), Novantum, Vd. Bookkeeping; order-processing; accounts payable; claims; liaison with principals; customer relations (phone and mail); direct-mail promotion; technical product evaluation; field demonstrations; emergency service calls.

8-55 to 8-56 *Assistant Building Superintendent,* Wine Medical & Professional Bldg. (60 tenants), Babylon Oaks, Ca. Night watchman and boiler engineer. Sole responsibility 72 hours per week.

Personal: Single. Born 3-21-35, Dogtown, Vd.

Memberships: Phi Beta Kappa; Atlantean Society for Optimum Bureaucracy.

3
ACORN
PASTURE

"*Come FORE!*"
At the command Ibi-Roy laid back hollow-pointed eagerly erect ears and came to sit upright before his master with lifted chin, smiling with pleasure at this quotidian session of attention, his brush slowly sweeping the cold dun grass, and allowed the leash to be attached to the pull-ring of the chain around his neck in the depth of his tawny ruff. He was happy to please his god, cheerfully submitting to the interruption of his princely freedom, aware without calculation that the tutoring would soon be over. "Come to heel!"

As docile as a dogface soldier the doughty saint obeyed, stepping neatly to his right and making an about-face counterclockwise, quick as a squirrel, proud of his perfect form, and seating himself again, now by the side of his stranger, at the ready for further orders, but unable to forbear looking up at the face above him with a surreptitious press of his cheek against the heavily clothed hip bone.

But today that dearest of humans was too preoccupied with first-person horror to pay attention to the feelings of his worshipper. As they slipped into the cemetery under the oak trees that bordered the back yard, through their private gap between the rotten board fence and the ruined barrier of piled stones from the original pasture, fear had returned to wither Caleb's zest for teaching. These days the shadow recurred with greater and greater oppression. He now marveled that it ever left him. How could he have forgotten for a waking instant the constant indwelling scratch of the crab at his throat?

Next week he was going to see the specialist and hear the pronouncement that would scientifically translate an idiopathy of acute angina into a doom still incredible. It was true that his mother had smoked cigarettes before conception, during gestation, and throughout his life with her, but he himself had discontinued the habit after no more than three or fours years long since ended. He didn't drink every day, rarely got more than mildly drunk, and then only on pure Scotch that left his head clearer than ever the next morning. Sometimes, especially in college years, he had been careless about salty fried food, and he always swallowed too voraciously, but ordinarily he ate with more discretion than the healthy people around him, and his weight matched his bones. Moreover he'd always done more walking than his peers, and nowadays with the tireless companionship of Ibi he roamed the Cape on foot—some small circuit nearly every day, and once every week or so an exploration across the interior one way or another, learning the variety of its paths probably as few other living strangers knew it in entirety. He was the last of the athletes who still avoided wheels whenever possible.

With the end of the leash raised to the level of his waist in his gloved right hand, elbow crooked, holding the middle of it slack in his left, drawn further back from his shoulder on the working side, Caleb walked slowly over to the cinder driveway and took the northerly fork in dutiful response to the saint's daily prayer for supervision. The cemetery tour had become so routine that he could rehearse the lessons in his most absentminded moods—even wrought with mortal dread. Ibi was learning well enough to graduate any day.

"HEEL . . ." Caleb mumbled automatically every now and then as he abruptly varied the pace in speed and direction to remind the dog of his relative place. It was continually necessary to test the subordination of this natural leader. His compliance wasn't wanting in intelligence: only sometimes still in mental concentration and perseverence. It looked as if he was at last reconciling himself to the follower's role, so different from the duty he'd been spared when the aloof blind man turned him over to this young one much quicker in his movements and redolent of the wide world.

But hitherto the training had been at night, isolated by companionable darkness from almost all distractions save the scents, concentrated upon cueing and sequences. It was now time to test in daylight the saint's self-restraint when under the sway of an instinct aroused visually from beyond the range of smell by the motion of mammals—not only other saints of reciprocal passion and curiosity, and insolently flitting squirrels who seemed exempt from natural law, but also, most difficult of all to resist, sly felines tempting him to the chase. Ibi was so quick and fast that to Caleb's horror (but affected ignorance) he had innocently killed one or two of these provocative sinners, to their astonishment, who perhaps weren't really teasing him on purpose. So far the schooling had more resembled Sunday catechism in the mere desiderata of a creed than successful exercises in the suppression of one's own judgment. At first a regime of unqualified obedience—voice-control without a leash—doesn't sit well with a prince. It was only gradually that Ibi had ceased to dispute the same rules of behavior when invoked during the intervals between these training expeditions.

"HEEL now, HEEL!" Whenever the noble head at his side thoughtlessly surged beyond its proper position at the foremost trajectory of his knee, Caleb slowed down and gave a backward jerk at the choke-collar hidden in the thick fur that was no longer needed to protect the jugular from the teeth of wolves but did serve to muffle the impassive throat against an irritable master's sudden yanks. In the beginning Ibi had been inclined to regard the leather line as a draft harness, or perhaps as a device for him to lead by. Even now it was tiresome for Caleb to keep his left arm alertly cocked with the slack of the leash, biceps contracted, ready to pull back from behind his own axis with a strenuous wrench of his shoulder. Or, more effectively, he would still sometimes stop in his tracks and jerk his pupil back to proper position by main force while repeating several times with scarcely suppressed annoyance and louder than necessary the key sound HEEL. This one word was supposed to prompt an entire pattern of behavior, guided only by the inattentive actions of the superior going about his business, whereby, among other observances, the private would drop into a regulation sitting posture whenever even the briefest stop was made, and in general would never find himself standing still in his officer's presence.

Today Caleb was too engrossed with the mortal craw between his heart and brain—the seat of an occasionally acute irritant of little apparent significance that has unexpectedly revealed itself as mortally chronic—to encourage with praise the lengthening periods of perfect performance. (Praise was the only positive inducement permitted by his propaedeutic doctrine to complement the negative chastisements of voice and noose, seeing that edible tidbits of reward would have fostered the vulgar motive for obedience that most strangers assumed to be the basis of a saint's love. Delicious morsels might well be an incentive for early studies, Caleb allowed, but only at the ultimate expense of disinterested loyalty and love of learning, for the inspiration to which, as advisedly as the elder Montaigne or the elder Shandy, he usually whispered murmured or cooed his approval, with emphasis upon the sound of GOOD as the superlative adjective.) Partly also because of the student's increasingly successful performance without tension or censure, the teacher fell back into his own thoughts. On a wintry gray day, with nothing new in that whole dreary field of mementos mori to extravasate his condensing selfcentered thoughts—not even some fresh horror of broken glass (which he'd long since accustomed himself to avoiding automatically, no longer mindful of Ibi's bare feet as if they were his own).

Mechanically he ran through all the tricks of heeling: unexpectedly swerving, randomly circling or twirling, braking to a halt, accelerating like an alarmed horse just when the dog was complacently attuned to the donkey discipline of neither lagging nor anticipating by so much as half a nose the slowpoking gait of a biped. All the while, with fewer and fewer words, less and less heedful of his pedagogic function, Caleb threaded lanes and paths among headstones and mausoleums mainly of dressed gray granite, up and down the unkempt slopes and curves, skirting patches of ice—only to abbreviate the return course to Cod Street by way of the permanently open iron gates.

Every day he still enjoyed hours of forgetfulness, especially when warmed up with sanguine work, and minutes of statistical hope; but once again, for the fortieth time that day, he warned himself that there was no mistaking his sullenly diurnal sore throat: he had cropped no mere culture of bacteria or colony of transitory viruses. Lodged in his gullet was the essential disease that could never be eradicated as long as human life metabolized. A foul pleonastic neoplasm had insidiously planted itself in harrowings less noticeable than the lesions of a scraped knee, and was now gathering into a formless polyp destined to throttle him at the stem of his existence, at the very node of body and mind. Once more, with pressed lips, he swallowed experimentally, and once more was unable to deceive himself with the faint and evanescent anodyne of speciously edulcorated saliva.

Fear was now and then displaced by mourning for his character. More than anyone else in the world he had abused sweet life in preparing himself to use it efficiently. Too late he understood Einstein's youthful self-admonition not to waste time on inessential learning. Under the ceaseless influence of his academic years, he'd thwarted his proper purpose not only by reading too much but also by slowing himself down to magnify every text in the pedantic mania for appreciating the work of others before pretending to his own—with neither the academic ability to apprehend rapidly nor the academic leisure to apprehend everything. His gullet's malignance was fitting punishment for having too well controlled his God-given appetite, for having rationalized his exuberance, for having fooled himself with study, for having shunned the dissipations of unprepared scholars, for having assumed his False Mask of Milton instead of envisaging Keats. Without longevity, elaboration was a vice.

The discipline of a dog wasn't academic. Like military drill its ceremonial and moral value was ultimately practical. Its parade-ground evolutions were but means to maximum survival. The syntactic elements of motion were not inculcated simply as discrete and separable reactions. Once trained, and the leash discarded, a saint's response to the single command of HEEL, uttered unemphatically and without repetition, without analysis into contingent components or ad hoc algorithms of instruction, would be obedience to a general idea under any circumstances—the principle of maintaining a certain relative position on the left, far enough behind to be aware of the god's every movement without turning one's head, close enough not to miss the slightest guiding sound or tremor of emotion, yet far enough forward to be able to sense danger from the right as well as from the left, whatever the speed or course, while never impeding the will or whim of divinity. This standard formation of parallel patrol had evolved for the convenience of a good right arm, leaving unencumbered space for the use of axe or sword or gun. The left flank was better defended by a supersensitive predator than by a cloak and shield; and if aggression was called for, no squire ever so fearlessly complemented a knight as did this leaping cousin of the wolf.

It is true the militant young saint had aspired to no vow of chastity; yet, though born into the house of a rich man, he had inherited the absolute poverty of his race (an unpropertied dependence upon the lords of the earth); and in his response to Caleb's primary commands (prerequisite to heeling)—SIT, LIE DOWN, STAY, and even (the hardest) GO HOME—he was already dedicated to humble obedience. (Inasmuch as the pupil had emerged from a genetic pool in which the concepts of FETCH and CARRY had never been bred, those bird-dog instructions were still too difficult for the tutor's skill and patience.) But not until he had acquired the habit of heeling under all conditions of boredom and provocation, immune to every distraction—sans leash, sans reproof or praise, sans reward—subordinating his will to arbitrary speeds and courses for as long as the injunction should happen to last, could he be taken everywhere as traveling companion and bodyguard amid the traffickings of mankind. The telic motive for training was to dissolve anxieties of the marketplace, especially those relating to Ibi's personal and social security, by symbiotic adaptation to the culture, rather than by segregation. It was a pity to suffer the pain of unnecessary separation during downtown errands and other excursions to distracting places.

Ibi's safety in commerce with strangers required above all his respect for the lawless ruling class of kilroys. It was Caleb's opinion that these dynamic artifacts were multiplying in Dogtown like freewheeling swarms of fucking fascists. Whether on the road or "down the street", the dog's life could be assured only as Caleb's shadow, flexibly attached, obedient at the speed of light. Their public companionship also depended upon the suffrage of strangers (including Puritans and cat-owners) for the continued freedom of such a formidable animal, and to this end the appearance of polite docility and benign gentility was important politically.

If they were permitted to mingle with the public as comrades, and walk the world together, they could share escapades anywhere, at any hour, without threat to the master's peace from any unarmed living creature.

But what skills a bond of love strength and courage in face of one's integral fatality? A canker beyond the reach of medicine or will was now eating out the very Adam's apple of the elder friend. For the first time it occurred to Caleb that he might escape the grief he'd dreaded by predeceasing Ibi-Roy and leaving the same for him. He suddenly recalled with shocking relevance to himself the painted face of a young Industrial Products Manager, with whom he'd worked at Zoroaster, lying in an open satin-lined coffin like a male doll on display before the stoneless and crossless altar of some Pauline sect in a suburb of Botolph, the air of the flat zinc-and-plywood room stifled with waxed flowers out of season.

Of course now there was no question of studying mathematics or improving his knowledge of other culture. But was there enough time left before the pain reached his brain to finish the only possible proof of the existence of his own thought-experience, which otherwise would vanish from the universe leaving not a single mind any the wiser? Was his head capable of functioning at white heat under the blade of an uncertainly retarded guillotine? Was it possible in a few months of remaining clarity to make up for all the time he'd squandered on mere reading? In a shorted life could Creative Mind compensate like Keats's for the curtailment of learning? Since the death of Yeats there had been no one else to extend the geometrical penumbra of literature.

But his vital column was competent to work only in the sleep of reason. The task of his life was anesthetic. With his face to the wall, would he have the strength to focus his entire Will, as well as merely rational clairvoyance, into a final flare of noetic illusion? Must not the terror of surd extinction waken him with morbid discomfit to the Body of Fate and undermine with truth the most precious hours of his life?

And now of course there would be no sea voyage either. Europe would go by the board—a goal far older in his thirsting soul than the determination of his work. Even the congenital hunger had disappeared. All differentiated desires had evaporated into black mist. When all appetites were obliterated in the approaching close of time, his only hope was for the primitive pleasure of clear thinking and painless breathing. To a dying brain the desire to tread the British Isles and Armorica appeared as trifling as a mania for football. Yet no other satisfaction could alleviate the pain of failure to prove his life.

He was permanently stranded halfway from the Pacific to the shores of the Eastern Atlantic. He would die no further East than the place where his life had begun, halfway from the frontier of his degraded civilization to its orient that he'd yet to see, perishing of thirst on an island he'd meant to revisit only for its cache of history, like a son of the pirate-woman Ann Bonney returned for the treasure of his mother.

He'd be buried within a mile or two of the point at which his umbilical cord had been snipped, but he knew he wouldn't lie in this familiar churchless churchyard. Shabby though it had grown of late, in the last century Acorn Pasture Cemetery had been designated Dogtown's elite alma metronecropolis; but it was a private corporation that no longer offered either lot or stock for sale to an outsider even if he had the stomach to negotiate his own disposal in advance. Despite having dwelt for many months at its salient corner, looking down upon it from the chair to which he was dedicated, and having become intimate with its architecture as the Lyceum of his daily peripatetics,

Caleb had even less claim to a patch of its soil than common folks, who were all his superiors in influence of property family or opinion. He had been tolerated in Dogtown, and perhaps even envied by a few for his possession of the city's most impressive saint, but he could never become a resident of this colony, at any price, though it was newer than its neighborhood and three hundred years younger than some of the city's forsaken burial grounds; for it was already saturated, after little more than a century of realized investments.

Acorn Pasture Cemetery had become the nearest thing to a park for the congested Harbor Ward, and its diagonal trails were shortcuts for school kids. On summer nights it served as a more convenient trysting precinct for motorless lovers than less populated but more distant beaches groves or fields to which they would have had to walk. But in winter, at least when there was no snow to soften the stones and shroud abuses, when oaks and maples were bare with cold and elms dying also of disease, the shrubbery undressed of its concealments—in winter this garden in the middle of the city offered nothing more comforting for cover than the old pasture walls of unmortared field stones around much of the perimeter, interior battlements of granite hoods and head-dresses, several unshaped mastodons of rock left standing exactly where primeval ice had dropped them dead, and ledges like petrified gray whalebacks upraising the land at the rear, where the Pompeian classroom was haphazardly planted with overgrown pillars of salt. In cold weather there was little dawdling by stranger or saint come to stretch his legs or piss; children and erotics only hurried through: but at this hour chosen by Caleb for the first daylight rehearsal most such pedestrians were kept away by school, jobs, or warmer scents.

Although it was a season in which they could see and be seen almost from any boundary of the cemetery to another, they were lucky enough not to notice or be noticed by even one of Ibi's kind. Not that he wasn't aware of individual spoor in whiffs from every upright they passed, all odorless cold and aseptic as they appeared to impervious strangers. Unidentified or specially interesting scents were his greatest temptations for pause or divagation. It was hard enough for a young marker full of joy and energy to learn not to lead the way, particularly nowadays when their time in the open together was so limited that he couldn't agree it was best spent in redundant schoolwork. To have encountered a fellow saint without breaking off the spiritual exercise would have been too much for the holiest flesh and blood at this stage of a novitiate.

"Heel." Caleb murmured from time to time with unreliable

patience as he gave a slight monitory tug on the leash with his weary left arm, "You're still at *heel!*", reminding Ibi to slow down or swerve in unison. Self-control was wearing off. The daylight conditions of the world were still too exciting for the perfect resignation he'd attained at night. Three or four times when throttled more violently than necessary by the noosed chain around his neck the scholar gasped for breath without resentment as he backed up to regain his proper position, his curled flag still fanning the air in uncontrite pleasure at the attention, even if it brought him further maledictions. As they resumed at a pensive pace he remembered for no more than a few seconds that his throat would remain comfortable if he continued to refrain from assuming the initiative; and presently again he was unable to contain the tireless energy bridled by acculturation.

It was particularly difficult for Ibi not to concern himself with what was to be seen on the right, beyond the skirt of his master's coat, because he was instinctively disquieted by the fact that the configuration to which the exercise conformed was originally devised for the benefit of dexterous masters. He was uneasy about Caleb's vulnerability as a southpaw ingenuously conforming to a convention determined by the chirality of common hunters and pastors. For not only was the right flank exposed without protection and practically blind withal, but the left's weaponry was ironically hampered by the presence of his protector! Teamwork so ill-suited to efficiency in sinister combat, venery, or herding could not but aggravate the divinity's neurosis as an alienated stranger. Ibi would have preferred to take the opposite side.

He understood however that in a time of peace, without prey to chase, without wilderness dwelling to guard, without sled to draw, without sheep to marshal, the chief of a chiefless people was destined to apply his hereditary quality simply as a private deity's body-servant from whom no economic service was possible and who had nothing to do in his time off but examine the local environment. It was his duty, principal pleasure, and inborn urge to express intrinsically precious love by demonstrating that "only a free rational will can submit or obey".

Nevertheless, for all his insight, the born prince had no notion of his god's feckless insignificance when among strangers without his squire. To the unselfconscious paragon of his species it seemed nothing but an attribute of identification that his man cast less shadow than other adult strangers, and nothing but a characteristic of benevolence that when at home he spent more time alone with his dog than any other owner would. Ibi suspected nothing impuissant in his master's voice, never wondering if it would have sounded frail and uncertain in a parliament. Caleb certainly did not try to conceal the truth from his best and faithful friend (as he did from strangers); but Ibi, blind to the astigmatic judgments of society, failed to see any shortcoming in his beloved person. Whereas in fact the little man felt voiceless in a land of voices, and knew himself to be a sourly colorless lip-pursing spuriosity in the sweet-soup culture, a bitter recusant in the noisy market of sugar cones.

Ibi's illusion often made the heart of Caleb ache with pity. The dog never gave a thought to his own death, and wasn't philosophical enough to question the assumption that his man was not only immortal but also invulnerable and unconditional; while Caleb himself worried all the time about their mutual insecurity in a society more truthfully reflected by its vicious mobs of kilroys than by its forthcoming new Catholicratic administration in Washington (disappointing Noxin of a somewhat more representative Presidency only by the flimsiest possible count).

But political victory and social insecurity were now absolutely overshadowed by the ephemerality of existence itself. For Caleb money was no longer convertible into time. There was to be no future leisure to save up for. Present leisure could no longer be squandered on learning. He must discontinue his study of the accounting equation and abandon all hope of mastering the mathematical theory that might confirm and enrich (if not professionalize) his quasimathematical methodology.

Yet even if there was to be no further development of his genetic potential as a savant, wasn't it still possible to realize his contribution to intellectual evolution by letting the devil take the hindermost, quitting his job instanter, and nailing his theses to some little door? Hadn't he always professed to be going for broke anyway? His money and credit might run out before night descended, but by forcing a quick deficit of time he could hope at least to epitomize like Heraclitus the texts he had in mind for his own tablet shards.

After Rafe Opsimath's departure his nominally freelance job as "Consultant" (a k a "Business Manager") at the Laboratory of Melchizedec and the Mesocosm had been tailored to his wishes by Father Lucey, whose tolerance for eccentricity seemed inexhaustible. It was the only job he'd ever felt comfortable in. The Fathers Lucey and Duncannon were the only employers to whom he'd ever disclosed his motives for earning a minimum wage. But now even with three days a week to himself, and a couple of hours before breakfast on the other four, there wasn't time enough to steal a march on the weird sisters. With perhaps only a few months to go, all day every day would hardly yield the hours of sweet silent thought that even a drastically simplified oeuvre would require—and his vocation lay in the direction of complexity!

Still, if only he could keep a clear head, and a couple of fingers nimble enough to strike the keys. . . .

"*HEEL!*—Why are you so stubborn, Ibi? You know perfectly well what's expected of you. The sooner you do it right the sooner we can stop wasting time on drills!"

Imminent fatality notwithstanding, Caleb's confidence in his vital purpose was precisely the product of nature nurture and accidents as particularly shaped by his own freewill (allowing for his limited ability and for the insuperable inefficiency of conflict between internal and external conditions). Despite the valuable pleasures he'd unnecessarily foregone he could scarcely admit that he had made any essential mistakes in laying and correcting the course that had brought him to his present position. But regret for choices that had led to wastefulness in his reading and aesthetic experience was another matter.

More readily than any other, however, he acknowledged his mistake in never having stopped to learn how to use a typewriter properly. No master had ever made him learn to type, and he had scorned his opportunities to submit to training voluntarily on the ground that it would have taken too much time from his education, and that he could always learn the skill by himself if as and when it became expedient so to condescend. In the beginning he'd fought rearguard for the pen in his left hand as the most sensitive stylus for finely shaping and articulating his reciprocating black symbols on indetermined fields of white. When mystical rationalization failed as a defense of backwardness, and he was sullenly driven to a typewriter by the tide of history, he'd at first given over no more than two digits to the practice of this technology and nothing at all to skill—though oddly enough in the interest of efficiency he had taught himself his own "touch system" for the opposite-hand operation of modern ten-key adding machines and calculators (so that he could use his pencil without interruption while reading sums remainders products and dividends). Even after he'd ventured the use of thumbs and other fingers than the fore, he grudged letters the kind of musical exercises to which he'd put himself for numbers; and submission to the rote of a night-school class in the vulgate would have required far too much time, quite apart from the generic humiliation of "taking a course", which was no longer tolerable at any level to a scriptor with his bellyful of pedagogic subordination. He excused himself from any autodidactic regime with the claim that he was too overcome by the highminded impatience for immediate expression that drove him to script in the first place, as his only means to immortality—whether in whirlwinds of conflicting impulses, in rockets of concentrated force, or in rolling freight trains of irresistible inertia. But notwithstanding this disingenuous exculpation of what amounted to sloth, he never denied that by halting his progress for two or three weeks in order to acquire the inestimably useful craft of touch-typing he might have increased his annual production by twentyfold.

So now, too late in life, he confessed his character irredeemably weakened by an ingrained "hunt-and-peck" habit that he repented more acutely than any of his positive mistakes. He had finally accepted as one of the irreversible changes in civilization the vital fact that no publisher would ever again take up a new handwritten manuscript. He justified his compromise with necessity not by the impure criterion of a reader's convenience but by the prudential need for carbon copies.

From his present vantage, therefore, having accepted the typewriter as an essential instrument, the old balks to his aspirations—such as the necessity of renouncing certain academic options in favor of others, or his inability to read all the books he'd quit the university in order to educate himself with—seemed minor tribulations of human frailty compared with the frustration of his communication between mind and page. The omission of typewriting in his vocational education loomed as large as a blackened radian in the full moon.

The workaday praxis of hunt-and-peck (to which he'd resorted for the first time when there was no admiring girl around to type fair copies of his college papers) had only reinforced its own bad habits—despite his continually renewed resolution to exercise more fingers and to keep his eyes off the keys. But of course halfway measures were no less futile in this selfdiscipline than in attempts to give up cigarettes. And now there was no time for the gestation, rebirth, infancy, and pupillage of true conversion. If successful, he'd be dead before he could surpass the accuracy and speed at which he was already limited. Even now, when his ideas raced—and he trusted that toward the end his thought would approach the velocity of light—with words thronging to the numberless queues in his head, his motor nerves were diabolically confounded by delay, error, and correction; no method availed to juggle or hoard the images and syntagms that clamored for space in his working memory. His head was pressed into use as capacitor or buffer when it was already overtaxed as oscillator and modulator: he was unable to sustain whatever resonance he managed to generate.

Thus in his aborted pursuit of geometry and mechanics—left with little Latin and less Greek; no more than a glimpse of Old English; not the foggiest notion of Gaelic; less than a cuneiform iota of the Sumerian alphabet; deficiency in German; incompetence in French; ignorance of Spanish, Italian, Norwegian, and Russian; nescience in chemistry, biology, geology, natural history, ornithology, architecture, and all branches of engineering—he found his remaining life frustrated by the most serious disability of all. But remorse for his lazy failure to master the world's commonest skill only aggravated his vow of terminal dedication.

His penalty would be levied not against the quality of his desperate accomplishment but against the quantity. Nevertheless, by sheer effort and self-control, could he not mount an arithmetical progression of average daily production? By taking rigorous thought before setting down every sentence, why couldn't he anticipate nearly every revision or correction? Would a constant vision of the Jolly Roger inspire him with sustainable bursts of the superhuman energy to transform imagination from the trigonometric to the theatrical?

Theatrical! Even from the lowest depths Caleb laughed aloud at the notion of his deathbed conversion to dramaturgy! He had been contemplating the metanoia long enough—but his preparation for it had scarcely begun. And under any circumstances of longevity the very proposition that his present self was within throwing distance of a stage production seemed slapstick. It would take a long walk to find anyone with less histrionic aptitude than Caleb Karcist! You'd have to go abroad to find a more timid speaker, or one so scornful of the qualities prized by Atlanteans, so contemptuous of the Limeway culture to which he was ridiculously unequal.

This funny reminder of his singular disaffection cheered him up as he came to the end of Ibi's lesson. "Good good Ibi-Boy, you're my noble pride and joy! Another month or so and you'll be a man of culture." The dog looked up wagging anew his unflagging flag of a tail. The indicative tone was always more comfortable than the imperative or interrogative because it expected no response. His clear brown eyes, deeper and more direct in assurance of loyalty than any human speech, expressed nothing but gladness to hear anything Caleb might say. He then passed the day's penultimate examination by following a sprightly figure eight without once tightening the slack of his leash or bumping against his man's leg, ending with a seated halt, looking straight before him like a proud Guardsman, as if he'd fallen into abstracted boredom at this simple childsplay, pretending not to care that the ensuing final test would be more subtle.

Near the spot they'd started from, their backs to the open iron gates on Cod Street and the gray stone funeral chapel on their left, they were now facing the knolls and monuments they had then circled at the far end of the cemetery, where the trees were more numerous and the plots more interesting. Caleb paused to gaze, affecting to forget his sidekick. This garden of graves had been designed by partners from the metropolis who later became famous in the art of landscape design and whose leader shaped much larger greenways in Botolph, New Uruk, Chicago, and other enlightened environments. Acorn Pasture was one of their earliest ornamental cemeteries, dreamed up under the influence of Divine Humanism to associate green and pleasant things with death; but it was a poor small job in comparison with the original such park, to which Caleb had often been taken as a child, Mount Olive Cemetery in Unabridge, an immensely rich arboretum and botanical garden, where he used to climb the crenelated Emerson Tower on a high place overlooking Norumbega University, Botolph harbor, and the whole Shawmut River basin. Such in truth was the cast of a brief reverie while trying to fool the dog with his stillness, who resting on his haunches betrayed no suspicion of further trial. But when Caleb drawled in his lowest and most casual voice (no louder or more emphatic than a whisper in its dying fall) "Come *Fore*", he found that Ibi had been reading his mind again. Before the second syllable was uttered the pupil had presented himself front and center in flawless form to await the benediction.

Caleb bent down to unsnap the leash. But the dog knew he was not yet released. His silkily pointed ears, ordinarily erect and twitching like gothic radar antennas, were delicately folded back in long soft waves smoothly curled against the side of his head where the fine fur was most satisfying to the fingers of sensuous admirers; and for a moment of suspense, quivering with the humorous expectation conveyed by increasingly rapid oscillations of his brush sweeping the sere grass, he suffered them to be quizzically cupped and stroked by both palms of the beloved comedian bowing over him.

"O-*KAY!* Ita, Ibi est."

Liberated in a trice by the wizard's magic word, Ibi-Roy bounded away, made a vaulting pivot on his forepaws, repeated the cycle twenty feet further along, and sped off in a beeline to violate one of the most scorned ordinances in the ibicity's code by marking the dog-marble of a highliner fishing captain as if he'd had his heart set on that particular stone since they'd first entered the vacant lists.

Suddenly for the first time Caleb was struck with a pang of

consideration for Ibi's welfare from Ibi's own point of view. How would he understand his master's treacherous disappearance? Father Lucy might take care of the undertakers and all that; and perhaps Father Duncannon would accept his books for the Laboratory's library; and there was his mother to think of: but what about Ibi, just beginning his mature life? Would Mrs Keith adopt him? The Keiths had once had a beloved dog of the fetching sort. Were they capable of cherishing and appreciating such a differently educated aristocrat? It would be well to prepare them for the responsibility, or make other arrangements. . . .

"What a magnificent wolfdog!" From behind his back sounded the charming low voice with a condiment of enunciation that might have been British. It was the first time a beautiful girl had ever noticed Caleb Karcist before he'd noticed her.

4
BELTANE
HILL

From her words Ibi-Roi knew this female source of scents to be no Puritan, and he was glad to meet her. He immediately presented himself, to anticipate his master by shortening all courtesies.

"The colonists set a bounty on his ancestors." Caleb replied after clearing his throat. "But wolves don't bark or curl their tails."

"Well he's not a wolfhound either. Nor a husky or an Alsatian. And he's certainly not a dingo."

"Viking Shepherds are bred on Cape Gloucester. My pride and joy."

"Is he friendly?" she asked, though she and the saint were already exchanging familiarities.

"He is now. The only trained dog in Dogtown."

"Can you tell me where to find the grave of Isopel Berners?"

Ibi had never been jealous of Caleb's talking friends; he was presently content to put this novel juxtaposition of human smells behind him and trot ahead in the direction Caleb pointed, making free with all the granite rounds and squares, not at all annoyed to be reexploring familiar territory on forward digressions from their course through the forest of stones, first to one side and then to the other, not without the presence of mind to look back now and then to make sure he hadn't lost his followers, not at all disconcerted that he himself was as often as not the object of attention.

Caleb wasn't jealous either. So limited was his success with women that he'd rejoice in the good offices of any third party while he calculated probabilities and weighed the best tactics for probing his strategic situation. He always needed all the help he could get, seeing that his proportion of failures was greater than most men's even though his attempts were few and nearly always carefully selected. Until episodes were reviewed in solitude he found it hard to believe that he did best when he wasn't trying. But a surprisingly comfortable liking for this first-class windfall soon drove from his mind the premeditation of a third-class hunter. There was no chase. The fearless pard had put herself in hand to start with. The entire burden rested upon the question of what to do to keep her there.

The girl understood that she wasn't much troubling her guides for this trifling service, considering the kind of leisure in which she'd found them. But in Acorn Pasture there were no path signs or other concise means of fixing the residents by address.

Her brow was smooth; her thin humorous lips bespoke intelligent self-reliance, and her lively black eyes gleamed with all sorts of intelligence. But he dared not steal much of a look at the rest of her as they walked toward the wooded ridge at the back of the wintering burial garden where it rose into a grove of oaks and eclipsed the row of shabby houses lining Pollock Avenue three blocks in from Cod Street. In elegant leather boots, long navy-blue coat of military cut with a fur-lined collar, and kid gloves, with no feminine accouterments, she made long buoyant strides at his side—but for spurs and saber, a bareheaded little Cossack with loose black curls—both frank and deferential with questions and answers, neither shy nor brash. Was she perhaps a little too comradely or cousinly to confer upon him the particular kind of companionship he preferred? He kept his mouth busy apologizing for the seasonal desolation and for the litter from juvenile drinking parties in the charming crannies of prehistoric boulders, as if her opinion of him depended upon a defense of Dogtown's civic pride.

At the far end of the cemetery, an irregular barrow of hewn

monuments among natural rocks, bordered by the dilapidated granite wall (incorrigibly breached at the corner by a worn dirt path toward the nearby school), they climbed vestigial steps of roughcut stone to ascend the steepest part of the bank beside bared grooves in the slippery grass where kids dove their bikes and sleds. Hazardous acorns were everywhere underfoot, whole and decapitated, cups and balls detached among musty brown leaves rotting in the frost. Caleb led the last few yards of the way in order to avoid the dilemma of whether or not to offer his hand. His cardinal principle of the first phase was to admit awareness of everything about a girl except her tactile qualities.

Ibi trotted up to glance at what they'd come to look at, a knee-high lump of rusty granite rounded by the glacier that had brought it but otherwise dressed only with a flattened panel large enough to bear the simple chiseled name, already almost illegible from weathering and mossy fungus, nearly overgrown from behind by a blackened bush at the lip of a drop too sharp for more easterly grave sites. But the object was of no importance to him, barely deserving the perfunctory micturition performed without haste or delay before he bounded off again to inspect the latest scents elsewhere.

"Here she is." said Caleb. ISOPEL BERNERS allowed itself neither colophon nor date. "George Borrow's Fayaway! It doesn't look as if many pilgrims come to see her."

"Well somebody left her some herbs. I should think the birds would carry them off."

"See how much space they gave her. She was taller than Maude Gonne."

"More independent too." said the girl. "She would have been a healthy match for Yeats. If he'd lived among gypsies instead of mooning for the fairies."

"The Gypsies never had a literature!"

"Isopel followed an Irishman here, they say."

"In her time the Casbah was full of Salt-Irish. But by the time Yeats got here for a reading in 1914 there were so few Irish of any kind left on the Cape that only three people showed up to hear him. He was so displeased that he omitted all mention of Dogtown in his writings. Of course that left T S Chittering with a free hand. But Yeats still refused to include the 'Three Griefs' in his edition of the *Unaford Book of Atlantean Verse!*"

Yet her interest in the gravestone was satisfied almost as soon as Ibi's. Nor did she pay much more heed to its environment than did Caleb who knew it by heart.

But she was embarrassingly attentive to his desperate chatter as he descended to the bathos of a local dragoman. "It's hard to believe, hemmed in like this by the whole shabby city, but they say you used to be able to see both bays from here. Imagine this pasture when it was still for sheep!"

They turned back toward Cod Street, having paused at the high point to scan the whole field of inert claims upon corporate memory. War veterans wore the boldest inscriptions. The most modest headstones were those of prolific mothers. The more ostentatious sculptures were imported marble angels with broken heads or wings, invulnerable granite obelisks and spheres, Roman and Celtic crosses, curbed enclosures with paved platforms, ceremonial fences of stone and chain, and one tree-tall gothic belfry spire mounted upon a hewn-and-fitted tripod in the precinct of the lately underlain Duke of Gloucester et ux.

"Don't they look like pawns knights and bishops all jumbled together with the royalty after an earthquake?" he offered.

While politely pretending interest in his temporizing smalltalk about the trappings of immortality, even as they scanned each other's manner for the telltales of personal history and attitude, she must have been taking in through the cheerful windows of her soul the melancholy import of the epigraphs they passed, for by way of returning him a baffling clue she made an inductive comment. "What I dislike about cemeteries is the way they insist upon the inequities of life." (He read her lips as frankly expressing the pleasure of his company.) "Look!" she explained. "Babies buried after nine days, little girls dead at fifteen, fathers gone at fifty. And the old maids lasting a century get added to the same tombstone. Or the widow of a young father lives ninety three years and an old maid dies at five-and-twenty. I'm almost that old already!"

Just the right age for him. "In our older burial grounds it was the wives who always wore out first." he replied. "But the thing to notice here is how many old men are cited for nothing else than the two or three years they spent in uniform!"

"Yes. It would be as if a woman's life were remembered only for the time she spent with a man." the girl said. "Poor Isopel! Even at that she probably would have left a blank."

Her remark was encouraging. On the other hand, the more easy a sophisticate's conversation the more crass it is to presume upon her latitude. "There are other famous people buried here." he told her, and then hesitated. "Famous in Dogtown." he added with a grin. "Sculptors, painters, Big League infielders, generals, aviators, solo navigators, ice and salt tycoons, opera singers, philanthropists, schooner captains, fishermen—"

"And druids?"

"Some of these are cenotaphs for men lost at sea. Many are for victims of Dogtown fires. Our newest cemetery across the river hasn't yet grown trees. It already holds too many kilroy fatalities."

"I'm not surprised. I've never seen such bad drivers, even in France . . . But this must be a pleasant graveyard in the summer. Where I live now there's so little soil that they have to scrape the earth up into heaps to make it deep enough. I suppose the Tudor Church used to forbid cremation."

By this time they were back where they'd started from. Caleb had put two and two together with sufficient confidence to hazard a more personal approach, perhaps too late. "You're not English then?"

"My father is. I was born in England but I've never spent more than a year there. Brought up in Australia, schooled in British Columbia and Acadia. I'm supposed to be an inhabitant of Terra Nova. Most of the people there still consider themselves British colonists rather than Canadians. Yet they won't let the Ottowa government change the name of our Province back to the plain English of historical Codfishland. The High Church party wants to keep Latin as the official language, and everyone else is ready to die for bilingualism at the least. But I don't think I can call myself English. I'm a gypsy."

She looked like an ideal one, save that the curls of her hair were short and fine. "Terra Nova's halfway to England!" he exclaimed in admiration.

"Halfway to the North Pole. Do you live around here?"

He pointed to the nearest house, at the end of a residential strip indenting the cemetery along its Cod Street border. "In the garret." From this side view his attic windows were not visible, but the white weatherstreaked clapboards of the first two stories were roofed with his chimneyed gable of gray shingles worn pale by the north wind. The granite block foundation was hidden by a wavily propped-up wooden fence of whitewashed vertical boards, and the ungainly house looked altogether too high for its length. From this angle it was indelicately exposed, like an awkward overgrown tomboy lined up with the demure little properties beyond it, not much less provincial than the buildings he imagined in Terra Nova. "It was once the Apostolic rectory, though this was never a churchyard. There used to be a strip of houses all along here. The others were removed to make this frontage."

"What is there to see if I keep walking the other way?" With hands in her coat pockets she directed her eyebrow down the street to the right, away from the tracks and the harbor.

Caleb's heart hesitated, but it was marvelously well served by his mouth. "Ibi and I could show you two or three interesting things, if you're not looking for pilgrim picture-postcard scenes. Without retracing our steps."

For the first time they looked at each other as if he'd read her mind. "I'd like that!" she said. "If you have nothing else to do."

It seemed to him that though more Parisian than provincial she was too careless of her beauty ever to have cared for the seductive arts. "There's no such thing as anything better to do." he lied.

She watched intelligently as Ibi eagerly obeyed the call, responding to the *Come FORE* command so that the leash might be attached for some adventure out of the ordinary. *"Come to HEEL!"*

The three of them headed down Cod Street, facing the afternoon traffic of kilroys streaming into town from the Squid Circle terminus of the Felly, Caleb in the middle and Ibi on his best behavior walking close to the curb on the left. But very soon, pausing for an interval in the otherwise ceaseless stream of noise, they crossed Cod and turned down toward the river on Coalyard Lane, where the half-industrial streetscape sleeping in the cold daylight below the railroad embankment was as quiet as a livery yard. *"Come FORE!"* Here it was safe to release their equerry from his bond. After a few romping gestures to the playful new stranger-female he assumed a roving patrol, almost always far ahead and ranging from one flank to the other, pioneering the trail that it might please his charges to take he knew not where, ever with an eye on their lagging progress, except when he was briefly too absorbed with special galaxies of scent or wafted whiffs.

By this time she'd asked their names and he knew hers: Bice Picory. "It's for Beatrice. I can't stand being called Bea." Her father was a Royal Navy liaison officer, "a sort of roving naval attache" posted for some time to the big Atlantean radar station at the northern tip of Terra Nova. "For the last six months I've been working and migrating in various parts of the States. I'm a Gypsy on two counts: pro tem, because of coming here in a gypsy truck; but also by blood. Back in Transylvania my mother's forebears made one or two of those marriages—I forget the story."

For the time being her envy of Caleb for the possession of Ibi, which seemed to endow him in her estimation with categorical superiority to truck-owners as well as to gentlemen, nearly compensated for the disadvantages of his inexperience. He suppressed his jealousy of the imperial cosmopolitan past that immeasureably enhanced everything he could see of her with his own eyes and concentrated on offering her the benefit of his commentary, that she might respect his value as a denizen.

At first his chatter was devoted to the purpose of convincing her that the Dogtown Smithy and Iron Works, to which he was now leading her, should be as interesting to her as it was to him. He escorted her past the finishing shop on the rise at the end of the street, two redbrick stories of factory windows lighting the single floor of Brobdingnagian turning-machines, and down a cindered drive to the bulkheaded riverbank where coal barges had once moored to the storage dock, on which an outside traveling crane, now as immobile and rusty as the contents of a junk yard, stood like a set of flying buttresses detached from the sheetmetaled side of the mammoth forging shed. Higher than its roof the railroad flung itself straight across the broad clam flats to lodge upon the island rock with one short leap of the drawbridge, spanning an artificial ravine through which the entire tide of the Namauche valley sluiced navigably back and forth between stilted spiles and bulwarks of heavy timber. The black grid of trestled double track rested in place above the visitors' heads as a slanted lattice against the afternoon sky. It drew their attention to an incipient unveiling of heavenly blue in the overcast.

They went to stand under the lofty corrugated shell just inside an opening at the inactive end of the earthen floor. The umbrageous structure focussed their gaze upon two or three distant apertures of dull orange fire partially obstructed by huge horizontal trunks of squared steel whose ends or middles were being softened for the titanic hammers and presses (now idling nearby) which would reshape them first into elongated polygonal prisms and then roughly into cylinders. Each of these heat or force machines with its own concrete foundation condensed and radiated a separate nucleus in the vast cavern. The broad telluric deck of clinkered oil-soaked dirt gave ample space to paved machinery platforms, quenching pits decked with steel grating, and the imbedded tracks for cradling dollies by which the work stations were interconnected, leaving room here and there for blackened worndown ridges of the Cape's earthbone where it hadn't been necessary to blast them level. The furnaces casting gloomy shadows in the immense clerestoried nave made the whole temple look to Bice like an antique hell with no mortal attendants.

To Caleb it looked like the inverted hollow of a flimsy iron steamship with daylight showing through its seams and with no partitions to divide the engine room from its empty cargo hold. This cracked aerial hull, trussed and rigged like a temporary tropical basilica, was no more weatherproof than a circus tent to keep the snow and rain from hissing into steam on its eternally blowing furnaces and rusting into dust its sporadic earth-thumping machinery. The mammoth skeletal shelter, uncaulked and uninsulated, barely enclosing the dim half silence of a resonant atmosphere, was meant to dissipate a fathomless waste of fossil heat, imported nowadays in the form of oil.

Caleb fell silent for a minute, appalled to realize that most of his guidance would be lost upon this girl from a sunny world of letters. He could hardly imagine what she or Ibi (who'd seen it many times) now saw. As in a Gothic cathedral, the patched corrugated curtain walls bore no weight; the internal architecture of the lightly framed hangar was unified in the upper shadows by a universal crane of cables and wheels which traveled orthogonally its entire three-dimensional coordinate system, defining the whole incarceration. The vigilant cab could move erratically on a bridge that itself rolled on tracks elevated above all the works. Mainly at what might have been called the transept, near the cliff-foot working portal, this dynamic arachnid gathered and transposed the masses within its span that occasionally attracted its alertly faceted eye, punctuating an irrational web of points within the matrix. Aroused to spates of predation, the almost invisible brain glided back and forth on mobile beams, spinning up and down its dangled claw in response to clairvoyant signals of its victims. The hunchbacked cyclops was now fetching some stock at the darkest end of the rectoparallelepiped, calling attention to itself not by any action that initially caught the eye but by the whirring rumbles with which it positioned itself, burdened or disburdened, to raise and lower its massively hooked tackle on six or eight counterspinning loops of smoothly sliding steel cable. Its hunting was ordered in abrupt simpleminded series, with no method of higher efficiency, disregarding the principle of least action in its slavish sequences of redundant motion between long rests, presumably subordinating its own convenience to the invisible direction of some more integrative mind that was privy to the requirements not only of all the organs within the integument but also of intercourse with outdoor units of the larger system. For outside the gloomy shed, on the bluff above, the derricked magnet manipulated the outdoor inventory of raw material and goods-in-process, intermediating between this spider and a smaller one within the steamheated machine shop on the high plateau of the yard.

Such was the forge of Aphrodite's lame husband, where anchors had once been made. But the postwar materials of the smithy were gigantic rather than Olympian, stepped and collared shafts tapered at one end or both, gradually forged from beams two feet square and sometimes nearly as long as the gondola cars in which they arrived. These products were never touched by mortal hands, except perhaps with the cautious pat of a gauntlet to verify their temperature when cold or cooling; but often they were shifted by small chanties of men wielding tools made for Paul Bunyan—such as monstrous antiquated blacksmith tongs with variously shaped prehensile jaws, manhandled by three or four pairs of hands to rotate cherry-red stalks between the earthquaking blows of a colossal hammer, which was not simply dropped like a weighted guillotine but in scorn of gravity driven downward by the hydraulic fist of Thor. Chocked up elsewhere on the ground they sometimes took a week to lose their heat in slow deliberation before they could be hoisted by magnet back up the precipice and trundled on the yard rails into the god's machine shop for final turning, where the more refined crane would lift them in and out of slowly laboring engine lathes.

It had taken Caleb many visits to figure out this scene; but by the lack of enlightenment on the soft pale shield of the girl's face he divined that she was no more interested than the goddess of love in his idolatry of the cave's shadows, which impressed her only as those of brutal undifferentiated powers. If she put her mind to the object at all it was only to seek human forms in the crepuscular noise of combustion. At least he had sense enough to keep fairly quiet after a stab or two at imbuing her with his unnatural vision of the reddened black pits. It was no less futile to attempt intimacy by taking her to a theater of smithies than it was to pique her feminine curiosity by asking her to admire the nearby cluster of gear-teeth by which a small electric motor was able to erect from horizontal to nearly vertical the drawbridge heavy enough to have borne at one time the weight of two steam locomotives. He glossed without confidence, in the colorless effort to carry out his misjudgment in bringing her here.

"You should see this purgatory at night! There's only one man here, checking temperatures. He lets us walk around inside. You can't touch anything, even if it looks cold gray. It's surprising how sensitive one's face is to radiant heat at a distance. Ibi must feel it in his tongue. You should see how he clings to my apron strings when we walk through that iron garden! The watchman likes dogs, but I avoid him as much as I can because he also likes to talk. Everybody in Dogtown wants to talk!"

"Are you a misanthrope?"

"Only a friendly recluse. Schopenhauer says that 'for the most part we have only the choice between solitude and vulgarity'."

"Do you live alone when you're not out with vulgar gypsies?"

"I'm a quasi-hermit." Though wishing to speak of his enthusiasms he hesitated to risk another mistake by telling her about his station in life.

They walked back up the road to its crest in front of the machine shop at the butt of Coalyard Lane. As he was leading her over toward the railroad tracks she interrupted his ciceronage by running a few yards down a hollow to peer into the lighted windows of the *Nous*'s recently installed printing plant. When they had passed it the first time he was talking too much about the neighboring coal pockets and fuel-oil tanks to notice that it was the one artifact in which she had evinced voluntary interest since seeing the orphan's grave. Before letting him show her any more of what he thought was remarkable she made him wait five minutes for her to examine the remodeled single-story brick building to which the newspaper had recently moved from its centenary quarters on Front Street. "That's a new rotary." she remarked of the machinery as she smiled at a couple of old men waving at her through the public inspection window of the quieted pressroom. The tourists had missed the hectic daily run and its distribution from the circulation dock; but the people at typewriters under a modern ceiling of fluorescent tubes in the new office wing were already typing copy for tomorrow's deadline. "The newsroom looks nice too!" she observed with all her attention.

"We have the best news photographer in the country." Caleb boasted.

"I studied journalism at Chebuctu. I've been a reporter."

Caleb's heart sank in disappointment. But only a degree or two. He remembered that she was practically a European, and that even as an actress she would have overcome his prejudice with the ironic charm of her refinements. He also reminded himself that from girls he had once learned to tolerate a little of the ephemera upon which national selfcongratulations were founded.

Before crossing the tracks (having resumed the tour he intended) they paused to watch the magnetic derrick move some of the rusty barkless logs in the courtyard of the Iron Works. His assiduity in pointing out causes and effects had temporarily abated. He didn't mind her giggling at the oversize toy.

Then treading splintered planks laid lengthwise over etiolated ties still pungent with creosote he steered her onto a private road across rusty rails of the siding and burnished tracks of the rubbish-littered right-of-way. She didn't seem to care that her stylish boots were scuffed by the crunching frozen dust.

He took her round the shabby clapboards of Buck Barebones's

machine shop. It resembled deteriorating feed stores on the Great Plains because it had originally been built for the same purpose. It was tall and narrow, with receding unfenestrated upper story, and still moored along its dock side was an overgrown spur of the railroad.

"That business is run by a mechanical genius who's also the most generous man in town. He lets me use his machines free, and even takes the time to show me how, even though it's not good for his cutting tools to get gummed up with wood."

"Are you a woodworker?"

"Would that I were! It would be the best way to earn a living. But I've never been able to get an apprentice job to start with."

"Then you make things as a hobby?" she asked. "Boat models?"

"Life's too short for hobbies. I've only made some special blocks."

"You mean toy bricks? And you don't call that a hobby? It must be fun at least. Or else you've invented something clever."

"In principle a Greek invention: equilateral triangles—only with holes in them."

"What are the holes for?"

"Sockets for steel rods. Among other things the triangles are connectors, based on sixty and a hundred twenty degrees. Real modules are almost all binary, bilateral, or orthagonal."

"Then yours aren't real? When I was a little girl my father gave me a kit like that, to build skeletons with."

"But those were round, and the angular unit was forty-five degrees, an even dividend in the rectilinear system. My little deltas—or you might call them wyes—are more organic."

"I thought they were supposed to be unreal!" She concentrated on his face. "Aren't you a numerologist? Your name suggests as much."

"God forbid! I wanted to make organization charts in three dimensions. And other models of reality."

"So they're not insignificant of what's real! You make molecules."

"Yes. I thought a circle was more naturally divided into three, and then subdivided into six and twelve, than into four right angles and their equal subdivisions."

"Why did you think that?"

Her aroused curiosity was beginning to make him uncomfortable. "From my own contrarieties. They are never simple binary conflicts. My motives never seem to be that clear. The Either/Or polarity of electricity falsifies the complexity. So do mathematical theories of decision making. A whole tree of rational dilemmas is just as simple-minded as the plain double-bitted axe I started with. Three's more truthful than two in analyzing complexities."

"And also more useful in creating them!" She laughed sympathetically, as if he had a rare talent for making her less indifferent to the abstractions under discussion. "But even if you divided the real globe into three it would still spin on two poles and have one equator. How can we help having north and south, and therefore east and west? What could be more natural—and therefore organic—than four quadrants? Not to mention the up and down of gravity, and all the bilateral flora and fauna. Would I see any better with three eyes?"

The two merry eyes now focussed on his thoughts seemed many enough to perfect the joy of a man, but he remained too uncertain of their perspective to risk any of the gallantries that might have escaped his lips enthusiastically. "Please notice that sometimes I've used the past tense. What you saw at a glance eventually sank in for me—that the binary's just as natural as a clover leaf, and more useful than the platonic triad in building things. You see how clever I was!"

"So all that shop work went to waste."

"No. My two-inch trinities are nice and tangible: good solid varnished maple, about a fifth as thick as they are wide. Each apex is truncated to flatten just enough surface for drilling a hole parallel to the face and straight through to the opposite side. And there's a perpendicular axle hole through the center. It's not easy to meet those simple specifications because wood likes to follow its own drift even against inexorable machines; the grain tends to deflect drills at any speed. But when you finally finish a few dozen unspoiled ones it's very satisfying to stack them up as circular staircases or fit them together in a row of alternating apexes and bases: either lying flat or standing on edge they make a beautiful rhythmic wall of holes and niches."

"Then they're play-toys after all."

"Well, you might say experimental objects in architectural aesthetics."

"Organic—and now aesthetic! That doesn't sound too mathematical for my appreciation."

They were so absorbed in this conversation that he failed to point out Fuckintired Rock, the blockhouse of lichened ledge and blueberry bushes between their rutted road and the river; but it appeared to him that so far he had been playing his few cards well enough in the geometrical suit. She asked him to continue.

He took a deep breath. "But now I'm trying to make isorectotetrahedrons."

"For God's sake, what are those?"

It was too late to retreat before the irritation in her voice. "An isorectotetrahedron is three congruent mutually perpendicular isoceles right triangles with a common point of origin and each sharing two of its sides. It's a special case of the rectotetrahedron, which is the essentially modern version of a general tetrahedron. Iso-recto-tetrahedron: I R T H—IRTH."

"It sounds less earthy than the trinity."

"It's a duodecimal device to reconcile my world with yours."

"So you claim to have succeeded in squaring the triangle! I want an exclusive interview. Even *The Newurker* might buy that story."

"The third dimension gets its equal due—and adumbrates the next, or the *n*th. I still have a trinity—as the fourth face of my IRTH—but I'm no longer confined to a single plane of choice. At the same time, any one of the Pythagorean triangles can be rotated about the origin to generate its own Cartesian continuum. Thereupon, by generalizing the special *iso* case and varying the lengths of the sides, the whole quintessentially European apparatus of trigonometry is accommodated—and, by extension, the graphic system of complex numbers!"

"It's already too complex." She picked up a stick and tried to illustrate his abstractions by scratching some dissimilar right triangles in the frozen mud. "You mystify me."

"I'm not a mystic. I reduce mysteries. I can show you how all mystical pyramids are merely compounds of simple rectifications in the three-space tension system. This system describes not only cubes and parallelepipeds of all sizes but also, by whirling a variable, any helix, gyre, or labyrinth!"

"To cosmic history—from the two-bit axe!" she chanted. "I could write a song about that."

"It's woman's optimum counterentropic resistance to the principle of least action."

"What do you mean *woman's?*" she responded sharply. "Is that more of your mystique?"

"I use the gender genetically and generically, as the general one." His cheeks burned with fatuity as he tried to smile while explaining his epicene language, regretting the premature relaxation of his guard.

Through an abandoned field that was once the Poor Farm's they came into Blithedale Place where a few low Highway Department sheds huddled in the lee of the surviving Old People's Home, a stately well-proportioned mansion with slated gables and a high brick facade of narrow granite-linteled windows for a handful of forgotten residents. Blithedale brought them up to Jubilee Avenue, a constricted shortcut artery over the rump of Beltane Hill to the esplanade, much traveled by kilroys avoiding the congested downtown end of Cod Street to get over to the Gut Bridge on the harborfront. The afternoon tide of students from the nearby high school had already ebbed. Caleb recalled Ibi and kept him at his side until they had crossed Jubilee and started to climb the hill itself by way of Governor's Avenue, steep as any urban ascent in the Old World and just as treeless, crowded with frame houses on both sides.

"Reminds me of Yerba Buena," said Bice. That was the one other city they'd both been to. Since all the kids were now out of elementary school also, the neighborhood was getting loud with voices, which she smiled at when they passed, as Caleb scowled. He was taking her to survey the harbor from his favorite vantage—the climax of their loop back to Cod Street. Luckily they found no children to disturb his pleasure in the neglected little park, a plot of jagged striated gray rock reaching for the sky with knobby fins and arched vertebrae, scantly awash in thin swells of dessicated winter grass. Few traces of former public investment shared the crown of Beltane Hill with a large private house situated at the peak of its naked earthbone, the spacious square cupola of which, an observatory twenty feet above the Harbor's highest geodetic point, Caleb coveted as much as any Irish tower with a winding stair. Other neat or tattered houses, for the most part likewise white, supported a rooftop field of old flues and new antennas that crowded the plunging trapezoid boundaries of the deserted little park below their vantage. Discrete undisturbing shouts of distant young ones rose up to them among all the blended noises of the city softened and purified by the filter of habitation. From this nexus of earth and welkin, now in taut pale sunshine, bracing their feet upon pinnacles of granite they beheld through disparate eyes the clear cold city and the windless seas.

"From here at least you can still see both the bays," Caleb pointed out "and ocean to the east as well!" And he insisted that she look behind the house at the Namauche River basin with wooded hills beyond the marshes. But she preferred to gaze at the outer harbor, obscured only by the clutter on its margins, spread out before them like a dreamt-up lagoon, separated from the limitless waters by the long arm of the Foreside with its baton of a breakwater poised on the surface of the blue. The forlorn boats abroad on the map of the offing seemed as motionless as differentiated dots of paint, and those underway inside the harbor moved no more perceptibly than the minute hands of an electric clock.

The sublimity of the prospect didn't prevent him from jabbering about its nearer homely features, as if it was her duty as a journalist to take note of what even natives hadn't been taught to see: the welter of asphalted wooden gables with white or sometimes green or yellow pediments, even pink, each facing the way it pleased though jostled by higher and lower roofs pitched everywhichway, such that many of the unseen streets must have been crimped and twisted to reach them; the brick powerhouse and its stack; the colossal brick armory with a red compass needle shingled on top to guide airplanes migratory birds and Monarch butterflies; the state fish pier and its massive freezer likewise brick; a half-abandoned factory of lofty fenestrated brick rising like a flat cathedral barracks above its gray wooden neighborhood; and warehouses mostly of old wood lining the waterfront in both directions from the new brick fish-factory of Mercator-Steelyard. He thought chimneys should interest her more than steeples, which however were what she asked about, starting with the Victorian Baroque clock tower of Ibicity Hall, which dominated the massed architecture of the acropolis even when viewed from above. He also made her listen to the approaching whistle of a train as the inland signal of liturgical hours that day and night regularly outsounded the unceasing pulsations of the inner harbor.

He pointed across that thalassic valley with irrepressible officiousness. "That's where I work. See that red building right down on the water with DOGTOWN NET & TWINE MANUFACTORY painted on the side? Now look just a little to the right of it and raise your eyes to the skyline: that roof with some evergreens around it. Can you see it? It's called The Laboratory of Melchizedec and the Mesocosm."

She pretended to distinguish it among tree and housetops on a ridge two miles away by the flight of a gull. "Sounds like a consulting firm."

"It's the headquarters of a Tudor-Classic order. But my job is temporary—only until the Feast of Saints Peter and Paul at the end of June."

"Are you religious?"

He blushed and hesitated, but resolved not quite to repeat Peter's poltroonery. "I'm not a member. But I'm anthropologically sympathetic. The Founding Father was ordained in England."

"I spent four years at a High Church convent." she said. And he recognized from her tone the scar of vaccination. He judged her impervious to any kind of bread and wine. But her intimate question gave him leave to change the subject by examining her in turn, and he found her forthright, with little of the reticence or delitescence usually to be met with in girls. From home, convent, and college she had fled across the border, eventually to join one of the gypsies, those goliards of Atlantean commerce whom Caleb most accused of irreligion on the road.

In their kilroy caravans a great many of them traveled to and from Dogtown for their living because it was the East's principal entrepot and processor of pelagic fish, one of the few commodities for which the rates and routes were still exempt from regulation by the Interstate Commerce Commission (following from the anachronistic tradition of administrative law that frozen fish was like the fresh in being too perishable to stand upon the ceremonies of common carriage). Since the big trucking companies operated like scheduled ocean liners, and none had transcontinental rights from Dogtown to all markets, the demand for specially expeditious refrigerated transport was met by individual worker-capitalists who could afford no payroll. But like the captain of his own tramp steamer, each gypsy negotiated loads of frozen fish for any port that had a freezer dock. His lucrative business was hauling frozen vegetables from the Messpot Valley to the Northeast, or meat from the plains, or citrus from the Gulf; but in order to compete for revenue to cover at least running expenses back to his heartland, he'd deadhead up to Dogtown from one of the metropolitan terminals to solicit a westward load of fish. If nothing else, gypsies held title to the tractors of their trailers, and usually they could pay off their mortgages on them only by serving as their own relief drivers; but some were liberal enough to carry pro tem assistants for companions and lumpers, or occasionally a wife. The cabs had bunks that one could sleep in while another was driving; and berths wide enough for two were beginning to appear on elongated chasses as the rigs were permitted to grow (with the frozen-food industry) from ten to fourteen—and even eighteen—wheels.

Bice didn't claim to be a helper and she wasn't married. Caleb was loathe to ask about the gypsy who'd brought her to Dogtown, or about her accommodations. For all his horror of civilization's devolution into dependency upon the infernal consumption engine, he was no less fascinated than most other males by the huge freewheeling locomotive cabins that towered over domestic kilroys like Western wheat combines over Montvert mowing machines. Intimidated locals were compelled to tolerate these horseless prairie schooners (and their vast boxes when parked continuously noisy with auxiliary refrigeration motors) by the doctrine that Dogtown's vitality required their services. The gypsies themselves, eyed with awe in bars restaurants and hotels, were wild and woolly cowboys off a cattle-drive, fearless sailors from the seven seas of Atlantean desert.

Bice might have enlightened Caleb about some of the human frailties of these fast nomads, perhaps allaying his fear of them as categorical fascists, if she hadn't felt her liberty so close to expiration.

The sky was well westered, lowering to the distant hills across the tidal valley behind their backs as they swiftly gravitated down the eastern side of the hill—though not before he pointed down through a gap in the immediate line of houses, across the obscured ravine of the railroad, to his own pair of roundtopped windows, winged by half-gothic blackened green shutters against white clapboards between steep eves. From this distal angle of his attic, with the owner's horizontally tined antenna lashed to one of the two rickety chimneys, a bleak backdrop was formed against the northern neighborhood of the cemetery by wintering crowns of the cemetery elms moribund with a vascular disease blamed on the Dutch.

"We're almost back to where we started." he assured her. "But from up here you've whiffed the essence of *this fouled exisle of dogs and gulls,* as Ipsissimus Charlemagne calls it. He lives over there beyond the armory. Have you ever heard of our great Director?"

She whirled in her steps and looked in his face with a smile of delight. "Why else would I have taken this ride to Dogtown? Isopel Berners was only a failure. Then you know him personally!"

Caleb inferred that some advantage was awaiting exploitation. He had met Doc only a few months before, when Rafe Opsimath took him to Leviathan Court, but now almost every week he spent a long Saturday evening drinking whiskey in that fabulous kitchen. All along he had been hoping to verify his original guess that Bice was a sympathizer with the Resistance. "Shall I take you to meet him?"

"Good God no! I'm not that presumptuous! I wouldn't know what to say to him. He couldn't waste time on an ignorant foreigner. That's not what I'm here for. But I was curious about the town he lives in, on my way home to Terra Nova. I'm waiting to get on one of the freighters."

"Working your way—?" Once again he blushed and faltered. "I mean are you trying to get a job? My mother's a stewardess on a Norse ship in the South Atlantean trade. Of course these are small reefers." Adding: "But big enough to come and go from Europe!"

"I don't have working papers. But some of the T N boats that come here have a spare cabin for passengers." She had been in town only a day or two, but notwithstanding her earlier mien of diffidence it now appeared that she already knew several key men of the local import trade, from Jason Anacoluther, owner of almost everything, down to some of the lumpers who worked for the stevedoring firm.

Abashed by her inside knowledge of Dogtown's port, and jealous of the rivals wielding its power, Caleb found himself in sympathy with the poor gypsy from Quadropolis who'd thought he was giving her a round trip. "But what about your brother!" he couldn't help protesting. Sister was what she'd told him the gypsy finally agreed to call her on the road.

"Oh he finally asked for a load this morning and by this time he'll be on his way to Pickawillany. He was a nice guy. A pretty good poet in the oldfashioned way—about 'coon hunts and Mississippi bluffs and truck stops and counter-girls who don't understand that he understands them. Very good with language . . ."

Caleb jettisoned his pity for the gypsy. But meanwhile the descent to Cod Street, at a corner well along her way back downtown, brought him to his second crisis. There was only one invitation he could fetch up without recourse to masculine vulgarity. "Would you like to come see my triangles?"

That pretext made her merry. "And have a drink too." he amplified in his confusion. They turned toward the grade crossing at the bottom of the little hollow that separated the foot of Beltane hill from the rise to Acorn Pasture—the route she had roamed by herself before discovering Ibi, who at her request was now permitted to lead her home by his leash as a new friend of the family.

"Some of the gypsy rigs are named and decorated." Caleb remarked as he gained confidence. "I suppose one of these days I'll be seeing BICE painted on a radiator."

"Oh I don't think he'll go that far. But he did say that during the holidays he hung a wreath with Christmas lights on his grill."

"I think I saw that one! They all go past the house."

"Now please tell me truly what an imaginary number is."

With their backs to the inner precincts of the post-Restoration city that lay between the tracks and the harbor, they walked up the right side of Cod Street on a narrow asphalt sidewalk along granite walls retaining the houses that crowded the narrows of the city's carotid. This artery had been overloaded with interurban traffic when the Felly's Eisenhower Bridge (bypassing the ancient coastal highroad to the Gut) was spliced into Squid Circle, its recently engrafted deadeye bulldozed onto the marsh half a mile to the north near an obliterated village green where the original adventurers had felt safest from Frenchmen and other pirates. After crossing the head of Acorn Street, which accompanied the dilapidated southern wall of the cemetery from behind the front row of white clapboards and picket fences, they returned to the gently swelling plateau of the Rectory, where Cod Street briefly broadened more generously than anywhere else in its twisted encirclement of the Cape.

Caleb's unlikely snare, the Keith house with its front stoop of synthetic granite, stood upon ground a foot or two higher than its neighbors'. He cunningly withheld the interesting fact imparted by his landlord the City Planner that just short of this gentle crest the city's sanitary sewer mains, imperfectly segregated from the flow of the "storm" drains, stopped or turned aside from both directions, and that therefore an obsolescent private cesspool remained in use out of sight beneath the rope swing hanging from a mighty horizontal limb of oak in the back yard, where its leaching field was drained by the cemetery. He thought he was doing well enough in keeping her attention, and the crucial entertainment was yet to come.

Just then the ambience of locative seduction was pierced and shattered—not once but twice, and then two or three times again—by the blast of the 4:08 "Westbound" to Botolph that was arriving and departing at the depot next to the grade-crossing they had just come over. He was more or less inured to these maddingly protracted horns of Roland sounding almost around the clock, but Bice started with primitive fear like a surprised cat. She whirled around in time to see the guard, by a coalpile outside his hut, crank down the prayingmantis barriers of white and black stripes. The close-up blast of a diesel threatens to split any unity of spirit, though not absolutely louder than the humane whistle of a steam locomotive. Caleb took her elbow in courteous gesture of reassurance. Until then they had explored each others defenses without so much as shaking hands.

5
THE
RECTORY

"I envy you the beaches. This town must be lovely in the summer."

"It's spoiled by swarms of mindless pilgrims all day long driving in and driving out and driving up and down, taking pictures of fishing boats and buying seascapes. Most of the stories in the *Nous* promote the needle trades."

"Not every visitor is stupid. Anyway, I miss the warm weather down under. I suppose you like cold and lonely winters."

"I don't know what I'm saying. You make me exaggerate. It isn't that I hate summer—just the pleasure-seeking traffic that smothers it. But I do prefer winter observations. There's more to be seen when the land takes off its clothes. Also the lull in abuse gives the perishable rubbish a chance to start rotting."

The opportunist chatted and laughed incontinently as he attempted to tidy up his quarters under her eyes while bringing refreshments from a larder ever unprepared for guests, flustered by the simultaneity of his efforts. Bice chose the swivel chair behind his writing table. With a half-turn its occupant could command the backyard cemetery oaks through one of the low twin windows, the tops of which were squared off no higher than the sitting girl's head, unlike the Gothical pair lighting Caleb's streetfront bedroom and kitchen, though all four of his sills were but a few inches off the floor.

She lowered her head to peer into the greater distance. "That split rock makes this corner of the sculpture garden look as natural as an arboretum."

He told her that the intentions of the national Garden Cemetery Movement for necropolitan sanctuaries of squirrels and birds had been more euphemistic than natural, but that here, despite the original Proprietors' subscription to its enlightened maxim denying in general everything grim and bitter about death's corruption, the horticulture was bound to have suffered also from the human nature of the Cape. The sites had all been numbered—almost four hundred of them—but for the lack of signs it was forgotten that the avenues dividing them into irregular sections were named after trees, and that the artfully ordained paths subdividing these were named after less woody species of vegetation such as the mistletoe. Once there had been optimistic rules against picking flowers and molesting wildlife.

Now the charming cleft in that boulder was full of broken glass, and few of the headstones remained undamaged. "As anthropologists our Georgios never had much foresight. The Vikings knew enough to leave rune-stone texts like land mines, incorporating self-contained lethal curses against future vandals."

"From what I've seen, nothing can intimidate the youth of Atlantis." she said. "I notice that even your royal dog is rather unscrupulous about desecrating deathsheads and crossbones."

Caleb was disappointed that she didn't notice the sleepy thump from the tail of the housecarl in response to her reference. Ibi was flung out on his side like a bearskin rug across the channel of egress where best he could doze without missing any significant movement of either stranger. The host ceased his hospitality-fussing and cleared for himself the only other seat, across his own desk from her, glancing whither she pointed in the low slanting winter light of the waned afternoon, but watching her sip the Scotch-and-water like a man of good taste, the only spirit in his liquor locker.

Playing with her position of authority, she swung forward to face her client from the chair she had spontaneously seized, innocent of the thrill of violation she was imparting to him who'd have angrily protested the possession of his most private place by almost any other human being. She nodded toward the books that rose six feet from the floor to make the long northern wall of the white garret by truncating its eaves—as if, as in a dream, the responsibility for them in her office was his. "Well, young man . . ." She began, like a mimicking child (thereby rendering her beauty less formidable), by asking with mock severity if he'd read them all, but made him blush at what might have been taken as an accusation of fecklessness inferred from his purchase of such means to evade the direct experience of reality. His voice quivered: "Just for reference . . . when I need to look up something." To many girls without the perspicacity to admire the collection as an honest confession of the slothful and procrastinating temptations to which he so often yielded this library would have been a sign of virtuosity; and to most others it would have been cause to disdain him for unmanly appetitions. Yet for the uppermost place in his emotions a delight in her apparently sympathetic intelligence contended with dismay at its possibly ironical application, however good-humored. She rose to survey the evidence, glass in hand, pursing her lips as she slowly paced, pausing at no point with special interest.

But her eyes scanned much more broadly too. Presently she was asking cheerful questions about other objects, darting from this to that, as though trying to keep him off guard while she completed a sketch. Her attention was arrested by a typewritten résumé of his business career on a corner of the table. Formally polite for the first time, she asked his leave to pick it up.

Returning to the swivel chair as she perused the document, she leaned back, crossed her legs, cleared her throat, and commenced to interview him. "Well, young man." she said again. "What kind of work are you looking for?" He had relieved her of the coat but she was still booted and a long black wool skirt concealed the other segments of her legs; under her unbuttoned purple cardigan however she wore a white blouse nearly disclosing the texture as well as the form of her otherwise unshielded bosom, which he made continual effort to keep his eyes from seeming to seek. The suggestion of a casual nakedness under clothes worn only for protection against the weather autonomically excited the imagination of his body; but his mind reminded him not to neglect the fluid in their glasses or fail to renew his offerings of tiny smoked oysters and cream cheese upon wheaten crackers, which delicacies by amazing good luck he happened to have recently laid in, almost for the first time in his life, as possible food for thought to keep him at the desk during the afternoons when his zest was like to wane.

"Anything but selling. Anything that requires no commuting."

"Why, do you hate driving as well as drivers? Or there are trains."

"I'd rather spend half that extra wasted time on whatever the job is."

"I guess it wouldn't last long if you didn't."

"You mean: to compensate for incompetence?"

"To abate their suspicion that your heart isn't in it. I too think you have ulterior motives, Mr Karcist."

"It's true that I'd rather convert money into time than time into money."

"Yet I see you have a sales background!" Her eyes were searching up and down the page. "Assistant to sales rep . . . Sales Correspondent . . . Sales Analyst . . ."

"The accident of necessity started me off in sales administration—not selling. In Cornucopia it was the only kind of job I could get. Even here in Vinland a degree in English stains the scutcheon of anyone not intending to teach it. You'll notice my artful stratagem in fudging that shame with 'Liberal Arts'—which may make it worse with totally uneducated Protestican employers, but when neutralized by my shirtsleeve business experience it may not stand so much in my way with personnel managers who've been to college. If people don't question me too closely I can give them to understand that some of my courses were useful. First I throw dust in their eyes by maintaining that management is an art, and emphasize the idea of 'science' in Hume's 'Faculty of Arts & Sciences'. Then I point out that Philosophy is the mother of Logic, which is now becoming respectable at least among data-processors. But of course I know that my academic blot remains almost as suspicious as a prison term by way of accounting for four years of my ambitious life."

"Still, sales managers must know that selling's an art of rhetoric."

"So what? I'm the world's worst salesman—even in the neutral communications of everyday life. That's why I'm lucky to get the menial work of mere sales administration. I'm the least persuasive man you'll ever meet."

"Oh I dare say you have some sort of charm."

"I can't open my mouth without betraying the conviction that I'll meet with resistance or hostility, and my mind goes blank whenever I have a good argument. Even in speaking my own ideas I lose the train of thought, and I'm useless in explaining anyone else's. I'm so conscious of my flat voice strangling itself in the effort that it deteriorates all the more with disgust at the futility of talking. To make it worse, in spite of my better judgment, I try to make up for my oral ineptitude by multiplying my abstractions—the very thing that my countrymen hate the most. But I'm supposed to act confident, so I keep talking with numb lips."

"Your lips don't look numb to me."

Caleb had no intention of dispraising himself unnecessarily, but it seemed important to make her understand why he had no profession. "Even if I had a normal voice I couldn't sell emancipation free of charge to a slave!"

"I rather like your voice. Maybe it's just that the stress of survival makes you tense, and the strain shows up in your throat instead of the guts, where most people absorb it."

With new admiration of the girl, but forgetting his immediate motive, he was distracted for a moment by a bit of authentically subjective speculation. "My mother says I was born almost strangled by the umbilical cord. No wonder my voice is so weak! I can't even shout with rage. I can't make a loud noise. I'm like a giraffe!" But the idea of Caleb Karcist browsing in the treetops high above the lions and wildebeests provoked them both to laughter, and at once restored his objective sense of purpose.

"Just because your fibres aren't made for braying? Nowadays we have microphones and amplifiers. Even a bosun's mate doesn't need to bellow. —Mr Karcist, I'm afraid the reason it's going to be hard to place you is that deep in your heart you think all communication is phony."

"Nevertheless I must be a communicator of some kind, you've read me so well!" He was contemplating an advance that he cautiously trusted she'd sympathize with; for, journalist or no, and despite the liking she had betrayed during their walk for demotic Atlantean entertainments, she was at least half educated as a common reader and claimed to have overcome an addiction to devilvision. Her speech was enchanting both in matter and in manner.

"But the worst of my economic problem" he said "is that from the earliest age I've never been able to accommodate the abuse of language. Even merely to listen to, the broadcast degradation of democratic speech is more painful to me even than the advertising. Ignorance of grammar among administrators appalls me as much as innocence of Ohm's and Kirkoff's laws among master electricians, or the fatuity of managers unable to read the accounting equation. In this country the only linguistic law is Gresham's, which even the dictionaries make a virtue of: the so-called living language! Overnight, from coast to coast, our audiences conform to novelty. Fresh deformities are stomached relished assimilated and avidly imitated at the morning coffee claque. True idiom is blurred into colorful ad hoc cliches. A hundred years of change is forced by an hour of broadcast. The mind-shunting appetite for imagery is ceaselessly stimulated vulgarized and stuffed. I don't mind the original metaphor of funny or poetic speech; but every teacher should be taught enough taste to winnow out the chaff, if not the intellect to criticize or the rear-guard courage to fight their retreat!"

"Tut tut, young man; permit me to suggest that in business interviews you conceal your passion. Leave those scruples to unpublished writers. Confine your precision to geometry. As for holding down a job, you can't even be a bookkeeper without treading the market's path of least resistance."

"No, once I've diverted them with numbers and diagrams they don't seem to notice that I can't bring myself to abet their philological disloyalty. They are subconsciously annoyed by my nonconformity, but they have no ear for it. They don't notice the absence of abuse."

"You surprise me, Mr Karcist. I thought that in the States all pejorative concepts of vulgarity had been proscribed. But in order to place you I must ask which is the more distressing, popular syntax or popular diction?"

"There's no hope to limit chronic damage from the latter, but the former is an acute cause of anguish. Almost any malapert construction, if only impudent enough to catch the ear, or insidiously smooth, is too powerful to be resisted by the words themselves, which are thereby captured declassified and prostituted. One more abomination of form becomes the latest convention. Even the lowest common denominations of currency may eventually be salvaged as particles of ironic poetry; but the functional relationships of elements that have been painstakingly differentiated by creative evolution are irreversibly homogenized by the insolent overheated agitation of chemical bonds in these promiscuous syntheses of meretricious compounds, especially when mixed or suspended in soups of music! Nowadays, with radio and devilvision, it's hyperentropic vandalism to slur or pervert evolved discriminations of thought out of whim or laziness, merely to meet the need of some immediate rhetorical effect. The artificial reduction of precision by misuse of God-given imagination—our undermanagement of language—is a particularly Atlantean vice. It's an artificially accelerated infection of society that has killed off the normal antibodies of literate culture and rendered it so susceptible to amusing or sentimental simplification, in the interest of show business or commercial persuasion, that the undeformed heritage of language is no longer tested and modified by the people's own truly natural linguistic experiments, spontaneous and unselfconscious. The corruption has already gone so far that in many locutions we are losing the distinction between objective and subjective indication. Take the term 'my guilt': the very faculty of thought suffers regression when we can no longer tell the difference between factual culpability and *feelings of* culpability. Thanks to uneducated psychologists, epistemology and ontology are likewise conflated in the typically solecistic use of the word 'frustration'—"

"Please, please! I am only a journalist!" she brought him up short. Caleb came to his senses without distinguishing the objective from the subjective in his mortification. He realized that her astonishment at his passionate abstractions, begun in playfulness, was more tolerant than any applicant had right to expect. But instead of offering to drop the intempestive topic she now extended it by challenging him to produce a concrete example of grammatical, rather than philosophical, horror—"or rather, object of horror!"

How could he stop making a fool of himself? Wriggling on her hook, he demurred at demonstrating his theme with instances, being as aware as she was that each case by itself would appear niggardly or pedantic even to a Brit, and that even in jest nobody but an old-fashioned schoolmarm would sympathize with his reactionary animus. Certainly he would have been laughed out of court by his friend Doctor Charlemagne, who made it a virtue to whip along the galloping vernacular, and who recklessly contributed to almost any demotic waywardness that tended to undermine the idolatry established by 19C grammarians, in preparation for a general anabatic revolution in the highest culture. Anyway, under the circumstances, in his own confusion of the epistemological and the ontological, poor Caleb couldn't remember a single one of the commonplace abuses that outraged him every time he read a newspaper or listened to the radio. His thoughts were exclusively divided between the misgivings he had so improvidently bestirred in himself and dismay at the connotation of self-righteousness in this unprecedented outburst of his simmered hatred for a pollution upon which neither the Sadducees nor the Pharisees wasted much breath. At the same time he hoped to revive his side of the fun. But "Never mind." was all he could find to say, his forehead burning with chagrin. "It's only my disinterested neurosis."

So the audition almost ended in self-defeat. He was overcome with the psychic paralysis that suddenly grips the losing favorites late in a championship game, whose irredeemable lapses have been brought on by nothing less inexcusable than overweening arrogance. What imp had made him so incontinently display a vexation far too intimate and delicate to impart even to a woman in whose speech he had not yet detected any of the labile vulgarity that he was too dumbstruck to itemize? Just because she seemed privately pure (though also catholic in her tolerance), why must he overreach himself in the premature delusion of rapport—and blunder into the expectation that this blown flower from a foreign convent school, acting as a personnel manager, would absolve him of his phobic chastity?

Such sinful pride should be confessed only to Father Duncannon, a classically educated scientific gentleman qualified to understand his pain at hearing, for instance, a noun like *loan* used as a verb, or a preposition like *like* as a conjunction like *as*. These distinctions hardly served to lure anyone with whom you'd like to play the jewel of games.

"I admire your morality, Mr K, but I fear it doesn't commend itself to employers. Not even universities. You may be too conservative for business in North Atlantis. Still, there's nothing in the résumé to give you away. I'd personally be inclined to give you a chance at any position. With a woman practice matters more than theory. But I'd suggest you refrain from honesty at your next interview with a man."

"Then must I conclude that I'm not getting any further here?"

"We have no cork-lined offices, you know. In any case you'd be only temporary." She paused, wrinkling her brow judiciously. "There might be an opening I could fit you into; but first I'd like to find out a little more about your true history. After all, I can't very well take on a stranger can I? Let's go back to the beginning. You were born here. Any brothers or sisters? —No? —That's your first disadvantage."

"But my mother says I incarnate one of each."

"Her conceits don't count. Was your father a wildeyed iconoclast, by any chance? Perhaps that's all there is to your neurosis."

"No paternal pressure." he said. "My origins are obscure."

"That doesn't make up for being an only child if your mother tied you to her apron strings."

Deep water again, but this time not of his own choosing, and he thought he could get ashore. "She took me on hitchhiking trips so that I could learn something about cars. It was our only travel, except when we were evicted to new addresses. It's still a thrill for me to cross a state line. But she didn't teach me to throw a ball properly, and to this day I've never been able to play any position but second base. When I was twelve, which she called the age of manhood, I was sent away to a work school."

"A borstal institution? What were you in trouble for?"

"Dutchkill School was preparatory, not reformatory. Our little town school in Montvert didn't have what I needed to get into a Laurel

League varsity. No Trig, no Chemistry, no Physics, no Latin, no German,—"

"Oh my goodness!" Mockingly she tapped her temple with four spread fingers. "So you had to board at a charity school for scholars?"

"For troublesome rich kids, over in another valley. My mother begged a full scholarship for me. There were only about twenty five students. I dreaded her visits. She called me her pride and joy in front of everybody. Thank God it was hard for her to get there, without a car." He fetched from a dusty corner of the room a discolored axe with two blades like the faces of Janus, holding up the flattened shaft of worn hickory by its throat just under the double head as if it was a sacred steel cobra. "This is my diploma. The school was a hardscrabble dairy farm at the end of a valley, surrounded by woods, and this Western axe is the kind we used for cutting lumber and firewood, along with wedges mauls and two-handled crosscut saws. See: both edges are sharp, but this blade for felling and trimming trees has been ground finely concave like the bow of clipper ship, whereas the other one's as convex as the bow of an East Indiaman and is used for hack work like clearing brush when no deep cut is needed and it's likely to get nicked by stones."

He showed her, and told her, up close, running his thumb over the biting edges. Now she nodded respectful indeed. The shapes of kindred tools in the Maritimes were familiar, but never before had they been explained to her. She said nothing to discourage him as he plunged into the maze of his passage to manhood, bragging about details of his rugged education that still excited his pride: the georgics he had acquired with the unfeigned sweat of manual work in ice and snow or sweltering summer sun, alongside mostly older prepschool boys who paid to learn responsibility. But he was there to earn his way by getting into college, for the sake of Dutchkill's reputation.

At first she compared him to the infamous football players attending famous U S universities on "athletic scholarships", and to mercenary knights. But he told her he'd been made a gentleman by walking half a mile at five AM every day of the week, even if in three feet of snow at thirty degrees below zero, to scrape manure and milk the cows, and by carrying forty-gallon milk cans back to the main house afterwards; by victualing and currycombing a team of draft horses in their stalls; by building wagonloads of hay with birdlike cunning; by forking dung, spreading fertilizer, and shoveling gravel; by digging post-holes and stringing barbed wire; by hammering and welding iron at a blacksmith's forge; by digging ditches and dislocating stones with pick and crowbar; by assisting at constructions with the tools of carpenter and mason; but above all by rhythmically swinging the doublebitted axe. Finally, when he claimed to have been a champion at the feats of Saturday night village square-dances, and hinted glancing at her merry black eyes that that proficiency, with all its chivalric overtones and innuendos, might be more interesting than his others, she compared him to a troubadour who couldn't sing.

It then occurred to him that she must be wondering why he was daft on all kinds of work, and whether he was trying to impress her with his adolescence because there was nothing in his résumé to be amorously admired. Unless the subject was changed she might think it about time to end the interview. Indeed, as if sharing that fear herself, she now asked "Why did you go out to Hume for college? I'd have thought Sir Galahad would despise Cornucopia as a land of lotus-eaters. Why not the laurels of nearby Norumbega?"

"Because my most vivid years were in Unabridge just outside those walls, among the peasant Franks and Doily Irish, who hated the university more for its culture than for its real-estate tax exemption. My mother also scorned that garrison, almost as much as our neighbors scorned us. She said it was full of 'softboiled stuffed shirts'—effeminate peacocks with no experience in real life!" He did not confess the banal motive for his emigration: an urge for westward travel and a plain desire for the milk and honey. "Out there the public servants aren't so surly. And at college you don't have to live like a college boy. Hume's more like a Continental university: sink or swim, without House rules or homogeneous social precepts; no High Tables or official dances or teas with the Master's wife. It's no enclave of superiority." He also refrained from mentioning the obvious incitement of lightly dressed student girls, cheek by jowl, ad libitum. But he did add: "Besides, I wanted to get away from my mother's territory, hoping she wouldn't follow me in pursuit of the sun."

"And did she go West to keep house for her stable boy?"

"Only much later—and without success. At first the only way she could earn a living was by selling Bibles door-to-door up in the redwood country. Then after half a dozen menial jobs in the labor pool of Babylon Oaks she went to sea on the ship running on charter up and down the coast between British Columbia and Chile. So it wasn't as bad for me as it might have been."

"I think you're heartless."

"You've never met my mother. She'd bowl you over at first sight with her openhearted admiration and affection, and immediately address you with some more or less impertinent soubriquet that she'd ostentatiously affix as long as you remained on speaking terms. Within half an hour she'd be guessing at all your secrets. And she's clairvoyant. At the Allenton Town Fair she used to dress up as a gypsy to read palms, and her success was disturbing. At that kind of merrymaking she hits the nail on the head so often that people are infuriated when she insists upon something outrageously wrong about themselves. But whatever she says, flattering or absurd, is bound to be embarrassing. She's lost hundreds of instantaneous friends. But the timid and the prudent usually sheer off in fear or disgust before they can be overwhelmed."

"Now I understand why you're so reserved." Bice remarked.

"Reserved! Who's the reserved one?" He'd rarely revealed himself so impulsively—yet his interviewer had told him practically nothing about what most interested him as an incentive for giving himself away. What kind of gypsy poets was she used to? He veered from the sense that this ravishing cat was trifling with his pride to the wonder whether she was flattering him with a depth of masculinity that granted all the liberty he needed to keep her intrigued. "It's my turn to do the interviewing!"

"But I'm not looking for a job here." She swung a complete circle in his swivel chair. "Of course I might not refuse an extraordinary opportunity."

"We'll go have dinner at the Windmill."

"No. I don't want you to spend any money. Are you hungry? Maybe we could find some odds and ends in your kitchen. Don't forget, I still haven't seen your trinities. But first I must see if I can cancel an appointment."

Caleb left her with the telephone for that purpose and went to search his larder, having laid his kit of triangles on the table. Then, risking the chance that she might vanish in his absence, or meditate without his influence on keeping her promise to another man, but with the hope that she'd feel more assured of her privacy than suspicious of the sounds made by running water, he stepped under the eaves behind his kitchen to take a showerbath briefer than a round of boxing, shave his clouded face, clean up the bathroom a little, and shift into fresh clothes. When he came back, hardly as soon as he'd hoped, slightly out of breath with apology but confident of his odor, she was rolling on the rug with his dog. Ibi was rather excited, crooning singsongs. "Your pride-and-joy is giving me a lick and a promise!" she called out with a giggle.

Kneeling close at her side he asked if she'd made her call. The ruffed-up dog had paused to lie with his head on her shoulder and all four legs in the air, one forepaw faineantly dangling, but with the arrival of a third party he became conscious of his undignified posture, twisted out of her arm, stood up with legs braced to shake himself all over, and went as if suddenly bored to sprawl near the door where he could examine his anterior hindquarters without disturbance.

"Yes," she replied. "Everything's resolved. We'll have time for your interview. But mine isn't quite finished. I have two more questions." Then she too rose, brushing dust and doghair off her skirt with the flat of her hand. "By the way, you've already disqualified yourself as houseboy or groom. I'd like to give Ibi-Roi a good brushing. I hope you did a better job with horses." She helped herself to more whiskey and hors d'oeuvres before returning to the official seat. "But your Scotch I like. I feel civilized in this room."

Caleb also went to the bottle, and then to his straightbacked chair. She had unpacked the triangles from their hinged wooden casket, which had originally been the packing case for Christmas cheese from Captain Ozone. It was subdivided into compartments and outfitted with hardware, including tiny piratical-looking padlocks wired to dangling keys with pipe-cleaner twists. Trinities were scattered and piled all about the place he had cleared for her on the big littered writing table, among steel connecting rods of various lengths and a few auxiliary squares like wooden tiles, dominated by one large cylinder with a hole in its center that served as a pedestal for aerial configurations.

But he was a little nettled to find that she'd taken it upon herself to draw this most embarrassing apparatus into her playground. With the quick irreverence of a chimpanzee she had discovered and seized from the top of the file cabinet his miniature skene for a theater, mounted on a breadboard. This model had been fabricated to help compensate his imagination for lack of histrionic experience. At the back stood a straight inch-thick wall four by seven inches in extent (standing on its long side), built with a dozen or two varicolored crudely shaped bricks of the children's clay that doesn't harden, various rectangular lengths of gray pink and green irregularly pressed upon each other; and to it was pinned an oblong of white card bearing across its top in relatively large letters the legend TABLET 1, beneath which, in colored pencil, proceeding from left to right within the rows and columns of a ruled matrix, was sketched like the schematic diagram for a construction project his idiosyncratic suggestion of a choreographic chart. Upon the platform representing the stage in front of this scene she was beginning a spiral staircase with the triangles fanned flat on top of each other, her head cocked from time to time as she inspected her rather clumsy work—which in fact she swept away more than once to reassemble.

"They make interesting stage-sets." he said, almost resentful of her presumption but hoping to divert her attention from the backdrop. "I like solid building materials for stage-sets. Nothing should be faked or imitated with paint. You should have real friction and inertia. That's why I'm looking for some kind of fine-grained plastic material dense enough to be machined like steel. I'd like to make my isorectotetrahedrons out of something as heavy as soapstone."

"Then you'd better have a deus ex machina in your stage crew. Or else never change the scene." she advised without looking up.

"And no proscenium, no curtain, no Limeway realism or fantasy-by-flies."

"Then you are a reactionary! But at least you write your plays."

"Mine go back to the oldest stories. Someone else must write the music."

"I should hope so!" she sighed with an enchanting plash of gaiety, adding, with a sidewise wave of her eyebrow toward his covered typewriter on its tiny castered table in the corner behind her, "But are you really even a typist?" She glanced once more at his curriculum vitae lying under the aesthetic mess, and found a certain line with her forefinger. "I come to the question of why you doctor up a plausible life-history by calling yourself a consultant. You seem to me a silent stouthearted axe-carrier no further along than the start of a theatrical career. To whom, besides those priests, are you inclined to give advice?"

"In these parts 'consulting' is a euphemistic mask for odd jobs and interrupted unemployment, or temporary occupations best left unspecified. It implies that one'll consider any offer. Moreover, since consulting is mysterious and confidential, it warns inquisitors that one's not at liberty to answer delicate questions."

"Hm. That's something to remember. No one can check up on your claims. I was just about to ask you for a reference. But please vouchsafe an example of the assignments concealed behind your window-dressing."

"I worked part-time with C R F automatic typewriters and programmed calculators for blind old Captain Ozone. He needed someone with an expressionless voice who could also read aloud in prosaic rhythm, without melody or timbre. My landlady, as the librarian who knows the city's readers, recommended me."

"Well what did you read to the client?"

"Technical journals and monographs that would never appear in

Braille, which he hated anyway. I was amazed at how easily he absorbed information. I was never asked to reread as much as a single word, yet he'd remember the exact context of all the figures and citations he had me record in tape."

"It speaks well for your scientific comprehension."

"Only syntactical intuition. It was an eerie experience, reading to a blind genius you never see, behind his black curtain. He was just beginning to relax the barriers when he was taken ill for the last time. But he'd already given me his dog." [Thump, thump from the floored tail of the forgotten third party stretched flat in dozing command of the egress.] "Ibi was considered too big and aggressive to be tamed as a guide, and they were going to put him up in the Taraville woods to guard the testing quarry, but he and I'd made friends at first sight."

But her pursuit of his career did not let up. "You could take a job in so-called technical writing. New electronic plants are going up all along the Massachusetts Felly. Don't you have a car? You could easily pay for it by making a lot more money out of town." Apparently she had already surveyed the local economy. Yet she guessed his motives: "You could earn enough to quit."

Gratuitous avocational suggestions coming from anyone less attractive would have provoked all his defensive emotions, and perhaps a bumbling cascade of excuses. But the same instinct for discrimination with which she had assimilated the diction of the States (from books or from gypsies) seemed to have distinguished him as worthy of her assistance. The sudden conviction of that goodwill served to remind him that he held no firmer ground in society than that entailed by entitlement to Ibi's custody, in the one place where his relationship to society happened to be more determinate than random. He was touched by her generous adoption of his perspective, to which she might be comparing her own alienation. But despite his persuasion of her kindness he hung back from exposing her to the deeper complications of his welfare without the maturation of an intimacy that naturally wanted either much more time or precipitate action. And in any case, at a moment when it was most important to be master of himself, he had no time to spare for the feelings (irrelevant to his present purpose) that he'd have to summon up for any effort to set forth his unique difficulties. On the other hand, he saw no advantage in withholding all his secrets from a polar opposite who might thereby be prompted to reciprocate with more exciting disclosures of her own.

Nonetheless, replying in kind and choosing words of epitome as coolly as her warm presence allowed, eschewing any number of other halyards to the truth about his peculiar rig of social motives, he cautiously raised his circumspect colors, neither Union Jack nor Jolly Roger. "All those firms have government contracts. You can't work for them without what's called a security clearance, which at the very least requires certain papers: and I'm an undocumented native. If I appealed for special consideration they'd start a dossier on me." As if there wasn't one already—Selective Service at least, about which he hoped she had the delicacy not to inquire! "If I'm brought to the government's special attention I may be refused a passport."

"You're a dissenter—or a felon?"

He was on the very point of confiding that he had been turned down for a job in the Strategic Intelligence Service after meeting all the qualifications, probably because someone had accused him of sympathizing with the Resistance, and perhaps also because his mother's record attainted his own; but he managed to stifle the impulse when he considered that civic fears in the U S A were not well understood by subjects of the British Commonwealth, who he believed took for granted the rule of law over that of public opinion.

It was a good thing that without waiting for an answer she took up only one component of his predicament. "Isn't the Occupation all over? Your new President will change all that. The whole world hails his election!"

"Maybe, provided he doesn't trust the public relations experts. But this is still a nation of Pauline meat-eating individualists who don't believe in society except when there's war or depression. Self-interest is our official virtue. In a year or two the antigen will be snuffed out by a reflux of dynacratic sentimentality. Even with a big majority of the popular vote (which Kennedy didn't have) it's much harder for a Catholicrat President than for a Protestican because he's automatically opposed by most of the country's taxable wealth. He must rely on people who want the things that taxes are for. Most of those are too bemused by opiates or Can deception to stir their stumps and vote, or even to discern their own interests when they do vote. And no more than a tenth of the enfranchised population cares less about their personal stake than about the commonwealth or the species."

"Jeremiah, do you really believe that politics have anything to do with your predicament?" Her quizzical friendliness, as she paused again in her creative occupation to add a trifle to the notes she'd been pencilling every now and then in the margins of his biography, made him feel as if all his sincere words were being upstaged by someone's mocking pantomime.

"If a President can't reform the culture he certainly can't buck public opinion by openly enforcing the laws that are regarded as protecting the internal enemies of Atlantis." Caleb retorted.

"If they think you're an enemy I should think they wouldn't want to prevent your expatriation. Good riddance! Go live among the law-abiding British, if you can find a place in one of their classes. You believe in Tory English."

"I said I was a loyalist to language, not a royalist!"

"Well you've converted me into an Ibi-Royalist." she replied. [Again a somnolent thump on the floorboards.] "But I do suspect you're a spy in this country. Atlanteans probably don't want you to tell the world what you know about Atlantis."

"I have no wish to become British Armorican Irish Manx or Madogian: it's only that I crave to tread the Celtic kingdoms and see the rest of the Continent. That's not expatriation, and it can't make me any more European than I already am."

Satisfaction with her mentality did not quite overcome his hesitation to venture the physical admiration to be expected from any Tom Dick or Harry. All afternoon he had taken as much pleasure in her firm quick movements as in her light catholic humor and her swiftly quiet cadences of antipodean speech (tinctured with the faintest echoes of Cockney English); but by this time, as they talked to each other with diminishing pretense of impartiality, his sensuous delight was giving way asymptotically to a sensual desire for chirosensation of the maidenly proportional forbiddingly tangible tumuli with tender-budded coronas all but revealed by her careless blouse, which to him was more inhibiting than Eskimo clothes in conventional deception of accessibility. On his side the conversation that had been so artificially sustained was now attenuating under the flaring onset of his one continual and categorical motive, which had been slightly diverted, even as it was intensified, by his object's subjective quicksilver.

"That brings me to the enigma." she said. "They say that all the promising youth of Dogtown leave home as soon as they're able to escape—the only reason they ever volunteer for the service or go to college. I should think this would be the last place you'd want to come back to, and stop at, halfway to the eastward. It's an unlikely port of embarkation. Why do we meet in Dogtown?"

"Because it's my *first* place! Shouldn't it be the last one to leave from? FILO, as accountants say: First In, Last Out! Besides, I'm not a promising youth."

"Good! I'm not looking for promises. Or secrets. But please resolve my final doubt about employing you."

"I came here for my birth certificate. I need it for a passport, even to file an application."

"Why should a little thing like that take so long? Are you saving up for the fee? I'll give you the money for that. Go and get all that Anglophilia out of your system. I'll write you a letter of introduction to the Home Secretary's daughter."

"There are complications. —But now it's my interview. How well can you type?"

"I'm a musician of the keyboard. Nuns are good at teaching things like that. But I don't know how to control your C R F player-piano gadgets."

"I can't even control myself." Caleb replied, encountering neither surprise nor hesitation when he rose from his inferior seat and came around the table to kiss her on the lips, which he found coolly affectionate and highly communicative, with tiny tremors like the nibbles of a doe.

"I like the way you interview." she whispered at last. "I was beginning to think you weren't interested in things like this." The calm willingness of her response helped Caleb keep his head, but as he led her to the door she forgot to relinquish the perforated triangle of varnished maple that she'd been toying with. It remained unconsciously in her left palm like a nut from the Tree of Knowledge.

Ibi scrambled up to follow, expecting his dinner.

6
POET'S CORNER

Never while working for Rafe Opsimath had Caleb closed the door of Room 36 at such an hour or so daintily. Whispering *Heel* but to take no chances holding Ibi short on the leash he walked swiftly and softly down the dim silent corridor that he had so often trod carelessly. But the dog was no feline, and since first staggering to his feet in the maternal litter had been walking on his toes without the slightest congenital or acquired inclination to retract his loose blunt claws, the clatter of which was now barely absorbed by the remaining threads of the hotel's antedeluvian carpet.

Descending the stairs Caleb breathed more freely, as the likelihood abated that he should compromise Bice if by any chance he encountered Shelly Schlossberg up from his basement at five in the morning. Though prohibition of false registration for unmarried companions was a dead letter of the law, especially for cosmopolitan innkeepers, the Schlossbergs would never have tolerated a woman who received another man after the first had left, and not merely because they wished to efface the CaraVANsary's former reputation on the waterfront.

With wrung loins and triumphant heart Caleb crossed the empty lobby and let the two of them out the latched door by which six hours earlier Bice had snuck them in. For the few minutes of the interval after Shelly had answered her ring and returned to his studio Caleb had lurked outside with Ibi, already well contented with proceedings in his own bed but greedily intent upon resuming them in hers, while not yet aware that it was the very one about which while arraying his stockmarket statistics he had sometimes daydreamed a fantastic adventure. That night he was even to realize certain secondary visions concerning the huge old bathtub.

Shelly was so pleased by Rafe's sojourn in 36 that he'd never removed the table. Inasmuch as the house was seldom full, that room could usually be reserved for writers. For the most part it stood hopefully vacant. Perhaps researchers and professional thinkers would start turning up next summer. Since Rafe's departure that favored space had been occupied almost exclusively by theatrical or literary artists paying off-season visits to Doctor Charlemagne, among them a poet who admired the Van itself as much as the broken view of the inner harborfront from the two planes of the room's windows. Thus the landlord had dubbed 36 his Poet's Corner, and even toyed with the idea of advertising it as such in the New Uruk trade papers. But he and Edie soon learned that you couldn't tell poets from fellow Bohemians or Beauts without preliminary inquiry so probing as to seem impertinent; and that some of the real ones, with their wives, looked more like insurance men than Ippies. It was to say the least impolitic for a commercial host to examine his guest's aspirations—worse than asking for both passport and Social Security card. So the Schlossbergs hit upon the expedient of merely mentioning the great Director's name. If the registrant responded as one of Doc's claque he was automatically assigned to the Poet's Corner.

It was a test they didn't bother to apply to gypsies, who could usually be recognized by an element of cowboy outfit such as hat boots or bandanna. But evidently Bice's poet hadn't looked like a gypsy, and of course his vehicle was not parked within sight of the lobby. Yet Caleb doubted that the man would ever have heard of Doctor Charlemagne. It must have been Bice herself (as pseudo-wife) who'd aptly responded to one of the innkeeper's hints. Even Caleb himself, the most prickly of strangers, had never resented Shelly's kind of overtures; to free and easy vagabonds the proprietor was doubtless irresistible. Edie sometimes jested that she would write a novel based solely upon what her husband elicited from the motley succession of visitors that crossed their front desk—not only goliards and gypsies but also drummers of the dispossesed sort, customs inspectors, migrant fishermen, beached merchant-mariners, fugitive women, and unfastidious pilgrims.

And wonderful to say, as Caleb now stepped out onto the corner of Loft and Front, what living creature was to be seen in the night (other than Ibi at his heel and a solitary gull flying low to some landward purpose) but Doc Himself! Even in the uncertain lamplight two blocks up the hill at Morality Square his leaning barndoor of a back with hands clasped behind it, costumed in an overcoat from the retreating French army of 1812, was unmistakable to anyone who'd ever seen him on the prowl. He wore a knitted Navy watch cap discarded from the late Atlantic war, and a seven-foot purpled muffler twisted over his shoulder in rakish academic fashion.

Enough snow had already fallen to capture the huge splayed footprints straying past the Van and up the acclevity of Front Street: a capricious line of skewly doubled dashes that maculated the whole empty blanket of swansdown and would have drawn any eye to seek the bear leaving such gigantic marks. Once or twice the track swerved from curb to curb, or mounted the sidewalk to loiter before a glassed display at either wall of the deserted canyon; but its line of regression was about halfway between the crown of the whited thoroughfare and the gutter on its left. When Caleb caught sight of the night-walker he was standing at the top, at the center of the city's main intersection, weight on one leg, bent forward like an umpire, peering by turn in the four cardinal directions of the crossroads, and skyward too, as if from a ghostly poop royal.

Caleb shrank into the shadows of Loft Street, still restraining Ibi, to keep from being seen by the very person for whose privileged company he craved whenever there was time to spare. Doc could be unmercifully short with anyone who came to see him at Leviathan Court when he was at his thinking or writing; but when not so engaged—especially if wandering about town—he was positively overbearing with talk at chance encounters, whether or not his interlocutor was at leisure for listening. He cared nothing for the fatigue and anxiety of a citizen who had to get up and go to work in the morning.

This time Caleb was lucky. Doc plunged down the steep narrow segment of Pleasure Street from Morality Square to the Oak Hill salient in the inner harbor shabbily crowded with commercial and multifamilied tenements that once had sheltered the fishery's red-light houses and many more taverns. The elephantine vagrant would now be braking his weight past the crumbling brick Court House (a lofty damp-stained box wafted with cold drafts and unventilated tobacco smoke, long since condemned by the city's own Building Inspector) on the granite steps of which a dim blue light marked the nightmanned Police Station on the first floor, whose shifting watches from the hillside office he believed were decided upon his innocence. By the time that Caleb resuming his way had reached the Square and relieved his anxiety with a cautious look down that one-way crevass in the ridge of business blocks, the browsing anthropologist had disappeared somewhere about the waterfront.

Turning up Pleasure in the other direction, he released Ibi for the rare sensation of running free among the city's central scents to scan the layers of news condensed and insulated under the thickening pile of an odorless white carpet before it was soiled by strangers. Darting soundlessly ahead in his own turn of joy, which put to shame the grunting recreation that had exhausted his owner, the explorer swiftly vanished, only to reappear in silence as a lustrous shadow of massless grace on either side of every street.

But Caleb himself was not singlemindedly savoring the freedom and safety of a silently cleansed city, practically vacated, where the only motion was their own against the dancing snow's. Though here downtown the winter ordinance against overnight parking on the streets (in favor of the snowplows, which were probably just then being rousted out at the Public Works Barn over on the other side of Squid Circle) was hardly violated at all as if especially for his aesthetic satisfaction, on this occasion his thoughts alternated between the tousled bed at home and the Poet's. Anyway, even as a zealot of law and order, he was too rapt in private peace to be disturbed by an innocent kilroy's motionless trespass upon the shrouded white night.

Heading north from the omphalic square with footsteps more brutal than his beast's, he desecrated pristine Pleasure Street by crossing diagonally to the block behind Pound's Drug Store in front of the Western Union telegraph office, which no longer remained open all around the clock or delivered its messages by any means but phone or mail. And then immediately left at the high-stacked Anabasic church clad in a peeling armor of scalloped white shingles on the eastern end of Halibut Street, a bent row of antiPapist fanes and likeminded mansions which paralleled Front Street on the brow of a ridge that had commanded the inner harbor before commercial buildings rose to occlude its eminence during the prosperous decades after the Great Fire of 1830. Brushing past the Dogtown Savings and Loan Association ("Mother of Homes"), the only business at the back of the Pound Block, which was dwarfed by the church crowding even more narrowly the opposite sidewalk of the cramped little street, but before reaching the wooden gothic synagogue Temple (purchased from the Divine Humanists when they merged with the General Individualists further down the street) he right-turned north again on Whale Avenue. Across from a perfectly 18C clapboard dwelling on the corner stood the Atheneum Free Library, in which his landlady was employed, a squared white box spoiled in the course of its 19C modifications. Thereafter loomed to his right the spacious brick pile of Ibicity Hall, where his landlord worked, its otiose corner pinnacles ruthfully veiled by nighttime snowwhirl, the lighted clocks of its snow-fringed Baroque tower faintly visible through the thickly descended sky, its beclouded weathercock higher than any roof in the central Harbor ward, lording it over the slates of the immensely weightier Grammar School (factory of legends) opposite the high steps of its main entrance, similar in masonry but less eclectic in style, and over the balustraded gravel roof of the monumentally pillared Post Office next door, humbly lower than its brick neighbors, with facings of granite too smooth and light in color, which had been built during the Depression (even before the New Deal) to make work for the dispirited building trades.

In contrast to the other old seaports of Gloucester County, especially Bethsalem a little to the south and Newessexport a little to the north, Dogtown's surviving architecture was largely undistinguished or downright ugly (and its generally visible dwellings of recent addition, outside the Harbor Ward, tasteless at best); but in this snow-laden quiet of softly yielding suspense, free of strangers and vehicles, free of all saints but one, Caleb saw nothing to complain of. In the warm musk of his clothes, his shoes not yet wet through, homing without criticism through the sleeping heart of what seemed all at once his own city, the aged homunculus that formed a metamorphic part of his constant character was again youthfully astir at the prestidigitatorial memory of what he and Bice had said and done together at both ends of this route, first in his own narrow pallet and then upon the high wide bedstead of Poet's Corner. He anticipated the evening of this propitious new day. In sybaritic thought-experiments he canvassed voluptuations that had quite properly been left unexplored in favor of the fundamentals, while looking forward to the occasion for repeating and excelling the extraordinary impression he had already made. He dismissed an undeveloped inkling that no impression would ever make as much difference to her as it did to other women he had known. But praise be to Inanna! Inanna be praised: there was something purely playful in their desire for each other; something playful and controllable, maybe even more on his side than on hers. He couldn't have dreamed up a more satisfactory conquest. There seemed to be no bottom to this casket of gems.

At the moving center of his reorganized world, smiling complacently, he stared ahead at the path he was pioneering through the snow with absent mind, never watching for its hidden curbs and pavements. He dwelt upon the object of his inward eye and ear in the secure awareness that his external senses were warranted and enhanced by the gliding outrider who scouted his progression in outflung epicyclic sweeps, periodically trailing across the whitesward course a warm black spoor of pentadic cuneiforms. The architectures weren't minded by Ibi; each and all he circled impartially, now on one side, now on the other—the public buildings and the private houses in back of them or in between, from one block to the next and probably beyond, never hesitating in the darkness, never blundering into pit or fence, always finding his way where no way was intended by the Puritan proprietors who calculated ways to thwart the saints.

Whale Avenue ran short straight and stout like a crossbeam bearing the socket of a mast and held the city together. Coming to the Back Street end of it he faced the Petrine Scholastic rectory, again of brick, flanked by the parochial school and backed by the rough granite apse of the Blessed Virgin Mary basilica, by far the city's most populous church, the huge rounded nave of which ruled over the wooden houses of its banlieu like a castle over its village and rendered inconsonantly slender the new aluminum flèche at the other end (which had recently been donated by a clan of Tuscan fishermen to replace the massive one demolished by a hurricane). As from all positions of the earth a constellation seems to lie in one plane, so in the spectrum of perspectives from the open bay and outer harbor the buildings on this civic hill—including the outlying Armory, Court House, office buildings, and department stores—are deceptively massed into one consolidated stronghold. Together the B V M spire and the Hall tower pierce the acropolis skyline like the two projections of a single cathedral.

"Some altar boy!" she had sighed. "Only a woman can know that our church has lost such a fine rectory priest." It was during the first lull after his interrogation of her in the garret, a few minutes after his trinity had dropped to the floor from her hand and as he was dozing for a second or two. Perhaps she was thinking of Christ's manhood. Before the interview she had noticed pinned low on the wall in a corner of his study a small black silvermounted crucifix (with some of its rosary beads still attached), and he'd told her that he too once did time at a Tudor-Classic convent there on the Cape, though only a year, at the age of five, and was taught to serve at the altar. "Who cares if you're not very good at preaching?"

Caleb turned left at the Scholastic enclave (where he and Bice hand in hand had turned to the right), and came at once to Parlous Square, now safe, at which Back Street continued west, Cusk ended from the south, and Pollock began to the north; but he steered forty-five degrees to starboard, half-right up Depot Avenue on a northwesterly course. It was a rare pleasure to traverse in silent solitude that distorted five-point star, which (especially when superintended twice a day in the school calendar by a uniformed woman who authorized the crossing of children) was the town's most likely locus for a traffic jam. At other times it was often another of the city's first-come-first-serve melees—pedestrian take the hindermost; and sometimes the impasse of kilroys disputing the right-of-way could be unknotted only by an irritably cooperative backing up. The sole rule usually observed was to keep to the right of a white wooden pylon no higher than a woman (now dressed as a snowman), which Bice had been amused to hear him refer to as a traffic *dummy*. "I call it a pruned scarecrow." she'd said, before the snow began: "But it might attract white ravens."

Caleb recalled her laugh and laughed aloud thereat as he kept precisely to the route she'd walked with him, between his bed and hers, recrossing Parlous Square from the plumber's shop labeled Sanitary Engineers to the gusseted lot of the untidy Tidewater gas station, heading for the yonder railroad properties.

For the Cornucopian visitor Rafe Opsimath this V & M R R freight yard had been the port's venerable ganglionic connection to the continental system of commerce, like the retina of an eye grown aged looking eastward out to sea. The low stoneless architecture of weatherbeaten sheds and platforms, moribund and gray, was no shelter for the rusting iron nerves. For Caleb, however, who lived in the neighborhood, this ground was the inner city's harbor. The basin that neither rose nor fell with Ocean's tide was a wooden moraine naturalized by the century of steam already receded, and the boarded-up freight houses and rotting docks were this night renewed by raiments of snow; the dead vegetation between the rails and windstrewn trash were vested with the same alb that now clothed all the roofs and statuary of Dogtown. The splintered and half-buried ties, from which time and neglect had dangerously loosened the rail-spikes, were obliterated in general absolution. Even the mapping tracery of the candelabra itself was about to be leveled and erased, if the snowfall lasted a little longer. Until the frosted moisture condensed under sun or rain, the lines of steel would be brought back into relief only when trustfully sought by wheels of steel forged to match them; and except for the single track continuing to Seamark most of them were seldom sought in any weather.

Yet still, a couple of boxcars and a reefer, two flat cars bared of their iron loads, a gondola emptied of coal, as well as a few tankcars for fish-oil exports or fuel-oil imports, stood shaggy with snow on several of the rundown sidings like frozen bison or extinct beasts of burden, attached and single, to prove that certain petering industrial traffic persisted more stubbornly than circus trains. Noah's Traveling Circus, which nowadays drove directly to Salt Cod Park in a convoy of kilroy trailers to rig its tents without marching the animals at all, or even to the Fair Grounds by the Land's End terminal in Seamark, had for fifty years disembarked and marshalled upon the quays of this interior groundlevel harbor three rings worth of exotic procession. Could he really believe his own eyes' memory of the circus parade down Front Street on its way to the Park, or was he recalling only his own local extrapolation from a storybook Sister Catherine read aloud? Likely as not it was one of the hypnotic pictures transferred by his mother in living words from her own experience, subject to his own interpretation at repeated times of telling and later gradually modified by his own visual experience elsewhere in literature or life. Yet circus trains to Dogtown were known historical facts.

Just then an almost Christmas joy of more masculine boyhood was summoned by the familiar clanking sounds of a railroad at its proper business. The yard engine from Bethsalem had worked its way up the line as quietly as possible to this penultimate knot of the Gloucester Branch. In consideration of the sleeping precinct it operated at an irreducible level of communication, signaling its intuitive crew (aboard or afoot) with faint inchoate whistles choked off apologetically at their very inception. It had been shunting cars on tiptoe, toning down the collisions of coupling necessary for all synapses in a permutation of rolling stock, moderating as much as possible the shocks of opposed inertias; and tonight—this morning—the heavenly filtration which had been bestowed upon the whole sleeping seaboard further palliated the creaking stresses of discontinuous acceleration, the sudden strains of passively enchained linkage, and the screeching pain of curved rails at almost obstetrical onslaughts of lateral wedging. The engineer, conductor, and two brakemen whispered to each other with the cryptic lantern signs of bootleggers rustling cargo both in and out. They had casual time to clear the Branch of its miscellaneous freight business for the day's preemptive passenger schedule to be set in motion from Botolph an hour before dawn.

What Ibi paid no attention to Caleb was just too late to witness. He emerged into open view of the track continuing to Land's End only to catch no more of the juggled five- or six-car consist than two red lights on the rear platform of a white-thatched caboose disappearing around the curve where it snicked clean through a thicket of multiple-dwelling units at the very center of Dogtown's population, the northern arm of a parabola that brought the double tracks into town as close to the waterfront as they were allowed to approach. Fifteen years after the establishment of this original terminus in 1845 the four rails of the right-of-way had been pinched into two and bent northerly in final extension of service to the tip of the Cape (though never quite as far as ocean wharves), where there was plenty of room for a turnaround loop and numerous long finger-piers of rail on which to classify and moor in their idleness the engines and cars of both kinds. The ghostly little freight train vanished with but a single muffled toot into the deeper silence of the Purdeyville cuts.

This dry-land dockyard in Caleb's own quarter was then left with more silence than ever fell upon the tidal port. There the pulsing susurrations of harbor industry never ceased, even when no one seemed at work. There all the stationary engines motors and compressors were never simultaneously still. And there, unpredictably, at any hour of the night, your psyche might be rocked on its beam-ends by blasts of the powerhouse fire-whistle in its very ear.

Tonight in fact it had startled Bice into spilling champagne on Caleb's bare chest. It was more deafening than any locomotive of the century. Like most Dogtowners, having formed efficient habits of cognition, Caleb had paid no attention to the coded signal once he heard the prefix that ruled out his own zone. He'd waited calmly for the long sequence of dots and dashes to repeat itself and stop (for it proved to be only an unimportant single-alarm) before instructing the scared girl to lick up her trepidated libation. Those unmanning but informative tocsins issued from the obsolete works of "the Traction" (Cape Gloucester Power, Light, and Traction Company, lately absorbed into the Vinland Gas and Electric system), which continued to keep up enough steam for that purpose while on stand-by reserve but was nowadays fired up in earnest only when peak loads overburdened an exiguous high-tension line from the big turbines down at Bethsalem Beach that transmitted the whole county's basic necessity. The Traction, though it had originally generated DC power for the Cape's trolley cars, remained a shipshape AC plant, almost academic in lavishment of space, its oldtimers cherishing a tradition of Bristol-fashion maintenance that generously overmatched the present rate of wear and tear. The reciprocating engine and dynamo were overshadowed by their huge flywheel, the center of attraction, enclosed like an archaeological exhibit of some whale's skeleton by a balconied gray deck with polished brass railings and sheltered by a building designed in the age of philanthropy. But the current function of the building, or rather of the ominous bank of transformers in the carefully fenced yard outside, was mainly to distribute imported electricity—no longer to produce it. This dendritic allocation of fungible energy was controlled by a switchboard of meters mounted upon a painted black-and-white schematic chart of the Cape all along one wall, grossly inconsistent in scale, which resembled less a map than some giant claviature. As an admiring visitor Caleb was welcome there at any hour, with Ibi, and he knew that Bice would be yet more cordially accepted. It was another generally overlooked cathedral that he meant to show her, with its tall stack and emergency pile of coal, only a few hundred yards from where she undressed.

They had made one slight divagation on their progression between dalliances, for the so-called champagne, a bubbling wine from the "Empyrean State" of Nether Land, excellent for auxiliary ecstasy. So in returning now as if on sentimental journey Caleb methodically traces in reverse the invisible footsteps of which he was quite reckless when making them with Bice. Having passed the baggage shed (now used only by the atrophied Railway Express), he crosses Depot Avenue to the little liquor store crowded with merchandise that they discontinued their sport to reach before statutory closing time. During their early games he'd called her his Gypsy Champagne, an effervescent blend of many different sweet and sour grapes, his own special devil's wine, delicately superfermented in her own skin, which he'd declared to be the most beautiful of her organs as he traced its surfaces for seams and boundaries. It was her vintage of mind, he'd said, that gave her eyes the merry sparkle. Again, he'd told her that from the first her face had raised in him a great thirst for the depths of her intelligence. "Champagne goes flat once you open the bottle!" she'd warned. Did she expect him to stay sober? he'd asked. "On your kind of toasting it's the champagne itself that gets inebriated!" she'd replied. And it was this talk that had at last aroused such a craving for the proper drink to pledge each other's health that it became one of the motives to get themselves out of bed the first time—along with hunger, and the yen for a double mattress suitable for throes of play and snatches of sleep. So he'd fed Ibi and made some scrambled eggs. Running like Hansel and Gretel they'd made it to the store just before lockup. At the Poet's Corner he got her tipsy, and felt as if his luck was well deserved.

But now he stays not to take in the winter scene of glittering Canadian whiskey bottles deployed in the snow-festooned window amid unmeltable snow of bitumen-based alabaster foam (reflecting only dim light from outdoors); blurring the cusp of his visible footprints, he turns on his heel, faithful to his reconstructive choreography, and recrosses the street, trailing behind him on the blanked page an inverted V of ephemeral signature.

Back then to the Dogtown passenger station, where in former livelihoods he's many a time purchased his commuter ticket and close by the stove on cold mornings read whatever book he carried, listening without intelligence to desultory traffic clicking through the telegraph key, which was apparently never heeded by the intelligent Station Master or his assistant. The long platform of cracked asphalt, under a roof cantilevered from its colonnade of squared wooden posts, serves as pedestrian shortcut to Cod Street at the crossing gates.

Ibi has disappeared ahead, beyond the parabolic divide, already ranging his home territory, ostentatiously demonstrating that it was unnecessary for his man to advise him of their destination. Much as he has delighted in the decadent adventure, he's as happy as ever to have been restored to the great outdoors, and happier yet to get back to his dish. Bice had protested Caleb's stern rule against allowing Ibi on the bed at home, declaring that such "discipline" (in her mouth a scornful term) was but further evidence of his cold heart; and in 36, where there was plenty of room and guests could forget the doghair they left, she defied the disciplinarian by inviting the saint to leap up and keep the bed warm. But the docile brute, settling down upon the bedspread as heavily as a lumpish duplicate of Caleb, soon felt too sheepish about enjoying the effete comfort of the violated taboo to remain at ease; if he was not to be the center of attention, moreover, he preferred to sleep on a rug that didn't jiggle—which he did after the first ten minutes, though still a little uncomfortable with Caleb's own lapsarian behavior. Now, having set his mind at rest with a quick reconnaissance of the manorial environment, he has blazoned himself on the front stoop, a snow-mantled leopard sitting on ground of snow.

He clears an arc of snow with his brush on the synthetic granite step, complacently smiling at the surprise of his laggard tutor.

But an elder too can fool a younger—for instance, by not coming up to the door. To Ibi's astonishment, Caleb hops up onto the small lawn between driveway and porch, flings himself down on his back, and, sweeping his own arcs with both arms stretched out straight, etches a winged angel in the snow. But there is still too little cover on the frozen ground for full intaglio; and the exiguous image isn't half completed anyway before it's mucked up by the transmogrified puppy cub bounding down from the escutcheon for his share of the novel fun, licking the supine face and prancing a dizzy dance with vandal's feet.

Brought up short by Ibi's slobbering officiousness, Caleb jumps to his feet, recovering the dignity of homo erectus, and mounts the steps to the tall double door (the rounded tops of whose frosted glass panels are repeated at his own windows two stories up under the eaves). Propping open the aluminum storm-door with his hip, while Ibi patiently awaits his usual fumbling at the common entrance to the cave, he turns to take a last look at the blessed silence. The darkest hour before dawn, under the thickest of soft skies, is illuminated as much intrinsically by the snow fallen and falling as by the electric nightlight which it can't absorb. On this white stage of the vicinage white houses now more luminous than in their open radiance under a full moon face each other (and a corner of the white cemetery) across the frozen river of Cod Street, which presents itself as an immaculate strip of unobstructed whiteness emerging from walls of white mist beyond the somewhat yellowed haloes of steadfast lamps on either hand that isolate and magnify statistical samples of the swirling downward-driven flakes not yet committed to the earth—ideal christian triangles countlessly conglomerated into globs of hebrew hexagons, all of them taking kaleidoscopic form by the two-to-one ratio of hydrogen and oxygen—not one among the myriads compatible with a single five-point star of Inanna.

Suddenly out of the darkness that invests the whole candescence—an aureate pair of headlights, framed by a square constellation of amber spots, preceding the sound of their source, comes up the narrow dogleg of Cod Street from the outside world. As the double beams boring the snowwhirl adjust themselves from a tangent of the rise to a parallel with the summit plateau, the engine is shifted with deep-breathen satisfaction to an even quieter ratio of gears; but the impinging motion adds horizontal velocity to the rushing drift of intensified cross-sections selected from the lowest atmosphere. A modest semitrailer from the West, first of the morning, rolling at respectful speed across a peaceful sector of observation, is comforting reassurance of the island's winter supplies, even if it happens to be a lone gypsy deadheading into Dogtown just to take a load of fish away. The benign rig glides gently down the other slope to the railroad tracks, its hollow square of red tail lights winking out of sight eftsoons and leaving the downy sheet of snow deflowered by only ten blunt treads.

Caleb turns the key. Led by his bodyguard he crosses the threshold twice crossed by Bice. Ibi has learned not to bound up the stairs ahead of his master, but as no degree of acculturated partnership can ever convert him into an indoor pard, especially on the bare hardwood floor outside bedroom doors on the second floor on the way to their private staircase for the final ascent, Caleb himself walks like a cat and shrugs his shoulders at the foot-muffling that can't be taught. He only hopes that Dexter and Gloria Keith were more amused than annoyed, before they went to sleep, at the booted extra pair of feet that crept down after so much silence when the night was young. But no matter what they guessed, that married couple could never imagine the adventure then just half begun!

Yet the warm security of this dustless castle reminds him of his gratitude to the Keith family for relieving him of the fear of fire that even the spilled champagne did not excite, or the fear of having missed one of the signals. All night he has taken for granted the safety of his wooden tower. Even coming back up Cod Street he forgot to look ahead for a shortening of the row of houses that is not supposed to end before the cemetery, or to look for broken glass and smoked clapboards on the third floor. Piously he blesses the proprietors for so well guarding his artifacts during that respite from worry.

As he finally lies down alone again in his tumbled bed, pretending to detect the lingering impressions of Bice's body, the first plow comes clanking by on its way downtown. But he falls asleep before Ibi has finished his noisy lapping at the water dish on the kitchen floor; and he's never conscious of the next truck, scattering salted sand that withers growing things along the curb: which signals the opinion of the Director of Public Works that the first little storm of the season is just about over.

Thus is Caleb floated upon the flood tide of his year in halcyon slumber as he congratulates himself for having brought his own storm to such a pitch without falling in love. In the bemusement of transitory gratification he feels the bonds of Inanna as no more fettering than an elephant's gyves of grass.

7
AVALON REEFER

"Good morning, Herr Talgrid Obelliminus! Have you sustinated your cambrones already? You must never forget to casticulate, whereinafter your immiscible octifier is so disrestitiously umbreous. Otherwise there'll be a new unspectaculation, as heterodyned by that busbee operator aforesaid hereinafter aufgeborgen sein werden." said Caleb an hour or so later when the dog stretched up off the floor to greet him first thing in the morning. "Or are you the wight I haven't yet excogitated?" he then asked. "Anyway, don't worry: it's only the hypersimulation of doubly unrecorded alteractions. Women are the better people."

Ibi's head inserted itself between hand and knee of the man seated on the bed preparing for action. The tail of the attendant wagged vigorously to hear the voice in such good spirits. Caleb leaned over to suppress the alarm threatened by his clock. His anticipatory recovery of consciousness was especially remarkable because at this time of year it was scheduled every day a minute or so earlier than the crack of dawn. Ibi had expected to the contrary that the nonce feast lately so exhaustively concelebrated would sanction the lenitive tendency to sleep at least until the normal hour of an officeworker.

For all his clarity of heart and tone of other tissue, Caleb had to drink an extra cup of coffee in the attempt to clarify and tune his mind. At his desk, shaved and dressed, he found his elation still encircled by an aura of haziness like a ring around the moon. He was unable to bend his thought to the angular concepts awaiting his attention, to say nothing of conducting new experiments; but it was no neutralization of libido that befuddled his insomnolence. This blithesome energy, not keen enough to recover and extend his anachronistic vision of words and action, was dissipated by the dreamy memory of Bice's precisely contemporary performance, which stimulated only a vague urge to write acutely. So he gave himself up to reverie, in lazy convalescence of intellect, satisfied with the disciplinary achievement of keeping to schedule. Moving slowly, he broke his fast with a good appetite but a dull taste.

The snow hadn't amounted to much. Kids were going to school, and everyone else to normal business. There was no respectable excuse for not going to the Laboratory. At his own request, as the nominal steward of The Trustees of the Classic Order of the Vine, he worked only four days a week, but was paid enough to sustain himself and Ibi, plus certain small perquisites and emoluments by which Father Lucey made sure it would cost him no more in personal expenditures to do the job in proper style than to stay at home like an anchorite.

Proper style was sometimes a style seemly to the worldly. Out of town the Father Economist bought him very good lunches, and he was reimbursed other expenses at a level befitting the dignity of a Tudor functionary. Indeed in New Uruk, once when they were walking in the District, he was steered into the Street's best haberdashery to be fitted out with a mouse-gray Homburg for special wear in and about Graveyard Street or its provincial colonies in Washington and Botolph, ostensibly half for the fun of it, though for him all fashionable hats were somewhat out of scale (like the caps of frail Navy officers).

Among his bonuses was free use of the Order's scooting little Autotod to commute the three miles between Rectory and Lab. By the time he took leave of Ibi outside, when the Keith family had already dispersed to its various public duties, he no longer felt fresh as the morning. It was always heartbreaking to say goodbye to the faithful saint watching his departure with philosophical resignation, his tail slowly asway in rapidly diminishing hope of reprieve or exception; but today, sadly surveying each other's face as Caleb warmed up the tiny air-cooled engine behind his back, his daily pang of sweet melancholy was overborne by a new sense of unforgivable culpability—for having been exclusively fascinated by a fairweather friend of eighteen hours whose sympathy was immeasurably less spiritual and whose loyalty was neither offered nor expected; for having practically forgotten the devotion of his truest lover in favor of one who felt that what good men wanted of her they probably all deserved.

Ibi escorted the car to the boundary of his messuage and halted to watch it back out into Cod Street at the first lull in traffic. But before the house was out of sight in the rearview mirror Caleb thought he saw his retainer turn away and trot off to tribal business in the cemetery, presumably intending to keep within sensory range of the property he guarded.

Caleb summoned the will to drag himself through the day. It was lucky for his dimmed mind that Father Lucey had taken the high boss Father Duncannon up to Bournemouth Bill for the day to visit the Order's senior Member Secular, a parish rector in the Diocese of Markland whom they consulted on all important matters—in this case the forthcoming Chapter to be held at the Laboratory in June. Nor should his ruminant psyche be disturbed by any company within the office itself, for Mortimer Ockham, the taciturn bookkeeper and scrivener (an insider, the oldest remaining charter Member besides the Father Founder himself), would be away on duty at the brokerage in Botolph. Considering that he was in no mood to work—still less to discuss anything that wasn't too private for discussion with anyone but Bice, and was scarcely in condition to reply to anybody else's inquiries—such a conjunction of absences was nothing less than fate's continuation of the good fortune that had brought her to the gates of Acorn Pasture Cemetery for the love of dogs at precisely the right minute yesterday afternoon.

At the same time this propitious hap fixed him with solo responsibility for the monastery and its Japanese houseboy. Oku required no immediate supervision, and was able to answer the telephone in half intelligible English; any excuse for Caleb's own truancy would have been accepted without a second thought: but the circumstances calling for a day of bleary rest at home only pleaded his cardinal point of honor not to malinger or fib with his godsent employers, who had appeared in his destiny at a level immeasurably higher than romantic chance. Gratitude to them and for them had indeed become so pervasive in his appreciation of life that simply in respect for their cloth he was secretly attempting to overcome the unimaginative habit of taking in vain the names of the Father and Son when complaining to himself, as he often did, about the cussedness of things—though he knew they would have smiled at the notion of correcting him in any behavior except his service at their Mass; and even about liturgical manners they were forbearingly didactic.

All the more was he determined to prove himself worthy of professional trust in the face of a virtually necessitous urge to return betimes to Bice's bed. It was only in deference to her recovery of sleep that he hadn't telephoned the Poet's Corner before he left the house.

Although he hoped for as much solitude as possible until they met again, his greetings were not morose to those others with whom he saw no danger of being forced into conversation. In a cloud of incense obscuring the habitual scenes before his eyes, insulated by the nimbus of lightheaded fecklessness that sloughed or diffused all his perceptions of ordinary weights and measures, yet at the center exulting in his memory and anticipation of an educated gypsy baring her skin to his in manifest desire for his particular ministrations, he smiled amiably at the curator of the Free Enterprise Education Library, his first stop of the day, where he often spent an hour or two augmenting his data before driving over to the Lab in East Harbor.

It was nonetheless with inveterate resentment that he ignored the two old codgers already devouring the day's *Graveyard Chronicle*, which served as national newspaper as well as official bulletin of the previous day's transactions for readers whose participation or wish for participation in the economy was fiscal financial monetary or Protestican, while they waited for the ticker to begin its discreet clatter under the little glass dome. He sank into his routine of mechanical research at the reference table in the back room, blindly recording certain routine facts, postponing the effort to understand their significance. He fetched and replaced various looseleaf books and newsprint journals without consciousness of having risen from his seat. The young scholaraster always acknowledged to himself, and indeed warned his friends, that he was an efficient acquisitor of knowledge only when the subject happened to suit both his bent and his coincident emotion; and today he was not surprised to find himself stupidly deaf to everything that knocked at his brain except the images of tumescence.

FEEL played a definite part in Caleb's job. He was entitled to use its facilities as a citizen of Dogtown, unlike the Lab's clerical drudge Mortimer Ockham, who lived with his mad wife in far off Norumbega and who despite astonishing ecclesiastical erudition was anyway not very interested in analysis. Whereas almost all virtuous Christians since Tertullian have discountenanced the involvement of churches in worldly affairs, and inasmuch as Father Christopher Lucey had become well enough known to be obliged to wear his round collar whenever he made appearances around town, it was convenient for the Trustees to have the agency of one privileged to the facilities endowed by Tybbot's charitable foundation. The majority of FEEL's utilities (in addition to the *Chronicle* and the ticker) were provided, as if to a paying subscriber, by Tybbot Financial Service (TFS) or its affiliates. There was *Tybbot's Market Service Reports,* a perpetually revised set of corporate character sketches in standard format; *Tybbot's Business Reference,* with its authoritative credit ratings; and *Poor Richard's Weekly,* known as the most thoughtful of business journals, which had continued to print the philanthropist's personal contributions until the last deadline of his life. But some were purchased from other financial publishers.

One was especially impressed by the tolerance of FEEL's periodical department not only for its clients but also for all the direct and indirect competitors of Tybbot's own enterprises. Dogtowners were given access to almost all the reputable publications that any Promethean or Epimethean investor might care to consult, some of them so expensive that they were regarded as esoteric, or so voluminous, so incessant, that only a staffed library could keep them contemporaneously organized in their countless loose-leaf binders: Broody's world-famous *Security Reports;* Uniform and Rich's *Reference Service;* Blockhouse & Garrison's *Tax-Dodge Rulings,* and their indispensable *Business Case Reports* (both of them full of loopholes for sleepless defense against Uncle Sugar's firebrands, but the latter with cautionary tales of skirmishes with redskin Labor too, and gazetted lawsuits filed by businessmen against their brothers, the index to which it was useful for Caleb to scan every month for the possible involvement of Parity companies in major litigation); the *DeSoto Reports* on what was brewing in the construction industry; for extraordinarily specialized financial specialists, even the *Sauer's Catalog* of manufacturers' prices and specifications for architects and builders; but most delightful of all, about a dozen of the "market letters" usually appearing only on the desks of affluent professional investors like Jason Anacoluther—including all volumes of the precious *Aggrandizement* advisories!

Today of course Caleb cared not a fig for this rich array of abstracts. It might as well have been the catacomb of a salt mine he'd long since been sentenced to. He was able to wield his pick and shovel like a dazed automaton only because he'd become so accustomed to the task that it now amounted to nothing more than filling old bottles with new wine by simple habitual procedure. Even in his fog he laughed to think that by yet another merciful grant of fortune he had put behind him all need for thought in FEELing.

In any event the work in question was a madman's dream. In the beginning—with the enthusiastic encouragement of Rafe Opsimath, his former employer, subventor and rightful owner of the original Parity Corporation chart—he had been hired by Father Chris primarily to keep that static molecular skeleton up to date. The great multicolored map of Arthur Halymboyd's heraldic web was donated to the Trustees under no illusion that it could continue to be very useful without occasional revisions of structure and periodic revisions of quantities. It took considerable diligence and judgment to maintain a synchronous representation of the empire's changing assets, seeing that most of the published facts were out of phase with each other or otherwise irregular, and were anyway more than three months old to start with. Even the most organic cross-section is ill suited to evolutionary description.

Yet the chart had at once established itself for Rafe and Chris as the syllabus of interrelationship for all their appraisals of real or fictitious persons who had been or might be associated with the house of Halymboyd. By means of annotated diagram an otherwise unenvisaged tangle of branches and creepers were brought to order as an intelligible labyrinth, and Caleb had sworn that his drawing could continue to serve the purpose of revelation and prophecy. Until the next major schism or anabolism, however, the variable dynamic details were recorded and organized by card file and columnar tables. He wasn't expected to develop the latest information into a new picture until the next special occasion for impressing someone.

Meanwhile therefore he was using the library to keep reasonably abreast of phenomena without immediately assimilating the news into his monstrous uncinematic icon. His depiction of Halymboyd's control had sustained all doubt about its general validity, but the proximate causations of that invisible hand were best traced by numerical monitors. The Father Economist's first strategic question was whether or not the enigmatic father of Parity was exploiting his structural power by arbitrarily or rhythmically manipulating its stock on the market. Chris thought he noticed an unobtrusive undulatory pattern of price history. A gradual rise and fall of a point or two attracts little public attention, but for penny stocks such a fluctuation signifies very large gains and losses of market value.

Which, in principle, directly or indirectly, allowing for lags in the dissemination of financial information, since PAR comprised interests in many companies themselves listed in several different stockmarkets (most of them at much higher unit prices), should have varied as a dependent variable with the net sum variation of the component values. Did it actually do so? More fundamentally, was the whole (fictitiously personified in the price of PAR itself) consistently greater or less than the sum of its holdings? Determining a correlation was the first step in attempting to falsify the hypothesis that Halymboyd was tactically controlling the price of PAR.

At any rate, Caleb had made it his business to follow and compare the daily closings of all securities that appeared to be in any actual or potential phase of ingestion digestion or excretion by the Parity Corporation.

If he hadn't been carrying out scholarship of his own design it would have been too much dogwork even for Caleb. The project was utterly unconscionable for a free-wheeling aristocrat like Chris (who would have cheerfully served God as a stretcher-bearer under fire)— and therefore extravagantly appreciated. The priest marveled uncritically at the huge matrix pieced together with rubber cement out of the largest available sheets of graph paper, which Caleb would post with a fine pencil when he got to the Lab office after mining the figures on Tybbot's premises. As a matter of fact, immersed in the details he had bitten off to chew, Caleb was almost ready to admit to himself that it was a little absurd to go back to the middle of the previous year for historical patterns that might well prove entirely negative in correlation with anything at all. Chris said nothing against the ambitious initiative, but they both partook of a growing nervousness about all the time it was taking. Which ordinarily made Caleb work all the harder to fill his vast field of blank cells—and discount the percentage of his time that should have been charged to the job.

Having spent an hour and more extracting information from all the reports he could find on the Nuncupative Mutual Assurance Society (NUN, an unexcitingly famous creation of Dr Capstick for the patronage of small consumers in which no Parity stockholder could help owning a small stake), he finally got hold of the morning *Chronicle* and made short work of the latest quotations, dispatching the numbers to his notebook with summary weariness.

Smiling condescendingly at the young matron on watch who little dreamed that this trim polite young patron (presumably born or destined to riches) had but lately come from the ineffably envied arms and legs of a perfectly desirable bachelor girl, he continued on his way to the Lab, murmuring experiments with half a dozen different greetings as he wryly wondered how long he would be able to resist the urge to wake up Bice by phone.

The clear day was just cold enough to prevent the sun from melting the snow, and even downtown the city's whiting was still clean. Caleb slowed down as he drove past the Van, but in the snow-accumulating gut of Front Street there was a dearth of parking space and the cars behind him were impatient with his hesitation; so the good soldier got the upper hand over his palpitating heart as he put the Poet's Corner further and further behind him. If necessary Bice could see the ships and boats without his guidance, but he wished to be her dragoman for the cityscape of houses with towers, fish plants, sail lofts, wharves, power plant, Leviathan Court, and the entire artifactual margin of the inner harbor, around to the spacious seascapes of the gentry quarter in which he worked.

But it occurred to him that tonight he'd have to keep her indoors still, both before and after, because there was no safe walking after any winter storm. The city's street-plowing left impassable windrows of snow over the pinched gutters and sidewalks, which no one ever took a shovel to—certainly not the merchants, who were forever bellyaching for outright snow removal by the Department of Public Works, as well as more parking pavement for their lazy-legged customers—despite an unequivocal ordinance requiring all frontagers to clear a safe footing for children and other poor people.

He also pondered the most convenient restaurant for dinner betweentimes, and wondered if he could somehow cop a catnap beforehand.

The little Autotod (with most of its weight on the drive-axle) made no difficulty of getting up the yet unsanded Moor Rock hill to the Laboratory of Melchizedek and the Mesocosm, which (except for the red cross over its foremost gable that some of the Members grumbled about because of the Petrine Classic taste it seemed to falsely suggest) was no more impressive than scores of other real estates preempting a prospect from one of the Cape's high places, each in its own incomparable situation.

Oku was not to be seen. Caleb went directly up to the office, a large upper room at the westerly end with windows on three sides. Sitting at his desk (separating two others), with the inner city at his back and the Crow Point lighthouse a mile off to his right, he looked out over the Eastern Ocean toward the Azores. There were almost always a few boats either coming and going northeastward up the coast or dragging unseen nets at imperceptible speeds more or less on the legal side of the three-mile limit that had been lobbied by the inshore lobstermen who more or less hostilely shared the port with proper fishermen.

The house had been built early in the century by a family of Father Duncannon's relatives under an eclectic influence. Above gray walls of roughhewn granite, Tudor stucco and half-timber adorned parts of the sunniest levels. Disregarding the pruned pines and cultivated shrubbery sown upon Moor Rock since the extermination of forests you could easily imagine the house as a comfortably fortified strong-point commanding from its hump of ledge the rockboned tail of the Cape known as the Foreside. Just to the south the attenuating promontory was hollowed by Nedlaw Pond, like the eye of a sailmaker's needle, pinched at the neck between Nedlaw Beach on the harbor side and Dilemma Cove on the outer shore, false haven for the wrack of ships.

But today Caleb paid no attention to the panorama that always lay below him to glance or stare at. The first thing he did was telephone the special number for Poet's Corner that had been connected for Rafe and never unplugged. Many rings but no answer. Well at least I can't be blamed for waking her up. She's out for breakfast. I'll call every half hour until she returns, or maybe twice that often, starting in ten or five minutes. He was cheered by a feeling of having reestablished communication, and the most competent part of his mind was again devoted to the composition of intriguing or beguiling phrases of reintroduction to please her with—to remind her of loveliness shared.

His IN-basket held nothing urgent: printed matter for the most part, which he tossed into the PENDING slot for later reading; but also a little unimportant mail that Chris had opened and selectively annotated, and a few messages about phone calls or accounts payable that could be ignored until tomorrow. There was little to prevent him from wading into the vast paddies he himself had laid out. Even today they could be hoed by laborious acts of will, though with thoughts so blurred that it would take more than a few hours of piddling to work up a clarifying sweat. While awaiting a word with Bice it was a blessing to have in the fire an iron of his own shaping. If the specifications of his task had been set by tradition or authority he couldn't have helped pacing the monastery like a caged lion, or running around town like a dog, or going back home to sleep.

He unrolled the great historical wall that he was continually extending as contiguous columns of uniform brick, the simplicity and repetition of which, troweled up so mechanically, was soothing slavery for a mind less and less able to keep its grasp on the veridicality of the priceless liberties that had befallen him. Without obligation or perfidy he had earned the unpremeditated delights of an amorous dryad! At a time like this the unidimensional games of philosophy and business were better left to married men. Yet the brainless procedure of laying the latest bricks so absorbed his thin attention that twenty minutes passed before he roused himself to try her number again.

Still no answer.

Turning then to indolent contemplation of more exciting work, he pulled from the file cabinet a thick folder of messy notes and sketches for a graphic rendition of the organization he worked for. This chart would map very few entities, and compared to the information of the PAR galaxy its simple delineations seemed ludicrously unnecessary. Yet with two coordinates and three colors it purported to represent values and interdimensional relationships infinitely deeper and more comprehensive than the simple monistic world of which Parity was but a transitory sample.

The Laboratory of Melchizedek & the Mesocosm served the international communitas known as the Classic Order of the Vine, whose constituents were Petrine communicants of the Pauline Apostolic Church of the U S A , or of other churches in the Tudor Communion; yet their theology, up to one point or another (but always scrupling at the Pope), was closer to the Petrine Scholastics of the Classic Church. To Scholastics who happened to hear of it, as well as to fellow Tudors, the Order's "antithetical" allegiance to the apostolic succession seemed no more than a manifestation of the puny feckless ambivalence that informed the entire so-called Tudor-Petrine ("High Church") effort to retrieve Petrine orthodoxy without cleaving to Rome. But few in either communion were aware of C O V 's existence—and fewer still suspected that its purpose was not merely to repetrify the Tudor liturgy but also (unlike other Tudor-Petrines) to revise the Petrine Mass itself, altering the form and a little of the content in order to restore its primitive function as the dynamo of Christianity. Father Duncannon believed that the Scholastics themselves had been misunderstanding the essential action of the altar at least since St Augustine, probably from as far back as St Paul. Little wonder then that his "revisionist" order was the beneficiary of very few tithers and had to make the most of its investments.

What saved the Order from ostracism disgrace and public condemnation was the politely aspersed High Church tradition in which it was justly but somewhat misleadingly subsumed. The Unaford Movement and T S Chittering were recognized in Atlantean ecclesiastical and literary circles; there were several High Church religious orders with monasteries and convents in the United States (including one by which Caleb had been nurtured as an infant), as well as a few dozen parishes scattered transcontinentally among Apostolic dioceses—especially where aesthetic wealth was concentrated—and a disproportionately large establishment of eleemosynary missions to the disabled and dispossessed of all races. Priests and nuns of the Tudor-Petrine persuasion were readily accepted by the general public in Scholastic vicinities because their habits and gestures got them mistaken for Classic troops. Thus in Dogtown the Fathers Duncannon and Lucey escaped definition as eccentrics (except among reactionary insiders and government investigators) because they were assumed to be no better or worse than patriotic papists.

But a sense that the piety of the Order was suspect, that in any common theologic it would stink of too much ritual or "materialism", had piqued Caleb's predilection for it as an antithetic cause within the church he'd left behind in his Boy Scout years. Yet Father Duncannon's writings stimulated his crude religious sensibility—or at least his philosophical passions—without overcoming his resistance to the orthodox spiritual obligations entailed by joining C O V . Short of bending his stiff neck, submitting to the confession of faith, and subordinating to religious rule his thirst for experience, he served the institutional needs of the tiny movement with most of his orectic energy that remained from artistic and erotic engagement.

Again. Still no answer.

At the moment of course his enthusiasm for Father Duncannon's revision of Christianity was in abeyance. In the sconce of his enervated body he felt separated from his own will.

To serve his time in the giddy haze, hoping that some intellectual motion could be evoked by uncognitive contemplation, he stared stupidly at the inchoate diagrams thus far evolved in his attempt to reconcile (and thereby to organize) all the confusing and apparently paradoxical attributes of Father Duncannon's vine as passim he had found them in the Order's documents over against personal testimony of the two utterly dissimilar Members Regular, the Superior (Father Founder) and the Father Economist. (Mortimer Ockham, the only Member Secular to whom Caleb had access, preferred not to express himself about any subject, least of all the one to which these twenty years he had dedicated the entirety of emotion and reason that remained unabsorbed by the insanity of his wife.) Caleb cudgeled his infirm spirit with reminders that the unspoken purpose of his organizational study was to justify Father Lucey's exploitation of unburied talents under the vow of poverty. By extracting rational concepts from the present modus operandi he might help Chris forestall the gathering complaints of certain anguished members who murmured vaguely about the Order benefiting from capitalistic investment exceeding the irreducible usufructification of a savings account. Though emulating many elements of Dominican, Cephasite (Society of Peter), and other Medieval or Counterdeformation precedent, the C O V Rule (as originally drafted by Father Duncannon, edited by clerical advisers, approved by the original membership, printed in the "Little Red Book", and of course ratified by all new volunteers) professed modern democratic principles, where reason and conscience permitted, especially in secular works. The opinion of members therefore weighed heavily even in financial matters beyond their competence, which were legally under the sole jurisdictions of the three Trustees. Most of these quasi-electors regarded Chris's operation as an important moral issue. Some thought the issue was simple and ancient.

He'd better reach her before lunch because she might be out all afternoon. He dialed again. She hadn't yet returned from breakfast.

He was nearly ready to work up fair drawings from the freehand jumbles into which he'd stuffed the captions and relationships he intended to convey. Because it was to be drawn on 11-by-17 paper (the largest size that could be conveniently photocopied), though the basic configuration was almost as simple as the Trinity, either the squares or their distances would be much magnified. Conceptual subtleties could be expressed only by labels and alternate dotted lines in various colors on two progressive incarnations of the same skeleton that would look all too busy, with satellite circles and other shapes meant to denote or suggest the categorical distinctions and functional complexity into which he was finally analyzing this unique social organism, as follows.

Item, the Members Regular (still only two): a partnership at the top of the chart. Item, the Laboratory of Melchizedec and the Mesocosm: a nonprofit charitable corporation which owned and operated all facilities. Item, the Trustees of the Founder's Fund of the Classic Order of the Vine: a trust charged with the possession and management of capital intended for the support of the Members Regular, for maintenance of their Laboratory, and for subvention of designated C O V projects or donations, said trust being constituted of the two Members Regular and an attorney from worldly society (in the person of a Jewish corporation lawyer—perhaps to recognize the anthropological foundation of the church). Item: the Management Agency, as Chris chose to dub the employees of the Trustees, principally one of the Members Regular ex officio, i e the Father Economist acting outside his dual capacity as a Trustee and a religious (who of course returned his remunerations to the employers), and his paid assistants or consultants from the secular environment. And item: as spiritual body and beneficiary of the aforementioned apparatus, the whole company of the Classic Order of the Vine (including of course the Members Regular), legally a mere association, whose scattered fellowship in liturgical mission was the ultimate subject and object of everything at the monastic headquarters in Dogtown.

The phone rang just as Caleb was making a move to try it again, slashing the silence, rending his nerves like the backfire of a kilroy at his elbow. As a veteran of urban life, like a dog, he had learned to recover almost wholly from violently disconcerting breaches of peace; still, although he hadn't thought of giving Bice the office number, he answered the signal trembling as eagerly as if he was expecting her initiative.

"This is Chris Lucey." said the warm soft voice that always identified itself in this unassuming tone, long after it was well known and expected by a familiar colleague. But even in the throes of his bewitchment Caleb wasn't disappointed to hear it. The Southerner's courtesy was unfailingly sensitive to the possible state of his interlocutor, sympathetic to any mood in the rainbow between euphoria and depression, masking his own. The messages he delivered were often calculated to bring pleasure in the form of interesting news or exciting suggestion. Although Caleb still called him Father Lucey in public (and in Father Duncannon's presence, whom he never heard address the Regular subordinate in any other form), he had soon succumbed to the custom of informal salutation that Chris had indirectly encouraged at Weatherglass, Neatherd & Company and in all his personal friendships.

"Chris! Where are you?"

"Oh we've been conferring with Father Davy almost two hours now." Unless he and Father Duncannon had started before daylight, or skipped breakfast, he may have been exaggerating; yet there was nothing false in his reputation as a fast driver. He professed to believe that the Father Superior as passenger turned a blind eye to his speed. But Caleb was used to Chris's poetic license. "It's been a fruitful visit. Right now Father Duncannon is hearing Father Davy's confession. I'm sorry I haven't had the chance to call before this, because there's something I wanted to tell you. I should have left a note, but we had a small contretemps in getting off this morning and it slipped my mind. I hope this isn't too late or otherwise inconvenient: feel free to ignore it as a matter of no importance:: we asked Oku to serve you lunch. It happens that we have far more turkey than we can use. Take the scraps home to Ibi. We told Oku noon, but if that's not the best time for you please let him know when. If you can find his shadow. I should think it'd be in the kitchen by now. Forgive me for bursting in with such a triviality so late in the day."

It was almost as if Chris had been informed by an angel. Caleb was not entirely sorry to be forestalled in his foolish plan to search for Bice during the lunch hour with waning energy and ravenous appetite. Chris's kindness frustrated the untimely urge to act. Turkey was his favorite delicatessen. A first-class solitary lunch at the Lab would furthermore spare the expense of hasty eating at a crowded counter, as well as the irritation of noontime traffic. Almost every day that he spent at the Lab had brought an invitation to eat alone with Father Duncannon (for Chris was almost always absent during market hours), and by now he was used to the gentle status of a paid companion; but this was the first time he'd been offered the role of an independent gentleman.

"Yes, it's been very interesting indeed." Chris continued. "Father Davy's wisdom is a great comfort to us. He does bring us down to the essentials." Caleb imagined Father Davy as a tough character with a rugged face, and he was apprehensive about the perspicacity of this celibate parish rector, mentioned so often as a paragon of shrewd simplicity, who had once earned a doctorate in philosophy at Norumbega. He often doubted that Father Davy much approved the hiring of an irregular staff mercenary too stiffnecked to profess interest in membership yet presumptuous enough to have been made privy to business which dedicated fellows of the Order were not privileged to.

"I think we've finally fixed the date for Chapter." Chris was saying. "The last week of June, when the academics will be free, yet early enough not to interfere too much with summer schools or vacation travel. The only problem is Pentecost coverage for the parish priests. What do you think?"

"As long as we reserve accommodations well in advance. Dogtown will be crowded for Gloucestermas, don't forget."

"Yes, the solstice!" cried the agreeable voice, as if Caleb's remark had brought it a burst of intelligence. "The Gloucestertide octave ends on the twenty-ninth—the feast of Saints Peter and Paul! —Perfectly symbolic for Apostolic revisionists!" it added with a jocund laugh.

"Is it too early to find out exactly what the city's calendar will be? I don't see why we shouldn't all take in the blessing of the fleet. And there'll be plenty of other diversions for camp followers! Most of the

Members need a holiday themselves, and some of them have never been here before. For children, and those who haven't yet put away childish things, there'll be elephants, carousel, popcorn, parades, bonfires, fireworks! Some of our members might be interested in the duodecathlon. I'll pass your suggestion on to the fathers right away. It's a pity we won't have cells and suites for everybody at the Lab. It's far too big for the two of us and yet not a quarter of the size we'd need for everybody's rations and quarters. We expect this to be our biggest Chapter yet."

"I'll start lining up reservations as soon as you give me an estimate. We'll have to steal a march on the pilgrims. But it'll be expensive."

"This is just the kind of thing the Trustees are in business for, and I wouldn't be averse to demonstrating our purpose to certain of our more doubtful members. This is going to be a definitive Chapter, maybe the most important we'll ever have—at least from my point of view. Thank you for pointing out Dogtown's secular advantages.

"By the way—I hope you don't mind—I took the liberty of showing Father Davy your choreograph of the Anamnesis. He was extremely interested. As you know, Father Duncannon is considering ways to use it for priests and acolytes learning our deviations from the Prayer Book and the Missal. Out in the isolation of parish churches one naturally gets almost incorrigibly habituated to the official eucharist. It's easy to make mistakes in either rite when you have to substitute one for the other."

Caleb was happy enough to drop the subject of Gloucestermas, but immeasurably pleased to hear his labor of love so pragmatically appreciated; yet he continued to suspect that Father Davy discountenanced the luxury of visual aids from a Laboratory intended to nourish the living Vine itself of Christ. The good priest may still have regarded the little scroll (tied with a red ribbon) as only another aesthetic plaything to divert the two religious from the essential business of their Order. Caleb had the feeling that Father Davy was more pious than the Father Founder himself, who greatly valued the chart at least as a birthday present meticulously created by a disinterested admirer on his own time. It was the tribute of a diffident layman to lifework potentially of incalculable importance to mankind's survival.

Not that his tracking of action in the mesocosmic liturgy of the Vine looked radically different from what it would have been for the standard Mass of the West. The component parts of the ritual revised by Father Duncannon and his advisors were classic, and few of the classic parts were omitted or revised. The Anamnesis was respectful to the Scholastic liturgy, defensible in terms of liturgical scholarship, and submissive to traditions of ceremonial decorum; but it harkened back to the primitive church in its structural emphasis on the Offertory.

Caleb had begun diagramming the rite merely to help himself learn his volunteer duty as the Lab's ordinary acolyte. Once a week he earned a good cenobite breakfast in the refectory by relieving either priest (usually Father Lucey) of the obligation to serve the celebrant at the altar (usually Father Duncannon) when they were alone in the chapel. When not officiating, both of them preferred to act as laymen of the congregation, wearing no vestments.

As the diachronic description of a dynamic procedure at any sacred place, this schematic, unlike his organization charts, was drawn not as a static set of geometric shapes but as a superposing delineation of motions and gestures. Interlinked lines of red blue and green flowed back and forth, punctuated or annotated with suggestive symbols of his own devising (such as a kind of truncated squareroot sign to indicate genuflection), on a ground of space defined in black ink, to trace the cooperations of priest, acolyte, and people. This 6-by-17 sheet, though curled and uncurled like a royal epistle, seemed to him an illuminated manuscript of sacred dance; but he hoped it would be downright useful to any performer simply as a mnemonic program from the perspective of the acolyte, who had no altar missal before his eyes with plenary text and rubrics. It was an attempt to communicate the whole dromenon as the action that provided the Word: his compendium and epitome of the basic Mass as reformed by Father Duncannon to reveal its vastly misunderstood significance. As both scribe and altar boy Caleb was precisely faithful to his teacher's standards of liturgical courtesy, yet he'd hesitated with reverent trepidation, as an ignorant craftsmen, before finally daring to lay his rolled-up offering next to the plate at the head of the refectory table one morning after Mass.

On the telephone Chris seemed glad to have escaped his seniors for this business chat, perhaps in part because it was his wont to make occasion for tactful withdrawal when he believed the company would like to discuss his behavior or himself. ". . . I don't know how we ever got along without a creative artist! I expect to find your organization charts quite edifying. They may be the charms we need to scotch an insurrection, on or before Chapter. At the very least they'll help prepare me for the thunderhead of criticism now gathering from gentle wisps all over the sky!" He laughed gaily at his spiritual predicament.

Caleb himself was sometimes uncomfortable to be the almost mutually exclusive confidant of both the Fathers—on the one hand as a pragmatic civilian companion, on the other as a theoretical disciple at reflective levels of enthusiasm. Though he was an eager accomplice in Chris's financial adventures on behalf of the Laboratory (sanctioned by frequent assurance that the Father Superior was deferentially consulted and fully informed of all significant options, even when no approval was required by the Trustees), Father Duncannon never mentioned investment or income to him, despite the fact that he functioned as the Laboratory's general administrator. By the same token, he had to rely upon Chris for all information by which to define, interpret, categorize, or label the functions and divisions to be denoted in his diagrams of the soi-disant democracy that the unostentatious old autocrat had created in Christian antithesis to the Christian world.

". . . And you were so skillful with the diameters and deployments of circles, and with distinctions of color, that your Parity chart suggests King Arthur's whole career by displaying the latest condition of his empire!" Chris's compliments of Caleb were often delicately reiterated simply by adopting his inspired assistant's sobriquet for the president of the labyrinth; but this was one of the times he chose to expatiate upon the hint in a newly interesting way. "That sheet of paper practically dictated our working hypothesis. Rafe Opsimath is a hardheaded businessman, and his opinion emphatically confirms mine. He phoned yesterday, and asked me to relay his cordial greetings. He'll probably call you today about some questions he thinks you can help him with. But he's coming East after the first of the year, you know, for his winter session up at White Quarry. That should be a good time for the three of us to go down to New Uruk again and at last barge in on the king in person. Rafe has done the Order a great service by bringing you to us.

"Likewise your clarification of our own picture will help him as well as us understand the circular chain of authority whereby money flows one way and complaints the other! Like everyone else the poor guy's still puzzled by the apparent discrepancy between our capitalism and our socialism! He says he could follow us into poverty or into usury, but not into both at once, because he can't shake off the perennial philosophy of spirit versus matter. He probably thinks we want to reform society without reforming ourselves. Who can say he's mistaken?" Chris spoke as always with cheerful respect for all stripes of opinion, which however were less important to him than the psyches of those who evinced them.

Hoping that Rafe would be too busy at Tubalcain to call him that afternoon, Caleb struggled murkily for professional words that might transcend his listlessness and acknowledge Chris's encouragement.

"There'll be dotted-line partitions to separate the domain of the Lab from the secular membership, and both from the realm of usury."

"But I'm more and more intrigued by your distinctions between our endocrine and nervous systems!"

This discrimination of Caleb's was becoming one of Chris's favorite metaphors in their contemplative talks while riding back or forth to Botolph in the Nicolet. But as they now continued to speak about this fanciful project so peripheral to the management of money Caleb was once again suddenly attacked by the sickening conviction that his glib models were abusing Chris's all-too-openminded appreciations. He felt as if he was giving the Fathers another overworked toy, too clever by half, absurdly complicated for its own sake—worthy only of scorn or dismissal by people of Christ, Antichrist, or art, and especially by women.

It wasn't an unprecedented self-perception. But although he knew this repetition of it would soon be forgotten, without permanently improving his essential character as a fool, the self-chastisement burned hotter every time he suffered it; and now it reminded him of the related fatuity in which he had regaled Bice with the Isorectotetrahedron and other conceits. Above all, it rubbed in the irresponsibility of picking and choosing the religious ideas he liked without renouncing the romantic theory of tragedy by which in his own mind he distinguished his opinions from those of all contemporaries and practically all other thinkers. This enlightening embarrassment once again seemed the only pure insight of his life, save for the faded intuitions of dependency in childhood and his elemental love of Ibi.

When he hung up, having tried to sound as cheerful as usual, he was very glad to find that it was time to turn aside from childish things and go down to lunch as hungry as a happy man. Of Oku himself neither hide nor hair was visible, but good crisp food and a pot of hot tea were neatly ready at one end of the long dark walnut table supposedly from a Tuscan Renaissance monastery. He was too tired and hungry even to read. Eating and drinking everything on the table, he did not linger, but on an impulse spawned of desperation he went into the gloomy "great hall" and lay down shivering on one of the rigid slightly musty old plush sofas that probably hadn't borne weight for a decade, huddled under a steamer rug from Father Duncannon's study. He slept tensely, but in an utter nothingness of time, for half an hour.

Back at his desk in a trance of cold silence he rotated telephone digits every few minutes, more and more mechanically, while he forced himself through the motions of attending to the easiest paperwork he could lay his hands on, setting aside not only his charts but also all correspondence with the outside world. The phone did not again sound its peremptory signal, and he postponed for the day all duties that would have required him to speak as much as a single further word to anyone but Bice. He kept fearing a genial call from Rafe.

Somehow occupied with cajoling his spirit through the afternoon, he was overtaken sooner than expected by the moment at which it might be judged late enough to liberate himself for action without inordinately abusing his warrant. He hoped that Oku wasn't noticing from one of the darkened windows as he drove away a little earlier than ever before.

There was only one thing to do. Cursing the premature rush-hour traffic that maddingly impeded the speed of his tortuous transit with its multitudinous self-centered stupidity and lawless arrogance, estranged from himself by his own exhibition of savagery against the kilroy masses, he arrived at the Van full of disembodied dread at the helplessness of his case. All his hope and desire was fixed upon a person whose position and momentum had both vanished from his unaided faculties of determination.

The phenomenon was resolved somewhat as he might have expected.

Edie Schlossberg sat behind the front desk anxiously darting looks in almost a circle around her, now at the inert dusty switchboard, now at objects under the counter, at papers passing through her hands, at the register book, the ledger, the cash drawer, like a bird that couldn't command its own cage. She'd just relieved her husband of that exposed nest and was still upset by difficulties upstairs or down. She finally settled down to paying bills or whatever she did while awaiting customers, but who could believe she'd once occupied a key space-buyer's desk in a tower of Babel?

"Caleb!" Her scrunched face, pursing with uncertainties, was all at once beautified by a reversal of care, her unfortunate buckteeth raised in cordial delight at her own unexpected pleasure. "What a nice surprise! You're looking for Shelly. He's gone downstairs to his shop." She invariably presumed one's preference for her husband.

Under the circumstances Caleb would rather have found someone less personally solicitous to answer his questions—if not no one at all to prevent him from bounding up to the Poet's Corner unannounced. "I'm looking for a Miss Picory. It may be Room 36."

"Oh! —Oh!" With Edie these two exclamations (the second ascending in tone from the first), followed by a pause, usually betrayed no more than her step-by-step comprehension of an astonishingly simple meaning. But the reply itself expressed no particular curiosity: "I'm afraid you're too late. She left early this morning."

"Early this morning!" Already weak with fatigue, surprised without the armor of pride in which he had trained himself to conceal the disappointments of life, and overwhelmed by the shock of impenetrable news, he was nearly brought to tears. With breaking voice he made a poor show of indifference. The good Edie would see that he had joined a chase, like any other dog. The best face he could put upon his inquiry was that of one who at least was not in love with the quarry. The one thing clear to him was that his pursuit of Bice could last no longer than her availability.

"I thought she might have decided to stay another day." he said, making shift to shrug his shoulders with a nonchalant curl of the lip.

"I wish she had. She was a very nice young lady. Such a lot of fun, and so generous. I'm going to miss her. She actually checked out yesterday in advance, so she could leave first thing in the morning without getting me up. But I can never sleep as late as I should—there's so little time in the day—so I was here when the captain came to pick her up in Sam's cab about six o'clock. I never thought a beautiful girl could get up early. But it gave us a chance to clean up her room before we got too busy, and that's always a help. She left the maid five dollars."

Caleb stretched and yawned. "Which captain was it?" he asked with a poorly shammed drawl.

"One of the Terrie skippers. I didn't get his name. The *Avalon Reefer*. I think they sailed before seven. "They're hoping this weather will hold."

"It's probably the last trip from St James's before the ice." Caleb remarked with his hand on the door, hinting that he'd been in on the deliberations.

"The captain was charming. I hope her cabin's comfortable. Those boats weren't built for passengers."

The captain, the cabin, the comfort! Caleb lurched home in stunned amazement without seeing anything as he drove. Perversely brusque and irritable with Ibi his one true sympathizer—in fact shutting the front door in his face—he bitterly rushed up the two staircases Bice had trod to throw himself onto his ironic bed.

He closed his eyes and tried to postpone further thinking of his unconscionable loss. Dull oblivion was his only recourse. He wished it could last until morning. But his spiralling bewilderment took up the pain that had at first been shielded by defensively ingenious hermeneutics. It struck him like a doleful gong that not twenty-four hours ago in that very spot she had sweetly reciprocated all his tender incursions of the natural boundary between them, surely bemused by little less than love of him.

But if he slept now he'd have to wake to desolation in the middle of the night, having cruelly passed his suffering on to Ibi without apology or explanation, who was now not only as griefstricken as himself, and infinitely more perplexed, but also hungry cold and absolutely innocent. His ineludible responsibility for the dog's love brought an end to his hope for an anesthetic hiatus. In less than three minutes, to stave off rapidly compounding guilt, he went down with tearful remorse to admit his best friend and sole comfort.

As he staggered up out of his aborted gob of sleep in order to relieve conscience in jolting pragmatic reality, like a besotted farmer whose dissolution is checked by moral obligation to his unmilked cows, he reasoned to himself that if her plans for departure had been laid before she met him there was nothing about her betrayal that reflected upon his worthiness.

He and Ibi were assigned the front door for their access to the house, whereas the Keiths used the entrance from the side porch or the one from the back stoop, but the two parties had to share the hall stairs for circulation to the upper floors. Fortunately it was still too early for the family to be gathering; he encountered no one. Even in his most sociable mood Caleb stayed out of the householders' way, hoping to remind them as seldom as possible of the awkward fact that a stranger walked some of their domestic passageways. He supposed that Dexter, as a professional man of some prestige, was secretly touchy about renting space in his castle, as if in financial need.

The doubly joyful dog accepted Caleb's contrition without prejudice or gratitude, as one of the dispensations of nature that followed another, forgotten like all the rest and never to be complained of. Bounding ahead upstairs with padded paws and clicking claws, Ibi led his man to face the kitchen again exactly as he and Bice had left it.

He fed Ibi and paused feckless with a glass of whiskey, while his will vacillated between the sentimental inclination to leave everything as long as possible just as she'd used it, preserving the invisible prints of her lips and fingers, forbearing to disturb the last position of the chair she'd sat in, and the angry urge to wipe out every reminder of her presence. But as a practical matter there was little free choice.

Listening with dazed indifference to airwave speculations about the forthcoming new administration in Washington, and closing his sense to all the other broadcast news, he cleaned up the mess, got himself a something to eat, and again cleaned up. By the time he'd let Ibi out for his postprandial evacuations, finished in the kitchen, and called Ibi back home again, he was unable to open a book, and he scarcely mustered the energy to brush his teeth before flopping into his cold disordered bed, thankful for the gravitational inertia of total exhaustion. In ten seconds he was asleep.

But why had she lied to him, gratuitously lied, starting at first acquaintance? Lying might have served a purpose if she'd been a farmer's daughter—and if it was plausible that such a poor seducer as himself could be mistaken as the innocent object of sex-starved seduction! It was not difficult to imagine that in sheer pity or cowardice she might have failed to disabuse his expectations of the affair once they were at play: but, if so, why should she have deceived him about her early debarkation—after telling him something of the truth about her interest in taking passage by sea, before he knew he was going to touch so much as her hand? Surely she'd been taking him for granted as another of her foregone conquests.

Not that she didn't mean well. No doubt she blamed herself for trifling. Those supple delicate lips spoke him such pleasingly shaped words of Queen's English as he'd never been addressed before. The gentleman couldn't be blamed for believing that an educated slavegirl had surrendered to him, nor she herself for briefly believing that she'd done so. But was she laughing now—or was she weeping? Or in the novelty of a voyage by freighter had she already forgotten her last lover? In spite of all the lovely sounds she'd learned to make, perhaps she was essentially impervious.

Amid all present enlargements of speculation he seemed to remember a faint feeling that her cooperative savor of his advances had been a little too prepared, and that it had been a little wanting in the sighs of transport which she would have rendered if he'd been the woman in her place. At the time her glamor had blinded him to the possibility that she'd learned to put up with the caresses of men the way many a girl puts up with their stories as a matter of course and cooks for them without being hungry herself.

Ibi seemed equally eager for oblivion. He too had missed a night on his own mat. Neither of them stirred for eleven hours, and then it was the man who woke the dog, not much past the usual time.

For a little while Caleb thought he'd dispelled his dismay by restoring his body. But pale cheer faded as soon as he went into his study with the coffee and turned on the warm light of his lamp. The trinities lay scattered on his desk like a child's abandoned playthings who knows nothing of an adult obligation to reverse the local entropy left behind by having fun. Considered together with her indifference to kitchen and bedroom shambles, this abuse of his citadel suddenly brought to light the clay in which the jewel was set that had passed through his hands while he was blinded with the illusions of greed. He had enjoyed her behavior in the belief that it corroborated an aristocratic superiority to bourgeois virtues. Yet as he wryly repacked the silly modules in their neat magazine his evidence of her earthenware character yielded the single carat of satisfaction that all along he had evaded the arrows of love.

Then he came upon a sheet of paper bearing the notes she had made while manipulating these very blocks from this very swivel chair. He studied every stroke of the small scholarly handwriting, meticulously cultivated, more precisely controlled than his own. Her markings seemed to be slightly expanded promptings for what she'd intended to say to him. "Sell Ts to dept stores for kids—500% markup . . . *New Ur* ads for Xmas carriage trade . . . more elegant than Linker Toys / Erection Kits . . . patent or copyright? . . . Mfrg looks simple, cheap: problem is pkg & mktg . . . "

He didn't like the way her mind had run on his behalf; but her hand suggested a competence with the written word equal to her oral charms. Were they the tracks of an advertising mind—or of a Dark Reader brimming with misguided intellect and groping for the kind of education that she'd missed?

But they were written on the back of his résumé, and when he turned it over he found the notes she had made on the face of it, later, during his interview. These abbreviated observations inflamed the smouldering ashes of her epiphany. The traveling saleswoman had left the farmboy with such precious experience that he wouldn't have traded his ruin for the concurrent favors of half a dozen local beauties happy to risk conception without an iota of claim upon his liberty or his income; yet in the reawakened storm his heart's mind whipped back and forth like a flag at the North Pole, execrating Providence as often as he thanked it for sailing her out of reach so fast.

For her pencilled recruiting notes—ostensibly unselfconscious, but not quite cryptic enough to disarm his suspicion that they were meant for his eyes—were equivocally provocative, scattered down the page without apposite correlation to the typewritten lines of his professional history: "Sentimental about U K , makes too much myst of geography . . . —Rare Atlantean, 18C Loyalist/ROIalist . . . Wishes understnd superiority of women. (*Find out more abt mother*) . . . Too well educated—but lousy French. Despises oral speech, even English (both Brit & Atl): horror of self-expr . . . Nice proportions; wld make good dancer . . . Belongs at Unaford—research in lost causes. Too theoretical for bus. Fixations on low-level tech details & loves bureaucracy—yet not pedantic . . . Excels with dog . . . —Admirable enthusiasm cum personal reserve. May be method in madness. *(Recmnd as cav servente for long trips.)* But idealistic—cld be romantic hero for certain type girl . . . self-consc abt lefthandedness. Prob a bastard and/or draft-dodger: talks freely abt self on all other topics . . . lst-class candidate for brother (or uncle or —???—). Too indpndent for marriage . . . "

It didn't look like the trail of a journalist. What would have happened to these precocious fragments if he'd been infinitessimally less bold and the interview had led to nothing? Were these crypticisms as calculated to stir a man's lifelong regret as the Valentine of her decolleted blouse in the event that after the interview he should have failed to overcome either scruple or timidity (if she didn't know which) to offer the necessary iota of male initiative? Or had she planted the sophisticated-looking marginalia with careless clairvoyance just to prolong the desire of him who was about to become a forsakable lover?

Yet on the other hand she may have simply forgotten to fold up his curriculum and take it with her as a cherished souvenir for herself. Or at least have sincerely intended to tear it into small pieces after the little interviewing game was over. Perhaps she was genuinely absentminded about her technique—indeed about all the procedures of her life.

Flogging an uneven memory for clues, he studiously assayed the true and the false. They'd both had their way, whatever her intentions; but it wasn't as if she thought she was yielding him anything very valuable. Her sexual complaisance was something to reckon as no less significant in his final summing up than the social fact, now borne home to him, that despite a thousand lovely signs of intelligence and taste he couldn't remember any words in which she'd evinced unusual knowledge or expressed an original idea.

But the spuriously consoling inference that her spirit dwelt on no mountain top did not much palliate this first matutinal agitation of his new life. It was too late to stipulate Creative Mind for a Beatrice already consummated. He had more than envisioned her. He had materially touched and felt from within an idealization of her limits. A truly extraordinary brain in that otherwise perfected organism could not have further enriched his mapping and sounding in as little time as half a day and a night.

He accomplished nothing at his desk. The act of rising with his empty cup perversely reignited a former train of recollections singularly intempestive for a man getting ready to go off to work. During their pillow talk at the Poet's Corner, for instance, he had lightly asked her if it was true (as the Hudson's Bay Company men were said to report) that the Eskimos of northern Cabotland shared their wives with overnight wayfarers; and only now did her short reply strike him as brutal: "What difference does it make?" And she had given no evidence of the slightest curiosity about his erotic history. When he'd hinted a casual question about hers she diverted his attention from the main object of his interest by launching into a rather boring account of symbolic dreams in cloistered adolescence.

By this time the *Avalon Reefer* must have been somewhere off Sable Island, the so-called graveyard of ships but not much of a hazard to a modern motor vessel equipped with radar; and in that sea lane it was still too early in season to worry about icebergs. She might be taking up the captain's spare time, but it wasn't a long enough passage for her to befuddle all the mates and steersmen too. Since the selfmade commanders of these little ships were supposed to be phlegmatic family men, Caleb reasoned, if this skipper had so egregiously departed from the norm as to fetch the applicant from her hotel for fear she'd change her mind or oversleep, he must be smitten well enough to keep a jealous eye on officers and crew.

A renaissance of mentally charged satyriasis had already succeeded the transitory satiation of his loins, but he no longer hoped to float above his fate like a man of the world deprived merely of a pretty piece of luck.

After shaving and eating, as he made the bed (reluctantly expunging the impressions she had made), while Ibi watched patiently with a bladder full enough to mark every stone in Acorn Pasture, he wondered if Edie's chambermaid had found five dollars worth of nuisance in the doghairs alone.

8
RIMA
VOCALIS

Caleb had been astonished to find that he no longer suffered his symptom. Listening to the laryngologist's "negative" findings, he smiled indulgently at the idiom of physicians, who by expressing disappointment at the absence of disease confessed a greater interest in sickness than in health. But physicists were less philological: their signs for electric charge perpetuated an early empirical misunderstanding of the direction in which current actually flows, thereby conveying to the common reader an impression that electrons gravitate from the less potent to the more potent state, contrary to the second law of thermodynamics and all other physical principles.

He couldn't recall the jaw-loosening collar of tight pain that had seared the inside of his neck, under his eyes, behind his mouth; but he wanted a cause for the vanished terror. For all his tests and diagnostic rays, the doctor could only tentatively suggest there might be "a wart on the true vocal cords" that kept the narrow slit between them a little too open when it would normally be closed, thus allowing the raw wind to whistle through his larynx when he was sleeping. So the angina would probably be nothing to worry about if it reappeared.

Shrugging his shoulders when Caleb pressed him for causes prior to the proximate, chronic or acute, the specialist fell back upon a lightly held generalization that might be called the idiopathic hypothesis, which clinicians found quite useful, once they admitted Psyche to the temple of Asclepius: any human body might serve as vector for a uniquely psychosomatic neuroendocrinal syndrome. Having long denied mental etiology in anatomical matters because it was too negative for science, even the remaining positivists of the medical profession were now giving way to the convenience of a diagnostic dodge justified only by radical philosophies still no closer than Descartes to any definite explanation of the nexus that is equally crucial in pathology and iatrics. But Caleb had learned to bridle his reasoning with doctors, and he was content to hear that the cause of his sore throat, like that of "soldier's heart" during the war, may have been "emotional". In the end he was not discontent to be left with the freedom to hazard his own theories of the case.

But was the verruca still on his reeds? After all, the doctor's reassuring inconclusion did not greatly astonish him, for he had always suspected a sort of globus hystericus from the feminine strains of his conflict-complex. It would take a negative cause to explain the mysterious disappearance of what had seemed to be its unequivocal presence. His relief might be no more trustworthy than the temporary sedation of a hermit crab maturing in the rima of his throat.

Even though he'd noticed no soreness since the moment he first laid eyes on Bice, the contrarieties of his life could hardly have been coterminous with the anesthesia of her company. Weeks after the cruel departure of his therapist, the pain had not reappeared in his throat. The shock of losing her as suddenly as he'd found her was thus not symmetrical with the cause of his unexpected negativity.

Yet the uncaused and uncured wart must be etiologically related to his practically congenital voice, which had neither improved nor deteriorated. For the chronic sore throat his occult excrescence was perhaps a necessary cause rendered sufficient by psychical tensions and compressions. The idiopathic organism of Caleb Karcist was then relieved of its merely superficial symptom by a tonal adjustment of his libido. Such a rebalancing of his heating ventilating and air-conditioning system (H V A C) could lift one special discomfort without touching the structural dyscrasia. For the abiding infirmity a wart might well remain both necessary and sufficient.

His introspeculation therefore reduced itself to the opinion that on the whole this pathological phenomenon was a protest against Atlantean civilization (as anticipated in the womb) by his speech-generator. At first he was happy to let it go at that, without troubling himself to define the particular circumstances against which he or his daimon was protesting.

Still, he was now feeling much better systemically also. In his nuova vita the wild fluctuations of his attitude toward Bice—as lover, as enemy—were dampened by steadily rising gratitude for the part she'd played in demonstrating that his manhood wasn't being throttled by the pain in the neck of having a voice that exposed his social frailty. She hadn't cured the voice but she had professed to like it; and indeed even to himself it had seemed quite manly when he was talking to her in bed. Between diminishing spates of oscillation from attraction to repulsion he seldom doubted the double success of having enjoyed an extraordinary adventure but avoided the distress of falling in love.

Nonetheless, this satisfaction notwithstanding, he wasn't yet rid of the recurring dejections during which he paid for his success by forgetting it—by brooding instead over the loss that had occurred so soon as almost to have canceled the gain.

Between waking and sleeping he often pondered the melancholy pattern of accidents suffered by his erotic substance. A girl to whom he'd once been most important, known too well in a long blaze of intolerable passion, had managed to remain a maid until just after she left him. The smattering of other previous loves weren't memorable as individual experiences; and thereafter, in his putative maturity, he seemed destined never to keep a woman long enough to establish his importance in the first place. He'd been lucky enough at approaching polar opposites over the past four or five years, allowing for the rather reclusive habits of his life and the dimness of his lure in the eyes of humanity's other half; yet for one reason or another he'd always had to start all over again in the general chase before learning much about any one female person. Why couldn't he keep a girl—or get a girl that he wanted to keep—long enough to get to the bottom of her feelings? Making love with a new one the first time is naturally more important than any one other time, being the necessary if not sufficient beginning of knowledge; but he had been surprised to find what a small beginning it always was, even when it loomed large in a short series. Certainly in Bice's case revelation eluded his maximum touch. It seemed as if for her their first and only two sessions were but flirting experiments.

Once while afoot in his study, reminding himself of the incomparable prize he'd lost and magnifying the details of her visit in sentimental review, he picked up his axe, remembering that he had elevated it for her like a St Anthony's cross to proclaim his woodsman's prowess as a youth. This time he was aware of the ridiculous disproportion. He imagined Gilgamesh holding it in one hand like a hatchet—or Dexter Keith or Doc Charlemagne—or the faceless gypsy-poet or a brawny Terra Nova sea-captain. Hefting the naked janiform toy even as tool and not as a weapon, he belittled himself in the cold solitude of her absence.

His mother sometimes used to blame herself for his diminutive replication of the dominant male sex, although it amused her more than it amused him. "It looks as if poor Caliban isn't going to realize his genetic potential! And it's all my fault! I was an impure woman. My lungs were sooty with the foul cheroot! I smoked like a puffinbilly while I was carrying you—in the selfish ignorance of my 'feminine fulfillment'—just to flaunt my flaming youth and defy Mrs Grundy! And then I blew my dirt into your precious little face who was and is my pride and joy! You're not going to be any taller than I am. But maybe it's the girl in you! Forgive me, my stalwart three-in-one . . . "

This was one of the terms by which Mary Tremont joyfully referred to her only child, who she proclaimed was divinely appointed to serve as all three children (boy—girl—boy) whom, while still a child herself, she had "ordered from God" with predetermined complexions of eyes hair and skin (sometimes under the names of Peedee, Hullabaloo, and Pog-dog—Redburn's terms for his first three productions), long before she considered the question of mating. At the earliest age of understanding he'd been informed that he was born almost strangled by the umbilical cord, his head traumatized by forceps and twisted on his neck like a dead chicken's, and delivered into the morgue as incapable of breathing—to be saved only by the grace of God, thanks to one of Dogtown's keen-eared nurses who happened to be passing that cold basement door when he uttered what might have been his first and only whimper. Thus had God punished and forgiven the mother's "sin of individualism".

According to the autobiographer, however, her sins of heedless self-assertion had continued, and after his infant infirmity was diagnosed as rickets she accused herself of failing to fortify him with proper nutrition against the world she had brought him into willy-nilly.

Nonetheless she was otherwise so delighted with her baby that she called herself the Mother of All Living; and when disappointments in her life of atonements accumulated to a critical phase she had decided to tempt Providence no further. If only to make sure that he could never evade his princely responsibility as Three-in-One (a couple of sons and a daughter), she had repeatedly told him in his childhood: "When I saw that through your afflictions God was warning me about my greediness for babies without renunciation of an egotistic preoccupation with so-called art, I went into the hospital and got my tubes tied, praying that He would help me overcome my selfishness. And He did! He gave me the strength not to try to make up for my sins by spoiling you! You've made your own character—infinitely superior to mine." Here she would hug and kiss him with quizzical laughs of joy and pride. "You've done it all yourself, Honor Boy! Kiss the Mum what loves you more than tongue can tell! My little oak tree! I promise never to stop you from cutting the motherbond! I was an only-child too, but it's much harder for a boy."

It was anything but true that he did it all himself, but after about the age of twelve he'd left off protesting his love and gratitude whenever she accused him of cold indifference, not because his love and gratitude had faded or diminished with the concentrating selfhood of youth but because he more and more resented the emotional extortion. Usually he refrained from any response at all, and then (at best) she called him her "strong silent man", the scornful reproach veering through satire into praise before the words were out of her mouth. "Pure women have bigger babies," she'd say "but I have God's *man-child*! I've always taken pains to make you two-thirds manly—but you've outdone yourself! Kiss the mother that bores you!"

A smell of burning cigarettes, especially in the open air, still attracted him to almost any woman at its source as if it was the incense of intelligence. But when he was in grade school her smoking was nothing to be proud of; still worse, she smoked on the street as openly as a man, sucking in the hot vapor with little gasps as she strode along attracting attention to herself as an intrepid mother. In Unabridge her public behavior had embarrassed him as merely eccentric; for during the war, even in New Armorica, especially near the ports, strange manners and customs were becoming acceptable (at least in thoroughfares and marketplaces) as almost nugatory idiosyncrasies of the international brotherhood united in resistance to Germany and Japan; but after the war, far from the cities, in a Montvert village where her ways were shocking or detestable to most of the inhabitants, and at an age when he was more sensitive to nonconformity, he had hoped against hope to escape identification.

Another boast was true enough, that she never spared her only child the castigation of reality—even unto knowledge of her own "white lies" of economic expediency or poetic license. Yet worst of all, in Allenton, she was too honest by half—preferring scandalous fiction to good clean falsehood by calling herself divorced instead of widowed. How he'd longed for her to marry, at every hint of the possibility, even as he was learning to despair of any stepfather half saintly enough to become her husband!

He couldn't remember ever being exempt from responsibility as the man of the house. He'd naturally shirked housework as much as he could, procrastinating errands and special assignments, hating everything he had to do for the partnership (which usually included a cat or two and a dog) rather than for himself, but he could never shrug off the threat of his duty as "head of the family". She called him head of the family, sometimes with tears and sometimes with laughter, when she was "tired of being a lorn lone breadwinner without protection in this heartless male world".

Staring down at the cemetery from his swivel chair he shuddered at the folly of having told a callow girl much too much about the origin of his sympathies. He was ashamed of having so forgotten himself as to heap upon a meretricious opportunist such confidences as would have been deserved only by a loyal friend of proven affinity. But he blessed his stars that he hadn't besmirched his hatchment to the extent of telling Bice everything, or any one thing that in an access of trust or enthusiasm he hadn't already told someone else. She had done well to abandon him soon enough. It was nonetheless irksome that she probably thought she carried away all his secrets like the virtue and honor of a debauched virgin.

It had been simply a clause of experience that would have seemed unremarkable in the curriculum vitae of a normal bachelor: nothing more than a picaresque adventure. But whose adventure was it—his or hers? She had called herself a freelance journalist. Looking for stories she was. Riding with gypsies, asking Dogtown questions, appropriating men's secrets. Caleb felt as if he'd added to his mother's sorrows by allowing himself to be exploited—deceived by the same blind desire that in other men deceived the woman.

Women are the better people! —Mary Tremont's whooping motto that she loved to make a big impression with, crying it out on any pretext. But she also maintained that women were the worst exceptions, and there were plenty of them that she hated. Indeed she attributed to the ill will of female enemies the fact that she was fired from all her jobs by the boss men; and in gossiped cases resembling this one with

Bice (which the son would sooner have made known to anyone else in the world than to his mother) she usually judged the woman worse, unless the man turned out to be one of the typical louts or prigs she herself would have spotted a mile away.

But Caleb bore the onus of being supposed to incarnate his mother's ideal of male character (if not of physique)—neither loutish nor priggish. According to her there weren't many real men nowadays. (In reply to a notorious magazine article titled "The Vanishing Atlantean Male" she had once called attention to herself with a long triumphant letter to the editor called "The Vanquishing Atlantean Female".) She teased her son by standing before him with her hands on his shoulders, attempting to catch his eye, which was by then higher than hers after all, and beaming shrill admiration: "The stouthearted runt of my litter! Yet taller than Churchill! If he had Churchill's voice the world would know why he's my hero. If it hadn't been for my sins he'd look heroic too! All on his own—without father, without riches, without charm, without a commanding presence—he's made his way through a life of hard knocks and the best schools as a perfect little gentleman. Even to begin his life he had to triumph over a Laocoöanian birth-trauma, survive exposure in a tomb, and cure himself of rickets with codliver oil when his mother had been too ignorant to feed him enough Vitamin D in the wintertime. Who knows how many other trials he's undergone in silent fortitude? He'd never tell his crazy mother. And all the way along his brilliant career he's had to drag her behind him floundering in the dust and kicking at the traces! Who can blame him for running away??"

As a ridiculously inept female righthander (having had no ball-playing father or brother to learn from) she never suspected the humiliations of a natural southpaw who'd had only her to misstart his throwing and batting; and then it was too late to master the basic knack of using his wrist. Considering the early malformation of his baseball habits, it was no wonder he had an arm also like a chicken's and never hit a home run. Even in some of his purely autodidactic initiatives he had abused his integral sinistrality—as for instance in boxing (solely for purposes of self-defense) when he adopted the dexterous stance that prevents a lefthander from cocking his natural knockout punch.

But in his own view the disadvantages of inadequately corrected feminine nurture were primarily spiritual: such as his tendency to go all for love. His gynotropic sensibility was too sympathetic. He often ascribed to a precocious intimation of women the failure to get his share as a predator. Yet wasn't it really the law of nature, rather than nurture, that accounted for the advantage women had of him, so obviously deficient in the masculinity of voice and stature that might have balanced the equation of desire? More than the accidents of tobacco and malnutrition it was the capriciousness of genes that altered the entelechy of one whose mind was successful enough to survive imperfectly.

Still, allowing for the circumstances of his gestation and all the formal causes thereafter, he was proud to have turned out proportional and hale—strong enough for his weight, nimble enough for his height. Doctors declared his "vital capacity" remarkable, despite all the smoking his mother and he himself had done. His athletic gift was stamina. In absolute competition his virtue was endurance. So valuable did he at last estimate this heritage that as soon as his angor animi had been pronounced unfounded (or at any rate extraneous) he made up his mind to enhance and prolong the prime of his imperfect life, which his next birthday was the latest symbol of, by becoming a solitary runner.

He took to flight as naturally as a cormorant to diving. He'd always run on his toes without any sense of special effort. This sport, if such it could be called, was a blessedly introverted self-discipline. It depended upon no cooperation but his own. And progress was easy to measure. It did the body more good than anything that might have been more fun and taken more time. Yet it was really for Ibi's sake that he finally overcame his laziness and actually began it.

The truth is that except for the summit of Beltane Hill, commanding the whole lively Harbor, and the innards of the Iron Works, where things might change from night to night, he'd been getting bored with the gray area of his quotidian walking radius. After the electrifying tour with Bice, moreover, it was painful to repeat the circuit without her, as if she was mocking the ingenuous enthusiasm with which he'd conducted her, or as if it was his failure to keep her under enchantment that deepened the winter blight of his precinct's landscape. He'd therefore become more and more remiss in giving Ibi the daily bread of active companionship for which his pinches of tutoring had been only the leaven. The saint had been growing sad on mere sourdough—with less and less even of that. His pleading eyes, too loyal to intend reproach, followed his stranger's movements about the house, counting hours, counting days. Caleb had begun to fear the weakening of faith—that Ibi-Roi might go native with his pack. It was bad enough for the master to be away from home so much; responsibility for the education and employment of that eager boundless energy, infinitely less selfish than his own, had weighed heavily upon the residual leisure of his guilt-ridden calendar.

Soon the new joy of running with his man (at first so bizarre and puzzling) seemed to Ibi no more supererogatory as a special claim than one of his inalienable civil rights. His expectant patience early every morning became an inescapable reinforcement of Caleb's sometimes flagging will.

But the regime became almost addictive for the biped too, who every morning—once he was on the road—blessed his four-legged companion for keeping him up to the mark. No matter how hard it was to get up in time and force his body to do the opposite of what it craved to continue to do at five AM —no matter how painfully his joints creaked at the very thought of setting out, or how hatefully the wind froze his face—after a course was half begun his gladness never failed. In the penultimate exultation of his showerbath, as he made the liminal passage from hot water to cold, transforming athletic to intellectual power, he looked forward to the catalytic pleasure of fullbodied black coffee—the means to mental work that in confused motivation he often mistook for its ends. In despair of adding a cubit to his stature, or volume and timbre to his voice, the simple ability to move further and more swiftly than a child—as if synecdochic of many gifts—inspired optimism about his other functions.

But it went hard to accustom himself to such stress each day before he was warmed up by the usual activities of life. It took a long time to train his muscles to match the efficiency of his lungs, and a longer time yet to force the integrated system to generate and sustain the glorious sweat of his hottest steady state. He could never get used to the frightening struggle against winter, but by beginning this development in the worst of seasons he could blithely contemplate the gradual alleviation of recurrent dismay as the mornings grew less dark. Whenever he came out under a clear sky there was a special pleasure in racing against sunrise.

Not that he loved the agony of urging himself to the apogee of zest so early and abruptly. But any other time of day would have been more unpleasant or less convenient. For one thing, it was difficult to find another space on the clock at which he would not have indulged himself with food or drink within the previous three or four hours, seeing that deskwork required liquid stimulus and made him ravenous for every feeding. He told himself that the artificial occupations at neither of his desks could brook distracting privations—not even in the name of salubrious longevity. Though admitting that it was possible to make himself get by on longer fasts between meals, he rationalized his unwillingness to assume that additional burden of self-discipline on the grounds that it would only have left him with other sufficiently compelling causes to rule out for his running at any other disposable time when a shower and clean clothes would not interrupt the diurnal rhythm of his schedule. Chiefly the traffic.

If it hadn't been for the traffic he might have reconciled himself to the public exposure of his crotchet during cheerier hours. You had to rise before dawn to avoid the kilroys, whose noisome emanations and kinetic interferences were more hostile than the littering strangers who drove and parked them. After dark, when they sometimes somewhere somewhat thinned out, their blindingly inquisitive headlights were insulting to a touchy athlete seeking peace for his ordeal, especially when snow or ice kept him off the sidewalks and he had to dispute them for his very path.

Caleb never doubted the salutary profit of his habit-forming efforts, but it was a long time before he succeeded well enough in the painful struggle against inertia gravity and friction to spare reflective attention for the ibicityscape he laboriously witnessed every morning (if he didn't have a cold or some other malingering excuse). Yet it was one of his motives and rewards to review more of the town in half an hour of swift purified silence than could ever be covered on prolonged walks in the afternoon or night.

His athletic hope was to become able at will, say on weekends, to extend the usual half-hour to three or more, and to circle the Cape on Cod Street, clockwise or widdershins, starting and ending at the wide place in front of the cemetery (where once there'd been a trolley siding, as at half a dozen other nodules in the highroad, for the cars awaiting and passing one another on the same periegetic route). He expected to realize this feat of symbolic possession within a year: to gather in a single loop all the Dogtown space that up until now he'd been claiming or reclaiming in slow and separate explorations, block by block or hamlet by hamlet; to drag the Cape into his otter trawl, collaring the whole of Purdeyville, drawing in the entire selfmade island by its cincturing settlements. Without the kilroy-sin of infernal consumption he'd tread for himself the circumference that pilgrims formerly rode on trolleycars dynamoed by steam from one external fire. Meanwhile, in preparing himself, he hoped to trace all the streets of the Harbor ward, protected by Ibi from sleepless populations of neighborhood saints.

Caleb's bond with his dog was strengthened by the frequency and intensity of this joint exercise, which, compared with lengthy hikes on the weekends, also left him with longer stretches of productive leisure during his three days of grace in every seven. One quick harmonious run served as compendium for half a day's walk. The man's doubletime pace accelerated the dog's epicyclic trots once or twice a week into far more satisfying gallops almost every day of the month. Thus, despite his disappointed weekend afternoons, Ibi remained unsuspicious of the sly efficiency in this daily dose of supernal kinesthesia, and he was vaguely surprised to find himself spending most of the week's holidays lying on the floor of Caleb's study. He was as happy as ever to be silently close to the one he adored, but failed to understand what had happened to nightwalks and hebdomadal rambles.

Whereas for Caleb each excursion, nearly as frequent as the sun's, was a burst of self-rewarding virtue that justified the body-sloth of all other hours. In practice, every faithful series of mornings earned him a surplus to pay in advance for a day or two off in a fortnight, when he could bask in indolence of the flesh and indulge the freedom of his will as soon as he got out of bed in the morning. On those days, and on the others when Caleb pronounced himself vulnerable to stress, Ibi mourned away the precious Hesiodic hours, not gladly suffering the divinity's cheerfulness at getting a lot of work done in his bonus-time, inasmuch as a young dog's day was lost on which he had no kinesthetic sport—the cultural end and purpose of evolutionary means like hunting and reproduction, the action of individual salvation that indeed in the wild had no existence apart from the chase for food or love.

As a dog of symbiotic civilization, for food Ibi had only to await nightfall and climb some stairs, or make eyes at the landlady. And the other pursuit was almost as rare as his master's, owing to the fact that most of Harbor Ward's bitches (of practicable class at least) had been denatured by surgery to keep them too cool or were kept in seclusion when hot. As a matter of fact, occasions were so few that he'd been a little backward in learning what that chase was all about. Much as he loved the competitive run, he was always bewildered to realize that he'd mindlessly joined it. But even in his nonage he'd succeeded to the leadership of saints and not long after taking over Acorn Pasture he'd been surprised to find himself humping someone he'd never seen face to face. He had discovered his proximate motive by doing what he'd seen done. It was a strange thing to be doing, unrelated to anything else he was interested in; but he had no choice, and the sensation explained his effort. Then too he felt much better afterwards.

Though Ibi never gave a thought to procreation it was obvious that his parts often enough wanted the necessary and coefficient cause of it, as Bice had gleefully observed—especially when he sat scratching his ribs with a hind leg. Without memory, image, or ideal, some dim proprioceptive metaphor called forth from its furred scabbard his tapered pink lance. In such instances Ibi himself didn't even notice that he was exhibiting an involuntary hope.

The homologous phenomenon also troubled his god, both before and after Bice, albeit his was usually a case of acute awareness and embarrassment, and more often voluntary than not. But on this score there was nothing for Caleb to worry about as long as he was running, preparing to run, or recovering from a run, when he was not buffeted by all the human cognitions and imaginations that continually reinforced his body's radical propensity to extend itself (even on long walks, which afforded leisure for promiscuous mooning about real or imaginary objects of desire).

But Caleb's running was amphibolous. Although it infallibly forestalled or postponed his epitome of the species *homunculus erectus* until the day was well begun, its hardening of the rest of him tended to androgenize his feminine frailty in the world of brutality. Without enjoying the peace of Abelard, or even eschewing incidental opportunity, he hoped to verify Dante's doctrine that love was only an accident appearing in a substance; and to demonstrate that the neutralizing sweat of his utmost effort against the flesh's indolence was more manly than the grossly male obtrusion that disturbed the frictionless psychical vigor of his rib-scratching leisure. Nevertheless, rather than reinforcing his occult self-confidence, the introversion of solitary exercise, to the contrary, might only have fostered the diffidence deriving from his inconsequential person, which had been left more disheartened than ever by his failure to prolong Bice's sojourn, if he hadn't gotten a letter from her that placed his character in a light favorable to his own most flattering mirror.

It arrived about two weeks after the *Avalon Reefer* had sailed, following his last consultation with the doctor, when his new regime was but a day or two old and already faltering under initial stress (his muscles stiffer and more knotted after half a mile than they would be in the future after ten times that distance). Any message at all from her would have invigorated his athletic determination. Once he saw her words in the small black handwriting fully equal to her style of speech, the program of teaching his body to move rapidly for the greatest possible distance could no longer remain under ultimate suspicion as a device for disguising a fated condition of his existence. It now seemed that his quality had been material cause for a unique accident to her substance.

For thus had she written:

St James's, T N . *[Terra Nova—half way from where I am to where I want to be. More romantic to me than green mansions. I'm jealous mostly of her places.*] Dear Caliban: *[She presumes upon my confidences, using the name used by my mother. Is this letter about to disparage me?]*

Now that I'm almost home (with the land still swaying under my feet) I think I can be frank with you—at last, and evermore! Yet I must have torn up six long letters to you while we were at sea. *[I wish I had the first. This one's much too short, and probably the most calculated—if there really were any others. She may have been too busy to write ten words. I wonder if she'll mention the Captain, or his officers and men.]* (If it hadn't been too cold to go out on deck I might have been able to see you in perspective.) *[I e , smaller than ever? But at least she wasn't so casual as to have forgotten me immediately. It takes some measure of interest to write a letter that isn't expected, even if you're half English and like to leave a literate impression.]* I can't bear to have you remember me merely as a wandering gypsy. I was too much in awe of you, the scholarly writer of geometry plays, *[Does she mean to mock me?]* to tell you the truth about myself. I never lie if I don't have to, but I didn't tell you everything. I was too embarrassed, because you're so clever (with a theory of tragedy and all the rest), and I was afraid you'd make fun of me.

No one else I've ever met has even heard of the Sumerians, not to mention imaginary numbers (which you never did keep your promise to tell me about). *[Is she ingenuous or satiric?]* Don't worry, dear hero (standing alone against the U S Government and Public Opinion): your time is coming. When you're famous, remember the little antipodean waif that discovered your talent long before the world paid you homage. *[My talent as a lover!]* I shall think of you whenever I see an erectohedron (if that's the right way to spell it)—or any angle of sixty degrees. *[Then she'll think of me often!]*

The truth I didn't tell you is that I'm a poet (though indeed not of narrative like your mother). Or at least I write verse. I mention it now because I'm feeling very guilty about not having been straightforward with you—when you were so open and unreserved with me. I fully intended to reveal my miserable little secret until it dawned on me how superior your work must be. I felt too ashamed to admit that I'd like to call myself an artist. I tell you only now, when it can make no difference—unless we see each other again, in which case you must promise never to throw this confession in my face.

Think of me as what I mostly am: just a special journalist. (I have real talent as a newspaperwoman.) Perhaps I'll never be able to write a decent poem, but if I do, wherever I am, it'll be dedicated to you. When you read this one about Dogtown that I've just finished, decent or not, don't be harsh with me. It would break my heart—drive me back to the nunnery—if you scorned me out of hand. So please be tactful when you reply—if you have any time to waste on correspondence with a half-educated provincial. (But I haven't yet quite made up my mind; maybe I'd better wait to see if you answer this letter, because if you're unsympathetic to the way I conduct my life there's not much hope that you'll take the trouble to look for what's good in all the dross.)

I'm a freelance, you know, and I'm pursuing my profession. Among other things, I want to do an article on Dogtown from our hyperborean point of view, which until recently wasn't even Provincial! (They say "Codfishland" was the oldest and most primitive colony in the British Empire. It was actually an independent country under the Crown for nearly eighty years, but when the Depression came along it went crying back to mother! And now after ten years the diehard protestors still fly the Union Jack in defiance of Federation with Canada. Anything with a Maple Leaf will always smack too much of the Fleur-de-lis!) The Captain and the mates and the engineers of the *Avalon Reefer* are all renegades from fishing families up and down the east coast of T N, and along with some pretty shocking local color I picked up many interesting stories about the old relations with Dogtown, which still represents civilization to many old-timers up here. It was the best known port of entry to the opulent U S A . Women would hear from fishermen that "the stars are as big as the moon in the Dogtown States!" *[Is that stamping ground acrawl with pillow-talking poets too?]*

But I'm not going all the way back up north to St Bede until spring. I'm booked for the A R when the ice breaks up and she resumes her rounds of the coastal fisheries. Captain Newf will be on leave, so the first mate will be acting skipper: he has his papers now. *[I bet old Newf cancels his vacation if the law of the sea permits. He must suspect the mate's a poet!]* Meanwhile I'm going to England on an Ulster liner I know that happens to be due in a few days. If you come across, I can put you up!! (I'll be staying at a friend's flat in London—while he's riding a camel across the Sahara in order to have something to write about.) I can show you the high points of our old isles the way you showed me the sights of yours—only you'd better give me a month and a half to do it in! It won't cost you anything while you're here: I have adequate resources in the old country.

Caleb's brain runs amok with flashes of wild surmise, reverberant with the coruscations of esemplastic hope—only to fling himself with a dull thud up against the glass brick wall between himself and the offing. *[Archipelago of landfalls beyond this horizon: my Orient, my Byzantium; my Marquesas:: my incunabular goal::: the green and pleasant font of my language::::: the timescape of my mind! Even urban Britain, to others the grimy womb of electricity and mechanics, is for me a tarnished crumbling diadem of jewels, theater of the globe, pledge enough (if no more be possible) for the whole "heaven of Europe"—without the tariffs of foreign Babel!*

It was folly to have told her so much that she can trifle with what poets would call my dreams. For she can't have forgotten that I'm no citizen of her Commonwealth with an inalienable safe-conduct to the Empire's metropolis. In 1787 my Vinland yielded up its power to issue the passport that I've been denied by the inimical pedantry of Protesticans in Washington, whose work can't be uncovered and undone overnight, even by President Kennedy. Perhaps she doesn't yet understand Stateside hatred of the Resistance. Or is she deliberately tormenting me with her liberty as a cosmopolitan? First it was her true mind that she falsely promised: now it's the guerdon of my heart's desire! This is not a paragraph that I should take seriously.] Yet—

But I know Ibi is one of the "complications" you spoke of (without telling me what the others are) that have kept you from crossing the Atlantic. Unfortunately it's true that they won't let you take him to England. I've already looked into the possibilities, and it's sad to report on the best of authority that no amount of bribery or influence will get a dog into the British Isles without six months of quarantine. Granted that England's the proper Dogtown of the Continent, would you and Ibi meet me in France instead? (It would dampen my enthusiasm for your brilliant company not to have the comfort and protection of that noble third party. In fact, I don't think I'd care for you without him. You're too intellectual for me to keep up with. Yet Ibi's well formed character suggests that you'd do me some good too! (Even so, I still think it's unnecessarily cruel not to allow him onto your bed. If he were mine I'd sleep with him every night.) For his sake I might even ask you to marry me. *[Her affection for Ibi is sincere enough. Right from the first she rolled on the floor with him, utterly oblivious to the doghairs on her elegant clothes.]*

I'll be thinking of you both when I get to work on my Dogtown story. But you mustn't be jealous if I cherish some of the other characters down there. They're all part of my scene. Jason Anacoluther said he'd look me up next time he's in St James's. I probably won't be here by then; but I'm not sure how I feel about it anyway. He reminds me too much of some of my father's old chums.

But the one I'd like to apologize to is Gepetto (. . . Something). He's the sculptor that earns his living with some kind of a machine on his truck, a friend of Dr Charlemagne's, and I believe a true artist. I think you'd like his shop, which is also his studio and his living quarters. It's over near the East Harbor Wye. Could you get me his name and address? *[No thank you, Mademoiselle: I have no intention of pandering to your amorous vagaries . . . But I may go look him up, just to see if he knows you as well as I do. Then maybe I'll send you his address, and maybe I won't.]*

I've decided not to enclose my poem after all, which is really about you. It could never be worthy of young Milton the Roi-alist of Dogtown. Anyhow, you're already too dangerous. I'm not yet ready to let a man break the glass bubble people see me inside of.
    Your distant admirer,
    Gypsy B.
P.S. My love and kisses to the Doge of Dogtown!
XXXXXXOOOOOOOOXXXXX!!!!!

It was not a loving letter, but it could be taken as generous and respectful. On the whole it elevated Caleb's spirits. It affixed an honorable period to the adventure, without much damage to his chivalrous sensibility. In appearing to balance the two parties emotionally it encouraged the proposition that he had taken a definite step forward in his womanizing career. There was no need to dwell upon the aspect of failure, which could be found in anybody's exploits. Nothing in the letter cast doubt upon his conviction that with a little further opportunity—another night or two—his kisses would have wakened the sleeping gypsy to a frenzy beyond her own comprehension. He deferred to no man in his understanding of a woman.

9
THE RESISTANCE

On one of his Saturday night visits to Doctor Charlemagne Caleb found a caller before him. Sneaking swiftly up the back way with Ibi on short leash lest the hounds of hell downstairs get wind of the outrage—he gave his prescribed three thumps on the boards of the outside landing with Doc's six-foot oak staff, which was kept there for the purpose so that knocks on the flimsy door wouldn't shatter its flimsier window. The glass was mounted too high for even a normal man standing outside to see into, but before he was admitted, as usual, he got a glimpse of Doc's suspicious downward glare before it dissolved into a welcoming smile, semipaternal—and later, at the table, almost maternal.

At first blush—before they were introduced—Caleb was annoyed at the prospect of sharing his host's attention with the earlier guest. In pilgrim season he wouldn't have been surprised at a preemptor, because Doc had no telephone by which to fend off visitors; but transpontine seekers, even to the Court of Leviathan, were seldom to be seen in the wintertime. Caleb hadn't reckoned on local friends, having none of his own and assuming that he was the only douzeper in town. Yet it might turn out to be one of the long nights on which to share Doc's attention was to share the burden.

As his Saturday night visits had grown customary the attention was occasionally shared only with Deeta Dana the housekeeper. Sometimes she'd sit with them for a time, listening quietly and speaking little, accepting neither proudly nor meekly the Director's peculiar deference, and then silently withdraw at some unnoticed point when the visitor's consciousness was totally absorbed by his host's clauses or his own, retiring to the windowless room just big enough for the giant bed that opened off Doc's harbor-lighted study, which occupied the lion's corner of the half-flat. But tonight she was not to be seen, and the royal kitchen table still required only the usual three of the whole domicile's four rickety chairs.

Charlemagne himself cared not at all for animals, except as symbols, but Deeta was a particular admirer of Ibi-Roy. She proved her affection with savory morsels gleaned and saved for his visits. When she wasn't on stage at his arrival Ibi would nose through the tiring-room arras to greet her in the cubicle his master was never shown. This time, after pressing past the table at the opposite end from the parlously trussed kitchen chair on which the royalty towered, wrapped in a shawl and warming his back at the range (a sole source of heat except for what wafted up through the floorboards from the brokendown actor's stinking hound-pound below), and squeezing apologetically around the foot of the board, he couldn't help frightening the swart restless fellow sitting there, who freely confessed that he was terrified even of dogs no bigger than a cat.

Though Doc and Ibi had grown easier with each other for Caleb's sake, after some slight tremors of reciprocal anxiety on first acquaintance when the visiting bodyguard had been startled into barking a warning at the colossal apparition that opened the back door, the polite saint (though himself as large as a jaguar) was still a little cautious about entering the cave of that toplofty shadow-casting stranger. His instinctive hostility had been so mollified by the emperor's own slowly abating chariness of his presence, and by the almost motherly voice-hospitality accorded his master, that nowadays, after searching out the housekeeper for a warm nuzzle in the bedroom (if not a bite of something in the kitchen), Ibi was confident enough of everybody's security to dream away the long hours stretched out sidelong on the worn cracked linoleum between Caleb's back and the woman's room all filled with the giant's smells, to whom he was now willing to entrust the protection of the cave at its mouth, having learned to discount any danger in the purely intellectual excitement that sometime agitated the blooming buzzing confusion of upper air.

"Maestro Gepetto DaGetto, this is Childe Caleb. He's okay." The very man Caleb was meaning to look up (even as he'd looked up Doc himself, when he used the name of Rafe Opsimath as his visa)! Since getting Bice's letter Caleb had heard more about the notorious worker of ferrous metals, magnet of avant-garde art-lovers, teacher of Shelly Schlossberg. The Tuscan sculptor made his living as an itinerant welder. He sat in stiff restlessness, like a gamin behaving himself in a formal school for revolutionaries, not much taller than Caleb but twice as old and three times as strong. He usually looked either bewildered or passionate, but now he let out a screech of delight when he heard himself further identified as "the smith of Dogtown's soul".

"Hey that's *good!* Very good, Doctor! You never called me that before!"

Without pausing to sniff Caleb, Gepetto immediately complimented him by resuming the interrupted conversation. "I thought it was stochastics he got rich on!" he exclaimed to his superior at a somewhat lower pitch, exactly as he was about to exclaim when Caleb had knocked. His part in the gossip was an openhearted cackle mingling the pleasure of uncertain surprise with the triumph of discovering another real-world paradox that could help undermine public confidence in the inherited conglomerate of logic. Doc had been talking to him about Richard Tybbot the late Duke of Dogtown his COSMOS "Antistochastic Foundation".

The newcomer was able to help immediately by dilating upon COSMOS as a branch of Frank Bacon's responsibility d b a the fund to Criticize and Oppose Stochastical Measures Obtaining in Science. But the issue remained a mystery to Gepetto (a k a Petto), who like most Dogtowners had trouble pronouncing the key words.

"No, my dear boy, *statistics* is what he made his money on; and the law of contrary demand—which he combined in so-called 'negative analysis'. Caleb could explain it to us. But Tybbot was fundamentally a fundamentalist. He left a lot of money to encourage faith in what he took to be Einstein's philosophy of physical determinism. It was the one cause that ameliorated his antisemitism." said Doc, swallowing more of the Scotch his first guest had brought (now backed up by Caleb's new bottle) and dragging jerkily on a cigarette as he stared through the upper half of his bifocals at the sculptor with great round eyes beneath shaggy gray brows in cogitation far higher or deeper than his friendly efforts in paraliterate communication.

Caleb considered himself more capable than others of matching at least Doc's articulate ideas—though he was sometimes not unaware of being a little too inclined to prove that he was doing so by actually disputing factitious conveniences in his senior's practical reasoning. In this case, which touched upon one of his own worlds of empirical experience, he was especially eager to engage his mentor, for no one within that world gave more than a grin for its metaphysics: Doc alone, without firsthand knowledge, was capable of understanding what he would try to say. Who but Doc could understand a young common reader's original contribution to metiers of which they knew little but what he himself told them in abstract briefs?

Caleb longed to make known to that searching capacious mind his grievances against the stochastic dogma that of late had presumed to compensate for the failures of accounting by enclosing and alienating, without foresight judgment or wit, the open pastures in which statistical data should be free to all kinds of graziers. He'd have liked to fascinate Doc with the problem of organizing the quantities ignored by accountants, who, like the declared victors of Medieval battles, were those who remained on the field overnight. On the battlefields of management stochastitians were as blind to geographical Gestalt as market technicians and lawyers, whereas Caleb their critic fancied himself descrying whole river basins and exploring all their ramifications, mastering trackless forests by index and cross-reference, anatomizing uncultivated commons with multiple subledgers, discriminating the several flowers of unfenced prairies, and otherwise expatiating the topography of thorough enumeration.

But he was wise enough to refrain from such vagaries at a drinking bout. In any event, his voice was too timid to intervene, and Doctor Charlemagne was already stringing barbed wire all over the landscape like one of the hyperanimated characters in Sault Diskey's Panantic cartoons:

". . . not because he was really pro-Einstein or anti-Bohr or anything as interesting as that—and he probably never heard of Schrödinger or Heisenberg. As a matter of fact the reason he endowed the original R O I nestegg—Reinforcement of Orismological Ideals, n'est-ce pas, Caleb?—is that he had difficulty reading even fragments of philosophy at Vinland Polytech. But he liked to see himself as the Pauline Prince Henry of a scientific neo-Deformation that would discover a New Atlantis of causality—reestablish faith where now there's only hope . . . " Here Caleb recognized in the use of a dichotomy that had been one of his own themes at this very table a second acknowledgement of his favored status as a selfsufficient pursuivant—the first having been Doc's jocular "Childe", adopted from his own enthusiastic references to himself as one who would be the sovereign's Childe Roland if he had the voice to wind a horn loud enough to reach anybody's ear.

". . . You hear what I mean? He swallowed Francis Bacon from an article in the *Reader's Indigestion* and made him into a reactionary standard-bearer. Have you ever been to the Bacon Museum he saddled his business college with? To give him his due, at a certain level of education it may have helped stave off some of the magic mistiness that feeds on the journalistic versions of 'Uncertainty' and Neognostic psychology; but he was a one-eyed prophet when he derived time from compound interest . . . "

As always, Doc's talk was largely an experiment of thought in progress, whether bounding through patches of tansy or mulling esoteric herbs, and no one was really expected to follow much of it (or to slow him up with questions revealing how far short any listener must needs have fallen); he left room for reply or interruption only when he was beginning to get bored, or to peter out in divagations too absurd, and needed a fresh handful of grist for the same or another milling.

As he sat wondering if there was any particular drift in tonight's play of mind Caleb's bemusement was suddenly arrested by an isolated coppice in the fecund marsh: " . . . The Chauvin of business wanted to make Dogtown into a new Geneva. He couldn't see that Paulinism has finished its mission. It's given us freedom and democracy, thank you very much; we'd never be here without it: but now it's just washed-out individualism . . . The Crats have squeaked by this time, but the Senator can't liberate us from the effects of the Occupation. Noxin has been checked for a little while longer, but he won't be put away, because eight years ago, with the war hero's official blessing, he showed the Protestican pitchmen how to radiate lethal doses of sentimentality into the body politic right between the eyes and disintegrate the sense of public virtue. And once he'd forced the Crats to take up devilvision too the end of party politics was begun. No one in the world is ever going to gather an army to liberate us from what Dostoyevsky might have named 'The Ray That Is Called Vision' . . . "

But the tide was aflood, between mud and grass, finding again the local shoreline from which it had only slackly receded. " . . . FAITH IS A GOOD IDEA. So Tybbot made it the climax of his maxims on the Purdeyville rocks."

Partly from fortuitously retained impressions of childhood's dimmest phase, or from earlier umbilical memories, partly from later hearsay published in the *Nous,* and partly from his own recent discoveries, Caleb knew some of the apothegms that Tybbot had caused to have incised in a string of random boulders along the south path to Purdeyville before donating to the city his ancestral moiety of the island's watershed. Indeed Caleb had been looking forward to Ibi's assistance in a springtime search for all the forgotten inscriptions, before they were again armored with the summer's overgrowth of brambles. "I seem to remember that it comes right after WHEN WORK STOPS VALUES DECAY." he remarked sententiously, as evidence that he'd been following the monologue as attentively as Doc's huge countenance demanded.

"Sure, you must know the Purdeyville scene, you and your pissing totem. Those graffiti chiseled into granite left naked by God are rapes that'll last until doomsday. Tybbot's idea of immutable morality . . . "Still, old Whitey was right: I used to corner him about his notion of Eternal Objects—but, as you geometers know, we've got to use certain categories of form. As a matter of fact they're categories of categories, probably proper to the human neural network. Keep that in mind, Mr Karcist, and you won't be so surprised that Alpha Norman Whitehead the greatest organic systems-man of them all is pleased to call himself an idealist. Nobody except maybe poor deluded Churl Marx has yet kept up a consistent fight against the archformmonger that started all Academies. Even those smart positivists at Vin Polytech are now positing entelechy in the optical development of frogs. And when it turns out that even instincts are prepossessive, you can't deny everybody's kind of idealism . . ."

Caleb was prepared to accept Doc's saltatory play of mind as long as it seemed potentially intelligible in terms of his own prejudices and predilections, even though he was convinced that the anthropologist often conflated nominalism with realism; but he wasn't clear enough in his own idea of the polar distinction between subjective and objective idealism to challenge the author of supraphilosophical dromenology, and he didn't wish to waste the night away in rambling argument secondary to the hopper of critical ideas he yearned to propound for approval of the only competent mind in the world that would not ignore an unprofessional fledgling outside all academic pales. But the waters of a mastermind move of their own will, and for the moment all he could do was ditch and dike a little here or there, without great expectations, little hoping that in the presence of Petto's offshore breeze tonight's tide would find its way to the floodline once or twice previously attained at luminous perigees of apsis.

Yet for any satellite of Charlemagne, even at greatest distance, the resonance of affinity was easily sustained by the larger body, whose powerful vibrations required no more for reinforcement than the tuned sympathy of intelligent admiration, however muted or passive its contribution; and there were occasions on which even Caleb could endure the role of a silent second fiddle. At such times he soothed his impatience with the reflection that after all he was one of the few who ever made bold to challenge the aulic assumption that Doc's ensembles, once the initial gossip was disposed of, were but apostolic gatherings of rapt ears and voices of *Amen*—not because polyphony was abhorred but because his true peers were too rare to turn up at Leviathan Court or any other but their own.

Still, this Saturday night became something more than soliloquy, and Caleb's nerves—supercharged with replies and propositions that might have rivalled Doc's propositions in wit or digression—were alert to his opportunities for interruption, which were somewhat liberalized by the Director's sensitive desire for harmony in drinking. The eyes of both Caleb and Petto were continually sought and scrutinized by those larger eyes, and even as the grossly expressive brows flagged down one's temptations to protest a statement here or there, a sudden acknowledging smile or nurturing gesture, with benevolent sounds of approval as soft as a mother lion's, spurred the intimidated responses of his two kitchen-cubs and renewed the knighthood of honorary interlocutors.

So once again Caleb was listening with joyful excitement to the talk that in talking to itself spun and stitched the famous "langue-Doc"—a species of discourse that only a sloppy orismologist could have claimed for the genus of communication rather than for that of selfexpression. The delivery—always in low and pleasant tones of voice—was loved by its partisans (and hated by its competitors) for a manneristic rhythm of parole and rhetorical ellipsis to which it is impossible to do sympathetic justice by literal transcription and conventional print, which perhaps can best render the gist of its signals on this occasion by the following filtered extractions.

"Until Darwin won out there was some excuse for a private intellectual to take idealism as the norm—say Guy Winthrop, who at least had the perspicacity and guts to acknowledge a struggle to keep it up. You couldn't expect him to overturn the Pauline culture singlehanded. Coming later, with all the civil and historical advantages of old Anglo-Ireland, it was a little easier for Yeats to recognize the tension, which he did by committing his still-Platonic triangle to 'a base of realism and an apex of beauty'. . . " Doc here teased Caleb with a happy grin. ". . . and analytical philosophy didn't liberate the academy: it only changed the metaphysical level of ideals. The substantive adjectives for the true the good and the beautiful are still construed as nouns.

"That much criticism was always possible, of course. But after all that's been laid open for us in these last sixty or eighty years by physics and anthropology, and now by biology, especially as the genuine ontology of the new Atlantis, it's no longer forgivable to subordinate verbs to nouns. Leaving aside questions of copulative and the existential conjugation, verbs are real. Even when abstracted from particulars by a noun, the elementary fact is an act—some sort of *action* in detail. All precategorical reality is at least active, whether transitive or intransitive. The gerund and the gerundive come before the noun.

". . . In *idea* itself, you see, the important thing is the seeing, not the subject or the object of seeing—neither the I nor the Thou nor the idol that the alternative idealisms latch onto. If ideals are no better than matching structures, like the forms picked out by those frogs at Tech, forget the *ism* . . . The question remains what an idea is. You can't get along without ideas. Even Marx couldn't. One thing you can say is that the vision in *idea* is as important as it is in *theater* and in *theory*. To *think*, on the other hand, is the metaphor. Think of that, gentlemen! It's what makes the idioms of a language—not to mention the idiosyncrasy of a poet or the idiocy of a critic."

"The id and the ego!" cried Petto helpfully. "Let's call it the *Io!*"

Caleb had opened his mouth and was about to propose that the difference between philosophical idealism and the ordinary projective imagination of (for instance) the political and economic reformers associated with the Catholicratic Party, who were scornfully called idealists by the Protesticans, was the latter's incorporation of time, hope, and relationship in the primary qualifications of an essence.

But his didact forfended this gratuitous observation by hitting him with an assignment: "Now there's something to apply your creative wits to, Caliban my childe: an unidealistic idea of ideas. I bet you could find an etymology to connect *idea* and *theater*. . . . "

The voice was so sympathetic and maternal, so sensitive to Caleb's vanity and pride (though probably underestimating it by half), that it palliated his annoyance at the idea of having his future tillage of ideas subsumed in advance by a leader who would not design to drive the stakes for terrain he claimed, but only stroll ahead on high, free of impedimenta, hardly motioning to his harried surveyors, while he waited for hunters and porters to pitch camp and roast some venison for his supper!

Caleb seized upon this impertinence however as an opportunity to change the subject, or at least to part the stream of his master's speech with some small obstruction, perhaps to stir up some white water and an eddy of true intercollocution. Despite the aggravating presence of a third party, he rashly decided to risk his position as a favorite (with reason to hope for that of confidant) by introducing the idea that there was another visionary in town whose real (not merely nominalist) opposition to Plato should do the teacher's heart good.

For many weeks he had considered tactics for the delivery of this good news, pondering the enormous difficulty of expressing all its interesting elements compendiously, without talking too fast, before it encountered the resistance of infant scar tissue. For any mere mention of a Father anybody would instantly evoke the entire culture of the Classic Scholastic Church from which Ipsissimus Charlemagne had made his well-known escape long before Caleb Karcist was born. Any apparent attempt to reopen Doc's cauterized theology would presumably meet with lofty rejection disguised in subtle subsuming condescension—and only exacerbated by the witness of an adoring anticlerical Tuscan before whom he would especially wish to maintain the spiritual aseity of an incomparable human. But sooner or later the impulse to expose emotional connections was always too strong for Caleb to keep quiet. Thus, ignoring his assignment, he chose this luff of the sail as a cue to lay his hand upon the governor's tiller.

"The revisionist priest I work for, who was once a physicist—"

"Revisionist priest!" Petto let out a whooping screech of mirthless laughter, in triumphant rejoinder, as if to an unwitting oxymoron, clapping his thigh and looking from one of his companions to the other in apparent expectancy of their less rapid intelligence. But then he changed his mind, to the effect that maybe Caleb's epithet was some ironical witticism after all. "Terrific! This kitchen is the only place in Atlantis for radical poetry like that. Keep it up, Caleb! How come I've never seen you before? We need more people like you in the Resistance!"

"How do you know he isn't a collaborator?" Doc mocked, putting a forefinger to his lips.

"Really!!??" Petto subsided, chastened at the height of linguistic imagination by his senior's realism, amazed at the possible truth. His averted eyes wheeled around the room like a bolting horse's. Then "Don't say that . . ." he muttered, as if Doc had trifled with a curse of the Mafia.

Himself nonplussed by an absurdity that for all he knew pointed to secret understandings between the two old friends, Caleb was unable to advance the connection he longed to make between the father of dromenology and the priest who seemed to him the Common Era's sole upholder of a fennel-stalk which preserved the spark of social counterentropy that had been snuffed by Paul and the Hellenists almost as soon as it was drilled from its Jewish fire-sticks. It was not the first time he had been turned aside from an attempt to catalyze a synergy between this large individual of extreme specific gravity and its less ipseistic peer of similar potentiality in what was taken to be an entirely different field of force.

For the sake of mankind, and to gratify his own cravings for catholicity, he would have taken great joy in the reciprocal enlightenment of Doctor Charlemagne and Father Duncannon; but his was not an evangelist's zeal: he simply wished that each could take the other's ideas into appreciative consideration. He knew that even if they recognized a community of values in the complementarity of their arcs, the like charges of the minds themselves would be mutually repellent.

Yet it often seemed to Caleb that these two men, so utterly unlike in origins, in person, in discipline, and in the typology of the Four Faculties—with antecedents and posterities of glaringly unequal importance to the history of humanity—were such momentously significant collaborators in the revolution of thought that it was his peculiar moral imperative to discover them to each other! They reminded him of the equation for information and counterentropy: the same formula for phenomena and epiphenomena that appeared to be unrelated to each other at any level of abstraction lower than that at which his own mind excited their unification.

They were both courteous men, to be sure. Ipsissimus Charlemagne would have received Father Duncannon with respect and pleasure—provided he himself wasn't committed to the appointment; but such a visit was of course out of the question. By this time Caleb knew that Father Duncannon, the elder and more dignified, was from long experience as leery of artists as the artist was of priests; and Caleb was unwilling to use up any of his credit with the churchman on a foredoomed attempt to interest him in paying a call on a neo-Bohemian genius. Pride and prejudice wore different weeds on the two sides of the inner harbor, yet at a certain level they too betrayed an abstract form in common!

What was true of their psyches was true of their writings. Vocabulary, diction, allusion, imagery, construction, cadence, punctuation, and other qualities for attention—not to mention subject and attitude!—all precluded even the cursory inspection of each other's work that might have led these Creative Minds to fruitful convergence.

Not that Caleb would have agreed to "lend" Doc his out-of-print copies of Father Duncannon's privately published books. Any documents left near Doc's maw were seldom seen again, or seen in the same condition: either lost in the middens of his cave, or carelessly tossed back with the first few pages savagely attacked with carpenter's pencil; or else unscrupulously consumed by the assimilative and excretive process of a stomach that affected poetic innocence regarding its peremptory appetites—expropriated without explanation. Doc never bothered to argue the crown's divine right to any grist for its mill, pretending to be oblivious of a poor man's claim to meal of his own. Indeed in his very youth, even when he was acquainted with Alpha Einstein (who he thought only expatiated what he himself already knew, leaving to Schrödinger and Heisenberg the honor of giving him what he wanted from physics), the mirror on his wall had sufficiently persuaded him that as an artist as well as savant he was the most highly organized one of all—which is to say the highest in the food chain.

And on the other side, although the great director was most famous among the unscholarly brotherhood of "further studies", largely by word of mouth, as the fountainhead of dromenology, his one available publication (the only one that had yet found its way to common readers by commercial distribution), an essay called "Quantum Prose", which Caleb had originally read with such powerful assent that he now felt obliged to give it wide berth for fear of its permanent magnetic force, was only obliquely pertinent to the common ground of the two savants whom Caleb yearned to connect, and in any event was hardly perspicuous enough to hold the eye of a scientist educated in the old school of lucid language whose patience for lesser work than that which addressed mankind's needless pain was running even shorter than his remaining time to elucidate the precious means for its relief, especially in view of the fact that through repeated disappointments of earlier hopes he had come to detest those who professed the lore of arts, most of all the dramatic, despite the fact that of all the world's recruits to the clergy he numbered among those even less prejudiced against what Tertullian called "the Church of the Devil" than the anti-Jansenist Cephasites of France.

Yet Caleb was too confident of the creative power in ideas to relinquish the hope that the West would eventually be released from "the spell of Plato" that bewitched its very language, and from the spell of Paul that implanted faith as the touchstone of its religion; so he was increasingly troubled by the frustration of his voluntary function as a sort of hiated coupling between the dromenologist blind to the most important dromenological praxis in human history and the one cultivator of that old yeast who ought to have been most enthusiastic about the dromenological interpretation of all culture. Sometimes this ambition seemed to himself as humorous as that of a Teiresias trying to mediate ineluctable imperfections in communication between the sexes.

"Or just another maquis manqué . . . " Doc had meanwhile added, using a substantive of the Resistance, which appeared to bewilder Petto in this context—though he knew the word *manqué,* familiar enough to all Dogtown marooners and sojourners of any education whatsoever.

"All priests support the government." said the art-welder. "I'd rather be myself." What he here confided to Doctor Charlemagne, as if in defense of his ignorance, he would shout jubilantly when alone with his own followers.

Now it was Caleb who did not yet fully understand. But Doc was still favoring his younger and newer friend over the anarchist, flattering him most of the evening by playing to his strong suits, like the chief rabbi examining a wonderful young Jesus, mainly by repeatedly veering back to the topic of Tybbot and his philanthropies, which for the nonce seemed to interest him extraordinarily—certainly more than it interested Petto, or even Caleb himself, a statistical youth of business experience who quite enjoyed the warm acknowledgement that he had contributed intelligently to some unrevealed subsumption of His Imperial Majesty (H I M). The allegiance of the fatherless boy was charmingly bolstered by caresses of the voice, his critical faculty soothed by a parental appreciation more characteristic of mothers than of fathers. As easily as Petto, Caleb was always reconciled to HIMself by a kind word, and conjured to forget that he would have preferred to talk about other engrossments.

" . . . Do you suppose Tybbot got wind of the resolution-of-uncertainty thing you told me about, and wanted to promote it for purging free enterprise of randomness?" As if by license of eccentricity at a colloquium of the best minds attended by peers, Doc thrust his face over into Caleb's. "The old man probably wanted to hire Shannon away from the phone company. Wouldn't that be something to his credit? My sense is that he was always uncomfortable with the trial-and-error stance of businessmen. Obviously the Can ideology could last longer if speculation were less indeterminate. Frank tells me Heisenberg was anathematized at Tybbot's official morning prayers. Was he trying to scotch all negative capability in his staff?"

Once again Caleb was astonished at how Doc seemed to get to the heart of a matter he couldn't know much about by attributing too much to the intellects of his subsumed characters. "Like all financiers," he replied cautiously, "Tybbot was more interested in forecasting than in systems or organization. But I admire his efforts to make marketing people figure things out through demographic analysis and rational imagination. Tybbot Institute is one school where you can't get a Master's degree by designing questionnaires and tabulating opinion surveys. A Geneva Chauvinist of the first water never confuses what *is done* with what should be done."

The last sentence was a mildly teasing or flattering allusion to Doc's definition of dromenon—who thereupon smiled and nodded but otherwise took no notice of the ambiguous reflection upon his influence. "So I take it you think that like many of his betters he understood indeterminacy as indeterminism: the primal threat?"

Petto was looking back and forth from one to the other, impressed by the novelty of Doc in deferential mode. Caleb as a man of business (despite his own proclivity) had grown suspicious of the mere palaver in which intellectuals were wont to squander their luxury of time; and anyway as a clandestine aristocrat he always felt degraded by demands to explicate affairs of trade: but now he was obliged to take a deep breath and continue the role of a bright young local in which the Director had apparently cast him for tonight's performance.

"Yes," he said "but Tybbot never understood that information theory is really only communication analysis. The COSMOS Fund in effect was to foster the resolution of uncertainty by finding new means of measurement. Advertising for example, which he thought was much too undetermined . . . " As Petto grew more and more pettish—visibly closing his ears, all but audibly agitated by the baneful influence these tales of money and power were infusing into the sacred atmosphere of his big brother's sanctum—Caleb told Doc that Tybbot would have become the richest man in Atlantis if he hadn't proved the courage of his convictions (which had already made him rich enough in anticipating the Crash of 1929) by disposing of his interest in Old Homestead Manufacturing just before the war simply because a majority of the board decided to support management in a new emphasis upon marketing that was for the first time to include advertising. In doing so he exhibited his solidarity with old Homer Rith, the original "statistical engineer", inventor and bard of the so-called data processing industry, who was selling out his share also on the same cue and retiring from the chairmanship of his own begotten firm. OHM soon thereafter became the most successful enterprise in the history of technology. (In all Atlantis there remained only one company that abstained from advertising, but its product was sugary and the main ingredient was addictive.)

Yet the poor old duke would turn over in his grave, Caleb told Doc, if he knew that Frank Bacon his own eleemosynar was already entertaining proposals for new deterministic methods that might undermine the entire free-enterprise economy of Atlantis. For if "information theory" could be applied to graphics and poetry, as well as to prose, said Caleb, it would logically be taken up also by the undisinterested professariat at the 'Bega Business School who pretended to mathematical scholarship in their unremitting campaign to professionalize the art of prostitution. Here was another boring game for their ludicrous imitation of science: to calculate the optimum amount of real information (true or false) per dollar of space or time.

But then across the Shawmut River in a tolerably disinterested (largely Catholicratic) department of Norumbega's veridical scholarship, he pointed out, it was but another step to propose the federal taxation of all billable dimensions in inverse proportion to the pith of a display. (According to Rafe Opsimath such a levy, based upon the calculation of entropy, had already been advocated by the Controller of Tubalcain, a deflationist Crat, on the grounds that it would favor the informative industrial advertising of genuinely superior steam cleaners.) Any such sumptuary legislation might not reform *The Newurker* or the Sunday *New Uruk Testament Magazine*—only enhance the conspicuousness of the consumption they catered to—but it would elsewhere encourage a slight elevation of broadcast salesmanship and contribute to interest in theories of criticism at vocational universities.

With huge eyes staring at Caleb above the horizon of his bifocals Doc nodded approbation, but he was no longer thinking about the Tybbot legacy administered by Frank Bacon, nor yet about the Resistance. His broad forehead, usually ridged in smooth uninterrupted waves like the formations of a gentle beach, was now divided with a caesura rising straight above his nose like a vent for smoke—in Zeuslike recollection, not in musing abstraction—as the cognitive brain played at many portals of the dovecote within.

Throughout the conversation Petto had been unintentionally silenced, but he wasn't slighted. His neglected presence was appealed to with glances no less courteous than any participating Hellenist or biochemist might have enjoyed at some White Quarry seminar that

Doc presided over. And Caleb politely acknowledged him as audience whenever he remembered to do so during his absorbing struggle for the esteem of his dominant interlocutor. In spite of the sculptor's anxiety and irritation, alternately rigid and squirming in his rickety chair, he remained on his good behavior, hardly opening his mouth for an hour—not entirely as an awestruck self-sacrificial little sister, but full of kinly pride and instinctive reservations. Most of his interjections were corroborative gestures, as if he was the emperor's companionable bodyguard, chosen for his expletives laughter and dramatic expression, during an otherwise private conference with some impecunious young vassal chafing at the short leash of hegemony. He always seconded Doc, whose attention gravitated to Childe Caleb, but he might as well have been polishing the hilt of his sword for all he cared about the art of managing information.

Elbows on the table, Doc had hardly moved all evening, shoving the bottle a foot this way or that when one of their glasses got low, letting his guests go to the sink for their own water and omitting reference to the barbaric amenity of ice (for the making of which there was no household machinery), from time to time sliding toward them the dish of cheeses Deeta had provided, though himself eating nothing so soon after his lunch. Suddenly he showed that his optical contemplation of Caleb's brief performance was due not as much to love of learning as to the separate pursuit of a rather endearing pedagogical comparison.

"That archangel of yours makes too much of psychology. Opsimath thinks he can manage anything: won't believe the history of his art—which is obviously less successful than any other, as the Bible emphasizes. The trouble with selfmade men like him is that they've never failed. They believe by definition that evolution's successful. I'm making him read Crevecoeur, but that won't do much good unless he sticks it out all the way to the end. No one understands failure until it's too late. You're the same way, for the time being," he said to Caleb "but you've got the 18C ambition for objective lucidity—just what's missing in his kind of management."

This accusation was of course absurdly equivocal—inasmuch as Laurence Sterne and Doctor Johnson were equally subscribers to the 18C (as were also Alexander Hamilton and Immanuel Kant)—but Caleb was annoyed to be reminded of the seasoned experience that distinguished Doc's whaling from his own rational and enthusiastic canoeing on the same ocean (as if seas were just for summer paddling). Doc was at least half right about the a priori persuasions of his junior's temperament, which subconsciously assumed an ultimate anabasis, if not continuous progress, in the history of both Atlantis and himself. Unless directly threatened, he secretly admitted, I'm nothing but a slightly imaginative apparatus for analysis synthesis and desire. Haven't I already forgotten my own death again? Haven't I always turned my eyes from the animal misery that overwhelmingly prevails?

Caleb hunkered down to weather the expected humiliation of having his sunshine mentality generously subsumed as a usefully limited Weltanschauung. But as the Languedoc wore on he apprehended that what he had at first mistaken for a critique of the pure reason exemplified by his geometrical inquisition into the human universe was after all no more damaging than kindly faint praise of his peculiar talent for diagram, "the third language".

"It wasn't until I got around to reading some of his homework that I found out you were the real author of the one idea in the appendix, which is actually the guts of his Disquisition. This is one case where communication really is a category—a pure principle of understanding; but he cites it as a mere conveyance, for my benefit as an ignoramus, failing to admit that if you'd rendered him your services only in speech or in math he'd never have whipped up from all that banal information any idea to *be* conveyed. A vector is its own burden.

"I don't mind his plagiarism; it's no worse than the collaboration and prelaboration called research assistance that gets the professors their grants and Noble Prizes: but I do take exception to the shallowness of his gratitude. It's too late to block his diploma, but I'd like to rub his nose in your chart. I swear I'll turn his own text against him. He's the dissenter who preaches to his old teacher that 'form follows function, not content, and the financial arts are purely formal'!

"I'm so fed up with correspondence-school humanism and regimental Convocations that I wasn't going to bother hauling myself up there again. The ordeal's already coming around again, in a couple of weeks—or maybe it's the week after. But I've got half a mind to show up, just to set that ambitious boilermaker straight!"

Caleb's mind did not follow the latter part of Doc's remarks. Vain as any actor (albeit less ingenuous), still savoring the benefit of a dramatizing layman's over-magnifying spectacles, he uttered the hint of modest demur that habitually came to his lips before he could frame a graceful acquiescence: "It was the only way . . . "

"Of course, it was a matter of necessity—the one way to get the job done. My friend Jim Jones the soldier says the only real strength is bred of necessity. Like courage. A man's method is also his necessity, when he's got something to make that hasn't been made before. In theater the right staging is the only way to get it done—not applied aesthetics. Too much unnecessary muscle or beauty in a dancer spoils the aerobic efficiency that makes good work out of mere motion. Of course everyone labels numbers with words and words with numbers—but you had the imagination to see all those bits and columns of information embodied in a single drawing: which in its outcome naturally seems to you no more than what you were paid to do."

Now Caleb the Roundhead Chauvinist squirmed under this overweening praise, which jarred upon his moral pride as far too cavalier, and upon his intellectual pride as too demeaning; yet it warmed his love of Doc's unfeigned sympathy for all manifestations of Creative Mind. But then at a ramble came the inevitable subsumption.

In accordance with what he believed was his late friend Alpha Whitehead's opinion of mathematics as a special system of logic (itself a special system of logos), Doc went on to assert that speech (logos in general) remained comprehensive of both number and geometry. In principle, though with considerable clumsiness, it could describe all mathematics, whereas the converse did not hold. Even the cross-sectional simultaneity of diagram (as an application of geometry), which wasn't much good without worded labels anyway, could at length be matched by poetic elaboration or simplification. Furthermore, contrary to prevalent doctrines, speech was not merely our metalanguage but also, in etymological justice, the only true language among all the sciences behaviors beliefs and other derivatives of dromena, not excluding music and the visual arts. This generalization implied that the speaker of it was a master of speech.

Yet this Indian-giving did not offend Caleb in the final analysis, inasmuch as he was himself a monger of the manifold logos—if only in its literate mode. He chose to save for another occasion A E's account of "pictures" as prior and more general in the heuristic intuition of undromenological theories like Relativity. He was pleased enough by the attention, and at the moment he offered no argument against any of the philology that Rafe's inquisitor seemed to maintain.

But it was hard to check his impulse to tease the casual instructor for grumbling about those remarkably light burdens (as they seemed to a veteran of the vulgar economy) that were imposed upon his independent personality by White Quarry College, which apparently suppressed or ignored any student complaints about his negligence or tardiness of response to mailed-in "weakly weeklies", and failed to insist upon the execution of his schedule once he finally did arrive at a Semiconvocation.

Meanwhile the ephebus heard himself warned against his praiseworthy talent as a "multimarginal twilight man". It appeared that he was in danger of succumbing to the insidious versatility that distracts the ablest of men from sinking singleminded shafts deep enough to strike the minerals rightfully their own. "Opsimath now, he's corrupt with rampant intelligence, and for that reason alone an artist-manque—in all the arts, even the mere performing art of management. But you—in so cagily guarding against the corruption that comes of cultivating aesthetic appetites—you've infected yourself with a conscientiousness about what scholars think. Your vice is to indulge a promiscuous appetite for learning."

Hapless Telemachus, nettled by the overweening reproof, suffered a flicker of jealous suspicion that Nestor found Rafe, the generous foil, more interesting than himself, the parsimonious jewel. Petto on the other hand was disturbed by Doc's criticism of that unconventional commercial traveler from Cornucopia, an affable gentleman of power who might come back to buy some of the welding he had imaginatively admired with a no-bullshit sensitivity to techniques of fabrication. But no more was said about Rafe.

"An artist" Doc went on "has got to contain his hankering for philosophy as well as for money—or, if he already has somewhat of them, must live off his capital by converting them both into art, instead of giving himself over to speculation, or trying to get by on the interest. You understand that I'm not speaking simply of mulling the 'cathedral of concepts' or 'regnant values', but even of your own deep tragedy-ontology . . ."

Petto was glad to hear this homily addressed exclusively to Caleb, as it were taking the words out of his own mouth, himself a preacher who'd never experienced either of these temptations.

Caleb listened advisedly, because he thought he recognized this warning from the artist of histrionics against too much philosophy as a reflection of intellectual conflicts that they shared, and because it implicitly alluded to their last conversation, in which the probationer had incontinently exposed certain romantic ideas. This ulterior tribute flattered the culprit far more profoundly than the earlier patronization of his businesslike abilities—while Petto, whose intuition excelled his perception, was a little embarrassed to witness a radically cruel analysis in the form of kindly-voiced chastisement.

But at last came tribute meet to Petto too, as oldest loyal friend, with whom (one was given to understand) there was no longer need for a lot of talk, but who battened on any acknowledgment of Doc's brotherhood and always lighted up at compliments to his vitality. It was Caleb's turn for embarrassment as a witnessing fellow. " . . . As for living," said Doc "our Benvenuto will do that for us."

By this time Caleb had tentatively recalled and organized around the identity of Gepetto DaGetto a few vague and scattered memories from cursory perusal of the *Nous,* and scraps of lunchcounter gossip he suddenly found he'd preconsciously absorbed, which were now entering into his composite picture of the character before him. Without doubt this was the individual shown on the Community News page declaring to the world "It's my life that's art—not the sculpture!"

The name DaGetto was still murmured among alert people of all classes to conjure execrations of the local Resistance, and it had once even appeared in the Botolph papers on a list of suspects bruited by an investigating committee of the Commonwealth's legislature (whereas Ipsissimus Charlemagne had been overlooked entirely!). But public apprehensions were gradually subsiding, as it became more and more obvious that the maquis had always been ludicrously weak pacifists and were losing their initial semblance of strength (supported only by some old folks' wan resentment of all the latest technology) with each year's new cohorts of birth and death.

Childe Caleb and Maestro Gepetto were still flushed with gratification (tempered by pity for each other) when they were suddenly dismissed, several hours before the customary time, in fact on the early side of midnight.

"Would you mind?" Doc scraped his feet, pushed away the bottle and glass before him, spread the flat of his hands to either side of the table, bent over until his chin was almost in the crumbs, and looked up at them from under waving brows with a charmingly apologetic grin. "I've got that inquisition to attend to, you know. Take the bottle with you." All at once he became a courtly host, apologizing several times again as he led his company to the door, mumbling also something about "an editorial" for *Dromenology's* latest overdue number.

Hastily responding, as if caught redhanded in an offense against civilized manners, too unprepared to manage any counter-apology, the three guests scrambled to their feet, Ibi the first among them, who was shamefaced at being caught off guard but delighted to be roused so early from his resigned repose, paws slipping on the linoleum in his rush to be the first outdoors. Doc humorously dodged the dog as he drew the bolt with pantomimic grace. They cleared out in less than a minute, coats and hats and all.

Thus, with a sense of release, both men of two minds (eager for Doc's company yet without much leisure for endless night symposiums),

Caleb and Petto found themselves in the fresh cold air of Leviathan Court savoring a windfall of free rest, one of them exhausted by the grilling, the other by sitting still so long to listen.

Whew! Caleb wasn't sorry that Doc had forgotten or delicately excluded from this evening's play of mind the problem of bringing an epic to the stage, which last week, in the abundance of his heart, upon happening to discover Doc's interest in the incunabular matter of Mesopotamia, he had incautiously advanced as a theoretical question. Almost in the same breath he had joked about the symbolic difficulties of trinary metaphysics, giving the doctor a taste of his own medicine in the art of mystifying allusion. He'd had no intention of betraying either the seminal hope or the barren despair that alternated in the germination of his orthogonal four-pointed acorn; but he did toss off the remark that "it's a matter of making the best of all tensely asymmetrical worlds with a single device for the unification of Pythagoras Descartes and Hamilton". Betting that Doc would never admit bewilderment or mathematical ignorance by putting him to the question, he'd indulged the pent-up urge to say something reckless about his motive: "I'd like to invent a pithy romantic technology for the generation of all worldlines, and apply it to all histories and arts in the continuum of complex numbers. My rectotetrahedral calculus would avoid the illusion of simplicity without forswearing reason!"

He'd won that hand, without being trumped, because Doc was for a different game that night. As if with the intention of beginning a relevant reply, the senior player had thereupon dealt out the theme that Dogtown's destiny was frustrated by the lack of art-drama. The city's unconscious yearning was evident from the blind evolution of cults and carnivals and parades and pageants. For a long time, Doc had declared, he'd been trying to interest Dexter Keith and others in getting the city to commission a production of *Bartholomew Fair* at Gloucestermas. He maintained that in Dogtown he wouldn't need professional actors to do it right.

But as he stood with his new friend at the top of Leviathan Court, Caleb was still marvelling, somewhat doubtfully, that he'd been addressed by Doc as an artist. Like the semiclairvoyant mother now safely exiled to South Atlantis, Doc had a way of putting two and two together without having the numbers, though he did so without cackling over his discoveries. Perhaps the secret had not been hard to guess, but Caleb had never gone so far as to mention that he was writing a play. He breathed more easily, however, now that his preoccupation could be tacitly assumed, omitting awkward explanation of his presumption in making such an attempt virtually under the very eyes of H I M , without requesting approval or advice and thereby avoiding the deconstructive criticism of a dramaturge who apparently had never descended to the level of text-scribbling.

But tonight both he and Petto had been spared the obligation of responding to Doc's monologues on sundry other topics they'd severally had other occasions to endure when they weren't in the mood. There'd been no talk for instance about dromenological matters in the Charlemagnian repertory, and scarcely anything about the Resistance or its oppressors: no mention of the "cathode-ray sugar cone" (C R S C), Idol of the Hearth and opiate of all classes; or the epidemic narcosis of Kaka-Koma and Sucro-Soma (viciously introduced and inflamed by advertising, the same immunosuppressive disease that DV had acquired from Atlantean whorehouses before its conception); not a word about sentimental Uncle Sugar patriotism; nor about the saccharin epicenity of a noveau bourgeoisie ruled by the nidification instinct and nurtured on ersatz folklore invented yesterday in the inanely fantastic panantics of Hanky Panky the Monkey picturesquely stereotyped by the bulbous blue nose of a buffoon; nor yet about the slurry of sucrose melos in which all other stories were dulcerated and slurped; nor even about "the popular muse of copycatting", as "the performing art of selection by anyone possessing an aperture . . . " They had long since agreed with Doc on all these matters.

Stamping with glee, Petto expressed surprise that tonight's play of mind had passed over the decadence of Dogtown culture. "He let us off easy tonight, Caleb! I could have relaxed!" The hornyhanded veteran addressed the tenderfoot as guilelessly as a simplehearted old friend, readily accepting his privileged access to the throne and never questioning whether he was an abolitionist meliorist nonjuror or recusant.

"He called me an 18C man!" Caleb moaned to the modernist. The winter ground was clear and dry, concealing nothing that could be seen in the city's artificial chiaroscuro.

"Don't feel bad. Prob'ly he only meant your style." replied Petto out of the corner of his mouth, glancing into the dark of all directions, never looking at the person he was talking to, as if guilty of conspiracy in lese-majeste. "You just happened to be the one who crossed his path when he was thinking about it. Sometimes he gives me hell too. But he doesn't mean anything by it. I can read his mind. You gotta learn not to take it too hard."

But now that he was let out of school he was becoming a very different boy, full of self-assertion. "He's my blood brother. I'd do anything for him. Anything! A prince of an intellectual. There's nothing he doesn't know. But don't expect to understand what he says!" His down-curled forefinger, roughened by burns and callouses, waved between their two noses and pointed obliquely toward the sky over Caleb's right shoulder, his voice rising under the tension of holding it low. "I'll tell you something—not his fault: he was an only-child. All his ego in the head too! He doesn't feel things at Leonardo's center, where all the axes cross. You know what I mean? With H I M it's all the Great I-AM—the Capital I!" He finished in an awe-inspiring whisper.

"Isn't that seeded at every man's center?" Caleb suggested, timidly probing for Petto's sense of humor.

But it remained inaccessible to assault. Petto's laughs came either at his own initiative or when least expected. His was an organism too possessed by its own impressions to detect the drift of another's, a characteristic which Caleb allowed was of great advantage to certain kinds of artist.

"You know why His Imperial Majesty is riding high tonight?" He waited for a shake of the head to confirm Caleb's dumb little smile of submission. "I'll tell you why! He told me about it before you came. This afternoon Jock Merrimac came to see him! Mohammed came to the mountain!" His cachinnations peeled off layer upon layer of imaginative appreciation, his arm flogging the air as he bobbed once around in a slow jig, doubled up with internal mirth. Luckily for Caleb he didn't again pause for response.

Suddenly Petto sobered himself. "Come and see my work. It's early yet. Have another drink. I'll ride you home afterwards. —Will the dog bite?"

Ibi could hardly believe the adventure he was embarking upon. Nothing loathe, he leapt up into the cab of Petto's truck before the door was fairly open. He rode in a seventh heaven redolent of machine scents, protecting his master side-by-side on the stranger's seat high above the street, enjoying from the inside a noisy motion of the kind that always before had been alien. It was a very pleasing revelation of strangers' adaptability.

Caleb told Petto that he'd often noticed this welding rig around town. To reach it they'd walked down the Court to Front Street, escaping the notice of sleeping dogs, Mrs Laplace now off duty.

"I park down here so I won't wake up Doc's neighbors. The muffler needs patching. Besides, I don't like turning around up there. Even in daylight I can't see when I back up."

Hugged by his fraternal master, basking in equality of station on tattered plastic springs, Ibi sat taller than either of his companions, with command of all the glass. But during the brief transfiguration, this fleeting Festival of Fools, looking down at the passing shadows strobed by glares and flickers, he searched in vain for sinners or other saints abroad.

On the short way to East Harbor Wye, veering up and careening down the house-clothed rock of Joint Hill that divided the peninsular from the central ward of the city—swaying through a succession of narrow bends for half a mile around the inner head of the tide, but screened from the penetrating waters by half a century's swaybacked roofs and gray decaying clapboard, apologetically coughing along the night-quiet street with a sputtering tailpipe—they seemed to pass not a single remnant of nature that could be brightened by summer's green. Yelling now at the top of his voice in order to make himself heard, bouncing up and down on the seat with the rhythmic reinforcement of his own muscles, Maestro Petto artlessly betrayed the rivalry in his subordination to the grand master: "You know what? He'll never be part of this city like I am!"

Caleb was too tired to strain his puny voice in polite effort to answer any of Petto's remarks in passage. The truck's violation of silence tightened his stomach and made his shoulders cringe, notwithstanding the fact that Ibi's far more sensitive ears, alertly erect, seemed perfectly able to exclude the noise that his own strangers were responsible for.

"Some of the Tuscans may say I'm an outsider. But my grandfather was the best forcola-carver for gondolas in Venice, see, where the best sailors came from. Besides, a lot of these fat golden-guinea fishermen that call themselves Tuscans mostly came down from the quarries when Key Square was still full of the Irish, and all the real seamen come from Trinacria. Some of them give me the fig when I go by. They don't always understand me yet. But they will, when they see my work! Don't get me wrong: they always call me when they've got a job they can't handle themselves, even when they know I won't work on credit anymore. You'd be surprised how many of them tell me their troubles. At least the woman like me. —Hey!" His pitch rose in a diapasoned scream of triumph: "Come to think of it, maybe that's exactly the trouble!" Flabbergasted (but not dumbfounded) by this delayed insight, he took his hands off the wheel to applaud the laughter of his own joy exactly at the first reversal of the East Front Street twist, and to knuckle the fragile biceps of the goodluck passenger without whose assistance he might never have enlightened himself thus. "When it comes to *semen,* those woman aren't happy without the best!"

Yet despite this asseveration of self-esteem the welder's delight was selfless, and his generous loyalty rose from its depths to displace his critical reservations about their beloved tutelary, who seen only on the street seemed mere ragged flaneur to fellow citizens though in truth a chosen demigod of many off-islanders never privileged to behold him so near. So before they reached their destination he was crowing that "the great Atlantean bard" had finally knuckled under to HIMself of Dogtown, the greater mind, bigger than any poetical football player on God's earth.

He was referring to his news that the narrator of "present-day national epic", Jock Merrimac, whose celebrations of places from coast to coast were admired even by Doc as "original passions not yet dissolved in sugar soup by the amplified rhapsodes", had come crawling in alcoholic stupor to pay his tribute to the artist of dromenon. The younger of the two luminaries (and much the more famous) had become the first to yield to the magnanimous impulses that eventually or occasionally override the dignified reserve of worthily lionized sovereigns.

Of course the erstwhile athlete and poetic champion of the Beauts could the more easily afford to be gracious, inasmuch as he enjoyed national success with a notoriously rising generation, the formation of whose emotions and opinions suffered little drag from the inertia of study. Yet on the other hand, leading a dissipated and dangerous life, Merrimac probably believed himself the closer to death.

Furthermore, though Caleb would not have argued the point with Doc, it was hardly an imperative of culture that the work of an epic poet nowadays be subsumed by the dramatic branch of dromenology simply because theater is an art of more dimensions. Or on strength of the theory that epic is always generated by yet earlier dromena that haven't been favored by coevolution with the conception of drama. For it was held by Doc's same doctrine that drama itself is given birth when fragments of epic descended from foreign dromena impregnate the matrilocal dromenon at an earlier phase of its own religious decadence but at a favorable time much later in history and in a peculiarly fertile situation. Dam and sire, heterogeneously descended from the same primeval dance, were equals in the procreation.

At any rate, although literary opinion had been much affected by Merrimac's poetic narrative, it remained almost wholly impervious to the works of the Director, owing only in part to the fact that the flowering of DV and the revival of popular verse had excused the public from reading complex prose.

Truth to tell, Doc's writing was too much for Petto also. But to him that failure of noetic communication mattered very little, seeing that he knew firsthand, without literate intermediation, that his friend the philanthropologist, THE LIVING MAN HIMSELF, had the heart to FEEL all humanity (as it was said that Shakespeare did). But Petto claimed to read a lot, and more than anything else he read the cantos about Atlantean places Merrimac was still and always passing through, and the women. Merrimac's long narrative always moved like a man's blood, Petto cried, beating out its own rhythm like a smith's at his anvil, pulsing like the sculptor's own life intensified in Dogtown. "I'm Jock's brother too!" he declared to Caleb. "And now maybe Doc will let me drive him up to Higher Falls so I can meet the guy myself!" Again he shrilled with violent amusement at a conceit of his own devising.

Yet this topic had hardly been broached when the welding rig rattled down into the waterfront yard behind the sculptor's shop. After a couple of perorational hiccups the hunchbacked truck fell into cold silence before some bushes outside the basement smithy. Caleb's feeble comment was therefore audible: "It's not his epic that makes him our best poet, but the lyric verse about his childhood in Higher Falls, which no one pays any attention to. Have you read the *Professor Hex* cycle—especially 'Mary Maciddy' and 'Mister Max'? That book was put on remainder in less than six months!"

Caleb and Doc had agreed that this was Merrimac's masterpiece, a glory of spontaneous New French imagination in English, availing itself of classical language only as represented by derivatives used in the artificial mill town built on the great Kerouac River by recent ancestors of the Greek and Latin poet Percy Higher, the cultivated anti-Jock of highest contemporary reputation. Unbeknownst even to the cognoscenti, Doc had acclaimed *Professor Hex* as the Ur-type of the "Quantum writing" that he himself had been prophesying. And he had heard from one poetic go-between (a commutable herald of both camps) that this book was Jock's own favorite—more to be treasured than all the scrolls of musical lines that had made his name so famous among readers and illiterates alike by spacing out his feverish celebrations of Atlantean narcosis over beds and jazz clubs from one seaboard to the other. Yet already the newest layer of unhistoried youth knew nothing of the embittered alcoholic (now hiding at home with his mother) who in true innocence had set afoot the infamously salubrious movement of Beauts (sometimes spelled as Buttes), and had inspired among transients the latterday custom of calling each other by the name of Mac.

"I don't know that one. But go ahead and read it if it really grabs you! You're still younger than I am. Epic poetry will come later for you. But don't ever forget this day! It's here in Dogtown that Ipsissimus Charlemagne and Jacques Merrimac came together for the first time!"

"Languedoc and Languedoui."

They climbed down with Ibi and walked up around the dingy building to enter by the front door directly from the sidewalk onto the floor Petto called his studio.

10
QUINQUAGESIMA
OFFERTORY

The Laboratory's snowplowing contractor had cleared the circular drive while the last of the flakes were still suspended, and when Caleb drove up for Sunday mass his way was lightly reimmaculated by the completed precipitation. The muffled sound of his four chugging pistons was absorbed by the coverlet of thick whiteness that softly comforted all the bare bones and undressed skin of the selfmade island and its main that preserved history above the level investment of the warmer sea. The first kilroy he had ever owned, an obsolete two-door Little King acquired only yesterday from the used-car lot of the Devonport dealer, seemed to be making tracks in a renewed age. Yet the deep snowfields were already beginning to gather earth's vernal heat of fusion, and in the civilized atmosphere of early March they were not likely to much outlast their own purity.

A double garage under the servants' wing, a vestigial coach house in the architect's design, had been converted into a chapel. He carefully parked where most room would be left for other cars. Later he would dig out the half-buried Autotod for Father Duncannon's quotidian use. The big Nicolet was gone with Father Lucey to New Uruk, or at least to the Botolph airport for awaiting him there.

Chris was known for being suddenly called away "on business of the church", but this was the first time such an excursion had spanned Sunday morning, the very time that two or three ladies were apt to show up for the liturgy. Caleb had previously served only at ferial Mass (before going to work upstairs), when outsiders were not especially invited to participate, and when the Father Superior was more likely to need a surrogate for his errant Member Regular to bear a hand at the altar as a trained representative of the laity. It would have been embarrassing to disappoint the ladies at the last moment with a note pinned to the door of a dark cold oratory, especially since they had been cordially informed of the Fathers' return from a long trip to the provinces.

Father Duncannon harbored no illusion that this unofficial little contingent of High Church dissidents from St Paul's Apostolic parish wished to understand the radical revision of significance in the liturgy to which they were resorting. These ladies were conservative Tractarians longing for Petrine etiquette at a Tudor altar. They sometimes had the Fathers to tea, and were occasionally invited to the Laboratory refectory in cordial reciprocation, but though they politely accepted the Order's introductory leaflets it was not to be expected that they would inquire about membership. They had a tacit inkling of the Order's odor in the nostrils of established churchmen both Low and High.

Caleb hadn't seen either of his employers since they started their fortnight trip of three or four thousand miles to visit various North Atlantean members before Lent set in. Their purpose was to obtain a certain measure of advice and prior consent in order to ensure a successfully democratic Chapter in June. If there'd been enough time, and if less money had been tied up in the market, they might have flown to England, Rhodesia, South Africa, Malta, Israel, Lebanon, India, Australia, Singapore, Korea, Japan, Jamaica, Trinidad, and/or Argentina to consult other members who would not be able to attend.

Short as it was, the time counted away from the throb of the Street, with nothing but a telephone credit card to maintain communications, easily sufficed for Chris to accumulate an urgent deficit of financial conferences and field investigations. Two weeks on the road cooped up with the religious savant to whom he had dedicated his life, and for whose sake he would gladly have died, was enough to have driven him into one of his selfconscious tantrums (to some of which the employee had became willy-nilly privy, as a separable lay companion for whom neither of the Members Regular was spiritually responsible). In any event Caleb suspected an impulsive desertion tantamount to disobedience. Despite the irregularity of sudden substitution, the gentle tight-lipped Superior was perhaps somewhat relieved at the prospect of being served at this public Mass by a distinctly smaller and more subordinate trusty.

Nonetheless Chris appeared to have objective cause. He had telephoned Caleb at home on Saturday afternoon to announce with his usual cheerful courtesy their return from the tour and his urgent departure for New Uruk on the very morrow. "Within forty-eight hours I think I'll have some good news about Parity. By the way, you'll be glad to know that those Polish bonds may be worth far more than they show on the books. But it looks as if something much more important is about to happen, or *is* happening. Maybe a clean break with Professor Capstick. Or possibly one of the acquisitions you predicted. Anyway, Hamilton DeCamp has all of a sudden managed to get me an appointment with Mr Halymboyd. Unfortunately it must be on Sunday afternoon—not in Ur but out at his place in Mussel Roads. If I'd had some warning I might have been able to manage an invitation for you to go with me. But anyway I guess we've already come to the point where you and I must divide the labor."

With tactful elaboration Chris was prepared to forfend or mitigate Caleb's involuntary envy and all-too-human resentment at missing out on the conference he'd so assiduously helped to bring about. "There may be further meetings at Parity headquarters on Monday. I don't quite know what to expect. But I'll be staying at the New Uruk Ascetic Club, in case you want to reach me before Tuesday. Meanwhile, if you don't mind, I'll report to you by phone on Sunday night. But please don't stay home on that account. I know you're interested, but it's not worth disturbing one of your Mondays."

Caleb was partly amused and partly annoyed that Chris would pretend to believe that he worked his whole day off in concentration too profound to brook such a fascinating interruption.

"In fact it's only out of dire necessity that I'm calling you now. Your long weekends are sacred to Father and me, as I promised in the beginning. So I beg exceptional indulgence for this intrusion—and all the more because I'm forced to request the very best hours of your well-earned solitude . . ." And so Caleb was asked to serve at the Sunday morning Eucharist if he found it convenient to do so. Before he could protest his unquestionable willingness (for he was always eager to divide a breakfast with Father Duncannon), the alleged inconvenience was sweetened by the superfluous reward of an extra day free of duty whenever he wanted to take it (unless he preferred overtime pay for equivalent hours). Hoping that Father Duncannon was not aware of this bribery to perform the most pleasant of Christian acts, he refrained from rejecting such a precious gratuity out of hand solely for the sake of his private time-hungry gestation of uniquely surplus value.

"But I won't deny that we also need you here at the Lab all the rest of next week to prepare for negotiations at this end if I'm successful in getting Halymboyd to follow me back to Dogtown. It's essential that he visit Father Duncannon in Dogtown—and that Father be in the right mood for receiving him! . . . Besides, Father has some ideas about Chapter that he wants your advice about."

Taking a shovel from his car Caleb rapidly cut a path through the snowbank to the french windows that had taken the place of garage doors in the stone arch which thereby admitted natural light to the west end of the chapel. The tiny cave was furnished with fewer than twenty simple chairs and kneeling pads on the uncarpeted half of the flagstone floor. The east end, where on another site the panoplied altar might have been lighted by a stained-glass apse, was butted up against a sloping whitewashed ledge of subterranean granite.

It was warm and fragrant inside the glass sashes. With a familiar pang of guilt, though almost as boldly as if he was a committed member of the church universal like any other communicant, he deposited his penny in the dish on a small Table of Prothesis at the door (homologue of the Greek prothysis where the slaughtering was done below Zeus's high altar of ashes, and analogue of the offertory sideboard behind the Screen of Iconstasis in the sanctuary of a Byzantine church), exchanging the coin for a weightless white wafer of unleavened bread that he took from the laity's wooden bowl and placed in the laity's ciborium. For contrary to the natural assumption of the Fathers when they learned of his pupillage at the Petrine altar of a Tudor convent, and of his later devotion to boys' activities on the Pauline horn of the Apostolic dilemma, including rather elite service in plainer Holy Communion at the famous St George's Apostolic Church in Unabridge (which Washington himself had attended when he came up from Parthenia to take command of the Continental Army and besiege the British in Botolph), he had never undergone the sacrament of Confirmation.

After a dozen years of heedless paganism, without the slightest sense of spiritual loss, normally preoccupied with peremptory desires that seemed totally at odds with the preoccupations of religion, and possessed of his own romantic theories, but never deliberately blasphemous or otherwise particularly rebellious, in his headlong enthusiasm for Father Duncannon's science-born revision of primitive Christian doctrine he had forgotten to mention that even as an older acolyte he had never been qualified to receive the bread and wine—until he was so entangled in the affairs of the Order that it would have been a scandal to raise the question of his own ecclesiastical status for the first time on the very step of the altar in flagrante delicto. At a very early age the manners of consumption had become familiar enough by studied observation to require no instruction.

At the same time, his life had been thoroughly clear of the church for so many years of intellectual adventure that memory of his boyhood churchmanship was very vague (the doctrinal content of which anyhow had been generally bewildering, for the Tudor-Petrines were almost as inclined as the Classic Scholastics themselves to educate their children prematurely), and he couldn't absolutely swear that he had not been submitted to a bishop at an age when one ceremony was distinguished from another chiefly by the number of candles or by the degrees of motion. To this day his catechismal lessons, though still tincturing his blood, remained confused and unmemorable.

Therefore, although Confirmation was no official prerequisite to the assumption of an acolyte's duties at the altar, he had chosen to ignore the preparatory ritual of Confirmation—as an elective merely adjuvant to one's personal participation in the sacrament proper—and to behave like an authorized communicant, letting any devil take the hindermost.

In the sacristy, formerly a laundry, after shedding outdoor garments he was hastily buttoning up his black cassock when Father Duncannon came down the winding stairs in his domestic soutane. Caleb dared not greet him cheerily, for the priest never acknowledged the initial presence of his acolyte with more than a faint nod, and this morning the mere fugacious hint of an ironic smile was sufficient to express the Superior's gratitude for discreet aid in bridging a contretemps that was slightly exasperating but certainly not worth an interruption of the sacerdotal routine. Caleb's veneration of Doctor Lancelot Duncannon the physicist was as nothing to his awe of the frail taciturn Father Duncannon about to say a Mass like any other priest.

At St Martha's Convent School there had been a sacristan to help Father Pole dress for the altar. In meekest silence, like a magician's valet, Sister Agnes would hand him each linen or brocaded garment according to putatively immemorial protocol, and otherwise wait upon him hand and foot, as the spiritual five-year-old boy watched with a ceremonial reverence that now almost twenty years later the worldly boy understood to be excessive. Here Father Duncannon needed no holy handmaid to vest himself with amice alb cincture maniple stole and chasuble (for each season a different outerwear of what Tyndale called "disguises"). With neither haste nor hesitation, standing at his dressing table, he solemnly wrapped himself in the green embossments of pure white for the classic office he shared with a million others around the world on Quinquagesima (a k a the last Sunday of Epiphany), while in accordance with Lab custom Caleb went out into the sanctuary to fold back and remove the blue altar cover, place the missal-desk on the Epistle side, and prop up the altar cards, twice returning to fetch dishes and linens for the credence table, as well as the cruets of water and wine.

And then one last errand on his own, a Promethean function in which since the age of Samuel he'd delighted more than any other among his services to God. For the acolyte's most proprietary duty was to set softly ablaze in luminary gold the crepuscular points which had once seemed very high in the shadows behind the perpetual sanctuary lamp that flickered only dim red light. Striking a lucifer on the granite wall of the sacristy behind the wardrobe (where charred scratches were least unsightly), he ignited the flat waxen fuse exposed on a spear-long handle at the end of a brass lumen curved like a swan's neck against the addorsed nape of its opposingly combined snuffer. It remained a childish pleasure to light the candles with punctilio, and he hoped with grace, his tight black tunic buttoned in military severity from neck to ankle (not yet surfluffed like a chorister's with his loose lace-trimmed cotta).

But now he shares the tiny nave with two or three ladies kneeling at the backs of chairs in front of them. Holding his torch delicately at port, he paces front and center to the foot of the altar (thus intersecting the longitudinal axis of the crucifix-surmounted tabernacle which normally contains the "reserved sacrament") and genuflects. Then steps he up to his right with arms outreaching and precisely kisses with flame the blackened wick of the brass-collared Epistle light. Whereupon, making his turn inward in reverence for the central mount, retracing the path to downstage center, he genuflects again and completes the line of a V by movement up to the Gospel candle at his left. Again descending, he bends his right knee to the floor, and walks back into the sacristy with rapid complacency, extinguishing the fennel stalk with a rabbit punch of breath.

The Mass-boy's aesthetical enlightenment has cheered the cella, and he is pleased to deceive himself with the illusion that his solo ceremony is an overture integral to the sacramental opus. Thereafter too he plays his part as elegantly as possible, considering that the effective words and actions are reserved for the priest.

By this time Father Duncannon was waiting to get started. Four-cornered black biretta on his head, his body carapaced in gold-embroidered green, one hand bore the stem of a chalice skirted in a flat tent of the same thickly threaded color, the other with elbow horizontal pressing lightly upon the green burse that capped the stiff brocade, like a steward's steadying the topmost dish in his stack. Facing off, priest and acolyte bowed to each other, Father Duncannon murmured some words of prayer that Caleb had never caught but to which he always said "Amen". They bowed again, and the bus boy turned to lead the way, supporting in curled palms the heavy red missal, obviously large for such a small operation, which leaned against his chest like Aaron's breastplate of judgment enjeweled with the names of twelve tribes.

Inside the portal Caleb tinkled a warning bell hung upon the granite wall to rouse an almost imperceptible stir in the little congregation, bearing witness to the vigor of their solemn swift procession. Almost simultaneously, without breaking his stride, he dipped three fingers into the granite-mounted stoup and stretching back his right arm passed the touch of holy water to the extended fingers of the priest, both of them for that instant balancing their loads with one hand while they signed themselves with the cross. In this manner they approached the small altar so disproportionately large for the room.

Even in a monastery on Sunday there was no reason to waste any time about a low Mass—said without haste but not sung. There was much to do before arriving at the first essential part of the sacramental action. (The synaxis as a whole, at one time called "the Mass of the catechumens", centrally devoted to Scripture, was usually much magnified by Apostolics and separately practiced as "Morning Prayer". Under the sway of idealistic individualism, according to Father Duncannon, the interpretation of biblical Word, along with exercises of personal piety, was emphasized and inflated practically to the exclusion of action—much as, according to Doctor Charlemagne, the merely verbal elements of Greek drama, to the exclusion of everything else, were emphasized and inflated in the New Comedy. Here of course the sermon would be omitted.)

By shedding some of Archbishop Cranmer's beautiful paragraphs and transposing other traditional elements, guided by the orthodox findings of Dom Gregory Dix and other liturgical scholars, Father Duncannon and a few learned advisors among the original Members had purged the liturgy of spiritually selfish Pauline corruptions. Still, one must get from the beginning to the middle of a thing if there's going to be an end to it, and to these radical critics of Tudor symbolism there was nothing otiose or sentimental about doing so with the courtesy of genuflections, kisses, signs of the cross, and other Petrine gestures inherited via Rome and Unaford, as long as the expressions were not syntactically illogical.

Both man and boy in motion, the initial tasks were divided cooperatively between the servant of God and the servant of the servant of God, but the latter so intent upon the perfection of his service that he was scarcely aware of what the former was doing. Thenceforth Caleb concentrated on his own signals and skills like a discreet maid at the proscenium blessedly unconcerned with the substantial behavior of the star upstaging her. Having relieved the priest of his four-cornered hat (taking it by a certain one of the three flanges of its crown and setting it down on the footpace), while the priest went up to lay out his service of silver and cloth, the acolyte took the book straight up to the Epistle side of the mensa and (with palms together before his breast) returned the long square way about the predella (genuflecting on the axis) to left of center (stage right), thus positioning himself diagonally opposite the Word; whereupon the priest redescended to stand in the middle closely to the right of the kneeling attendant.

Side by side, facing the crucifix, they speeded deliberately through the Preparation, the leader quick and perfunctory, the inexpert follower laboring as the sanctuary representative of all the people to remember his responses, taxing himself not to slow things down, almost blushingly conscious that his as yet unnimble tongue hobbled the rhythm of this unvaried antiphon. But he had learned his lines well enough, resuscitated from the uncomprehended memorization of his institutional infancy.

. . . *Holy Ghost.*

"Amen." he said.

. . . *altar of God.*

"Even unto the God of my joy and gladness."

. . . *O deliver me from the deceitful and wicked man.*

"For thou art the God of my strength; why hast thou put me from thee: and why go I so heavily, while the enemy oppresseth me?"

. . . *unto thy holy hill, and to thy dwelling.*

"And that I may go unto the altar of God, even unto the God of my joy and gladness: and upon the harp will I give thanks unto thee, O God, my God."

Though making fewer errors week by week, Caleb was not yet quite easy with his role in the subsequent action of the revised Anamnesis, still relying upon mnemonic visualization of his choreographic chart, and when his mind went blank the habits of his formative years tended to obliterate the distinctions between the new "antithetical" and the old "thetical" Christianity that manifested themselves in certain rejections reconstructions or textual corrections of the ritual's component parts. But there was no change in Psalm 43. Father Duncannon had never presumed to fool around with quoted translations.

Why art thou so heavy, O my soul: and why art thou so disquieted within me?

"O put thy trust in God: for I will yet give him thanks, which is the help of my countenance, and my God." It was the word *disquieted* that used to fascinate him when he'd finally made out Father Pole's mumbling of the verse, still understanding almost nothing else of what he had been taught to hear and reply.

In casual conversation, with the same uncensorious drop of tone in which he spoke of the Pauline "confusion" that frustrated the so-called Social Gospel and other liberal doctrines driven by the noblest motives, Father Duncannon intimated that little ignorant altar boys were sentimental Tudor-Petrine decorations on the ultra end of the spectrum. But there had been few other boys at the Convent, fewer still any bit older, and none so responsible as Caleb. All the rest were girls (some as big and beautiful as twelve years old, awe-inspiringly privileged to Confirmation Class). For a year Father Pole had been about the only man that Caleb ever saw, whom he judged a tyrant to the Sisters but who was nevertheless especially kind to him—who baptised him, put him to work at the altar, and kept him at his side after Mass when he walked in the garden before breakfast to water flowers in the crannied walls with a long slender spout of burnished copper. Caleb now knew that Father Pole had founded the school under suffrance of the Bishop of Vinland, as a mission of the High Church from Unaford to Cape Gloucester; but in the first grade a priest's authority seemed no less than that of a Pope.

Later Caleb played Samuel in a pageant at St George's. Samuel the boy was called from his cot at night by a voice that at first he mistook for Eli the Priest's, Father Pole's. Even now at the altar, remembering both those strata of the past, Samuel he remained, and the *disquieting* voice of God was still expected to sound like the small voice that called Caleb's name in the convent dormitory when everyone was asleep, which at the time he'd taken as a vocation for the priesthood, when Betty with the golden hair should become a Sister and his wife.

Glory be to the Father and to the Son and to the Holy Ghost.

"As it was in the beginning is now and ever shall be: world without end. Amen." The prime hope beyond faith since August 1945.

But here again: *I will go unto the altar of God.*

"Even unto the God of my joy and gladness."

Our help is in the name of the Lord.

"Who hath made heaven and earth."

Wilt thou not turn again and quicken us, O God?

"That thy people may rejoice in thee."

O Lord, show thy mercy upon us.

"And grant us thy salvation."

. . . hear our prayer.

"And let our cry come unto thee."

. . . with you.

"And with thy spirit." That is, Father Duncannon's—and Father Pole's, and Eli's, and Melchizedek's. All this, along with the essentials that follow, Father Duncannon's Anamnesis respectfully retains from the common tradition.

As priest goes up to start main public business at altar, boy sidles a few feet to the left on his knees to gain Gospel corner of footpace.

. . . Through Christ our Lord.

"Amen."

. . . fellow citizens the kingdom of your Son.

"Amen."

Priest says Introit for Quinquagesima, and then *Kyrie, eleison.* (The pagan *Lord, have mercy upon us* advisedly kept in Greek, betokening one root-system of the Holy Classic Vine.)

"Kyrie eleison."

Kyrie eleison.

"Christe eleison." Christ have mercy. A small pleasure here, to take the lead by introducing Gregory the Great's variation of the prechristian form.

Christe eleison.

"Christe eleison."

Kyrie eleison. As always the priest has the last word, and tarries not for any further suggestion. The exordium is over that was devised to eke out itinerant presbyters' long procession from the front door to the altar of the basilica, before they were established by the state and could afford houses of assembly (designed for the regular service of large numbers) with sacristies for handy storage of their own vessels and wardrobes. But when the world's most important work may be done repeatedly and continually with small resonant masses of little more inertia than the altar boy's, no time should be spared for ceremony adrift between actions. Thus on an up-breath without pause is briskly begun *The Lord be with you,* as if an uninterrupted coda to the foregoing but actually the next step in ascent toward the Word that will prepare us to join the sacrifice.

"And with thy spirit" too.

Then in somewhat overbearing hustle, before Caleb and the ladies can well finish their four words of response to the versicle, his lagging voice is overborne by the quick command of *Let us pray.*

For a while, during his breathing spells, starting with the collects, he listens for little but his cues as leader of the chorus:

. . . *for thine only Son Jesus Christ's sake.*

"Amen." The most common Hebrew element, retained (with different pronunciations) by all branches of Christianity.

. . . *Through Jesus Christ thy Son Our Lord.*

"Amen" say all to the priest.

Then comes the boy's unrehearsed performance of the Logos. Rising with the small missal that is kept by his knee on the step, he genuflects at the center and crosses over to the Epistle side. Standing behind the priest, he reads aloud, attempting the rapid clarity of a professional. "The Lesson from the Epistle of St Paul in the first book of Corinthians . . . " Even in his own ears the best of his utterance is a more or less smooth monotone spoken faster than he can breathe yet trying to the patience of a priest for the time it takes. His own comprehension of the unrehearsed message he's mouthing is all but nil: it's success enough to get each word right, make the phrases cohere, finish the sentences where they end. "Though I speak with the tongues of men and of angels, and have not charity . . . "

Years of unripe exposure have made most of these jigsaw phrases as familiar as insignificant images that are fixed passim in childhood, but the hurry of sounding them leaves him none of the slow-witting leisure he would require to form a synthesis from the fragments. Yet even his mother from whom he's absorbed his prejudice against Paul can't criticize the point of today's passage, of which he knows he most needs to be reminded. Here he cannot chafe at doctrine or rationalize his insubordination. It's the article of panchristian solidarity that transcends all intellectual confusion and even the willful stupidity of those who cannot feel it. "And now abideth faith, hope, charity, these three . . ." Of the three it's only hope that he too easily summons, and only faith that he neglects; but he has no quarrel at all with the Christian love that's nominally common to the most selfish fundamentalist and the most superstitious papist. There isn't a rampant or esoteric heresy that doesn't at least mildly profess and faintly profit from the same by virtue of individual souls. And even anarchistical life-artists like Gepetto DaGetto sometimes commend western religion in their dim apprehension of love as its enzyme. And those who would truncate the organization of humanity at the level of their own hierarchical dominance, rejecting further integration of society as inessential to personal aggrandizement or salvation, often seem to believe in some such affinity with a few other members of their species as an almost supreme desideratum, for the family is often rated above the self even by Protesticans. "Here endeth the Lesson."

Thanks be to God, say priest and people for Caleb's contribution as he goes over to lay his little book on the credence table and stand facing the priest at the Epistle horn of the altar. How triumphantly would phalloanalytic Petto caper if he heard it called the horn! "The pizzle-horny priests!" he'd guffaw, imagining only the unicorn, not a handle of the Ark—never bethinking himself that a cow has horns too, and the moon; or that the drinking horn, the Deerslayer's powder horn, is also the vessel of perfumes and anointments; and a woman's cornucopia as well as the male's trumpet. The horn was Hannah's strength. Men sport poor evaginations of that hollow, Caleb has been told by his mother. Genesis and Paul got it backwards when they said that woman came of man. But Caleb reminds himself that in his conflict tree these are horns of only first-order dilemma.

Before the priest quite finishes intoning the short Tract following the Gradual, as he turns away from the text his acolyte snatches the propped-up Missal, stand and all, and makes a V-line down and up the single step, before and after genuflecting at the center, bearing it to the opposite horn of the Lord's table where the priest can effortlessly avail himself of the transported Gospel located by a ribbon elsewhere in the massive red volume. Caleb steps down to his rear and politely waits with straightened hands demurely joined. Again, *The Lord be with you.*

"And with thy spirit." likewise.

A portion of the Holy Gospel according to Saint Luke.

And then, down on the side, facing the priest but ignored by him who's looking diagonally at the open pages on the altar, the Mass-boy follows his leader in making the triple sign of the cross with his right thumb at forehead mouth and breast. "Glory be to Thee, O Lord." Caleb murmurs. Whereupon, bowing to the master, he returns on an L-line around the footpace to his position on the Epistle side, diagonally facing the diagonal back of the priest, this time having simply bowed to the cross as he passed the center while the priest was already embarked upon the Word. Again with palms together in front of his chest he stands alertly waiting to jump into his leadership of the people's subjoinder whenever this excerpt of Gospel may abruptly end.

Then Jesus took unto him the twelve, and said unto them, Behold, we go up to Jerusalem, and all things that are written by the prophets concerning the Son of Man shall be accomplished. . . .

For Caleb these words prompted a return to his old search for diction to replace the term *tragedy* so often abused in reference to the death of Christ (as well as to half a school of lesser calamities disasters and fatalities—real or imagined, caused or chanced—that seemed to escape the boundless seine of comedy, human and divine) because of its pathos. *Catastrophe* might be the least unsatisfactory, if it didn't have a certain mathematical denotation, and if only one could find some aptly limiting adjective to modify it; but even then, that word properly applied to but a single point or phase of a whole dromenon, much as *Offertory* and *Consecration* and *Communion* applied to respective phases of a whole sacrifice. From Father Duncannon he had learned to avoid the confusions and conflations of the latter pure term, *sacrifice* itself, thereby further inhibiting his communication with contemporaries. Christ's sacrifice was uniquely effective—but the tragedy of Prometheus Oedipus Hamlet and Cuchulain nevertheless fell into a far narrower category. *Tragedy* and *sacrifice* were perhaps not the most abused words in the language—and Caleb suffered under scores of catachreses much more vulgar—but they were the two most important words abused. The distinction between them epitomized his apology for a sacrilegious career.

. . . a certain blind man sat by the wayside begging. Imagine Captain Ozone begging. Some said there were pearls in the eye-sockets behind his black glasses. He was working on radar eyes to replace them, hoping at least to sense shapes darkly. He'd then bestow the pearls upon his favorites. At Joyous Gard (which in my presence he never called Chateau Noir) I wasn't the apple of his eye, but I understood what I read to him better than what I've said aloud to Eli in the temple, and he liked my weak undramatic monotone well enough to give me Ibi, worth the price of a thousand pearls, in whose utility he had such little faith. But to society at large the engineer was a man without the

charity of his means. When all is said and done, who were his real darlings? Doc was annoyed to find that he'd left no legacy for *Dromenology*, to say nothing of Dogtown College. He probably thinks Ozone played him for a fool, buying on a rich man's false credit the status of an unsubsumed peer. The rumor is that the Captain kept changing his will, until there was a deathbed conversion by the "Blind Priest" (who apparently doesn't mind being so called, whereas of course any priest must be a whole man), the Scholastic chaplain to the blind at Beacon Institute, which is now supposed to be endowed with Ozone's CRF stock and his punched-tape machines. If so, the rich man's theological confusion still ended in blind heterodoxy, because it's said he never changed his mind about seeing that the Alterian Neognostics got the Chateau: a crying shame that stinks of viciousness as well as gross insult to the earnestness of both the Blind Priest and Doctor Charlemagne, who—come to think of it—has lately been calling Dogtown a city of the blind, like Florence, factious and incautious in plain view of besiegers bearing gifts. The one consolation is that Noxin presumably will get no more annual slush funds from the sugarcone daddy . . .

And they which went before rebuked him, that he should hold his peace. . . . Captain Ozone was probably never in his life rebuked—except by his father, for pedagogical edification, and by the Gestapo—he who had sympathized with fascism!—for extreme reasons: least of all by the underlings of an impecunious itinerant rabbi! From the blueblood side of his family, nearly purple, descendants of old planters, the Lord of New Albion continued sole claimant to the rights of a landgrant extending due West between the parallels three leagues north of the Kerouac River's mouth and three leagues south of the Shawmut's, from Europe's Western Ocean all the way to the Great South Sea. It was as if he owned a Northwest Passage. Till death, blindness was his only failure.

And Jesus said unto him, Receive thy sight: thy faith hath saved thee. The object of faith is the promise, Milton says, meaning perhaps the infallible means for fulfillment; whereas that of hope is the thing promised, meaning the end result. With what faith was Captain Ozone possessed if not that of technological capitalism? But even in blindness he seemed too sure of his own wizardry to feel the need of hope—except for the extirpation of F D R socialism. Did he begin to see green pastures when he closed his eyes for the last time—before the last election?

And all the people, when they saw it, gave praise unto God.

"Praise be to thee, O Christ." says the automatic acolyte, with the ladies behind him, as the priest kisses the Gospel and steps to the center of the altar. Since here the homily is skipped (low Mass in a monastic church being no particular occasion for interpretation of the Word, the main purpose of an "invisible church" for Pauline reformers, who used to spend the best part of the Lord's Day in the inaction of listening, not primarily to the Gospel itself, as disconnected from its ritual source, but for three hours at a stretch to the fulminations and exhortations of a preacher expounding the Chauvinist contrary of what Father Duncannon calls today's narcissistic psychologism, not even jacked up by instruments of music), there's no time for the people to sit down or for Caleb to relax.

Indeed, "Go to sermon", rational counterpart of the superstitious "Go to Mass" for which Frenchmen had been notorious, was the sabbath motto for the real-estate priesthood of all believers, those most educated of all history's colonists who took possession of Vinland; but Caleb would have wished for both word and action if Father Duncannon did the talking, whose kerygma would have elucidated the myth with the ritual, and helped him ascertain the degree to which his own interpretation of Christianity was too primitive for the liberal revision. Despite this revered priest's exposition of orthodoxy which excited Caleb's whole mind and all his hope for humanity, he regarded himself as no worthier than a theoretical inquirer into the Classic Order of the Vine, still too provisional to call himself sincere about the personal means which the corporate instrument was supposed to apply to personal ends. But aside from questioning final causality, as between individual and society, wasn't it possible to further reduce the supernatural in Father Duncannon's essential faith without succumbing to symbolistical hermeneutics?

No wonder Caleb looked forward to the Chapter conclave. It would be his duty to record on magnetic tape all open debates (some of which Chris had been warning him of), as well as all the allocutions and other addresses not too delicate for an unprofessed private secretary. Those who build churches like courtrooms, or synagogues separate from the Temple, weren't the only ones in this city on a hill to cultivate freedom of conscience. There was a time when Classic Scholastics themselves allowed even for dialogue from dual pulpits and for contributions from the floor. It didn't require a modern Deformer's discovery of "Christian Realism" to excite Petrine appetites for economic and sociological criticism heretofore unevolved in the boundless body of Christian speculation.

Caleb hungered for the clarifications that he feared would have been untimely or unseemly to ask directly during his precious hours alone with Father Duncannon, of whose personal attention he as a mere friend of the Order hesitated to take too much advantage, and with whom in any case there were always more secular matters to talk about than they would ever have the leisure to dispatch, not to mention the interminable details of Laboratory housekeeping and maintenance. It seemed to him that there was as much to learn about his own received religion in a new light as there was about all the branches of literature and science which had generated the light. With Chris, by the same token, mutatis mutandis, various ecclesiastical questions would have been at least equally intempestive—or the answers too subjective for reliability.

For instance he longed to hear Father Duncannon's deep explanation of the mysterious Melchizedec. Why was this corporation and charterhouse named after that ur-priest? *Laboratory*, yes, as a place of work and prayer; and *Mesocosm* in reference to the crucial middle range of structure at the disposal of mankind—the world of molecular organization, actual and potential, between the entropy of quanta and the entropy of macrocosmos: the realm of society, love, and brains. But who was this king of prejewish Salem who appeared out of nowhere in *Genesis* as high priest of the Most High God bearing bread and wine for Abram, and later seen as the antetype of Christ, in whose name all priests to this day are ordained forever? Whose beginning and end remain unknown. Who as both king and priest was superior to Abram (father of half the world's religions). Was he a royal seer from some golden age of Indo-European oak trees—"Druid priest", as Guy Winthrop called him? A wandering Sumerian *lugal* displaced by Semites? Or on the contrary some royal Babylonian wiseman epiphanizing a prophecy handed down through Eber from prehistoric Arrata and Lake Van? To Caleb the name of Melchizedec was indeed as romantic as Nimrod's: as equivocal as Balaam's, unfixed, free of orthodox determinations, still available to legend—charged as yet with unreleased energy. Like the names of Semiramis, Prester John, the Wandering Jew, King Alfred, or Morgan le Fay.

In earliest Christian days the sermon (culmination of the synagogical Synaxis, as it has remained the culmination of Pauline "worship" since the Deformation) would have sent off the catechumens to consider what they might be getting into, leaving the baptized to begin the Mass of the Faithful with a precis of the one true myth itself. Now, marking transition from the Liturgy of the Word to the Eucharist proper, the stately bellwether stands before the cross and, with a composing flourish of the wrists, abducting elevating and rejoining his outspread hands, starts off the tough and finely hammered

Nicene Creed, insisting that his tiny herd chime in after the first line to disavow any lingering trace of the Arian heresy that once dominated the church, not to mention all the gnosticisms that still seduce sophisticated Christians.

We believe in one God—
His mother, though now a believer, by her own account had remained silent at the age of fourteen during the recitation of these few words in the chorus of her girls' Confirmation Class at the altar rail, and the bishop hadn't noticed. What does it mean, to "believe *in*"? Caleb asked himself for the *in*th time. Under the influence of Father Duncannon's ideas, and Doctor Charlemagne's too—though neither would have approved his fusion of them—he believed *that* the purpose of Christianity was to save mankind by improving the world, and that at present the prerequisite for improvement of the world was an appreciation of the Gospel myth that would rehabilitate everywhere the one liturgy that can perpetuate for such purpose the world's only successful sacrifice, source of that myth. Universal understanding of Christianity's special dromenology could keep the news as good as ever by clarifying the open system of four dimensions that incorporated both the essential myth and its sacramental ritual. But if faith was required to believe *in* the Gospel, he was obliged to qualify himself as no believer-in.

"*—the Father almighty, maker of heaven and earth. . . . And in one Lord Jesus Christ . . . Begotten, not made, being of one substance with the Father. . . .*" History's most tested ontological convention settled this orthodoxy even before Julian the Apostate (regarding himself as Alexander the Great the Second) tried to dissipate the whole shadow-empire, heresies and all. Here, at "*. . . came down from heaven*", priest acolyte and people genuflect in unison, lower their voices likewise, and give pause to speech, as if performing their single step of dance in the midst of a hymn. "*. . . and was incarnate by the Holy Ghost of the Virgin Mary: and was made man.*" Of all the scandals to inductive reason for one whose Christianity was of little faith but who had no doubt of female priority in sexual evolution, the virgin birth (and even an immaculate conception of the B V M herself) was least miraculous and easiest to believe. To this layman a bit of atavistic biochemistry was not inconceivable if it brought about the unique excitement of Christmas. To Caleb the well-defined event of the Annunciation was scientifically interesting, and therefore less of a scandal than was the other horn of the theological dilemma to spiritual souls.

For the stumbling block to gnostics and most idealists was the crassness of incarnation. Humanity in Trinity still boggled the minds not only of Docetists but also of Socinians Nestorians Monophysites and Monothetelists in modern dress. That the thoroughly divine Son of Man really existed as a manchild who squalled and whimpered like one of their own was the doctrine most difficult of all for theists to believe.

Arius tried to solve the problem of Incarnation by introducing an iota into the crucial Greek substantive, declaring Jesus to be merely of *like* but lesser substance with God. It was a world-historical shock to all branches of idealism when Nicaea insisted that this manhood was of the same substance—an edge of the same equilateral triangle—as the ineffable idea than which nothing more perfect could be conceived. History's greatest objective mystery—the ontological crux at the year Zero—was reduced to its minimum articulation in the only slightly less mysterious process of that amazing parliament (illustrating the epistemological principle of least common incredibility), simply by expunging the imaginary number *i* that would have doomed Christianity like a sunflower. Caleb marveled that once the distinction had been hammered out between *person* and *substance*, the Athanasians could simply remove the Arian iota. *Homoiousian* ("of *like* substance") was syncopated to *homoousian* ("of the *same* substance"). The Trinity was preserved by differentiating the Son from the Father and from the Holy Ghost in terms of his *hypostasis*. By translating the Greek synonyms *ousia* and *hypostasis* into the complementary Latin words *substantia* and *persona*, Father Duncannon had explained, the Council's stroke of collective metaphysics illustrated no more metaphorically than models in chemistry the function of language in pinning down the truth.

Arius died in a privy, after getting a bellyache from the disputation, according to Montaigne; and his Antipope Leo also died at stool. (Dante mentions the analogous death of an heretical Pope Anastasius.) St Hilary, on the other hand, the great Classic enemy of Arius, successfully prayed for the death of his own beautiful daughter before she should lose her virginity in lawful marriage to one of her many suitors; whereupon her mother's wish to be united with God in a less intact beatitude was also granted.

Such were the outmoded follies of Christianity to which Gepetto DaGetto unwittingly alluded in bursts of threadbare hostility, the maker of what Doc called "fearless anti-icons", without getting the names straight, when Caleb had probed for his apprehension of the ancestral idols he liked to kick in the face. "But I don't need organized religion to feel the spiritual symbols of Dogtown!" Petto crowingly laughed, bouncing six inches into the air after a spiraling stomp of both feet, again drawing a contrast between his robustly primitive sense of sensation and Doc's overcultivated culture. But he was instantly sobered, and revealed his complaint to Caleb, when his own words fetched up the memory that the leader had also dubbed him Homo Faber.

Mistaking Petto's distress for resentment of a Latin epithet connoting mere technology, or else sounding like faker or fibber, Caleb had offered the bold opinion that Doc would have done better to call his friend Homo Poeticus, inasmuch as the Greek root suggested both imagination of making and doing of action, but was taken aback by the welder's violent rejection of his flattery. "Hell no! Not a homo! Don't say that! I'm a working man! I'm one of the people. Their woman know!"

But the virile artificer was proud to accept most of Doc's labels as recognition of his living art. Thus he boasted of such appellative obiter dicta as "the smith of Dogtown's soul". It was under this curious inspiration that he contemplated doing the Pope as Monkey of God, and had asked Caleb if he knew anything about Scholastic beliefs that might give him a detail to start with.

But the vibrant sculptor was fondest of being hailed as a blithe Ariel chained by his passions to the gross art of an anvil. His god was not the Davy Lawrence Christ (whom he nonetheless praised for hyperhuman carnality) but a spirit too ethereal to mind the world. He knew of the Gnostics, and he liked the idea that the world had to be brought into existence by a begotten demiurge who was also privileged to harrow hell. If he'd been born in a more religious era he probably would have fallen for any heresy that claimed some combination of the Dionysian Eleusinian Manichaean and Cathar, humanistic or ideal, provided that it hinted at angels of God succumbing to the daughters of men on the underside of pure being.

Caleb doesn't pay attention to the rest of the Creed he's saying because he picked it up by rote too young. ". . . Amen."

The Lord be with you.

"And with thy spirit" too.

In the presence of the whole Church, let us confess our sins to almighty God. It has been Father's Duncannon's moral and intellectual pleasure to dispense with Archbishop Cranmer's "improperly emotive, rhetorical, and legalistic" version of the General Confession, especially the reference to provoking God's prechristian "wrath and indignation" by merely personal misdoings. In C O V 's new Anamnesis the position and composition of the confession and absolution are radical revisions of the Tudor Eucharist, according to Father Duncannon's reasoned interpretation of ancient tradition and Christian logic.

Contrary to the Pauline bias of the official Prayer Book, the purpose of this penitence and mutual absolution, here advisedly integrated into the liturgy of the Offertory, is to invoke the relative and contingent cure of imperfection in individual modulations of the corporate oblation, which is collectively produced in the four-dimensional environment created by society. The following two confessions, unlike Cranmer's, are not intended to prepare individual souls for pious reception of the gifts that are to be returned by God in the functionally different liturgy of Communion, which comes only after the forthcoming Consecration; and they distinctly refuse to except the priest's spiritual treatment from the commonalty's. Since "there are no strictly private sins", the appropriate general confession retroactively purifies or rectifies the personal freewills that have corporately produced (through purchase, by exchange of work) the bread and wine about to be offered, in order to make the oblation as worthy of sacrifice as humanly possible in the actual society brought to pass through an historical system perverted by violence, mental confusion, injustice, hatred, willful stupidity, malice, selfishness, and all their disordering superorganic effects that frustrate the counterentropic possibilities of Christ's church. This rite furthermore demonstrates the democratic principle of the priesthood of all believers by ensuring that the priest be absolved by the people before he presumes to absolve his equals.

First therefore the priest kneeling before his standing people confesses the shortcomings and defects introduced into history by his fault since last participating in the offertory. *I confess to God almighty, to the ever-blessed Virgin Mary, to blessed Michael the Archangel, to the whole Company of Heaven, to all the Church, and especially to you my brothers here present, that I have sinned exceedingly in thought, word, and deed, by my fault, by my own fault, by my own most grievous fault* [striking himself on the breast three times]. . . . "This generic public confession can be very useful as an omnibus bill for sinners like myself." said Chris with a gallant laugh, as he cruised home easterly on the Felly after a good day of trading, dropping one hand from the wheel and reclining half his back against the driver's door so that he could keep an eye on the road while lounging in the corner and directly addressing Caleb. He no doubt finds a way to make it cover the sin of not mentioning all his sins in auricular confession, Caleb thinks. Maybe he confesses things to me that he doesn't mention to any priest, but it's likely enough that he tells us all enough to present a plausible personality.

On another occasion, belting down a couple of drinks at a Chinese road house hardly after they'd put the Bot city limits behind them, Chris predicted with a stiff upper lip that he'd end up in the Seventh

Circle if Dante was any prophet. "But he was no Church Father or Confessor, you know, let alone a martyr. His personal opinion doesn't carry any more weight than Milton's—or mine, for that matter—as to what sins are more or most irredeemable."

Chris can be as Arminian as a Divine Individualist when it suits his casuistry. *Have charity and do as thou wilt* might as well be blazoned on his shield. He remembers the exculpatory clauses from all the theology and canon law he's forgotten or never learned. In certain conversations he can sound quite clever. "No need to confess what is not a sin," says he with a wry laugh, calling himself the Order's Cephasite. He pleads that even in the Scholastic church for such matters conscience is the ultimate authority. I'd like to hear him deliver a homily on the modern probabilism he wrote his thesis about. Like most charming talkers, he's a lousy writer, and he knows it; but he's proud of that one paper. It seems that morals is the only academic subject besides psychology he ever took to heart. He tries to extend the principle that denial of absolution bears the burden of proof beyond all reasonable doubt to cover the prior selection by conscience of topics for confession. If there's any reason at all not to nominate a sin to one's confessor, then one need not do so, even if there are more and greater reasons for scheduling it. But in case there's any sinful flaw in the rationalization, it will be tacitly assimilated in the public penitence and mutual forgiveness of the liturgy!

Still, Father Lucey is the only member of the Classic Order of the Vine who's ever been at once qualified and willing enough to take vows as a religious priest and live under Father Duncannon's personal authority.

. . . *he may forgive my sins, and so perfect these offerings, making them worthy of his holy sacrifice. Lord, I am not worthy that thou shouldest come under my roof, but speak the word only and I shall be healed.*

"Almighty God have mercy upon thee, forgive thee thy sins . . . " The celebrant is thus contingently absolved by Caleb and the ladies speaking in their own royal priesthood as representatives of the whole church. Whatever Chris may do in mufti, in or out of domino, in Botolph or New Uruk, his works by these words (when he celebrates the Anamnesis) join the supplication for community of atonement.

Amen, this time says the priest.

Who now rises, as acolyte and people kneel in turn. "We confess to God almighty . . . and to thee, Father . . . " They too strike their breasts three times, saying what the priest has said, only changing the first person from singular to plural and the second person from plural to singular. And the shy altar boy must admit that corporate confession isn't so bad. These pronouns are not too humiliating, and it's obvious that our unnecessary contributions to the general imperfection should be repented and remitted to whatever possible degree. Words like these do not seem to bind one's future freedom for experience. They don't renounce the Dionysia. ". . . that we have wounded the body of the Son of God on earth, and that these his offerings of bread and wine are marred though our neglect and our wrongdoings."

Yet foremost among the assumptions of the church that Caleb remains too uneasy to discuss even theoretically with Father Duncannon is the sacrament of penance as practiced in personal particular and peculiar confession of the actual variables: an entirely secret act which nevertheless would be unbearably degrading to his stiffnecked dignity, like consulting a psychoanalyst. Deference to another's prehension of his psyche, as if his system were subsumed, would violate a gentleman's hypostatic pride. Caleb takes no pride in the fact that this stumbling block to classic orthodoxy is more deeply embedded in the path he halfheartedly explores than the intellectual barrier to faith, but he's too proud to be candid about his shame in taking advantage of the Vine's ideas.

Once or twice with Chris, before he began to understand that neither of the Fathers was much loathe to have a loose fish with whom idle or fallible thoughts could be trusted, he did attempt an explanation of his attitude toward the unspoken question of why he shouldn't be expected to try himself as a Postulant Secular, hoping that since it was not a canonically secret confession his halting declaration would be delicately and sympathetically transmitted to Father Duncannon. It was a problem that nobody seemed to expect on the table as he grew enthusiastic about the Order and its membership, which represented both the solidarity and the responsibility he excused himself from.

"Why isn't the sacrament of Mass enough?" he asked the latitudinarian.

"Perhaps it is, for you. Your calling is to dedicate yourself to work that the rest of us haven't the gift for—besides what you're doing for the Order as our most useful friend. It's perhaps precisely because you're not a member that you can be so useful. We don't want a business manager who can't see through us. And Father Duncannon needs an educated young companion to comfort his lonely old age. Obviously I'm no intellectual. He should have relief from my simpleminded psychology. And those of our old members who can converse with him on his own level are seldom at hand. There are times when it's good for him to forget the problems of an abbot. Please not to worry about your artistic conflicts as far as we are concerned!"

"But I've got a stiff neck."

"If the foreskin of your heart is uncircumcised, let you remain a Gentile. Whatever you consider your cross is the cross you should cheerfully bear. But I must say that a man of your originality shows remarkable modesty and generosity in devoting so much precious time to an Order that's not your vocation. It's as if you do your own work with one hand tied behind your back."

And so, as usual, the selfsufficient young buck was disarmed of his feeble religious honesty. He never got around to mooting with either of his employers the other sacraments he doubted or self-servingly construed.

"Therefore we beg the ever-blessed Virgin Mary, blessed Michael the Archangel, the whole Company of Heaven, all the Church, and thee, Father, to pray for us to the Lord our God: that through the atoning action of his Son, he may forgive our sins, and so perfect these offerings, making them worthy of his Holy Sacrifice . . . but speak the word only and we shall be healed."

Almighty God have mercy upon you, forgive you your sins, and bring you to everlasting life.

"Amen."

The almighty and merciful Lord grant unto you pardon, absolution [†] *and remission of your sins.*

"Amen." [By which, yet again, with the Hebrew word used by BCE Jews and Jesus himself to say "Would that it might be so.", AD Christians mean "So it is." Neither Greek nor Latin nor English can express it all at once: "Fixed and settled but not yet already."]

Blessed art Thou, O Lord; teach me Thy justifications: with my lips I have pronounced all the judgments of Thy mouth.

Because the ensuing action of the Offertory—neglected by Scholastics, suppressed by Tudors, scorned by thoroughgoing Paulines—was being restored to the rite after eighteen or nineteen centuries only by the praxis of tiny scattered congregations, much smaller than aggregations of molecules visible to the magnifying glasses of almost all searching Christians, the revision seemed insignificant even to most of the fraternal professionals who axiomatically defended the Book of Common Prayer against its insolence. Almost every adherent of the Order came to understand that the Mass they called the Anamnesis was in effect unwillingly clandestine, and that to any layman stumbling upon it the variances at issue seemed either pedantically esoteric or merely aesthetic. Unless you stopped to study these words and rubrics, which reshaped the very logic of the old but far from primeval ceremonies of the ritual, you'd never suspect that the whole of Christianity was thus remounted in its social foundation.

Again and again Caleb marveled at his accidental privilege.

Yet realism often sounded a lot like the old subversive idealism, and when his thoughts wandered, or when his back wearied from kneeling upright without support during the longer stretches of inactivity later on, comfortable rhythms and echoes of Cranmer's brilliantly compromising language sometimes rose from the devious infancy of the Tudor Church through the neural channels of his earliest training to carry him momentarily off course in his reformed behavior at the altar; his new dromenological habits were not yet perfectly proved against the drift back toward those that were never quite forgotten. But this time he made no mistakes in the interesting nexus of innovative action that now followed as the laity's visible participation in the Offertory. This part of his service (as one of the people) was more than a mere convenience for the priest or a footman's embellishment of the amenities:

He steps to the center, his back for once to the cross, and takes the silver ciborium of wafers from the lady who has volunteered to bring it up from the back of the chapel, bowing to her as she bows to him. (Martin Luther once more turns over in his grave who cried out that any Offertory at all "stank of oblation", and Cranmer shudders angrily.) Then like a quarterback he turns about to find the priest standing behind him with the paten to receive the people's offerings—in this instance just a pitiable few featheryweight discs from the granaries of the economic system. The Anamnesis has no place for collecting tithes of money in an alms basin to finance missionary and overhead accounts: this is an oblation to be perfected by grace and returned to the givers for consumption at the altar.

Priest and acolyte also bow to each other. Then the one swings round in turn to do his work at the table and ask the blessings while the other moves like a butler up Stage Left toward the sideboard; and while still on his way to the credence table Caleb and the people in unison with the priest (or rather in a degree or two of lag behind his lead) intone the basic notes of prose:

"*Receive, O Holy Father, almighty and everlasting God, this bread of our lives, now made spotless by thy Son's atoning power, and which we offer unto thee, our living and true God; and may this offering here be lifted up to thine eternal kingdom within the resurrection and ascension of the same thy Son, Jesus Christ our Lord. Amen.*" Caleb is compelled to agree that it takes something less natural than the incarnation and death of a divinity to make the sacrificial method work, and for the time being his negative capability is robust enough to let the Gospel ride.

For him right now there's a welcome flurry of stage business ancillary to preparation of the wine—a more spiritual product of human industry than daily bread. His greater part in the ceremonial of offering in this kind arises however not from any unequal veneration of blood and flesh but simply from the priest's need for more help in getting the cup ready and setting the Lord's table. At the little buffet against the wall Caleb removes and lays aside the stoppers of the two cruets, takes up the wine in his right hand with the lip toward himself, the water cruet by its handle in his left, and steps to the Epistle horn of the altar, where he is met by the priest with his chalice. Boy having kissed wine cruet, priest makes small blessing with his fingers and takes it by handle to pour supply into holy drinking horn. Meanwhile boy transfers water cruet held by handle in left hand to obverse clasp of neck by right, thus freeing left to accept by neck on lip side the wine cruet returned by priest; who now blesses water, which boy kisses, having meanwhile also kissed wine a second time. Priest takes this second cruet by handle, mixes a little water into the chalice, returns it to solemn boy for final kiss. Who takes the cruets back to their stand, replacing the stopper of the wine. Draping a narrowly folded linen napkin over his left wrist like a mock-waiter's, he picks up the lavabo with that hand and the water cruet this time by its handle with his right, and goes again to wait for the priest.

This intricate pas de deux with four hands is the high point of Caleb's competence. Before the end of it he's repeating with all the others [priest in offertorial stance before the cross]: *"We offer unto thee, O Lord, this wine of our lives, humbly beseeching thy mercy: that thou make this offering to have its portion in the eternal humanity of thine Incarnate Son at thy right hand in glory. Amen."*

After some further small business of his own, while the expectant dog stands alert with his hands full, the priest making appropriate signs of invocation and blessing recites in a lowered voice his Epiclesis of the Holy Ghost—the Spirit of triune God required not, as the Byzantines have it, for the ensuing transubstantiation (which is really the creative act of the Second Person, Christ himself), but for the engracement of the community here bringing oblation—just as the Apostles, against all odds of despair and dissension, were inspired at Pentecost by the counterentropic descent of that Third Person to start the church in the first place. *Send down, almighty God, thy Holy and enabling Spirit, to bless both us thy people and our lives within this sacrifice.*

And as by his power thou didst open the way for the creation of the world, for the Incarnation of the Word . . . [in view of the fact, as my mother Mary would put it who hasn't any notion of the liturgical connection, that in order to improve the world women need more collaboration than men can provide] . . . *that this thy Son, our Saviour, may move our present gifts and creatures of bread and wine into the glory of his ascended Body and Blood. Who liveth and reigneth with thee, in the unity of the same Holy Spirit, God world without end.*

"Amen." Nothing works for long without a holy spirit, even when only two or three are gathered together for a local purpose.

Swayed by his own frailties, encouraged by his tendentious reading of Yeats, Caleb generally preferred things said to things sung, being of opinion for instance that in opera and its congeners word as well as action is arrested suspended soused subjugated stupefied distorted disintegrated or bent out of shape; and he secretly dissented from Father Duncannon's variorum rubrics (a lover of opera withal) to the effect that a Solemn Mass was the sung norm of ceremony even for this revivified Anamnesis. Caleb thought it behooved high church to keep Mass low—as by rights a workaday practice of dynamic information and communication—unless congregations are too large to hear the spoken word. (An optional Scholastic version of the quotidian celebration, recovered after many centuries of purely passive observation on the laity's part, was distinguished from the traditional show by the term "Dialogue" Mass—which of course described all Tudor versions.) Yet at this point in the Offertory the senses of this acolyte remembered a delight in special ceremonies which he'd been too young to have explained to him, and he found himself sniffing for sweet-smelling puffs that the hierophant might now have been censing the oblations with—by the light of a dozen candles!

Twenty years ago at festal afternoon Benedictions—he knew not how often or seldom—Caleb had carried the little brass incense boat with finely hinged lid. In a cloud of holy smoke he proffered the aromatic fuel as reverently as if it was the granulated Host. Dipping its tiny brass spoon Father Pole would once or twice recharge the great brass censer, ornately tiered, hot as a samovar, which was too tall and heavy for a small boy to swing and not easily opened for fueling by its hoist of complicated chains. Some grown-up thurifer must have been there to serve as the interchanger of that burden. Standing at their skirts the altar boy had almost swooned with pleasure at the burnt offering per fumum. It dimmed the glorious candlelight of the convent chapel's sanctuary as with sweet savory mists from a burning bush. In the Temple frankincense must have overcome the stench of slaughter like spices countervailing the spoilage of unrefrigerated foods.

(But now surely it was one of Father Duncannon's private sorrows—and perhaps Yahweh's too—that he couldn't on any day of the year celebrate or concelebrate his vision of Christ's ecclesiastical intention with the solemn support of deacons subdeacons and crucifer, as well as thurifer and boat-boy, and other specialized acolytes deployed in ranks like sub-waiters at the Royalist Club, all directed by a Master of Ceremonies, accompanied by choir, perhaps in a cathedral.)

Here and now however it's only a matter of assisting the priest as he whispers Psalm 26 to himself: *I will wash my hands in innocency, O Lord: and so will I go to thine altar.* . . . Caleb pours water over the curled thumbs and forefingers into the bowl—a preprandial cleansing that doesn't call for the kissing of anything; following which the lordly master rumples the daintily pressed strip of linen towel with ostentatious carelessness and tosses it down again upon his servant's sleeve, turning back to his important work. Caleb puts aside the lavings and returns to stand at his place down to the right of center (Stage Left).

Meanwhile priest acolyte and civilians together say the final offertory prayer: "*O God, who didst wonderfully create, and yet more wonderfully renew the dignity of human nature: grant that in and through this sacrifice we may be made partakers of his divinity who emptied himself to share our humanity, Jesus Christ thy Son our Lord: Who liveth and reigneth with thee in the unity of the Holy Spirit, God: world without end. Amen.*"

Pray brethren—the priest alone continues, turning to the people, in one motion extending and joining his hands as they kneel—*that this our sacrifice may be acceptable to God the Father almighty.*

And they respond: "The Lord receive our sacrifice at thy hands, to the praise and glory of his name, and both to our benefit and to that of all his holy Church."

Amen, says the priest to them, now again with his turtleback turned, and silently reads from the missal his Secret Prayers for Quinquagesima, which Caleb in the lovely quietness never tries to guess at.

A woman's secret thoughts were not written anywhere, but Gepetto DaGetto's were patent. Inasmuch as it seemed that for all the celibate or even merely chaste makers of Christian dogma, virginal or rehabilitated, starting with Paul, everything thought or done to please homunculus erectus for his own sake (to say nothing of his cunicular mate) was more infamous than any of the cruelties frauds or injustices that infected society, the church had a bad name among those not disposed so to identify the origin of sin if there was such a thing. On the other hand, Caleb asked himself, what health is there in a proletarian of middle age boasting like a sophomore of his scorn for the narrows of a marriage bed? "She leads her life and I lead mine!" Petto had proclaimed in his only allusion to the wife living half a mile from his shop, who still boarded him, along with the resident children.

You didn't have to be a prig not to occupy your speech with the obvious concerns of il cazzo, or not to adumbrate your savoir faire by verbal pinches on the ass of every woman courteous enough to give an artist the benefit of impersonal respect. If Benvenuto's virility is so successful, why must he insist upon recognition of his purposely exacerbated and perpetually renewed mania? There was a big enough bed in the room above his studio. "I'm oversexed!" he smugly groaned to crescendo, the same harpoon of humor cast over and over again, like a satyr for whom no bevy of men's daughters could be wild enough to tame his spirit, under the impression that he was psychosomatically distinguished from other men—as if there weren't about thirteen thousand other homunculi in Dogtown alone—some just getting started, others retired, but none of them inert.

"Fuck Mrs Grundy!" Petto added, surprising Caleb with that Giorgio name for bourgeois oppression that he'd thought was forgotten by nearly everybody except his mother. This Tuscan must have read something historical. Or else he'd been tutored by one of his liberated patrons on her Dogtown fling.

But Petto worked hard for his family, and no hope or achievement in the blended realm of art and sex ever obliterated his inherited conscience of responsibility as an armslength pater familias, or his innocence as a welder doing what he hated to do with fabrications he didn't understand. Yet never in triumph or failure was commercial impurity allowed to taint the conscience and innocence of his plastic imagination, which was misguided only in its apologia pro vita sua.

Caleb credited Bice with having discerned from the first, in the bar at the Van, while her poetic rig-driver was talking to Shelly, the deeply wick'd flame at the core of Petto's flares. But at twice her age he seemed to Caleb categorically more ingenuous than she who was so honorable about the secrecy natural to a feline creature. Was it safe to believe that on her one brief visit to Dogtown she had not been enticed as far as his third floor—before that first glimpse of Ibi in the cemetery, before the attraction of Caleb himself, before her deal with the captain of the *Avalon Reefer?* Had it been otherwise, Petto would have boasted the particular adultery.

As to the sculpture, which the artist called his "Ironry", it revealed his imagination through passionately forged grotesquerie and welded humor, with dwarf skeletons and dismembered body armor on Caleb's own scale. At the first sight of it an indefinite artistic excitement was aroused in him like the tumescence of a swan's folded wings that are stirred without a scintilla of resentment by the behavior of a rival. These definite figures of inchoate ambiguity suddenly erased his skepticism of Doctor Charlemagne's poetical theory that Dogtown strove unconsciously for a proper theater.

But Caleb's sense of erotic competition (more personal than a swan's) was not long displaced by artistic emotion. As soon as an opening presented itself, while he was gazing at an iron frame in the *Nude Teiresias* series by which Petto's formal conception of female experience amazingly disabused his expectation of mere realistic fantasy, he tossed the bait as offhand as a dropped handkerchief. "Did you know the reporter who wrote you up in the *Nous?*" he asked, stooping to examine a weld at the stem. "It was the first time I ever noticed that by-line."

There was an alarming pause, which it seemed to Caleb might have signified anger or bewilderment or disappointment at his blatant disingenuity. At length he was compelled to look up at the artist. But the silent interval proved to have been characteristically rhetorical. It was broken by the quiet hiss of suppressed energy indicative of a search for the best channel of explosion. "A stranger, just passing through town! I guess she didn't know my Premature Antifascist reputation. I thought I was still on the blacklist. It was amazing they finally got around to printing it."

Then staring in all directions, whirling full circle with clasped hands in his hammer-throwing crouch, as his fierce frown burst into a happy smile, the actor's mounting pressure found dramatic outlet. "Freelance writer! A Georgio too! Yeah, what a beauty!" His gesture suggested with surprising austerity a girl's head torso and center, not by a vulgar symmetry of curves but by delicately separated ideographic strokes quickly ending in a toss of the hands. "What a sweetheart!" He kissed his pursed fingertips. "Bice Picory! Bice is for Beatrice. I'm half Florentine: she's my Beatrice! Only she's the poet and I'm her ideal!"

Rose once more the long-drawn undignified cackle that endeared him to Caleb. "Said she was just a little Zingara and wanted me to be her tinker. I thought she said *thinker!*" Rotating with another screech of laughter at his own difficulty in pronouncing the distinction, Petto made Ibi's ears twitch who had long since finished his exploration of the room and was lying alert in tolerant judgment of the stranger's friendly intentions.

The lover of women wandered away for a moment, eyes focussed on the past, touching tools on his bench, grasping bars of iron, smoothing surfaces of stone. "Man oh man, the smartest girl I ever saw! She got my story out of these speechless lumps of iron and stone. —Hey: next time she's going to stay with me! (That's a long way off though.) I told her she didn't have to worry: I had a vasectomy!" Renewed peal of high-pitched glee and bent-over slapping of his knee. "Who could resist a mouth like that?"

Caleb found himself at a loss for words of sympathy that might have encouraged further revelation. After two or three swallows high in his throat, he faintly asked "Would she make a good model?"

Petto instantly became stern and masterly, scolding the young man, to whom he'd previously been so deferential, for the kind of vulgarity with which a maestro is sadly disappointed. At one stroke Caleb was demoted from peer to apprentice. The elder forgot his almost awestruck gratitude for the sweet savor of Caleb's warm appreciations, to which he had delightedly responded with praise for the visitor's extraordinary perception, especially as expanded into a rare admiration for the whole range of his livelihood—the irony of his situation, the value of his heritage, the romance of his business, the vigorous imagination of his armatures, the realism of his created ideals. Caleb knew nothing about the kind of electric welding Petto practiced in his outside trade; but whose praise was of greater worth than an educated young scholar's (as it appeared) who had warmed to the cold iron-smithy in the downstairs shop, having had some experience with the use of a forge, and actually knew the horn of an anvil from a tuyere? (When Caleb had rashly offered his services as a helper in hand-wrought ironwork, carried away by the idea of an East Harbor Etna, he was told that there wasn't enough of it to pay for the coal. The shop had gradually been absorbed by the studio, and the smith had to rely on the portable rig for all his income, mostly in the form of bad debts.) Yet Petto's moral fibre was softened by no man's praise.

Caleb had simply said the first thing that came into the poverty-stricken smalltalk region of his gray matter. He was now reproved, as if angrily, for a callow fantasy about the nature of a serious sculptor's art. "Naa, naa!" Petto turned all around in disgust, doubling up in scornful pain. "For crying out loud, I don't do figures from life! Can't you see? I don't copy anything, not even Beatrice! I express what's inside *me* —not what I can see or fuck! You don't understand what it's like to be creative first last and always! Didn't I tell you—I'm *her* idol—she's not mine!"

But he suddenly relented: his own words had struck a new connection to the motor nerves of exultation. "Yes, that's it: she's the *ideal,* I'm the *idol!* Let her write poetry about *me.* It's about time woman started worshipping men . . . " Obviously there had been no personal disgust in his attack upon Caleb, whose gaucherie was immediately forgiven or forgotten. "Besides, models are always getting pregnant."

Caleb tried again to make light of his interest in the subject. "If you're fixed, all you've got to do is keep away the Holy Ghost."

Petto stared in alarm. "Don't get me wrong—there's nothing wrong with me! No one would know the difference. I'm not even circumcised. In fact I'm a better stud than ever, being more de-sired!" He was so delighted at having found that way of putting it that he forthwith lost interest in the defense of his honor.

With wooden lips and stiffened rima vocalis it was impossible for Caleb to correct misapprehensions or call attention to his own sense of humor. As he was making motions to take his leave disquieted, he noticed a small shape of heavy copper wire fastened by solder, incongruously pliable in a studio full of rigid ferrous metals, brittle surfaces of granite, and jagged splints of driftwood. Already aware of the representational significance Petto attached to the titles of his nonrepresentational objets d'art, he asked with admiration what it was called.

He had clearly restored himself to Petto's good graces. *"Study Without Flesh.* Most people don't even notice it. It's so small and skinny I couldn't even get one *S* onto it. I guess I should use a tag." He loved "Simplicissimus" as his nom de main—often simplified to *S-s* or simply *s,* which he called The Snake, the savior of woman: his caducean sign of a mental health and guilelessness somewhat inconsonant with his equally sincere claim to be "the Hermes of good news who teaches knowledge of good and evil!"

Continuing now in a powerful low voice he slowly emphasized certain words with punctuating motions of one forefinger: "It came to me when the old Pope died. It was a good sign that they didn't try to cover up his death. But I was hoping the church would finally abolish Popes and turn to spiritual democracy. But then they went and picked another one. Jesus Christ, what a blow! My religion has more to offer, but I was ready to give them my respect, and this piece was my suggestion for their great opportunity: showing them what their Holy Ghost should be. The only contributions I can make to anything are sex and sculptor." As Petto did not distinguish *women* from *woman,* neither did he sound a difference between *sculpture* and *sculptor.* "And I can't very well give them my sex, can I?" he added, again stamping his feet with a wail of selfcongratulating conceit.

"If I were a collector, this is the one I'd pick first." said Caleb sincerely.

"No kidding?" Petto took the piece from where Caleb had set it down and handed it to him. "Take it. If you like it you should have it."

"But I can't buy it. That's worth a lot of money."

"Why can't I give it to you? I got the copper free, and it didn't take long to make. I can do another one any time. Who cares about money, when it's for a friend? I've got money to live on. As long as I can convert copper into art I don't need to convert the art into coppers! All an artist wants is *recognition!"*

"But who am I to give you that?" All Caleb's unvoiced judgments of Petto the man were put to shame by this generosity, which seemed truly the outward and visible sign of charity. There was nothing mean or ambitious about this rival. Even his lechery wasn't jealous. "But I'll label it for posterity and keep it in my study. What did you say the name of it was again?"

"I don't care what you call it. It means whatever you want it to mean."

Though he knew of no precedent for converting a coil of copper directly into bread, Caleb decided that after a decent interval he'd ask Petto's permission to give his sculpture to the Laboratory in which it really belonged.

. . . *Throughout all ages, world without end.* The priest finished his secret prayer aloud.

"Amen."

11
EMBER WEDNESDAY
CONSECRATION

he Lord be with you.
"And with thy spirit."
Lift up your hearts.
"We lift them up unto the Lord." Caleb began to inquire why indeed his heart was so high. In part because it was the start of a mild day already gathering heat from a new cloudless sun in the marches between ice and water. By the time he finished breakfast with the Fathers and walked upstairs to the office, rivulets would be running downhill beneath the snow, undermining the shelves of ice that still bordered the streets, and the crusted molecules of unmarred snowfields would be sparkling with the cheerful effort to collapse in the general dissolution of crystalline winter.
Let us give thanks unto the Lord our God.
"It is meet and right so to do." Partly also in a wave of admiration for the subtle kalendar of the church that was gradually emerging

from his confusion of movable and immovable, feast and feria, proper and ordinary. Considering the relativity of all motion, it was only geometric predilection for solar fatherhood that presumed the less rational half of the Christian year to be "variable", when in fact simply lunar. According to a more local scheme of earth and satellite, Christmas and its dependencies—the pairs of equinoxes and solstices celebrated by ember days—might be considered the eccentrics. But though the dates themselves were rendered as Caesar's, fixedly resistant to feminine principles, the church reckoned signal acts of Christ from the Semitic dispensation. Caleb was learning to discern the intricacy with which these complements of calculation were alternated and interwoven like two rhythms in the same verses.

Today was St Patrick's by the sun; and the last of these three ember days, codetermined by the moon, would fall practically on the equinox, his own birthday. In two days, fixed by solar date, came St Joseph's the artisan, the man most of all whose faith was tested, probably without the kind of warning Abraham had with Isaac. The Lenten fish business, advented like a pregnancy of its lunar mother by the lead time for national distribution, was already at its anticipatory peak, with scores of solidly laden trailer rigs daily grinding westward out of Dogtown. Twice in a fortnight he'd glimpsed the gipsy kilroy that was decorated on its radiator with the name of BICE.

It is very meet, right, and our bounden duty that we should at all times and in all places give thanks unto thee, O holy Lord, almighty Father, everlasting God: —

Careful now: don't get caught daydreaming:: the Sanctus is at hand. If you miss the cue you'll lose some of your action, and the Mass will go right along without you. All you need is one more chance to wake up that all-too-wakeful princess by putting her to sleep. It can be done, with a certain kind of dissembled patience, guided by the experience of Poet's Corner—as interpreted in subsequent reflection upon secondary communications.

Who by bodily fasting dost overcome faults, dost raise the mind, and dost bestow on us virtue and its rewards: through Christ our Lord.

Spiritually he was feeling good also because he'd gained an extra hour at *The Isorectotetrahedron* by skipping the morning discipline that made his body feel so good when over with and was so gratifying to the saint who shared it as a pleasure no matter how early and dark, no matter how wet or cold and windy.

Before he was well awake, to Ibi's disappointment, he had persuaded himself that the streets were too cluttered with carbonized snow and rotten ice, harshly congealed in nocturnal suspension of the thaw, for a frail white-collar wight to run the risk of injury on arduous dawn patrol. Gladly therefore had he jumped from bed, omitting all less joyful pain, to make for his coffee more or less directly, and never noticed that he came to Mass any the worse for his indulgence. As he was warming his typewriter keys, ahead of schedule, unsweated and unbathed, all the surplus energy of his lazy aerobic system seemed to flow unobstructed to Creative Mind. Though afterwards there wasn't much to show for his euphoria, dereliction of the supererogatory means to longevity on this occasion had somewhat served the end for which longevity was purported, instilling him moreover with a temporary conviction of limitless capacity for all the lesser duties and pleasures of the long day ahead.

Through whom the angels praise,—
Raphael Opsimath had recently reappeared at a party to which Caleb had been invited by Tessa Barebones, his new voice teacher, in celebration of a successful return from her first two weeks of "Semi-Con" at White Quarry College in Montvert; whence too the Cornucopian, perched for a night or two at the Poet's Corner, was on the way home from his last, as if to escort or pursue the venerable Doctor Charlemagne likewise repairing from the academic sojourn to his Dogtown nest. As Rafe had previously introduced Caleb severally to Doc and to Tessa (who had been led to White Quarry by Rafe's example), so also it was through the archangel's good offices that her new hometown professor had finally been delivered by taxi all the way out to the old granite Powerhouse in North Village, no more than three hours late.

the Dominations adore, the Powers fear thy Majesty. The heavens and the heavenly Virtues, and the blessed Seraphim together sing thy praise with exultation. With whom, we beseech thee, bid that our voices also be admitted, with suppliant thanksgiving saying:—
Miss Starling, so briefly his "voice coach", a respectable descendant of Merry Sterne and sister of a famous organist, after starting Caleb on her primer of exercises for a singer (despite all his protestations of strictly prosaic purpose), had quietly gone to her rest in a family lot almost within view of his window. She'd been pleased to find her reputation locally remembered so long after retirement from service to a clientele of aspirants and stars behind the scenes in Botolph's international circles of civil and performing arts (including famous politicians who came to her secretly for their lessons).

On Father Lucey's recommendation, he'd been accepted as a last and unpromising pupil. He got round her retirement with the presentation of himself as an impecunious neighbor whose polite and intelligent career was blighted by a piteous defect which she alone in all of Gloucester County might be able to correct. Furthermore, as a childless old lady evidently indifferent to riches and blessed with soft spots for boys and saints, having noticed Ibi through her parlor window as he waited with his master for her response to the doorbell on the porch of the big old house inherited from her deceased brother, she had greatly reduced her long-outdated fee.

His present remorse for having thereupon displayed his trust in her by gratuitously blurting out a declaration of hatred for organ music was hardly mitigated by the memory of her gentle amusement at what she had at first taken merely as an unskilled jest. It was perhaps therefore, and for similar reasons relating to discordant traits of his otherwise agreeable and sanguine outlook, that throughout the few introductory sessions before her last illness, despite the uneducated maternal instinct he stirred in the little spinster (whose bones seemed much too frail for her career), she had always comported herself with him in a seemly professional manner.

Yes, unlike Father Chris.

"*Holy, Holy, Holy,*"—but behold, Caleb was not lost in reverie! Scarcely having listened, he nevertheless found himself precisely ringing sanctus [***] with the small brass sacring bell kept by his knee, while voicing with the priest and people—"*Lord God of Hosts. Heaven and earth are full of thy glory. Hosanna in the highest.*" He rose to go light the candle on the credence table, genuflecting [√] on the way both out and back to his place, as Father Duncannon proceeded to the canon of the material sacrifice by which Christianity was generated and regenerated at unexclusive altars from one millenium to the next.

Therefore most merciful Father, through Jesus Christ thy Son our Lord, in this our Eucharist and praise, we humbly pray and beseech thee that thou accept and bless these [†] *gifts, these* [†] *offerings, these* [†] *holy and unspotted sacrifices, which, first, we offer unto thee for thy holy classic Church:—*

Oblations now absolved from the unintended evil caused by people of goodwill and their accomplices in stupidity, ignorance, incompetence, pride, specialization, laziness, insanity, overwork, or concentration of vision, as well as by the selfish or passionate entropy of tribal fear hatred and vengeance. Joyful in his sense of private accomplishment, this morning Caleb has been too oblivious of the whole world's want of what Father Duncannon called "atoning eupepsia". But when endeavoring to chasten himself by taking to heart the disorders and dysfunctions of the United Nations, he was driven toward sinful skepticism by the confounding apprehension that even sweet-tempered Christians of good digestion and rational mind, in whose power it might be to save the world, were allowing themselves to be defeated by the same kinds of intellectual disability that astronomers and experimental physicists would be laboring under nowadays if they had remained Platonists or Aristotelians, rejecting quantum mechanics and Relativity.

that thou vouchsafe to keep it in peace, to guard, unite, and govern it throughout the whole world: together with thy servant our Bishop Richard—
Accidental namesake of "the first high-churchman", surnamed Cheyney, excommunicated Archbishop of Gloucester, ground down between Paulines and Petrines and buried unmarked in his own cathedral, who had advisedly ordained Edmund Campion yet himself settled for a Lutheran-like doctrine of consubstantiation anathema to his colleagues in the "pestilential sect" of Tudor. But this was Richard Bishop Derwent, who successfully strove to be "a relator of men to each other", whose gentle good works were tirelessly ecumenical and famously opposed to the bigotry of races: still Vinland's Apostolic diocesan in Botolph, still the single authority respected High and Low; unlike many of those who had elected him, Broad enough in person to tolerate both incense and whale shit.

It was a name not only recently incumbent. Long ago at the convent "The Bishop" with hardly any civil identity had been as high and remote beyond the dominion of the Mother Superior and even the supremacy of Father Pole as God the Father was beyond the Son of Man visible on crucifixes. Caleb marveled to hear him mentioned by his Christian name, and to find himself under the same episcopacy after returning to Vinland from the land of milk and honey where he'd never given a thought to bishops. He did not remember ever having seen the great man whose visible hand would have been laid upon his head if he'd ever been confirmed during his childhood days of churching; but from what he'd heard since then he couldn't help revering the old prelate's benign opacity.

Anywhere from Hobart to Hudson's Bay the merely conservatory management of ministries in the Tudor Communion called for political equivocation and humanistic psychology; but by the wisdom of his organized charity this bishop of a deep-rooted but otherwise unnoticeable minority had greatly multiplied the quiet per-capita influence of a tiny Pauline Apostolic republic within a democratic Commonwealth dominated by the green eminence of Patrick Cardinal O'Neill, whose properties were immensely greater and whose nameday was the year's most patriotic for the raucous swarm in the metropolis. Richard however was a friend of Patrick's, and they were said to be humorous with each other, especially in considering the ironies of their respective historical vantages. Yet Bishop Derwent's little brick palace at One Freud Street on Governor's Hill, crowded by townhouses, overlooking the paradeground of the Atlantean Revolution like an anachronistic publishing house, was stuffed with blue-blooded investment portfolios and idealistic tracts, and seemed as well established as its antecedent fifteen years before the Declaration of Independence; and it was probably as safe as the golden-domed New State House nearby above it, until the last peak of the Hill is finally leveled all the way to meet the demands of aircraft for more fill in Botolph Harbor. Caleb never heard either of the Lab's dissident Fathers (themselves undoubtedly even more humorous and ironic) complain about their obligation to report to this inconspicuous address for ten minutes every year, during which theological and political topics were religiously avoided.

and all the orthodox, and those who profess the classic and apostolic faith. Remember, O Lord, thy servants and handmaids . . .

Commemoration for the Living, a string of Christian names representing personal troubles or special situations, mostly of C O V members whom Caleb had never met, including residents of such Oceania islands as Typee and Truk, and one or two he recognized as worker-priests in England. He wasn't told why they were mentioned, but he knew that lay members were usually in difficulties with their parish clergy, and clerical members sometimes in more difficulties with their bishops than with cannibals; and he gathered that Members Secular in general, none being bound to special celibacy or obedience, were nearly as likely as the run of neurotic population to be in difficulties with themselves. The ones in England were poor, and probably lived where there was little of the green and pleasant ever to be seen.

With the detachment of resignation he now calmly took notice of the quickening in his heart peculiar to the thought of England—a disturbance less insistent than that of homunculus erectus, but never assuaged, and far more sentimental. It was the avowed goal by which he had been drawn this far east from the lotus-eating land of Cornucopia. He'd gone West for freedom of education, but it was as a graduate on the opposite way to Britannia Antiqua that he found himself stranded on the self-made island of his birth. Thus he thrilled to the locus even of Labor's urban missionaries in the isles of Europe, where a thousand years ago (according to Francis Bacon the Tudor ancestor of his Scholastic friend Frank in Dogtown) the English branch of the Vine had been planted by the right hand of God "that it might stretch her branches".

In his chronic hopes for ultratlantic pleasure this nostalgia for all the places he'd never seen everywhere in Britain and Ireland, and the Isle of Manannan between them, prevailed over all the rest. The dull pain that betrayed continual frustration of adventure in goodly states and kingdoms, muffled for the most part by erotic economic or theoretical preoccupations, might at any moment flick its salty tongue across his naked skin (as it did right now) like the goad of deprivation and impotence suffered by some life-prisoner at a sudden image of the grassy lane to his hometown ballfield; as poignant as Mallory's dream of the legendary past, as patriotic as Virgil's—especially now that his most acute desire was in abeyance, leaving only the congenital inclination of his undiscriminating cuniculagnia. It was impossible for Caleb to imagine a transport more satisfactory than that by water to the island of industry and empire (to whose flag, whilom, by a custom the revival of which Samuel Pepys was assigned to ponder, the ships of all nations were expected to dip their own, as acknowledgment of her "privilege in the seas"), where you could get within walking distance of any house by canal or rail, where no farm was very far from the waves, and where the art of brickwork was a drab commonplace. Yet it was a vulgar fact that almost every literate Atlantean occasionally yenned a European vacation for prestige or pastime, and that most of his peers had made transatlantic visits (without discernible edification from the experience thereof); wherefore, among other reasons, he had grown too ashamed and proud ever to describe or explain his unsatisfied craving simply to see the civilization he belonged to—to touch it, to walk it, but above all to look at it and look and look: silently, solitarily if not contentedly, to contemplate its artifactual nature from moving windows or on his feet:: not so much to see its spires and flying buttresses as to feel its cobbles through his soles, to tread not its museums but its footpaths, climb its stiles, find its water locks, study its railway platforms; to touch the mineral and wood of its ordinary places, and relate its 19C things to an archeology about which their familiar owners were generally incurious.

And also, after Britain (where a lone timid alien could make his necessities known without great difficulty), in old Armorica; in all the overlaid provinces of his Celtic, Hellenic, Teutonic, Norman, Romantic Europe. But not for the languages. In the Cisatlantic babel of New Uruk he could have heard any of the world's dialects, and almost anywhere in Atlantis he could have learned vernaculars from books and soundtracked films of adequate facsimile. There was access to more of European production in both Hume and Unabridge than he had ever cared to avail himself of, and it would have taken too much time energy and discipline from more important work to seek pleasure through philology. Whereas to ride and walk the outdoor heaven of Europe—his Orient, his East Indies, his South Seas—he thought would be headier adventure and more tireless than dalliances with Fayaway or Riolama: in half a dozen countries of the Continent simply to see things and places more interesting than comfortable, the territory of history—where day and night a lust to see would for the nonce obliterate his lust to read and his lust to make. Like a colonial Icelandic saga-man, tongue-tied, finally setting foot in Norway . . .

and all here gathered round, whose faith and devotion unto thee are known and manifest: who offer unto thee this sacrifice . . .

Could it be entirely of his own free will that he had adopted as his categorical desideratum this delight for which he was famished—for which in any clear and straightforward choice he would have sacrificed all careers except the unrewarding toil of his imaginary theater, and all reward except the guerdon craved by all homunculi? Was this spiritual craving even preformed in the cells of his ancestors—if it was not perhaps a characteristic acquired as late as gestation? "Mummy, have I ever been to England?" Yes my darling, so she did say, you saw England through the porthole of my navel. She liked to joke that she'd almost killed two birds with one stone by combining mal de mere with her morningsickness. Of course the tobacco she smoked was Atlantean. Thus he had been conceived Atlantean and retarded by the Atlantean drug, but by epigenesis had waxed two thirds European before being born in Atlantis.

. . . Joining in communion, and reverencing the memory, chiefly, of the glorious and ever-blessed Virgin Mary . . .

The common name Mary had so many different contexts that he hardly ever associated it with Mary Tremont of whose womb he was the only fruit. His mother, as unlike the B V M as was the never-virgin Magdalen—thank God she has found sheltered amity with the Brotherhood of the Peaceable Kingdom. For the present at least, Orellana is far enough away, in the margin of a jungle-bound savannah on the mysterious slackwater capillary that joins the Amazon with the Orinoco, the Lusitanian system with the Hispanic conquest. It took her a week to get there even after disembarking from the old Mississippi steamboat on the Rio Negro.

Only after her last letter has he begun to believe that there's no longer danger of her suddenly jumping ship to fly "home" to Dogtown on her last dollar. You can't walk off in a huff when your nest-egg has been contributed to a green mansion invested by anthrophagite boas and patrolled by sullen anti-Pauline descendants of the aboriginal cannibals. Of course she's personally determined to "make friends" with the people of the black jaguar; but such propinquities of habitat in an isolated ecology instinctively hostile to any sect of "separated brethren" can only reinforce the unity and agape of a Massless "church-based intentional community".

It's really too comforting to be true. But woe to the peace of her little oak tree when she changes her mind about the "brothers and sisters" by whom she's at last been accepted! How will the stormy spirit fare when her enthusiasm runs afoul of "the listening ear of consensus" in that democratically authoritarian enclave of self-forswearing communitarians who caution against "hasty decision" and deem unity more important than theology itself—where unity is the very end and purpose of all policy and corporate self-discipline? How long can she continue to renounce or disguise her cherished powers of selfexpression?

. . . as also of the holy patriarchs and prophets of Israel, of the blessed apostles and martyrs of our fulfilling faith, and of all the saints: by whose prayers grant that in all the work which thou hast given us to do in earth we may ever be defended by the help of thy protection. . . .

—from the likes of Father Chris. Out in the secular world that iatric gentleman, generous discreet and gracious, seldom made ostentation of his cloth, yet was always prepared to offer himself as an honorable pastor of young men psychically awry. Only when led into the immediate danger of seduction did Caleb realize (though by then with no great astonishment) that in his employment and on their travels Chris had been treating him as a woman is like to be treated. According even to Dante, "courtesy and honor are all one." Like a well-read maiden of limited erotic persuasions, on the occasion of trial he was frightened by his predicament, ashamed of his awkwardness in apologetic self-defense, and chagrined in general at the incompetence of his own courtesy. But enlightened rather than disillusioned. Friendship survived the rebuff, and with greater intimacy, because the revelation of intention (which in their personal relations thereafter was tacitly acknowledged to have been scotched and displaced) actually liberated the professional confessor and therapist for an easier off-limit role, vis-a-vis this uniquely situated associate, as a cheerful and unselfishly narcissistic penitent.

It was on a warm October Sunday afternoon in the early days of enthusiasm that Caleb and Ibi had shown Chris the heath of Purdeyville, with the yellows and reds of a few hardy sumacs and scrub oaks, which in a whole century gained little over perdurable junipers and rocks even though there was no longer any livestock to crop the billows of faded pasture that thinly clothed the granite vertebrae and clavicles of old Lady Gloucester and upraised many of her internal shoals and reefs to the yet more ancient sky. In somewhat selfserving fashion Caleb was confessing the timidity and infirmity of his voice: since he'd never been able to shout or make a commotion, to say nothing of bellow, he did not possess the competitive benefit of confidence in voice even at the volume of ordinary persuasion or telephonic conversation:: otherwise he might have risen in any number of glittering careers—anyway to half the level of his competence! Yet then, he intimated, essential energy would have been sorely diverted from the one job worth all his intimidation.

It was the first time he'd ever talked like this to anyone but girls in love with him, or maybe about to be, two or three at most. But now he had a priest all to himself, and one who seemed to understand everything without glossaries. At the time he was hardly aware of being as solicitously ministered to as he himself would have ministered to any susceptible girl he'd managed to lure out for a wholesome look in broad daylight at the most deserted available landscape. He was accustomed to being the one who heard and sympathized with confessions of weakness—including Chris's!

In this private hour of holiday from their mutual and separate businesses, Chris laughed softly at Caleb's complaint. Speaking very little in a low unemphatic tone, only very very faintly Southern, soothing with the dulcet cheerfulness of faineance feigned, and utterly without psychological unction or psychopompous cliche, he devoted himself to the encouragement of Caleb's revelations on any pathological topic; but in this case the lack of simple manliness in voice was the only deficiency conceivably amenable to the personal cure of an unintellectual psychiatric social worker.

Chris offered the opinion that Caleb's declared difficulty was purely contingent. "The voice is strained because it's not your own. Yours can be found if we look for it. Your genius has always had to disguise itself in order to make its way alone in the world. Any other artist would have misplaced much more than his voice! We'll pray for you on St Blasius day, of course, but there's no need to wait until February. I think you can be healed quite soon without divine intervention. Would you like me to try? By the laying-on of hands for a few minutes every now and then, I'll teach you how to relax your viscera. Most of the time you can practice by yourself."

He thinks I'm neurotically repressed, Caleb had said to himself with a wry twist of the lip as he lay down on the grass in a sequestered space behind a boulder and among some juniper bushes, thinking what a shame it was that he'd never used that moorland with Bice, or with any other girl for that matter, as he uneasily allowed Chris to rub his stomach without listening closely to the soft talk about somatic relaxation. Too embarrassed to betray distress at this sophistication of ostensibly pragmatic friendship, he tensely suffered the therapist to unbutton an opening in his shirt and find the bare skin. But he could no longer cherish any doubt of the obvious motive for the laying on of hands when the circular motions of the fingertips, pretending at first to center on the diaphragm and span the ribs (as he himself by similar tactics might have pretended a disinterested approach to the chest of a girl), gradually slipped down beneath the waistband of his underwear in circulating asymmetry.

Now Caleb accepted Doc's theory that priapic cults were only superficially biased in favor of one gender. Though reproductive injaculation required ithyphallic initiative, in corresponding states of hydrostatic pressure the sanguine solid was simply congruent to the haptic dilation. Nothing indicated its superiority in attractive power to the delitescence of the rima veneris which excites and exhausts it. And if anything, though a necessary cause, it contributes less to generation. Fertility may have been the *instinctive* evolutionary motive of sex-cults—as indeed, a fortiori, perpetuation of the species is the final cause of religion in general—but even half-understood procreation isn't usually the formal or *conscious* cause of phallicism. The appendage of outward and visible significance happens to be masculine. Like priesthood the part had to fall to one sex or the other. But according to Doctor Charlemagne as anthropologist the occasional ostentation of its metamorphic motility is mutually fascinating to male and female. In the function of satisfaction its efficiency is reciprocal. This conjoint sensor serves sight and touch as private if not public totem. You might call it an ideal talisman of inconstant desire for both sexes at moments of secret or festal expectation, when lives between infancy and dotage are most intensely concrescent—at least if free of hunger thirst and pain, relieved of work, and free for recreation. But to Caleb the lingam stood for the yoni from which it had derived by eversion as an equal and opposite salient like the outside representing the inside of a reversible mask. For him, as erotomaniacal as any other swain, the instrument of reciprocal sympathy had even less to do with affection for men than with desire for progeny.

He was sympathetic enough with the homuncular plight of whalers three years on a voyage, or sailors on L S T s dawdling for even a few months in the womanless Pacific, or other celibates still young enough to suffer under the tyranny of their gonads; the solecisms imagined of these sufferers could be attributed to the old law that when you drive the devil out the front door he comes in at the back: yet knowing nothing of other men, uncircumcised or not, his epicene curiosity was simply anatomical—on the order of architectural, in terms of base shaft entasis and capital—rather than mechanical, in terms of dynamic function—never disturbing enough to overcome the propriety of what he regarded as dignified behavior. But he was horrified by the very thought of Greek love as a means of serving his prurience.

In fact, notwithstanding his loyal admiration and affectionate gratitude for extraordinary kindness and generosity, he felt nothing but aversion for the body of this ungainly middle-aged ostrich, insalubriously white and hairy beneath the cloth, who did violence to its own vows. Distressed by the lack of norms or precedents, perplexed about appropriate manners, and hotly ashamed of his failure to resist Chris's blandishments from the very beginning of his employment, he yielded to alarm. Scrambling to his knees, looking away from his friend as he fastened his clothes, he croaked "I'm much too ticklish to relax", and made no further attempt at courtesy.

"It's something that bears getting used to." Chris assented, smoothly resuming his usual good cheer. But with long swift strides he was soon leading the way back along the path on which Caleb had been the earlier guide, forgetting or pretending to forget their ostensible destination much further along at Cynosure Rock (which he had long professed a wish to visit), as if the introductory lesson had come to its intended end and rain was about to overtake them.

Thereafter no further mention had ever been made of continuing the treatment. Only a day or two later he referred Caleb to Miss Starling. "A man of your talent shouldn't despair of his voice." was all he said.

It was rather of Bice that Caleb did still despair. With the air cleared between himself and Chris that was seen in retrospect to have been so charged with uncertainty, he had begun to speak of her to his tacitly confessed confessor, who readily responded to the cue—almost with zest—as if it entailed without offense a perfectly face-saving explanation of his rejection.

Thereafter in their conversation with others, at the brokerage office or on trips, Chris generally contrived to divert suspicion of their companionship by alluding to Caleb's natural interest in women, as neither a member of the Order nor a religious. Caleb hardly cared that he was now used to neutralize public perception of the priest's gravitation toward the young men who flocked to the investment business, or who were selectively encountered in volunteer social work. Now noticing that his protector always made a point of mentioning or even celebrating the wives and children of married acquaintances, and the women among his friends, he found it surprisingly easy to speak of his Beatrice. Not that he took much advantage of his opportunities to do so. It served no purpose to cast off honorable inhibitions simply in order to say a small part of what he said to himself, save perhaps charitably to prime the pump for one who had begun to do most of the therapeutic confessing.

The vivacity of the merry black eyes already eluded his memory anyway. Few impressions of her audible words remained, snagged at random by his neural nets, to put the best face upon his unperfected attempt to loosen and unstring the self-sufficing integrity of her body. Yet now and then the sensations of her imaginary presence still brought his breath to a halt, and unintentionally recalled feelings of the loveliest tenderness. His anger was lost in the perpetual revision of inferences about her character. But he still brooded over the qualitative question of how many men she had awakened from the sleep of reason, or of work, or of faithful service, only to leave them in turmoil bitterness and confusion. In his global assay the tincture of her presence, an antipodal stranger roaming the northwest shores of the Atlantic (and perhaps right now its northeast islands too), varied between the tonic and the toxic. He had come to believe that by shunning local bondage Beatrice Picory contributed neither artifact nor art to the scenes she visited. Yet perhaps the moments of joy conferred by the touch of that transient at each station in her wandering really did atone for the aggregate pain she left behind in the fraternity of desire. She was so amiable and debonair, as well as beautiful and intelligent, that probably by nobody but herself would she be judged as troubled a product of civilization as she was producer.

This oblation, therefore, of our bounden duty and service, as also of thy whole family, we beseech thee, O Lord, graciously to accept:

With his spread fingers cradling the back of her scalp, his thumbs spanning her delicate ear lobes beneath the short finely touseled locks that enwreathed her face as if attracted like curling black smoke, he had believed himself in control of her entire body. In truth, her pitch and rhythm were not distinctive, nor even the melody he played. It was the instrument's timbre that in retrospect had distinquished it for his unquenched desire, like a firmly hollowed cello's, sounding itself without the touch of a bow. Yet the whole taut integument was as soft and unvarnished as promised from the first by her half opened blouse and her long loose skirt that hinted itself negligibly less liftable than commonplace short ones.

Firsthand unbuttoning laid bare no essence of the spirit thus embodied, which successful caresses had made him all the more ambitious to discover. It was the gay mentality that kept urging him to music even after learning that her envelopment of his half-live corpuscles was on the whole undistinguished as purely sensual experience, and after guessing that its envelopments of others' were equally warm and easy—less distinguishable from each other in her memory than incidents of preliminary attraction. Perhaps others also craved sensation of their own less than her nervously shielded psyche's. They too wished to modulate that mind and impress its history by fostering and reaping its immanent talent for the gift it advertised.

Anyway, he for one had been wild to possess its knowledge, having divined that she wouldn't let men touch her who weren't magnetized enough to seek the consciousness she was proud of, or whose own consciousness and knowledge at least in part hers did not seek. Concluding from internal evidence that all her musicians were intelligently insane, he nearly sighed aloud at Mass.

and order our days in thy peace, deliver us from eternal dereliction, and keep us in the flock of those who do thy will . . .

So as its vector that was how the phallic haunted him at present— not as object but as subject; not for its maleness but by its maleness: autonomic and inadvertent, but acute. Whether bow or plectrum, the lower case *i* is often enlarged to capital ego even without an object of imagination, but in this case there were particular recollections of experience. Drawing blood from his head, that stylus shifted to itself the center of his intelligence, which had become simultaneously as directed as love's arrow and as promiscuous as chronic famishment, by disputing the weight of his cassock, as if to rewrite its story. Though the sensuous sensibility of the vector's vector sometimes separated itself from the blind sensuality of homunculus erectus, this was an instance of painfully harmonious reinforcement. It was the intellectual Caleb who attached such great value to the female mind he was after. There seemed to be virtually a soul inside—a spirit, at least—but only one way to reach it.

Upon which oblation vouchsafe to look with favorable and gracious countenance: and to receive it even as thou didst vouchsafe to receive the gifts of thy chosen people within the covenant of our patriarch Abraham: the sacrifices of thine ancient priesthood Israel.

Caleb lifted the bell from its place by his knee. The only woman who had ever really tried to tell him her mind was his mother—full of knowledge and feeling that he wished not to hear. Her critical imagination had always been tormented with feminine knowledge and feeling. As a boy he had wanted only the knowledge and feeling of technology; his desire was for knowledge and feeling of athletic military and political power, as leader or lone wolf, always as a citizen of the greatest nation. He believed in the vert and venison of Robin Hood, and in the benefaction of the Catholicratic Party.

It wasn't until the age of twelve that he'd begun to interest himself in the phallic knowledge and feeling that had little to do with power, only with the powerful desire of which all men are victims. He found nothing in it to dominate others.

So while still subject to his mother he had come to desire girls along with organized artefacts, while resisting the feminine sensibilities she forced upon him, whether fine or gross. She who had planted images of unspeakable knowledge in her unwilling son-confessor was the last woman in the world of whom he would have asked questions (which would have been much to her triumphant delight) when his interest in feminine knowledge was germinated by lovely feelings for particular girls. He had practiced the craft of dissembled incuriosity about her erotic folly, which in the principal affair during his childhood she told him was inflamed by the phallic enormity of her faithless Lusitanian "fisher-of-women", whose elusive presence had darkened several years of his struggle for social innocence purged of consanguine shame.

Nor had he wished to hear about himself as her "little oak tree and only-begotten son" representing all three children (including the daughter) of her own childhood desires; about the gutless perfidy of men and mean-minded deceitfulness of women; or about the lorn loneliness of a "discasted female family breadwinner—neither maid nor wife nor widow". After reading the autobiographical work of Rousseau (with an enthusiasm that forever blocked any appetite her son might have worked up for that authority), she had called him a child of Melchizedec. (As they used to say in Europe, "son of a priest", or "nephew" of a Pope.) "Children of Melchizedec", she liked to quote—tearfully or laughing—were "persons about whom nothing was known."

For after all—thank God or the Devil—she wouldn't tell him all her knowledge, even when she knew he didn't want to know it! Or she'd tell him such moody facts of quantum-possibility that like a classical scientist ignorant of her eigenstate he habitually rejected them as veridical only to the feminine brain that had been psychotically scored in the 1918 epidemic of encephalitis lethargica. At some point in his youth he had unconsciously begun to believe that she had no truth to tell him. Though in most matters her purpose was to expose too much—to force upon him and other human beings, in spite of themselves, what she called truth—in the matter of his origin she was strangely opaque, sometimes absurdly inconsistent, often playfully fictitious: perhaps in this one case embarrassed. Seeing that he could never bring himself to question her, he had gradually learned to appreciate the epistemological advantages of his practically unilateral descent, and to evade or forestall her accidental elucidations.

And do thou, O God, we beseech thee, vouchsafe to render it in every way—
Caleb rang the bell once, without noticing that Adam of Eden had relapsed.

blessed, ratified—Melchizedec at the altar thrice made crosses [†††]—*reasonable, and acceptable*—and again, once over the bread itself [†], once over the grail [†]—*that for us it may in turn be moved into the ascended Bo*[†]*dy and Blo*[†]*od of thy most dearly beloved Son, our Lord Jesus Christ.*

The Mass was now in its making. There was a time in England that at this point it became illegal. It was the moment of qualitative discontinuity at which works of the world were informed with the uniquely counterentropic energy to jump their otherwise gravitated orbits in relative time and enter into the coherent order that otherwise could never be attained by a society of ignorant selfish and quarrelsome wills. Unless this reasonable and unbloody mactation was repeatedly performed by the cells of Christ's church, the suicidal species could neither evolve nor survive. Thus the climax of the one true *muthos:*

Who the day before he suffered took bread into his holy, venerable, and creative hands—the people's surgeon here doing all these things himself, not as mere dramatic actor in edification of an audience but as factor of their own sacramental work, in the way that things have been done since the original Institution—*and lifting up his eyes to heaven unto thee, O God, his almighty Father, giving thanks to thee, he bles* [†]*sed, brake, and gave to his disciples, saying: Take and eat all ye of this.*

For this is my body. An actual metacosmic leap of matter known as the Consecration: mankind's perpetuated revolution.

The priest genuflects [√] with both hands on the edge of the altar. As authorized technologist he has instantaneously altered the phase-state of bread entrusted to his office. It is for the acolyte to catch up the drama here: first by ringing once [*] his sanctus-bell, a merely ceremonial embellishment of the essential action, but nonetheless a satisfactory bit of his ancillary part at the altar and a harmlessly pleasant signal to the congregation.

Caleb rings twice [**] as the priest in heave-offering raises high the host to show it. It was said that in the dark times of this religion a glimpse of the Elevation, even at a distance through the porch door, was enough to count for annual attendance at the Mass, sufficient for a sinner's salvation. On Easter Day in the Philippines, in preparation for setting up a cross on the nearest headland, Magellan saluted this wave of his priest's holy bread with all his ship's guns and a volley of aquebuses. The degeneration of liturgy (or "Masse-game", "theatrical sights", "idolatry", and "masking", as the old reformers called it) into a rite little less goetic than the ritual of witchcraft was morally as repugnant to Caleb as the spiritual selfishness at the opposite end of Christian confusion in which Paulines had sought private salvation by hearing an individual's abuse of kerygma for three hours twice a week.

But the focal dromenon had survived all its distortions. Even in its most degraded forms it had always followed Jesus the supreme liturgical genius in preserving live sacrifice without violence. Once more this thought quickened Caleb's heartbeat with the renewed access of hope that by benefit of Father Duncannon's analysis the whole church would finally become aware of why and how its liturgy was root and branch of Word and works—perhaps not too late to save society from its fatuous self-reliance.

Again Father Duncannon [√], hands on altar; but this time Caleb thrice [***]. Mactation not of meat but of vegetable protein, planted reaped transported manufactured and distributed by men and women in order to participate in history's one successful offering of flesh. But in fulfilling the Jews' efforts to traffic with God by transforming natural organized matter into supernal gifts of thanksgiving (as Greeks and barbarians also tried to traffic with their grosser gods), the Christian priesthood had almost everywhere disavowed or neglected the social organism for which praeternatural grace was ultimately intended.

Likewise after supper, taking also this excellent chalice into his holy, venerable, and creative hands, and giving thanks to thee, he bles[†]*sed and gave to his disciples, saying: Take and drink all ye of it. For this is the chalice of my blood, in the new covenant: the mystery of faith: which shall be shed for you and for many . . .*

Starting with his earliest incomprehensible Masses at the convent, these and like words of "memorial"—originally and now again meant to invoke divine action for the transit of dedicated material from its historical state to that of holiness beyond the time of "all this middle-earth" (as our sphere is called in the Wakefield *Noah*), by virtue of Christ bloodied on the Cross—had fetched up a vague but horrifying vision established even earlier by the confidences of his mother. "I shed my blood for you in childbirth," she'd said from the beginning. "I was going to die for you. I already loved you more than God."

As oft as ye do these things, ye shall do them as Anamnesis of me.

The priest adores [√] the consecrated wine, elevates the cup, sets it down, and once more sinks [√] to one knee before it, as Caleb again signals once [*] and twice [**] and thrice [***].

Still on his own two knees, activity at a pause, the bell-ringer stiffens his spine and braces himself for the last long stint of upright kneeling, which seems not much easier in manhood than in childhood. The muscles of his back begin to ache.

Wherefore, O Lord and heavenly Father, we also thy servants, joined together as an holy people, a royal priesthood, according to the institution of our Lord and Saviour Jesus Christ, making Anamnesis of his blessed passion and precious death, his mighty resurrection and glorious ascension, do offer unto thy divine majesty of thy own gifts and bounty: a pure host, a holy host, a spotless host, the holy bread of eternal life; and the chalice of everlasting salvation.

Here, in Caleb's opinion, if anywhere, supernatural action has been reduced to its one objective miracle. There's nothing exclusively subjective or spiritual about breaching the limits of the secular system and dispatching quanta of society's work to the ground of being, where our ontological continuum comprehends any construction of the human universe including that of itself. In his rationalized adaptation of Christianity, no other mystery than this dromenological sacrament was admitted to the metasystem, not even the original paschal miracle that made this one possible. His secret heresy, formed in the pride of an unfledged Promethean, he dared not disclose to Father Duncannon, whose orthodox theodynamics it narrowly limited.

And we humbly beseech thee, almighty God; command that these gifts now be brought by the hands of thine own angel of mighty counsel, the High Priest of our profession, to thine altar on high: that as many of us as by this partaking of the altar shall receive the most sacred Body and Blood of thy Son may be fulfilled with all heavenly benediction and grace. Through the same Christ, our Lord . . . But in Father Duncannon's regeneration of doctrine, all but ignored by almost all his own Tudor churchmen as well as by the Petrines of other communions who most needed its explanation of the liturgy's central importance to betterment of Christ's commonwealth, "transubstantiation" was no mere symbolic substitution of the moral for the material or of the ideal for the actual. Among all the real and immemorial symbols of human life, Jesus Christ arbitrarily chose the commodities of bread and wine as sacramental. Now, ensubstantiated by the Offertory as sacred products of society, reflecting all its systemic causes and effects, individual and collective, they were presented to God for him to perfect, so that in their ensuing consumption by members of the corporation they might nourish the human economy with supranatural reinforcement of the church's efforts to expiate and renew the feasible components of its stupid disorder.

Remember also, O Lord, thy servants and handmaids who have gone before us . . . Why commemoration for the dead precisely at this point? It would seem better to have mentioned Florence [Starling] back among the intercessions, as sainted highchurch lady and arm's-length "Friend" of the Order (for lack of local highchurch parish). Caleb reminded himself to test Father Duncannon's advice on this point. Of course no mention of Captain Ozone that I've heard. That old warlock was never here, probably had hardly heard of the C O V , would have scorned its belief in society, its realism, its hope for the future. Having been brought up Tudor-Petrine in lovely brick Gothic at the foot of Governor's Hill in Botolph, and always having considered himself a member of the Antidisestablishmentarian aristocracy (yet not above a willingness to enhance devilvision and encourage Noxin), the great inventor, it was said, had finally comforted his soul by soon enough denying all his atavisms and sacrileges (such as the private celebration of certain fantasies promoted in Gnujian neognosticism) with the most reactionary profession of his mother's faith.

Satisfied so far with his own nearly flawless performance (though far from relaxed in body), and for the present alert only to his cues for a few *"Amen"*s, Caleb thus found himself led to an allusion usually suppressed in a welter of memories and phantasms—most of which were ironic, none unequivocal, and some nothing but idle red herring. Among his mother's skeins of retrojection, which she herself called intuitions and which were typically contradicted by other equally convinced speculations, was the occult tale that the cold and reclusive blindman who'd inherited the New Albion Grant and possessed the means for putting any number of natural daughters through college and establishing any number of grandsons in unremunerative professions, had been her own mother's creative seducer. That lady's surd refusal to respond to the accusation, no matter how wheedling or provocative with alternate taunts, only proved the suspicion to her contumelious daughter.

On account of the "hypocritical arrangements" under which she had been brought up, of which in this case Caleb never heard any evidence for doubt, Mary called her mother Mrs Grundy. As he read aloud to the smooth high forehead above Captain Ozone's closed black visor, and listened occasionally to the cultivated accents of St Grottlesex School that were so inconsonant with brilliant success in the very swim of vulgarized technology, Caleb had not been spontaneously reminded of his origins. He was so accustomed to disowning familiar facts that were beyond an egalitarian boy-child's span of interest in the future that it had taken him a long time after first going to work at Chateau Noir to recall that immemorial allegation in his vaguely registered personal lore, which was long since neutralized by empirically acquired skepticism, and to match it with the identity of his accidental employer. Even yet, if his mother's claim ever came to mind, amidst all the jetsam afloat in neglected backwaters without the burden of verification or reconciliation, it was with a flip of amusement lasting no longer than the glance of a sunbeam on an inaccessible offing.

To them, O Lord, and to all that rest in Christ, we beseech thee to grant thy mercy, light, and peace . . . In life, during their brief and reserved association, Captain Ozone thought well enough of his reader when it was a question of bestowing the dog, but otherwise betrayed neither partiality nor aversion. Caleb smiled at the thought that not even a reactionary wizard of electronics whose leisure was devoted to carnal pleasures could have been so loveless and self-absorbed—so callously blind even to his own defense against embarrassment—as to have remained deliberately uninformed of a misbegotten daughter's history, unless he had so many by-blows that he was utterly indifferent to progeny; and such proliferation seemed unlikely of a man who by all accounts had been queerly reclusive by condition and temperament long before the trauma of reflex amaurosis. The adventitious employee's sparest account of the time and place of his origins might have warned any possible grandfather. But it was plain that the inventor's will named no Tremont or other Mary for compensation or acknowledgment, bequeathed a Caleb no mention, and left nothing for the maintenance of a Viking Shepherd. The alleged grandson's disappointment of a legacy had been as casual as the imposed imagination of it. It was the balk of a fantastic thought-experiment, no more to be noticed than any other preclusion of the innumerable estates obtained by others in the best of all possible worlds.

Father Duncannon strikes his breast with the right hand, the very gesture of Father Pole that had been most dramatic to five-year-old Caleb looking for landmarks in the longest tedious stretch of his uncomprehending service at the altar. *And to us also, thy suppliant servants, trusting in the multitude of thy mercies, vouchsafe to grant some part and fellowship with thy holy apostles and martyrs, together with blessed Patrick, thy Confessor, and with all thy saints: within whose company we beseech thee to admit us, regarding us only in the body of thine incarnate Son, and pardoning our offenses.* The Church through time and space; the quaquaversal church of all dimensions. But today the streets of Botolph are vainglorious with brogue, parades, and rodomontade, the vaunted green substituted for every other color: blague enough to make you hate the Diskeyized Irish and despise the shamrock plucked by St Patrick to illustrate the Trinity. It must have been a Gypsy who started the search for four-leaf clovers, or a Jewish geometer who sought the tetrahedron. Yet so great was the first Patrick—twelve times imprisoned and condemned by the druids: Patricus the Latin Briton, British patrician, student of the French Faust, converter of all Erin without force or bloodshed—that it was easy to believe he drove all the snakes into the sea. The first time in Ireland, as a boy called Sucat, pirated into slavery as cowboy or shepherd, he had escaped to the Continent with a shipload of Irish wolfhounds.

Through the same Christ, our Lord: through whom, O Lord, all these good things thou dost ever create; dost sanctify [†], *quicken*[†], *bless*[†], *and bestow them upon us.* The priest is now very busy with his hands, making many different signs of the cross with or over the wafer and cup, before and after another genuflection [√] *Through* [†] *whom, and with* [†] *whom, and in* [†] *whom are unto thee, O God the Father* [†] *almighty, in the unity of the Holy* [†] *Ghost, all honor and glory.*

He covers the vessels with their pall, genuflects [√] yet again, and raises his voice in thin tag of song: *Throughout all ages, world without end.*

So far. Our sacrifices have grown scant. Too long we've been confused. Yet, still in hope: "Amen." In Caleb's Christian hope sanguine irony was substituted for Mary Tremont's defiant mockery of the patriarchal commandment that "No bastard shall enter the assembly of the Lord, even unto the tenth generation." But a Dogtown birthday on the vernal equinox, nine months after Gloucestermas, was always best unmentioned.

12
LADY DAY
COMMUNION

Commanded by saving precepts, and taught by divine institution, we are bold to say: Our Father—
This Wednesday, feast of the Annunciation, the voice was different; the priest was too large for the scale of the chamber. He carried himself with a bent head as if habituated to the effort of adaptation yet now selfconsciously repressing an urge to dramatize his Mass. It was the first time Caleb had served this big jerky bird at the altar. Chris's acceptance of today's duty seemed to represent some attempt to revive the discipline, like the new leaf of domesticity turned by a contrite husband whose guilt has been exposed. For once Father Duncannon had taken his place among the laity, as he often longed to do, not in the part of auditor or inspector general but perhaps reproaching himself for anxious feelings that may have resembled those of an actor (Shakespeare for instance) with the rare opportunity to see his own usual role in a drama of his own creation.

But this scheduled alternation of celebrants was as nothing to the astonishing alteration of Caleb's private sentiments. Since last week the tone of his vibrancy had changed by whole octaves. In his head right now there was no amazement to spare for the ironic symmetries of the two practically idiorrhythmic cenobites he worked for. It was still the dawn of too many marvels; his brain was too busy with speculations displacing each other in an endless round of insights.

The cusps of exhilaration were somewhat broadened by the peaceful aftermath of an hour's running; yet the assault upon his composure would have been intolerable if the Mass itself hadn't endued his armature with the inertia of a flywheel converting bursts of tangential energy into the rotary power that kept him from jumping out of his skin. The twitching big-footed movements of the gallinaceous stockbroker, all decked in ill-fitting armor of the Lord, made a Mass as stabilizing as any other priest's.

"*Who art in heaven, hallowed be thy name. Thy kingdom come. Thy will be done, in earth as it is in heaven. Give us this day our daily bread . . .*" The bread of the historical present carries work through time.

Thus briskly, following the quietly intense action of the Consecration, several voices join the celebrant's in sounding this robust prayer for one communiy of free wills. In this logical placement Caleb gives it credence. As one vital syntagm of the rite, no longer a merely personal devotion, it states the purpose of ensuing action.

In the Middle Ages Communion was usually reserved to the clergy, forgotten for the spectators; then, almost to the exclusion of everything else in the canon of the liturgy, it was afflated by the Deformers: expurgated, rarified, disembodied. And of the Scholastic Mass it was all that Cranmer really wanted to save. So in helping to correct the Pauline reaction from magic to idealism, the Lord's Prayer in this position binds the Communion to the Offertory and unequivocates the social foundation of Christianity. This last third of the Anamnesis completes a cybernetic circuit returning the eucharist from God to all communicants as free persons, who otherwise lack the cooperative grace to repair and develop the chosen species to which He has entrusted his hope.

Caleb too hoped for the City of God. He was glad that this short collective invocation diverted hope from the rewards of individual piety—personal immortality in particular—by connecting the sacrifice to the whole City's counterentropic love, and love to its works. And he loved Father Duncannon because by simple change of focus from Christian mythology to its ritual source, through analysis and revision of the theodynamic sacrifice itself, he provided the church (if it was willing to hear) with the means for understanding the frustration of its theological efforts to integrate "Scripture" and "social ethics". Since St Peter's death the church seemed until now to have been casting bread and wine into the sea merely as pledges, like the Doge's wedding rings for Venice.

Deliver us, we beseech thee, O Lord, from all evils, past, present, and to come; and at the intercession of all the Saints [†††] *favorably grant peace in our days.* . . . The Peace. The Kiss of Peace and communal supper every once in a while was about all the Brotherhood of the Peaceable Kingdom had left of Christ's dromenon—they who called themselves primitive Christians! But the birthday letter from his mother had been specially interesting and uncharacteristically peaceful, as if (except for letterwriting) she'd happily sacrificed to "unity" the last passions of her creative energy, though he was guilty of hoping that her submission would lessen the danger to himself of her unbridled personality, which threatened the peace of mind required for his own cool edifice as fire threatened the library of Alexandria.

Through Jesus Christ, thy Son our Lord. The clumsy smoothtalking leader of today's celebration was surprisingly adept at the silent Fraction, gently snapping his large white host (the Levite's own bread) first into two ragged half-moons, and then into a small third piece that would be dropped into the wine. This breaking of bread was often mistaken as a representation of the mactation, or breaking of Christ's body on the cross, and Cranmer had placed it earlier, in the Consecration, as merely a symbolic memorial of the crucifixion; but Caleb had learned that this overt surgery at the altar rightly began the priestly work of distribution: it was the first step in sharing the food of grace for a commonwealth. He found himself with faith enough to rely upon Christ's perfection of his offering, which had been purchased for a penny in the relativity of a particular world-line, and was now about to be fed back to the communicant as that which has been fostered by all law and prophecy, both means and end of amalgamated righteousness. *Who liveth and reigneth with thee in the unity of the Holy Ghost, God.* . . .

At the Annunciation today commemorated, within the octave of the Greater Dionysia, Mary was covered by the shadow of the Holy Ghost. In an earlier religion it would have been beatitude without atonement! For Beatrice Picory there are probably a thousand atonements without beatitude. At least until recently: apparently she's been trying to make up for lost time with her new carpenter—if he's still the only one she can beatifically atone with. Her last letter, from Unaford: "I'm beginning to grow up. With this man Jude I've finally found the experience that I was born for but only you had led me up to. (I now know why you so much value it for women.) But he's too violent in other things to understand me as you do—corrupt and hateful, most of the time. I've come to hate the guitar, and arrogantly uneducated patois. English slang makes less poetic sense than the Atlantean. I'll probably leave him soon. But the Englishmen at University are all stupid, at least the ones at Belial College, where I've been hanging out."

It's oddly flattering and degrading to become the confessor by mail of a woman you thought you loved and loves others with her body, when you know she's using you as a mirror. But at least you can be sure of your distinction in that category of furniture. It's less painful than the part of Joseph.

Throughout all ages, world without end.
"Amen." After all, I've had the privilege of her thigh.
The peace [†] *of the Lord be* [†] *always with you.*
"And with thy spirit." Without responsibility.
May this commixture and consecration of the Body and Blood of our Lord Jesus Christ be to us who receive it the means of his redeeming work.

"Amen." Everyone knows that on the female side there have been billions of conceptions without beatitude. Perhaps even the Minotaur's. Not so on our blithe part in the transaction. Of necessity homunculi are promiscuous with quickened bliss. Back in Hume, didn't I earn remittance money for the old lady by beatitudes without atonement? How she'd laugh Alleluia and Hosannah if ever she who'd shed her blood for me got pneuma of the idea that I shed semen for her benefit when I was almost still a virgin! In performing the most generative act since Creation the Holy Spirit at least covered with his shadow; but I, as one of the chosen vendors to Annunciator Laboratories of Cornucopia Inc, without so much as an artificial cow to abuse me, was as unscrupulous with my aristocratic paroxysms as the Gypsy with her atonements.

But that faceless prostitution of my half-vital minims may have compensated the ecosystem for the entropy I made as janitor of the medical building when I burned book fossils all those nights just to keep the furnace going. I got royalties as bonus for three of the fresh emissions that were started toward term by hidden Pasiphaes waiting for them two doors down the hall in the customer conception room. But how many more specimens from *I,* frozen in vitro, have since been warmed up to $310K°$ and revived in vivo, mostly at other places, to test the yet more remarkable displacement of my corpuscles? How many dozen little legal Minotaurs of world-lines unbeknownst to me have borne or will bear the pedigree of my anonymous dossier as grandchildren of Melchizedek?

O Lamb of God, that takest away the sins of the world:—When loaves of bread were still being used for communal distribution in the early Church, the Agnus Dei was sung at length while all the people waited.

"Have mercy upon us."

Caleb almost chuckled out loud: It was one in a million that the Selector liked me. She was a motherly doctor of forensic anthropology, maybe wistful for her own student days, wishing she'd met a boy like me. Putting her faith in academic records, and believing I'd soon be a well balanced intellectual, she thought there were clients who'd overlook my specifications as a runt—those anyway whose husbands were no bigger than I.

O Lamb of God . . .

There must be a son or two among them; it's unlikely that I've engendered daughters only. Yet perhaps it was thanks to some especially feminine quality of the beatitudes in which I am instrumental that all three of my spuriously conceiving atonements have come out female: the one I know, the one I'm pretty sure of, and the one that was simply possible.

O Lamb of God, that takest away the sins of the world:

"Grant us peace."

But the one I know certainly I learn about last! It's astonishing that in a nation of transcontinental gossip I didn't get wind of her existence until yesterday! Of course I'm glad I was so blithely ignorant. Now that destiny has ceased shielding my conscience, the danger's past. Lilian will be stalwart still. I love her for it more than ever. She doesn't want me to take responsibility.

Caleb had never been interested in babies or children. But this revelation and other amazing new concepts had suddenly spawned a simultaneous variety of broods.

> His brain was so loaded, it nearly exploded,
> And the poor girl would shake with alarm.

The words of the song endlessly circled the rim of his brain. Unrelated ideas kept climbing upon each other like magic acrobats making an unsupported ascent—while his ability to apprehend and possess seemed unlimited. This morning the zest of his body, the play he was writing, the work of the Order, the new President's formation of a government, and other exciting promises of the future, all at the same time, had bidden to disconcert his motions at the altar with regenerating waves of mutual interference.

His renaissance seemed to need no sleep. Love, astonishment, perspicuity, Creative Mind, and sweet tender desire (as if assured of forthcoming appeasement) concurrently extended and expanded all kinds of feeling that normally alternated with each other and deferred to reality. It was a mystic trove of actual passion and passive action of such a molecular cohesion that he warned himself of disintegration if he ever paid it out in linear sequence.

Who could have surmised that the little servant kneeling there so meekly was engrafted with scions of Prometheus and Faust? He was no enemy of God, but he jumped with joy at the latitude of his freedom. In the poise of his ability to read and write about everything at once, he could hardly breathe. With what seemed an equipollent grasp of every essential he wanted to organize all learning; and all at once he had become equipotentially confident in prospect of the exclusive and undiminished love of more women than one. For the time being he made no attempt to distinguish such prehensions from concrescent success, or his personal manhood from that of the homunculus. Still, though he felt himself master of everything commanded by the English language, the manic density of his desires was frightening. Far from repelling spirit, it germinated dragons' teeth of contending ineffability!

O Lord Jesu Christ, who saidst to thine Apostles: Peace I leave with you, my peace I give unto you; and didst pray to God the Father that all thy members should be one in Thee. . . . This Anamnesis not only dispensed with Archbishop Cranmer's most beautiful (and least Zwinglian) Prayer of Humble Access—which had been famously written into the Book of Common Prayer at this point as a substitute for several Latin prayers of personal piety for private salvation, yet which unfortunately required what Father Duncannon called "an almost abject grovelling", a "misplaced wallowing in self-deprecation", which was inappropriate to religious confidence—but also, stimulated by Eber Durkheim, lighted by the works of such scholars as Don Tawney and Dom Dix, driven by theodynamic logic, and reacting against individualism, introduced its own bold precommunion prayers.

Caleb was sorry that Father Duncannon—as a diachronistic and nearly inaudible revolutionary, a scientist without academic office, a priest without prelacy, barely on suffrance of the broadest authorities, and of course without a primate's powers of promulgation—in the effort to restore primitive genes of communal sacrifice without presumptuously overturning venerable formulas of language, had accepted the literary advice of two or three archaistic amateurs. Indeed those "thee"s and "thou"s, and "didst"s and "saidst"s, and the like, not to mention a plethora of printed capitalizations, when used in modern self-explanatory text at junctures like this one as well as in the old elements that formed most of the reshaped liturgy, sometimes stuck in Caleb's craw. The Father Founder's native Atlantean resistance to such inflectional piety had no doubt been weakened in youth by long steeping in the German language, for the sake of reading Leibniz, Kant, Goethe, Planck, Nernst, Schrödinger, Heisenberg, and Einstein.

Father Duncannon was sensitive to the fact that even some of his most admiring followers grumbled that the traditional manner of his revisions was sometimes a little too aesthetical, despite the radical materialism it conveyed, four hundred years after institution of the Tudor rite. Young Turks among the Members were obliged to indulge him in his lifetime, but Father Davy (no youngster) was known to be urging a second edition in due course of revolution. Perhaps at Chapter the founding Superior would appoint an advisory commission on the vernacular.

. . . by this Holy Communion of thy Body and Blood, create anew among us in thy Church true peace and unity according to thy will . . . The first of these three prayers expressed hope for the grace of unity, or solidarity of social freewill—in what Durkheim called "the fusion of all particular sentiments into one common sentiment", a communion of the people in consciousness of moral fraternity—as a gift of the Holy Spirit bestowed on and through the works of society wrought from natural energy and matter. This tikkun for superorganic disharmony was what pre-sacrificial clans had sought in their totem feasts, as did the totalitarian republic of the B P K in Parima, which philanthropically disavowed individualism without retaining oblation and sacrifice but merely holding corporate communions at occasional suppers of grape and agape.

"Amen."

Peace be with thee. Does peace mean absolution too?

Suddenly, but not for the nonce only, the erstwhile lover of one Lilian Cloud besobered himself at the thought of her stoic hardships in consequence of his pagan selfishness. So stupidly had he left her with child! And so indifferently, as late as yesterday afternoon, had he glanced at the daughter, while all his analytic faculties were confounded by the stunning reappearance of the mother—and by the sudden resurrection of his desire for what had been a nulliparous embodiment. Four years ago, following the last catamenial relief of fear for his bachelorhood, which he forgot to renew in the next fortnight of farewell, he had taken leave of her dreamy atonements and mountainous beatitudes to seek his retrogressive fortune in the

East. He'd hardly noticed when there was no answer to his last three or four letters. Now for the first time he knew that in silence she'd travailed and borne the aftermath. Nor was she bitter or sarcastic. A radiant apparition of friendliness, she'd seemed almost as surprised as he at their intersection after three thousand miles of diverging time.

"And with thy spirit."

His dark moon he had called her: with moods ever waxing or waning, always heavier or lighter in spirit, but never frivolous or popular, and never attracted to the crowd. But that successful contrast to an earlier romance (immaturely passionate in its cascade of frustrations, violent to his soul) had amazed him from beginning to end. Loving him well, she had reserved nothing expressible, raised no claim, and strengthened him enough to leave her, uncomplaining about his insensitivity even to the pains that he might have guessed in her.

O Lord Jesu Christ, who through this sacrifice hast graciously received the bread and wine of our humanity here offered, into thine Incarnate Life . . . At the moment Caleb was more concerned with the miracle of simply mortal coupling. He was inclined to cherish the ecstasy of one or both in the dual atonement of man and woman as more mysterious than a mere profane by-product of the instinctual drive for relief that perpetuates the species. In the superfluous beatitude of a woman, aside from evolutionary function, it was more effective than pure metaphor at breaching the boundary of the system we live in. But at least he was levelheaded enough to acknowledge that the Jews in their long intelligent search for successful sacrifice had proved that even on the highest places neither sexual oblation nor sexual transport nor sexual communication was the way to the Holy Spirit in mankind's desperate appeal for grace.

His appetite for the illusions of erotic experience was not abated by understanding that the satisfaction of private valences occurs between self-serving gametes which can bond to each other only intermittently at best, in pairs, never to all the others, even in the grossest of orgies. The immaculate conception of Jesus Christ and his celibacy as the perfectly normal Son of Man (exactly six feet high, Yeats kept reminding his readers) were plain indications that the sacrament for humanity's salvation from its own progressive fatuity was chosen without regard to the device of natural evolution. A communion so exclusively dichotomous, enabled only by the extreme sensibility of gender, so unevenly available to young and old, so unjust to the ill-favored, so subject to the biochemical condition of individuals, so psychically delicate, and on any particular occasion so uncertain of consequence—whether as brute limbic act of reproduction, as impudent display of lust, as jewel of games, as epithalamian friendship, or as lovely mystic romance—would never have been assigned by a perceptive god to serve as the transcendentally effective sacrament for a whole church.

. . . return now, we beseech thee, thyself to us within this Holy Communion of thy Body and Blood; and with thyself entrust into our hands our own lives again, here consecrated and made one with thee: Who with God the Father, in the unity of the Holy Ghost . . .

Lilian's formerly broad face was now thinned and more refined in animation. She seemed more slender overall, as if at his desertion she'd shed the flesh of childhood and disclosed the underlying independent beauty. Wasn't she lighter in tread, lither in movement, tauter in speech, and less diffident in gesture? Parturition must have ended all her somnolent gestations. Or perhaps the subsequent burdens of maternity had provoked a latent competence for outer life. There side by side in the bustle of Harry's Delicatessen, with a daughter tugging at her sleeve, he hadn't dared ask if there was a man making her look so happy.

The astonishment of seeing her had evaporated the years, dissolved the mountains plains and rivers of continental space. At the pang in his heart, the blush in his face, a fog was clapped over his brain like the benighting hood on a hunter's hawk. For a moment he was dumbfounded at the stranger. But nothing dampened the lightning that instantly rehearsed long-forgotten chains of sensation at the sound of her voice.

As they descended from their stools at the lunch counter and walked down to the waterfront, hobbled by a child who might grow fretful, her story was rapidly hinted by the significance of her obvious news, and her reticent information was enough to recast the long slanting light of his memory. Seen ex post facto, she'd been heroic all along. Taking his leave as she got into a car immeasureably more respectable than his own, he wondered at her entirely new air of self-sufficiency, which, in persuading him that he'd loved her without interruption, deepened his jealousy of her unknown adventures. Her friendly reserve only inflamed his guesses.

"Amen." of course.

Next, the third commensal prayer, unequivocal antidote to the martyred Cranmer, now said by Father Lucey as Father Duncannon modestly listened, along with the Irishborn lady Theodora Cibber, local friend of the Laboratory (yet adherent to High Church piety). Some of the pragmatic Members are impatient at a devotional explanation right here in the Anamnesis. Father Davy would like a faster transition to the liturgical business at hand.

Let the partaking of thy Body and Blood, O Lord Jesu Christ, to which, by the enabling action of the Holy Ghost, we now draw near, fill us with that power which belongs alone to thee; that going forth in the eternal virtue of these Holy Gifts, to garner more of human life within the blessed order of thy Kingdom here in earth, we may return a richer and more perfected offering when next we bring our bread and wine to thine Anamnesis: Who livest and reignest with God the Father, in the unity of the same Holy Ghost, God, world without end.

But Caleb constantly fears that the degradation of mentality has gone too far for corporate regeneration. In ad hoc unity of interest, under benign leadership, it has been possible to put down waves of fascism; but it's too late to invoke even the Holy Ghost in offering to withstand the irreversible tide of the Atlantean plague infecting every hearth and inn with mental sloth. There's no hope in resisting the overwhelmingly unopposed epidemic of anti-autoimmunity when it's spread by devilvision. Our Antichrist is no mere prince of reversible darkness or whore of perishable Babylon, still less a rebel leader outcast in the cause of Promethean liberty, but the Evil Eye itself: disembodied, inorganic, ubiquitous, artificially replicated, more prolific than Sin the daughter of Satan's head (bred in incest to her father), more virulent than the money in it.

Still, what Caleb dreads more absolutely, sometimes to the point of all but immediate terror—what no one not only would be unable to resist but also could not abstain from or recuse as a dissident or surreptitious individual, whether critic, consumer, child, or dog—is that the gradual corruption of sensibility will be cut short by the sudden catastrophic consummation of dispirited matter's proclivity for disorder. He half believes the Fall of Man is yet to come. Mankind's final artifacts, though not demotically contagious like the seeping sugary Atlantean disease, already exist in the possession of two history-hating enemies: fabricated Zero-coefficients that will all at once reverse and undo all evolution since axe and Babel. The agony of all living things will instantly become infinite for as long as it can last, first equalizing and then canceling all miseries with practically unlimited concentrations of entropy.

Although it turned out that Jewish physics hadn't been necessary to save Europe by the skin of its teeth from Nazi application of the same science, in the summer of 1945 it had been psychologically impossible to refrain from forestalling fate in Japan. But from now on E-bombs will need no time to reverse the growth of time. They will dispense with time when they disintegrate all works—even the works of Jews for Pharaoh and for Hitler. Nothing will remain but unread signs, like the legend over the gate at Auschwitz, "Arbeit macht Frei", or Dogtown's granite memorial:

WHEN WORK STOPS
VALUES DECAY.

History and all the arts will be coterminous with me.

The Anamnesis as memento mori. He confesses himself possessed like almost everyone else with little private eddies of hope while all together the nations have only a last few minutes of warning to look for the gift of grace long since offered by the Son of Man. Our sublunary gyre will end, and soon, if its Christian beneficiaries continue to abuse their privileged theophysics. He's ashamed that he can't keep his mind on the grand hope and despair, because he believes that it will take "the whole state of Christ's church" to dismantle the ultimate products of Novum Organum before all our works are timelessly annihilated by the White Death of humanly determined entropy.

Nothing secular alone can save us—not even government by women. They are by instinct the better people, as the old lady professes; but intellectually they're no less confused. Without common theory, the means to coordinate all kinds of hearts, even femininity will come to the end of time. But the Vine needs time, as much as soil and light, for phylaxis and growth, just as I need more time than I can ever be granted to finish the idio-work I already have in mind.

He tries to imagine what the Father Founder feels so late in life about his apparent failure as a leader of Tudor counterdeformation. Long ago it was the question of anti-entropy that led Lancelot Duncannon step by step from his boyhood love of the Cape Gloucester Power, Light, and Traction system to the friendship of Ezra Schrödinger. Only in Christian metanoia after youth was gone did he see a way from the philosophical chiasm of a physics mesmerized by polar interests in elementals and universals to the irreducible mystery of theodynamics—like Sadi Carnot, an engineer, seeing the bottom of thermodynamics before even the First Law was discovered, to say nothing of the Second.

It seems to Caleb that Father Duncannon has anticipated a quickening in the waters of the stream ahead that someday will give way to the thunderous precipice which no merely scientific "raft of reason" can negotiate. The practical scientist arrived at priesthood by identifying God's perpetual metacosmic grace as praeternaturally organic energy, the topical will to order and growth which is ordinarily recognized as "negative entropy" but which is axiologically even less negative than Keats's poetic sensibility, and which he therefore redenominated as *counter*entropic. He liked to jest that Maxwell's Demon had been his guardian angel during the years of estrangement from the church of his fathers.

"Amen."

But there will be no response to the celebrant's silent (not secret) prayer that finally initiates the physical act of communion: *I will receive the bread of heaven, and call upon the name of the Lord. Blessed is he that cometh in the name of the Lord, Hosanna in the highest* [†].

And with *The Body of our Lord Jesus Christ,* Father Lucey consumes both parts of the broken host. My awkwardly courtly friend, too large for this tiny altar and low ceiling, bowing and genuflecting [√], pauses in caesura of motion between the two elements of his communion ex officio. He eats bread and drinks wine for love of all the world—while I stir up fire from the image of a single broken moon-wafer. I summon up memories of a certain female body's genius for lunar possession. I'm enthralled by my merely personal existence.

But now I know the girl herself was not enthralled. Alone in poverty, already frantic for the time and space to do the work in art she lived for more than love, she chose to bring her woman-child into the world. That supreme impediment could have been sloughed off as a bit of blood and mucous, with the clandestine assistance of the lecherous old scholar in Hume who'd once been a lecturer at the medical school across the Bay and practiced for the smallest of fees in vengeful defiance of the State of Cornucopia.

Indeed Caleb is finding that the ashes he raked had only been banked, no more extinguished for lack of draft than quiescent fuel for hell. "The moon-coals blazed!" he immediately wrote her last night, hoping to evoke in her prevailing memory the slow indolent sensuality with which she'd always approached crescendos immensely more vivacious than any other happiness she showed. (One of the few things he got out of her was an address in Taraville.) But he tore up the letter because he knew she would not trust poetic words.

Unlike Bice, she wasn't the sort of girl who always had a flock of men after her, and was therefore chary of man's praises—presumably of his especially, considering that he'd given exceedingly abstract reasons for leaving her. In those days she'd had no confidence in her allure, except when her clothes were off and he could examine the full extent of it. Now that most of the abstract reasons no longer obtained, having been satisfied forgotten or revised, he felt too fatuous to ask if it was simply joy in the daughter that made her look as if she was never depressed.

But even if there were no man in her bed, she'd not easily be won back by an unreliable opportunist who has as little intention as ever of asking her to be his wife. She knows instinctively that the small problem of desire overshadows all my anxieties about human suffering and culture, and in my most spontaneous response even takes precedence over my evaluation of absolute work. My perspective is so shallow, my selfishness so colossal, like Faust's, that miscalculated attempts at carefree wenching have occluded proper worry about the whole age of the Last Testament! And now may it be that I'm falling in love for the very purpose of escaping impersonal responsibilities? If so, it has happened more than once, generally to my discomfort—yet never to my regret! But a woman with a child unclaimed by any other man! How suddenly my aversion has been overturned! How quickly a younker's categorical distaste can be converted to craving curiosity!

Having eaten his bread and paused, ostensibly for a little space of meditation, Father Lucey now uncovers the cup, genuflects [√], and with the traditional Petrine prayer prepares himself to drink: *What return shall I make unto the Lord for all the benefits that he hath done me? I will receive the cup of salvation, and call upon the name of the Lord. I will call upon the Lord which is worthy to be praised; so shall I be safe from my enemies.* [Motioning † with the chalice itself.]

Caleb is not caught dreaming of love: with his bell [*] he calls the congregation to communion, rises, and steps over to stand at the gospel side, as the priest announces, for himself: *The Blood of our Lord Jesus Christ.*

While the other communicants are coming up to kneel at the altar, the ungainly priest in undersized vestments performs his part with surprising felicity, speaking his lines in sweet unostentatious tones modulated by the simple humility of his special case. Caleb's affection wells up with gratitude and pity.

No doubt Mrs Cibber the sole outsider was aware of sacerdotal charm in the performance of Father Duncannon's wellspoken but kinetically ungraceful coadjutor (known to her from tea parties) celebrating as smoothly as he could a rite somewhat too formal for his personality: withal a youthful-looking officer of the church who chose to dedicate his maturity to a special cause which she admired without appreciation. But Father Duncannon, now coming forward at the summons of the congregation: what did he hear in the voice that he had led to that holy office? How much did the mentor know or suspect? Of how much had he repeatedly absolved this psychologist he'd brought into the church despite a neurosis that might embarrass his Vine's respectable antithesis to the institution?

But you couldn't have a monastery inhabited by an abbot alone. Chris Lucey had been free and willing to utter the classic renunciations. He clove to his privileged position, without rivals, in fated love for a childless father just weak enough to bless a prodigal against better judgment and in the face of exasperation at every level.

Yet, after all, Chris owed his unique position in the Order of the Vine to his ordination in the global holy order of the aboriginal Melchizedek which "forever" entailed a broader obligation and a universal power. After the "Druid priest" who founded that brotherhood all but one of the fathers (including Aaron and David)—all but one, who took upon himself the total burden of sacrifice, not for power or glory, or even for salvation, but for the humiliation of love—remained imperfect. Who could draw the line from which to throw a stone? But whether or not Father Lucey should be found worthy at the last, the Mass he made was good.

Chris assumed a boldness in working his irrevocable responsibility. "My Christian name is Christopher." he told Caleb as he drove the Nicolet with one hand at seventy-five. "I don't have to be a saint or martyr to do the job God gave me. My personal redemption is the least of his concerns. According to the twenty-fifth Article of Religion, the sacraments must be worthily received; but the twenty-sixth allows that one need not worthily dispense them. The church can relieve a priest of active duty—depose, debar, defrock him, or accept his resignation—but his commission can never be invalidated. The priesthood happens to be my only way to the Eucharist." Laughingly he added one of the Order's mottoes: "And *How shall we escape if we neglect such a great salvation?* —Besides, Father Duncannon's branch of the Vine needs me as a money-pump." The mollification in his voice effaced the self beneath it, and disarmed analysis of its spiritual logic. Caleb wondered if his friend ever dared thus confess himself to ecclesiastical colleagues or extramural superiors.

The priest having partaken himself of bread and wine with his back to the people, and having prepared to housel them with the same, he turns to show the bread as a fragment of wimple-white moon held between thumb and forefinger above the silver paten supported by his other hand. *Behold the Lamb of God; behold him that taketh away the sins of the world.*

"Blessed is he that cometh in the name of the Lord, [†] Hosanna in the highest." Caleb leads the response of the people now kneeling by him at the altar—Father Duncannon and Mrs Cibber, whom he'd immediately admired for her sympathetic mien and educated speech, for her Celtic maturity beautified by fine wrinkles of patience gentility and unassuming wisdom—and was prepared to love as an exemplary mother, without disloyalty to the stronger one who'd brought him into the world. But this calm and gentle grandam had no need for another and slighter son, no matter how sympathetic, in her big sturdy family.

Over cupped palms of acolyte and visitor (both of whom hold to this bit of Low tradition), and the extended tongue of the Superior (who undogmatically prefers the symbol of immaculate consumption), each in turn, three times in all: *The Body* [†] *of our Lord Jesus Christ.*

During this distribution and reception the wonderful silence was solemn and intimate. The unleavened bread for these communicants was not a piece of the fractured disc that the priest has displayed, nor was it a shard torn from one whole loaf (the original practice, preferred in principle), but a small circle so light that it looked as bluish as skim milk and tasted like a dry snowflake. As they swallowed in turn it occurred to the participating attendant that a communal manducation of crusty crumby bread, if not deafening to the chewer herimself, would have sounded funnier than a row of cleaned-up cows munching grain at their stanchions in the peace that follows a milking.

Hastily, for fear of giggling, he turned his thoughts back to the human particulars of the present company that he (by far the youngest and least faithful) felt honored to serve. Kneeling at a right angle to Mrs Cibber, as she bent to eat from her hands the wheaten coin placed therein by a priest whose life would have been incomprehensible to her if she'd heard it suggested, Caleb covertly observed the lovely lines creasing her eyelids and the refinement of her delicately aging mouth. Perhaps she was not the only educated wife of a Dogtown fisherman; but in youth her lips like those of Irish scholars from time immemorial had learned to exchange with native speakers all the languages of Switzerland. Her waggish husband Wat was rarely expected to appear with her on public occasions, or to share her tastes, let alone religion. This morning she had walked to the Laboratory through wet snow brought by the full moon's equinoctial storm, along with brimming high tides and surf above the breakwater.

Then there was the Father Superior at his unaccustomed turn on the people's side of the footpace, humbly kneeling next to Mrs Cibber in his plain soutane, the undress uniform he loved. After his scientific career was well begun he'd taken to the cloth partly out of a determination to renounce the silver spoon of provincial aristocracy that had served his quietly brilliant headstart in education. Yet, he'd told Caleb, "until I decided to study for holy orders in England, I was a docile student and conventional worker. I didn't learn to think for myself until I was forty. My learning had been merely acquisitive, almost totally passive, and I wasn't much more than a high-church aesthete even when I took to hanging around with Chittering and all those literary people. When I met Gregory Dix, and then got to know Schrödinger, I realized I hadn't been taught to criticize symbols. I'd always been interested in thermodynamics, but I was really aimless in doing science of my own. Until I began to find connections and see the larger system of things, almost too late, I was no wiser than any other precocious dilettante." But what precocity! The providence of his erudition! As an amateur philologist expatriating himself from a culture of steam and electric power, Lancelot Duncannon had wandered into theoretical physics because Mark Planck, a friend of his uncle's, suggested to him "If you're going to study languages, you ought to learn something about scientific terminology here in Berlin". Thus he was referred to Waldemar Nernst, and began to devote his mind to mesocosmic energy.

Now Father Lucey held a silver drinking horn before his flock: *The Blood of our Lord Jesus Christ*. This priest—companion and aide to the other, but no epigone in culture—was far less concerned with thermodynamics than with endocrinology. Though some medical friend had provided him with the latter term for his one span of interest in science it was on his own that he recognized and expanded its behavioral significance. On the literary side a fortuitous intersection of fascinations had fixed his otherwise careless memory on the third ring of the Seventh Circle, that annulus of endless toil for suicides as well as usurers and sodomites—whereof he proposed the hypothesis that at least two of the three proclivities therein represented could be explained by shared biochemical characteristics. He continually sought ideas to account for their assignment to a category in common.

"I know that suicide will be my final sin." he once remarked, this time driving at eighty. At the moment Caleb himself was feeling too little pain to be scared, and anyway remained confident of Chris's motivation to persevere in the service and protection of Father Duncannon as long as the concurrence of both their lives was possible. That coexistence made Chris's life not only bearable but also useful and exciting.

In any case Caleb had learned from childhood the futility and danger of arguing against suicidal histrionics. Such words were not to be protested; he pretended to pass them over as metaphorically expressive of Chris's less cheerful feelings, as if the priest was a poet. In truth the young confidant was temperamentally still too buoyant to have developed his own poetic sensibility along any lines at all (except those of a troubadour-manqué); and he had grown rather callous to the concept of that sin, as of certain others—notwithstanding his rare analytical efforts to recall the premature cicatrization of his psyche that seemed to have blunted his perception of other psyches' suffering.

They taste the cup, sweet and warming. After only a morsel of diaphanous bread the single swallow of communion wine is distinctly alimentary.

Owing perhaps to the unbounded ebullience set afoot by yesterday's astonishing revival of an old love, for the second time that morning, in the short silence of refreshment, Caleb had to suppress an outburst of untimely imagination. This time he was trying to ward off the memory of when, as cosmopolitan schoolboy at a Montvert village church, he had fought down his convulsive snicker at an amazingly solemn communion of grape juice, uneasily endured in the hard pews by a sparse cold congregation of strictly individual souls for whom it was an annual elective gesture. The vestigial ceremony, as a token acknowledgment of one event recorded in the all-important Word, was sufficiently purged of priestcraft, dumbshow, and bibulous pleasure; but the disjunction seemed to embarrass even the minister, and wasn't explained by any of the prayers. After the tiny half-filled glasses were mutely passed around in the sockets of a chrome double-layered tray, man woman and child waited for the silent cue to raise the thimbles to their lips, as if, strangers gathered for the first time, they were toasting an unfamiliar cause with champagne too good for their stations in life. In the silence, who among them did not fear a solitary fart? Then, with a prolonged quiet clinking, the tray was passed again to collect the empties.

Caleb forces his thoughts to avert laughter by attempting to compare the present comedy in which he sincerely plays the part of a classic worshipper. But self-examination isn't much his wont, and today there's no use trying to think about what he's there for. At times he has at least in part succeeded: the action of some Masses has engaged his heart and mind. But he believes himself well enough committed even when heart and mind are absent. So long as he attends regularly, the liturgical flywheel will carry him through to the next time—him and the whole world. The corporate act will take care of itself. At this Eucharist Mrs Cibber may be the only one now concentrating on the sense of the rite. There has been no sermon to make the rest of us think about what we're doing. Yet to think is not the purpose of doing. Should I rather say that the purpose of doing is not to think? Or, if often done, to think of something else?

The other day Chris chided me with his praise: "You're brainy and neurological, seldom at the mercy of your chemistry. You control your emotions electrically. That's why you can be objective about your subjectivity. That's how you're able to imagine things with discipline. Your mind is analytically synthetic, like Leonardo's." Caleb didn't much like the lefthanded comparison with one incapable of writing a play.

Yet Chris wasn't boasting about himself, as one of his secular companions might have been, when he said "I'm merely chemical and emotional, nothing but a creature of my blood stream. Hormones are certainly a man's humours—only I think there are combinations of more than four!"

At that moment Chris was probably thinking of the most public of his three secret "proclivities". If he's able to interest Arthur Halymboyd in Paraclete Biochemical Corporation—or maybe especially if he isn't—I'm afraid he'll sell all our Parity and put everything directly into that hormone outfit. Of course such a divagation of investment by Parity itself would spoil my pipe dream of systematic industrial management. I almost wish I'd never called that company to his attention. Still, he's right: we may have discovered the greatest growth-stock of the decade. I shouldn't let my electrical proclivity for schematic organization stand in the way of an adventitious speculation that might vastly profit the Vine in benefiting the whole world order. Of course he's not interested in contraception for the same reasons I am; but the way he's begun to rave about steroids, you'd never suspect he doesn't know any better than I why they're called that.

According to one of his casuistic hypotheses, the Trustees' equity in Paraclete, which he describes as a high-risk property not unlike partnership in a Venetian argosy, would be less susceptible to the stigmatization of usury than the present diversification of its investments through Parity, which regularly issues dividends. Above all, such an investment could never be reprehended as even partially militaristic or socially deleterious. On the contrary, nothing can do more than birth control to reduce poverty and stave off the Apocalypse. People will never stop fucking.

The pharmaceutical industry is naturally the one to concoct pseudopharmacals; and within the industry a laboratory that specializes in fertility steroids might be expected to invent an anticounterentropy-wafer for keeping women as rhythmic as the moon. I've always believed that carefree atonement would be a harmless boon of magic. The alleviation of anxiety might breed more jealousy, not less; but generally the aggressions of society would be somewhat mollifed. And little I in particular might be at less of a competitive disadvantage if girls felt freer to experiment.

On the other hand, if women's suffrage is thus enhanced, it seems equally possible that my kind will lose all the claims it's staked.

Grant, O Lord, says the priest under his breath, beginning the prayers of ablution as he clears the table and cleans up his dishes, *that what we have taken with our mouths we may receive with singleness of mind and heart: and in this temporal gift may we partake of thine eternal power,* assisted by his acolyte, who has swiftly risen to fetch the two cruets by their handles and step up closer to the middle of the altar than at any other time. Without deigning to turn his head the lordly servant of God extends and lowers the chalice in his right hand; his own server pours a little unconsecrated wine, as detergent or disinfectant for the sacred vessel, and steps back down off the dais as the drops are swished and quaffed. *Let thy Body, O Lord, which we have taken, and thy Blood which we have drunk, cleave to our members: and grant that no stain of sin may again find place in us, whom thou hast refreshed with this pure and holy sacrament: Who livest and reignest, world without end. Amen.*

In this Caleb's most complex spate of action, inessential to the liturgy yet important to the style and pleasure of practical routine, the duty of a footman renders him officious in spite of himself. As a bowing servitor it seems to him he seems to onlookers excessively ceremonious. But there's no more seemly way to get the job done.

The lofty priest turns to lurch in his direction, now bowing too, and depresses the goblet between his palms, pairs of Aaronite thumbs and forefingers curled across the diameter in order to be rinsed by the wine and water which are thereupon poured by the lesser Levite— first a little wine from the cruet in his right hand and then more than that of water from the left: a pragmatic dash of life's general solvent to wash the hands of the priest. Then there at the step, briskly addorsing themselves, the master swings back to the center and drains the scourings like a thirsty housewife as he tidies up his formal mess, while the butler returns his less hallowed vessels to the little pantry table, replaces the stoppers, blows out the credence candle, and returns to stand at the Epistle horn. And this is not the last of it; nor is there time to savor its kinesthetics. It's not yet rote for Caleb: he must summon consciousness for every step of the procedure.

The priest of course has learned much more intricate business for this interval of cooperative housekeeping during which his helper's service has reached its petty climax. His tasks screened from layfolk by the encrusted purple turtleback of his poncho, the officiant at the altar wipes his mouth unhurriedly and then cleanses the giant silver eggcup with a flatworked strip of starched linen, which having been crumpled must be lightly refolded (like other napery spoiled during the meal) and built into the dressed ensemble to which the vessels are restored for their journey back to the sacristy on a single stem. The brocaded purple corporal lies flat on top of the chalice, like the mortarboard of an academic cap—a lid to steady the tent that clothes the assembly in stiffly triangulated skirts of matching device and color.

But first the server must shift that heavy opaque veil, because it still lies folded lengthwise on the Epistle side of the Lord's Table (or Tomb, as some Scholastics hold), occupying just the place that will presently be required for the missal. So Caleb steps forward to take up the thickly purpled cloth of gold, retreating meticulously to the horn he's been working from, and carries it all along the rectangular perimeter, genuflecting [√] at the center, to lay it on the opposite side, only three feet from whence it came, for the minor convenience of the priest in finding it at his left.

Yet suave busboy's rather long trip also serves a reciprocal need: for he thereupon lifts the opened missal in its portable lectern, and with both hands bears it on a V-line all the way back to where the veil had lain, setting the book exactly where the priest can step over to read the Communion Sentence without separating his devoutly steepled pairs of fingers. (It's presumably in consideration of his burden that the server is allowed to cut the corners of the predella and at the invert of his return merely to bow his neck in reverence to the tabernacle). But then once more Caleb crosses the stage by its apron, past the center [√] as usual, in order to stand at the Gospel side with his own hands at the gothic and listen for cues.

Meanwhile: *Give heed! A virgin will conceive and bear a son. His name will be Emmanuel.* Which means: God with us. The priest moves to the center of the altar, bends to kiss it, and again faces the people, as if to acknowledge society's claims by returning to the secular world after finishing his sacred duties. *The Lord be with you.*

"And with thy spirit."

Let us pray. [Again the acolyte leads the people in kneeling.] *Pour forth, we beseech thee, O Lord, thy grace into our hearts: that we, to whom the incarnation of Christ thy Son was made known by the message of an angel, may by his passion and cross be brought to the glory of his . . .*

Why is the resurrection so damned necessary?

Having once more swung around to kiss the altar (devilishly low for a man so high), Father Lucey again addresses the people: a priest off duty, a fisherman's wife, and a server. *Dominus vobiscum.*

A Latin element had been advisedly retained by the generally revisionary scriptwriter. As in the matter of vestments, without denying the incidental comfort of mere tradition, Father Duncannon cherished this allusion to the vernacular of the primitive church for its convection of historical substance, notwithstanding the mild objections of some Members who would dispense with all such remnants of Scholasticism. But the hereditarily privileged savant, lacking a common touch, insisted that social democracy was one of his liturgical principles, and he could hardly have been less aware than the radicals of his own susceptibility to the archaism he deplored in the High Church, or of his equally unwarranted vulnerability to charges of the very sentimentality that he soundly attacked in the Low. Yet he fastidiously grieved that Greek and Latin would soon be swept away with Cranmer's English beauties in the spirit of liberation that he himself was stirring up.

"Et cum spiritu tuo."

Ita, Missa est. Go back to work in the world, for the Mass has been made. The repast of sacrifice is over. Once again we assimilate common metabolic substance.

"Deo gratias." For the means and ends of sacrifice, the Eucharist.

When we're on our good behavior we not only give thanks before a meal but also say grace afterwards, in courtesy to both provider and companions, affording ourselves time to savor the moment's ease from need and appetite, and to compose ourselves for the profanity to which we must return. Thus the propriety of a coda to the liturgy, in which the representative of Christ affirms its myth theologically, without redundantly or gratuitously blessing those who are plainly blessed already by the matter now consumed: *Let this our bounden duty and service be pleasing unto thee, O Holy Trinity: and grant that this sacrifice, which by thy grace we have here offered, may be acceptable to thee, and through thy mercy obtain thy gracious favor both for us and all for whom it has been made. Through Christ, our Lord.*

Just as the priest bows at his concluding kiss of the altar, the acolyte, having risen with perfect backfield timing and stepped to the right, sinks [√] to one knee; and continues to the Epistle side as the priest, his manual work completed, moves stage right in the opposite direction a pace or two across the front of the altar, hands pressed palm to palm beneath his chin. The work is all done; yet lo, a traditional antistrophe has yet to run its course! The acolyte turns forty-five degrees half-left-face to honor the Last Gospel, standing diagonally below the purpled mock-turtle, who towers over an altar-card text known practically by heart even to ministers with overburdened memories.

But these first fourteen verses of John the Evangelist—Greek echoes of the first lines of the Hebrew book—are here read without all the signs and flourishes that embellished this anticlimactic prolongation of the Dismissal by Tudor Classicism. At this point the five-year-old in the convent chapel had assisted Father Pole much more ceremoniously, as he now remembered. Then there'd been yet another shifting of the missal stand for a bit of variable lection to introduce this invariant Gospel; and he'd held the card up to those kindly old eyes rimmed by stern circles of black horn. But now at a distance he only stands and waits—except at the pause of reverence for the mention of Christ's incarnation, an illustrative as well as obeisant genuflection just before the end, when he dips in perfect unison with the penitent confessor, and they tarry for a moment in the slow flex and reflex of fully bended knee without quite interrupting the continuity of movement, to observe the keynote of Christian doctrine:

In the beginning was the Word, and the Word was with God, and the Word was God. The same was in the beginning with God. All things were made by him: and without him was not anything made that was made: in him was life, and the life was the light of men: and the light shineth in darkness, and the darkness comprehended it not—i e , never subsumed it. *There was a man sent from God whose name was John.* An earlier John than the author, but of course also a Jew, an Essene, who saw like the prophets before him that Jewish sacrifice had failed even in the Temple. *The same came for a witness, to bear witness of the light, that all men through him might believe. He was not that light, but was sent to bear witness to that light. That was the true light, which lighteth every man that cometh into the world. He was in the world, and the world was made by him, and world knew him not. He came unto his own, and his own received him not,* seeing that he held no doctorate or even master's degree and hadn't been elected. *But as many as received him, to them gave he power to become the sons of God, even to them,* circumcised or not, *that believed on his name: which were born, not of blood, nor of the will of the flesh, but of God. And the Word was made flesh,*
[√]
and dwelt among us. The priest slowly turns toward the center, finishing from memory, while the acolyte mounts gravely to take the missal from its stand. *And we beheld his glory, the glory as of the Only-begotten of the Father, full of grace and truth.*

And so with the book at his chest Caleb begins the exodos of his service before the purpled Lenten altar by converging at the center with his purple-clad master who bears the chalice purple-panoplied. Together they execute their respective rightangles and descend from the platform of the tiny chapel side by side. On the flagstones, facing again toward each other, they turn about elbow to elbow and curtsey [√] joint farewell to the tabernacle, as the little bird, freeing his right arm from the ventral burden, picks up the biretta by one of its flanges and with a sidewise inclination of his head hands it to the ostrich. Perched upon the pale bald skull, noticeably narrower than the ludicrous winglet ears, it makes the lofty priest all the more impressive. The small one, gliding rapidly on smooth knee and supple ankle, though he prefers Father Duncannon's more dignified pace, leads the long loping strides of softly galumphing feet out through the arched stone doorway, low enough to require a further ducking of the head that's always inclined, wherever it goes, to downplay the conspicuousness of altitude.

In the sacristy Chris mumbles half a sentence of prayer, and they bow to each other for the last time in their first altar service together. Father Pole used to have Sister Agnes the sacristan to help divest him of chasuble, amice, stole, maniple, cincture, and alb—to the best of Caleb's recollection exactly reversing the private ceremony that had preceded the Introit; but here with Chris in the cold and slightly dusty liturgical supply room, a stony closet of the underpopulated monastery, procedures are fast and in this case almost sloppy. The Laboratory of Melchizedec and the Mesocosm provides no special wardrobes clothespresses or other commodious furniture to be kept immaculate and fragrant by a handmaid. The celebrant undresses himself while his one servant undresses the altar.

Caleb hung his cotta on a hook. In his unadorned black cassock, the skirted garment of priests, snugly buttoned from neck to toe, he took the half-arched brass candlesnuffer back into the sanctuary with an unctuous grace he was unable to disguise despite the effort to show himself as a plain and simple servingman. The arena was a little warmer than the tiring room, but Mrs Cibber in worn and shapeless storm clothes was kneeling with straight back and bent neck behind one of the chairs that was exposed to the draft kept in motion by outward conduction of heat through the french doors.

He knew she was called Teddi by Mrs Keith and her friends. He was again struck by the beauty upon her, the slight smile made by small folds at the corners of her level lips, and smitten with a pang resembling jealousy: envy of her sons, even platonically fanciful rivalry with her husband. Was it absurd to respond so deeply to a middle-aged matron's face with whom he was so slightly acquainted? A Theodora whose features after all bore a certain typological resemblance to his mother's Mary—to whom twenty-five years ago no angel would ever have said "The Holy Spirit will come upon you, and the power of the Most High will cover you with its shadow; therefore the child to be born will be called holy, the Son of God"—but whose behavior was surely very different.

Smoothly [√] smoothly: Gospel candle first—the light that must never burn without the escort of another; stage right, reach to extinguish the flame of the Evangel. Then at the foot, in recrossing the center, dip the knee [√] again, and rise up to smother with pungent puff of smoke the valiant Epistle. [√] He turns to leave once more.

Mrs Cibber was stirring now. Even Father Duncannon hadn't waited for the altar boy to douse the yellow flames; like all the pragmatic professionals and busy communicants of the world hurrying off to duty or pleasure who annoyed this fastidious acolyte everywhere he attended Mass, the reverend mentor had taken his leave as soon as the celebrant disappeared with his grail. Caleb grudgingly understood that this apparent discourtesy was a trifle of homely custom, smaller in importance than many another point of manner or syntax, and he realized that his lone objection could hardly proclaim it egregious; but to him it seemed incongruous to preserve the protocol of lights so punctiliously and yet to abandon the living candles to a lackey's euthanasia—indeed to desert them instanter, scarcely waiting for the door to close upon the celebrant's recession, even before the servant can reappear with his snuffer. It was a disrespect he vowed never to join, like one of the standard new solecisms of language against which he remained personally stubborn. He would never abuse *loan* as a verb or *real* as an adverb; it went against his grain, like painting white trim on colored houses, or like leaving a woman, as if having lost interest in her, before the minutes of beatitude were over.

But Mrs Cibber had the delicacy to wait for Samuel not only to put the quietus to the Epistle fire, leaving the chapel colder, but also to put the altar to rest under its unfolded blue dust cloth, and to slip away at last! But of course it may have been that her private devotions just happened to come to an end as he made his final exit. It may have been nothing but the gathering of skirts that postponed her earlier departure.

He thought of raising the question with Father Duncannon, to whom it might not be entirely unworthy of discussion as a point of minor heraldic significance. He was bound to be offered some systemic principle by which to dissolve this unmomentous pedantry of scruple. Once more he would be obliged to convict himself of making distinctions that made no difference even to the most differentiating master of ceremonies. No doubt the highest of his authorities would dispel this compunction of etiquette as easily as a false point of genteel grammar. It would turn out to be another straw target of obsession, much too fussy for healthy operation in a world of cultural evolution. He blamed it as another symptom of his timidity. He had always been too polite—even to Lilian, when he hadn't been bold enough to remember to ask about a last disproof of dread annunciation before he went and forsook her.

13
LENT

Both the Petrines and the Paulines of Dogtown, homines economici alike, were afraid the Pope was going to lift the sanctions of Lenten fasting, which as far as they were concerned differed from Elizabethan sumptuary law for fish chiefly in the calendar of consumption and only secondarily in motive; but he hadn't done so yet, and the presence of a Scholastic in the White House might stiffen the Papal resistance to modern indulgence. In any event, the peak of the city's daily domestic transport of frozen penance-food, for orders anticipating the necessary lags of distribution, came as far ahead of Easter as Ash Wednesday did. In public and private inventories all over the country refrigerated food warehouses were normally too full of meat and vegetables to accept much of this underrated merchandise any sooner; but now Mercator-Steelyard's stockpile of frozen fish, which had been accumulated over the first three quarters of its fiscal year, mainly in Jason Anacoluther's warehouse, was being rapidly discharged over the road.

Forty percent of a fish-packer's annual sales were billed in two months. Therefore the Yard's primary management problem was to maintain year-round production, which on a large scale was much more efficient than the old production-to-order custom of buying and cutting fish, and which had become technically possible when Frank Bacon the Elder led most of the fish processors from fresh to frozen marketing. His methods of preservation had made feasible not only reservoirs of finished product but also steady international supplies of raw material. Seasonal fluctuations of payroll were beginning to smooth out, much to the satisfaction of the Vinland Department of Unemployment's local office, where the off-season waiting lines for benefit checks were getting shorter, on the average, year by year.

Yet this objective remained in conflict with the extremes of seasonal demand. No genius in marketing was able to reduce costs by selling fish at a constant rate over twelve months, and the economics of inventory management—working capital and storage both supplied by Jason as principal banker and warehouser—still weighed nearly as heavily in accounting equations as the productivity of steady employment. Thus the problem of Lent continued to complicate Thad Kryothermsky's progress in industrial engineering, as assisted by his brother-in-law Buck Barebones the independent toolmaker.

This year Easter fell at its latest possible date; gypsy kilroy traffic hadn't yet subsided to its base level by the first of April. One Saturday afternoon Caleb and Ibi escaped the noise of Cod Street, which sometimes got on their nerves even at the back of the house when its most pronounced constituents were left isolated and particularly annoying after the recession of steady weekday components, by walking down to the river to see what was going on for the weekend at the nearly deserted Iron Works.

Almost always on his strolls about Dogtown Caleb gleaned one or two new ideas, simple or complex, to enrich the significance of the city that Doc sometimes called a "microtopopolis of dogs and gulls". Today he noticed on one of the mighty Iron Works presses a plate bearing the name of Lake Weary Steam and Hydraulic Machinery Manufacturing Company, which he recognized with a thrill as one of Parity's adopted children in the Laclede Aircraft cohort, thereby discovering yet another linkage in his network of Dogtown prehensions. And then, climbing the steep flight of wooden stairs up the face of the enclave's cliff to cross through the lumberyard of iron, he suddenly recognized the braced mast and boom of the electromagnet derrick as a swivel-rigged evolution of the rectotetrahedron.

Superexcited by these two "sentences of thought", with nerves already stimulated by the recent rediscovery of Lilian, he paused for the nth time as a repatriated topopolitan to contemplate the perspective of double railroad tracks expanding in his eye from the opposite shore known as the mainland—straight through the marsh to span the island's moat of laving brine. The embankment stretched like a dam across the estuary, a viaduct leading level rails onto the short naked deck of the drawbridge that bore trains high over the deep narrow sluiceway right into the heart of Dogtown. At the bottom of the canyon formed by spiled and planked abutments the channel of the Namauche River was constricted into one of its two narrowest and swiftest straits. But the exposed tracks on this draw, without balustrade or superstructure, were so much higher than the pavement of the Gut Bridge on the esplanade (just out of sight to the south) that it was opened far less often for small craft of business or pleasure.

Just then, however, by happy chance, though the tide was ebbing and the ravine nearly at its deepest, the bridgetender in unhasty response to the polite toot of an approaching horn emerged from his shabby little gray cube on the far side to cross the tracks and set his machinery agrinding. To Caleb's childish delight and Ibi's mature indifference, a heavily laden dragger was returning to the Harbor from John Smith's Bay. Rounding from under the high-flown arch of the Eisenhower Bridge (which carried the Massachusetts Felly clear above the most celestial masts), still trawling a dozen gulls by invisible lines in the air, it chugged into the foreground of Fox Hill and plowed down the reach for its sharp swing to starboard at this aperture in the causeway's long barrier.

As Caleb watched (and Ibi tried to figure out why he was standing still) the single bascule, hinged on the far side, began to tilt upward with a steady clanking groan, breaking the transcontinental circuit. From a distance it resembled the opening of a switch knife; but from here, accompanied by the unharmonized rumble of gearwheels in a fixed train of individual speeds pitches and circumferences, the grid of tied rails rising against the sky was more like the lattice of a castle's portcullis. In its brief pause of apogee the fishing boat glided under its tracery with none of the caution prescribed by official rules of inland piloting. Without a glance at the defile they traversed, a couple of Laodicean crewmen were gathering up their net on tackle suspended from the foremast.

Reversing into relaxation, with a polyphonal whine of interconnected gears and pinions now driven by weight alone, the drawbridge spun down to its clanking rest like the clamping jaw of an upsidedown sperm whale. As the bridgetender walked over to make sure the rails were properly rejoined the Medieval apparatus fell into lovely silence against the general background of softly woven sounds. Faint throbbings of family motors, shiftings of Cod Street traffic, cries and beats of children from Saturday households, the isolated barking of unhappy prisoners: all were almost mutely absorbed—not by the superconducting distances, not by the thickets shrouding the playground in a nearby hollow, not by the trees and overgrowth in a nearby colonial cemetery or the dwindled swamp between, nor by the mound of embrambled living rock and withered blueberry bushes also within the perimeter of tracks, river, streets, and wage-earning properties—but by each other.

Now Ibi was roaming ahead across the tracks in search of natural scents; but Caleb, looking both ways, once more analyzed with a traveler's pleasure the clever switches that gracefully connected the two parallel pairs of track and their sidings, precisely by the same devices—with the same binary options—by which the myriads they replicated made nodes for the network everywhere else on the continent. With his foot on a rail he felt interstate expectancies through the sole of his shoe, as once again he lamented the want of a spur track to the harbor.

Yet it was the sea that made his island European. Glancing also right and left, toward one ocean on the same plane at either hand, Caleb knew not whether he looked up river or down. He wondered just where in this Janus-mouthed cut the tidal race met and parted from itself. Where did the two opposing currents simultaneously begin and end? Did the null point shift, from day to day and moon to moon, like the channel midpoints of the Mississippi before it was fixed by the Corps of Engineers?

Turning toward home he noticed working lights in Dogtown Machine & Design. Impelled by interest and affection, he soon found himself and Ibi welcome at the shop. Buck was never too busy for a friend. Despite Caleb's acutely sympathetic compunction about encroaching upon a creative man's rare moments of solitude, he gladly accepted the opportunity to involve the master artificer in his own sculptural problem.

Neither by immaterial imagination nor by projective geometry on paper had he been able to satisfy himself whether or not six congruent isorectotetrahedrons could be made to occupy a cube. As a maker of customized machinery Buck's fancies and skills better qualified him for the challenges of complex articulation than for the abstract simplification of volumes; but he was a sweet man who never scorned unfamiliar arts merely on the grounds of inutility, and he asked no questions about the reasons for his young friend's crotchet.

So in all generosity, by way of empirical experiment, Buck was at once engaged by the practical problem of manufacturing from solid metal a handful of perfectly identical triangulated quadrants. The inventor was so piqued by this simple difficulty as a serious recreation, or as at least temporary relief from complex tasks of mundane design, that Caleb was embarrassed not to be a paying client. Even with the machine tools of a job-shop it was no easy challenge. They discussed alternatives of material and possible sequences of operation by saw lathe milling machine and grinder. Circles of power must convert rough bars or ingots into smoothly exact wholes and thirds of orthogonal corners!

The consultant's seriousness put the author's playful interest to shame, who began to regret his comparatively frivolous invasion of a busy brain's rare and precious meditation. Certainly for himself such fooling around was a seductive divagation akin to "creation without toil", like systems-theorization or literary criticism: the illusion of outflanking real work. But for Buck it was intrinsically important enough to displace a little of the utilitarian thinking he lived for and his family lived on. After nearly an hour of rather technical conversation Caleb unsuccessfully attempted to withdraw his request for suggestions, reiterating a conviction that his symbolic shapes better lent themselves to thought-experiments. He and Buck finally agreed to let the matter rest in their respective subconscious ateliers until next they met.

Meanwhile Ibi had found a tolerable cave in the darkened space between the cast-iron legs of an old drill press, which he preferred to all the idle lathes and milling machines along the same inside wall, not far from the pan of water that Buck kept fresh for random visitors willing to pay a call despite the smell of burnt oil and curled-up hot-shaved steel; and there he lay stretched out full on his side, his lips trembling and paws twitching in happily active dream, unreservedly confident of everyone's safety in Mr Barebones's curtilage. Ibi and Buck would have liked each other in person even if Buck had been a penniless bum and Ibi a starved stray kurdogge, notwithstanding Buck's manifest inattention to dogs as persons and Ibi's insensibility to artifacts. Ibi had not yet met Praisegod the family collie always left at home for wife and kids on the wharf in Seamark, who objected to mechanical odors, but he immediately detected the existence of some such male individual from the whiffs on Barebones' clothes and was favorably predisposed toward all elements of that olfactory family.

At last, though in disappointment of Ibi's hope to go home the long way (by Beltane Hill), Caleb was proceeding back through Coalyard Lane, approaching the *DT Daily Nous* property, when he heard characteristically intimate yelps. He hurried around to the forepark of the building—and, sure enough, discovered them to be ecstatic salutations worthy of himself. Ibi wriggled in undignified jubilation on the nearly green grass, rolling and laughing under the caresses of a touseled blackhaired friend, flushed with delight, crouching in her elegant greatcoat and high-heeled leather boots—none other than Bice Picory!

With a single pang of astonishment this epitome of Transylvanian beauty instantly benighted Caleb with the dotage of mingled triumph and jealousy that he had believed was dissipated like a morning fog. He'd thought himself finally freed of this succubus by riding the hopes of a new anchor to windward in the person of his old Lilian. But in a flash he was as besotted as his dog, oblivious to complications.

As soon as she rose to face Caleb, Ibi knew his jig was up. Cheerfully accepting the abrupt cessation of attention, he affected to be escaping a perfunctory social duty and trotted off across the deserted pavement to resume his wandering investigations of the small fences and gardens on the residentially adulterated side of the business byway. A hooting train just then intruded above their heads, rumbling and screeching along the embankment; but the behemoth left behind the same mild Saturday afternoon sounds of peace, muffled as before in the infinity of different distances and modulated by a spectrum of faint rhythms, human and mechanical, which either canceled each other or gently pulsed in passing reinforcement: for lovers the equivalent of privacy and silence.

"Ibi-Roi remembered me!"

"No one forgets you."

"I just got a job on the paper!" She kissed his nose. "I'm going to settle here."

"As an alien?"

"I have a Social Security number. They didn't ask for a passport. Keep it a secret that I still belong to the British Commonwealth and I won't tell anybody that you write plays." Seeing that there were no windows on that side of the Nous building, she took his hand and exuberantly swung it in hers as they walked up the Lane toward the slackening stream of Cod Street kilroys. Mr Ghibellini had taken her out to lunch, and on Saturday afternoon they had the office all to themselves. "I've got the chance to become City Hall reporter, with my own byline. Meanwhile I'm Community News editor and featurewriter." Her ambition seemed well defined. "A couple of years on the *Nous* will be good for my curriculum vitae when I make it to New Uruk!" She squeezed his hand like a sisterly hetaera, lifting the back of it to her lips, which felt like the nuzzling of a doe.

As they were passing the fuel-oil dealer's lot she came to a stop and turned to him affectionately, opening her coat. The blouse was nearly as unbuttoned as her sweater. "See what I'm wearing!" The wooden triangle that she had taken from his ingenuous box of platonic equilaterals hung by a leather thong barely higher than the soft twin heaps he always envisioned with his sense of touch. She stroked the talisman with her fingers. "Feel how warm I keep it."

The half-star of David, pierced at its center, suited the lines of her face; its scale was not too large for her body; its grained varnish harmonized with the colors of her skin and clothes. He hardly remembered that the plane shape and trilateral symmetry no longer satisfied him; unlike the isorectotetrahedron it did not provide the lines for a cross, or the axes for all variables: but, resolving to scotch his nostalgia, he only asked "And where may Sister Carmen be living?"

"I'm staying in Gepetto DaGetto's loft until I find a place of my own. Then I'll be able to see my Childe Caleb more often."

Inasmuch as "Childe Caleb" was a dubbing of Doc's, it appeared that she'd already been gossipping with Petto—and perhaps telling more than hearing. Caleb's minute of unforeseen elation gave way to premeditated resentment.

"He's going to teach me how to drive his welding rig, so I can get a license." she went on. "Some judge took away the staff photographer's license for six months. It's pretty hard for him to get around by taxi, and Mr Ghibellini says he's much too good to lose. So I've got to get a car for my work. Teaming up will be a good way for me to learn the city."

The name Flash Silver was now another one to look for. Caleb could learn the warp of his city from her deceptions about the woof. Pride prevented any utterance of his personal questions. But he enjoyed the advantage of not envying the career she presumed enviable. Probably she envisaged herself, after intense microtopopolitan experience, sitting at a cosmopolitan desk of the *New Uruk Testament*. Yet as a fantastic literary ambition it was not necessarily stupid or corrupt. He allowed that his mother had once entertained illusions about the glory of journalism. And it seemed to him that

Bice's purpose in getting the job might be laudable as an intention to put herself on a new footing—to be free of bondage to the men in her mirror.

Whereas Ibi served as the incidental mascot of her euphoria, his master felt more like a scapegoat for the foolish romances of her past, which she was now kissing goodbye—in the security of her prospective independence. Her sparkling dark beauty was still firmly mercurial, still infused with quietly intelligent gaiety; on the surface it remained too desirable to resist: yet now divining the depth of her professional motive, he marveled that such a journalist had ever been his correspondent. It was hard to remember that he had ever been banal enough to praise her in the light of the same moon by which he now admired Lilian's authentic reflection.

In the days that followed the reappearance of Bice, which did not embarrass the love for Lilian that had already repossessed his most imaginative desire, his unsubstantiated erotic confidence was so enhanced by the double appropinquity of sexual friends, whom he was in a position to contemplate comparatively in alternating hopes of second chances, that he was left with little time to dwell upon apparently contingent and surmountable disappointments of sexual privilege—especially whenever both women were displaced in the foreground of his mind by the bread or wine of his work, or by public news of the new administration in Washington. A complex of hopes was easier to tolerate than an exclusive desire.

But it was to Ibi that he owed his incipient social confidence. More and more often he found himself addressing the dog as his "pride and joy". This elliptical scrap from Sir Walter Scott's table, alluding to "A mother's pride, a father's joy", had been applied to himself as a child, not only in private crooning but also in mortifying public proclamation when Mary Tremont was referring to her high expectations of the stunted messiah. Nowadays the phrase sprang to Caleb's lips when he was rejoicing in his one comfortable liaison with Dogtown society at large.

As combined ward and warden, client and protector, Ibi knew no shame, nor was any required of him. He was no respecter of persons, no envier of place. Yet on his account Caleb felt respected and envied by those of all nations and sects who did not hate all saints. Ibi was admired by any male or female stranger not overly defensive of feline sinners or neurotically terrified by canards about ferocious instincts inherited from wolves. Without class distinction, at all levels of wealth and culture, the beautiful young Viking Shepherd was hailed as the finest kind. Leaving aside the economic and spiritual community to which Caleb was enjoined in the catholic rite of the Mass (although he belonged to no congregation of Paul or parish of Peter), and except for some partisan emotions in national baseball and politics, his only sense of sectarian solidarity in matters of taste and feeling was embodied in this powerful mediator.

Captain Ozone had been a man of the people no more than Caleb was, but in very different respects. Had it not been for Ibi's personal role as pharmakos in converting some cold objective compassion to a generous impulse, Caleb would have remained almost as uncomfortable with the blind patrician as other citizens were. The Cathode King's liking for dogs as a species was hardly more pronounced or constant than his attraction to women as a gender, and in fact he preferred the company of cats; but he seemed respectful enough of sacred values to show a touch of largesse in making Caleb the gift of his intended bodyguide and watchdog of the Joyous Gard estate.

At an age too young for consent Ibi had been perhaps the only representative of the Dogtown public (save for a pride of house cats) to witness the tactile experiments with his private associates in which the blind man found diversion from his natural magic. If the grown cub hadn't been banished from the loveless aristocracy, to live in small rented quarters with the otherwise friendless youth of obscure origin and uncertain competence who was so intelligently intrigued by the CRF technology of reading and writing eight channels of tactile holes, he probably would have been relegated to marking the remainder of the New Albion Grant (the Prudence Point messuage plus one quarry tract), which was now being probated as the testator's only real asset between the coast of Mr John Smith's explorations and that of Sir Francis Drake's. Or instructions might have been issued to dispose of him as a nuisance.

That order would have been received by Sidles the butler, the same who'd done duty as nursemaid and stern disciplinarian for Ibi's puppyhood of housetraining, straight from the kennel of the gardener (subsequently retired to Poncedeleon), who had taken it upon himself many years ago to perpetuate the Viking Shepherd bloodline on his own premises, whether or not the Captain gave a damn up at the Chateau itself. Once the days of puppy-messing were left behind, the taciturn major domo had discovered in himself the eyes to see and a heart to feel the affectionate beauty quickly maturing with energy too ebullient for the gloomy Great Hall. He'd made a good start in domesticating this superfluity of life by teaching such unnatural customs as that of lying down with cats (an acculturation of Ibi's that was later to prove very fortunately conducive to peaceful symbiosis in the Cod Street household, where Ibi readily familiarized himself with the Keiths' sinner, distinguishing it from those on other property that invited his chasing).

In any event, when the Captain decided to dedicate the seeing-eye born on his own grounds, Sidles had colluded with the gardener in procrastinating arrangements for the castration prerequisite to a dog's outside professional training as a guide for the blind. Meanwhile, fortunately, the Captain's electronic invention took the good turn he'd almost despaired of, and he changed his mind about learning to rely upon an animal. So before it finally came to emasculation and boarding school—or to turning the big dog out, fenced or chained, for permanent duty as brute monitor of the rocks—Harley Craigie was one day called to take the all-but-fated eunuch four or five miles south to Caleb's address, who at the time had no car to fetch him in. Sidles loaded the cab with uncharacteristic signs of tenderness in his equable melancholy.

Then it was Harley's turn to be swayed. You'd never have suspected that he was a stranger to his alert passenger, who sat on the front seat like a democratic officer inspecting new territory in his command car, as trusting of the vehicle as if he had conjured it up himself—questioning the mechanical apparatus no more than the driver's goodwill or the destination. That taxi ride became the subject of Harley's most anthologized poem, wherein Ibi was first called "Our Present Prince of Saints", long before his virtues had fully taken form.

He'd next endeared himself—and Caleb along with him—to the late Duke of Dogtown's functionaries on a payroll supervised by Frank Bacon the Younger. When Caleb led him on a leash into the Front Street office of the Viking Shepherd Society to get his indenture altered, this avatar of the royal bloodline was rendered homage like a perfect phenotype who might be the last simply because he was too debonair for self-preservation among the wicked.

Then too Ibi had spread joie de vivre along the way up to the Hotel de la Ibicité, where he met and conquered the heart of Mrs Sirius the gruff Registrar of All Saints, whose perfunctory business it was to catechize every applicant about the civil behavior code vis-à-dos the town's innocent sinners. At the first glimpse of his pedigree she invited him behind the counter for a personal audience, and was no less delighted by his courtesy than by his size and beauty. "No longer need we fear the mainland Danes!"

And with like pleasure the Dog Warden on his Harbor beat in the paddy wagon had immediately recognized the kingship of the odd little roadrunner's companion. As eagerly as Sergeant Proctor spotted recalcitrant saints a mile away and identified the strangers responsible for them, he also loved to start around town the praise of exemplary citizens. It was no black mark against a landless bachelor's prestige to be seen under the escort of a totem who took his degraded circumstances in stride with as little mortification as if he'd been born of Harbor crossbreeds. Though seeking no civic honors, and conspicuous he hoped only to patrolling policemen, Caleb was pitiably pleased to have his peculiar reputation neutralized by the company of a dog with a triangular brass tag on his collar chain, better identified than a military serviceman with a round aluminum license.

The C O V Fathers were sorry that the prince of saints could not be allowed even into the sunporch vestibule of the Laboratory where Caleb often sipped sherry with them late in the afternoon—an exclusion not so much for reasons of monastic discipline as in consideration of the doghairs for Oku to clean up whose irritable nerves were already balanced all too delicately. But Father Duncannon was always kind enough to wrap and save for their acolyte's acolyte the bones and scraps he was worthy to have gathered up for himself under their table, and when homeward bound on road trips never failed to ask acolytes at restaurants to do the same for his mascot. Sometimes the sympathetic priest went out of his way to buy a solely dedicated soup bone. He of course made no attempt to let his left hand know what his right hand did, but when these treats were not to be consumed on the doorstep of the Lab, Caleb their conveyor took care to give the credit where it was due, and generally made every effort to encourage this especially precious loop of interspecial affection.

While it was true that Father Lucey for his part paid no more intrinsic attention to other species than to children of his own kind (his filtered consciousness of Ibi thus resembling Doctor Charlemagne's), his courtesy and Christian charity were a match for Ibi's; and anyway he reflected the Superior whenever not absorbed in his own peculiar concerns. Yet it should be remembered that he had spontaneously saved Ibi's life before even meeting him.

Each of Caleb's friends felt a special bond with Ibi. In the case of Shelly Schlossberg it was exceptionally respectful, arising from conflated admiration of Jack London's two symmetrical protagonists—the great dog of Golden Bay who went to lead the wolves, and the great wolf who came down from the North to champion human culture. But both the Schlossbergs would have liked him anyway, as they liked without fuss all congenial or interesting Jews Gentiles and barbarians. They accorded him the private hospitality due an original of any shape or color, leaving him the options of bold or shy initiative in furthering the cordial acquaintance, which was strengthened chiefly by chance encounters on the street. Although the two innkeepers were often dutifully distracted by poorly governed details of business, their joint interest in Ibi was no more impolite than their cordiality toward Doc, Petto, Buck, Levi Nathan, or the Mayor. It happened that Bice became their favorite; they were both particularly fond of her, as if they'd have preferred her as a daughter to Caleb as a son: but they always remembered tidbits for Caleb's dog when he chanced to stop at the Van.

Almost without exception Ibi was beloved of women—no less the ones who worried about doghair or muddy feet than the ones who could make light of housekeeping. But the attitude of Deeta Dana was unique, Doc's orphan "housekeeper" and "secretary" whose wages if any must have been provided by *Dromenology*. Not for an instant had there been a trace of her master's cynophobia, which she ignored. Caleb wondered if Ibi's friendship behind the curtain was her compensation for the boredom of Doc's Saturday-night symposiums—unless those diversions in her kitchen would have been a blessed relief even without the presence of a dog. But her love of Ibi was immediate and uncondescending; and he'd have telepathically responded even if she'd kept him at arm's length and never given him her food.

Early one Sunday morning not long after that hebdomadal routine had formed, as Caleb scraped his chair and rose to leave, instead of the usual upward scrambling in the back room he heard a two-stage slithering thump on the floor, and the whirr of Ibi hastily shaking himself for the manful journey home. He said nothing to alarm his host, but by chance a few days later he found occasion to confirm his suspicion.

Shopping for groceries on his way home from work he met Deeta emerging from the Great Aristotle and Plato. She carried by the handle two sturdy net shopping bags stuffed with victuals for Doc. It was the first time he'd ever seen her at liberty, and if she hadn't spoken first he wouldn't have recognized her, shining in the public daylight. Previously he had sensed only thick dull braids over ungroomed and eccentric costume; but he now discovered the bright yellow hair of a healthy young face, as fair and cheerful as a boy could wish for.

"Caleb! It's so nice to see you! But where's Ibi-Roi?"

The liberality of her greeting amazed him. He had thought her diffidently disdainful of all that was common and ordinary, of young men in general; but now she was as if happy to regard him off-duty as her only common and ordinary friend. She even accepted a ride home, though it was less than half a mile and she hated kilroys of every kind.

"He's not allowed into monasteries or A & P s, so he usually stays home to guard the house."

"Against the Little People? They don't really steal down to the cemeteries from Purdeyville, you know."

"No, the landlady's babies are safely in school while she works at the Library all day. I suppose he just musters the saints and keeps an eye on prowling sinners."

"He'd rather be helping herd your sheep." She raised one of her bags. "I've got something special for him."

"You spoil him. It makes me look hardhearted. I think you've been letting him up on your bed."

"Shshsh!" The fairhaired servant put finger to lips with a banal playfulness he hadn't expected to find dwelling with her solemn sense of Parnassian responsibility. "Please don't tell the master. He'd start coughing and sneezing if he knew. I always brush Ibi's sheddings off the blanket. So why should you care?"

"Because he knows it's forbidden and he's not sly by nature. It makes him deceive me, and then he feels guilty."

"But why do you forbid it?"

Caleb was nonplussed for an instant. "Because I'm too lazy to wash and brush."

"Try to turn a blind eye when I'm the housekeeper." she demanded. "Perhaps I'm less puritannical than you are, but I'm certainly not corrupting your saint! He's quite capable of making a distinction between luxurious furloughs and the regular barracks discipline."

"I grant you that he's a good anthropologist. He tolerates exotic customs as easily as his own. Anyway, I'm always glad to share a witch's secret."

Again, Ibi met yet a different want in the Keith family, which had lost its own beloved Saint Sucat to a vicissitude of old age. The landlady herself, Gloria Keith, was ten or fifteen years older than Deeta, but her hair was lighter, short and finely upcurled like the youngest's of storybook princes. At first glance her bones looked comparatively delicate; but in her Montvert high school she'd been key cheerleader as well as class president. Bucolic freshness had not yet faded from her small undignified face, nor boundless energy from the blue of her eyes, which were still hardly more creased in their setting than her highschool daughter Deirdre's. Even now the palely freckled skin was only invisibly weathered by the burdens and anxieties of her centric responsibility as an Atlantean matron of incessantly spontaneous humanitarianism and a profession of her own. Her husband Dexter was of a different Celtic type: tall as Doctor Charlemagne yet athletic and darkly cleancut, a veritable hero, more prominent than his wife as a leader in cooperative citizenship. Though to Ibi both of them were pillars of security, the homemaking woman was his alma mater. He remembered no other mother.

Thanks to deepening familiarity with the mise en scene, Mrs Keith gradually gathered idiosyncracy in Caleb's eyes. Like many others, the Curator of Legends at the Atheneum Library (and history consultant to the Lyceum), formerly teacher of Social Studies at Harbor Grammar, was fascinated by the fabulously deserted pastures of Purdeyville. Yet whereas the maidservant Deeta Dana was able to spend most of her free time on that junipered heath, snowshoeing through dingles for winter herbs, dipping spring water, or picking blueberries like the scores of seasoned oldtimers who were unwilling to abandon pastimes that were once elements of livelihood, the overworking housewife had no leisure to walk the fells and go aberrying, or to saunter among the sites and features she nonetheless studied from the rather bookish vantage of an enthusiastically naturalized marooner (or so-called "denizen") who happened to have been born to scenery without the sea around it. It was with words and pictures that Goody Keith counseled countless children composing Gloucesterbooks for school. More than their classroom teachers she got them to enrich with the fourth dimension whatever kind of geography they toiled over in the three easy ones.

Busy with the normal comforts of her household, naturally full of its own history, she wasn't likely to invite Ibi onto her bed even in the improbable event that she should find herself alone therein if his master were out of town when hers was. Any empty hollow was usually claimed by the Persian O'Hair, survivor of a twin called Burke that had been killed as a kitten by some militant saint when unguardedly scratching dirt beyond the cemetery fence.

Ibi did in part take the venerable place of Sucat, namesake of St Patrick, a retrieving pointer-setter of auburn Anglo-Irish descent, who had grown old among the Keith children and without being taught had made himself useful. Many a motorist waiting in line for the railroad crossing gates to open (including Flash Silver, whose witnessing photograph was once published on the front page of the *Nous*) had admired Sucat marching home with Dexter's briefcase suspended from his mouth by its handles—like Berganza bearing the portfolio of the merchant's son to the Cephasite school in Seville—

followed by the then commuter himself who needed both his hands for the two little kids who had awaited his train. The Keiths made fun of Ibi's aristocratic refusal to learn such servile duty, and boasted that Sooky would even carry a parcel of hamburger in his mouth without yielding to temptation.

"There are a thousand species of beetle." Caleb once said to Mrs Keith when they both happened to pause at the same spot for a look at Ibi as he lay curved on the ground patiently awaiting chow call. "I wonder why dogs of a thousand sizes and shapes are all under one label."

"Because they intermarry." she laughed. "Like men and women." Like Gloria the golden pony and Dexter her big black stallion, Caleb thought: not only of one species but also of the same Celtic breed!

They discussed the racial distinctions derived from the respective motivations of hunter and shepherd, the differing vocations that are still of interest to their genes. Sooky had been a willing servant to the limit of his powers; but without special schooling Ibi would chase and carry only for his own amusement, as for instance in swimming for a stick flung into the water but refusing to recognize the provision that to get it thrown again he had to bring it to the thrower. Caleb admitted to his landlady that he was disquieted by this obtuseness in royal intelligence.

"I can't believe that natural selection has had time enough for such refinement of behavior." he remarked. "Two different acculturations must have been acquired from the doctrines of their ancestors. But without language how do they inherit the acquisition?"

"Through their mother's milk?"

"Sometimes it's only the father's characteristic."

"I must look it up, since I'm the reference librarian! But don't worry about Ibi. The same thing's true of us. Some of the most intelligent people are blind to what the majority can see without trying. But we don't attribute insensitivity to race—so where shall I find the answer?"

"Under 'Matriarchy'. You were right the first time."

Thus does Ibi make for conversation between the timid little incast, who habitually shuns smalltalk with citizens, and the official champion of topopatriotism, mother of children perfectly integrated into social institutions, wife of the eminent City Planner who isn't allowed to do much planning but whose determinations are worth a great deal to many Knights, especially to owners and developers of living rock—while Ibi remains unaware of Caleb's inferiority in the estimation of strangers, still believing in the absoluteness of his master's power. It is through Ibi that Caleb begins his limited civic accommodation: not real assimilation, to be sure, but tentative ingratiation; a camouflaging adaptation to common expectations in almost everything except language.

Caleb wasn't quite the first of his lineage to depend upon a saint for mediation in the society of strangers. His mother Mary had owned a Viking Shepherd queen by the name of Sycorax, the most beautiful dam in Dogtown annals. In nostalgic monologues from the cradle onward he had heard that name like some legendary precursor's, when background memories were formed without framework or articulation—certainly without psychological conceptions. Unlike her son, Mary had never needed a dog to attract the favorable attention of an opposite sex; if anything, along those lines, the Shepherd was duenna against the same in her exposure as a girl. But Sycorax was primarily her best friend and severest critic, the only one who would listen to her narrative poems.

Though as a boy Caleb had never regarded his mother's prehistoric female famulus as an element of his heritage, now, at this late date, his genealogical attitude was altered by the pride of similar possession. For if he chose to muster the courage, research of the public archives would probably disclose that one of his dog's ancestors had belonged to Mary Tremont. The very possibility that the fabulous bitch had played a part in the royal pedigree aroused in Ibi's owner, almost for the first time, a definite interest in his mother's preconceiving past. Before he was old enough to escape his mother all the lore that seemed to have no bearing upon his own life had been too boringly feminine to pay any attention to.

But he did remember the claim that the fiercely protective Sycorax had understood everything her mistress said or read to her. One assumed that those confessions of the human rebel to her interspecial sister were less reserved but more rational than those she was to make in the future to her child; surely they were less suicidal: for she too in youth, even as a female, had been full of totally convincing joy hope and ambition, if but only half the time. The life span of Sycorax now represented for Caleb the range from innocence to experience in his mother's years of nubile freedom, during which the agony was creative and romantic—before the annunciation.

Gazing down at a cemetery that may have been one of those in which she'd had what she once referred to as "many initiations", he picked up his pen to fill a long overdue letter to her with the only news he was willing to tell—his acquisition of Ibi—like a scholar awakening to the ritual origin of a baffling myth. Although Lent 1961 began his twenty-seventh year, and he still could not bring bring himself to imagine the liminal events of Gloucestermas 1934, he now conjured up his faded image of Sycorax from the mist-shrouded chronological disorder of the prior decade that had rather symmetrically spanned both sides of his mother's twenty-ninth. It was hard for him to imagine any real life before F D R's second term. But some sense of the dog's existence had been vaguely fixed by a single unfixed photograph which was later lost with the "Family Album" during an Unabridge eviction. The vanished icon of Ibi's matrilinear stirps called forth drifting speculations that he ordinarily neglected or postponed.

Now that his mother professed incommutable commitment to the community of the Brotherhood of the Peaceable Kingdom, he breathed more freely in informing her of his situation than he had since the age of twelve. Anyway he could hardly have concealed his Dogtown address, which would naturally excite her proprietary imagination despite his pointed asseverations that it was a mere transit point on the way to Europe. Although she still had pen ink postage and gall enough to write any personage on earth, and it was therefore still necessary to guard his expressions, he now felt safe enough to confide in her a little of what he would have openly related to any other acquaintance, namely his association with a V S who understood everything he said; but also to confess in a few words the love of her at the foundation of all his (unspecified) endeavors.

Not until after his letter was posted to the hinterland of Orellana did he remind himself of the most pertinent incunabular vocative from which he had striven to free himself. From the dawn of his linguistic consciousness in her arms, as the companion presumed to understand everything said to him, he had been called "Caliban, my little Cubie, full of puppy love for the bitch what bores him!"—especially when he was a Cub Scout "winning awards right and left as the Honor Boy". And in another humor she sometimes called him the "whoreson of a fisherman's niece". Of all locutions in the habitual abuse of women that had offended him throughout his life in the world of men, the one he most abhorred was "son of a bitch".

In his letter he took care to omit mention of Ibi's provenance; for he would no more have mentioned Captain Ozone in a letter to her than he'd have spoken to Captain Ozone about his origins. Karcist was a surname apparently unknown or forgotten to the blind technologist who remained the incarnation of equivocal power in Mary Tremont's demonology. She didn't know that he'd gone blind. Allusions to the Captain had not appeared in letters since her rebirth at Vernalia, nor many other old themes of her hardship and humiliation;

but her son was none the less fearful that any mention of people she had known in Dogtown would revive her unchristian rancor, overwhelming the inhibitions of her conversion, if only while she was writing.

Caleb's native habitat had been hers long before it was his, and for a much longer time; and she had lost little confidence in her judgments of the past, despite all the gentle chastisement to which she voluntarily subjected herself under the tyranny of prayer-meeting socialism. Though now bathed in communal peace, as she declared, her well-wrought criticisms of mankind were not as easily forgotten as the enthusiasms, sacred and profane, that had led to all her previous disappointments.

Yet it was as much to her own chagrin as to the pain of her corporate supervisors that she was unable to expunge all manifestations of her incorrigibility. She was determined to conform to the Spirit. When she repeated in his birthday letter "You will probably never see me again," for the first time in his life she did not mean she was going to kill herself.

He was accustomed to thick envelopes of cheap paper densely covered on both sides with her compact roundly flowing hand, the unhesitant script lavishly punctuated and emphasized; but now she met the constraints of airmail by cramming almost as much onto fewer and flimsier sheets. Sometimes he had to put them aside while he gathered an appetite for the reading.

She got little enough response. He believed it was an effort to alleviate the dissatisfaction of unrequited jungle communications that had prompted her request to the Sunday Circle (spiritual directorate of the democratic plantation) for permission to write an autobiography as her assigned self-discipline—in addition of course to her regular duties in the laundry and kitchen that were always performed with the humble and faithful competence she had learned perforce through menial "breadwinning" in the profane world—on her own private time (generally allotted for siesta and recreation), which was little enough for any kind of solitude. She hoped it would be printed by their publishing house in England (The Milk Press). A book of repentance would serve as her personal "outreach"!

It was almost inconceivable that the unostentatious selfsurrendering pureminded Brotherhood would even consider the idea of "individualistic" confessions, even if they could be expurgated of scandalous contrasts to the ideal outcome of religious life. But news of the mere petition struck familiar fear in the pusillanimous heart of Caleb. Thank God that Captain Ozone was dead; and Richard Tybbot, and many of the others that might remember her in Dogtown. But the *Dogtown Daily Nous* was still publishing literary announcements. And Theodora Cibber, an old friend she never criticized, was bound to be sent the apology for Mary Tremont's life—in which Caleb Karcist was sure to figure unmistakably.

His mother's standing request that he look up Mrs Cibber was but a faltering remnant of the old stream of demands that he make himself known to people she knew wherever he went. By mail it was her custom to badger both sides about getting together; but in this case she was almost conventionally tentative, as if she no longer dared write her old benefactor directly—maybe in part because her heart was becoming inured to her son's apparently disdainful neglect of suggestions made for his own good, and perhaps also because of her preoccupation with the immediate problem of her own redemption, but especially because of the unique awe that was inspired in her by that good lady.

"Teddi Cibber stood by me in all my adversity, and she once kept you and me alive in simple unhesitating charity when her own family was struggling to keep bread on the table. If you see her, convey my eternal gratitude (and yours). Send me her address, and give her mine. Ask her if she'd like to hear from me. It will be a long time before I'm worthy of her gracious friendship. Her husband Wat was a hardworking fisherman and stalwart provider, who had dangerous troubles with the corrupt Tuscans of the waterfront, going back to rum-running days, but he was afraid of me and of all awkward feminine truth. He did not approve of me at all, nor of any 'Bohemian', nor of Catholicrats, nor of urban life beyond the Gut Bridge. Even in the irrevocable sacrifice of an education deemed superfluous for her condition, by slaving her life away for a family and neighborhood that knew quite well they were burying a jewel of great price, Teddi always carried herself with the cheerful dignity of an Anglo-Irish Themis. She was the only one I could turn to for help in getting you into the convent when they sent me to the looney-asylum and tied my tubes."

Caleb had been bold enough to become a friend of Wat Cibber's without revealing that he was Mary Tremont's baby. The shame of belonging to a deranged woman who confessed to "indiscretions B C E " (Before Caleb's Era), who remembered herself as "infamous" for irregular maternity, and who flattered herself on being known thereafter for her socially dangerous initiatives, was still keen enough to prevent him from mentioning her name within earshot of any Dogtown oldtimers.

Her next letter somewhat allayed his anxiety about publication. There was no further report of either imprimatur or proscription; and for the first time her fearfully enviable creative energy began to seem repressible:

"I'm getting old and ugly now. My 'liver spots' are changing to unsightly moles; the flesh on my arms, legs, body and bosom is sagging more and more. The 'very pretty face', which people of this world used to compliment me on (and which I could always use as a mask to hide my guilty self-knowledge), is now no more! I *am* old and ugly! But I don't mind. I only hope God can still 'do deeds' with me, because that is what I am here for.

"This morning (Sunday) I woke up elated by the thought that *I never again need take another job in all the rest of my life!* Such a comforting thought (after my miserable years of work-history—so disillusioning, so stormy, so varied!) started my day off beautifully, befitting the weather, for once so clear, cool and perfect (within three degrees of the Equator) that it reminded me of Cornucopia! I don't think I shall ever want to leave Vernalia. Mount Duida, our distant and mysterious sundial, is now my Sinai."

It's the Amazonian land of El Dorado and Green Mansions, where Lusitanian law and vernacular merge with equally invasive Hispanic, drained by the Casiquiara "canal" that connects the Amazon and Orinoco basins by slack water responding alternately to the welling and sucking of two swamp systems, like the abyssal currents of Lake Van (in the shadow of Mt Ararat) which were anciently reputed to respond in turn to the variably unequal drafts of the Tigris and Euphrates at their sources underground. But it is said of the Casiquiara that the imperceptible changes of its tide obeys no discernible law of seasons or decades, nor mankind's arbitrary regulations, unlike the canals that once connected the Tigris to the Euphrates in lower Mesopotamia, where Nimrod had to raise one of the rivers and there was nothing but his Tower of Babel to cast a shadow.

"This place will be lovely to me always. I still feel 'translated'—'unreal'—perhaps 'dead'! And why not? After all, I have forever left behind me the world and all my old tensions, worries, struggles, conflicts, sins! And I am here doing God's will in order to prepare—with all my Brothers-and-Sisters-to-be (when I am admitted to the inner Circle)—for the Kingdom of Christ on earth! I fervently pray that God will call you too, and that you will have ears to hear Him. Take up your bed and walk!

"What is happening here to my prized 'gift' for poetry (my second gift, which He allowed me to acquire after vaporizing all my Satanic talent for graven images with the death of Sycorax in that horrible fire: my beloved brave loyal dog-sister, the only true friend I ever had, and the most beautiful of all His own creatures, who should have been the only model allowed into my studio) differs little from what has happened to many people of the Brotherhood who come from the arts of music, theater, dance, painting—probably to their like amazement: *I can't seem to write any more!* Now that in itself is phenomenal, considering my notorious production of words! But what is more remarkable, *I don't care!* I, who have always been compelled to 'express myself' in order to live and be lived with, have been struck dumb—even with plentiful paper and a good fountain pen in hand! I, who for years past have written, edited, and rewritten 18 unpublished fascicles of epic and bales of shorter narrative poems, plus boundless (forever *un*bound) volumes of personal verse, suddenly *have nothing to say*—and no words to say it in! I, who eagerly worked at the 'profession' of journalism for the sake of supporting my 'creative soul', and once was even able to pay out from my salary the wages of housekeepers to do 'the dirty work' and take care of my three-in-one child, am now living in the greatest tranquility and earning my stoneground wholewheat bread by folding threadbare clothes in the community laundry.

"Before I ever heard of the B P K I had realized the empty vanity of a life of 'letters' (such as you, poor foolish youth, secretly aspire to, I know); and long before that I knew what 'tinkling cymbals' the 'Great' poets really are—as human beings. Still, just think of it: *I*, the person 'dedicated' of yore to write REAL things, eschewing the hollow pretense of fellowship with other vain 'artists' (in all branches of the 'ARTS')—who swore to cherish my integrity as a *creative* individual while protecting myself from the taint of mere Bohemianism or other Success—have grown so *dumb* that writing a letter to my silent noncommital son has come to be a chore!

"*The explanation:* Self (Ego) IS dying! PRAISE GOD FROM WHOM ALL BLESSINGS FLOW! I am well out of the world, where there never was a place for *me!*

"But I hope there will be a happy place for you, my sturdy staddle-oak. Last month when the local half-Petrine Guaicas (not the still mysterious 'white Atlindians' of Esmeralda whose territory the Lusitanians and Hispanics have been disputing for hundreds of years) were superstitiously celebrating Saint Blasius, I prayed with thanksgiving for your survival. (Poor little dogface! After four days of traumatic labor to get out of my womb, with your head brutally torn by the steel forceps of a *male* doctor, your throat was strangled by *my* umbilical cord, and for two and a half hours you were left as dead in the morgue—until God sent a blessed *female* nurse to hear your valiant whimper for breath.) I ask God's forgiveness for all my 'plain talk' about passions and obsessions and false 'beatitudes' that I now know were sinful, which no woman should ever speak of to a man of any age, let alone her own innocent child. You were burdened with my wretched misguided 'psychology' before you were old enough to close your ears and rebel against my overweening 'feminism'.

"And *you* must forgive me for for all my 'sophisticated' smoking—from before the beginning of your infancy until you escaped from home! (I haven't had a cigarette since I met those wonderful B P K Schumachers when I was their passenger stewardess on my last ship. God sent them as angels to save me from blind self-absorption!)

"Forgive me for feeding you *pasteurized* milk, just because it was out of fashion to be a natural mother! For a clever careerist like me the way of Mary with baby Jesus was just a nuisance! I was still more concerned with my own precious pigheaded SELF than with yours—despite the conviction that my God-given child was the most important gift of my life!

"Forgive me for the lousy board and room that gave you rickets, before I overcame my thoughtless self-indulgence and learned the rudiments of child-rearing like any ordinary good mother. And all that time I was boasting about my maternal instincts! (Every kind soul who glanced at my baby carriage was told that you were going to be a great man of one kind or another!)

"Forgive me for tossing you up in the air and catching you to express *my* joy in your existence, heedless of your tiny delicate fragile little flower of a brain. It's God's miracle that you had the will to overcome all your damages and become my Honor Boy!

"You were *justified* in refusing to give up college in order to support me. I was selfish and shortsighted to rail at you like a fishwife, and for that I pray forgiveness too.

"I hope you will find Dogtown less mean-spirited than I did. Though most of its inhabitants were hateful evil-minded dullards, I love it more than any other *place* on earth. Its sea-rocks and quarries and Purdeyville boulders are the firm foundation of all my memories, always the scene of my important dreams. But I can never set foot there again, knowing that the city fathers will have me committed once more to that Medieval county hospital where the 'therapy' *makes* a prisoner crazy and the *male* doctors lord it by force over the Bedlam of their creation. The vulgar *male* judge told me: "There's no room for you in Dogtown." His injunction still stands as a warrant against me (which fortunately the Coast Guard never got wind of when I was issued my pass to work at sea).

"But it seems almost a vindication of my mutinous life there that the 'quickening humor' of Dogtown's original Viking Shepherd has passed into your *appreciative* possession through my very own well-bred(!) Sycorax, who lived and died for me after having twenty-seven puppies in three litters, the last two of which were miscegenations of her own choice! Your Ibi-Roi must be a descendant of her firstborn, 'the pick of the litter' who opened her womb. I had to sell or give them all away. I hope you can teach Ibi to wipe his feet before coming into the house and not to wolf down his food."

Caleb had no more confidence in his mother's fear of returning to Dogtown than in her interpretations of objective fact, but his anxiety was gradually allayed by the long distance and lengthening duration of her present sojourn. After long probation as a resident inquirer, and prolonged hesitation on the part of Vernalia's sanhedrin, she was formally admitted to the Circle as a Novice. By then they must have had an inkling of what they were risking. He almost prayed for her full and permanent membership—a boon equivalent to miracle.

The letters continued to come from her "jungle veranda, written during the sabbath hour of solitude" when she savored relief from all cooperative work and worship. In new serenity her memories gravitated to the "illiterate vanity" of what she regarded as her preliminary youth, rather than to the "sinful passages" that marked departure from that age, and she seemed successful in her effort to silence the unforgettable pain and bitterness of the "struggle against jealous Puritans and miserly Protesticans" by which to a large degree her entire history had thitherto been dramatized.

Nonetheless, before opening certain strictly epistolary questions (without encouraging any hope that his interest might connote a wish for reunion), it was necessary to remind himself of her many previous disappointments in briefer and less sheltered longanimities. It was the better part of wisdom to grant time a further testing of her new roots (or tendrils) in the "isolated peace" of that Christian commune on the edge of a campo in equatorial South Atlantis. It was hard to believe that a mind like hers, so creatively active in the discernment of human stupidity, could henceforth proscribe its own consciousness of the social reality opposite and more than equal to the truth picked out in euphoria.

Yet even in reviewing a life's plight of hope and failure in which the latter actually predominates, one often selects only what is relevant to the pleasant mood; and he found within himself, palely perpetuated in a more cautious and rational frame, the same corklike bobbing of an optimism that more than half the time ignored the warnings of its own praeternaturally critical insight.

Meanwhile in Dogtown he never spoke of his birthday. He half doubted yet did not care to test her old teasing allegation that any of its natives born about March 21 (even if not on the spring equinox exactly) was vulgarly presumed to be a by-blow of the last Gloucestermas. Out of ineluctable pride he had always pretended to pay no attention to her baited hooks of information, not in fear of biting the truth but simply in aversion to the degradation of playing into her hands with questions she wanted to answer; for he hated above all her pouncing interpretations of his interest in anything she told him. But his brow grew hot and his cheeks inflamed whenever he was obliged to give the date of his birth even to acquaintances or officials who knew nothing of local folklore. To himself the implication of Midsummer's Night was quite as glaring as the analogy in an equation of ratios.

And so, even as the danger of her apparition seemed to recede, he waited to see if there was going to be some sort of postal interference before promising himself to start methodically cudgeling his tenuous memory of her cradle-rocking autobiographies. He now regretted all the letters over the years that he had rapidly scanned and never preserved, most of them longer than the latest. They had always seemed to be rehearsing the same kind of trusting joy, mystic yearning, heartbreaking love of the loveless, jealousy, disappointed hope, hostility, reproach, humiliation, resentment, failure, wasted works, shame, unremitting poverty, and intellectual hardships shared by no class of the populace. In those letters the stories songs and prophecies of her life, from which it had always been his instinctive motive to flee, were continually retold, with variations and contradictions, like centuries of emendation and conflation in the stemma of a biblical canon.

And so he still refrained from asking about Sycorax or the Year of the Dog.

To her disgust, he wouldn't even say where he was working. Despite his increasing curiosity about the Brotherhood's attempt to achieve Pauline charity by means of economically organized community, which invited comparison with the communal economy envisioned for at least one monastery of the Classic Order of the Vine, he told her nothing about the right good news of Christianity emanating from East Harbor.

But it wasn't only her to whom he was incapable of evangelizing: with all human beings he was as incapable of persuasion as he was of confession.

14
MOONFEATHER

Thus personal recompense to his mother was the one social responsibility that most threatened Caleb's ability to circumvent the realism of Atlantean theater as a closet playwright. Guilt, shame, aversion, pity, admiration, love. But she guessed nothing of his inchoate drama.

Lilian Cloud, on the other hand, had been informed, and never lost faith in his determination. Fortunately he had been relieved of responsibility for her motherhood before she informed him of it. Compensatory gratitude in this case inspired love in all his works.

She later confessed that a few weeks before her presence was made known by their accidental meeting at Harry's she'd had a first glimpse of Ibi walking on Cod Street with Caleb, and was overtaken by surprisingly emotional memories of her childhood wolf-love. Yet it was her unforgotten admiration of Caleb's mother that willingly readmitted him to the porch of her temple. The rencounter was a confusion of pleasure and dismay that she might otherwise have made sure to avoid, in the delicatessen or anywhere else in the city.

Anyway, for them both, discovery overwhelmed rediscovery. New developments so thronged into the consciousness of each other that reminiscence was practically dispossessed. Lilian especially appeared to find no necessity for reminding herself of the lovers they had been when four years younger. At that time of life any number of superseding nostalgias might have been crowded into a term as long as Eisenhower's second Occupation.

Their briefly shared past (felt at the time as a whole life-cycle of youth), three thousand miles to the west, now seemed little more significant, at least on Caleb's part, than any of the accidents that introduce men and women to each other before their lives begin to intertwine: symbolically fatal in early retrospect but then remembered only as remotely contingent, or relegated to a sentimental category of the dim past by the succession of alarums and excursions that afterwards disturb the two courses on which they seem to become different persons entirely. In his sudden edification the original knowledge of her remained no more visible than a sunken cornerstone long since obscured by superstructure and landscape. By starting with the ruined foundations he nevertheless spared himself a thousand hesitations and delays in building a much larger new castle.

Yet although his old leman was transfigured, the transfiguration was inaccessible. She did have a man, whether to be ridden of, or still to be ridden by. At first he was told only that the man's name was Gil, a computer programmer. Later he learned that Gilbert Algo was the name to look for. But she was ambiguous about her situation, and seemed overtaken by ambivalence.

Lilian's worth to him was so intensified by this immediate barrier that he almost totally forgot the nexus between them in the person of their daughter Monday. The little girl was called Mooney because she had come out from behind a Cloud, her mother said, but the baby had been named Monday in the first place because in nulliparity she herself was sometimes addressed by the future father as Dark-of-the-Moon. This humorous remark was almost the full extent of Lilian's reference to Caleb's knowledge of her past. Thus Mooney seemed no more than an inconvenient but historically enriched possession of the woman he loved, simply a donnée of her present condition.

Before he could stop himself Caleb bluntly asked her if she'd intended to settle in Dogtown.

"No, of course I'm not here on purpose! Not until Gil was already going full-tilt at Dogtown did it dawn on me that it was the name of your hometown that you'd spoken of stopping at when you left me for Europa."

"It took a couple of years to get this far."

"I remembered it was the place that Ruth Chapman said Michael wanted to come back to. Ruth was very kind to me. She gave me a job at her nursery school in Londonbridge after I had to leave the bookstore. But to me in those days the East was the East, just a vaguely fascinating jumble of cities and villages with confusing names all crowded together."

"Doctor Charlemagne says the Cape is dogged by coincidence."

"I didn't resist the idea when I realized. The town even looks like you. When are you going to resume your journey? —No, I take that back. You're a new friend, and it's not proper to question your intentions, past or future. This must be the last time we see each other if you don't agree that we're new acquaintances."

"Nothing could be truer."

"Then no more of the past!"

So it was Gil who had brought her here. She had refused to consider any menage with him that did not provide for what she wryly called "all my baggage", which comprised her mother as well as her daughter. The mother had come down from the mountains of Cornucopia to see her through travail and successive migrations. The alienated old widow was otherwise bereft of relatives, and prematurely infirm, but still able to do some of the housework and take care of her grandchild during the work-week while her daughter earned their living.

Since Lilian believed that metropolitan residence would be disadvantageous to Mooney, Gil had scanned the north shore for a cheap semi-rustic establishment that was convenient to St Botolph by commuter railroad and not too fussy about appearances. The search had so won him to Dogtown's apparent way of life that he was glad to rent a house near Prudence Cove even though it was five miles from the station. He hoped for recreation with the Cape's boats and beaches.

"It looked like a town I could find work in, and it was shabby enough for my taste. I saw plenty of dogs around. Folly Road seemed an appropriate address. It's safe for Mooney to play on because it goes nowhere—just dwindles off into Purdeyville—and it's full of potholes to slow down the dead-end traffic. I remembered your mother's advice—when you took me aboard her ship at the pier in the Estuary—to walk the world before settling down to a dead end. Well it was long enough Mother and Mooney and I'd been pioneering backwards without a covered wagon, and by the time I walked in

Norumbega Square I'd seen enough of the mountains and plains. But I always wanted a dead end on the Atlantic Ocean. We can hear it from the house.

"—But why are we here? What are your present intentions?" she asked with a humorous twist of her upper lip that he didn't remember from the old days. They were now skoaling glasses of Scotch, safely escaped in Newessexport, to begin what turned out to be the first and only dinner of what he was regarding as only the first of many at the very outset of romantic discovery.

"Because we elect unique affinities." he replied, not wishing quite yet to call attention to his less unique opportunism. "It's destiny, that the only two needles in the haystack should find each other without a search."

"I'm afraid I've been pricked by other needles." she replied. "So it must be the haystack that's unique."

After an instant of hesitation he took her to mean that when a man and woman each drift with at least one current or even countercurrent of contemporary civilization, if not actually swim along without reservation, all other things being equal, they are less likely to fall in love with each other for reasons of the mind than those hitherto isolated in idiosyncratic criticism of their culture. In any case, head over heels with risible enthusiasm, it was primarily by expressing his own mind that Caleb beamed his love of hers.

But she too was enchanted. In an excited language complementary to the erotic they interjected thoughts of this and that about art and reality, skipping through forests, leaping rivers, and instinctively finding the same passes through continental divides. There was no need to dwell upon their opinions; nor did they feel called upon to confirm the apprehended meanings of their glancing allusions to pell-mell ideas separately steeped. A couple of fleeting hours wasn't enough for questions anyway, to say nothing of explanations.

As far as any one of her ideas was concerned, as it transpired, for want of time together Caleb would have to content himself for the most part with subsequent retrospection of briefly flashing hints and clues. Even allowing for the forbidden fact that he couldn't help being influenced by what he'd learned of her in a previous life, Lilian's intelligence mystery and beauty seemed new and incomparable. But in this beginning he spoke only of what her mind would speak of, and said nothing in praise of her person.

Evidently such behavior was seductive; for later, on the way back to Dogtown in her car, she took it upon herself to park in a certain spot off the road where they could talk more privately. There she made the first move to kiss him, much to his astonishment who'd been prepared for a long siege—all the longer because it must have seemed to her that without assuming responsibility he was again taking advantage of a sweetheart whom he'd once valued so little as to abandon merely for the sake of travel.

But his scruples were nothing to her. That night it was as if she'd never dreamt there might be such a wonderful man of the world and didn't care that she couldn't help indulging her impulse. In two seconds her abandonment to the present and oblivion to the future were fully shared. They kissed and talked for another hour like flowering children so delighted with tender first kisses that for the time being they wanted no more of each other than to sit without limit side by side and face to face.

She was compelled to steal those few hours from her domestic duties on the exceptional pretext of retrieving some utensils that had been left with former neighbors who'd carried them to Newessexport when moving up there from St Botolph. Thereafter Caleb was to learn how rare and precious her freedom was, and how lucky he'd been to get her away at all. It was difficult to so much as signal by telephone without the knowledge of her protector her mother or her employer. Even Mooney was getting old enough to spill the beans at home if they weren't discreet in their exchanges when her company was a condition of fortune's brief blessing. The only third party in whom they could confide was Ibi. But he too was a danger to this kind of love, for Mooney was so glad to meet him on the street that with none of the real or pretended fear of saints imbued in many little girls by their mothers she'd throw her arms around his neck and hug him (much to his embarrassment); and the innocent lovers feared she would also remember him in babble at home.

Lilian worked at Loathey O'Toole's public house, and her exotic face could hardly fare unnoticed on the streets of the Harbor (especially among downtown workers like the Keiths), or of course in the Taraville neighborhood, where she was presumed to be a Mrs Cloud-Algo. If she and Caleb were to be seen together as anything more than polite fellow citizens casually sharing a sidewalk, it must be "off the Rock", and that was extremely difficult for Lilian to contrive, despite all the clever calculations of Caleb's proposals. On certain occasions she was extraordinarily resourceful in finding the hour or two required for a few minutes at some rendezvous which he could never have engineered; but otherwise (as he expressed their plight) the only chinks in the wall between Pyramus and Thisbe were for telephone wires, on which their conversations were usually constrained either by time or by auditors at her end of the line.

Under these conditions his most immediate yearning was for her words, which became more and more dear. He longed for expatiation on any of her perceptions that he'd detected from perhaps no more than a whiff during one of her swift obiter dicta.

The next possible meeting after those introductory kisses (sweeter than the loveliest consummation of unconstrained desire) was narrowed down to Newessexport in daylight. That northern venue with pleasant taverns for anonymous strangers was preferred for public privacy to more populous Bethsalem, the Cape's county seat to the south, as less attractive of Dogtown busybodies. Its architectural beauty survived its other interests, unlike that of Dogtown, where poverty and fire had scotched almost all manifestations of its lesser Georgian or Federalist wealth. Having fostered no vital fishery to replace the mercantile clippers and whalers that had made it rich despite a poor harbor (no more than the barred mouth of the Kerouac River), its past was realer than its declining present: but a fine locale for cerebral lovers on the verge of melancholy.

He found this new Lilian deft and decisive. "I'll scoop you up from your front steps at ten after two." she told him, and proved as good as her word. She drove without hesitation and, when he wasn't too exclusively absorbed by the whirlwind in his head to pay attention to what she was doing on the road, worried him a bit with her cavalier indifference to the hazards of speed. No religious conversion could have astonished him more than the apparent transformation of her very temperament—which in fact was so advanced that it often made him forget this wasn't an entirely unknown face. As accompaniment to her quietly rational manner of discourse, the breathtaking new tempo of motion and verve of meaning nearly expunged his recollection of the slow brooding store-clerk in Hume whose passions had been so unworldly and volcanic by virtue of prolonged reservation.

At a bare red table in an almost deserted barroom not much different from ten thousand others in towns that had no architecture or waterfront he made his last feeble attempt to apologize for desertion, to show that he was not now unmindful of how he had interrupted her life as an artist. But again she forbad such talk, thenceforth and evermore. "I felt like the B V M : it was exhilarating to become pregnant without a lover's claim! Childbirth rid me of ancestral heaviness and phlegm. Mooney was the greatest gift of my life. But it's awkward to keep thanking you. We're both reborn Easterners now—strangers afresh."

And truly she seemed to suffer no echoes of grievance. Instead he heard coolly pronounced sentiments even more exciting than the physical response to his attraction. The new man found to his amazement that he was distinctively fascinating, respected and desired by a free spirit critically experienced of exceptional men. His presence seemed to dwarf her estimation of Gil (which however might be expected in any case of a woman disaffected by her consort), for she believed that Gil appreciated nothing of value in her mental life. But Caleb pointed out to himself that Gil remained in possession.

She did however return to the one subject from their mutual past that she still sanctioned. The unfaded impression of her meeting with his mother brought more questions about Vernalia than he liked to spend such stolen time upon. Besides, he felt it slightly dishonorable and humiliating to bind her to him by exploiting his sinister nobility like some dependent morganatic heir.

But Lilian never forgot that Mary Tremont had once been an artist as well as an illicit mother; and after all he did not regret that in the old days (when Dogtown seemed so safely distant in the past, and her ship touching along the west coast of North and South Atlantis probably wouldn't return even to Golden Bay in less than half a year) he'd naively told the girl too much about the nurture he was proud of. He hardly noticed that it was because of Lilian's sympathetic interest in his mother he felt free to mention almost anything.

"Has she seen any of the Atlindus around Vernalia?" Lilian asked. "I wonder whose territory it was."

"Guaicas, Riolama's people, from the River of Seven Stars. They used to be called the 'white Naturals', because their skin was lighter than the others, from having lived so deep in the rain forest of El Dorado that the sun hadn't reached them. Amazonas is still mysterious. My mother thinks it's a pure Guaica family that sometimes comes to the Brotherhood hospital, among the Iberian Atlindus, and she walks out of bounds trying to get acquainted with them when they leave. No doubt she's generous and ostentatious about it. She admits that she still hasn't overcome her exhibitionism."

"Ten thousand years ago those people were related to the Atlindus of Cornucopia. My great-grandmother was probably a distant cousin of Ishi, and I'd probably be a squaw of the Yahi tribe right now if Yankees hadn't scoured the Cordilleras so fast. Gold is so cruel that it makes iron seem innocent."

"Down there the ghost towns were made by rubber."

"Does she go far off limits?"

"Not in this case. She's too terrified of snakes. But she's always looking for the local black jaguar to make friends with! The Brotherhood isn't amused when she calls the Guaican Lucifer 'a splendid god'".

"My father shot the she-wolf I was making friends with. He liked to call himself a rancher. That's when I began to understand I was divided between two kinds of people. But I wasn't sure whether it was male against female or white against color. I'm a quadroon, and I feel about a quarter masculine, so the confusion persists."

Lilian Cloud was the daughter of a halfbreed daughter of a locomotive engineer. Her father was a stingy far-from-penniless 'skin-keeper'—innkeeper for hunters and skiers—near Los Dados in the most famous pass of the high Cordillera. She was never dedicated by either parent to the toils of education, but turned up first in her highschool class and insisted upon going down from the mountains to the University, until drawn to the nearby Cornucopia School of Art by the academic freedom of pottery and weaving.

Now the girl who'd been spared most of her mother's drudgery was discovering in herself a practical energy and urban grace that never failed to earn her immediate promotion to the top of restaurant staffs, whether as leading waitress, cashier, or "hostess"; and without being won over she'd gradually taken enough ironical interest in commercial ceremony and management to learn something about buying and bookkeeping. For Mooney's sake she limited her acquiescence to Loathey's demand for her time, and to a diminishing degree she therefore remained partially dependent upon Gil for the comfort of her mother's decline and the happiness of her daughter's environment.

Caleb was told little about the vinculum that bound Lilian to the unimaginable Gil in person. Her fluctuating hostility toward the incumbent was less veiled than the countervailing desire, remaining or recurring—whether cooled or inflamed by the man's absences, an outside lover could scarcely guess. He learned that the susceptible programmer was now keeping bachelor quarters in St Botolph without relinquishing his Taraville key. She evaded none of Caleb's questions, and he admired the frankness of her replies, though they tacitly dispensed with the most interesting details as unnecessarily petty or time-consuming to recount. But he was too sensible of his culpability as both debaucher in the past and opportunist in the present to press any of the curiosities that would have found their way to his lips if there'd been leisure for delicate conversation.

This temporal poverty frustrated questions more maddeningly than it did the advancement of his touches. Afterwards, measuring in minutes each of their times together, he would marvel at how much he learned about her thoughts and feelings toward himself, and toward Mooney, without much furthering his knowledge of her erratic life with or without her lover in the flesh.

As the hemisphere's tide gathered speed toward summer their shared time became more and more exiguous, yet was so magnified by Caleb's lens of convex but clouded feelings that every moment of Lilian's auricular presence brought hours more of solitary rumination. Circumstances and social logic were so unfavorable that almost every meeting she announced as final. But her crises of passion were always expressed in a voice tempered and low, without emphasis or cadence—yet so subtly poetic to his ear that for weeks he could perfectly rehearse sentences otherwise unremarkable in diction or word order. He was enchanted by her monotone, not incompetent and boring like his own, but articulated with the instinct of a self-determined mind equally resistant to ordinary melody and rhetoric.

Near the beginning of their new love she'd calmly said "I never felt anything like this before. You've put me in upheaval." Meaning with her level gaze straight into his eyes that as a numinous stranger he was sweeping her into a surf of love as turbulent as his own. But later, at a fevered front-seat tryst, without potion to sip or light to see by, she declared his courtship absurd: "Mooney is in a good neighborhood. Gil loves her and she loves him. Furthermore I'm a tainted woman. There have been a number of other men. Before Mooney was kicking in my belly I took up with Dave Wilson back there. He wanted to marry me. He and some of the others. Even Gil tried to make me bear him another child legally. As it is, now that he's moved back in, his heart is set on adopting Mooney, for some financial reason, I suppose.—Of course I'll never let that bastard get her away from me.—I was glad to have a baby, but I never wanted a husband. I'm not fit to mate for life. But one has parts, like a bitch in heat."

"Let me join the suitors." Caleb quickly replied, hoping not to betray fastidious pain at her abrupt but unemphatic disclosure, which he believed wasn't calculated to surprise him. At the same time he was pathetically grateful to her for trusting him with this glance at a truth-lode that he had no right to inquire into, and no opportunity to approach obliquely in satiated whispers.

"You're not a suitor. You never were and never should be. Your work brooks no competition."

Caleb admitted to himself that he was no more decent than

Rousseau in his regard for marriage or offspring; but it was necessary to suppress a peculiar mixture of dismay with his excitement at her ironically unillusioned attitude. It seemed impossible to pursue and disentangle any of her themes or narratives until he had her to himself for more than a hour or two, especially when suffering such long and uncertain intervals of anxiety from one interview to the next.

"So why are we here?" With the characteristically wry tender smile upon which he often meditated in her absence she again took up that superfluous question. Ever her spoken or unspoken refrain, *Why are we here?*

To him it sounded Russian. Lacking love's proper occasion, he could find no response that didn't sound too fatuous before it reached his tongue. *Why are we here* indeed!

"Why keep this up?" she pursued. "We can live without seeing each other. As long as I know you exist."

He trembled in alarm. Fear instantly blighted his brain. He could think of nothing honorable or even feasible in answer to the reasoning he knew was unassailable. With cracking voice, nearly in tears, all that he could utter was "It's infinitely sad."

"No:" she said "Sad. Very very sad. But not infinitely sad."

"Well, half infinitely." he conceded.

So they both laughed; and on their way home in what she called a last farewell they delighted each other more than ever with sweet daylight kisses, reliving with assimilated wisdom youth's rosebud dawn of body over spirit. And then, though he never denied that he was not a suitor for her hand, she offered no objection to the idea of another assignation—as circumstances might permit.

But once or twice, despite her fascination with Caleb as a man of words, she spoke as if her body still loved the one of bytes and algorithms (which she had no interest in). Caleb dared not ask if Gil had returned to her bed for good or was blowing back and forth in tempests. As Lilian's domiciliary feelings veered with winds that were opaquely subterranean from Caleb's ethereal vantage, little by little he improved his diagnostic guesses, though never forgetting the proviso that he might be wrong about every symptom by as much as a hundred and eighty degrees. It was understood without special asseveration that her variable love of bondage did not exclude a deeper love for Caleb. "You're inaccessible." she said evenly. "All my life I've most desired what I cannot have. It's like being in love with a Cephasite voyageur."

That was one of the blows to his heart as palpable as contempt in proving the folly of its desire. He'd heard something like the same from others, even from Bice—with more vivacity and less passion. But they were sitting face to face at another chrome-rimmed table in such satisfaction at the sheer presence of each other that nothing she said could seriously dampen his good spirits as long as she remained in sight and refrained from foreclosing further communication. Despite all his foreboding, and ostensibly without so much as presuming that she would ever speak to him again, he took manifest joy in the quiet irony of her equable voice—humorously cool yet almost clinical, in contrast to what it said: in no way belying the overt blazes of feeling with which in greater privacy her mouth would press his.

Those the two instrumental powers of her lips—scarcely ever experienced at once but perfectly teamed in Caleb's imagination—whirled his chariot toward either an unbearable loss or an incredible glory, neither of which he wished to define until he could win the one prize craved by all lovers as the first milestone of any course—all the while he tried to tell himself how necessary it was to prepare for the decision he feared absolutely. Reflected in his distorting oscilloscope, her dielectric tension raised the significance of every word and gesture to exponential powers of information.

Never but once did he give her important cause to reproach him for violation of their treaty, or to deny him an answer to his curiosity; and even then she didn't take exception. That was when in desperation of success he took his life into his hands by breaking the pledge to ignore their history. "Have you forgotten that Mooney is my daughter?" he timorously ventured. It really seemed as if she had put that fact back behind the cloud.

"Not at all. I well remember the act in which she was conceived. There weren't a great many others."

At first blush he was stunned, as if by an insult to his chivalry. But then he teased her: "Other acts or other men?"

"Other acts with you under a full moon." Divining one of his misapprehensions, she added: "I've never had overlapping lovers."

Afraid to breathe, he waited for her to say more. They both looked at their glasses, or at the little squares of paper napkin that in Atlantis serve as saucers on surfaces of plastic. Then at each other, with rueful smiles.

But her statement was not the premise of some awful or imperative syllogism. Instead it turned out to be a theme for his own sole development in the long anxious stretches between the rewards of her actual presence, before and after episodic adventures of parking in deserted kilroy groves near some highway, too soon broken off in her tardy haste to get home and make the family supper.

"And you?" she then asked.

"Neither have I." In afterthought he chuckled: "Except at the Annunciator Bank, you remember?"

"I hope somebody's being nicer than that to you now."

Suddenly enjoying an almost unreserved freedom of confession, he told her a little about the Beatrice-game with lighthearted self-mockery. To be sure, he put the best face upon its ignominious aspect; but the torments vanished in an objectivity induced by Lilian's cheerfully pragmatic attitude, which made him forget for a while his infinitely superior torment of unfulfillment by the twenty-five-percent masculine sympathizer herself. Then and thereafter she appeared thoroughly innocent of jealousy—either of his amours or of Gil's (whose infidelities she seemed to accept rather as symptoms of weak character than as offences of equity); and Caleb was secretly so put to shame by what he referred to as her "maturity" that his emulation of her outlook was as good as a provisional cure of soul. Her astonishingly disinterested concern for his celibate strait deepened his impression of her purity.

His ensorcellment to this sister seemed aristocratically incestuous, the snares of Bice's flirtatious eroticism almost vulgar. But the aristocratic quality was Lilian's, and the vulgarity of the other case was his own. Respectfully, as weakest of the three, he compared the intellectual maturity of Lilian, which inflamed his love of her skin and bones, with Bice's philosophical immaturity, which undoubtedly played a part in her infatuation of homunculi. Both of them were women whose critical mentality electrified the natural magnetism of gender-beauty; but Bice's field of electromagnetism fascinated a much broader spectrum of men, including those who would fear or disesteem the true wit of either.

To Lilian, aloud, he made no denial of loyalty at least to the memory of his initial adventure with Bice; and he was sure that if she had known her, or heard his description of her attractions, it would have made no difference in her encouragement of his hopes for an equilibrium of desire perhaps comparable to her own with Gil. But Caleb believed that even without having her fill at home the idea of "another woman" wouldn't have been alarming to Lilian, and that the only particulars she cared about were those of affect upon the quality of the man or men she loved.

Thus, though not displeased to hear of his unexceptionable lust for the surfaces and crevices of the human entity formed with her shape, endowed with her feelings, and labeled with her name, she commiserated him that the frustration of his carnal intention could not be assuaged as was her corresponding desire for him by such relief as she was extrinsically accorded in her own bed often enough to remove the deprivation of a lovelier similar sensation as cause for romantic folly. "As for us, 'tis a consummation devoutly to be wished." she said. "Maybe sometime chance will favor us out of thin air with a night together—a weekend, a fortnight, even a whole moon! You'll finally have the benefit of my maturity!"

Lilian's last sentence did not at once register in his memory. Confidence in his own qualities having been bolstered by her deportment in his arms, he was more struck by the cordial advice that followed, which seemed at the time as practical as it was funny: "Meanwhile, overwhelm her!"

Their respective displacement of objects did not indicate that the subjective relations between Caleb and Lilian were less profoundly sexual than they had been four years earlier, or than those of Tristan and Yseult. But sensual matters, like the many other pursuits of mind expelled or forfended by the chronologic of their exigent encounters, were hardly touched upon before abandoned; and for each of them it was necessary to allude to things surmised as if they were things known. Most of their pains and delights had to be left for guesswork after parting, for they met only in giddy dives of exploration to the bottom of an insulated sea where they preferred to save their breath for kisses. Too soon, always too soon, the oxidation of time forced them to the surface! They were both too buoyant to resist the rule of reality.

He did take time however to caution her with the parable of Axel and Sara up on a crag, where even in the castle's deepest treasure vault the atmospheric pressure was much too low. It was not such eternity that Pyramus and Thisbe wanted, but only a little more of time—or times less seldom, less distant, and less uncertain.

Lilian's twin raven braids were no more, and he forgot them, which formerly he'd caressed like heavenly snakes; her skin was now as clear and translucent as a nun's, except when furrowed vertically between the brows like Ibi's asking guidance; and the storms of experience had left her trunk as supple as a birch. Yet what had been simply smooth in her face was now refined by further differentiations of feature, an admission of lines within the outlines, which excited his sense of beauty as never before by signifying a personally quickened fusion of sex and intellect. She was to him as the same goddess envisaged by a more discriminating cult.

Caleb was aware that he made too much of every moment's adventitious symbolism. Consciously and involuntarily, when he was not with her and free to brood (neglecting his toils of analysis or creation), he spun unceasing conjectures about her apprehensions of the common English language which alone to some degree directed men and women to the same sphere of understanding, which both she and Bice remarkably appreciated, but of which her usage took his breath beneath the waves. He identified her as his unique anti-material binary, differing from him in polarity and dexterity, but otherwise only in knowledge and perception that complemented his own. With her he wished to investigate the essence of gender in feeling, in proprioception, in all six senses—beneath and beyond the thoughts of speech that kept male and female in communication with each other. Was it possible that even Lilian's demisemi-masculine psyche shared more with Bice, and with all their sisters, than with himself her missing half?

Failing more festal means of neutralization, it was absolutely necessary to speak his mind to her. Knowing where she lived and where she worked, he would have run amok with indiscretions if he hadn't been able to make surreptitious use of the postal service.

His letters, enveloped without return address and traveling little further than a schoolroom lovenote, were successful as contributing influences. They fostered a certain curiosity about what he would say next, and perhaps a taste for the appreciations they expressed. She loved him the more for his written word. For some time, and then from time to time, all his other writing ceased.

It seemed odd that Lilian did not reciprocate in this auto-narcosis. At his increasingly importunate behest, who thirsted unto madness for exposition of her mind, she repeatedly promised to write. Yet she never replied to his letters. He begged her to take pity upon him.

Her silence may have been an ill effect of his sleeplessly roving salt-mill, which ground out alphabetic symbols from the sea beneath the waves and concentrated them upon her head like broadcast messages reversed—as if transmitted from all points on a circumference to the single receiver. He began to fear that his means of overwhelming assault—added to quotations from his mother's salty horn of plenty—defeated half the purpose by daunting Lilian's weaker penchant for the writing of words. It seemed a crime against humanity to reinforce her diffidence as an abandoned woman who'd never felt welcome within the society of "intellectuals". Only in a kind of tacit compromise (which did nothing to satisfy his thirst for sentences from her concerning himself) was he able to learn something of her expository skill, when he finally managed to extort from her portable file a few poems and essays that she had cared enough to preserve from incomplete "extension courses".

On the other hand it was plausible to argue as explanation of her graphic silence a penury of leisure in nursery kitchen and bedroom. Yet the woman herself never tergiversated with any such excuse. She refused to admit that she was ever tired or overworked, however much he speculated that she was too busy for amusements of any kind, often suppressing his imaginations of her dalliance with Gil as the background of her mental adventures with himself as well as of her domestic quarrels.

Or else, he thought, her pitiless false promises to write were symptoms of a refined scruple that was too embarrassing to offer in defense against the reproaches of her voiceless troubadour: that it would have been an immoral violation of Gil's good faith to put her hand to paper for the man she really loved.

One evening, in reckless hunger for the sight of her, not long after their first two or three clandestine conversations, he went to the Doghouse for his dinner without permission. He hadn't made bold to inquire into her schedule there, but as the fantastic luck of a beginner would have it, he found her not only on duty but also assigned to his table. It happened not to be one of her scheduled shifts as hostess, but she had responded to the emergency of several staff absences by coming in to serve as a waitress, dressed in one of the new white uniforms that Loathey O'Toole had recently imposed upon his maidservants simply to relieve the ubiquitous green of his ultra-Irish establishment.

Fearful of Lilian's annoyance at his foolish temerity in showing up merely with the hope to observe her for once at her trade as she might appear to other men's eyes from a distance, Caleb was quaking in his boots—when she surprised him with a smile of unexpected pleasure! Far from showing anger, her signs of happy recognition (it seemed to him) recklessly unmasked the acknowledged adoration of an ostensibly casual new customer.

But they immediately suppressed the ebullience of sudden joy. She was being paid for her impartial efficiency and he was in dread of tempting providence.

Owing to the incandescence of his delight as he covertly watched her come and go in the course of combined primary and semi-supervisory busyness, the special impression of her angelic competence did not clearly emerge into consciousness until the next morning when he woke to the half-dream. At the time, while he was feverishly assaying the words they might or did exchange so sparingly (though fully to the permissible limits of an employee's coquetry), which probably were rendered more than prudently conspicuous by sotto-voce intensity, her virtuoso food-service would have been even more striking if he'd been clearheaded enough to compare this quizzically bright and romantically disguised woman of the world, so nimble in improvisation, so light on her feet, to the thicker darker brooding antisocial artist who'd been his girl at Hume. His modesty always vanished at favorable attention from a woman, but she had then excelled him in gallantry, at which she wasted no words.

"What would you like to drink, Mr Karcist?" she began. Then murmured "You look just the way a man should look."

Now he was the last sort of male specimen to expect this kind of tribute. In any case he was so dumbfounded at not being frowned upon that he almost didn't hear her add "I could follow you anywhere!" Instead of being exiled he was merrily promoted! Or at least his hopes were temporarily exalted.

He wasn't misled as to the ultimate significance of this fine talk, whether it represented a lucky reading in the random librations of her equivocation or a resolute conviction at the heart of fervent indecision. He never doubted that she was continually balancing two protean quantities in an uncalibrated pair of scales. His was obviously the lighter. It was only right that she should weigh his most valuable qualities with an adjustment for the gravid plight to which they'd led her in the still not quite disconnected past. But his deepest vanity was elated by this spontaneous proof of the recent evolutionary jump in her feeling—of the objective correlative that it warranted of his person.

"Scotch and water, please." They laughed too loud together, remembering that at the outset of their signal dinner in Newessexport he had ordered the same thing for them both; but their befuddled young waiter had brought him a small glass of whiskey and set the tumbler of icewater down before her.

"I hate to wait on anybody else." she interpolated into her recitation of the jour's menu. "I can't keep my eyes off you." But to an onlooker now who didn't bend an ear too close she might have appeared the soul of businesslike propriety—indeed far less effervescent than Loathey preferred in general. But Caleb dared not overburden his triumph by ordering a second drink.

"Whenever you walk away I'm torn in half." he told her, averting his eyes from the placket of her ornamental apron.

"I've always walked in half."

"Even with Gil?"

"He'll never get up from the bed and walk! Gil doesn't yearn. He's not the stuff for my other half."

"Am I, do you think?" he asked.

"You won't be, of course. But you're what's missing." The sadness in her debonair tone excited all his nerves without distinction. The next day he sent her his praise:

THE CANDID WOMAN OF THE DOGHOUSE

In paling sky
this morning's moon
sails upright at half.
Has she been cloven—
or is she not yet joined?

(Here's the Scotch
and there's the water.)

The chord grows feathery
like cloud
before the reach of sun.

The candid woman
fades by day
as I pay homage
to her silent course.

(An unknown woman clad in white
plucked me from the morgue.)

He hoped Lilian would remember the story of his life that had won her to him at Hume: how Mary Tremont's pride and joy—Son of Rahab, her trinity of babies—having been agonized by slow labor, torn by the doctor's forceps, and strangled by his own umbilical cord, was put away for dead:: until retrieved by a passing nurse whose ears were tuned to the faintest whimper.

15
MAGIC
MOUNTAIN

For many weeks between winter and spring Caleb's love for Lilian flared as hotly as he could bear. Then little by little, for lack of oxygen commensurate to fuel, it began to steady itself. It was never banked or extinguished, and the coal bin was kept as full as an ever-normal granary. He shoveled as much anthracite as that furnace could burn. But there was plenty of soft coal for other combustions in the boiler room. In the carbon dioxide of true love his bituminous friendship with Bice Picory sometimes prospered.

At first the general effect of Lilian was a clarified reduction of all his experience to sympathetic emotion. He marched through his daily pursuits in a web of feeling. Yet because his skeleton had taken shape in the service of intellect, and was therefore calculated to support the rigging of unreduced mentation, his happy feelings about her, as they reinforced his fundamental resonance with the woman herself, stimulated masterful concepts of the objective universe; whereas the unhappy feelings in his hours of suffering took possession of his fused endocrine and nervous systems fully and exclusively, abhorring the company of extraneous thoughts—and at such times he looked for no merely aesthetic space between the net of joy and the tightrope of dread.

He had never before been so alive to the fact that even his most abstract constructions were emotional. All discrete intelligence, received and stored in oscillating crescendos by the capacitor in his head, pulsed as metaphor into the heart's continuous analogues of pure meaning. Despite the protracted intensification of diverted desire, the prevalent difficulty even of practically innocent assignation, the meager meed of exiguous speech, and unrequited communication by paper, he associated her precious existence (whether or not it would be lost to himself) with all his concurrent excitement about Father Duncannon's vision of the City of God, Doctor Charlemagne's dromenology, President Kennedy's opportunity to organize a Catholicratic government, and above all the proof-in-progress of his own imagination. Like so many trains claiming a single track (in the same or opposite direction), these simultaneous projects steamed and whistled for his time; but every engine steamed to and from the turntable of pure feeling.

Most of the time when he wasn't so absorbed in something he had to do, or in sleep, as to forget Lilian for a while, his passion for her, whether in the seeking or the suffering, felt more like frustrated transmission than thwarted reception. Either leading or trailing the momentum, creative or aesthetic, it dominated his mentality for spans of the calendar that seemed far longer than they really were. The whole sentience comprising these feelings seemed concentrated at the crest of one composite tsunami—not yet breaking, but bound to crash upon beach or rock (if not turned to selfdestructive chop by pelagic Sturm and Drang): a gathering of wave-power that with less providential fortune might have been anatomized as corpuscles gelling in pain.

When he sang the Moonfeather Blues it was Lilian herself who urged him to make the most of his advancements with Bice. For there did come times when some of his love for Lilian had to be frozen for preservation. But the journalist's company was always fresh, after she was rediscovered hugging Ibi outside her new office of employment, and (if he didn't wait until too late in the day to bid for her leisure) she was often accessible for libertine conversation.

He replied truly enough when she remarked on one occasion that he seemed downcast: "I'm not depressed. It's only a little Weltschmerz and angor animi."—because, he told her, Adlai Stevenson had not been appointed Secretary of Imperialism; but he did not mention that Lilian (of whom she still knew nothing at all) had excused herself from two hard-won appointments in succession.

Since from Moonfeather he never got answers to his questions, big or little, personal or cosmic, unless they were fit to be asked point-blank in short telephone calls, or unless they were so pressing that he remembered to ask them during the rarer and headier propinquities of her real presence (when all his wits fused in a superconducted torrent of sensation too centripetal to make space for unsensational information), much of his overstimulated urge to converse with a woman of sympathetic intelligence was sidetracked to Bice.

Not that he'd meanwhile forgotten the mercurial gypsy as unique instructor at an intermediate level of evolution never to be perfected or regretted. The atavistic (rather than Christian) dissolution of his resentment of her had been instantaneous. The pleasure of her company was no more to be denied than an interesting British movie. With Lilian's love in reserve, like the greatest defense of all, notwithstanding postponements of consummation, his selfconfidence in gallantry was revived. Nothing foreclosed his hope for carnal success with both or either.

In the course of time his sketch of Bice's character resolved itself into a few variant hypotheses of tolerable uncertainty—tolerable not only because her part of his cortical eroticism was factored with a coefficient that kept it less than half by far, but also because he was beginning to accept Lilian's doctrine with gratitude: that a lover could love more than one lover at once; the arcane second-order heresy that heretical troubadours and their ladies usually kept from each other.

But before Caleb was reassured by Lilian's implication that her principle applied as well to him as to herself, he'd undergone faint qualms of self-contempt for the complimentary salute to Bice's reappearance by homunculus erectus. First there was the continuum of jealousy recalled like an unpleasant dimension by the news of her cohabitation with Gepetto DaGetto. To this distress was added his feeling of guilt for the renaissance of an unscrupulous desire that dishonored the anomalous love, both older and newer, which for several weeks, until that very moment outside the Nous, had obsessed every axis of his passions. Could he so blatantly mock the lunar devotion he professed to the mother of his strange little daughter—as if for a second time, and so soon, forsooth!—simply because he was still disappointed by her honorable disallowance of the access generally most valued?

To the commoner's eye Bice was perhaps more beautiful, more

liberally magnetic in attitude mein and manner; but his allegiance (as distinguished from the prepossessions of his nether ego) was often inversely proportional to the agreement of other men, and even Bice's uncommon popularity would have counted against her whether or not it entailed competition. On the other hand, her specially attractive verbal intelligence (less profound but correspondingly more ambitious than Lilian's) was an extremely attractive ingredient of the physique that distinguished her from all the other sportive beauties he was ever likely to encounter.

Thus Lilian's rather urbane tolerance eased him into a lighthearted duplicity and divaricate despair. Soon his reignited candlelight love for the wandering siren—yes, not merely commonplace lust, but the priapic cultivation of mutual intelligence: love of that kind at least—steadied itself almost comfortably, like an errant knight's on his second time around to the same enchantment. For the present then, play of mind being virtually out of the picture as foreplay to definitive atonement with Thisbe (owing to her wall of circumstances), Pyramus amused himself with Beatrice by discussing such ideas as imaginary numbers, about which no one else had ever excited her.

At the middle distance of loosely chemical relations, initially half free of jealousy and destined to become all but wholly so, little vulnerable (he thought) to other pain on her account, like one who flinches but exults that he hasn't cried out, he now found it possible to converse with her almost freely about many matters that would have been tactically avoided or impatiently put aside as impediments to perfected recreation if he were still as defenceless against her charms as when he'd written the letters to England and Terra Nova that intensified and prolonged the first shock of her constitutional treachery. After that first questioning glance up at him from her crouching cheek-to-cheek hug of Ibi in Coalyard Lane, and his own speechless gaze of uncertainty, they had implicitly settled upon a new plane of intimacy without bothering to determine whether or not it would intersect the level formerly occupied by their intercourse.

He'd gotten wise enough not to resurrect the dead hope of traveling with her to Britain and other lands of his heart's desire, having come to understand that what she had to teach him was less European than Atlantean. Contenting himself with day-to-day fortune, he affected to accept the beauties of her personality disinterestedly; while for her part she gave him to understand that she regarded herself uniquely privileged in disciplines beyond her competence or vital interest, by virtue of luckiness and good taste, as the discoverer of him as a future celebrity.

Caleb presumed that her operational loyalty to Petto was transitory. At any rate it didn't rule out gayly lipped kisses or playfully palpating response to the provocation of her slitted blouses. Transitory or not, and irrespective of presumptive competitors (whose success may or may not have been grosser than his own), his extreme importunity was mostly forestalled or diverted by the senior love of which Bice had no inkling. And he gradually realized that the diplomatic deception on his part was serving his manner in such a way as to render her more affectionate, on the strength of what seemed to her his core of ultimate indifference; for being pursued to distraction was usually taken by her to indicate a pursuer's boring obtuseness.

"So—the Imperial Gypsy has returned from the old country!" He raised aloft his glass of ale, once more at home with her.

"But the Goliard has not yet resumed his journey to the East!" she replied in kind. "Prosit!"

"To brother and sister! Our kinship appears to be too close for marriage."

"That's why I was afraid of loving you too much." she laughed. "But I'm still in love with you. Can't you tell? I wish I'd had your mother, and no father. Of course you're a gentleman of the word. I'm not educated enough to reply to your ideas; I can't speak like an equal; my habits are bad and I haven't the constitution to refrain from keeping up with the times: but I admire you for never abusing a preposition as a conjunction. And in spite of all that you're the only one who's ever really understood me!"

Caleb smiled at finding himself so soon repeating the pastoral role that had become all too familiar to him as a complementary lover of women, meanwhile wondering what it was he'd told this girl that made her envy him his mother, a person of very different schesis (outside the congenital core of womanhood), despite certain resemblances he found in the younger's good humor, fledgling courage to claim her own adventures in a world made by men, and susceptibility to the cacoethes scribendi.

But with Bice especially he always kept an eye open for his cognitive goal with women—an end, inseparable from the concupiscent, which most of the intelligent women he'd approached with lesser expectation mistook for the designation of themselves as "mere" objects—some inkling of her feminine experience. For Caleb clung to the hope that he would have the opportunity to induce by natural magic the metamorphic beatitude which he properly could not share but only defer to and fall away from (though feeling it happen beneath his belly), yet which in afteraffect might make her speak the truth, opening pericopes of her history and somehow exposing the mystery beyond a man's imagination that he could only touch off and observe from an irreducible distance. Even in the words taught by men, even using the epicene language that necessarily misrepresents anyone's truth, her communications would be more informative than the wise silence of less denatured sisters—or at least more fascinating!

She probably knows more about men than I do, he thought. About their metamorphoses anyway. But how much more than she do I know about the transfiguration of women? All I really sense is their effect upon me, which in most cases is less subjective than what at best is my perhaps accidental affect upon them. Further than that, my knowledge can be no more than privileged hearsay.

What he actually said to Bice was "Women may understand men better than men understand women, but they don't understand themselves as well as men do."

"That statement is grammatically ambiguous; but it's true that I don't understand myself. The important thing is that you understand other things better than anyone else. I know you can't tell me all you understand, but there are two subjects I can learn to understand only from you: one is your mother; the other is imaginary numbers."

Then and thereafter, for most of their continuing conversations, like Paphnutius and Thais on opposite courses through the Harbor ward after a day's work, they were meeting at Leonardo's, the most cosmopolitan of cheap eating houses in the microtopopolis—he on his way home westward from the Foreside, she on her way from the *Nous* office to her quarters in East Harbor. She was still commuting by taxi or by "getting lifts" while she kept sporadically to the promise that she would save up money for a car and patiently learn the impatient craft of Vinland driving so that she could become a reporter worth her dole of salt, presumably aware that Gary Ghibellini should have been uneasy about the appearance of their deal.

Leonardo's "House of Pizza, Spaghetti and Fine Foods" was next door to Mercator-Steelyard's Main Office and not far from the City Lights Theater, across Front Street from the line of dingy stores and tenements concealing jagged basement wounds in the cicatrized rock of the Spirit Hill massif. Here the south side of the street was a level margin that once verged a tidewater cove, but now a broad flat separated it from the waterfront, upon which, beyond smaller yards and buildings, the tall-stacked steam plant of "the Traction" had been founded, whose whistle blasts still produced all public signals, obliterating all voices from Watch House Point to Joint Hill whenever they sounded. Leonardo's was the only restaurant in town (not excluding The Windmill or any of the other carriage-trade establishments) that favored European art over the local seascapes and fishing-wharf gauds which were believed by pilgrims and marooners alike to substantiate Dogtown's national importance as an erstwhile wellspring of painting; for in all its low-backed booths, which were separated from each other by vertical bamboo segments sparsely strung like beads, altogether resembling the curtains in Owhyhee pleasure domes for sailors, the wall bore one of the framed prints of a French Impressionist. It was also the only place in Dogtown that served the Canterbury Ale typically preferred by the class of people who called for Scotch when they wanted grain distilled. But the lighting, though sufficiently subdued and well enough blended not to discourage private conversation, was kinetically variegated by red yellow blue and green projections from constantly rotating chandeliers of stained glass which depicted with panache the four-pair teams of Clydesdales that once drew wagons piled high with the beer barrels of vulgar Hindenburg or Blitz.

Nor were patrons shielded from other wavelengths of the comparatively unobjectionable ambience. To Caleb's secret dismay (which soon dissolved into his general liking for the unpretentious tastes of the place) Bice recognized and welcomed most of the music ceaselessly sounding from a hidden vent. This passing but recurrent disturbance in his estimation of her discrimination arose not from a sense of her aesthetic limitations but from the reminder of his own secretly fastidious prejudice against all enzymatic fluids in which, by aural edulcoration, doses of language were well enough macerated for Atlantean digestion. At Leonardo's however the artificial sound was soothingly restrained to a volume no greater than what was necessary to mask the living voices that populated the chamber in averaged confusion.

Thus for Caleb these meals with Bice were events of humbling edification, at least as illustration of what Doc Charlemagne asserted to be Dogtown's uneven rear-guard stand against the national commerce of entertainment, to which the unselfconscious proprietor would never have dreamed himself renitent. The residual Tuscan sensibility that tempered the atmosphere of the room was a sampling of perhaps the most generous single element in the city's compounded peculiarity. It sometimes seemed to Caleb more remarkable in present Atlantis than the quattrocento genius of Tuscany. Yet the discreet nickelodeon and cheap dimmed prints offsetting the nostalgic vigor of dashing dray horses were equally charming to Bice, who liked nightclubs. They both also relished the quick service and good prices for the best of pizza, which was served off its circular cardboard trencher onto paper napkins without platforms of crockery. Together they took repeated swigs of ale in toast to Leonardo and his namesake.

"He was a sinister lovechild too." Caleb smugly pointed out.

"Nacht und Nebel, you're not the only bastard on this beach! My father was too amorous to marry my mother until legal entanglement with a Transylvanian Jewess could no longer damage his prospects for promotion as much as keeping a mistress and baby."

"But weren't you a changeling of the Gypsies?"

"At least I'm right-handed! According to Sancho Panza you must be too wayward to learn anything from teachers, or else you come from humble parents. Karcist sounds like a Jewish name."

"My mother thought it was Greek."

"But you told me you were born circumcised."

"They still baptised me when I was five, right here at St Martha's Convent."

"I suppose that's not too late. Abraham was ninety-nine. After 1391 many of the Marranos were dragged to the font by force—just so that the Inquisition could take jurisdiction over them as heretics!" Her merriment carried them into a second round of prosits.

"I usually feel more like a Jew than an Irishman or Greek."

"What's your middle name?"

"Distinguished people need no middle name. But I used to be ashamed of having no middle initial. It made me all the more conspicuous as the minim of all my grades. Finally my mother said 'Let it be *I*.' So I started signing myself Caleb I Karcist. That sounded good. After a while I thought of asking her what it stood for. 'Why not Ichabod?' she said. 'It means *Where is the glory?*' That was her allusion to the Purdeyville rock-maxim she chided me with when I was lazy: DO GREAT THINGS, DON'T DREAM THEM ALL DAY LONG. She told me to write it with a little *i* until I became a man. I experimented with that autograph in private. Only after leaving home did I learn that the imaginary number *i* was a constant in the square root of negative capability!"

"So at last you're going to tell me about the little demons! It's obvious that the big *I* stands for the great I-AM of your male arrogance, a k a Number One! Therein lies the tail. But why does a man need the lower case?"

She never forgot his promise to explain the universe generated by the square root of minus unity, as he had only started to do in the big bed of the Poet's Corner, just before putting her back to sleep in the last hour of their memorable dalliance, which now seemed as distant in years as it really was in months. "It's a phantom number that would have horrified the Greeks. It seems to account for the fact that counter-girls never notice me. I would have made a good spy if I hadn't been rejected by the Strategic Intelligence Service. In public, as an anti-actor, I'm always overlooked!"

"I'll take your word for what you are in public; but in private you minimize yourself quite falsely."

"The imaginary numbers are like an ocean—not very interesting when there's no land in sight. But they can be very exciting when they're not alone. When combined and coefficient with real ones they express complexity."

"You mean perplexity."

"A complex plane is made by an axis of reals and an axis of imaginaries. I'm imaginary and you are real. Together we produce complexity!"

"Only a Minnesinger like Ichabod Stylites could lead me such a light fantastic! Teach me this complex number!" She took up his hand, as if to lead him to a dance floor, and then dropped it. "But perhaps this is the wrong music."

"For instance, some 'directed line segment' if multiplied once and then once again by little i—"

"Little me, you should say, my dear."

"—by the square of the square root of minus one, is converted into the negative of its original vector. But as constituents of an IRTH-continuum, complex numbers symbolize the counterentropic modulus of human free will!"

"Male freewill! Not Mother Earth's!"

"Masculine, not male. The IRTH-molecule is a masculine egg."

"Made up of Ego-atoms—capital or not!"

But he only threw more dust in her eyes by setting forth the difference between what he called his technologically symbolic geometry and the magically symbolic geometry of platonists and neognostics, and by explaining how its multidimensional triangulations, both infinite and infinitesimal, were meant to express disparate civilizations, ancient and modern, in a universal system relating structure machine and power!

Caleb was well enough aware that to disburden Creative Mind upon a journalist, howsoever intelligent and sincere, was to avail himself of meretricious sympathy. But the ale was heady, and there was no one else at leisure to entertain his conceit. With Lilian he had no time to expound monological abstractions. Father Duncannon he feared was too much of a scientist, and Chris too little of one, to take his metaphors as much else than frivolous. Doc was the one to whom he'd most have liked to make the exposition; but with Doc he must either listen and respond to Doc's agenda or open himself to invidious subsumption which might sour the whole scheme, seeing that Doc himself was a creator of images whose animus was engaged with the same kind of matter.

Even in his cups Caleb was reminded of the self-indulgence he grudged Doctor Charlemagne: dilating upon wanton ideas with overawed admirers patently baffled by his topic but complying with the pretense of bilateral discussion and offering to uphold a fake appreciation. But in his own case the satisfaction was rare of holding any listener in thrall, and he was glad to swallow even Bice's quizzical version of admiration as a blessed placebo for certain passions of the intellect that excessively disturbed the work they infused.

Caleb and Bice frequently thus met in that Spring of 1961, which was to be a year of reconciliation, politics and all. But the Gypsy was utterly indifferent to the national affairs of the U S A, and her interest in Dogtown was no more political than necessary for the pursuit of her assignments at the *Nous* in preparation for city-hall reporting. All her spontaneous attention was personal—in the sense that except for Ibi all its objects were either individually human or conceivably pertinent to her first-person singular career.

She had been trying to persuade Gary Ghibellini to give her a second page, so that News of the Arts could be separated from Community News and expanded with photographs and reviews. Caleb now attributed her ebullience to the job rather than to Petto, despite her impatience at having to serve a pedestrian apprenticeship while awaiting her driver's license. She was learning to drive under the incoherent instruction of that ultra-virile antinomian—probably the most heedless driver in a city of heedless kilroys—who must not have been especially motivated to further her independence of locomotion. Indeed the thought of Petto teaching Desdemona how to drive his welding rig would have a brought a smile to the lips of Othello. Caleb found himself less annoyed than he had expected to be at supposing the sculptor's hands all over his model by way of guiding her in the use of arms and legs.

As for his own prospects with that torso, it seemed to him (recognizing her preoccupation with the journalistic ambition that was about to be advanced) that she was becoming almost as inured to his own banal chiropractic as to that of whom it was only to be expected. Yet at the same time he was enjoying progressively intimate distinction as what he modestly called her "incestuous brother confessor"; and she declared that in fact it was he whom she cherished as "Number i in petto"! He was said to be the only swain whose sagacity she deferred to. At any rate the latitude to which he was accordingly entitled relieved enough tension to free him for other opportunities without discouraging this particular hope of the upper-case I.

Speaking about her tasks at the *Nous*—for which she said Gary kept her on the payroll, despite severely limited mobility, simply in preference to suffering an ignorant graduate of some journalism school that turned out the only kind of person willing to grub for wages less than a fish-packer's in order to get a foothold on the first steppingstone to practicable literacy—she already alluded easily to Dogtown offices and institutions that Caleb was either ignorant or afraid of. Whenever he tentatively teased her for precocious savvy of local skeins, especially insofar as they involved male personages whom he suspected of being piqued or picquable by the narrator, from Jason Anacoluther on down to the youngest of lumpers, she merrily doffed the mask of professional objectivity, which oftener seemed false than true.

But as far as expanding his knowledge of Dogtown was concerned her descriptions and hints were soon outdoing the contacts he made through Ibi as illuminating coefficients of his own restrained observation. If only he could keep in touch with her on warmly progressive terms (while his former infatuation grounded itself to a more pragmatic intimacy), as an armchair spymaster, without spending time in bars, he might be able to vicariously acquaint himself with contemporary marooners generally unaware of his existence. She told him everything—or at least anything—of what she discovered that wasn't fit to print, and somewhat more of what was generally known without the newspaper.

He would have had to admit that this amplification of his worldly experience through the medium of a private reporter was more intelligible and exciting (albeit no more valuable) than the cognitive benefits of his association with the chief of saints, if it weren't for the fact that without the prior benefit of Ibi's mediation he'd never have even known she existed. So his ulterior though not ultimate motive was to keep this genuine androphile talking freely, and as much as possible to reduce her wariness of his discretion to the irreducible level of sexual reticence rarely violated even by the loosest tongued of promiscuous misandrists. Lover or not, he hoped to become the most confidential friend she'd ever have.

But of course Bice's tangible presence never failed to elicit in Caleb the same reckless urge she aroused in all men susceptible to gleaming intelligent beauty as governed by a boldly affectionate temperament of the Central European type. And one morning he awoke from an evaporated dream that left his feelings in a nostalgic vacuum suddenly remembering the living image of her innocence, by which she had long ago been prophesied.

At Leonardo's he examined her perfectly unblemished face anew: humorous dark eyes vivifying a smoothly curved escutcheon of luminous white loosely enwreathed in unsymmetrical waves of finest black, an obvious transfiguration of any parental bloodlines, endowed by himself with the heavenly nimbus of Europe. Yet no longer incomparable! For between sleeping and waking that morning two currents of memory, one as old as childhood, the other as fresh as incessant desire, had merged as they welled to the surface like purest brine. Only then did he learn why Bice's beauty had never really surprised him; and why in his inmost heart its tender sweetness had survived all his lust and anger.

During the last summer of the war he had begun to suffer a primitive phase of the most common mania without the comfort of knowing that it was merely sooner conscious than that of other boys and not otherwise egregious, precociously predisposed by the anecdotes of his mother to which he pretended not to listen, before he was bold enough to make active acquaintance with any girl he thought wouldn't be horrified by sexual attention. Secretly and unscrupulously he had been moaning for a sister in the house. Neither then nor thereafter, until he knew it was possible for him to win through to the body of a stranger, did he hold as aught but superstition or doctrinal convention (like marriage) the taboo he'd have violated with as little compunction as he omitted his prayers.

It was at this stage in his spiritual development that his unversed concupiscence had been purified by the first of love's first arrows. Fifteen years before laying eyes on Bice he had been pierced by that joyful shaft of pain at the very instant in which her living image had been wholly prefigured without premonition or predilection. It was the almost forgotten girl who had prepared him for the foreigner in Dogtown. Chronologically and physiologically, if not geographically, it might have been young Bice herself, going by the name of Eva—at least as he now recalled the secret brief and hopeless impression by which his lustful disposition had been prematurely civilized with the inklings of romance.

His veteran heart trembled with the memory recovered by his brain of an unfulfilled love that had first sublimated his desire to learn the gross mystery. The same hair eyes lips and merry sophistication, vivacious and unjaded! He marveled at the epiphany of Eva as a woman of the world, and eagerly forgave Bice the extraneous causes and conditions of her intervening life. His earliest ungained loss now explained his extemporaneous success from Acorn Pasture to the Poet's Corner.

In the booth at Leonardo's facing the absolutely independent person shared by his innocence and experience, he sought to alter her provenience—almost ready to insist that she recollect the other side of that fleeting encounter of childhood—if only to deny her free escape in the future. Excitedly he interrupted her chatter about the newspaper business; enthusiastically, he tried to explain the sense of destiny by which he was so wondrously possessed, refusing to grant that the unearthed archetype might have been even slightly reformed under the influence of its present embodiment like an anecdote in the New Testament. But then he found how little there was to tell her.

Accidental glints through rustling bamboo from the rotating Clydesdales prompted Caleb's reminiscence of the sunlight glancing through aspen leaves astir above the path to the ball field at the moment he'd been smitten by the god who torments instantaneous lovers of dryads—not Priapus the wanton quail-hunter, but the discriminating Valentine-archer Eros who never wastes a shot and often retrieves his arrow. He forgot all the other interests of his summer, and childish things were dropped away like all the graduated grades of school at once. Behind the trees along its banks the Gansevoort ceaselessly purled and gurgled across a rocky stretch of shallows between deep pools of unseen trout. Until his natural heartbeat was mutely disrupted by Love's civilizing trice of lancination the most absorbing pursuit of his vacation had been to launch upon that monotonously irreversible descent of savorless waters a variety of twigs matchsticks and scraps of lumber that might carry his spirit west across the state line, down to the great North River, and at last return it to the great sapid ocean of the rising sun whose alternating currents and autonomous ships he'd longed for more constantly than the nakedness of a girl.

"Eva was one of the 'Austrian refugee kids' we'd known were quartered for the summer with rich people across the river on mountainside estates we were never invited to. Someone arranged a softball game. They already knew the game. They were very self-confident, and good at everything, including English, as if they'd picked up our idioms without being taught—far better educated than any kid in Allenton: which struck me with as much awe as the cosmopolitan affluence that intimidated my friends. None of those refugees yet knew that their parents were burned to ashes.

"There were six or eight of them. I suppose half were boys, but they looked to Eva as their natural arbiter. They were all intelligent healthy happy and handsome but she was furthermore cheerful wise and beautiful—the most bewitching girl I'd ever seen. That's why I knew you at first sight!

"Up until then I'd looked only at blondes. Just to hear her speak, with that charming foreign accent, never raising her voice! In fact she didn't talk much at all. Yet there was nothing selfconscious about her. I played second base for their side and she was right behind me in the outfield, but even more than the other village kids I was silenced with reverence for her aura of maturity. She was nice to everybody, and never opinionated or bossy with her followers. I made a fool of myself showing off in front of her every way I could think of, practically taking over her team with my infield hustle, but I would have done so to better effect almost anywhere else, because I never did very well except at savvy chatter. Needless to say, I didn't dare say a word to her or let her catch me looking at her, and she didn't seem to distinguish me from the other yokels."

Bice listened without laughing. Was she assuming the identity of Eva according to his wish? What vital dark bright beauty therein confounded!

"Those 'Austrian' kids were all democratic enough, and willingly deferred to our customs, but they were ruled by their unseen guardians. It was hard to bear that they went on picnics without us locals, and always went swimming by themselves in a private pool up on the hill, never in the public river. It was said they wore no bathing suits." Caleb said nothing to Bice of the fortune that a lascivious ten-year-old would have forfeited for a glimpse of the soft vernal buds concealed by the delicate swelling of Eva's jumper.

"I would have stalked her if she'd gone to our school or been otherwise less inaccessible to plebeian childhood. The only thing between us was that one ragged inconclusive game, and I never expected to be thanked for serving on her side, she seemed so far above me, to the manner born—in cultivation, graciousness, worldly selfconfidence—as clever and dignified as a Prussian landgravine. She couldn't have been more than twelve, but I was much too young for her, and of course even gaucher than the peasants. All those foreign kids were apparently quite at ease in Atlantis. I was the one who behaved like a Displaced Person. But I don't think I saw Eva more than three times all together."

"You've already seen me more than three times, and without my clothes on too!" Bice whispered, now with a giggle. "Would you rather have had your history the other way around?"

"The last time I saw her I was struck dumb with confusion as our two gangs unexpectedly passed each other on the path. I probably seemed hostile, and she didn't look at me: as if we'd never seen each other before."

"I thought you were antisemitic."

"But I played on your side, didn't I?"

"That was before you found out that we weren't really Austrian. Sometimes all the Hungarian and Czech Jews were loosely called Austrian by refugee agencies. To Georgios it sounds less Jewish."

"I can't remember what we knew at the time, but it never occurred to me that you and the others might be Jewish. You seemed rich and aristocratic. Yet I knew from my mother that to grownups 'war refugees' was usually a euphemism for 'European Jews'. Even in Unabridge she'd been one of the few who were much aware of the official Nazi persecution, but she still didn't know about the camps with chimneys. Anyway, 'European Jews' included Einstein, and they seemed better esteemed than the Jews of our own cities."

"Eva was a poor Gypsy-Jew from Transylvania." Bice explained. "and only eleven."

"I'm still not sure that you haven't just changed your name!"

"No, I had my mother with me in Australia, and she was the refugee, not I. She got out of Hungary to England before the country Jews were betrayed by the city Jews—if that's true. And I had the Royal Navy to father me. That was the only reason I may have seemed haughty when I passed a certain colonial boy who paid me no attention."

"Grown up, you look more like a little British Cossack, in those boots of yours!"

"I can give you Eva's point of view, now that you've suffered and atoned for your cowardly bashfulness. I too had presentiments of love, and I wouldn't have paltered about a kiss or two. Europeans kids aren't any higher-minded than Atlanteans. But you've been forgiven for ignoring my kind feelings. You were more interesting and sympathetic than any boy I ever met on any continent, and even this itinerant scribe remembers you after fifteen years. You knew a lot more than anyone else and you could learn anything you didn't know. You looked like a faun but you walked about like a dog reading all the scents except mine. When I seemed cheerful and gregarious it was because I'd learned to protect myself with gaiety, but I was lonelier than my friends. Bereaved, in fact, of I know not whom. To you I was exotic, but I felt like a Gretel who never had her Hansel—the untabooed cradle-stolen sister of a forest creature!"

"Suffering boys never suspect that girls like you have pitiful feelings. We assume that as their bodies are inaccessible they must be invulnerable, and they seem to despise everyone they reserve themselves from."

Bice snorted, but not with surprise. "They're the most vincible of all. They don't know when to believe a boy."

Yet there in Leonardo's it still seemed to Caleb that she was referring to lovely girls less worldly than herself. He calmly granted that Bice's unreserved body had never yielded the mystic sweetness he'd loved the refugee for; but if the premature imprint of Eva nonetheless explained more practiced sensations by which he had been stricken at the first sight of her avatar—new expectation prophesied by the old—what explained the sense of sympathy and affinity that instantaneously inspired in Petto's undiscriminating predacity the nearest equivalent of love, and in the gypsy poet's before him, and probably in the others' to whom she responded? Was there an elite class of dogs, not to be defined by breed nurture or estate, fated to share a special sensibility to Bice's particular set of black bands in the spectrum of scents?

"Listen to me once and for all, Cubie-Calebeeney, my true love." she went on. "I promise not to embarrass you in Dogtown. Your mind exceeds my reach, and your future is too important to let it get complicated by a mundane wanderer. But I always love what I cannot deserve. You're not just my long lost brother: I want you to be my priest."

Temporizing, while he pondered what she meant, he corrected her metaphor. "I'm only the servant of a priest."

"I love you for your vows." she went on unjestingly. "Your personal work is sacred to me. Despite appearances, though I may sell my body to journalism, I'm really a poet. Not a real poet yet of course, probably just a jongleur. And maybe I'll never be able to write like a real woman, because I don't have the guts your mother has—I like to have my own way too much, I'm too selfish. I play roles, and then I fall for opposite numbers that I should know are also playing by the Method. In fact I have no character at all: it's simply that I'd like best to do the part of a poet; whereas actually, as far as ability goes, it turns out that I'm better at stories, which do get published—"

She interrupted herself, one finger raised, both eyes lifted toward the ceiling, a faraway smile slowly forming on her lips. "—Oh I love that song! I haven't heard it for weeks!" All at once she smiled the smile of a shy amoret against which the most churlish of misogynists would have been as defenceless as Caleb; but toward such ones it never would have been directed, for Bice penetrated the minds of fools and did not gladly suffer them, nor did she deign to ingratiate herself to those who despised her. "I know it's what I've heard you call 'Franco-Prussian nightclub music'—but a classic recording nevertheless. Now don't you really like it?"

"It's a nice melody." Caleb replied agreeably, making an effort at demotic appreciation, though before she demanded he hadn't in truth distinguished one from another the emanations of the remote jukebox. Now that he noticed this singing, however, the woman's throat sounded alluringly relaxed, and its lyrics in the Atlantean vulgate were not inappropriate to certain feelings he himself would have liked to evoke in a woman with a voice like that. "It's not as inane as indigenous sugar-soup." he conceded. Once again he resolved to pay more attention to what he was thought to be missing in the refinements of popular art.

But again he was swiftly presented with a succeeding phase of her strangely sinuous humor. Absently rubbing the tabletop with the bottom edge of her thumb, Bice stared down upon its glossy sanguine plastic. "What a pity you and I never had a song to call our own."

"We never had time." he replied with an atrabilious sentimentality that he immediately regretted for appearing too ready. "But we didn't need anyone else's tune."

"It still can be Vivaldi's 'Four Seasons', if you like. When I have my apartment I'll play you my selection of imperishable stuff."

"And I'll allow Ibi up on the bed!"

"Next month I'm moving into my own place at Apostles Dock. My mother's sending down my things. It's about time too. Simplicissimus is getting to be a bit of a bore with all his talk about the comeliness of il cazzo." Her tasty lips pursed judiciously, two fingers at her chin. "My analysis is that I'm not fit to possess or be possessed by any man."

"Still it must be gratifying to know that in every case you have both choices."

"Don't be ridiculous!" she expostulated somberly. It was the first flare of her anger that he'd ever seen. Expecting her to add *It's just like a man to say something like that,* he backed off in alarm—but also in an odd thrill of pleasure at this hint of familiarity, which he instinctively intended to put to the proof, against such time as he might experiment with hardening fraternal detachment in teaching her to appreciate the delicacy of his pleasantries.

She continued her complaint in querulous timbre. "I can't stand being blamed! I'm nobody's doxy. Why can't a girl have friends without everyone assuming she sleeps with them all? Just because I was fool enough to take a professional interest in Petto without being unfriendly! I should have dropped him after I wrote that one article; but when I went to work at the *Nous* I saw some interesting pictures Flash had taken of his work last year and never used, so I decided it would help them both to do another piece, for the little magazine in Unabridge that rejected my premature poetry. Flash is a genius in his way, and poor Petto deserves some recognition after all those years of poverty and toil. The only trouble is that a little recognition isn't enough for Maestro Simplicissimus. He's an authentic artist, compared with all the phonies—but his vanities are misplaced. He says his life is the most important work of art, and he fancies himself as a hotblooded sage! I've told him he's got to stop writing letters to the *Nous* about creative spirituality. Like many talented illiterates, as Doctor Charlemagne says, the 'Smith of Dogtown's Soul' prides himself on his manifesti."

So even Doc had not escaped her dragnet! "Doc can be pretty cruel with his own idolaters." Caleb said absently as he rapidly sketched to himself various hypotheses by which to organize and augment the fragments of feminine journalism she was offering him.

For a moment she reassumed her roguish gaiety. "If it were only with you, I wouldn't mind being under suspicion: fraternal incest is the prerogative of royalty. It's not half as shameful as being reputed the model for a Nude Teiresias series!" But she allowed these words to fade as she plucked lightly at the tweed in Caleb's sleeve.

"—Let's get out of here." she suddenly broke off. Her voice was now both decisive and pleading, with an import quite unfamiliar and puzzling to him, whether brave or passionate. "Take me for a ride somewhere, where we can talk without lights. I'll explain how it was your aftereffect that persuaded me to come back here instead of taking that Codfishland coastal trip on the *Avalon Reefer* this spring."

Therefore saying little, speaking softly, lest he becloud and reverse the crystalline precipitation for which he was hoping from this new intimacy, Caleb drove with her through the starless night to Dilemma Cove. She was talking all the way, and long after they got out of the car to walk in mist on the secluded beach.

"I had really intended to do a freelance on the fisheries and freezers that the Dominion government has been financing in the settlements north of St James's all the way up to the Strait. The Dogtown schooners used to go up there to bait up with weather-frozen herring, and that was about all the fish the Terries exported to the States; but now, with mechanical refrigeration plants along the coast, the Terra Nova cartel lands thousands of tons of fresh cod from their own small boats and ships most of it it down here in the freighters as frozen slabs. They also supply Mercator's salt fish, mostly sold in little oldfashioned wooden boxes, but some of it's cooked into fishcakes and canned right here at the Yard. There are still diehard customers in the hinterlands who won't have anything to do with frozen fishbricks, especially the old Scandies in Itasca. But you may not know that Terra Nova fishmeal and codliver oil go over to England."

The purpose of Caleb's passivity seemed balked by this strangely professional exordium; but he held his peace in patient admiration, remarking to himself that such commercial geography would have escaped the attention of Lilian Cloud even if she'd chosen to serve the public information system.

"It's an endless shoreline." Bice was musing with her mind's eye. "Some of the parts that I've seen only from the air are dreadfully boring, where the coast is low and dull; elsewhere the sea cliffs are black jagged rocks; but everywhere the ground is like tundra, with forests of dwarf trees where there's any growth at all. But the big desolate Bays are as beautiful as Tierra del Fuego—Annunciation, Atonement, Whitsun, Circumcision—each with innumerable small inlets, where they drive herds of whales to slaughter, and where the working coves are barely large enough for reefers like the *Avalon* to nose into the landing jetties and back out again at high tide. They say coastal seamanship like that is almost a lost art."

So they boasted, Caleb muttered in his envious heart. I'm sure you got an earful from more than one mouth under Captain Newf's command.

"You'd like the Terra Nova austerity—all dreary hard work, and no snakes anywhere on the whole island! They showed me pictures of the naked little artificial harbors I wanted to see for myself from the *Avalon*: treeless gray hamlets built around tin-roofed fish plants. And the destitute old settlements of tiny buildings huddled together under a weathered gray church on a bare gray hill, with a cemetery scraped up from the topsoil around it to make the graves deep enough. The miniature houses were made of very dear timber brought in a hundred years ago and never painted since. You can see that the wind is always blowing. I hate to think of children growing up in one of those places. The cramped beaches are steep shingle, and it's too cold for swimming at any time of year. The gray cliffs are blackened to their knees by the enormous high tides. Apparently there's nothing on the bleak east coast of Codfishland to remind you of this Cape's tawny rocks and civilized seascapes. No wonder Lord Calvert lost no time transplanting his colony down to rockless Port Campion where shallow-water crabs and oysters could be picked up for the asking!

"But they say a few of the Terra Nova landings are in lovely little coves of rock right inside the villages, where the water is so clear that it magnifies the tin cans and rubbish piling up on the bottom. Those imperishable middens must seem like imitations of the Dogtown States...."

Imperishable middens, indeed! This bit of unjournalistic orotundity suggested to Caleb the question of whether she had previously composed these ostensibly ad lib descriptions or had only purloined by professional ear the diction of some native poet in the crew. He never doubted her gifts—only the spontaneity of her rhetoric. But in the suspense of waiting to find out what all this geography was leading up to he held his tongue, for fear of distracting her from a perhaps fragile train of associations, while nonetheless apprehensive that the objective narrative might carry her too far from the subject in hand. Therefore, having wracked his brain for the most auspicious spot to park in at the Cove, though delighted at the more romantic prospect of walking down the beach with her, he sat motionless beside her in the car until she came to a pause. As the promise to open a secret to him was her own, it was not as likely to be altered by delay as if he'd offered the suggestion, and meanwhile he wished to risk not the slightest dissonance. Above all he was trying to steer clear of any word or gesture that might remind her of the banal tactics practiced by all the men she'd accepted or rejected in the last seven or eight or nine or ten years.

It was also necessary to callously dismiss from his foremind the certain knowledge of Ibi's disappointment worry and hunger (which however he hoped would be in some degree alleviated by the mother of the Keith household), and his more acute regret that Ibi was missing the adventure. Petto's disappointment worry and hunger at Wye Square were of no concern; for all he cared, the sculptor could relieve anxiety about his roving ward by fulminating at his night work under cool fluourescent lights.

As for opportunity, Caleb resolved not to touch Bice unless she touched him first. Indeed he was temporarily more ardent for her honest words than for the feel of her body—though the charming possibility did fleetingly occur to him that it was a sudden farfetched wave of desire for his touch that had impelled her to fabricate such modest reason to accompany him into an automobile (which to most Atlantean girls offered more equivocal protection than bracken beach or sofa).

But he needn't have expected the conventional, for in the U S A it was one of her faintly exotic distinctions not to have formed habits of emotional expression in the seats of kilroys. Like Caleb himself, and unlike the generality of damsels, she had never required an upholstered steel enclosure as a condition for the loosening of communicative inhibition. Nor at this point in her cultural development, if mere amusement had been her drift, would she have tolerated the postures to which a horseless carriage more or less limited its occupants.

It was not too cold to walk the small beach slowly, their hands comforted by the pockets of half-buttoned coats, insulated by a fog less dark than dense, thanks to a moon known only from the almanac to be somewhere overhead. At low water a crescent tympanum of smooth strand offered promenade below the windrow of popples braided with seaweed. A priestlike tide laved the orchestral arc in a continuous series of swishes as the gentle crest of each sussurating swell obliquely intersected with the marge of sand, sequentially from end to end between unseen horns of reef, repeating its quiet impulse down the beach like a slowly undulating rank of elfin seahorses ceaselessly tempting mortals to a contradance.

At last he hazarded to prompt her. "But why do you say I kept you from that coastal seafaring?" Adding slyly: "Especially since the love of me didn't prevent you from crossing over to Unaford!"

"Because on its last call the ship would have taken me to St Bede, and that's the place I've learned to dread from knowing you. It wasn't until I got to England that I understood what you'd taught me."

With a suddenly incontinent sense that she trusted him more than anyone else in the world Caleb risked his advantage as a confessor by indulging his wit before he could stop himself. "I was under the impression that you were well versed beforehand."

"Don't joke about our passion." she mechanically riposted, flushing a mock-coquetry drawn from her repertory of defenses. He believed that she would have scolded him for his callow levity if her authentic impulse of anger had not been forestalled by the kind of involuntary mannerism that one acquires out of habit in intersexual society yet blames oneself for using when a shield is uncalled for. "It should be left just the way it was—neither solemn nor shallow."

So it wasn't passion he had taught her! Not surprising. But these days, with Lilian to love him, Caleb's confidence was robust. No longer being unilaterally enthralled was like having an anchor to windward. He was content to accept Bice's delimitation in grateful silence. It was no time to further divert the questionable confession to which she seemed to be trusting for the sympathy that she perhaps hoped would some day take a famous place in his creative imagination. The artifice itself of ever so briefly raising the decorated shade of her window, while he alone was allowed to watch, assured him of her partial sincerity at least as journalist and poet. And surely his own behavior since her return—while biding his time like a motionless cat with a hopping bird, recognizing her persuasion that the spectacle of her dance would entertain him at a safe distance—had demonstrated that he felt no humiliation as mere confidant.

Yet in what she then told him he detected fewer signs of reminiscence for his benefit than of a resolute attempt to prepare for self-exposure in her poetry:

"Bear in mind that St Bede is further north than the wastes I've been talking about—an outpost beyond the beyond. It's where my first love happened. I was just out of the Acadia convent, but not a bit worried about pain or guilt, and no one would have called me a Gretchen. The sisters at Chebucto had failed to make me like my innocence, and I never believed in sin. None of the girls who hadn't spent their childhood there took any morality very seriously; but I was the only one that ever let anyone suspect we shouldn't be taken at face value. The others acted as if each Communion was our first.

"Still, I didn't want to spoil the great adventure by rushing into it, because I still believed in romance; I wasn't merely curious. But I was always three or four years older than my age, and there are some things you can't learn within the walls of a nunnery. I had a notion that I might get deformed if I didn't limit myself to superficial until I came of age.

"But home for summer holiday 'on the Rock' in Ultima Thule I forgot all such fear when I fell for David. He was the first Atlantean I ever knew—a flyer, shot down over Cipango during the War—and nothing like the other men up there. At least not since the Vikings abandoned their settlement at Turk's Cove, which wasn't far from St Bede. He looked like a thin Norse bard without the beard."

More than once that night in early spring, sealed off as well from time as from the space around their fog, Bice and Caleb paced a dark hollow of whitish wisps at the lowest level of living tide, dimly aware that the whole three-quarters rim of invisible land was higher than their footing. The salted sighs of Oceanus willingly gave ground to the quiet metronomic breathing of two biped wraiths among all the billions he strove to drown. Absorbed in the illusion of communication ever attempted by pairs of opposites, each in a different mood of heart and mode of brain, they trod the hard palate of a jaw that in contrary weathers had crushed with its granite teeth and buried in its maw the bones of God's leviathans and men's vessels driven between Kraken Ledge and False Point Rock by southeasterly tempests, or lured thereinto from the north or east by specious resemblance to the true Point of safety, before there was a Foreside Light to guide ships around the long tongue of rocks less than a mile further down the shore. Then were the soothing ripples roiled into juggernauts fighting one another like sharks to storm this treacherous niche in the fortified eternal Cape.

"I suppose your wandering Ossian just happened to be up at the top of the world hunting seals from the air with machine guns?"

By a squeeze of her hand, which had already taken his unbidden, like a brother's, Bice chided him for discordant jealousy. "How did you know he was poet? I only said he looked like one. He had a job flying supplies for the Mission Association. St Bede is more civilized than I've been making out; it's the headquarters for Inuit schools and medical service all over Cabotland and Vikland."

"A sky pilot then, born-again to the High Church in Shinto prison camp? High-church outreach in the missionary position!" Caleb was unable to deny the evil spirit in his heart.

But Bice ignored his malice. "May it please your lordship, I was a volunteer and he was a professional employee. My father was posted in St Bede as liaison officer to the Dominion Defense Force and the U S Strategic Air Command at Magic Mountain, the first big secret radar station and still the North Atlantic headquarters of DEW-LINE—the Distant Early Warning System—our Great Wall of China. It's an eerie eyrie that you'd understand much better than I did: a kind of electronic colony in the clouds, high above a little fishing port that isn't connected to the rest of the Province by road. Up in the military reservation one lives on color-coded spaghetti in a space ship, while down in the village they still hook fish from the sea and cut it by hand, collect cod livers in blubber barrels, breed sled-dogs, and preach the Gospel. There are all sorts of cabalistic screens that look like repellant targets radiating pulses of arrows. The cartographic carousels up there are supposed to detect Russians sneaking over the top of the world. The whole damn hive of watch rooms and command centers and rotating mirrors has no more to do with life than a cosmic game of chess.

"David had never resigned his commission in the Reserve, so he had privileges at the Officers Club, which is up on the peak right in the middle of all that paraphernalia but doesn't lack nightclub music. The banal Atlanteans liked to call it The Top of the Mark, because all the radars were Mark XYZ Something-or-other. To me it was a hotel atrium inside the devil's planetarium; I couldn't take in anything but the music. David called it the Abomination of Desolation, a high place for the cult of disintegration, totally devoid of soul. The library was a magazine of magazines, not a book in it except the Jerubbaal Bible and an ODE Dictionary.

"What I hated most were all the pompous drinkers full of self-righteous patriotism simply because the Russians had copied your E-Bomb. None of them looked less Communistic than David, but I began to listen to him because at the time I was trying to understand U S politics and he was the only one who criticized the President. He didn't speak very well of the Catholicrats either, I'm afraid, but he liked Stevenson, who was despised by all the swilling warriors. At that age I didn't care what his opinions were, or what they were about, as long as they weren't like everyone else's! He called himself an Independent."

"I hope you know that in this country the Mugwumps aren't like your Liberals." Caleb remarked with didactic contempt. "They flaunt their opinions as independent variables; but their choice is totally dependent upon variables determined by the parties they scorn. . . ." He stopped, reminding himself that even with Bice Picory it was no occasion to betray on his sleeve the invidious green eye of a timid little draft-dodger.

"I don't think a fairminded foreign correspondent should trust a partisan like you for political tutoring."

"The Catholicratic Party is the closest I can get to any solidarity." As usual when among infidels he forgot about the theoretical community of his church.

Through the salt-misted darkness her pale face glanced at him in the self-forgetful manner that deserved all his joy in her coherent uncombed beauty. The half of his love for her that remained alive was growing more stable than the whole had been, and much healthier; but it was still the thudded target of darts feathered like the arrows. "He didn't look like you at all; he was much older, and he knew how to command a bomber," she mused, "but he had your voice; and he was just as serious about life. My point is that you reminded me of him."

Caleb was glad of her respect but surprised and for the most part displeased to hear that she judged him characteristically longfaced. He considered himself as playful as Merry Sterne.

"He was a born New World gentleman. Like you. For a week or so after that lovely night here, when you made me forget about everything in my life that hadn't been sweet and tender, there wasn't much to remember before David—or between David and you.

"Outwardly he must have been an ideal all-round athletic engineering student before he went into the Air Corps and got to be a Captain. But then he was captured in his parachute not far from Hiroshima soon after the bomb was dropped. That's when his poetry started. Compared to you he was always innocent; he didn't know as much about literature or other things that I was interested in; and of course he hadn't had a mother like yours." She laughed: "But he would have agreed that women are the better people!"

Caleb was almost silenced by shame, yet cautiously balancing her words on the scales in her mind by which he measured himself against admirable men of the world, allowing for temporal perspectives of weight. In what dimensions of irony did her feelings reside? But even under the sway of humility he facetiously goaded her on. "So the precocious schoolgirl walking through the Officers Club with some redneck shavetail snuck a look over the shoulder of this veteran drinking alone. You were curious about what he could be writing in an official lounge full of pin-ups and slot machines."

"No," she replied tolerantly "I met him at the Mission store where I helped sell 'Eskimo artifacts' while I was waiting to start college in Acadia. Our trading post was a sort of art gallery or museum, combined with warehouse and mailorder office—the only commerce in native fur and ivory craftwork that wasn't monopolized by the Hudson Bay Company, which is the East India raj of British North Atlantis. I wanted to study anthropology and go live for a summer or two with Inuit artists."

Caleb was pleased to hear of this intellectual motive in Bice's history. It would be interesting to research all personal influences upon the course of her ambition in veering from disinterested service among people who persisted in determining when to work and when to sleep by the vicissitudes of weather (rather than allowing themselves to be ruled by institutions of clock and calendar) to stardom in the pressurecooking urban regime of word-production on tightly horological deadlines. But he also wondered with a snigger if she was remembering and assuming he had forgotten their previous exchange on allegations of the comfort offered benighted traveling men by the heads of Cabotland households as a matter of decent hospitality—and if she relied on the ethnological fact that Eskimos indulged all kabloonas for the childlike immaturity of their ethics. But now he carefully refrained from making any remark that might be construed as worthy of an armchair lecher or that might otherwise remind her of his incorrigible habituation to normal everyday associations of the collective male psyche, conscious or unconscious.

"The St Bede colons could make snowshoes and embroider mottoes, but until the military base was built they were too ignorant of technology to make up for the poverty of their own culture. They didn't know enough to separate the offal from the fillets in their cutting sheds. Most of them wouldn't read anything, even the Prayer Book at their own funerals. But I sometimes wished I could be trapped there by the winter, without an airplane, when the harbor was frozen solid and the road closed, so that I'd have to escape by dog sled. Imagine curling up under the snow with a team of warm gray Huskies! That would have made up for all the boredom, military and civilian."

"But now that you know what it's like to sleep with Ibi—"

"David was twice my age, sad, and obviously rather repressed. But before he said a word I knew he was sent from heaven to save me from suicide. At first I assumed him to be a mission doctor, or a priest in mufti—charmingly shy, or at least reticent; but almost immediately I guessed he could be purely passionate at some point no one would ever penetrate to. It turned out that he really was quite calm, almost all the time. Not that he tried to conceal his feelings: simply that he was unable to express them in person. But when he realized that such a disability stultified poetic development it had become the purpose of his life to try. I may have been too young to help very much, but I think I was good for him at just those months in his life.

"Anyhow, at that first meeting I knew only that he was looking for something to send his mother in Cornucopia. All those beautiful sealskin and ivory things were hard to choose among. I never considered the brutality of my beloved docile Inuits slaughtering those poor trusting silkies and godly bears with kilroy boats and guns."

"Hunting for food isn't as bad as nurturing domestic animals on purpose to eat their meat, which is much less efficient than farming protein directly from the grain."

"David didn't talk about efficiency, but he attracted me with his gentle ironies. I'd say he was idealistic in an oriental sort of way. Philosophy was all new to me. It turned me against all organized religion."

Organized religion! In the dark Caleb's lips compressed and nose twisted at this pejorative sniff from Mugwump individualism, which coming in unassailable cliches of allusive deprecation were always impossible to oppose without engaging in total war. Although the form of Bice's language was superior to that of other contemporaries, he judged its content as no better than it should be. At bottom he suffered less from the aesthetic pain of grammatic misbehavior than from moral anguish at abuse of meaning. Yet he knew that those two aspects of decadence were inseparable, and that single minds, unless heroic, were ultimately inextricable from the language producing them. He had found at an early age that if he was to have any pleasure with anybody he had either to cense or to muffle his censorious olfaction of both semantic and syntactic corruption, for together in them was reflected the kind of sin that most depressed him.

"What thrilled me most, fresh from the convent, was David's iconoclasm. For instance he was the first person I ever heard speak against Churchill, an idol I'd been born to revere—in fact my father happened to have been at his elbow on the battleship in Placenta Bay when the Atlantic Charter was signed with Roosevelt. But David called my Prime Minister all sorts of names and recited the misfortunes of two world wars as if they were all his mistakes, stupid or vicious. It was practically a personal hatred—almost like fear—perhaps Irish, against all Limeys. Yet otherwise, leaving aside a few tiny fissures in the latent volcano, David seemed as calm and rational as the best of bomber pilots. It wasn't until he was gone that I realized how little I understood masculine hysteria."

"Did he take off for India?" Caleb asked, less painfully jocular, bringing to heel the instincts of rivalry. He was overcoming his antipathy for the ageing Western adept who'd apparently deflowered the girl with a tenderness his own behavior was to remind her of, after a plethora of disappointments following her expulsion from the Garden of Ararat. He felt a mild waft of triadic affinity tinctured with homosexual as well as incestuous affection.

"He never loved me, but that didn't matter much. I doubt that he'll ever be able to love anybody, much as he may wish. I don't know where he went. Pilots can get a job anywhere in the world. Maybe he went home to take care of his mother, who had been dying for many years. But I do know why he went at that particular time. He left for my sake."

Her voice was little more distinct than a whisper, but not because she mumbled. Her words were evenly delivered, without pause or hesitation, through thin lips as quick and motile as ever. By now the cyclic rustlings of the sea were absorbed into the unheard rhythms of their own parallel breathing, and the only extrinsic sounds they heard—also assimilated postconsciously into the concentrated hush of communication—were an antiphony of pulsing moans from the foghorn over at the breakwater, beyond Nedlaw Pond on the other side of Crow Hill, and plangently monotonous knells more faintly across the notch of the peninsula from an equidistant bell on Parliament Island that guided the ghosts of ships to Dogtown's Inner Harbor. Yet by sunlight, from Caleb's upper windows at the Mesocosmic Lab, especially in the leafless season, this cove, now so covert, lay like a crescent jewel at the center of a lucid panorama filled with views and navigations.

"The Picory family lived on base, half way up the mountain, far enough from those electronic bedsprings and windmills not to hear their squeaks and groans, but not far enough down to be spared the incessant wind. There wasn't a tree within sight of our Hyperborean bungalow. Most of the time my father was away on trips to Washington or London or Ottawa or Tahosa, when he could help it, or Aleutia, Yukon, or somewhere in the Northwest Territories when he couldn't; or Hudson or Vikland or Iceland or some other godforsaken place under the hegemony of NATO. My mother was usually too busy juggling lovers right there on the mountain to worry about my initiation. The townspeople would have petitioned Parliament in outrage if they'd known about the kind of information that was exchanged under those waveguides and onion-domed antennas.

"Late one midsummer's night my father flew in unexpected and I had to intercept him practically naked at the door to slow him up for a couple of minutes so that David would have a chance to get out the back way. Thank God St Bede's wasn't as far north as God made it seem: there are a few hours of darkness at that time of year. I made my old man a drink and kept him company to divert his attention, especially because I'd neglected to close the door to my room and the bed was in a terrific mess; but it was hard to ignore the sound of David's jeep starting up outside.

"For a long time my father didn't ask why mother wasn't home, but I finally had to tell him I didn't know where she was. He said nothing much while I got him some food, and I hoped he'd be just too tired to care about anything until I could concoct a story. I wished that in the morning he would somehow wake with the painless intuition that his daughter had grown up and that a girl's love-life must begin somewhere, and better at home than on a kilroy seat.

"But more than death I dreaded his anger, though it had never yet been turned on me, because I loved him as the one power I knew would always be on my side against all the other powers of the world—as long as I was loyal. I used to try to imagine him in his youth as the parfit gentil knight sans reproche who had lost caste and sacrificed professional advancement when he had duty at Whitehall during the war by marrying a penniless Jewish refugee to acknowledge her bastard, and by persistently reminding the Government of all the horrible intelligence about the Final Solution on the Continent—which the F O at best wanted to ignore. To me he was the most honorable of unsung heroes, who one day yet would be recognized as a Captain at least. But even when I was a little girl I think I understood that by other officers Commander Picory was pitied or despised as little better than an official remittance man—despite Winchester and Sandhurst or Dartmouth and Portsmouth and Greenwich on either side of his lineage for many generations—who otherwise by then should have been given a command of his own, or at least posted to some really important staff. That was a big knot in my rosary.

"Well he had a couple of more drinks. I had never been acutely conscious of his drinking, even though my mother claimed it made him impotent. Anyway he never showed his liquor, and to me he looked old enough to account for her complaint. I'm sure he's still a very impressive man to most women—certainly more so than any of those subalterns who used to try to crawl all over me. Jason Anacoluther looks a little like him, though not as slim and handsome."

"I've never had a close look at the old philanthropic philanderer." Caleb equably remarked, encouraging her gaze into the past yet alert to the hazards of local competition.

"Oi Schlecht! Don't be deceived by Jason's wandering eyes." she retorted. "His generosity is subtle, but he's no Mephistopheles either. There's something sympathetic, like Doctor Charlemagne's paternal nature."

Although it seemed to Caleb that in Doc's case she mistook a maternal quality for the one she sought, her reply suggested a comforting image of her beefeating father with an element of resemblance that he bore to Roosevelt; and he liked the way she dispatched the digression, with a characteristic alertness that was instructive to behold in comparison with Lilian's, in whose greater depth of both wisdom and humor there was more to study. At present however his chief interest was crassly ignoble: to determine whether or not Dogtown's chief moneyman was in the running—beyond which his own gratuitous interjection had hardly been worth risking any irritation of her confidential mood.

But his self-interest was forgotten when she told the rest of her story, staring at the unilluminated shells and pebbles imbedded in the sand beneath her feet. "Suddenly my father said 'He's old enough to be your father!' It was clear he already knew who it would have been. Later I found out that he'd seen my diary, but even then I knew there was no use denying anything, or refusing to answer his questions. Without raising his voice he dishonored David with a bill of treachery and cowardice based on the accusations that he was a Yank, slandered Churchill, and defended the Japanese for their pacifistic attitude toward nuclear entropy-weapons.

"Then he started on me, in language I'd never heard before—all the while he was making me drink with him. Finally he shouted 'Why do you think I married that bitch? Why do you think I tried to save you from her kind of life?' I was petrified, like the victim of a snake before it's swallowed: I think what he said in the kitchen was almost as shocking as what he did when he dragged me into my room to revisit the scene of the crime. You can't bite and scratch your own father."

Caleb held his breath. She paused, absently stooping to pick up the empty white labyrinth of a sea-snail no larger than a dime. "Later he wept in my arms. After a while he must have dressed and left the house. My horror changed from terror to pity. I thought he was going to kill himself. For days afterwards, before I found my anger, I was so numb and befuddled from the devastation of everything that had kept me living, and so ashamed of myself, that I was glad David had disappeared. He never knew what happened. He quit his job without notice and went back to Cornucopia. I got one awkward letter saying he had gone too far in ruining my young life.

"My father never touched me again, or referred to his crime in any way at all—I suppose on the tacit understanding that I wouldn't tell my mother. Since then I've never taken his part against her, as I used to do. Sometimes I think she senses a deeper reason for my hostility toward him than his disapproval of my behavior with David, which I thereafter made no secret of. A few months later, after she took me to France for an abortion, my mother and father got divorced. But I doubt that it ever occurred to her that the fetus might not have been David's. I know it wasn't.

"So you see: I wear my own brand of the Big I, and it's much less romantic than Natty Hawhaw's sister's." She tapped her chest. "Now you're the only one who's ever seen it."

16
MATTER A PRIORI

Standing out in the North Atlantic, Dogtown is often disappointed at the cunctation of land-born Spring. In winter Lady Gloucester goes almost naked, all her bones are seen; the cats are exposed, and when there isn't much snow on the ground one must look at what the dogs have dropped, as well as all the rubbish in her hedges. Yet when the longed-for greening came at last—brambles first—Caleb hardly noticed the hundred-throated birds gradually rejoining the resident crows and gulls hungry all year round, muffled by the urban noise that lent comfort to the cemetery ruining under lowered or restive skies like the scattered wall of a fallen cathedral. Doubtless there was song far aloft in the King's pine-tops, or amid the Gothic ribs of dying elms, and closer-by in the burgeoning vaults of maimed and tangled Norman oaks. But only over on the grounds of the Lab, more closely enwrapt by the sea, did he remark the season. There on grassy slopes and pineneedled ledges, amid evergreen shrubs in an open grove of resinous masts, the sun and rain brought forth clumps of purple and yellow crocuses, making a roofless sanctuary of the entire high place in which Father Duncannon had hung his nonsectarian birdfeeder.

Lent for Caleb had been chaste withal. He could not foresee that before the quarter was half over he would be able to laugh at his struggle to overcome Lilian's busy virtue and Bice's caprice. But that was the start of his transition from bathos to pride.

* * *

More than once while waiting for jobs at sea Mary Tremont had sojourned at the Guest House of the Convent of St Agatha, an hour or two above New Uruk on the west bank of the North River. On the last of these retreats, before her final withdrawal from the Church of her nurture, she had begun her latest diary. This "patchwork journal" carried her all the way to Primavera, and there it evolved into an introduction to her intended autobiography, more dispassionate in style and restrained in volubility than any of her previous confessions, as if purged of self-indulgence both by the clarity of renewed religion and by the weariness of wisdom won by failure, yet composed as discontinuous fragments of memory, revelation, and events in progress, as testified by the motley variations of inks densely covering the disintegrating sheets of her disembounding notebooks, which would have discouraged a casual scholar.

But her literary self-castigation was confounded by the spiritual discipline of the Brotherhood, which informed her that it was just as "inadvisable" to accumulate pages about herself as to amass other private property. The Sunday Circle had no objection to the poetry she wrote for recitation or mimeographed publication at Primavera weddings and other festal events; and she was granted the liberty to ease her heart with letters to loved ones in the outside world—so long as she continued to improve her internal condition by gradually gaining control of the disuniting urge to do so. In the end she was "advised" to pack up her miscellaneous manuscripts and send them in the "diplomatic pouch" to the B P K's Outreach Family down at Manaus for transshipment to her son at Community expense. And so at length the bundle of cheap manila sheets had come into Caleb's possession friable and moldering, anticipated by her airmailed behest to read it. And for the first time in his life he felt at least an intermittent appetite for such research.

He did not expect to find any clues to his own occult genesis (albeit that in his postgraduate independence he was imperceptibly growing less hesitant to venture disguised and circuitous Dogtown inquiries); but now that he was privileged to a rational vision of classic community, he was eager for knowledge of his mother's contemporary life as a matter of comparative ritual. Father Duncannon found much to admire in the Utopia of the B P K, and was always willing to discuss ramifications of the crucial difference of theodynamics that separated even the most socialistic progeny of the Pauline Deformation from the primitive church, and to unravel with his retail informant the ever more entangled sleave spun by idealistic Christianity in its anthropological confusion.

Near the beginning of his mother's day-book Caleb found this passage:

> *The years and concentration I have spent* WRITING—*! Yet, even if there has been a wealth of personal experience and sharply remembered beauty to draw upon for "material", nothing is worth writing about! Prophecy is being fulfilled with alarming accuracy today: it is clear to everyone that the end of the world is not far . . . Could one's sympathy be better invested than upon the Early Christians who, so long ago, waited for the return of their Christ to rule this world in peace and justice? They were told by Him that He would come—! warned that His coming would be "sudden and swift". They who had known Him as a man upon earth among them lived and died still awaiting his preciously cherished promise to return. He is not yet here!*
>
> *The Serpent rules us still, and every day more slyly, more triumphantly. We know about the parable of the fig tree in the Spring—we have heard the Promise; reason tells us that eventually it must be fulfilled; and all current history confirms the expectation. We know all the warnings against being caught by it unaware, our "lamps untrimmed". —Yet blindly we go on with our stupid sinning, in league with the Tempter, whose triumphant glee is all but audible to us. "Generation of vipers", indeed we are! Hosts of vipers have lived and died . . . The world still is waiting for its own destruction. Picture the mass of humanity alive today—and the silly moron's smirk upon its collective face as it idles the "little time" away, beguiling itself with all that was twenty centuries ago forbidden by Him who is to be the Judge!*
>
> *We know; and we care not! When the warnings He gave are repeated to us, we "pooh-pooh" them.*
>
> *"Each man for himself" is the spirit of our time. This week I*

saw seven old ladies, in a "home" where they are being sheltered in spendthrift creature comfort until Death overtakes them. They sat at their dining table, eating succulent food, expressions of indwelling discontent and jealousy contorting their wrinkled faces. One, seventy-six, stared off into space as, with costly dentures, she masticated her food, thinking about her unhappiness and small debilities, a plate of muffins before her, covered with a snowy napkin. She was asked: "Will you have a muffin?" She replied, "No, thank you." Never glanced to left or right to see if others near her would *have a muffin;*—went on chewing and pouting, sorry for herself because her petty desires are not all *fulfilled.*

To her left, a bitter old woman, cursed with a weight of wealth she means to dispose of before she dies, somehow, *without* giving one cent of it to expectant heirs, lunged across the decorous table, grabbing the muffin plate for herself. "Oh, for God's sake," she cried hoarsely, choking over the morsel between her teeth, "loosen up on those muffins!" She put two on her own plate, replaced the napkin cover, and fell back into the visions she sees of lurid and lewd occurrences that are ever before her deranged mind's eye.

A third old woman, this a British lady, reached for the muffin plate and passed it to her next neighbor, a devout Churchwoman of ninety. "I don't eat hot bread," she remarked. "But I say, wouldn't you *like one?"* The ancient Churchwoman, shaking her head, replied: "I don't hear what you say. I'm getting very deaf, you know." The British lady, angry, muttered "Idjot!", and made no further attempt to pass the muffins.

After the meal, the muffin plate was returned to the kitchen untouched, except for the two on the plate of the wealthy one. These she carried out to the garden to feed to the birds. The cook had labored an hour to make and serve hot muffins to the "dear old ladies" of the Guest House.

New Uruk has a widely accepted slogan: "Mind your own business." If at any time there was virtue in the idea, none remains in it now, for it is today no more than a formula in defense of selfishness.

I have seen dreadful incidents on the public streets to which the citizenry, hastening on its individual greedy way, paid not the slightest attention. If prodded into noticing them at all, the public evoked its sacred motto: "I mind my own business."

On Third Avenue are many bars and taverns. One day—in gray cold winter—two angry men, very drunk indeed, were catapulted *through the swinging door of a dive by its bouncer. On the sidewalk they continued their altercation, fiercely and loudly. The people passing merely separated into a divided stream around them, frowning at the annoyance but not interested in the event.*

One of the two was a great brute of a man, with hands like hams, clenched in fury. The other, a slight, weak-chested figure, had strength in his tongue, and in drunken fearlessness spoke up to the first, who bore down on him savagely. The huge belligerent sprang upon the small one, grasping him by the skinny throat. After a short tussle the weaker man was flat on his back, the giant sitting on his body, squeezing his neck with both hands—while passers-by continued on their way with heads averted.

When the great clenching fingers had all but pressed life itself out of the little man, I cast about for help to prevent murder right there on the public thoroughfare. "Will you *stop that fight?" I asked a smug little Irish lawyer in cheap new clothes who carried his briefcase like a standard. "They're killing each other!"*

"Not my *business, ma'am," said he, pushing by me. "I'm due at court in ten minutes."*

Then I caught a glimpse of a face in the window of the barroom, opened the door and called inside: "Somebody come! Hurry!"

A half-hearted growl of protest rose from the dim interior. "They ain't on my *property, lady!" the bartender called. "We just t'run 'em outta here."*

In desperation, I acted on my own. I rushed over to the great hulking figure whose brutal strength by now had nearly forced the last breath from his supine victim.

"Look, Mister!" I hissed into his red, hairy ear. "Your wife wants you!"

Instantly the enormous hands relaxed; the bleary eyes of the monster took on a glint of terror. "Where's she at?" he muttered, managing to stagger to his feet. (I could see blood returning to the cheeks of the beaten one on the pavement.)

I pointed to the nearest corner. "There!" I lied to him. "She's after you, coming around the building!"

"Jee's!" said the brute. Without another word he hastened away. I had saved a life in the City that "minds its own business"!

On Avenue A many children, and dogs and cats, were hungry. They were so hungry that they had to steal off pushcarts propelled by angry peddlers at a loss to defend their wares.

But in Central Park an overfed Pekingese with a flannel band around its belly minced along the walk, self-consciously deliberate in its leisurely self-interest. At the other end of the leash was a wispy, faded old lady, beaming pridefully at the fat little dog, casting timid glances at passersby to elicit admiration for her pet.

In compassion for her deluded weakness, I obliged her. "Nice pup," I said, conquering my aversion to the unnatural-looking beast, which permitted me the liberty of scratching its ugly little head. "Gentle, isn't she?" I remarked to the gratified owner.

"Gentle, yes!" She blushed. "Her name is Genevieve."

"Intelligent, too." I hazarded. "Nice Genevieve!"

"And ever so discriminating!" boasted the proud little human woman whose life centered round the odious dog. "My cousin brought in a pint of Sherry's chocolate icecream last week. Since then Genevieve just won't eat any other brand! She's a fussy little thing!"

We parted. I had done my "good deed" for that day.

One beautiful Spring morning, across from the Art Museum on Vanity Row, a green bus charged up to the curb and let off a passenger. She was a heavy-set, middle-aged woman with a seeking look on her lonely face, obviously intending to visit the Museum. After the bus had departed she crossed the street and started up the broad steps in the wake of other visitors. Then I saw her look back over her shoulder, an eager expression lighting up her weary face.

Following her gaze, I saw its object. In a handsome English perambulator, pushed by a uniformed nurse, a baby had appeared from a mansion doorway on the side street opposite the Museum. Impulsively, the woman on the steps hurried back down to the curb, hastened back across the avenue, and approached the baby-buggy.

She spoke to the infant in a pleading tone. "Hello, darling!"

Possibly she was dimly aware that the nursemaid, trying to get past the barrier of her thick body planted in the path of the carriage, suspected her sanity or her motive; but I don't think she consciously cared. Her eyes filled with tears, and her mouth trembled, as she said to the baby, with a half-sob: "All my children went and grew up—!*"*

Then she swung about on her heel and recrossed Vanity Row, to climb the flight of steps into a Museum full of paint-and-plaster representations of Humanity and Love.

* * *

Caleb read these passages one Saturday afternoon as he was fighting the compulsion to make a further fool of himself by writing yet another letter to Lilian. The same day's mail had still brought none from her, but another one from his mother—which without mentioning the journals had put him in mind to take them up as diversion despite his entire self's demand to think of nothing but what he wanted to say to the Atlindu girl. But of course he found that the feelings and judgments roused by what he read only swelled the clamor for Lilian's attention that continually summoned all his powers into a single irresistible force of expression. Everything in his world must be made interesting to Moonfeather—especially if it wasn't explainable to Doctor Charlemagne or Father Duncannon!

Allowing for the probability that adolescent encephalitis had cracked the insulation of some of the criss-crossing jumpers in Mary Tremont's brain, to liberate her imagination and weaken her rules of evidence, but also guarding against his habit of therefore taking everything she said with too much salt, he was increasingly impressed by what he learned from her latest writing. Her suspicions and conjectures, presented in the same grammatical mood as history and news, had always to be entertained with a measure of masculine skepticism until the apodictic inductions and truly intuitive deductions could be precipitated from a creative welter. Lacking independent verification—or one's own instinctive corroboration!—it was unwise to accept any of her statements as anything but unreliable revision of vivid experience. Caleb took it for granted that Mary Tremont's plasticity of perception and fertility of supposition were dangerous to society because those who did not know her very well (and yet did not hate her) were quite likely either to dismiss all her facts in general contempt, thereby rejecting serviceable edification, or to accept her stories whole, deceiving themselves as to the actual relationship between truth and reality.

Still, for want of contradiction, seeing no harm in his own romantic rendering of the South Atlantean equatorial zone, he was glad to believe that indeed Vernalia lay in the region of Riolama's birth, and was haunted by a sacred black jaguar, as Mowgli's territory was haunted by Bagheera, his supreme hero of the books she had read him. (He wondered if the reverent young couples at Vernalia provided their children with that anthropomorphic fiction about the jungle of subcontinental Asia, far to the east and surprisingly north of christian El Dorado, notwithstanding the unified piety that seemed to leave no room for imagination or compassion of purely animal nature.)

And he was beginning to believe in her submission to the "modification of ego" demanded by her new sect, which remarkably shared the ultimate hope of Father Duncannon's Order without sharing its liturgical means, and especially without appreciating the distinction between individualism (abhorred by both) and liberty. But he continued to bear the guilt of withholding from his mother the key to the kingdom of heaven offered by the Classic Order of the Vine, simply in the interest of keeping her happy right where she was. But in sparing himself the duty of proselyting her his conscience was mollified by two persuasions: first, that the Brotherhood of the Peaceable Kingdom, in spite of its ultimate otherworldliness and its misguided attempt to find in corporate transcendentalism the effective solidarity of liturgical sacrament, stood in much less need of C O V's message than did other Paulines—or than even the great majority of Petrines also, who always to varying degrees had misunderstood the implied principles of their own doctrine for nineteen hundred years; and second, that her present faith was too firmly applied to admit the influence of any incongruent teaching whatsoever, in her conviction that she had finally settled her course toward eternity only after experiencing many other varieties of religion.

He rose to cook his dinner and feed the dog, looking forward to the usual Saturday evening with Doctor Charlemagne. But Ibi was nowhere to be found, inside or out. For the first time yet, the saint was missing for his daily meal. Caleb hesitantly decided to put aside his uneasiness and go to Leviathan Court alone.

When he returned at one in the morning, deliberately earlier than usual, pricked by anxiety, drawn by expectation, his guardian still was absent. If it hadn't been for the anodyne of whiskey, he would have gone out again to patrol the streets in his car. Instead, asserting to himself that his was only the commonplace worry of a growing youth's superannuating parent, he tried to sleep off his dread.

He awoke alertly to the clear light of a lovely mild morning. While still asleep his mind had formed the project of a run to Purdeyville, now that the loosened bonds of winter were probably dried out on most of the paths. If the ground was firm enough, he might venture a longer run than ever, propelled by love, all the way across the Cape and down from the woods by Lilian's forbidden road, risking a thrill of erotic disobedience, which only she herself would recognize—if she happened to be watching the stage during his three seconds of passage through the scene. In any event the Cape's trails and streets were virtually deserted early on Sunday mornings, and quiet exertion worthy of an Atlindian would merit Ibi's panting gratitude. —Ibi! Before even sensing the maceration of his muscles from an evening of Scotch he suddenly recalled the special condition of anxiety from which oblivion had protected him for the last five hours.

He lurched out of bed and quickly stole downstairs in his bathrobe, through the peacefully breathing household, only to find hope erased by a smudge of fear expanding toward an unexampled circumference of grief. Though disappearances were by no means abnormal for a young dog in springtime, it was a long time now—long enough for temporary exhaustion of the quickening humor, and long since long enough for hunger to have reasserted its sovereignty. Yet hunger itself might lead Ibi into the most reckless of dangers on street and highway.

One would have believed Ibi extraordinarily satisfied with his homelife; he could hardly have run away on purpose. But in Dogtown there were always rumors of saints being lost to methodical pirates, who sold their captives not only to faraway pet stores or police academies but to laboratories and vivisectionists. Ibi was not a silly dog, but he was a most conspicuous prince of the blood, and perhaps too noble to be suspicious of strangers.

Caleb's cold horror was again shunted aside for a few hours by chirographic expression of the passion that had been dominating his soul almost week after week. Neglecting his proper work—indulging the spontaneous energy that nowadays was always simmering or boiling like steam in his rib-cage—he spent most of the morning writing to Lilian. Quite apart from his general self-reproach for resorting to the written word, not for a moment did he quite dispel the sense of guilt for doing so when he might have been actively scouring the landscape; but with such scant privilege to Lilian's conversation, with so little mutuality of time—despite ingenious schemes on his part and apparent willingness on hers—facts topics themes anecdotes and opinions were always accumulating in his brain much faster than they could be remembered for release on some problematic occasion in a honeymoony future.

For the most part he had to be contented with being carried along by hope no more presumptuous than expectation of the next communication. Certainly there was patience enough on her side. Neither of them could have said what they were waiting for. But in him the steam for action rose at every stimulus without falling quite to its previous level between refuelings, and it tended toward explosion for want of channeled work. For Miss Cloud simply was not free. Would what he called her servitude come ever to an end?

But neither in truth was he himself free. Did he even wish his selfishness would cease? Once or twice she spoke of their putting away the things of adults, packing up her daughter and his dog, and running away like young fools (but in a little troop), as if to prove themselves capable of romantic violence. But usually they talked as if she was the one who refused him the elopement he'd never volunteered.

And in all conscience he couldn't urge upon her less than that. He wasn't brazen enough to argue forthrightly for the limited bourn of his present hope. Owing to his past irresponsibility—though she never betrayed a hint of regarding it anything but the natural termination of a nearly forgotten temporary partnership—he felt disqualified to urge upon her the favors he craved. He was now a seducer with one hand tied behind his back.

Caleb allowed that her ambivalent and fluctuating evasion of what he truly desired was wisely honorable for Mooney's sake—to whom (as he did venture to suggest) she unnecessarily subordinated her own spiritual welfare in puzzling out the landscape of a future. She and he both had peculiar reason to believe that a self-reliant kid was the better off for some little irregularity of circumstances; and most of the time neither of them pretended to believe that one ever wanted to cooperate even in an irregular menage. Moreover, his picture was so immediate, so large in scale, so fully occupied by the woman as subject and object of passionate knowledge, that it scarcely had space for any third party except a bodyguard dog (who complicated it only slightly), despite the known fact that Mooney had displaced all Lilian's arts and sciences, taking precedence over all personal satisfactions as long as life might last—though not of course at every single moment.

Their mutual past in Hume held them motionless in the present like taut chains under the tension of teamed imaginations pulling on skew vectors, male and female, against the Body of Fate's overloaded stoneboat. The ugly duckling of the High Cordillera, ironically called Dark-of-the-Moon, Primary and Objective, to whom he had given the books of Yeats, was now the beautiful Moonfeather, daughter of the Yahi, sole remnant of Ishi's tribe, dwelling at both edges of the Antithetical and Subjective. But in working her way across the country and making a new name for herself she never lost the courageous independence of mind which he had not fully appreciated as her first lover.

Neither the despairs of adversity nor any other suffering could make her join the trendsetting renunciation of Western physicism. That's where I come in, Caleb said to himself. However enviable the features of Gil Algo that he tried to guess and envisage, the man evidently remained wholly insensate to Lilian's yearning for critical philosophy as well as art.

Only because it seemed obvious to her, Lilian refrained from suggesting that their present "natural affinity", to him so amazingly revealed by coincidences of thought, might have followed in part from his own influence in the old days, when she was a plastic student and his ideas were predilect in her artistic brooding. Caleb failed to discern her self-effacing persuasion that he, having originally suited her inchoate proclivities, had crucially prejudiced the preconscious criteria by which she subsequently sought or accepted studies pleasures and friends—which in turn reinforced the influences he had initiated—even unto attraction of later lovers.

In beauty she was no insipid Miss Atlantis, nor in motion voluptuous; but the finely shaped planes of her face perfectly reflected an originality that always brought to her suit the kind of men in whom she took interest—clever or educated, usually older enough than herself to approach her desideratum of maturity, either successfully professional or half starving in poverty. Caleb might well have wondered if he had been misled as to her present consort's intellectual qualities by her laconic and ambivalent allusions to the domestic abuse that often seemed to be leading toward final estrangement.

To other lovers her child had been no more than a minor drawback, since in most cases they'd had preemptive obligations that set limits to the extra liaison. No doubt some were even thankful that she had a Mooney, along with some job or other, to keep her occupied while they were busy with their own families or other loves. Without effort in manner or adornment, without modification of attitude, her unassertive intelligence and dignity had attracted men she liked; she never paltered for terms or expected improvements of behavior. And Caleb rightly guessed that on her part she had offered no more commitment than a scientist passingly absorbed in some sympathetic study. As he was told with droll stress on one half of her mouth, she had grown accustomed to men's clandestine or unofficial attentions; and it was rather comfortable never to be possessed—to be able to keep first things first, to separate maternal devotion from partial urges.

Among those other urges, the ones most frustrated were intellectual. It was no wonder that, in Caleb's opinion, she overestimated the value of academic achievement and belittled her own noetic ability, granting herself no credit for the art-discipline of her principal formation, and was more given to overawe at educated inferiors than at fine princes charming, many of whom, successful or affluent, would have been ready and willing to marry her, Mooney and all, docilely submitting themselves to her moral authority. Thus in the beginning Lilian always listened carefully to her elected tutors.

At their one epochal dinner in Newessexport, when Caleb enjoyed beginner's luck, heady with sweet surprise—as if of entirely fresh acquaintance—in sensing her present interests (which obviously were neither scientific nor historical) by means of touching upon many of his own, while lacking time for exploration or argument, he had glimpsed exfoliations and involutions (later to be magnified) in a realm of her experience that was of secondary concern to him at the time of his former passion. For instance, in speaking of their affinitive allegiance to "William Plato Yeats, as against James Aristotle Joyce", she delighted his heart by confessing the irony of nevertheless coming to dislike idealism. Without tutelage of dromenologist or priest, her discriminations had evolved in parallel with his own!

She had kept some of her night-school papers, one of which was titled "The A Priori As a Relative Concept". It became the focus of his demand for a gift—some provisional substitute not only for her reserved body but also for letters that might have borne such privileged information as he thirsted for nearly as sorely. And at last she did yield to this particular importunity. Leading him to his dinner booth at the Doghouse one evening, she bowled him over by slipping the stapled pages inside his menu folder. And another paper too, from a different facet of her efforts, called "Catharsis". With those were also several poems, faintly typewritten under various conditions.

By this time Caleb was allowed to seek her at the restaurant (which he could afford to attend about once a week), provided he didn't abuse the privilege of stealing looks at her near and distant movements by turning his head like a Viking Shepherd, or by lingering indiscreetly. But that night she played his stage quite cordially as hostess and cashier, recklessly darting him hints of esoteric gladness whenever she found excuse to openly acknowledge him as a regular customer. It was a happy hour for the incognito cavalier.

But he was astonished to hear that she'd been angry about his "bribe" when he'd last found her at the Doghouse, the night she was filling in as waitress for this same table. After anxious deliberation throughout his dawdled meal he'd left in lieu of a tip the booklet of postage stamps originally intended for delivery to her by mail, hoping it was an inspired alternative to the flat diplomacy of leaving no insult at all. He was seeking the courtesy appropriate both for his obligation not to ignore the irony of her role as his servant and for this opportunity to communicate one or two of his feelings with an arresting symbol. Delicacy required a tactful balance of meaningless custom, commercial appreciation, secret gratitude, presumption of intimacy, guilt-offering, gallantry, jest, and lugubrious pleading.

Was she displeased because his gratuitous act was too publicly performed? Or because it seemed a practical joke indicative of the puerile soul she preferred not to see in an intellectual admirer? Or, as one might expect, because his callow witticism struck her as a blatantly disrespectful attempt to manipulate her epistolary freewill?

But the memory of anger made no difference in her astute good humor now. Neither the world nor a man required her forgiveness. To Lilian the behavior of all beings seemed natural; pleased or irritated, she never bore grievance—only interest or indifference. And the papers proved she was interested.

It was too dark to read close-packed philosophy in Loathey O'Toole's public house, and reading manuscript verse would have been too conspicuous; so he buried his priceless windfalls within the folds of his daily *Nous* as uncounted treasure. For once he was looking forward to departure from her sight, ravenous to peruse the written word that would take the edge off his raging appetite for personal letters. But in two hours, on her way home, before relieving her sleepy mother of the night watch, she would scoop him up from the sidewalk in front of his house and take him somewhere for what was intended to be no more than twenty minutes of personal kisses and words of mouth. Such trysts were most likely to be granted when Gil was spending the night in Bot.

It was therefore in the triumphant conjunction of Creative Mind and Body of Fate—ineffable physicality of spirit forgetful of objective lust, the scent of her neck still in his nostrils, the tenderness of her breast still in the cup of his palm—that Caleb spent most of his Saturday morning writing her a disputation called "Dialogue of Self". Not until he had done so, irresistibly inspired by her Muse, could he summon the patience for philosophical study of her essay.

Caleb's dialogical plaint, as follows, was inspired by the first of what he later dubbed her Verses for White Men—"Haiku Times Three", a short poem of three speeches by ID, EGO, and SUPEREGO, which began with ID's lines: "I walk like a cat: / I am the joy of my animal kingdom."

"Peace, heart! You promised to act your age. Supposedly a small measure of love's unpossessing possession was all that you could ask in honor. You swore you were prepared to endure the sadness of knowing her through the wall."

"Look who's talking! You're the one that assured me, hope to die, fingertips in holy water, that a little appeasement of objective curiosity would set us both at rest."

"But last night was a kaleidoscope of amazement! No wonder i could only marvel at the matter a priori! A man's calm induction can't get going until the complex facts are clear."

"Serves you right. You took up far too much of our time talking about yourself. I would have made her do all the talking."

—i had to point out affinities and correspondences—hypotheses that she and i both have instincts for."

"We had too few minutes for such aesthetic luxury. You might have shut up and just listened to her and me. You shouldn't have been tagging along anyway."

"Who was it—you or i—could negotiate the fine distinctions that allowed us to her table?"

"We both coped with the circumstances. Mine was the willpower. I had more to gain than you."

"Like hell you did! To say the least, my unexpected discoveries were more numerous than yours."

"But not as deep."

"Delving has hardly begun."

"You mean your delving. You make me laugh, you dynamic crypto-idealist! Even putting the best foot forward you're too excited about the character to meditate upon the person."

"Much you know about the boundaries of analysis! Besides, you can't deny that her character is equally valuable to you. For both of us that's the beauty deepest of them all."

"I'm with you there, brother! It's just that I perhaps need appropinquity more than you do."

"An old wives' tale, no truer than your claim to seniority! i can't get along six miles away from her any better than you can."

"How well is that?"

"It's too early to predict."

"And too late to repent!"

"Shake, man! Put it there! But we should be fair to her."

"What do you mean by that?"

"It's two against one. We're not dealing with twin sisters. Her being and action are an integer. Naturally she resists moduli like us—were it only because we have alternate theories about her kinetic location."

"I agree that to do her justice you and I have got to get together. We see she sees that our disunity is after all a mere traditional convenience. Beyond that, it's simply that you're less fearful and I'm more wise."

"Right now we're about to explode separately! Can we ever both have peace?"

"What counts is the joy. We each know that she exists, and can each keep trying to remember the details of her beauty, which comprises but does not consist of details. And even for me her loveliness is governed by mentality—hers, not yours. But God forbid you should lay your burden on her!"

"We both devoutly wish to be disburdened in her. But you're more at fault than i. i'm capable of philosophic disinterest, i'm more concerned with what's good for her."

"Hypocrite! The marriage of true minds is no less concupiscent than the joining of hearts and spines."

"Do you think i wasn't the one who taught you that? At the unforgettable Newessexport dinner you weren't the only one who didn't taste the food we ate or failed to notice our route home. Were you aware that i never went to sleep that night? You dozed off at 4 AM."

"I have no patience with all these analytical distinctions. What would she think, to hear this childish argument? She may not understand that we're sanely Siamese."

"Methinks she's never doubted that. Wisdom is a primary attribute of the esemplastic qualities we call her character."

"Of course. But I mislike that abstract way of expressing ourself."

"To express what we are blessedly fortunate to witness, new language must be extended by the old, both of which are necessary and insufficient."

"I need no language."

"Redneck prig! What else have we in common with a woman? How else maintain a modicum of peace between now and then?"

"Between now and when?"

"Dear heart, between now and when she makes herself more manifest."

"Peace! Peace is all you have on the brain!"

"Not peace like death! Do you think those kisses are all for you? It's on account of them that i can't remember all the things she's said any better than you do."

"This could go on and on!"

"For life."

That Saturday letter would reach her on Monday. On Sunday morning, for Tuesday delivery, he meant to do justice to her essay. And it turned out that the academic exercise he had so fearlessly begged to read, at the risk of finding mediocrity (easily enough to be excused in an unevenly educated artist), only multiplied his delight by the factor of a new dimension.

"The A Priori As a Relative Concept" was sometimes syntactically crude, strewn with misspellings, oblivious of literary solecisms, and occasionally servile to putative authority in matters that remained as unauthoritative as they were two thousand years ago. Since it betrayed slight acquaintance with philosophy beyond the topic of the book assigned for her discussion he was all the more impressed by her appreciation of the technical points at issue, and above all by her critical independence. Despite his general aversion to responsible effort in epistemology, he found novel relief from a residual scholastic conscience in writing his libidinous response.

Since he had never read the book in question, he was not obliged to wonder how much of whatever she did not quote directly was uniquely original in perception, or whether her comments would have been recognized by other readers as the conventional tropes of certain specialists. But he was just educated enough to guess that some of the author's paradigms were drawn from the repertory of modern analysis—especially the presumably famous crows that were always black.

Whatever the matter, Caleb exulted that by taking possession of the thoughts she had once seriously wrought in brief respite from the world of struggle and desire, he knew her mind a thousand times better than any merely privy carnal lover—better in fact than she knew herself, who was so diffident about what she regarded as her infantile intellect. For him she was a black swan, natively superior not only to all the ducks that populated Cornucopia campuses but also to the superior geese of Unabridge; and to himself as well, the fancy-free gull with advantages of gender and schooling—who now however claimed to be the only absolutely sympathetic quasi-suitor. The difficulty in responding to the impersonal prose of her unknown past was only that it provoked many too many more ideas of his own than did the febrific presence of her voice.

Most of her oral words to him, personal and spontaneous, were spoken at the terminus of a telephone route while extraneous entities were clamoring for her attention. For Mooney's sake, otherwise an only-child, she participated in a "cooperative child-care" arrangement that often entailed a houseful of responsibility far more demanding (though she never said so) than the defense of a wistfully half-forgotten academic paper. With an hour or two of leisure in her week she might have gotten excited again about the subject of it (or its like), Gil or no Gil, failing the greater boon of sufficient time and space for painting. Caleb had yet to bethink himself how he might have seemed to lord it over her with the wealth of time permitting him to exhume and throw in her face the cold attenuated statements of her past that fetched up as almost satirical in the hard light of breadwinning maternity yet still represented the intellectual life for which she had more talent than most of its professors; but he wrung and rang so many themes from those precious few pages (for lack of other texts) that he began to fear she would think him a maniac preacher. At the same time he imagined her smiling with amusement at the way her immature trifling with formal discourse had undermined his judgment.

But prudential wisdom scarcely found a place among Caleb's critical faculties when beglamored by the metaphysics of this sometime student. Issues that he thought he'd graduated from, or long since decided to proscribe as philosophical interference with his chosen learning, were suddenly vibrant with sexual intensity. So for the moment he put aside his chronic problem of anachronistic Sumerians and once more yielded to his idioerotic cacoethes scribendi with as much energetic selfindulgence as if it was the sole purpose of literacy, in this case free of vice by virtue of love.

May Day, 6:15 AM

Dear Thisbe:
The second time we met was under the other half of the moon, Phase 8, when it feathered the opposite way. For people like us the Antithetical phases are all more auspicious than the Primary. Now it's at the full, governing unified lovers.

But you are like a wartime sailor: at sea, too deprived of gentle talk, too endangered for poetry, too buffeted to write, too duty-bound even for reading perhaps; your only relief, random liberties ashore, brief intoxications. My wits have been permanently moonstruck by the total of eight hours now logged in your aura.

I ache for the armature of your body. Every minute we're together I forefeel the perfect conduction between our bones when the distance between us will be negative. Voice and touch multiply the delimitations by which I fix your reality in comparison to mine, disturbing it with my disturbance.

But we need night after night even to name the tributaries of our Amazon. In the lightning flashes of croquis conversations I have probably mistaken some of your remarks. I know I have misstated some of mine. So the longing for mutual time altogether exceeds the sum of my comparatively discrete desires for your comparatively discreet parts. That's what Keats might call my "sense of beauty", which "overcomes every other consideration, or rather obliterates all consideration".

Yet what you have thought in the past about others' thinking—most of all, what you have found to think about unbidden—must needs have entered into what you now are, and what you will be, even if the matter of it falls further beyond psychology than any of your present feelings. It would have taken an infinity of hours to fathom your existence if you hadn't given me this trove of thoughts.

The reason I can quote K so precisely is that your black crows {". . . the function of the a priori is classificatory or categorical", and "by the law of the excluded middle we proclaim our determination to make an unquestionable dichotomy of experience rather than a tripartite or other division . . ."} reminded me to look him up. You would appreciate his reaction to the kind of mentation you and he protest. In the original enunciation of "Negative Capability", a letter to his brothers, he speaks particularly of Shakes as "capable of being in uncertainties, Mysteries, doubts, without any irritable reaching after fact and reason."

[After breakfast:]

It's astonishing how many parallels to the bent of my thought I find in yours. It appears that in your unvocational wandering (a rather deft route through the realms of gold), and on my idiosyncratic itinerary of overwrought lucubrations, time and time again we've paused at the same images and keystones. As sole survivors of two lost tribes we cleave to cognate values and even fix upon the same terms. Despite all differences in nature and in nurture, and the alienation of gender, our twinship is betrayed by a priorities! For according to Professor L, as you put it, "the a priori is much like an epistemologically pristine net the nodes of which represent our concepts and the lines of which represent the definitional relationships between these concepts that are wholly analytic in the sense that they make no claims about the nature of data but merely reflect our active attitudes. . . ."

As for you and me in particular, our common locus is reckoned in n dimensions—n different continua, n degrees of freedom. It might be possible to talk about them if we could find two pillows together somewhere out of the rain, a posteriori.

But instead there's barely time for glancing allusions to what I think you've thought. So all alone I must bear the amplification and extension of my horny lemma . . .

[I've just been down to look for Ibi. He's disappeared for much longer than ever before. I hope it's nothing but a passing infatuation. If so, it might have taken him as far away as your neighborhood. But if he doesn't come home today I'll have to call Sgt Proctor, whose news or opinion I'll always dread to ask.]

From your account it strikes me that your author misses the radical significance of Kant's categorical Time, Space, and Causality (T S C)—according to what I vaguely remember of *Prolegomena to Any Future Metaphysics*. They aren't "concepts" at all (except in the apperceptions of philology or philosophy), but the psyche's necessary contribution of form to all experience—more prior than any of the a priori conceptions reticulated in the sieves of definition and logic. Kant's radically subjective T S C are not knotted and meshed in relationships like even the most universal percepts; and they can't be torn or mended. K is therefore not susceptible to L's criticism of what I would call the objective idealism implicit in traditional notions of the a priori . . .

But my heart leaps highest at your piece on tragedy. "This irreconcilable tension between intelligence and passion is the soul of tragedy." For me the main interest of philosophy is its service to the understanding of tragedy by examination of the freewill question inevitably called up by the collateral problems of chance and determinism. Most of the fundamental questions in metaphysics, science, and psychology then become relevant. . . .

Perhaps she forgot his own paper "The Mask of Prometheus", which despite its insolent dismissal of scholarly authority had been well enough received as a theory of tragedy to have drawn him into a career at Hume if he hadn't been extricated by other hope. In those days she hadn't given herself credit for reading it with any sort of comprehension.
But Caleb's loveletter was still far from exhausted:

. . . Thus I come to the praise of a third K. I've read only one of Kierkegaard's books, *Concluding Unscientific* [i.e. Unprofessional] *Postscript,* but it was enough to make him one of my nontragic heroes, and to justify one of my enthusiastic, temerarious, and highly exclusive opinions: that he was the first and almost only theorist of irony—oddly anticipating Yeats. *Ironic* is the term for you—if I were allowed but a single abstraction to describe subject, object, and circumstance. Irony announced itself in your interrogative brow . . .

But I can't let your matter rest at this level of agitation. You have inspired an exciting new connection in the network!

Skip all three of the K K K , if Mother Necessity leaves you no choice; but even if it takes time from Mooney (or from anyone else but me), you shouldn't omit Fayaway Morgan. Her *Liberty and Responsibility* was written for the few like you. It took a feminine philosophical anthropologist to escape idealism in all its subversive varieties—neurological, mystical, nominal, and real—and to put T S C in its relative place. She tactfully corrects certain a priori habits unwittingly inherited from the Greeks by all her colleagues and predecessors!

Like Auto Drang she has suffered the penalty of guild ostracism and bibliographic neglect. (He was the philosophical psychoanalyst who questioned the preeminence of fathers in Tristram Freud's imperial psychology, properly acknowledged freedom of the will, and distinguished creative action from aesthetic passion.) Therefore she too is almost unknown even to the younger radicals of the profession who are beginning to discern some of what she was long ago the first to discover.

One of the local systems she studied, as field philosopher and speculative anthropologist, was the nearly forgotten language of your own mothers. You may suppose what she found: "Yana philosophy in general had no law of contradiction. Where we have mutually exclusive dualistic categories, the Yahis had categories that were inclusive, but not mutually so . . ." That is to say, your people got along without a priori axioms of analysis like ours; they did not exclude the middle, and never had use for a Razor!

But her most radical essays in this book are on the Mardians of Polynesia. With them she dissolves K_2's T S C —the metasystem of the entire Western world and of all its products, including history. The hardest culture to analyze is the one you learn in. But her inferences are not the result of merely observational and self-deceptive sojourns among the subjects of objective study. They reflect both exotic and maternal experience, and interpret the ethnographic information that escapes the a priori nets of those who have reported the undisputed facts. "When we read about another culture," she says "we have to remember to read every word; we have to forget our habits of fast reading, because when we begin a sentence, we can never predict what its end will be."

Her insight—what is so far from being obvious that it was overlooked by the great men who had made study of the Mardian Islands particularly in search of cultural distinctions—was that these people have *no causality*. It's not just that they deny this or that cause-and-effect: they simply do not perceive any such function of T and S as C, dynamic or not, anywhere at all! They *un*assume the very essence of Western genius (now being realized everywhere as the necessary mode of progressive technology).

If Fayaway Morgan weren't such a gentle maverick, if she didn't refuse to suppress feminine sensibility in order to succeed in the Common Area of scientific discourse (arbitrated by men), and if she didn't therefore content herself with the hindermost reputation among great minds, her work would long since have undermined much of the prevailing nonsense about myth and ritual. In her utmost alienation she sometimes seems to have gone so far as to accept the a priori antilinear acausal nonhistorical "pattern" of the Mardians as an alternative to T S C even for us; but in her more equable mood she suggests a sort of epistemological complementarity between T S C cultures and those others that are disappearing.

Strangely enough, her writings were recommended to me by my revered friend Father Duncannon, the world's most metanoid T S C thinker, who never pretends not to be constrained by the a prioris of his classical nurture but is alert and unprejudiced enough to have found and admired her obscure monographs (amid the torrent of publications he's scanned in a savant lifetime), and not to have despised her morphological reasoning as he has finally come to despise the "irresponsibility" of most disestablishmentarian writers and "singleminded existentialists".

She says that the Mardian (and the Yahi) "can indicate that an action is completed without implying that the action is past; it may be timeless in a present-perfect tense . . ." That statement reminds me of the difficulty Christians have always had in explaining the ontological operation of the Mass as an anamnesis of the Last Supper. She often mentions problems in using our T S C language to describe worlds in which the epistemological nets are no more like ours than a cat's dream is like a king's.

When I raved about her ideas, after reading the old *Journal of Philosophy* offprint Father Duncannon lent me, he mentioned that she'd once lived here in Dogtown, working at the hospital as a nurse in the maternity ward, her pre-academic vocation, while her husband labored at his Norumbega doctorate. (Before the war she left Dogtown for the Pacific in the topsail schooner *Omoo* with a poorly subsidized crew of biologists and social scientists, and later had kids of her own.)

Now behold the most recent wonder vouchsafed me in anticipation of your causal existence! Only yesterday I read my mother's remark in a letter from Vernalia that she'd heard her "dearest lost friend Fay", whom she's always referred to as her "midwife", had published "a book on Atlindu customs". Suddenly I remember from my childhood, among all the names and anecdotes excessively familiar to a boy impatient for his independence, that "Fay" had now and then been coupled to a surname which I'm now quite sure was Morgan! Fayaway Morgan must have been the *candid woman* who rescued me from the morgue! Yet another instance of Lilian Cloud as my center of unbounded signification! You can see why I'm so daft on Destiny! Mysterious prehensions in T S C show up with every shovel I turn!

There isn't enough time to add how much I like your ragged little fragment on the Gilgamesh myth—pondering your own kind of "uncertainty". It proves once again that our coincidence of freewill—yours and mine, when loose in realms of gold—is no less praeternatural than a miracle.

I hope you aren't more irritable than I about the uncertainty of the hope you give me. —But right now I'm irritated by the grunts and toots of the May Day bands assembling down in the cemetery for the big parade. And my worry about Ibi rises again to strike at the joy of thinking about you. Let's hope he's downstairs waiting for me.

17
LUSTRATION

In the aftermath of writing to Lilian he felt as if he had buried her with words by consoling himself with feckless mooning. His desire was neutralized by disgust at having resorted to the unmanly expediency of overwhelming her with floods of futile prose merely to alleviate her blank inexorable absence. Casting doubt upon his most elemental self-reliance, and indeed gorged with revulsion against writing itself, the voiceless troubadour went downstairs with his thick letter, which he would have torn up in loathing of his infantile behavior save for the ingrained conviction that such a sacrifice would prove the morning absolutely rather than only comparatively wasted.

Above all he reproached himself for the selfindulgence of writing anything at all while time was crying out for utmost action up and down the earth in search of his most selfless friend—even though it was difficult to suppress at a lower level his naively sanguine expectation that in another three seconds he would find the dog lying patiently at a spot on the grass where all three doors could be watched at once.

But yet again it was disappointment that awaited him. Ibi still wasn't there.

As he walked along the iron fence of Acorn Pasture toward the mailbox, scrutinizing every living motion, scanning the asphalt pounded by ceaseless ranks and files of rushing kilroy wheels, his sense of irresponsibility faded into renewed horror of the inhumanity everyone is born into, the knowledge of which is ordinarily suppressed so that one may be able to pursue happiness. His consciousness suddenly opened to the suffering of dogs in conditions worse than death. By comparison the miseries of human desire were sniveling bathos.

Saints of the earth imprisoned in tiny private zoos without legal counsel or bill of rights; deprived of natural movement, sensory experience, and any kind of fellowship; chained, caged, frozen, or starved under repression by petty militarists or heartless utilitarians; tortured by idle experimentalists—if not abandoned by treacherous families, poisoned by vandals, overfed and undereducated by destructive sentimentalists, choked and bewildered by stupidly wielded leashes (all instinct and reason throttled by oxymoronic rote or capricious inconsistency—like mute orphan children suffering without the benefit of pedagogic intuition or primitive animal sympathy, without a language even for their pain—able at best to resist or beg but never to make a complaint or suggestion): always beholden to the mercy and intelligence of a master species! For any such fate Ibi might have been kidnapped.

And he thought of his crying brother-child held fast in some steeljawed trap, gnawing at a broken paw. Or knocked fifty feet off the road by a speeding kilroy, maimed and paralyzed. Or even sliced and crushed by one of the trains he'd gotten too used to hearing up close. Imagining himself in the languageless dependency of his fraternal animal, wholly vulnerable to mankind, Caleb began to weep that it was better to be already dead than stolen or maimed and still alive in ignorant agony of flesh or spirit. Dropped into the box with a counterpoising clang of the iron lip, his letter now seemed an irrevocable folly truly insignificant of love, though it reverberated like the hollow closing of his cell in a common tomb. His arms and legs began to tremble.

But it was nearing noon, and he regretted that he had committed himself to a special Sunday invitation, for which, lacking more definitely preemptive bad news, it was now necessary to get into the car which Ibi loved to ride in and make his way across the Harbor. The gathering fountainhead of Dogtown's May Day parade, which would soon block the exit of his car from the driveway, urged him to be early. Sanguine sunshine was just then breaking up the cloudbank that had seemed to presage a return of April, and he was encouraged to take advantage of his generally eastward course by divagating in an active search.

His sense of duty—if not of probability—compelled at least that much expiation on his way to pleasure. Under the influence of opening blue sky, on a morning about to turn as mild and windless as any marcher or watcher could wish, he mechanically explored a good sampling of the streets on either side of the route between Acorn Pasture and East Harbor that avoided the normal Sunday traffic from the highest Masses at the BVM and the Espirito Santo, aside from which the Harbor Ward was mostly emptied by the migration of spectators to the thoracic thoroughfares used for the public procession. But it was so unlikely that Ibi would have been led to seek his fortune in this direction that by the time he stepped on his gas for the Joint Hill watershed dividing the wards he was reduced to his habitual daily course and consciously occupied only with thoughts of his destination.

Which was Bice Picory's new quarters. For his first visit he had been bidden to lunch. "I have something to tell you. You'll be the first to know—if it meets with your approval. If it doesn't, dear brother, you'll be the last and only one." Then she added: "But don't come before twelve!"

He was still pondering that gratuitous qualification, which at the time had rendered him almost churlish, considering his exceptional acceptance of an invitation that called him away from his desk on a precious day before the sun was in decline, and which made him yet more sullenly suspicious when it dawned on him that this was not May's Eve but the day of rest that followed it. Still, though heartsick about Ibi and peevish about her impertinent summons, he was powerless to resist any kind of intercourse with the cheerful halfbreed beauty of the British Commonwealth who had become the nearest thing to a female companion.

Meanwhile, since it was always possible that Ibi would follow a bitch to the east, Caleb drove slow, with no kilroys whipping him on from the rear, and continued to scrutinize both sides of the street with perfunctory hope, searching the spaces between or beyond the houses raggedly populating his familiar passage through East Harbor, even pausing to peer at the shrubbery and scrap heap down on the shoreside flat to the rear of Petto's shop, where the welding rig was parked as usual. But there was no sign of animal life. From the base of the Wye Square triangle he looked up the hill on his left to inspect the descending throat of Skate Street—likewise with neither expectation nor reward. He couldn't search much further, for just beyond this junction East Front banked down along the railed seawall a little above the high tides and ran a hundred yards to twist past the gray wooden pile known as Apostles Dock, on an upper floor of which Bice now occupied a "studio apartment".

That rambling terraqueous barn was a conglomeration of fused or blended wings and annexes, roofed with gables of many an angle, averaging in height between three storeys and four, and more or less integrated in an L-shaped superstructure as the shoulders and one arm of a U-shaped wharf. The elevated residential nests of the cote were built into former commercial lofts like separate gas bags within the envelope of a dirigible, sharing the skeleton with a congeries of nautical and industrial workshops, not all of which were confined to the main deck. The ark's landward facade, hard upon a concrete sidewalk of tapering widths, was bent into several segments to fit the curve leading East Front slightly upward into the straightest reach of its crooked career. At this elbow the Harbor's main artery narrowly separated the tidewater Dock and adjacent wharfage from one of Lady Gloucester's inner thighs, a bramble-clung bluff of lichened granite. Here the earliest settlers had hewn the wagon track which was now almost too narrow for its double stream of motored wheels, following the Natural path trod by Champlain's men-at-arms when the waters that licked the uncut mother-rock were still of purest brine and when Mother's Neck across Argo Cove was still a tidal island.

The basin of the Dock was a horseshoe pool, slowly rising and falling with the rotation of the moon, haven to a variety of working boats moored to its spiles at perpetually cycling levels in all kinds of weather. This barnyard court was balconied on three sides by the broad four-inch planks of the street-level deck and at its headwaters by two tiers more of supervising timber terraces carved out of the pitched roof of the original warehouse for the convenience and pleasure of mostly bachelor tenants unconnected with any of the businesses they lived among.

Opposite the spar sheds of the long pier-borne wing that sheltered the fleet from Boreas the U's flat left arm blended with a broad wharf on the south side to provide a spacious operating platform for the Dock's stout swivel crane, which when called upon did the will of pygmies like a stationary elephant. This triangulated machine had long been admired by Caleb on his daily passings to and fro. It had not yet launched the densely jumbled toyboats still cluttering a large waterfront pavement that would be claimed by kilroys in the summer.

Stranded high in their sledged cradles with bottoms exposed, these hibernating amphibians were magnified by intimate views of their keels and propellers in the mazey hollows one could walk among. Not yet in season—unrigged, unable to respond with motion, each hull lashed into its own stagecrafted tarpaulin and lumber—the conspicuously unproductive vessels huddled together to shade the parking lot with their flaring topsides, darkening the sidewalk and dwarfing the vehicles that passed or parked on wheels. In winter, when not frozen into stillness, the wind flapped canvas and moaned among their naked underparts; but cats and dogs were no more baffled by this cavern of crutches and scaffolds than by a permanent preserve of forest.

Caleb envisioned himself henceforth haunting the Dock, which hitherto he'd only passed with envious curiosity. The labyrinth of shrouded bottoms, each chocked and trussed to the shape of its own curves on a separate brace of skids, cunningly set at any angle to make the most of its irregular dimensions in minimum space, invited a boy's investigation. But this seasonal warren struck a contrast to one it recalled. Every spring in Unabridge, after ice and mud finally vanished from the Norumbega Garth, sections of boardwalk were detached from each other and stacked up in an unpaved storage yard between the Divinity School and the yellow clapboard Psyche House, just inside the Varsity's pale in his backside neighborhood, to aestivate in a square of gridwork like columns and rows of cohorts in some shrunken godforsaken castra. Here in Dogtown every boat crib was carelessly daubed with a name, but there each unit of rectangular gray planking, prefabricated to standards without being fungible, had been branded with complex illiterate symbols—as if after decades of campaigning it still required dog tags to assign its underfoot articulation at winter's muster. Boardwalks were stacked high above your head like a legion of shipping pallets or toy traintracks, with fissures and crevasses in which kids could play Cowboys and Atlindus without too much fear of being noticed by the colly cops.

The crane that hoisted and launched these boats in a great sling was underpinned by reinforced pilings on the wharf itself. Its framework was a tetrahedron of steel girders, horizontal vertical and oblique: an isoceles right triangle laid flat upon the deck to support two others in planes normal to itself and to each other, sharing the one vertical member as their common useful edge, a swiveling mast which in turn supported by multiply pulleyed steel cable a longer boom of the same construction, hinged at its base in a swinging vertical plane, whereby lifting tackle could be suspended at angles varying between the limits of zero and ninety degrees (but probably averaging forty-five), in a horizontal sweep approaching three full quadrants over an area centered near a corner of the basin.

Although a few fishing boats were still berthed afloat within the haven, as well as a large old winter-rigged schooner (which served a small subsect of Pauline evangelicals for living quarters but no longer for missions), Apostles Dock had undergone the charming corruption befitting a Temple of marine pleasures, and it was famous among people like Owen Leary up and down the coast as an Inn of Yachts. Thus the great derrick was now used for little more than lifting whited luxuries in and out of a tidal dingle.

To Caleb Karcist, entering for the first time as a possible performer upon this stage redolent of naval stores and creaking with hawsers, the entire theater of the Dock was as stimulating as an Elizabethan playhouse—yet chiefly because enfolded here within the inner harbor it faced, just across the narrow vestibule of Argo Cove, instead of spectators, a fishermen's counterpart. Over there at Simon's Point Marine Railways, on the inner tip of Mother's Neck, working boats were hauled for repair; and many of the city's largest draggers tied up at its piers whenever they weren't fishing or unloading. At the extremity of its broad wharf, directly opposite the Apostle's, stood a similar crane, like the other foot of Colossus. The function of that tetrahedral machine was to raise and lower not the sybaritic craft of fair weather but heavy marine engines, large masts, whole assemblies of superstructure, pilings, and other necessary fabrications of the productive economy.

Climbing to the third outdoor deck by a narrow companionway, suddenly exultant in anticipation of occupying the scene from which he could survey the harbor's pit—one of the city's constantly respirating auditoriums—Caleb knocked on Bice's corridor door, which he found slightly ajar.

"Come in. I'm a little late taking my bath." If one could believe Petto, she was one goddess who wouldn't mind a man boasting that she had reserved none of her beauty from him. He'd been told by her erstwhile host that she liked to walk around naked in his studio. But Caleb was astonished, still pondering the psychology of such incestuous trauma as she had secretly confessed. He locked the door behind him.

Her new nest was small, and most of its furnishings were presented at first glance, especially a double bed, panoplied as a Bohemian sofa in crimson gold and aquamarine, counterpane tightly smoothed, pillows freshly plumped. Nothing else was neat. The kitchen was an alcove beyond bathroom partitions, which looked as flimsy as a summer hotel's. "In here." The one interior portal was open wide. "I wish to tub you Knight Commander of the Bath! Close the door: it's getting cold. Don't worry, your lunch is all but ready. I'll be out of here as soon as you wash my back."

Caleb rolled up his sleeves and knelt to the task, which he soon extended to take in her front. She lay back under his hands in the hot suds as complacent about the surfaces of her body as a house cat. But at the outset her mind was elsewhere, merrily displaced, as he saw by the bright black gaiety of her eyes, which nevertheless remained as alert as ever to him as the individual with whom they happened to be engaged.

The gypsy was almost always gratefully susceptible to the verbal teasing he found natural and convenient for keeping countenance with desirable girls; but in order to avoid the appearance of banality in his lewdly gentle manipulations, and divert attention from his salacious attempt to inspect the patch of moss awash in foaming bubbles, he affected a dispassionate fraternal attitude, deceitfully solicitous only for her happiness, while he wondered if this was an opportunity to dissolve the glass that sealed her essence—to teach her the crisis of beatitude that in his opinion was better known to Lilian and some other reserved or detached women lacking gypsy sparkle.

The interlude was blessed by her ignorance of his presumptuous hypothesis. "What are you doing?" she shrieked in humorously stifled outrage. "Just looking for your little delitescent rubicund horn." said he. "Never mind my ruby cund!" she hissed, altering her complacent posture. The silky black tumulus disappeared in a shifting firth. "I invited you for a special reason." she continued amiably. "This is my birthday." [He gestures embarrassment at not knowing, or not remembering.] "It's a surprise party because I didn't want you to bring anything except good counsel."

That seemed perfectly true. Her attitude toward properties struck him as not half unlike his mother's inveterate lily-in-the-field trust to the Lord's provision of next month's rent. Bice was generously improvident with her pittance-pence from the *Nous*—and had lavished all sorts of small gifts upon him in genuine concern for his material welfare as her most deserving friend, even unto some of his meals at Leonardo's, on the strength of what she called his Attic poverty and his expectation of being reduced to unremunerated self-employment after the Chapter in June. Yet she exhibited annoyance or indifference whenever he attempted to reciprocate. He had come to believe that she was morally unable to accept anything from one whose estimation she valued. But on this occasion he would have liked to signify his congratulation with a single five-petaled rose.

"Today is also the birth of my Vita Nuova!" she eagerly announced. But it still was not her smile that most beglamored him. Though her nimbus of jocund locks was somewhat dampened by the atmosphere of a hot bath, ringlets of sable garland clustering in shreds against the winter pallor of her heart-shaped face, even now (when his eyes and hands were making free with the budded torso that seemed to be especially craved by men of poetic imagination) those insouciant thrums of loose curls remained for Caleb the most lovely feature of her intelligence. That fairy crown of raven foliage embowered with tossing asymmetry the glade of cheek and brow, which was ceaselessly illuminated by a pair of living black jewels that like magic wells gathered and absorbed all colors of enchantment.

But their conversation was not romantic. From the beginning she had been an interesting general informant about local affairs, and since her Magic Mountain confession, which temporarily neutralized his most inciteful visions of "overwhelming" her and thereby instinctively encouraged her confidence in his friendship, she had become quite open with him about some of her feelings; yet, despite the tenor of Petto's unreliable defamations, she was always ambiguously discreet about the particulars of her relations with the men she spoke of, and Caleb was generally unsure of the degree to which she was intimate with them—to whom perhaps she spoke of himself. He could hardly admit that his curiosity was as tantalized as a celibate parish priest's.

For instance, what sins of hers was he now washing away? One at least must have been quite recent, for why else had she so pointedly warned him not to arrive too soon? The bed was too trimly tidied up. As little as an hour ago he might have ascertained by gross examination the state of her nerves, but at present nothing was evinced by the delicate tumescence of her proudly juvenile paps except perhaps a chronic dilation of vascular molecules when under the scope of an observer.

Quelling the all-too-familiar impulse to test her with impudent questions in the form of joshing banter, he subrogated the circumstances of his libido. "Twenty-one years ago today, give an hour or two, I was dancing around a Maypole at St Martha's Convent within a mile of here. It was the high point of the year. We practiced for what seemed like weeks. The boys' ribbons were blue; we twisted them in and out of the girls' reds and greens coming in the opposite direction—at least as I now remember the choreography. That's how I got my first impression of Betty. It was that round-dance that gave me a taste for squaredancing ten years later."

"No dancing in between? I had to go to dancing school." Pursing her lips and contracting her eyebrows, Bice improvised her comment:

Ichabod, ichabod, ichabod—i,
If I had then known you
I would have been shy!

"There was a Maypole at my convent too, but no boys. That's why I'm ten years behind you in maturity. I hope to catch up. When are you going to take me a'Maying at the Doghouse?" She already knew he wasn't willing to waste time showing himself as a dunce at nightclub dancing.

"I think of those May Day dances every time I see a bare flagpole or one of the old quarry masts."

"You know what!" she interrupted him and sat straight up in the soap suds, suddenly remembering a professional interest. "The other day going through your landlady's historical columns in the *Nous* files I found out that the Dogtown tradition of May Day parades started only about forty years ago when the Ibicity Clerk got his dates mixed up and confused it with Memorial Day at the other end of the month. But any excuse was good enough to institute the custom of another parade, and that's why there are two in May. I'm going to cover the other one for the paper. They say it's rather moving."

He told her that Dogtown had suffered many more fishing deaths than killings in all the national wars. "Something like fifty thousand, all by the sea, none by the fish. One of my earliest memories, before the convent, was standing near the Gut Bridge with my mother to watch them cast wreathes of flowers onto the outgoing tidal current. But I don't remember at all the parade that led to the ceremony. I can't bear to see the ceremony again, for fear of dismay at the words that probably now go with it. I wouldn't be surprised if they sang 'God Bless Atlantica'."

"Yet you might hear truly universal grief for death in livelihood." she protested.

His rejoinder sounded callous. "I haven't time to experiment with tolerance." Or with humiliation by the crowd. But why humiliation?

"Ibi would love to go. I could put his picture in the paper."

Thus was his awful fear recalled. He thought it would be a little eased by sharing the burden: he told her what was wrong. In dismay as instinctive as a mother's for some child, she at once rose from the water, offering to help him in the search, to telephone Sergeant Proctor at home, and to call the watch commander at the Police Station, that all patrols be put on the alert; even to put a boxed notice on tomorrow's front page.

Alarmed by her extravagant and impracticable reaction, he was able to restrain and calm her—keep her from stepping out of the bath—only by asseverating the probabilities of a false alarm, arguing the futility of random action, and promising to call for her help that very afternoon if Ibi didn't show up for his supper a second time. Yet while reassuring himself withal, then and theretofore, he was so bemused by the flawless nude at hand (neither fleshy nor skinny, neither wrinkled nor seamless) that he soon again forgot the fearful news with which he had interrupted her purification. He also forgot about the impenetrable integument of the inner woman, and made her do so too. On his part everybody else in the outer world was forgotten. Even of Lilian no concept or image arose in comparison or in stead. Fate had not appointed him a Paris, to make judgment of Aphrodite Hera and Athena. Anyhow, the body of this renewed virgin, as she stood hesitant above the foam with one foot on the edge of the tub, looked more like sylvan Artemis. The color of her shoaling ogive breasts was smoothly continuous with all the other tawny skin of twenty summers, but there was a narrow band of white around her loins, cusping at the dark scutcheon.

"Little nook and crannyberry!" he apostrophized, still crouching at the side of her pool, after a brief intermezzo without ill effect. If only I had a tongue like Ibi's!"

"What you couldn't tell!" she giggled. "I think you'd like to circumcise me! But I'm like Queen Elizabeth—cloven, not crested. You may be the jot—I'm only a tittle. But this is no time for linguistic sport. Let me dry off! I've got to get dressed and explain why you were invited to lunch!"

In exchange for leaving off his nearly inconsequential worship of chaste venery's Rima Veneris he was allowed to wield the towel; but he said he could hardly see her for the steam in the air. Since she refused to let him cool off the bathroom by opening the door, he launched into a sermonette about the human heat-exchanger as he scornfully dabbed and muffled her superhumid skin. "Even in cooler air it takes much longer to get dry after a hot bath than a hot shower finished off with a cold one. And it uses more hot water."

"*Cold* shower! Why do you think I came south? I'm not a wild Atlindu or a Purdeyville Finn! If you take cold showers before the weather gets hot you're even more of a militarist than I suspected!

—Besides, I don't pay for the hot water; and I like to take my time, drying off the Gypsy way!"

Caleb didn't pause to imagine the Gypsy way. Having already discovered that (though an admirer of Eskimos, not by any means an Atlindu) she was impervious to ecological morality, he abandoned the efficiency argument and embarked upon a physiological explanation of his theory that cold water, especially on the back of the neck, approximate to the hypothalamus, by making the brain think it's cold outside, instead of hot, immediately closes the pores and constricts the blood vessels, thereby conserving the body's heat that a warm environment otherwise makes it dissipate by cooling the blood. The skin's rise in temperature evaporates moisture more rapidly. "Also, the pores close quickly; they don't gradually suck back the dissolved dirt."

"There's nothing wrong with my complexion."

"La belle dame sans souci! You can't see the fungoidal microbes. —I won't dry between your toes; you'll have to do that all by yourself: so you won't pick up athlete's foot from somebody."

For this suggestion he was rewarded with a push and a snort. "Ugh! —Okay! Now's the time to try your ordeal, if I'm ever going to. I want to see you practice what you preach. You've got to suffer with me!" She reached down to haul him to his feet and unbuckle his belt. "We'll start all over again with a hot shower, and little by little I'll mix in the cold."

But he insisted that the changeover be instantaneous. "So I'll take the controls. It won't hurt, especially if the cold water hits you headfirst. It'll make you feel so much better that—"

"Never mind feeling better than good. I want to talk to you. Let's get it over with. Show me how a brave Natural takes his mind off nature. Just be sure to start with the hot."

In a trice the panamorous herm took his stand with the Naiad under her Arcadian fountain, the shower curtain enclosing them translucently like a modernized hydria. Not for long did they play under the tropical stream like infant brother and sister; for him at least the torment of taboo was no mimic affectation. It was some time more before she stopped them from fooling around toe to toe, of nearly equal distances, the warm waterfall plastering flat the hair of their heads and distorting sights of each other. "Your ego is much too ostentatious!" she called through the boisterous hiss.

"It's because I don't think hard enough." he shouted back. "Aristotle says the function of the brain is to cool the blood."

"You've told me that before." She then recited him a jingle she'd been thinking up:

Doctor Foster
Brought to Gloucester
Dogtown's itchy dance.
It-chy, ic-thy,
Ithy-phallic prance!

Her precise enunciation was tanged with honey.
"Yet your hermaphroditic little iota is nowhere to be seen." Caleb licked her palm, naturally procrastinating the execution of his vow to reach over her shoulder and switch to shocking icewater, his will and reason both occluded by the immediacy of her slippery skin at every level of his own. His purpled erubescent salute was no offense to her; but her riant complaisance was not in phase with his intent, which apparently was not reciprocated to much degree at present. Aside from the subliminal sense of guilt for silly dalliance during the crisis of Ibi's very existence, however, pride alone saved him from the folly of pressing for a dance that might not enthrall her.

So at last, without warning, when she'd forgotten the agreement, he abruptly twisted the faucets in opposite directions. She was the first to feel the catastrophic reversal of temperature, on the back of her head and shoulders—so shocking that it might as well have been an instantaneous inversion of gravity—so stunning that at first she felt nothing but the kinetic energy beating down upon her (as if it had not been doing so when hot and uxorious). All at once her whole pelt was overwhelmed by the apocalyptic mass of liquid hail. She shrieked. He laughed; but it was worse for him, like harlequin, being half shielded from the numb transition by her penumbra. He forced her to pirouette fully under the cruel force of the sluice. As she escaped, without finishing her lesson in thermodynamic virtue, recklessly flinging open the curtain before he could turn off the water, her anger came and went, yet for a quarter of a minute she remained displeased with her fanatic trainer.

The same cold water had of course reduced the satyr himself to a decent gymnastic attitude, tingling with Apollonian exhilaration, when he stepped out into the blessed silence, putting the best face upon his resolution to persevere in the slightly daunted exposition of his theory. She looked at him and laughed. "Now get me dry, Mr Strawberry-orchids! I must admit I'm already warm."

Opening the door, he trampled the old towel to absorb the puddle, and demonstrated his rigamarole with a fresh one. "Lightly first, take off the top strata of drops where the water's thickest. Otherwise it takes too long to evaporate the moisture, like patches of snowbank that the Spring sun can't get rid of—except that here the heat comes from underneath: their bulk is too much for their surface, and the skin's heat is wastefully absorbed by the water without being able to vaporize much of the mass. Once your towel gets the lumps of H_2O down to the last few layers of molecules, evenly distributed, your warm skin evaporates the residue very quickly . . . "

"I'm sorry my anabaptism is disrupting your regular dry sabbath." With an almost maternal smile, taking his didactic efforts for a quaint displacement of erotic disappointment, Bice offered her own condition as a self-mocking apology. "I don't have a big-*I* branded on my chest for incest, but you make me conscious of what's sinister in it. I'm not speaking of the taboo; with you I feel more innocent than with anyone else on earth—and yet you haunt me with everything that happened on the Magic Mountain—perhaps because you're the only one who knows about it. I'm glad I told you. By listening you helped undo the bad part as well as revive the good memory of David. So you know more about me than anyone else does. But I must learn how to get out of the lobster pots I swim into. I'm afraid I'll be trapped in a net by some crazy Hephaestus . . ."

He guessed that she was anxious to express her respect for him as a man and to acquit her gaiety of the coquetry which she realized it might seem to have led her into, yet that the plea in her deeply sobered eyes also conveyed gratitude for his apparently unresentful bravery in keeping up what she half thought was mere pleasantry about the conservation of energy and time.

"I know there's nothing extraordinary about my confusion." she went on. "Nowadays everyone may be knotted up. But most people are only strings of knots, like comboloi, or looped like rosaries—at worst a tangle that can be unraveled with time and patience. But I'm one endless knot, like the Druid's Claw that trapped Mephisto in Faust's study as a black dog because it was imperfectly drawn. I forget whether it's called a pentagram or a pentagon."

"Schoolmarms use stars to mark their praise. But yours is the five-point star of Inanna."

"Yes, it's not crassly powerful like a Magen David of two simple trinities. Sometimes I feel like the Parlous Square traffic dummy. When you counted out the five ways meeting there—on the way between Rectory and Poet's Corner, holding hands on our halcyon honeymoon—it was as charming as a lighthouse; but now I know it's the daily butt and bane of all the city's traffic!"

Her expiation was unselfcentered, however. With a beguiling smile she added inconsistently: "I'll never use the cold-water method voluntarily, but I do admit that your efficiency makes me feel good afterwards. Amorous, even." First, clad in a peplum of damp towel, as if regretting the nakedness that had falsely elevated his hopes, drawing from her linen chest yet another giant sweet-smelling deep-piled cloth of Egyptian cotton, she took her turn drying him as tenderly as a priestess doting upon the baby Eros. This time she assisted at the shapeshifter's metamorphosis. "I once read—in the Chebuctu—library—that circumcised homunculi—are more irritable—than concupiscent.—Is that—really so?" she asked, rounding prehensile lips with fictile babytalking kisses of the air, like a fish nibbling its excogitated bubbles. "Sister Helen, the outspoken biology teacher at the convent, told me that Catherine of Siena thought the nuptial ring of marriage to Christ was neither gold nor of silver but the foreskin given in blood and pain by his holy circumcision—a term which only she would explain. She herself thought it was in atonement for the curse of women, especially the BVM's. To me the cylinder seal of your covenant is more fascinating as an order of architecture—capital—and column—." She said no more. Not every corner of his brain was yet irrationally disturbed by the ecstasy he supervised. With an unseen smile he remembered randomly registered words of Montaigne: "some poet in need of this delight and famished for it". Her playfulness gave way to speechless evocation, and his amusement was overwhelmed by the practiced skill with which she slowly drew the bow. Even unto the egocentric limit, and past it, after all his liminal radicals had been gathered by her solicitations, the quickening of plasma was temporally magnified by a transcendental sensation of the donation in progress. At length, as supplicated, emissa fuit. At its very catastrophe the arrow's flight was muffled by his maidservant's rapture.

Though she had taken full charge of the quietus, he ignored the feeling of ignoble selfishness bestowed by her waiver of bilingual justice—the unrequiting shamelessness of his exclusive gratification. In a few minutes his displaced spirit repossessed its dignity. The mollified satyr was able to eat with an appetite as keen as ever, and to listen with friendly attention as his hostess finally brought him to the intended outcome of her May Day invitation. Sitting at the double window giving out upon the irenic cove scattered with small argosies at rest and lined with structures and machines waiting to serve them, which were likewise looked upon by thronged galleries of higher and lower estate, he was particularly grateful for her victuals as he fortified himself for the extrasexual conversation that he supposed was her ultimate expectation of him.

She pointed to the wooden triangle hanging at the neck of her nakedly underclothed and half unfastened fresh white shirt. "You see I wear this pectoral delta. And now you've anointed me in baptism for my new name!"

He raised wine glass and brow in query of hers. Creative Mind was recaptivated by the black luster of eyes that again seemed windows to a Psyche less ephemeral to inmost Eros than were the dazzling graces of her several other parts. At the same time, by abstraction from the person, he noticed how she was wont to speak in minor keys—like Lilian! Without much emphasis on pitch anywhere among the words, her utterances were wont to fall as they came to a pause or ended. "You mean you're getting married?" he laughed.

"Listen and advise." And then by means of further statements—hers declarative and imperative, his interrogative and exclamatory—they finally got around to the day's premeditated communication.

As Bice stuck to her job on the paper, running the Community Page and introducing The Arts, while she learned ibicentric language and worked toward her driver's license, in expectation of the star news beat with its customary by-line, she had begun to take fright at the public appearance of her distinctive name in awkward places. To Caleb the embarrassment required no exposition. If BICE appeared in colored lights on the radiator grill of a reefer rig rolling in and out of town every two or three weeks, if it manifested itself more persistently by eighteen-inch letters painted in luminous white on the granite crag at Mount Azimuth, where a cresting curve made it conspicuous even at night to every kilroy-driver on the Felly, and if it was advertised in bright new yellow (amidst faded Helens of past generations) on the sunless smoke-blackened wounds of the ravine between the Draw and the Depot traversed twice a day by hundreds of musing passengers (not to mention the crews of freight trains too), how ubiquitously must the name have been bruited throughout the *Nous*'s circulation by private smirks?

It would have been a vain attempt at professional deception to use the name Beatrice; for in a city full of Tuscans none would fail to recognize the famous contraction, just as the name of HELEN was once commonly evoked by NELL. And few were the men that once actually saw the person denoted by legendary BICE who wouldn't make it their business to learn PICORY as its complementary determinant—as in the case of TROY. In any case, once male antennas had been made alert to her presence somewhere in Dogtown, neither a secret new address nor an unlisted telephone number could obliterate both her names at once; and it was unlikely that any interested reader or colleague could have been put off the scent by the pharisaical expediency even of a married cognomen.

"I'm starting all over again here. Now that I'm articled to this profession I need a new name. Of course it's too late to change my Commonwealth identity for people and dogs who already know me; and anyhow I'm not a cat to change her spots. Let Bice Picory remain my otherworldly pen name. I've got a few copyrights and my curriculum vitae to consider. My father never reads anything, but he cares about the family reputation, even if literary or theatrical respectability is the only hope still left for the name he's damaged by being passed over in the Service. He's the last of his line, and the only reason he ever wanted children was to uphold family tradition. I could never bring myself to renounce his name entirely, any more than my mother did, though she came to hate his guts, when she got to be a credited Holyrood player, seeing that he'd sacrificed an excellent career for her sake. His steadfast defense of Jews indemnified the snobbery and much else. For some reason he's always been awestruck by people who respect high culture. Otherwise he would have sold his soul for a knighthood. He'll go to any length not to seem *provincial.* I think that's why he was so comfortable with the ruling class of Australians. The free settlers and Emancipists used to make a diet of fresh meat and salt fish simply because the convicts were fed salt meat and fresh fish.

"In his mind Dogtown's still a stinking little hole full of superstitious Irish bogtrotters and dirty foreign navvies—a Yankee Doodle refuge for renegade herring-chokers and all kinds of other traitors to the Empire. It represents everything his Victorian parents were trying to separate themselves from in England. So he'll be glad enough to have me keep the Picory out of local journalism. To him, by definition, *local* means *provincial.*" She stopped to laugh at a new thought: "To me Dogtown is local but not provincial—and he admires the worst: provincial but not local! —Besides, I hate the name Beatrice. It smacks too much of the Cenci. Give me a local name, Mr Melchizedec. Locate me a given name! I already have the surname!"

He was then told that she had already chosen for pseudo-patronymic the term *Cingani,* Tuscan equivalent of the Transylvanian *Tziganes*—Gypsies, as the operators of kilroy rigs were called behind their backs by townsmen of fixed abode, or by more sympathetic fishermen to start a fight. It occurred to him that this arbitrary appellation might have been calculated to encode her identity for certain of the same *Nous*-readers from whose recognition she sometimes said she wished to escape, whether itinerants, lumpers, fishermen, Roundhouse Knights, pilgrims, financiers, or artists.

"Preciosa." was his first suggestion. The infinitely talented little gypsy girl of Hispania, like Helen, had been universally desired as a child, and at about the age of ten chastely abducted by a hero to await her menarchy.

"But she had golden hair and emerald eyes! And she wasn't really a Romany. —Nor more than half am I. Gypsy women are always true to their mates, canards to the contrary notwithstanding; and they have no written language."

"Then Belle—for Isopel. It doesn't matter that Isopel Berners was blonde too, and tall to boot. She traveled in her own solitary caravan, and gave the tinkers as good as she got." He supposed she wouldn't accept any name that didn't hint at revelation, like her unbuttoned clothing.

Bice was delighted enough with the ironic parallels in his suggestion, but especially with the private sentiment it piqued, much to his surprise. "*Belle* will always remind me of our graveyard meeting! I won't answer to any other name. Belle Cingani—*Isopel* Cingani! I'll use Iso*b*el for my signature. *Bel* is Babylonian, and *Iso-* also seems to be a syllable you like."

With some exasperation she discountenanced his warnings about a passport and immigration papers: "There's no need, if I've stopped roaming."

At his leavetaking she nestled into his arms like a happy bird with folded wings. "Goodbye, Lavengro. Call me about Ibi. I bet he too's settling down by now."

He asked her with as much indifference as his voice could contrive if she had seen the welder lately.

"I think he's angry at me. I'll have to make it up to him."

He carried home the conclusion that she had celebrated May's Eve with some other man; and he shouldn't have wondered if the poetic Romany Rye was just then pulling out of town for the Middle West with thirty thousand pounds of frozen redfish, shrewdly labeled "Ocean Perch".

18
LORE OF THE ANGELS

Caleb's epochal assuagement by the woman repristinated as Belle Cingani lessened not at all the loss of Ibi-Roi. Such indulgence indeed could only stress his spring of conscience to the limit of its elasticity; two or three hours of merely feckless desistance from the search would have been sufficient guilt for a good master, who under the circumstances should have canceled his appointment entirely. But on his way home even the most remorseful foreboding did not prevent him from smiling at the idea of allowing foreplay to turn into endplay while tutoring on the efficiency of bathing hot and cold.

During his absence the weather had veered again to Spring, for the first time that year with definite promise of maturity. It was no wonder that Beltane had been the first day of Celtic summer as well as the birthday of Mordred. The wisteria choking the porch and drainpipes from soil to roof still showed little promise of its writhing livid efflorescence, but most of the arrested traceries in sight had thickened in one afternoon. Close to the cellar granite on snake-green spears half a dozen unruffled tulips had opened, delineated vermilion flames against the rough-hewn gray. In the dooryard buds of lilac burgeoned in advance of their leaves, like small lavender blackberries soon to become thyrsi of grapes. At the arbor fence unkempt golden forsythia led all the rest, precociously decadent and already half blown, on pulpy mottled stalks; but other bushes everywhere were barely afuzz with delicate color. The exotic young catalpa over the driveway was still gracefully stark, but all about the cemetery the naked filagrees of large native trees were aburst with the efforts of tiny spiked aspergillums: the twigs of oak in yellow algae-green already transcending their shy tints of autumnal red; the maples bearing unopened verdure still almost hidden in sprays of dull scarlet.

But in his anxiety Caleb paid no more heed to Spring's lines and colors than did Ibi himself, who (especially as a late resident of the earth, still unable to distinguish the fluctuations of nature from the novelties of experience) responded to sounds and scents always lost on a man. The sunny scene to which the human returned was reproachful and desolate. No dog awaited his car.

Beyond the bare hedge of rose bushes with latticed arborway that sketched a demarcation between lawn and back yard Mrs Keith was sitting in the sun on a bench against the whitewashed wall of the postern shed. Under ordinary conditions Caleb would have discreetly avoided greeting and entered the house without disturbing her rare leisure; but now on artless impulse he stepped through the open gate to seek advice that might qualify his absolute despair.

There at her feet lay Ibi, stretched flat on his side! And still alive! The pennate tail thumped like a drowsy fan in apology for the lese majesty owing to exhaustion only as he raised his head and offered to rise in homage. But Caleb forestalled that effort, flinging himself down upon his precious friend, abandoned to unmanly sobs of love that he instinctively felt no need to suppress in the presence of his landlady.

Ibi was greatly embarrassed by the emotional abasement of his master, which prevented the recovery of his own properly subordinate dignity. For half a minute Caleb made no attempt to repair this spontaneous betrayal of his private sensibility, while Mrs Keith's eyes were called up and away by some crows working the trees of Acorn Pasture. Yet even as he stood up, sweeping his eyes with the back of his hand, determined henceforth to savor and remember every moment of the dog's companionship as a tenuous and exceptional privilege immeasurably more mysterious than death, he was already half habituated again to Ibi's selfsufficient presence as a limb of his proprioceptive existence.

He rose to take the place that with a slight inviting movement Mrs Keith made for him on the seat beside her, but his averted face remained bent over the animal they now contemplated together. As he ruffled the warm thick fur of the mighty neck he remembered the special reason for his shameless confidence in Mrs Keith's sympathy. One stormy day, when the house was so astir with the wind that she didn't hear him come in, he had blundered upon her weeping at the foot of the stairs. Her tears had been quieter than his present ones, and instantly converted into a self-deprecating smile, but they were those of a woman's superior sorrows, explainable by no overt event of calamity or relief. Nothing had been said at the time, and as a matter of fact he had forgotten the occasion until this moment. It had come as a surprise to him that such a happily situated mother—all but totally different from his own!—at peace with society in what seemed the fulness of her maturity, should find reason to be so moved in solitude. At any rate he was now less embarrassed with her than he would have been with a younger woman accustomed to nothing more pathetic in a man than his frustration or disappointment.

Unlike Raphael Opsimath, slightly her elder, whom she had struck as immaturely vivacious in her attractive enthusiasms, Caleb looked up to Gloria Keith for the kindness prudence and comfort presumptively elicited by polite youth from maternal schoolteachers and librarians. He was therefore all the more astonished to hear her laughing before his tears were dry. It was no mere chuckle of compassionate gladness, but rather a gleeful revelation that had been briefly deferred in respect for his unmanly emotion. "You thought he was lost—!" she began; but bethinking herself at once, like one who suddenly understands that an amusing dream of her child is really a nightmare, her laugh ended with a smile of appreciation.

"You forgot about Walburga Eve! Didn't you notice the wild sky last night? The Thing of the Night-Mark convenes at Cynosure Rock under the full moon before May Day, and this year the fixed and movable were in jubilee conjunction! Furthermore it happens to be the year for a new Doge to mount the stone! He's a dogs' dog—aren't you, Ib?" She touched his majesty with the toe of her shoe. Ibi's tail thumped once or twice but he was too weary to open his eyes for compliments. She laughed again. "He's pretty bedraggled. Downright emaciated. But he seems to have suffered no wounds. Probably no one dared challenge him." The tail stirred again in confirmation.

"I've never seen him look so contented." said Caleb, fully recovered, kneeling once again to stroke the noble profile.

"He was as thirsty as a steam engine, and ate like a potbellied stove. But I thought he'd be gone a week! It goes to show how much he loves you!"

At least it argues quick success abroad, Caleb thought. "Now that I think of it," he said "I didn't see another dog on the streets! I knew the Pied Pipers had drawn away the people, but I vaguely wondered if there wasn't something more than simple peace and quiet to account for the eerie feeling!" He joined her laughter at his enlightenment.

"Sergeant Proctor says it's his easiest twenty-four hours of the year. There's an old May Day song that says 'This is the day the dogs are off!' But my people are busy. Dexter took Robert to review the parade on the Esplanade and Deirdre's over in Seamark helping Tessa Barebones run the Scandie Maypole festival. Since the little kids can't stay up at night, they celebrate the Eve on the morrow, with a snake dance of masked monsters goblins and jesters, before they reveal their white dresses and put on garlands to weave their fairy web around the pole. Afterwards they sit on the ground in a ring with open palmfuls of cracked corn and a chicken is put down in the center. Sometimes the stupid bird won't even look up, it's so busy pecking at nits in the grass under its feet. Then the kids have to keep contracting the circle until she notices that she's surrounded in silence by a horizon of offerings. The little girl she finally favors is paraded around the park in a wheelbarrow as Queen of the May, under a gonfalon of flowers, followed by all her peers. The second procession is an inside-out transformation of the first. It made me cry to see it, like an ideal wedding."

Caleb told her about his convent Maypole and Betty the blonde who'd been appointed Queen for her good conduct.

"I was once a High School Queen of the May—frog of the day in a very small pond of generous electors, because Dexter was the chosen King. But there was no Maypole. Here the saints have their own customs for celebrating Beltane. Not a pole but a rock."

Ibi drowsily attested to that statement also.

"I have a hard time remembering everybody's rites." said Caleb. "And all the different landmarks!" This was a fact he often emphasized and even exaggerated, lest he be taken and questioned as a troglodyte or aborigine. "Isn't there a Vision Stone?"

"Vision Stone, Marking Stone, Cynosure Rock—those three are the same thing, named by different sects. The vision was a woodcutter's, who one night saw an angel ascending from the rock on a golden ladder. He also heard organ music."

"Ubi petrus, Ibi ecclesia." Caleb boasted. "I think this Doge has had more than one vision in the last twenty-four hours. And he's marked the boundaries of his Dogtown See."

That too the saint confirmed, more than half asleep with smiling flews, but not without warning himself against overconfidence in the future. [It's not from ambition I'm imperator. I can't help getting anywhere first, when there's something in the air and I naturally run with the pack to find it out! There was never any serious fight, but after the Thing Dance none of the others disputed me anything. I suppose I was crazy to join the howling; but I must say it felt good as long as it lasted to find myself humping like an old cynic. It turns out to be a good deal more sensational than symbolic micturation! But from now on I can take it or leave it. Meanwhile it's nice to get regular meals from my ishi and this nice houselady, with fat and bones from the altar of the Levites. I don't wish to hunt like a wolf for field mice and grubs, just for the sake of autonomy. I'd rather be a worshipper all my life. If only I had some work to do for god . . .]

"I don't know about marking, but according to statute the Mayor must walk the whole city's boundaries once a year—which of course he never does." Mrs Keith replied. "Most of our law has gone to the dogs all over Vinland, but here the old Doglaw has been going to the Puritans ever since the first May Day parade, which originated spontaneously when they tarred and feathered Meriwether Sterne and rode him out of town on a rail, as 'a Tudor clergyman of the grossest tendencies and totally unfit', for introducing his asherah-dance as a civilized version of the Irindian May Day's Eve celebration. It's not commonly known that that grievance against him was only the last straw of hatred for his having invented Gloucestermas ten months before, which they wisely feared would become an annual custom in spite of their anathema. In lobbying the Crown for a patent to take over the Casterbridge Colony the Puritan party had reported the 'ill-carriage of the men', 'ill-commanded'. They hoped the new scapegoat procession would forestall any repetition of the Midsummer's saturnalia. But getting rid of the Reverend Sterne didn't scotch the merry evils he had hatched."

"I thought Doctor Foster started Gloucestermas!"

"Doctor Foster—the magus of lies! Some even claim that he taught the dogs their Ma'eve Thing, or at least was the only man who ever attended it. Others say he's the one that was tarred and feathered! There are dozens of jingles about what Doctor Foster brought to Gloucester! Old wives' emendations fly around this town like the prices of fish. His falsifications have infected Dogtown legends like bad blood. His phoney renown has overwhelmed Sterne's reputation just the way Faust's has degraded and suppressed Roger Bacon's. I'm trying to foster a critical attitude toward all the Foster stories! The hardest part of that job is to make kids distinguish fantasy from imagination."

Mrs Keith's indignation was less just than cheerful. As a sporting proposition she quoted Ben Jonson's definition of true History:

Time's witness, herald of antiquity,
The light of truth, and life of memory.

"Doctor Charlemagne thinks Faust was much misconstrued by Goethe, and even by Marlowe." she continued. "He says that the artificial hand of the DV marketplace has been installing Panky the Monkey as totem of our culture without the slightest awareness that he descends from Faust, or Foster, and that because of advertising Panky and his ilk are far more pernicious than Punch and Judy ever were, or any of the other clowns before DV. But here on the Cape we still have Doctor Foster himself to contend with too. Irresponsible tales only abuse Dogtowners' historiographical freedom—as undocumented mongrels in a libertine melting pot!"

Despite Caleb's chronic discomfort at anyone's innocent freedom with references to the institution of Gloucestermas, at this moment of euphoric relief from acute apprehension about his closest friend's very survival he was surprised by a perverse impulse to tell Mrs Keith why he was sensitive to her canine simile for Marooners, as well as to Doc's dangerous strictures on DV culture. He also felt like confessing everything else that misfitted him for social life.

But he found a safer means to fix her attention upon himself. "I must admit that Goethe was a great lyric poet; still, as a lionized romantic pundit amalgamating corrupt folklore from the Pauline age with allegorical fantasy from decadent Hellenism, he waxed too operatic to resist spectacle and too pompous to forswear his public. In Part II he gets his characters mixed up and then pretends he was being subtle. Not to mention his unexceptional notion of Christianity."

"Somehow he always reminded me of Benjamin Franklin." she replied inconsequentially but with great apparent interest in whatever he wished to say. "I can't read German."

Caleb understood that her contrastingly modest words were not meant to check his overweening opinionation; she wasn't admonishing him to judge not that he be not judged by unenglished Germans of the future. Nevertheless her comment reminded him that he was more influenced by the competence of Eckermann and his translator than by what he could construe in comparing Goethe-text with foolish Goethe-English; for he remembered little enough of Das Deutsch from three years at Dutchkill School—perhaps no more than a few hundred common syntagms, and certainly none of the modal auxiliary subjunctives for verbs strong or weak, separable or inseparable, in any of the countless tenses.

Anyway, theories of art hadn't figured in his crescent acquaintance with this official historian so learned in the Matter of New Armorica. She had gotten wind of the secret that he was using her house to shelter his work on the Matter of Sumer, but he knew he should not presume too much on the strength of what he knew she liked. Let it suffice that they were both pleased to find solidarity in talk of national politics, heretofore the leading topic of most conversation between them, from which she had probably accustomed herself to his sweeping abstractions. Then too she seemed to take pleasure in his fierce partiality for the Sterne tradition and his admiration of little John Smith her favorite hero.

Otherwise Caleb's only contribution to the Celtic Gemütlichkeit of the community under this Cod Street roof was the wolfdog less lonesome than himself. Thanks to Ibi, whose attractive and attracted self-confidence had all along mediated the otherwise divergent lives of the householders and their tenant like a shared entertainer, the occupant of the garret was less timid about betraying his true colors to the matron of the family than he would have been if he'd had nothing to offer but the rent (which he sensed was becoming of less concern to Mr and Mrs Keith than the space it preempted).

His little apartment had been fixed up to let when the Dexters' joint salaries were still inadequate to prudently afford a modern marriage with the privacies and conveniences required by two professionals and two decently thriving yet acquisitive and lordly children; but it was now obvious to Caleb that the landlord and his lady might both have availed themselves of the rooms and bath on the third floor, especially as the first two levels were more frequently invested with the expansions of youth. The giant Mr Keith's closet at Lilliput Hall was hardly a studio for his studies in design (which remained his avowed means of personal salvation even while they shrank into abeyance as he was drawn further and further into the web of municipal government). And at the Atheneum Mrs Keith had no office at all, malgré her unlimited responsibilities as combined Reference Librarian,

Curator of Muniments for the Ibicity Clerk, and Counselor in History to the School Department; she had to use a multipurpose corner of a family room for her homework.

Housing was thus one of the anxieties that beset Caleb less immediately than the fundamental question of what he would do for an income after his job at the Laboratory was finished halfway through the year. By keeping to himself as inconspicuously as possible, relying upon Ibi's personability rather than upon his own congeniality, and by bringing home guests no more audibly or often than might further his deepest desires—seldom enough, alas, and never once since the short honeymoon with Bice—he hoped that goodwill and ordinary inertia would tend to postpone indefinitely any initiative by the Keiths to get rid of him. But of course the same general policy, inconsistently pursued, had been serving his vocational purpose ever since he returned to Dogtown. Well aware that his habitual intention to shun the jejune conversation ordinarily expected of a familiar could not but invite suspicion of an antisocial attitude, he veered between trusting and doubting that without suspecting his fear of entanglement in customary wastes of time they understood his general reticence and his anxious refusals of their small invitations to fellowship as the timid delicacy of a paying passenger through corridors of their intimate household. To a point verging upon horror he had dreaded their assumption of his assent to their enlightened tolerance of devilvision, and it was hard to ward off their hospitable urgings to share occasional time-cells of broadcast edification—productions of Shakespeare for instance.

Still, it had always been advisable to stay on mutually obliging terms with the chatelaine upon whom he relied for Ibi's welfare when he himself was prevented from attending to it; and he'd gradually found that it was less difficult to keep on proper terms with her, despite her ebullient generosity and undiscriminating enthusiasms, than with her awe-inspiring husband, whom he seldom encountered. The Goodman Keith couldn't help looking arrogant; yet in his castle he was surprisingly amiable, like Lancelot perhaps, as if to make amends for the physical condescension with which a talented godlike man of overshadowing height necessarily addresses small younger men of much weaker voice. He accorded Caleb's remarks and opinions even more courtesy than the little Goody did.

Who, quickmoving and far from Olympian, often seemed more like an authoritative senior sister than a mother to her tall fair children. When the progenitors were seen together—rare occasions, owing to the fact that they were both counted among the busiest of public citizens, each in an intensive assortment of activities that seldom coalesced or overlapped with each other's, even though the Atheneum was just across the street from 'City Hall—she gave the impression of an as adoring foil to her husband as a younger sister. They had been highschool sweethearts, and college too, long before settling in Dogtown with their offspring.

With Mrs Keith it was the easier to keep a variable distance of least discomfort (accommodating her taste in interior decorating as well as everything aforesaid) because Doc Charlemagne so often cited her work with the rare semi-unsubsuming warmth reserved for exceptional marooners and unsung heroes overlooked by the intelligentsia. That praise persuaded Caleb that she was at least open to critical conversation and might appreciate the originality if not the importance of Doc's work. It was significantly to her credit that without in any way sharing Ipsissimus's way of life she was unafraid to own to his acquaintance publicly whenever the Atheneum Free Library was astir with his disturbing presence (as if at the unscheduled docking of an ocean liner)—maybe in part because she was used to the propinquity of a man almost as huge. Dexter was Doc's one admirer in city government, and sometimes called upon him as a respected peer when he could spare a few minutes at Leviathan Court; yet the planner was not wholly uncritical of the Director as a chorographer of the polis, and Doc was never heard to praise Dexter as an expert at anything, subsumed or otherwise. Doc pegged both the Keiths as "theater-lovers" of more or less musical stripe, but the wife's counterweighing virtues were pronounced: "She's a honey. With all the regraters of parlor history around here, she's the only one who goes right to source. She finds, like, where it really was at."

Doctor Charlemagne's distinction of persons in the Keith dyad after all was perhaps not much more disinterested than Ibi's preference for the female who often fed him; and thereby in absentia Doc unwittingly allied himself with his nemesis the saint (no respecter of persons) in encouraging Caleb to cultivate his one most promising nexus to the place of his nativity. What a sympathetic detective she might be!

So even in the Keiths' aura of economic political and social advantage that had at first oppressed him on his furtive way up and down the front steps of molded "composition" granite, to and from the attic door at the top of the second flight of stairs, Caleb was already somewhat eased in his fluctuating discomfort, at least with the parents, who were still half conscious of the spiritual danger to their family from the flickering electronic hearth installed in their living room—albeit mainly because they were severally too busy to sit down before it often enough to addict themselves.

And therefore Caleb was not entirely unprepared for this abrupt shedding of reserve. If the traffic out in front was not still in May Day remission, for all he knew it might have been noiseless. Happy birds made the only extraneous sounds to reach his mind in the backyard. Overcome by trust and gratitude for a kind of friendship sweetly strange to him, he emerged from the inner hedges of his maze with suddenly jocund heartiness.

When he was alone with Ibi in Purdeyville, or elsewhere unwitnessed, by way of uttering physical joy or intellectual elation he was wont to caw at crows, screech at gulls, bark at dogs, or meow at cats—sometimes succeeding in his attempt to puzzle them—and more than once he had done so on this very spot when no one else was home. It would have been madness now to exhibit such outright foolishness to a landowning stranger, but he had to throttle just such an urge as he bounded upstairs to fetch his doublebitted axe.

For it happened that a few days before Dexter had brought home from a barn auction the old cyclopedal grindstone of a Taraville dairy farmer finally dwindled out of business, and it now stood in the yard quaintly bewildered by its incongruous new environment. Caleb had spoken of it to keep Mrs Keith from returning to her flower-nurture right away. He told her about his school "diploma", and how it needed touching up from years of disuse, and asked permission to try out the rusted mechanism.

"I haven't seen a real axe since we left Montvert." she remarked with an almost masculine nostalgia when he'd rushed back again with his workable cachet. She had filled the reservoir with water and was musing over her husband's vagary, as if paying attention to it for the first time. "My father called these headwheels. I used to watch him grinding his axe just the way you are. It makes me homesick. But even growing up on the farm I couldn't tell a motor from a pump before I was sixteen. I don't think my father wanted me to. But I've always loved Tristram Shandy for saying that he was as unable to understand the principle of motion in a 'common knife-grinder's wheel' as any other clockwork mechanism—and not for lack of trying! I think I'd have preferred the old Irish sharpening stones, whatever they were like. —Just listen to those two crows!" she interrupted herself in a more thoughtful voice, glancing up at the pines in the cemetery.

Caleb launched into a selfconscious explanation of double-axe woodsmanship, distinguishing the grinding requirements of the two edges (one for felling, one for trimming). As a matter of self-respect he tried not to echo the lecture he'd delivered to Bice many months ago upstairs. Perched astride the forked bench in which the heavy sandstone circle was mounted—stained and chipped in its idle old age by a hundred frosts and a thousand dogs, bleached in the hottest of suns, mottled and slurred, its abrasive edge warped and smoothed by long disuse in open weather—the ostentatious amateur pumped its squeaky treadle with halting unaccustomed motions of his lightweight legs. "A sharp blade is safer than a dull one." he said. "It won't bounce off and cut you."

"The pushcart grinder-man who comes around here once a year with his come-hither bell is a pirate; he zips through the job at high speed and only puts an edge on the knives. Maybe we can sharpen our own blades from now on."

"You won't need him anyway: we have no Dulles anymore." Caleb was referring to the political exchanges that had furthered their introductory acquaintance soon after his installation on the third floor, and to their joint satisfaction at the electoral removal of Eisenhower's Secretary of State, whose misguidance especially in the Middle East had so presciently dismayed Adlai Stevenson as signally irreversible. Any reminder of the Occupation's end was a contribution to solidarity in the Keith demesne.

Mrs Keith's laugh at his pun was as shrill as a college girl's, and her riposte was just as silly: "I see you have more than one axe to grind!" Then after a pause she added more sedately: "But the damage has been done. The world's going to need God's help even under Kennedy!" They hadn't yet recovered from their disappointment that Stevenson had not been the one to replace the chauvinist elder (erstwhile Graveyard lawyer to Hitler's bankers) who'd compassed the fearfully simplified anticommunist policy of the Protestican administration.

Caleb made little attempt to check a voluble warmth welling up in the midst of the ice he relied upon to support his weight as an unobtrusive tenant and invisible citizen as he took a few halfhearted passes at burnishing the cheeks of his twin blades, but he was no longer much interested in an axe for neither edge of which he could find any present or prospective use. His performance was nothing more than an ineptly theatrical hint of the woodland skills he had learned in a vale of limited hardship separated only by a few years and a single range of mountains from the one in which her family had brought its farming to a devolutionary close. He gradually gave up his somewhat artificial enthusiasm as an outlived sentiment, but she didn't notice the desinence of his activity; she was still listening to the crows signaling each other from the tops of high trees.

"Are those crows or ravens?" he asked. "Are they cawing or croaking? If they aren't crows or ravens they must be rooks or jackdaws. I've never known whether those are all the same or different. Some of them seem to hang around in pairs, even within a flock." He wondered with sweet melancholy at this auspice of his unpaired match with Lilian. It required a definite decision to refrain from confessing that plaint to this senior woman. Despite his continual thralldom to sexlorn love (which seemed to him quite obvious, forgetting as he did that neither his landlady or anyone else was an observer of more than a very small section of his behavior), he believed he was entitled to pride himself upon Lilian's perturbation.

He had chanced upon a seam in Gloria Keith's uniformly opaque energy. She sat quietly, gardening tools laid aside, her toe gently rubbing Ibi's ribs at the dreamy tempo of her own half-attentive reverie. For the first time he discerned her fresh youthfully freckled complexion as ground and field of faintly incipient creases darkening and extending her eyelids with maturing refinements; yet almost at once these elements of his dilatory clairvoyance, reminding him of Mrs Cibber, and of his own mother in times of kindly wisdom, evaporated like morning mist and gave way to an unageing meadow clovered with buttercups and daisies. It was understandable that she should be glad of his company as a unique release from the responsibilities of citizenship and maternity. Drawing no conclusions from his insight, he threw off his remaining armor, as if he had discovered in her maiden blazon a permissive consanguinity.

"I was just thinking the same thing." Her musing mind, vacated by children and properties, seemed to be drifting between mythic sadness and optimistic redirection of boundless hopes. "Ravens may have served the angels when they fed Elijah, but these crows are common cacodemons."

At his mother's knee, doglike, in Unabridge and Allenton, Caleb had never been able to distinguish much of her expatriated acroamata from Dogtown's genuine folklore; since attaining the age of skeptical reason he had therefore rejected and almost forgotten, as merely fantastic, the metempsychotic doctrine that was cryptically reflected in Doc's characterization of the city as "a selfmade island of dogs and gulls"—the corollary to which Mrs Keith now referred: that it was also an island of cats and crows. As saint to sinner, so angel to demon; hence, as saint to angel, so sinner to demon. But not quite in

Manichaean symmetry, for some of Dogtown's Christians loved its sinners more than saints. In the analogy cats and crows might be antithetical counterparts to dogs and gulls, like terms in an equation of proportionality, but neither pragmatically nor axiologically were they much better balanced than entropy and its negative. Almost all marooners preferred the cause of angels, despite their own proverb (perhaps too awkward to be carved into a Purdeyville rock): "If all men were birds, few would be smart enough to make it as crows". Yet whatever one's bias Caleb now learned from the custodian of corporate lore, every native of Dogtown at least unconsciously absorbed the basic principle (subject to historical qualifications) that the blatant population of soaring fouling spirits with bodies parts and passions was some function of the population of dogs, with a corollary relationship for cats and crows. The emunctory gooney-birds that exuded white entropy-lumps all over the wharves and roofs of Lady Gloucester's Cape were mortal souls of the canines from which according to the maimed Cervantes men learned gratitude and vomiting.

By this time Caleb trusted Mrs Keith so well that he didn't mind admitting to his prepossession by this lore, which was always kept pretty quiet by grownup troglodytes and aborigines, who affected to regard it as a childish remnant best suited for unintelligible poets. He felt little danger in giving himself away by revealing to a lately naturalized citizen—even such a studious one as this—the fact that he knew too much not to have been born to local science.

She was talking like a new denizen now. "It's the gulls that made me want to live in Dogtown even before I saw the place. When I was a little girl in South Swindon sometimes one would fly over in a hard winter. Even then they seemed angels to me. I knew they had saved the Latterday Prophets from a plague of crickets out in Great Basin. But it wasn't until I went on an eighth-grade student government trip up to the Capitol at Montaigne and they took us over to Champlain to see Lake Van that I got a good look at them. All the other kids were after the Sea Serpent—which then I didn't know came from here, even though I'd read all the maritime stories I could lay my hands on."

"Did you ever make angels in the snow? Once I tried it out front this winter, but Ibi spoiled it all. In Unabridge we used to make them whenever we could find a flat patch before it was sullied. You stiffen yourself, with your arms at your sides, and fall flat on your back. Then you sweep your straight arms upward over your head on the same plane. If you also spread your legs there are tail wings: then the shape you leave is like a Sumerian god. The hardest part is getting up without spoiling the cameo."

"Oh!" she cried. "I'll try it at the beach!

>   A crow
>   in the snow
>   I know

—but not an angel! Wouldn't it be fun to make angels next to someone else, or in a chain, like paper dolls! Next winter I'll try it with the whole family!" She pointed to the middle of her back yard. "There's a good place—right over the cesspool!"

"You have the whole cemetery to work in." he suggested. "But first lock up this saint, or he'll horn in on the picture and lick your face when you can't protect yourself. He thinks it's some kind of playful submission." He glanced down for corroboration, but the dog was now soundly asleep. When it became clear that the exchange of irrelevant mouth-sounds would continue for some time without change of venue, Ibi had temporarily shrugged off his last shred of responsibility for vigilance with reasonable confidence that in broad daylight these two were capable of watching over each other and himself.

Unlike the ashamed natives of Dogtown, Mrs Keith felt free to discuss the natural history of angels. She told Caleb that the old burying ground, down near Cricket Field, had angel pictures on the gravestones, but that the visible saints ceased getting any burial at all when the Puritans put a bounty on them for helping the Irindians resist enclosure. The gull population grew very rapidly in the 17C. The ring of settlers was always squeezing the Purdeyville commons—especially in winter, when they themselves were oppressed on three and a half sides by freezing storms from the dogfish commons that surrounded them all. Yet it was thanks to the company of carnal saints, continually providing the sky with a superflewity of audible angels, that even during the least secure times no Atlindu raiders or French pirates ever caught the Cape unaware, and no rape of Dogtown was ever successful. 'If the dust of dead saints can give us any protection,' as a Puritan divine ironically remarked, 'we are not without it.'

"One of the Cynics in Merry Sterne's flock was sentenced by the court to have his tongue pierced with a red hot iron for the blasphemy of vowing to christen his dog. But later the same man carved a grave marker with a gull on the rise from his dead dog's mouth."

Caleb quickly fled that image. "I'm surprised that gulls aren't more partial to fresh water than to salt. Maybe only when they drink it, like dogs. Every day a lot of them take their siestas over on Nedlaw Pond—even when it's sealed with ice."

"What surprises me is that our two Lamentus species seem to tolerate each other more amicably than their own kind. At least I've never seen a spat on the ground or a dogfight in the air between a Maxwell and a Cosmo. They snub all the other birds." She paused thoughtfully. "But they haven't always ignored the crows! All crows are black, but gulls are not all white! Only one third of the angels fell with Azazel; during the war in heaven another third were neutral!"

Caleb had known that the Maxwell gull (known taxonomically as Lamentus marinus and vulgarly as the Great Black-back), sometimes mistaken at a distance for the osprey or the Atlantic bald eagle and often identified by children as a seagle, was believed to be gaining on the smaller and much more populous Cosmopolitan one (Lamentus argentatus or Herring Gull) all along the coast, as well as in Dogtown its provenance; but what she now taught him was its genesis as a zambo angel:

"The founders of the Maxwell species were half Cosmo angel and half demonic Corvus corax. Originally they were as hybrid as everything else engendered on this island. As you must know by now, Dogtown definitions exclude no middle: from earliest Irish times there's always been *either, or,* and *both!*"

By this time in their friendship Caleb hardly blushed at unwittingly personal remarks. None of her lore was prejudiced or opprobrious. In fact he was growing rather bold. "We still exclude the middle between male and female. But which was the Adam and which was the Eve?"

"That's one of the vexing issues! Most people are brought up to assume that Adam was the gull and Eve the raven. Maybe the next generation will be a little less gullible. I'm always contending with spurious legends—like the one that Doctor Foster bred the first pair in his study: obviously suggested by Faust's good and evil angels in the authorized standard fable. Sterne's orthodox refutation of that story was lost with his original Gloucesterbook manuscript, along with many of his heterodoxies; but even the Norfolk Chauvinists who hated Maypoles—the ones who came over in the second wave and dominated the West Country people who were already here—really believed that rooks could change their sex at will, and therefore were not inclined to perpetuate gender-biassed versions in this case. To my mind it was probably Merry's wife Perdita who bred the first nestful of Maxwells, simply by keeping a male crow and female gull in her kitchen until they realized they had no alternative. Still, I don't entirely discount the more venerable theory that it was Brendan's pet raven (neither dogmatic nor gullible): he outwitted the monks who were guarding his chastity against indigenous birds only of his own kind.

"Of course there are countless variations of all these attributions. I think I need a vacation from the whole endless uncertainty of history!" She laughed, but for a few seconds the glow of health dimmed on her face at this reminder of the stratospheric cloud by which the eye of scholarship is darkened whenever it looks out the window. "Anyway," she sighed, as if by rote, "Doctor Charlemagne says that the greatest Atlantean contributions to zoology, next to the grizzly bear and the rattlesnake, are from this Cape: the Sea Serpent and the Maxwell gull."

"He forgets the Viking Shepherd!" Caleb protested. The eyes of both strangers returned to the prince of that sainthood in his Mayday slumber, whose uppermost ear even then was erect and all but twitching. "But he calls you Dogtown's Clio and compares you to Hesiod."

Mrs Keith blushed. She was not one to accept either a compliment to herself or an animadversion upon another. She evaded embarrassment by suddenly releasing the pent-up urge to confide a new enthusiasm which, after two or three days of selfcontrolled induction and speculation, had risen to such a pressure that it was bound to burst its envelope of prudence at the earliest excuse.

Yet simultaneously, brightness restored, the sense of resolution flashed everywhere in her many-mansioned network, and by the act of jumping up she remembered the purpose of springing into action. The greeting first of Ibi and then of Caleb had made her forget a basketload brought from her washing machine to pin upon the clothesline—her family's towels and bed linen, including two huge conjugal sheets, four smaller ones, and a dozen pillowcases. "Since getting my gas dryer, I've been too lazy to come out and use these nice clotheslines Dexter put up for me; but open air and sunshine makes everything smell fresher and sweeter!" She accepted Caleb's help with the job while she told him what was exciting her mind.

"Wonderful school children do most of my research. Almost everything I work out is based on their legends. I'm mainly compiler editor and caretaker. But I'll tell you a secret if you promise not to tip anyone off before it comes out in the paper. There's a windfall from the High School! It's about the Matter of Lusitania! The missing link I've been waiting for! It fits perfectly with other stories we've known!

"When it comes time for Inez Canary to apply for college she's going to get the best letter of recommendation any admissions office ever saw! I just hope she'll apply. She ought to go to one of the Nine Muses. The guidance counselors want her to settle for secretarial school. As it is, her parents think she's wasting time on 'academics' at the High School. They think she should be working in a fish plant while angling for a husband. I may pay them a call. Theirs is a typical Dogtown attitude, and in her case it's particularly sad. She could easily get a scholarship . . ."

Caleb acknowledged to himself his indifference to the wasted lives of young girls for whose acquaintance he was ineligible, who mostly seemed to him the callous proprietors of pleasure reserved for other boys; whereas Mrs Keith was famous for her active interest in existential cases. Many a graduate or refugee of Dogtown education sent her cards with news of achievement or disappointment from dormitory or nest in the north south or west, whom she may have helped once or twenty times, for five minutes or for five hours, though for the last few years she hadn't been paid for teaching.

But Caleb was sensitive to ethnic considerations. In Unabridge his mother had hoped to marry her Lusitanian lover, like herself a Dogtown native, yet of a different world entirely. For a time the fatherless boy had yearned for the respectability even of an uneducated protector—whose expectations of a step-son he nonetheless dreaded. Fortunately it was not for nothing that the inveterate bachelor Tony Porter (anglicized from Porto), erstwhile manager of Dogtown's one motorized livery service, quondam cook and engineer in family boats, had shaken the dust of his hometown—if not the curses of fathers brothers and husbands—to escape the traditional version of connubial contentment.

Yet since Caleb still felt a certain affinity to the Loosies, who had not always been admitted to the highest circles of Dogtown commerce, and to females anyway, he was glad to hear of Inez the underdog her intellectual achievement, as follows, and all the gladder that it would help revive the glory of her underdog ancestors.

"You remember the story called 'The Twelve of England' (which should have been called 'The Twelve *in* England'), told in the sixth canto of the *Lusiads* by one Veloso, just before da Gama's ships are hit by the typhoon Dionysos has called up against them? Its chief hero is the great Magrico, an anachronistic Lancelot in the time of John of Gaunt. (John was grandfather of Prince Henry the Navigator as well as patron of both Chaucer and the poet who wrote about Gawain and the Green Knight.) But the story breaks off without finishing the chivalric biography of Magrico. We've always been tantalized by the hope of finding out what happened to him on the Continent.

"Well it turns out that on the way back home from India the story was recorded in Arabic by Monsaide the Moor, the interpreter and faithful double agent that the Lusitanians had found there, who'd saved their necks from the evil Moslems ruling the mind of the Hindu emperor, and whom da Gama was converting to Christianity. Thereupon Monsaide did very well back in the old country as a convert and trade consultant. But, like the Jewish 'New Christians', many of them, he and his direct male descendants were too proud to marry outside their race, and thus it happened that his grandson was the only full-blooded black student at the University of Coimbra when Camoens enrolled. They became literary friends.

"By that time Monsaide's family had become so rich that this grandson was encouraged to devote himself to scholarship. After Camoens went off to court (and had all the troubles that forced him overseas) this dilettante Moor, whose given name I haven't been able to determine, began to cultivate his ambitious personality, calling himself El Moro and regretting that he had shared his Arabic legends with his old friend the poet. El Moro wanted to burst upon the Western world like Avicenna, with bombshells of esoteric learning about its own cultural history that had been obliterated by idealistic reactions to the troubadour tradition, such as Catharism or the Grail fantasies, and then by Renaissance sentiments or their parodies, but preserved in the Arabic. He would account for Morris-dancing, mummery, Robin Hood, witch-religion, and Courtly Love!

"Meanwhile Camoens had been making himself pretty learned too. His purpose was to extend the matter of chansons de geste more than Virgil extended Homer, hoping to forestall inevitably decadent works like *Don Quixote,* yet he couldn't find any way to get everything he knew into the *Lusiads;* so on the way back from Goa, when he was stuck in Mozambique for a couple of years, he wrote a prose *Parnasso.*

"It started with the career of great Magrico in the 14C, but worked backwards through all the doctrines and lores reflected and obscured in Veloso's innocent version. Camoens was trying to integrate all the Matter of Rome and Matter of France that had been unknown or repugnant to people like Nennius or Geoffrey of Monmouth—although of course the Inquisition required him to reconcile his history with Saint Thomas."

Caleb asked if it was a theological epic.

"No, but Diogo do Couto, a Lusitanian historian who saw the first part of it when he was helping Camoens raise money to get back around the Cape of Storms, called it philosophical and extremely impressive. Otherwise its content has remained unknown, because the manuscript was stolen before its author could take ship again. Strangely enough, the thief overlooked the companion manuscript of the *Lusiads* itself—or else was just looking for the one particular story that was otherwise unknown to Westerners!"

"Is that what you found out?"

"No—and not I anyway, but Inez of the sophomore history class. What she's uncovered is that it was El Moro at home in Lisbon who'd gotten wind of Camoens's prose narrative and had it stolen by some secret Arab agent of his family's. It was brought back to Morocco by way of Cushite caravan—not simply to prevent its publication by Camoens (who by this time had earned the reputation of a half-criminal roughneck) but to make use of the material in a great opus of his own, which he was getting nervous about because all but the title of it remained unwritten. Of course he still had to wait for the death of his friend in 1580 (who had only the *Lusiads* to his credit); and then for the demise of witnesses too.

"In the meantime his auctorial excuses in the name of indolent Lusus (Lusitania's eponymic son of Dionysos) were wearing mighty thin. But at last in 1588 he was saved from ignominy as a literary fanfaron by the patriotic opportunity to take service as a gentleman-observer in the Lusitanian component of the Great Enterprise against England while he finished copying Camoens's text. He finally completed the plagiarism just before he would have been prevented from doing so by the irrational terror of Francis Drake that overtook even the bravest in the brave Armada."

As it transpired, El Draque had insured defeat of the Iberians by amphibious raids, before they even weighed anchor: he destroyed their supply of barrel staves. The failure to preserve wine water and victuals left their fleet especially expugnable in prolonged heavy weather and protracted actions when Drake began to chase them.

Caleb remarked that the real hero of the Enterprise was the good Duke of Medina Sidonia, Admiral against his will, who knew he'd be seasick from one anchorage to the next and catch colds from beginning to end. "Nothing was his fault, but he took all the blame."

"I agree." she eagerly replied. "He seems to have had all the rectitude fortitude and wisdom of a George Washington! Indeed he salvaged Philip's empire. But he couldn't save El Moro, or whatever his name was, who all the way to Calais was a sort of journalist aboard *Florencia* (née *San Francesco,* the Duke of Tuscany's capital ship, which had been impressed into the Lusitanian squadron as the best galleon in the whole Armada). He got rid of the incriminating Camoens manuscript in the heat of battle by donating it to the gunner for wadding. His almost finished copy of it he had the foresight to sew up in oilskins and seal inside a small casket made for him by the ship's tormented cooper.

"Unfortunately, in an attempt to advance himself with the Hispanic nobility, he made the mistake of getting transferred at the Calais rest-stop to de Leiva's ill-fated carrack *La Rata Santa Maria Encoronada*.

"During the storms that subsequently devastated the Armada all around the British Isles he was cast ashore in Galway Bay, one of many Moors and Lusitanians stranded along the Irish coast because the successful rescues made by surviving ships naturally favored white men. Since the few English soldiers on the shore had trouble enough keeping down the Firbolgs and Milesians, and were already nervous for their own lives, they slaughtered all the enemy they could find, even when they would have won good ransoms by taking some of them as prisoners instead."

"It used to be said that it's easier to find flocks of white crows than one Englishman who loves a foreigner." Caleb commented.

"Well the Irish helped these wretches whenever possible and sequestered as many as they could until the English gave up searching. In fact the refugees were more than welcome to fisherfolk widows. That's how the 'black Irish' strain got reestablished. Dexter's mother's people—by way of Scottish detour.

"But El Moro himself couldn't have been one of Dexter's ancestors because he wasn't as lucky as the less conspicuous ones who escaped massacre on the beach. The English had seen him, and he couldn't be concealed well enough to get to Scotland on the underground railroad. So he was harried right off the mainland, and he took refuge on the Aran Islands. It was from Inis Mor that he was finally smuggled into one of the clandestine Irish fishing expeditions to Atlantis. You can guess the rest. The first black man in New Armorica! For his own good they put him ashore to find his way to the remnant of Irindians in Purdeyville that later escaped the notice of both Champlain and John Smith.

"To Perdita, El Moro was an angel from heaven. He became the black Jesse of Purdeyville. When the Lusitanians immigrated in the 19C they sensed a faint kinship to their Irish predecessors. It's a libel to call this town lily white. Local blood was inoculated with good Moorish naphtha before Georgio bigots were here to prevent it. Troglodytes and aborigines can claim any tincture, even this one, without much risk of contradiction."

Caleb was always happy to hear of pride in crossbreeding, obscure lineage, irregular heritage, or outright genetic mystery.

"But I should get to the point of this unwritten monograph. El Moro still had the manuscript capsule. It was sewn into his jerkin like a beerbelly and had floated him ashore in Galway Bay. He must have looked like Othello playing Falstaff. As the consort of Mrs Sterne's grandmother, and no longer an effete prince of luxury, he gave up literary pretensions and devoted himself to the part of mortal May King, like Ossian in Tir-na-Dog. He never unsealed his lifejacket. Among those illiterates of high culture it served as his pledge to their queen, an unopened ark of covenant. And so it eventually passed into the possession of Merry Sterne as lawful husband of the converted Perdita."

While Caleb pondered this news Mrs Keith fetched glasses of ale, forbidding his assistance in solicitude for Ibi's peace, which would be broken if they both left the spot. Her prose resumed its sweet soporific for the alert ears of a dreaming champion. To his prosaic master it was sweeter still, but not as a lullaby. It seemed strange to be drinking with a matron in the peaceful sunshine of an urban glebe.

"So that explains the famous Merry Sterne manuscript. He was translating El Moro—or rather Camoens—into English?"

"More than that, sir! Much much more than that! Even before he took holy orders, back in Unabridge, in his study of ancient Celtic languages Merry Sterne had come into possession of the lost 'British book' that Geoffrey of Monmouth had based his history upon! So, toiling in colonial poverty, having been unable to find a patron he'd be willing to trust with secrets unflattering to the English aristocracy, the Reverend Mr Sterne was already working on a sequel to the *Kings of Britain,* based on the *Book of Armorican Exiles* (which had never been translated into English or Latin), starting with the torments of Arthur as the leader of an oppressed people who briefly became emperor of Europe while suffering the infidelities of Guinevere, Lancelot, and Mordred. He had done a lot of research on the British Christians driven out of England in the subsequent civil wars that culminated in the Saxon-conspired invasion by Gormund the King of Africa, the contemporary occupant of Ireland.

"It was his determination to make some kind of an independent living while pursuing his precious historical leads that had led him to don the cloth and get a job over here as chaplain to the fishermen! He was about as Arminian as a Tudor priest could be, but imagine what a sense of predestination he must have felt when the El Moro manuscript fell into his hands as an apparently divine dowry for his pagan marriage! Everything fell into place! The sequel to Geoffrey now became merely his *Prologos* to a *Historie of the Dogtowne Plantation!*"

Mrs Keith stopped to take a breath and laugh at her own trance-like concentration, but remembering the glass in her hand she quaffed some refreshment and immediately resumed her impressive in vitro composition of history. "As a son of the West Country, Sterne had more than a double axe to grind. In tracing the Christian remnant of Merlin's Britain, he'd become bitterly disgusted with the Welsh branch—'degenerating from the nobility of the Britons', as Geoffrey had said; but his imagination was greatly excited by the British who'd fled across the Channel to the Armorica of Arthur's former conquest. It was them he followed to Vinland—not the latterday Englishmen who'd come for fish and free love, and of course still less the Puritans who resented his assignment by the Archbishop.

"But aside from all that, he hoped his great work of the New World would neutralize the Latinizing influence of the Anatomy of Melancholy, which was just then being widely acclaimed by intellectuals, and at the same time justify the natural philosophy of Francis Bacon."

Caleb asked what happened to all the Reverend Sterne's manuscripts when he was hounded back to England.

"That remains to be seen—I hope. Someone like Doctor Charlemagne should organize a systematic search. We only know that Sterne's widow returned to Cape Gloucester from Yorickshire, leaving behind all the children except her oldest daughter. It had been his dream to found a Gloucester University in New Amorica, transferring the defunct Gloucester College charter from Unaford. All along he wanted to frustrate the Norumbega institution, which he'd known would be hostile to broad churchmanship as well as to the Irish!"

"The College is three centuries overdue. Doc wanted it to be the nucleus of an ultimate Quaquaversity of the Atlantic. I'm sure he would have sponsored your research if Captain Ozone had lived up to expectations."

"Yes." she agreed. "He told me Dogtown College would have known no bounds! That's just the school for me: coterminous in all outdoors with the New Albion Grant—all the way along the forty-second-and-a-half parallel to the other end of the Northwest Passage! By the way, that's all called into question now, you know. Who knows, maybe even Joyous Garde itself, and all the rest of his estate."

"You don't mean to say Ozone's will is nullified?" They were drinking second bottles now, leaning against the wall of the back shed, gazing down at Ibi or up at the nearest oaks on both sides of the cemetery fence—when not looking at each other in wild surmise.

"Not his intention. Only the land titles, I suppose. It now appears that old man Tybbot"—she gestured toward the tripod mausoleum in God's ten acres, invisible from where they sat, not far from the grave of Isopel Berners—"may indeed have had better reason than Captain Ozone to call himself our duke. At least his ancestors wrested their domain from Mother Earth and worked it with their own hands. I now have reason to believe that the Queen's grant to Sir Anthony Beacon was falsely dated by Lord Burleigh after he heard from one of his Irish spies that El Moro had escaped to New Armorica as a commissioned officer of King Philip. It wasn't until late 1589 or early 1590 that he drew up the document, purportedly a 1564 codicil to the royal charter for the Merchant Adventurers. Whether or not in Gloucester County Probate Court the discovery of a phony terminus a quo for the whole Grant could retroactively invalidate for successive heirs and assigns all the later registrations in Dogtown's Doomsday Book, if I took the case to a Federal judge I'd argue that the transpontine parcel of the Claim should be voided pro bono publico in favor of the redskins!"

Caleb asked why Burleigh should have bothered to fake the date.

"Have you got time to hear the answer?" replied the shanachie. "I don't want to drive you loco by harping on local matters—especially when you're so busy working with the Ur-text of all history!"

The ale was going to Caleb's head. "Your time is scarcer than mine. I could listen all night to your legends. One can well understand that for Europeans this Cape was the combined Fortunatae Insulae, Garden of the Hesperides, and ultramondane Land of the Young, long sought across the Western Ocean, where earth and heaven met in the Cave of the setting Sun! But there were also Atlindus from lands beyond the West. Doc says some of them searched for the source of all purity in the place where the sun came up, when nothing else seemed pure—least of all the muddy moody Father of All Waters. On their pilgrimage they found the Eastern Ocean right here at Namauche. I too have come out of the West to face the unattainable Land of the Dawn, like Vasco Da Gama when he found The Island of Love! Pray continue."

This giddy reply so perilously close to insolence was overlooked by the ebullient yellowheaded landlady. With a brief uncertain smile she returned to one of the stories that were keeping her awake at night.

"There was another meridian for East to meet West, where Islam closed with Christianity. In 1564 the Philippines—or the Lazarus Islands, as Magellan the Lusitanian had christened them on the Fifth Sunday in Lent—were formally appropriated to Hispania, which already had Papal title to half the world's circumference. It wasn't until 1579 that Drake claimed New Albion; and by 1589, the year El Moro landed here, nothing more than a few piracies had come to Queen Elizabeth from the northern South Sea. Mind you, this was more than a decade before Champlain landed in our Beauport to harvest hips of the wild rose, which Cartier had heard about from the Naturals as the wonderful Ameda plant, to make ascorbic 'tea of arborvitae'. And it was more than another ten years before John Smith documented the entire coast of Drogeo—the territory of Vinland when Markland was part of it. His Generall Historie of Norumbega would put to shame the flimsy geography of Papist explorers.

"But Good Queen Bess had been too stingy to send an official expedition anywhere over here in Drogeo, even when its shape and importance was very well known from the unofficial commerce of her fishermen—who were then just as chary about committing facts to writing for the benefit of revenue agents and rival colleagues as they are to this day, but who were nevertheless quite aware of their need for naval protection from Iberians and especially the French, not to mention the Naturals ashore. Elizabethan freebootery wasn't yet scraping low enough in the barrel of free enterprise to divert capital for commercial speculation on a coast that still awaited John Smith for its proper valuation in English.

"Lord Burleigh already had more than enough foreign competition in Atlantis. Without Crown colonies or investments there, what he now dreaded was that Philip would press the Hispanic claim to all of northern 'Florida'—a k a 'Virginia'—on the strength of El Moro's consortion as a squaw-man of Dogtown. The defeat of the Armada gave Burleigh a stronger hand in diplomatic negotiations, but legal arguments still counted for something between Christian nations. Maybe the Beacon grantee himself was leery of a provocative patent issued with such retroactive celerity by a court in which all boons were reluctant and difficulties were usually allowed to 'enjoy the benefit of time' while working themselves out.

"Anyhow, it's not surprising that such a document wasn't eventually registered at any Colonial courthouse, because back in London it was never even sent to Chancery Lane or attested by the Master of the Rolls with the Great Seal. You see, that would have required copying it into the capitularies, which were not organized files of looseleaf parchment but a single continuous journal of Time's relations with the Throne, and therefore would have given the lie to chronological falsification!"

"But who was Sir Anthony Beacon, and why was he given measureless leagues of Natural forest and prairie?"

"That was not exactly the name originally inscribed. 'Beacon' was the deliberate respelling of the family name when it finally crossed over to the Vinland Bay Colony with the claim some years after its disgrace and attainder. The grant had been made to Anthony *Bacon,* Francis Bacon's close and beloved elder brother. Lord Burleigh was their uncle by marriage, William Cecil. Both the Bacons had long been disappointed of his patronage, in spite of their assiduous service to the government. As the Queen's lord high treasurer and secretary of state for diplomacy, Burleigh had made good use of Anthony's secret intelligence and counterintelligence, especially on the Continent (where he was acquainted with everybody who was anybody, including Montaigne and Henry of Navarre), but also at home, at Gray's Inn, after leaving the foreign service. Elizabeth herself remained peevishly fond of Francis, although she never forgot his one ingenuous protest of a tax levy, but speedily quashed his notion that a revolution in the arts and sciences could be set afoot without upheaving the affairs of state.

"In any event, the brothers got little or no preferment under her reign—save for that unsolicited New Albion grant, sometimes referred to as the Vinland Instauration Charter. A queen who enjoyed the cunctation of time was very fortunate to have a chancellor who knew how to employ the statics of documentation in an ironical Star Chamber solution to the ministerial problem of importunate and highly deserving nephews as shrewd as himself and as clever as his mistress. But the basic policy of the award betrays the Fairy Queen's own fine Italian hand: typically oblique, ambiguous, multifarious, cautious, and humorous. It cost her nothing, served to rebuke loyal servants of the Crown without alienating them, while honoring the faithful service of their deceased father, and might yet prove useful in future contingencies—for Philip's empire was as ambitious as ever and showed no signs of retrenching.

"So the grant was her sop to Anthony. But it also mocked Francis for pestering her to found a new university—neither Scholastic (as Unaford tended to remain, at the very center of her England) nor Chauvinist (as Unabridge, which she preferred, tended to become), but broadly Tudor and empirical. She certainly had no love for either of the deviations from her religion; but her heart was not to be won by a promise to revolutionize the Re-learning she and her father were so good at. This desolate refuge of uncouth witchfolk disputing a heartless band of superstitious Irish degenerates and savage Naturals—potentially profitable only for fish and timber, and as yet unable to repay even a summer's staging—was just the sort of hotbed to start a scientific school that would overturn Plato as well as Aristotle!

"Of course she might have been less acerbic toward the brothers if she had known how much of Anthony's analytical statecraft her Lord High Treasurer had stolen the credit for.

"Anthony died before she did, but Burleigh's paperwork, which mentioned the possibility of New Learning in an obscure subordinate clause, remained in Jacobean times the legal justification for Merry Sterne's great hope, though he'd been promised nothing by any of the surviving Bacons.

"So you see, there are at least two fundamental flaws in Captain Ozone's New Albion Claim: first, it's not registered; second, it's in a different name! But it hasn't yet been dismissed by the Supreme Court!"

"Is there any evidence that Bacon equals Beacon? Our Frank Bacon deserves a stake in the Claim. If the inheritance were his, you can be sure he'd get an Instauration going! He'd begin by endowing Dogtown College—"

"The Claim and the estate were severable, I'm sorry to say; and long since severed."

Momentarily overlooking the distinction between a claim and a deed, Caleb contemplated Doc Charlemagne's institutional aspiration. During the centuries spanning Roger the Franciscan (Unaford 1229) and Francis the Tudor (Unabridge 1576)—as well as Archbishop Cranmer (Unabridge 1504) and Archbishop Laud (Unaford 1589), Chaucer and Shakespeare (common readers c1356 and c1580)—a fomentation of dromenology would have been gratuitous, whereas today the same might be said of encouraging the kinds of art and science that the Bacons have long since instigated. With the usufruct and borrowing-power of a three-thousand-mile swath across Atlantis, Frank Bacon would have put up the funds withheld by the Cathode King (even before he took leave of his senses) for a college differing from Francis Bacon's dream in its objective but not much in its attitude toward idols of the theater. With someone like Frank as patron, whose personal opinions were so much more diffident than the catholicity of his generous encouragement and admiration, the new keys of philosophy, which Caleb believed he could distinguish in the cluttered key ring represented by his wall of books, might have opened a dozen posterns to the kind of Charlemagian symposium that had never been funded by the Foundations—no more or less dromenological than metaphysical scientific aesthetic poetic and political.

No one resented the legacy of CRF shares to the Blind Priest on behalf of the Beacon Institute, not even Doc himself; but it was bitter to swallow the fact (if fact it really was) that the alfresco Theater on the Rocks, along with Chateau Noir, the living granite of Prudence Point, and the wherewithal to maintain it all, was falling into the hands of Alterian Neognostics—the "Gnujies"—those occultly reactionary platonists fundamentally inimical not only to the dromenological philosophy but also to the new physics and biology, to the primitive religions they patronized, and to human society itself. No open worldly enemy could be so pernicious to the maternal selfmade island that for the most part was jealously hospitable to physicalists and orthodox Christians, and Christian physicalists, and idoloclastic marooners of all stripes.

At the end of her account Mrs Keith turned to Caleb with pleading wide eyes and a finger to her lip. "But please, all this is still a secret hypothesis. I would die of shame, and maybe get fired, if Doctor Charlemagne or Mr Bacon or anyone else got hold of it before I've either refuted it or written it up with proper citations. My indiscretion might jeopardize Dexter's position too. Please? I was foolish to mention it prematurely. You're the only one who knows how crazy I am!"

Caleb was always delighted to accept a lady's confidence. "But what about him?" He motioned to the pointed ears at their feet.

"Oh, he and I have already tested each other with secrets—haven't we, Ibi!" The sleeping animal with the unsleeping antennas thumped his drowsy tail once or twice without opening his trustworthy eyes. "A saintly gentleman will honor secrets he hasn't witnessed even more scrupulously than the ones he has."

Both strangers as of one accord bent over to caress the noble head. The one exposed ear folded itself back like the wing of a mourning dove into silky charcoal-streaked fur smoothly continuous with the refined muzzle and silken crest. In the deep tawn of the ruff Caleb's little finger happened to meet Mrs Keith's. His hand withdrew itself with an absurd reflexive jerk, as if he'd seen a snake. It was a ridiculously catastrophic reaction to an inadvertent touch. As he quickly sat up straight and looked away, his brow and scalp swollen in a pulse of fever she gave no sign of having noticed either disrespect or gaucherie. But with that incidental thrill the reflection of his light had suddenly altered, as when without warning the harbor's bluest surface darkens at a puff of summer breeze.

"I hope he won't forget me when he's a soaring Maxwell in the sky." Mrs Keith voice on without missing a stitch as she lengthened her strokes of the deep shoulderless chest. "There will always be something for you on my back stoop—do you hear that, Ibi? I'll shuck your clams: you won't have to go through all the trial and error of cracking them open one by one like the eagle that had to get at the meat of a tortoise by dropping it on the bald head of poor old Aeschylus. But of course you'll be smarter than other angels about where to smash your bivalves."

Fractured shells were of course to be found on Dogtown rocks and pavements, but strands and greenswards were littered with unopened mussels abandoned by angels failing in their repeated experiments. She turned to address Caleb directly. "Wat Cibber says their stupidity's no surprise, considering that most animals lose their wits at death. The acquired simultaneity of birdseye vision makes up for their mundane inefficiency. As saints on earth they could only smell out the Cape over time, stone by stone, tree by tree."

Still embarrassed by the hot-stove retraction of his innocent hand, Caleb's inner man scarcely heard the words that followed his involuntary anticipation of the thoughts it caused; but his social mechanism seemed still to be working without supervision, for at a higher level his symbol-mongering mind listened and replied, superstitious as ever about admitting fatal ideas through careless words. Her reference to the transmigration of Ibi's soul was no more welcome than a sick man's raven. He had exorcised not only the idiopathic malignancy of which he believed himself cured but also all the mementos mori to which it educated him during those months of depression before he met Bice in the cemetery. So once again he turned away from the particulars of felt reality to cast abstract ideas upon the chessboard of theory. "You've just struck me for the first time with the obvious explanation of why we have so many more gulls than dogs! Life goes on, but there is no second death! Like the crowding of graves on our island even after the living population has ceased to grow!" On all his churchyard walks why had such a simple correspondence never occurred to him?

Mrs Keith's sleepless mind was given no pause by his vagrant speculation. She had described to him the lonely vale she grew up in, with a tiny ice-pond uniformly retained by the fieldstone-and-timber dam of a small abandoned sawmill—in contrast to this lowland setting of the grownup woman fearlessly alienated to a tidal polis, with a mighty husband and a clientele of children (her own and countless others); but it was as if from the elevation of that inexhaustible source that her energy came purling down bosky hillsides from rock to rock as an indomitable brook that yet was never loathe to pause at trout pools in its course through whatever meadows befell its terrain. She never dawdled, but sometimes slowed up—as right now—before finding her way to the next rapids. It seemed to Caleb that by resting in eddies she only accumulated power for any millwheel geared to saws or grindstones, before taking up her way again down a broadening valley below the millrace, forever gathering smaller streams, yet always remaining a thousand rocks and a hundred miles and dozens of dams from her energy's sink. Thus she wasn't fazed by his digression. "Getting the city to lay out more cemetery space has been one of Dexter's priorities! But no voter wants to plan on her own planting! We may have to start reusing some of the old graves, as they did at Elsinore."

Haply she was unaware of his confusion. He assured himself moreover that there was no harm in vaguely fanciful desires as long as they were not committed to thoughts in words. "But why don't we have an arithmetic progression of angel population?" were his words. "There's plenty of garbage and gurry going to waste."

"Dexter says that if we clean up the Harbor and the dump in South Parish, Dogtown may lose first place in the census of angels and forfeit some of its financial aid from the Feds."

"A fortiori then," he persisted, "why do we seem to have reached the maximum sustainable yield of angels? Saints are dying every day." The body of this nimble woman with a cap of feathery yellow hair was more definitely formed than her longer-legged daughter's, yet almost as weightless; though now floating quietly, as always it looked alert and indefatigable. Despite its deference to Dexter's professional opinion, whom it habitually credited as an officially reliable source of information, readier to hand than Doc or Wat or Tessa or Inez Canary, he would have sworn that it had forgotten all about husband and children as undissevered from itself. Yet Caleb the stranger among strangers was ever conscious of its family as the sun and stars of all its gravitations. To Gloria Keith this discussion was merely an interesting conversation with a disinterested meteor.

She was answering his question about the population of the Dogtown sky. "Beyond a certain ecological density the gulls get irritated with each other. The undiscriminating Cosmos are given cause to emigrate. Mr Opsimath says he's seen whole colonies of them congregated in the rice fields as far away as the Eucharist Valley in Cornucopia. The Maxwells that leave are the recalcitrant and footloose ones, or vegetarians; and like Englishmen they know that they will be honored anywhere as expatriotic heralds of an elect breed."

The sky had clouded up again. She noticed the dimmed light just as he shivered with the chill of it. "The weather deceived me." he said, falling back to the topic never stale in Dogtown, which has always wavered unpredictably between or outside the northern and southern moieties of the New Armorican climate. Cape Gloucester is by one virtue both a salient of continental rock and an inlet into the thermal sea-bath. On a frontier of winds and temperature, its warmths usually linger behind the land's in vernal hysteresis, and lag accordingly in the golden blue halcyons of September and October. Caleb had learned to exploit such shameless smalltalk by way of adaptive self-protection in his business career, but it was serviceable in all the higher walks of life as well. "I thought it had skipped from March to June. Spring's already been awarded an honorary diploma!"

"This is only Indian Spring, as Evelyn Dickinson said here. I get fooled because there's no mud-time. In Swindon County that was always the worst season for getting anywhere: no snow and ice for sledges or snowshoes; no firm dirt for wheels."

Caleb's somewhat more recent memories concurred. He told her that where he'd worked in his schooling, at the dead end of another godforsaken valley, to the westward almost to Yorick just a few miles from the Nether Land border of Montvert, the roads were sometimes so bad in mud-time that they had to crawl out with the tractor to get their supplies.

"My father could never afford a tractor. On the hardscrabble farms around there we didn't even bale our hay. There were a few good fields above the pond, but the whole township wasn't much more than a pocket of rocky pastures at the bottom of cussed little mountainsides. Maybe the cows wouldn't have minded baled hay—it's no worse than fishbricks I suppose—but the horses deserved it loose and sweet. We had a beautiful little team of Salics. They seemed big to me until I went to my first county fair. The Gallic stallions at the horse-pulling contests must have weighed twice as much as our gelding!"

Smoothing her skirt, she rose with a sigh that he doubted whether to take as nostalgia or as regret that their interview must come to an end. Her example was instantly followed by Ibi. All along in deepest sleep he'd been listening on the qui vive. For a moment he was stiff-legged, shaking himself from head to foot; but then he trotted off to relieve himself somewhere at the front of the house, as if glad of release from formal duty, his feathered tail upcurled, the wisps at his elbows and pasterns handsomely strewn by the motion.

But Mrs Keith was in no rush to end their reminiscences. She pointed to the rear edge of her property, which crossed their view as the ruined stone wall that narrowly divided her oaks from the trees that stood over graves and boulders in the near end of Acorn Pasture. "That precious tumbledown wall reminds me of home, where every field was cleared to make boundaries of loose rocks like those. I loved all gatherings of natural stone when I was little, but hewn stone was as wonderful to me as exotic seagulls. Until I went to Junior High I don't think I ever saw a building that wasn't made of wood, except for the cellars. My first conversation with Dexter was about foundations. Even in the seventh grade he wanted to be an architect. It was the high granite foundation that first attracted me to this place." She nodded toward the main part of the house. "I must have been destined for Dogtown."

Standing at his side she turned again to the scene they had been facing. "Still, this is my favorite spot: only crows to listen to, and except for graves no cut stone in sight! —But speaking of this dooryard paradise, it's going to return to nature if we don't pay more attention to it. This summer I'll insist that Robert come back here with the lawnmower once or twice at least! And I swear I'm going to do as much with these valiant perennials as I do with my public flowers out front—which I'm afraid has been little enough these past few years."

Caleb hardly suspected that she was renowned for casual gardening. In the course of a season her flowers seemed to make their appearances spontaneously, clumped here and there along fences and against the beloved gray granite that raised the house above its basement. Her son's greenskeeping of ground visible from the street left irregularities as charming fringes, and the informal curves of bare earth trodden across the lawn were bared without shame at every mowing; with clippers Mrs Keith herself on hands and knees would trim the edges he was too busy to be bothered with. By virtue of its situation the outer yard, sloping upward to the vestigial summit that based the house several feet above the street, and above the cemetery too, was almost obtrusively conspicuous, like a lighthouse on the main channel of a busy port, what with all the traffic streaming by, and the neighboring houses white as sailboats at the sidewalk level. Thereto a family better known than most for positions of responsibility and leadership was well advised to keep its property respectable.

"But I've missed a back window in my kitchen. It was always hard to keep an eye on the kids playing out here when they were younger. But I think of this yard especially as dear old Sucat's. He'd lie out here with his nose on his paws watching the stories Deedee or Rob made up, like St Patrick listening to Oisin's tales of the Fianna. He's buried over there in the corner as close to consecrated ground as we could dig. The wooden cross that Rob made was knocked down in a football tussle, and I'm sorry to admit that we never got around to putting him up an angel stone.

"Nowadays I'd like to be able to see the oak trees while I'm working in the kitchen. That's something else from books I used to long for when I was growing up. By then almost all the oaks in our area had been wiped out by blight. The timber was mostly maple, ash, birch, and softwood. Of course that was before chainsaws turned woodlot-cutting into vandalism."

"I hated to see the pulpwood trucks." said Caleb. "Millions of trees slaughtered every year for fashion advertising in the Sunday New Uruk Testament!"

"My father snaked every log out of our woods with the mare. She was the intelligent one. But if it was too big he'd have to hitch them both up as a dancing team. I'd cry when I saw them suffering at that kind of confusion. It was heartbreaking to see how hard they tried to please him, jerking their way through all the rocks and stumps, but only made him curse and whip the harder! In comparison, their usual work like plowing and haying was all peaceful sweat and patience, in softspoken cooperation, with hardly a gee or haw required. I was allowed to drive them in the hayfield, and standing on the rick with my man-size pitchfork I learned to build a tight load, like a nest for a Roc, layer by layer of sweet dry bunches as big as myself, starting with a hollow but ending with a dome, rising on my own slippery platform until I could see over some of the treetops and I felt like a rooster! I loved to hear my father boast about his child labor!"

A few years later in the lagging technology of rocky little Montvert farms, as the smallest and readiest of his haying gang (second baseman of the team) Caleb had learned the same special skill—with simple pitchfork receiving slithery collops of hay from forks below, binding them by gravity and friction alone into an imbricated stack that without cinch or fastening could sway through slanted fields like a freighted camel. At the time, treading his bowl as it rose, he had repeatedly recalled from a much earlier childhood adventure in Purdeyville the archetype of his mother tossing a pillow into each hollow center of two juniper bushes—prickly to the touch, pungent to the smell, yielding to the weight—and spreading bedclothes, to make nests for sleeping overnight under the first sky of stars he ever took a good look at. Now, sympathizing with Mrs Keith's bucolic nostalgia, he remembered the contingent memory that had also come to him then—in mature youth, a hundred miles from salt water—of the little boy's exciting train ride from St Bot to Land's End station, and a climb up through the woods to learn the joy of camping. And he wondered (as he had wondered so many times before about this case history of egregious maternal initiative) if any other single woman, even one as energetic as his landlady, could ever have summoned the courage for that kind of excursion with her city-cooped child on a couple of dog-days in August.

A sheltered mother could study history and was of course more charming. "Our process didn't differ much from salt-grass haying over in West Marsh after about 1880," she said "except that their horses had to wear bog-shoes. But in earlier times they built fixed hayricks inside a circle of staddle poles set up in the ground on the marsh itself, which they ditched for draining when they cut their peat during summer low tides. They ended up with thatched beehives that were as snugly weatherproof as the ones still being made on the downs of old Wessex. It looked more like Holland! The ditches served as canals for their gundalows, to sail the hay away on flood tides when they needed the fodder. But what we called a bullrake they called a loafer!"

Thus like her beloved Crevecoeur Mrs Keith now spoke of Hesiodic georgics from a past very little distant, in Vinland and Montvert, in fells and fens. But she didn't forget the woodlander yearning from which she'd digressed. "At least the spruce grows back in a generation. Even those lovely old white pines"—she pointed beyond the oaks—"could eventually be replaced. They're social trees; they're like each other. You can just plant and let your grandchildren wait for them. But oaks like this one"—the outreaching tree that dominated her yard—"are personalities! Silent characters for posterity! Can you imagine what a thrill it must have been to walk through whole groves of noble oaks in English parkland? I used to tell my dolls I'd been a Druid priestess in my other life."

"Aren't you still a dryad?" Caleb ventured.

"But not a hamadryad, I hope!" she laughed. "Most of the time a lazy gas dryad!" She waved a finger at her laden clotheslines. "When Deirdre was small, playing under that tree and making up stories for her private theater, I thought of her as the dryad."

She was speaking of the great oak that Caleb so often gazed upon from his garret chair, where he had grown accustomed to the backyard view unavailable to its owners. As they now stood together looking up at the long arm of the tree suspending the wistful swing forever awaiting a return of the Keith family's childhood, the dryads' wash to their left hardly stirred under its wooden pins—most of it bleached pure white, but some striped with lavender or lightly printed with thornless roses—screening the buckled whitened fenceboards along the cemetery side of the houselot, which had been intended to discourage at least the short people of funeral corteges or drum-and-bugle corps assembling in the 20C forepart of the public grounds from prying into the householders' private court. The foreground was homely with details of disused implements and abandoned playscapes—constructed mostly by Dexter Keith during his early years of enthusiasm for house and family, before the kids outgrew his own lifelong interests—notably an Ozymandian sandbox (now used by cats and dead leaves) once fitted with pole and awning like the afterdeck of a steam yacht, and, imbedded in amaranthine concrete, the weathered two-by-four towers of a suspension bridge two feet high and eight feet long, with deck now missing but rusty dog-leash catenaries still suspended. From here at ground level the cracked and lichened boulders behind the dilapidated wall, exactly unmoved since the glacier had dropped them, loomed like shapeless mastodons, by contrast rendering all regular curves and angles oversimplified, even the headstones of carved dog-marble.

But it was the far-reaching muscular oak that framed this stage at its rear. Caleb saw in it an effluence of conflicting desires from the same stem, none of which had yet been amputated. The few limbs that had withered were minor and lost to sight, or lofty unimportant twigs indistinguishable within the ribbed canopy greening and thickening almost before his eyes in the Maytime air. The budding leaves seemed impervious to the fluctuations of temperature that made a deceived human hug his shirtsleeves and complain to his fellows. Three or four stately evergreens in the stage-right background, which might have been destined for the king's masts, were tall and straight, well balanced with topgallant spars, but the deciduous oak, in the prime of its age, was asymmetrical and gnarling, more suitable for ships' ribs and knees; its main branches stemmed from the beautifully agonized bifurcations and trinary crotches of a tortuous striated trunk, establishing themes for all the ramifications that crowned them, whether arrayed with fresh green fans or still naked to the very digits: altogether preferring experience to eminence.

The great level yardarm, nearest branch to the roots of the tree, was as useful and nakedly vulnerable to mutilation by the edged tools of power as the trunk of a Carthaginian elephant to Roman swords. Without brace or counterweight, without guy or stay, yet somehow cantilevered underground, it faithfully suspended the outgrown swing of billet and hemp a foot or two above the dirt-worn grass. Who knew the span and depth at which this live post of sinew was grasped and stabilized by the earth? Was the visible complex of twisted torques and stresses exactly compensated by the chthonic anchor of knotted roots—outrigged to sanitary drains and sodden graves, extending downward like a keel of filaments deeper than sunless rocks subterraneously afloat, reaching for Lady Gloucester's abyssal bed, as its main trunk reached for Olympus?

Under daily contemplation from his window the mighty pachydermic bough, so serviceable and protective, had made itself the main branch of his conflict tree—equivocal tree of will, tangled tree of desire, triadic tree of choice, forking tree of pleasure: no sprig as simple as a binary decision. Perhaps from that angle it best represented his longing for the Anglo-Goidelic Isles of his language. But now from down below it loomed above his eyebrows like the main boom of a highline schooner, more impressive to a groundling than the bole no thicker than itself (the European Continent) from which it separated with the xylemic strength of a thumb spread from the forefinger.

But Caleb spoke to the geographer's wife of another conceit: "I call it the Mississippi Oak, and that's the Missouri branch, longer than the main river." He paused at the thought of anabolic nutrients rising from the soil, adding more humbly: "Except for the entropic flow of topsoil to the Delta. The current flows in the wrong direction!"

"Is that what you'd call an unmetaphorical image?"

"Or maybe homology without analogy."

"It's a fine tree, but it chokes our leaching field. One of these days we must get the cesspool pumped out. When we bought the house we were assured it was on the city sewer line, but nobody's got any drawings of what's under the streets, and recently poor Mr Clifford the Reality man was extremely apologetic to Dexter when we raised the issue ex post facto; he'd been so confident in remembering when a main was put in thirty years ago that he never thought of checking his assumption with the selfserving old sewer foreman who keeps everything in his head. It turns out that only a storm drain was extended to this part of Cod Street, and that this house isn't even connected to that! An honest mistake, and we would have taken the house even knowing there was bad cess to it, because we were feverishly determined never to crowd into another shoebox. Dexter says our underground garden is irrigated by effluent and fertilized by septage. I hope the tree doesn't die of it."

"A dead oak might attract an owl," said the devil's advocate, "to scare the paracletes away."

"Does their cooing bother you up there under the eaves? I've got it on my list to have some chicken wire tacked up in the corners of your pediments. I must admit the woodwork up there's a little sullied! The wisteria will never hide the whited white eyries of those pigeons!

"But right now I've got to go in and work on Deirdre's dress for the Junior Prom. It's a funny thing that only this week did it finally strike me that 'Prom' must be a contraction of *promenade*. To me that suggests something more than ocean liners or boulevards. When I was fifteen I went up to Joppa to visit my spinster great aunt, the town's only English teacher. She told me that in her day there was a custom for young people called 'walking to music'. It was a sort of rhythmic promenade in the town hall, the nearest thing to dancing they were ever allowed. That's how they did their courting. I guess things were always much different down here in these cosmopolitan seaports!"

Caleb wished it was possible to tell Mrs Keith more of the truth: Naturally I've noticed the inchoate selfconscious nubility of your daughter, growing like yonder slim catalpa tree, closer to me in age than I to you. At my typewriter I watched her as she sat for two minutes slowly twisting the ropes of her childhood's favorite seat, believing herself absolutely unobserved as she daydreamed without regret of the innocence she has been abandoning with desultory sound and motion. That one scene of unselfconscious meditation erased my resentment of the pert sovereignty with which such a body is endowed by a normal self-confidence. It made me jealous of the boys in school who can touch her, if only at the elbow, and look forward to further caress. But now also my malice has vanished toward those who enjoy Proms (of which I was deprived by an unsettled youth and several social handicaps) because I have become the friend of one whom Deirdre loves, to whom she is usually docile and obedient. I see her unripened beauty generously comprehended in the person of that one who made her, fused with the experienced beauty of faithful love and the selfless beauty of public service.

Still less could he say to the lady whose character had been formed before he was born: To you, as to me, the festivities of youth were seldom freely afforded; we found most of our delight in special skills of work: but judging by your verve and ankles I'm sure we also share a special faculty for the art of square dance, formerly my one communal virtuosity. Dancing to music! I could have swung you by the waist faster than any Su'fi lumberjack, fairly off your feet in a gyre à deux of light fantastic toes! Together like a dipoled dynamo we'd have whirled the corners of the hall out of sight, and all its interfering couples! Thereby advanced in your maiden estimation, I'd have become the first secret of your life, cherished even now beneath your pensive volubility and popular authority, beneath your conjugal privacies and multiplied cares. We meet again, all anachronism dissolved, and you are qualified by sympathy and knowledge to put me in touch with a topopolis that disdains the Resistance. With you there is much to learn; much also to explain and entrust. How it would relieve me—yet spare my reservations—to join by secret friendship the two worlds in which we differ!

Thus his welling affection for the steadfast New Deal woman from a land of Protestican individualists, who enchanted him with history made "shipshape and Dogtown fashion," and raised the absurd hope that she might dissolve some of his barriers to ordinary society. But on his private staircase to the top of the house he was beset by the new loneliness only to be expected from his insight into the lares and penates of a regular well-adapted family.

Turning again to his one true companion from the company of saints as they clambered to the top of the house, he whispered with a sigh "Women are the better people." The women to whom he referred were now represented by a communicative unblemished matron. "But tell me what you were doing all that time!"

No. Ibi was the dashing kind of gentleman who took things as they came, with never an afterthought. His reflections were immediately proleptic only—of the dish and bed just ahead. It was with remarkable self-restraint that he curbed his pace at the man's heel ascending this staircase. He had no intention of reviewing his first Walburga Night.

Printed by Libri Plureos GmbH in Hamburg, Germany